LEGACY OF ASH

Katya took up position at the bridge's narrow crest, her sword point-down at her feet in challenge. She'd no illusions about holding the wayfarers. It would cost them little effort to ride straight over her, had they the stomach for it. But the tightness of the approach offered a slim chance.

The knight raised a mailed fist. The pursuers halted a dozen yards from the bridge's mouth. Two more padded out from the surrounding alleys. Not horsemen, but the Council's simarka – bronze constructs forged in the likeness of lions and given life by a spark of magic. Prowling statues that hunted the Council's enemies. Katya swore under her breath. Her sword was useless against such creatures. A blacksmith's hammer would have served her better. She'd lost too many friends to those claws to believe otherwise.

"Lady Trelan." The knight's greeting boomed like thunder. "The Council demands your surrender."

"Viktor Akadra." Katya made no attempt to hide her bitterness. "Did your father not tell you? I do not recognise the Council's authority."

By Matthew Ward

The Legacy trilogy

Legacy of Ash
Legacy of Steel

LEGACY OF ASH

MATTHEW WARD

www.orbitbooks.net

ORBIT

First published in Great Britain in 2019 by Orbit
This paperback edition published in 2020 by Orbit

1 3 5 7 9 10 8 6 4 2

A CIP catalogue record for this book
is available from the British Library.

ISBN 978-0-356-51337-9

Typeset in Minion by M Rules
Printed and bound in Great Britain by
Clays Ltd, Elcograf S.p.A.

Papers used by Orbit are from well-managed forests
and other responsible sources.

Orbit
An imprint of
Little, Brown Book Group
Carmelite House
50 Victoria Embankment
London EC4Y 0DZ

An Hachette UK Company
www.hachette.co.uk

www.orbitbooks.net

For Lisa, whose light never fades

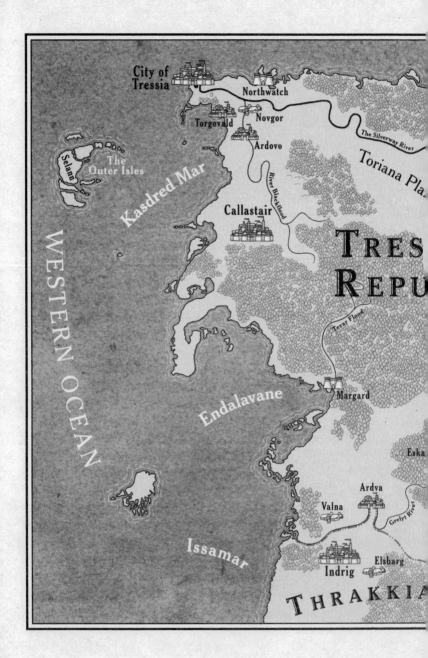

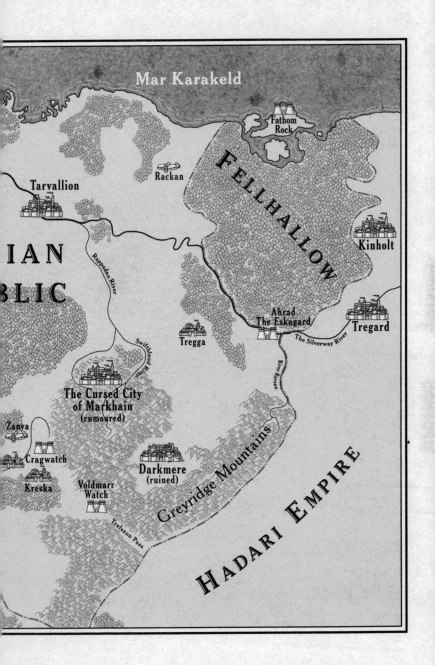

Mar Karakeld

Fathom
Rock

Rackan

FELLHALLOW

Tarvallion

Kinholt

IAN

BLIC

Rappadan River

Swiftblood River

Ahrad
The Eskagard

Tregard

Tregga

The Silverway River

The Cursed City
of Markhain
(rumoured)

River Lavsan

Zanya

Cragwatch

Kreska

Voldmarr
Watch

Darkmere
(ruined)

Greyridge Mountains

Trelszon Pass

HADARI EMPIRE

Dramatis Personae

In the City of Tressia

Viktor Akadra	Champion of the Tressian Council
Roslava Orova	Knight of Tressia
Kasamor Kiradin	Knight of Tressia
Malachi Reveque	Member of the Tressian Privy Council
Ebigail Kiradin	Member of the Tressian Privy Council
Hadon Akadra	Member of the Tressian Privy Council
Abitha Marest	Member of the Tressian Privy Council
Anton Tarev	Member of the Tressian Privy Council
Apara Rann	A vranakin, a cousin of the Crowmarket
Sevaka Kiradin	Officer of the Tressian Fleet, daughter to Ebigail Kiradin
Elzar Ilnarov	Tressian High Proctor; Master of the Forge
Aske Tarev	Tressian Knight, daughter to Anton Tarev
Marek Nomar	Steward to Ebigail Kiradin
Vladama Kurkas	Captain of the Akadra Hearthguard
Lilyana Reveque	Tressian Noble, wife to Malachi Reveque
Sidara Reveque	Daughter to Malachi and Lilyana Reveque
Constans Reveque	Son to Malachi and Lilyana Reveque
Stantin Izack	Captain of the Knights Essamere

In the Southshires

Katya Trelan	Dowager Duchess of Eskavord
Josiri Trelan	Duke of the Southshires, son to Katya Trelan
Calenne Trelan	Daughter to Katya Trelan
Revekah Halvor	Wolf's-head; Captain of the Phoenixes
Anastacia	Seneschal of Branghall Manor (when it suits her)
Drakos Crovan	The Wolf King
Arzro Makrov	Tressian Archimandrite
Shaisan Yanda	Governor of the Southshires
Valmir Sark	Captain of the Tressian Army
Elda Savka	Calenne Trelan's foster mother
Callad Vorn	Wolf's-head

Of the Hadari Empire

Kai Saran	Hadari Crown Prince
Melanna Saranal	Hadari Princessa, daughter of Kai Saran
Sera	Lunassera; a devoted servant of Ashana

Divinities

Ashana	Hadari Goddess of the Moon, known as Lunastra in Tressia
Lumestra	Tressian Goddess of the Sun, known as Astarra in the Hadari Empire
The Huntsman	Ashana's equerry
The Raven	The God of the Dead, Keeper of Otherworld

Gone, But Not Forgotten

Konor Belenzo	Hero of Legend
Malatriant	Tyrant Queen of Old, known as the Sceadotha in the Hadari Empire
Kevor Trelan	Duke of Eskavord

Fifteen Years Ago

Lumendas, 1st Day of Radiance

A Phoenix shall blaze from the darkness.
A beacon to the shackled;
a pyre to the keepers of their chains.

from the sermons of Konor Belenzo

Wind howled along the marcher road. Icy rain swirled behind.

Katya hung low over her horse's neck. Galloping strides jolted weary bones and set the fire in her side blazing anew. Sodden reins sawed at her palms. She blotted out the pain. Closed her ears to the harsh raven-song and ominous thunder. There was only the road, the dark silhouette of Eskavord's rampart, and the anger. Anger at the Council, for forcing her hand. At herself for thinking there'd ever been a chance.

Lightning split grey skies. Katya glanced behind. Josiri was a dark shape, his steed straining to keep pace with hers. That eased the burden. She'd lost so much when the phoenix banner had fallen. But she'd not lose her son.

Nor her daughter.

Eskavord's gate guard scattered without challenge. Had they recognised her, or simply fled the naked steel in her hand? Katya didn't care. The way was open.

In the shadow of jettied houses, sodden men and women loaded sparse possessions onto cart and dray. Children wailed in confusion. Dogs fought for scraps in the gutter. Of course word had reached Eskavord. Grim tidings ever outpaced the good.

You did this.

Katya stifled her conscience and spurred on through the tangled streets of Highgate.

Her horse forced a path through the crowds. The threat of her sword held the desperate at bay. Yesterday, she'd have felt safe within Eskavord's walls. Today she was a commodity to be traded for survival, if any had the wit to realise the prize within their grasp.

Thankfully, such wits were absent in Eskavord. That, or else no one recognised Katya as the dowager duchess Trelan. The Phoenix of prophecy.

No, not that. Katya was free of that delusion. It had cost too many lives, but she was free of it. She was not the Phoenix whose fires would cleanse the Southshires. She'd believed – Lumestra, *how* she'd believed – but belief alone did not change the world. Only deeds did that, and hers had fallen short.

The cottage came into view. Firestone lanterns shone upon its gable. Elda had kept the faith. Even at the end of the world, friends remained true.

Katya slid from the saddle and landed heavily on cobbles. Chainmail's broken links gouged her bloodied flesh.

"Mother?"

Josiri brought his steed to a halt in a spray of water. His hood was back, his blond hair plastered to his scalp.

She shook her head, hand warding away scrutiny. "It's nothing. Stay here. I'll not be long."

He nodded. Concern remained, but he knew better than to question. He'd grown into a dependable young man. Obedient. Loyal. Katya wished his father could have seen him thus. The two were so much alike. Josiri would make a fine duke, if he lived to see his seventeenth year.

She sheathed her sword and marched for the front door. Timbers shuddered under her gauntleted fist. "Elda? Elda! It's me."

A key turned. The door opened. Elda Savka stood on the threshold, her face sagging with relief. "My lady. When the rider came from Zanya, I feared the worst."

"The army is gone."

Elda paled. "Lumestra preserve us."

"The Council emptied the chapterhouses against us."

"I thought the masters of the orders had sworn to take no side."

"A knight's promise is not what it was, and the Council nothing if not persuasive." Katya closed her eyes, lost in the shuddering ground and brash clarions of recent memory. And the screams, most of all. "One charge, and we were lost."

"What of Josiri? Taymor?"

"Josiri is with me. My brother is taken. He may already be dead." Either way, he was beyond help. "Is Calenne here?"

"Yes, and ready to travel. I knew you'd come."

"I have no choice. The Council ... "

She fell silent as a girl appeared at the head of the staircase, her sapphire eyes alive with suspicion. Barely six years old, and she had the wit to know something was amiss. "Elda, what's happening?"

"Your mother is here, Calenne," said Elda. "You must go with her."

"Are you coming?"

The first sorrow touched Elda's brow. "No."

Calenne descended the stairs, expression still heavy with distrust. Katya stooped to embrace her daughter. She hoped Calenne's thin body stiffened at the cold and wet, and not revulsion for a woman she barely knew. From the first, Katya had thought it necessary to send Calenne away, to live shielded from the Council's sight. So many years lost. All for nothing.

Katya released Calenne from her embrace and turned wearily to Elda. "Thank you. For everything."

The other woman forced a wintery smile. "Take care of her."

Katya caught a glint of something darker beneath the smile. It lingered in Elda's eyes. A hardness. Another friendship soured by folly? Perhaps. It no longer mattered. "Until my last breath. Calenne?"

The girl flung her arms around Elda. She said nothing, but the tears on her cheeks told a tale all their own.

Elda pushed her gently away. "You must go, dear heart."

A clarion sounded, its brash notes cleaving through the clamour of the storm. An icy hand closed around Katya's heart. She'd run out of time.

Elda met her gaze. Urgency replaced sorrow. "Go! While you still can!"

Katya stooped and gathered Calenne. The girl's chest shook with thin sobs, but she offered no resistance. With a last glance at Elda, Katya set out into the rain once more. The clarion sounded again as she reached Josiri. His eyes were more watchful than ever, his sword ready in his hands.

"They're here," he said.

Katya heaved Calenne up to sit in front of her brother. She looked like a doll beside him, every day of the decade that separated them on full display.

"Look after your sister. If we're separated, ride hard for the border."

His brow furrowed. "To the Hadari? Mother . . . "

"The Hadari will treat you better than the Council." He still had so much to learn, and she no more time in which to teach him. "When enemies are your only recourse, choose the one with the least to gain. Promise me."

She received a reluctant nod in reply.

Satisfied, Katya clambered into her saddle and spurred west along the broad cobbles of Highgate. They'd expect her to take refuge in Branghall Manor, or at least strip it of anything valuable ahead of the inevitable looting. But the western gateway might still be clear.

The first cry rang out as they rejoined the road. "She's here!"

A blue-garbed wayfarer cantered through the crowd, rain scattering from leather pauldrons. Behind, another set a buccina to his lips. A brash rising triad hammered out through the rain and found answer in the streets beyond. The pursuit's vanguard had reached Eskavord. Lightly armoured riders to harry and delay while heavy knights closed the distance. Katya drew her sword and wheeled her horse about. "Make for the west gate!"

Josiri hesitated, then lashed his horse to motion. "Yah!"

Katya caught one last glimpse of Calenne's pale, dispassionate face. Then they were gone, and the horseman upon her.

The wayfarer was half her age, little more than a boy and eager for the glory that might earn a knight's crest. Townsfolk scattered from his path. He goaded his horse to the gallop, sword held high in anticipation of the killing blow to come. He'd not yet learned that the first blow seldom mattered as much as the last.

Katya's parry sent a shiver down her arm. The wayfarer's blade scraped clear, the momentum of his charge already carrying him past. Then he was behind, hauling on the reins. The sword came about, the killing stroke aimed at Katya's neck.

Her thrust took the younger man in the chest. Desperate strength drove the blade between his ribs. The hawk of the Tressian Council turned dark as the first blood stained the rider's woollen tabard. Then he slipped from his saddle, sword clanging against cobbles. With one last, defiant glare at the buccinator, Katya turned her steed about, and galloped through the narrow streets after her children.

She caught them at the bridge, where the waters of the Grelyt River fell away into the boiling millrace. They were not alone.

One wayfarer held the narrow bridge, blocking Josiri's path. A second closed from behind him, sword drawn. A third lay dead on the cobbles, horse already vanished into the rain.

Josiri turned his steed in a circle. He had one arm tight about his sister. The other hand held a bloody sword. The point trembled as it swept back and forth between his foes, daring them to approach.

Katya thrust back her heels. Her steed sprang forward.

Her sword bit into the nearest wayfarer's spine. Heels jerked as he fell back. His steed sprang away into the streets. The corpse, one booted foot tangled in its stirrups, dragged along behind.

Katya rode on past Josiri. Steel clashed, once, twice, and then the last wayfarer was gone. His body tipped over the low stone parapet and into the rushing waters below.

Josiri trotted close, his face studiously calm. Katya knew better. He'd not taken a life before today.

"You're hurt."

Pain stemmed Katya's denial. A glance revealed rainwater running red across her left hand. She also felt a wound high on her shoulder. The last wayfarer's parting gift, lost in the desperation of the moment.

The clarion came yet again. A dozen wayfarers spurred down the street. A plate-clad knight rode at their head, his destrier caparisoned in silver-flecked black. Not the heraldry of a knightly chapterhouse, but a family of the first rank. His sword – a heavy, fennlander's claymore – rested in its scabbard. A circular shield sat slung across his back.

The greys of the rain-sodden town lost their focus. Katya tightened her grip on the reins. She flexed the fingers of her left hand. They felt distant, as if belonging to someone else. Her shoulder ached, fit company for the dull roar in her side – a memento of the sword-thrust she'd taken on the ridge at Zanya. Weariness crowded in, the faces of the dead close behind.

The world lurched. Katya grasped at the bridle with her good hand. Focus returned at the cost of her sword, which fell onto the narrow roadway.

So that was how the matter lay?

So be it.

"Go," she breathed. "See to your sister's safety. I'll hold them."

Josiri spurred closer, the false calm giving way to horror. "Mother, no!"

Calenne looked on with impassive eyes.

"I can't ride." Katya dropped awkwardly from her saddle and stooped to reclaim her sword. The feel of the grips beneath her fingers awoke new determination. "Leave me."

"No. We're getting out of here. All of us." He reached out. "You can ride with me."

The tremor beneath his tone revealed the truth. His horse was already weary. What stamina remained would not long serve two riders, let alone three.

Katya glanced down the street. There'd soon be nothing left to argue over. She understood Josiri's reluctance, for it mirrored her own. To face a parting now, with so much unsaid . . . ? But a lifetime would not be enough to express her pride, nor to warn against repeating her mistakes. He'd have to find his own way now.

"Do you love me so little that you'd make me beg?" She forced herself to meet his gaze. "Accept this last gift and remember me well. Go."

Josiri gave a sharp nod, his lips a pale sliver. His throat bobbed. Then he turned his horse.

Katya dared not watch as her children galloped away, fearful that Josiri would read the gesture as a change of heart.

"Lumestra's light shine for you, my son," she whispered.

A slap to her horse's haunch sent it whinnying into the oncoming wayfarers. They scattered, fighting for control over startled steeds.

Katya took up position at the bridge's narrow crest, her sword point-down at her feet in challenge. She'd no illusions about holding the wayfarers. It would cost them little effort to ride straight over her, had they the stomach for it. But the tightness of the approach offered a slim chance.

The knight raised a mailed fist. The pursuers halted a dozen yards from the bridge's mouth. Two more padded out from the surrounding alleys. Not horsemen, but the Council's simarka – bronze constructs forged in the likeness of lions and given life by a spark of magic. Prowling statues that hunted the Council's enemies. Katya swore under her breath. Her sword was useless against such creatures. A blacksmith's hammer would have served her better. She'd lost too many friends to those claws to believe otherwise.

"Lady Trelan." The knight's greeting boomed like thunder. "The Council demands your surrender."

"Viktor Akadra." Katya made no attempt to hide her bitterness. "Did your father not tell you? I do not recognise the Council's authority."

The knight dismounted, the hem of his jet-black surcoat trailing in the rain. He removed his helm. Swarthy, chiselled features stared out from beneath a thatch of black hair. A young face, though one already confident far beyond its years.

He'd every reason to be so. Even without the armour, without the entourage of weary wayfarers – without her wounds – Akadra would have been more than her match. He stood a full head taller than she – half a head taller than any man she'd known.

"There has been enough suffering today." His tone matched his expression perfectly. Calm. Confident. Unyielding. He gestured, and the simarka sat, one to either side. Motionless. Watchful. "Let's not add to the tally."

"Then turn around, Lord Akadra. Leave me be."

Lips parted in something not entirely a smile. "You will stand before the Council and submit to judgement."

Katya knew what that meant. The humiliation of a show trial, arraigned as warning to any who'd follow in her footsteps and dare seek freedom for the Southshires. Then they'd parade her through the streets, her last dignity stripped away long before the gallows took her final breath. She'd lost a husband to that form of justice. She'd not suffer it herself.

"I'll die first."

"Incorrect."

Again, that damnable confidence. But her duty was clear.

Katya let the anger rise, as she had on the road. Its fire drove back the weariness, the pain, the fear for her children. Those problems belonged to the future, not the moment at hand. She was a daughter of the Southshires, the dowager duchess Trelan. She would not yield. The wound in Katya's side blazed as she surged forward. The alchemy of rage transmuted agony to strength and lent killing weight to the two-handed blow.

Akadra's sword scraped free of its scabbard. Blades clashed with a banshee screech. Lips parted in a snarl of surprise, he gave ground through the hissing rain.

Katya kept pace, right hand clamped over the failing left to give it purpose and guide it true. She hammered at Akadra's guard, summoning forth the lessons of girlhood to the bleak present. The forms of the sword her father had drilled into her until they flowed with the grace of a thrush's song and the power of a mountain river. Those lessons had kept her alive on the ridge at Zanya. They would not fail her now.

The wayfarers made no move to interfere.

But Akadra was done retreating.

Boots planted on the cobbles like the roots of some venerable, weather-worn oak, he checked each strike with grace that betrayed tutelage no less exacting than Katya's own. The claymore blurred across grey skies and battered her longsword aside.

The fire in Katya's veins turned sluggish. Cold and failing flesh sapped her purpose. Too late, she recognised the game Akadra had played. She'd wearied herself on his defences, and all the while her body had betrayed her.

Summoning her last strength, Katya hurled herself forward. A cry born of pain and desperation ripped free of her lips.

Again the claymore blurred to parry. The longsword's tip scraped past the larger blade, ripping into Akadra's cheek. He twisted away with a roar of pain.

Hooves sounded on cobbles. The leading wayfarers spurred forward, swords drawn to avenge their master's humiliation. The simarka, given no leave to advance, simply watched unfolding events with feline curiosity.

Katya's hands tightened on her sword. She'd held longer than she'd believed possible. She hoped Josiri had used the time well.

"Leave her!"

Akadra checked the wayfarers' advance with a single bellow. The left side of his face masked in blood, he turned his attention on Katya once more. He clasped a closed fist to his chest. Darkness gathered about his fingers like living shadow.

Katya's world blurred, its colours swirling away into an unseen void.

Her knee cracked against the cobbles. A hand slipped from her sword, fingers splayed to arrest her fall. Wisps of blood curled through pooling rainwater. She knelt there, gasping for breath, one ineluctable truth screaming for attention.

The rumours about Akadra were true.

The shadow dispersed as Akadra strode closer. The wayfarers had seen none of it, Katya realised – or had at least missed the significance. Otherwise, Akadra would have been as doomed as she. The Council would tolerate much from its loyal sons, but not witchcraft.

Colour flooded back. Akadra's sword dipped to the cobbles. His bloodied face held no triumph. Somehow that was worse.

"It's over." For the first time, his expression softened. "This is not the way, Katya. It never was. Surrender. Your wounds will be tended. You'll be treated with honour."

"Honour?" The word was ash on Katya's tongue. "Your father knows nothing of honour."

"It is not my father who makes the offer." He knelt, one gauntleted hand extended. "Please. Give me your sword."

Katya stared down at the cobbles, at her life's blood swirling away into the gutter. Could she trust him? A lifetime of emissaries and missives from the north had bled her people dry to feed a pointless war. Viktor's family was part of that, and so he was part of it. If his promise *was* genuine, he'd no power to keep it. The Council would never let it stand. The shame of the gallows path beckoned.

"You want my sword?" she growled.

Katya rose from her knees, her last effort channelled into one final blow.

Akadra's hand, so lately extended in conciliation, wrenched the sluggish blade from her grasp. He let his own fall alongside. Tugged off balance, Katya fell to her hands and knees. Defenceless. Helpless.

No. Not helpless. Never that.

She forced herself upright. There was no pain. No weariness. Just calm. Was this how Kevor had felt at the end? Before the creak of the deadman's drop had set her husband swinging? Trembling fingers closed around a dagger's hilt.

"My son will finish what I started."

The dagger rasped free, Katya's right hand again closing over her left.

"No!" Akadra dived forward. His hands reached for hers, his sudden alarm lending weight to his promises.

Katya rammed the dagger home. Chain links parted. She felt no pain as the blade slipped between her ribs. There was only a sudden giddiness as the last of her burdens fell away into mist.

Josiri held Calenne close through the clamour. Screams. Buccina calls. Galloping hooves. Barked orders. Josiri longed for the thunder's return. Bravery came easier in moments when the angry sky drowned all else.

The church spire passed away to his left. Desperate townsfolk crowded its lychpath, seeking sanctuary behind stone walls. People filled the streets beyond. Some wore council blue, most the sea-grey of Eskavord's guard, and too many the garb of ordinary folk caught in between.

Ravens scattered before Josiri's straining horse. He glanced down at the girl in his charge. His sister she may have been, but Calenne was a stranger. She sat in silence, not a tear on her cheeks. He didn't know how she held herself together so. It was all he could do not to fall apart.

A pair of wayfarers emerged from an alleyway, their approach masked by the booming skies. Howling with courage he didn't feel, Josiri hacked at the nearest. The woman slumped across her horse's neck. Josiri rowelled his mare, leaving the outpaced survivor snarling at the rain.

More wayfarers waited at the next junction, their horses arrayed in a loose line beneath overhanging eaves. The town wall loomed through the rain. The west gate was so close. Two streets away, no more.

A glance behind revealed a wayfarer galloping in pursuit. A pair of simarka loped alongside. Verdigrised claws struck sparks from the cobbles.

To turn back was to be taken, a rat in a trap. The certainty of it left Josiri no room for doubt. Onward was the only course.

"Hold tight to me," he told Calenne, "and don't let go."

Thin arms redoubled their grip. Josiri drove back his heels.

Time slowed, marked out by the pounding of hooves and the beat of a fearful heart. Steel glinted. Horses whinnied as wayfarers hauled on their reins.

"For the Southshires!"

The battle cry fed Josiri's resolve. The widening of the nearest wayfarer's eyes gave him more. They were as afraid of him as he of them. Maybe more, for was his mother not the Phoenix of prophecy?

Time quickened. Josiri's sword blurred. A wayfarer spun away in a bloody spray. And then Josiri was through the line, his horse's greedy stride gobbling the last distance to the west gate. The mare barely slowed at the next corner. Her hooves skidded on the rain-slicked cobbles.

Calenne screamed – not with terror, but in wild joy – and then the danger was past, and the west gate was in sight.

The portcullis was down, its iron teeth sunk deep. A line of tabarded soldiery blocked the roadway and the branching alleyways to either side. Halberds lowered. Shields locked tight together, a flock of white hawk blazons on a wall of rich king's blue. Wayfarers filled the street behind.

Thunder roared, its fury echoing through the hole where Josiri's heart should have been. He'd failed. Perhaps he'd never had a chance.

"Everything will be all right." He hoped the words sounded more convincing to Calenne than they did to him. "Mother will come."

Calenne stared up at him with all the earnestness of youth. "Mother's already dead."

Spears pressed in. An officer's voice bellowed orders through the rain. Josiri gazed down into his sister's cold, unblinking eyes, and felt more alone than ever.

Endas, 25th day of Wellmarch

Our souls are but motes of light, stolen from the Dark. Lumestra's love wakes us to life, and the hammer of duty tempers us upon the forge of our waking days.

from the sermons of Konor Belenzo

One

Preparations had taken weeks. Statues had been re-gilded. Familial portraits unveiled from dusty canvas and set in places of honour. The stained glass of the western window glittered in the afternoon sunlight. Come the hour of Ascension it would blaze like fire and cast an image of divine Lumestra into the hall so that the sun goddess too would stand among the guests.

It would not be so elsewhere. In the houses beneath Branghall's walls the part of Lumestra would be played by a doll, her limbs carved from firewood and her golden hair woven from last year's straw. There, her brief reign would not end with the fading of the sun. Instead, hearth-fires would usher her home on tongues of flame.

The chasm between rich and poor, ruler and ruled, was never more evident than at Ascension. Josiri strove to be mindful of that. For all that had befallen his family, he retained comfort and privilege denied to many.

But a prison remained a prison, even if the bars were gilded and the guards polite.

Most of the guards.

"That will have to come down." Arzro Makrov extended a finger to the portrait above High Table. "She has no place here, or anywhere else in the Tressian Republic."

Josiri exchanged a glance with Anastacia. The seneschal's black eyes glimmered a warning, reinforced by a slight shake of her head. Josiri ignored both and stepped closer, footsteps hollow on the hall's flagstones. "No place?"

Makrov flinched but held his ground. "Katya Trelan was a traitor."

Impotent anger kindled. Fifteen years on, and the wound remained raw as ever.

"This was my mother's home," said Josiri carefully. "She would have celebrated her fifty-fifth year this Ascension. Her body is ash, but she *will* be present in spirit."

"No."

Makrov drew his corpulent body up to its full, unimpressive height. The setting sun lent his robes the rich warmth of fresh blood. Ironic for a man so pallid. The intricate silver ward-brooch was a poor match for his stolid garb. But without it, he could not have crossed the enchanted manor wall.

Josiri's throat tightened. He locked gazes with Makrov for a long moment, and then let his eyes fall upon the remaining "guests". Would any offer support?

Shaisan Yanda didn't meet his gaze, but that was to be expected. As governor of the Southshires, she was only present to ensure Josiri did nothing rash. Nonetheless, the slight curl to her lip suggested she found Makrov's behaviour tiresome. She'd fought for the Council at Zanya, and on other battlefields besides, earning both her scars and the extra weight that came with advancing years.

As for Valmir Sark, he paid little attention. His interest lay more with ancestral finery . . . and likely in broaching Branghall's wine cellars come Ascension. Josiri had heard enough of Sark to know he was present only to spare his family another scandal. The high-collared uniform might as well have been for show. Sark was too young to have fought against Katya's rebellion. And as for him standing a turn on the Hadari border? The thought was laughable.

That left Anastacia, and her opinion carried no sway.

If only Calenne were there. She'd always had more success in dealing with the Council's emissaries, and more patience. Where in Lumestra's name was she? She'd promised.

Josiri swallowed his irritation. He'd enough enemies without adding his sister to the roster.

"The portrait remains," he said. "This is my house. I'll thank you to remember that."

Makrov's wispy grey eyebrows knotted. "Were it up to me, I'd allow it. Truly I would. But the Council insists. Katya Trelan brought nothing but division and strife. Her shadow should not mar Ascension."

Only the slightest pause between the words imbued challenge. Josiri's self-control, so painstakingly fortified before the meeting, slipped a notch. He shook off Anastacia's restraining hand and took another step.

Yanda's lips tightened to a thin, bloodless streak. Her hand closed meaningfully about the pommel of her sword. Sark gazed on with parted mouth and the first spark of true interest.

"It is my hope," said Josiri, "that my mother's presence will serve as a message of unity."

Makrov stared up at the portrait. "I applaud your intent. But the lawless are not quelled by gestures, but by strong words, and stronger action."

"I've given what leadership I can."

"I know," said Makrov. "I've read reports of your speeches. I'd like to hear one for myself. Tomorrow at noon?"

It was an artful twist of the knife. "If you wish."

"Excellent." He raised his voice. "Governor Yanda. You'll ensure his grace isn't speaking to an empty square? I'm sure Captain Sark will be delighted to assist."

"Of course, my lord," said Yanda. "And the portrait?"

Makrov locked gazes with Katya Trelan's dead stare. "I want it taken down and burned. Her body is ash. Let her spirit join it. I can think of no stronger message of unity."

"I won't do it," Josiri said through gritted teeth.

"Yes, you will." Makrov sighed. "Your grace. *Josiri.* I entertained hopes that you'd lead your people out of the past. But the Council's patience is not infinite. They may decide upon another exodus if there's anything less than full cooperation."

Exodus. The word sounded harmless. The reality was punishment meted out for a rebellion fifteen years in the past; families divided, stolen children shipped north to toil as little more than slaves. Makrov sought to douse a fire with tinder.

"Your mother's memory poisons you. As it poisons your people." Makrov set his hands on Josiri's shoulders. "Let her go. I have."

But he hadn't. That was why Makrov remained the Council's chief emissary to the Southshires, despite his advancing years and expanding waistline. His broken heart had never healed, but Katya Trelan lay fifteen years beyond his vengeance. And so he set his bitterness against her people, and against a son who he believed should have been his.

Makrov offered an avuncular smile. "You'll thank me one day."

Josiri held his tongue, not trusting himself to reply. Makrov strode away, Sark falling into step behind. Yanda hesitated a moment before following.

"Tomorrow at noon, your grace. I look forward to it." Makrov spoke without turning, the words echoing along the rafters. Then he was gone.

Josiri glanced up at his mother's portrait. Completed a year before her death, it captured to perfection the gleam of her eyes and the inscrutable perhaps-mocking, maybe-sympathetic smile. At least, Josiri thought it did. Fifteen years was a long time. He saw little of himself in his mother's likeness, but then he'd always been more akin to his father. The same unruly blond hair and lantern jaw. The same lingering resentment at forces beyond his control.

He perched on the edge of High Table and swallowed his irritation. He couldn't afford anger. Dignity was the cornerstone of leadership, or so his mother had preached.

"When I was a boy," he said, "my father told me that people are scared and stupid more than they are cruel. I thought he'd handed me the key to some great mystery. Now? The longer I spend in Makrov's company, the more I suspect my father told me what he *wished* were true."

Anastacia drew closer. Her outline blurred like vapour, as it always did when her attention wandered. Like her loose tangle of snow-white curls and impish features, the robes of a Trelan seneschal were for show. A concession. Josiri wasn't sure what Anastacia's true form actually *was*. Only black, glossy eyes – long considered the eyes of a witch, or a demon, bereft of iris and sclera – offered any hint.

The Council's proctors had captured her a year or so after the Battle of Zanya. Branghall, already a prison in all but name, had become her new home shortly after. Anastacia spoke often of what she'd done to deserve Tressian ire. The problem was, no two tales matched.

In one, she'd seduced and murdered a prominent councillor. In another, she'd instead seduced and murdered that same councillor's husband. A third story involved ransacking a church. And then there was the tale about a choir of serenes, and indecency that left the holy women's vows of chastity in tatters. After a dozen such stories, ranging from ribald to horrific, Josiri had stopped asking.

But somewhere along the line, they'd become friends. More than friends. If Makrov ever learned how close they were, it wouldn't be the gallows that awaited Josiri, but the pyre.

Pallid wisps of light curled from Anastacia's arched eyebrow. "The archimandrite is foolish in the way only clever men are. As for afraid? If he wasn't, you'd not be his prisoner."

Josiri snorted. "My mother casts a long shadow. But I'm not her."

"No. Your mother lost her war. You'll win yours."

"Flatterer."

The eyebrow twitched a fraction higher. "Isn't that a courtier's function?"

Genuine confusion, or another of Anastacia's little jokes? It was always hard to be sure. "In the rest of the Republic, perhaps. In the Southshires, truth is all we can afford."

"If you're going to start moping, I'd like to be excused."

A smile tugged at the corner of Josiri's mouth. "If you don't show your duke a little more respect, he might have you thrown from the manor."

Anastacia sniffed. "He's welcome to try. But these stones are old, and the Council's proctors made a thorough job of binding me to them. You'll fail before they do."

"You forget, I'm a Trelan. I'm stubborn."

"And where did stubbornness get your mother? Or your uncle, for that matter?"

Josiri's gaze drifted back to his mother's portrait. "What would she do?"

"I doubt she'd put a mere *thing*, no matter how beautiful, before the lives of her people." She shrugged. "But she was a Trelan, and some-one once told me – though I can't remember who – that Trelans are stubborn."

"And none more than she," said Josiri. "I don't want to give up the last of her."

Anastacia scratched at the back of her scalp – a mannerism she'd picked up off one of the servants in her frequent forays to the kitchens.

Her appetites were voracious – especially where the manor's wine cellar was concerned.

"Might I offer some advice, as one prisoner to another?"

"Of course."

"Burn the painting. Your mother's legacy is not in canvas and oils, but in blood."

The words provoked a fresh spark of irritation. "Calenne doesn't seem to think so."

Anastacia offered no reply. Josiri couldn't blame her for that. This particular field was well-furrowed. And besides, good advice was good advice. Katya Trelan had died to save her family. That was her true legacy.

"I should tell her how things went," he said. "Do you know where she is?"

"Where do you think?" Anastacia's tone grew whimsical to match her expression. "For myself, I might rearrange the window shutters on the upper floor. Just in case some helpful soul's watching? One who might be agreeable to expressing your annoyance at the archimandrite where you cannot?"

Josiri swallowed a snort of laughter. Regardless of what his mother would have done about the painting, this she *would* approve of. Humiliation repaid in kind.

"That's a grand idea."

Anastacia sniffed again. "Of course it is. Shall we say nightfall?"

That ran things close, but the timing should work. Makrov was due to hold celebration in Eskavord's tiny church at dusk. Afterwards, he'd make the long ride back to the fortress at Cragwatch. It all depended on whether Crovan's people were keeping watch on the shutters.

Still, inaction gained nothing.

Josiri nodded. "Nightfall it is."

Each creak of the stairs elicited a fearful wince, and a palm pressed harder against rough stone. Josiri told himself that the tower hadn't endured generations of enthusiastic winds just to crumble beneath his own meagre weight. He might even have believed it, if not for that almost imperceptible rocking motion. In his great-grandfather's time, the tower had been an observatory. Now the roof was a nest of fallen beams, and the walls stone teeth in a shattered jaw.

At least the skies were clear. The vistas almost held the terror at bay, fear paling before beauty. The town of Eskavord sprawled across the eastern valley, smoke dancing as the Ash Wind – so named for the cinders it gusted from the distant Thrakkian border to the south – brushed the slopes of Drannan Tor. Beyond the outermost farms sprawled the eaves of Davenwood. Beyond that, further east, the high town walls of Kreska nestled in the foothills of the Greyridge Mountains. All of it within a day's idle ride. Close at hand, and yet out of reach.

But it paid not to look too close. You might see the tabarded soldiers patrolling Eskavord's streets, or the boarded-up houses. The foreboding gibbets on Gallows Hill. Where Josiri's Uncle Taymor had danced a final jig – where his mother had burned, her ashes scattered so Lumestra could not easily resurrect her come the light of Third Dawn. It was worse in the month of Reaptithe. Endless supply wagons crept along the sunken roadways like columns of ants, bearing the Southshires' bounty north.

Duke Kevor Trelan had never been more popular with his people than when he called for secession. The Council had been quick to respond. Josiri still recalled the bleak Tzadas-morning the summons had arrived at Branghall, backed by swords enough to make refusal impossible. It was the last memory he had of his father. But the Council had erred. Duke Kevor's execution made rebellion inevitable.

Another gust assailed the tower. His panicked step clipped a fragment of stone. It ricocheted off the sun-bleached remnant of a wooden beam and clattered out over the edge.

"I suppose your demon told you where I was?"

Calenne, as usual, perched on the remnants of the old balcony – little more than a spur of timber jutting at right angles to a battered wall. Her back to a pile of rubble, she had one foot hooked across her knee. The other dangled out over the courtyard, three storeys and forty feet below. A leather-bound book lay open across her lap, pages fluttering.

"Her name is Anastacia."

"That's not her name." The wind plucked a spill of black hair from behind Calenne's ear. She tucked it back into place. "That's what *you* call her."

Calenne had disliked Anastacia from the first, though Josiri had never been clear why, and the passage of time had done little to heal the one-sided divide. Anastacia seldom reciprocated the antipathy, though whether that was because she considered herself above such things, or did so simply to irritate Calenne, Josiri wasn't sure.

"Because that's her wish. I don't call you Enna any longer, do I?"

Blue eyes met his then returned to the book. "What do you want?"

Josiri shook his head. So very much like their mother. No admission of wrong, just a new topic.

"I thought you'd be with me to greet Makrov."

She licked a fingertip and turned the page. "I changed my mind."

"We were discussing the arrangements for *your* wedding. Or do you no longer intend to marry at Ascension?"

"That's *why* I changed my mind."

"What's that supposed to mean?"

A rare moment of hesitation. "It doesn't matter."

"I see." Steeling himself, Josiri edged closer. "What are you reading?"

"This?" Calenne stared down at the book. "A gift from Kasamor. *The Turn of Winter*, by Iugo Maliev. I'm told it's all the rage in Tressia."

"Any good?"

"If you admire a heroine who lets herself be blown from place to place like a leaf on the wind. It's horrendously fascinating. Or fascinatingly horrendous. I haven't decided yet." She closed the book and set it on her knee. "How did the meeting go?"

"I'm to make a speech tomorrow, on the topic of unity."

She scowled. "It went that badly?"

"I didn't have my sister there to charm him," Josiri replied. "And . . . he reacted poorly to mother's portrait." No sense saying the rest. Calenne wouldn't understand.

She sighed. "And now you know why I stayed away. If Makrov reacts like that to Katya's image . . . I didn't want complications. I can't afford them. And I *do* want this marriage."

Josiri didn't have to ask what she meant. Katya in oils was bad enough. Her likeness in flesh and blood? Even with Calenne at her most demure and charming – a rarity – there was risk. With every passing year, his sister more resembled the mother she refused to acknowledge. Perhaps she'd been right to stay away.

"You think Makrov has the power to have it annulled?"

She shrugged. "Not alone. But Kasamor's mother isn't at all pleased at the match. I'm sure she's allies enough to make trouble."

"Kasamor would truly let her interfere?"

On his brief visits to Branghall, Kasamor had seemed smitten. As indeed had Calenne herself. On the other hand, Josiri had heard enough of Ebigail Kiradin, Kasamor's mother, to suspect she possessed both the reach and influence to thwart even the course of true love, if she so chose.

"On his last visit, he told me that I was the other half of his soul. So no, I don't believe he would. He'd sooner die, I think. And I . . . " Calenne shook her head and stared down at the book. "It doesn't matter."

Josiri frowned. "What? What doesn't matter?"

Calenne offered a small, resigned smile. "I've had bad dreams of late. The Black Knight. Waking up screaming doesn't do wonders for my mood."

The Black Knight. Viktor Akadra. The Phoenix-Slayer. The man who'd murdered their mother. He'd taken root in the dreams of a terrified six-year-old girl, and never let go. Josiri had lost track of how often in that first year he'd cradled Calenne as she'd slipped off to broken sleep.

"Is that why you're back to hiding up here? He'll not harm you, I promise."

"I know he won't." Her shoulders drooped, and her tone softened. "But thanks, all the same."

She set the book aside and joined him inside the tower proper. Josiri drew her into an embrace, reflecting, as he so often did, what a curious mix of close and distant they were. The decade between them drove them apart. He doubted he'd ever understand her. Fierce in aspect, but brittle beneath.

"The world's against us, little sister. We Trelans have to stick together."

Two

The kraikon loomed through the trees, as implacable as the colossal bronze statue it resembled. Burgeoning moonlight revealed an angular, stylised form more than twice Josiri's height. Golden magic hissed through lesions in an antiquated frame, crackling across the king's blue tabard and segmented steel plate. Empty, expressionless eyes swept the undergrowth from beneath an open helm.

Josiri held his breath. He pressed against the black oak and willed the kraikon to continue its patrol of Branghall's overgrown gardens. There wasn't a curfew as such. As ever, the bars of the cage were carefully hidden to ease cooperation. But to be caught beneath the estate wall at so late an hour? That would provoke questions he didn't wish to answer.

The kraikon stomped away through the night, the tip of its horsehair plume scraping against overhanging branches. Josiri allowed himself a sigh of relief.

"Evening, your grace."

The whisper was so close that the breath of it fell warm on Josiri's ear. He jumped, the involuntary yelp forming on his lips. A gloved hand stifled the cry, then slipped away.

"Careful." The whisper returned, leavened with amusement. "Don't want to upset the lummox."

Cheeks warming with embarrassment, Josiri pulled away. Revekah Halvor offered a toothy grin and sat carefully on an exposed root.

Anastacia's teeth gleamed white. She cut a ghostly figure so far from Branghall's foundations. The bark of the great black oak was clearly visible through a faded dress and translucent skin. Her fingers danced, shadow coiling in their wake. The oak sank silently into the soil, collapsing the arboreous tunnel that was Josiri's only connection to the outside world.

The tree's roots had always run deep, and far further than the estate wall. Under Anastacia's influence, they ran farther still, weaving the passage by which Revekah had broached Branghall's imprisoning wards. As notorious a soul as she had no hope of gaining official entrance through the main gate – the ward-brooches that allowed visitors to breach the enchantment were carefully and rarely doled out.

But there were other magics in the world than those pressed to the Council's service, by whose grace Anastacia had woven the hallowgate from the oak's gnarled flesh. Old magics, learned from forbidden gods. Or at least forbidden in Tressia, where Lumestra held sway. Remnants of temples to her heavenly sister, Ashana – or Lunastra, as she was named in the oldest scriptures – remained out in rural areas; shrines to Jack, the King of Thorns, in places wilder still.

Not for the first time, Josiri wondered where Anastacia had learned her magics. And where the Council had found her. "Demon", Calenne had named her – pejoratives aside, it suited her well.

"Where's Crovan?" he asked.

"Where's Crovan?" Revekah snorted. "That's how you greet an old woman who's travelled hard to be here? No respect, Josiri. None at all."

The twinkle in her eye belied both words and tone. Revekah's sixtieth year lay long behind her. Nonetheless, she'd not softened an inch since the chaos at Zanya, where she'd heaved Josiri onto her horse and ordered him to flee. She still wore the phoenix tabard over her leather jerkin. Like her, it had faded and worn thin with the passage of time.

"Crovan's away to the south. Might even be across the Thrakkian border by now."

Josiri frowned. "What went wrong?"

"A raid went sour." She shrugged. "It happens. He'll be back. But not tonight. I saw the shutters, and feared you'd be lonely."

They'd settled on the shutter-code years before as a way for Josiri to communicate with those southwealders who'd not yet given up the fight. Some, like Revekah, were survivors of his mother's doomed rebellion.

Crovan belonged to a younger generation. Together, they named themselves the Vagabond Council, a bitter jest aimed at the "noble" men and women who ruled the Southshires' fortunes from Tressia. The law named them Wolf's-heads – creatures of the wild, not the civilised world – and like wolves they were hunted.

The Tressian army, honed to the bloody craft of massed battle and border skirmish, was too blunt an instrument for rural insurrection. Wolf's-heads harried the occupying soldiery; ambushed grain convoys and prison wagons. They took shelter in abandoned villages, and in the Forbidden Places, where the magic of the Council's simarka and kraikons guttered like candle-flame in a storm.

"How are things out there?" he asked.

"They've been worse."

Which also meant they'd been better. "Are we any closer?"

"The weapon situation's improving. Between the Thrakkians and our sympathisers back in Tressia, we've enough blades for a small army."

"And armour?"

"That's harder – to get hold of, and to conceal – but we've quite the foundry up and running in the Larwater caves. Gavamor got his hands on a simarka amulet. It's damaged, but he reckons he can make copies, given time."

That *was* good news. The simarka were simple-minded, and took instruction from proctors, or else from the wearer of an amulet. With enough amulets, the resistance could neutralise one of the strongest weapons at Governor Yanda's command. Maybe even turn it back on their oppressors. "How long?"

"Weeks. Months. Maybe never. You know how these things go."

"We could bring Gavamor here? Anastacia could help him."

"Anastacia could *not*," said Anastacia. "She's more sense than to mess with caged sunlight."

Revekah shot her an unfriendly glance, but nodded. "And how would you explain his presence? To your sister, if no one else. I take it you've still not told her?"

Josiri shook his head. "Better she's kept out of it."

"It's her fight as much as it is yours."

"Not as far as she's concerned."

"Only because you've cosseted her," Revekah snapped. The lines on her face smoothed. "I shouldn't have said that. My apologies."

Josiri grunted. "For speaking your mind? But Calenne's chosen her path. I won't interfere."

"It may not matter anyway."

"What do you mean?"

"The Hadari are massing beyond Trelszon Pass. Crovan thinks they're preparing to invade." Shrewd eyes read his expression. "You've heard nothing?"

"Not a whisper." No wonder Makrov was on edge. Every blade the Council had in the Southshires was pointed in, not out. If the Hadari Empire made passage west over the Greyridge Mountains ... "Why did no one tell me?"

"Because they're worried what you might do," said Anastacia.

Revekah nodded. "The Council aren't fools. They're keeping temptation from you."

Josiri's stomach lurched. "They think I'd sell our people out to the Hadari?"

Another shrug. "Crovan thinks you should. When enemies are your only recourse ... "

" ... choose the one with least to gain," Josiri finished. "I know."

She drew a dagger from her belt and set it point-down in the soil, turning the blade this way and that. "Could be that Crovan's right."

"What do *you* think?"

Revekah flipped the dagger's point skyward. "I think I'm Tressian, even if those inbreds in the north have forgotten that. First of the Emperor's Immortals sets foot over the mountains gets my steel in his heart. But plenty agree with Crovan. They're tired, Josiri. They want a way out. They think the Hadari will give them one."

"A year. Eighteen months. We'll be ready."

"You said that last year," said Anastacia. "And the year before. And the year before that. Dawntithes come and Dawntithes go. And still you wait."

"She's right," said Revekah. "There'll never be a perfect time. You've worked wonders these last few years – even Crovan acknowledges that."

"I did little more than bring you together. Kept you focused on the goal."

"You've brought us hope. Leadership. If you step out of the shadows, others will follow."

Josiri scowled, lost in memories of clandestine meetings. The fear of discovery. The elation of new alliances, and growing opportunity. The fear returning as the prospect of uprising brought with it the spectre of defeat.

"Too many still think I'm collaborating with the Council."

"All the more reason to end this pretence. I'll vouch for you. So will Crovan. You'll prove the rest through actions."

Josiri strove to ignore that familiar, gnawing frustration. "The Council will crack down harder than ever. Makrov's already talking about another exodus."

Revekah's eyes flashed. "Good. It'll remind our people of what they've already lost. They'll rise up in their thousands before the first transport ship sails north."

"My mother thought the same. And look what happened to her. We're not ready."

Josiri paused. Was that true? Or was he speaking out of fear? A Trelan had led hundreds to their deaths less than a generation ago. His failure would seal the Southshires' fate. It weighed on his conscience. Never more so than in the long, dark hours before the dawn when Anastacia was snoring.

His mother had spoken of the loneliness of leadership, of holding sway over decisions no other could make. As a boy, he'd thought it nothing. As a young man struggling with Zanya's aftermath, he'd dismissed her sentiment as arrogance. Only now did he feel the aching truth.

If only he'd someone to confide in. Dignity forbade he confess his fears to Revekah or Crovan. Anastacia wouldn't understand. For all that she appeared mortal flesh – for all the warmth of her embrace – she never grasped concepts of uncertainty, and consequence. Maybe that was why she fascinated him so.

Perhaps he should have confessed the truth to Calenne. At least then the burden would be shared. But no. She'd made her decision. He'd have to make his. Before events made it for him.

But there was time yet. Or so he prayed.

"We're not ready," he repeated. "The Republic's done too good a job of keeping the people docile. *I've* done too good a job. We need to shake them from complacency first. I need you to understand that. And I need you to convince Crovan."

"Of course." Disappointment coursed thick through Revekah's voice. "I stood with your mother. My loyalty's yours until the day I die. But when that day comes I want to face it free, not hiding in the woods, haunted by what might have been."

Anastacia's lips curled into a sneer, though she had the good sense to say nothing.

Josiri laid a hand on Revekah's shoulder. "You won't. The Phoenix will rise. You'll be there to see it. I promise."

"And the Hadari?"

He stared up at the moon. Were the Hadari even now pleading with Ashana for swift victory in the Southshires? Everything had its reflection. Night and day. Ashana and Lumestra. Empire and Republic. All save the Southshires. Where did they belong? And what part did Josiri Trelan have to play?

"The Hadari remain the Council's problem, until they become ours."

Revekah set her hand over his, her bony grip firm. "I suppose that will have to do. But you didn't venture out here to offer a pledge to an old woman. What did you want of Crovan?"

Josiri blinked. Lost in the perils and possibilities of the future, he'd quite forgotten. His wants seemed trivial – even childish – when set against the prospect of invasion. But perhaps – just perhaps – they were precisely what was needed.

"To ask a favour," he said. "It concerns Makrov."

"Our good archimandrite?" A smile gleamed. "I'm listening."

Everything chafed. The shirt, the leather hunter's coat. The britches ... the britches most of all. Melanna longed for silken battle-robes. Even one of the embroidered dresses she wore when taking her place alongside her royal peers in the Hadari Golden Court. The latter wouldn't have been practical among the briars and branches, but at least she'd have been comfortable. She couldn't conjure how Tressians marched in such constricting garb, much less fought battles.

Melanna was to do neither that night. This was merely another step in familiarising herself with the lay of the land. It was more than her father had sanctioned, but it was far less than she longed for. She enjoyed more freedom than any other princessa before her – let alone one of her tender eighteen winters.

Branches crackled on the darkened slopes. Too much and too often to be creatures of the night. The wind bore voices through the moonlit trees. Urgent. Strident. Pained.

Melanna crouched, hand on the dagger at her belt. She'd have preferred a sword. Alas, such was denied to her.

Motionless, she let the sounds weave colour and form into the silvered nightscape, savouring the soft, damp fragrance of disturbed soil. Four Tressians. Maybe five. Walking with their usual graceless tread. Following the streambed at the hill's foot, two score paces distant. Not arrayed as hunters – at least, not hunting her. Ashana be praised for that small mercy.

The commotion moved off to the west. Good sense dictated she withdraw. Garbed as a Tressian though she was, there was no hiding the olive skin that was so rare in the Republic but so common beyond its eastern border, nor her loose, black tresses. She refused to plait her hair in the style of Tressian nobility, let alone crop it in the fashion of their pauper-class. Were she taken, her captors would soon deem *what* she was, even if exactly *who* remained beyond their wit.

But then Melanna had never been one for caution, even that born of good sense.

She threaded her way through the undergrowth, skirting tangled or muddied paths in favour of ground that would bear no sign of her passage. An old game, practised as a child beneath the eaves of the sprawling forest of Fellhallow.

A thin cry and a crash of branches heralded the hunt's end. Dark shapes converged on a fallen man. He lay on heels and hands in a tangle of ivy, scarlet robes muddied and torn, and his heavy jowls taut with rage. Misplaced defiance when confronted by four drawn swords.

"Wolf's-heads!" The man's fury did nothing to hide a northwealder's immaculate nasal diction. "You'll hang for this!"

Laughter pealed through the night.

"Brave words, my lord archimandrite." The woman shouted to be heard above her fellows. "You weren't quite so bold in the fight."

Keeping low, Melanna crept towards the confrontation and sheltered behind a stump. The speaker was an older woman; thin, with cropped white hair and a patchwork phoenix tabard belted tight across her chest. Her companions were men, heavyset and rough-shaven. They waited on the woman's lead, expectant and respectful. Melanna envied her that. In Tressia, a daughter was every bit as respected as a son, not a commodity wrapped in damask.

"I am a servant of Lumestra, not a soldier." The man spoke with haughty pride.

The old woman's sword-tip tapped the underside of his chin. "I know who you are, Arzro Makrov. You've blood enough on your hands for a hundred soldiers. Someday, that debt will come due, *eminence*."

"Better it be now," muttered another wolf's-head. "Save the bother later."

Agreement rumbled about the group.

The woman shook her head. "Kill him, and they'll send another. No shortage of worthies."

A wolf's-head stalked closer to the man, a grim smile on his lips. "All of 'em bleed."

"No." The woman's tone brooked no argument. "There's more than one way to deliver a message."

"I still say we kill him."

"And if they send Viktor Akadra in his place?" The woman shook her head. "What then?"

The wolf's-head spat. His face paled beneath its thick stubble. "Then we kill him, too."

"You're a fool."

"Then why'd you have us do this?"

The woman grinned. "Why else? For the coin in his saddlebags. And because even so humble a functionary as his excellency can be humbled further." She turned her gaze on Makrov. "Strip."

A muscle danced in Makrov's cheek. "I'll do no such thing."

The woman flicked her wrist. The sword-point prodded the fleshy folds of the archimandrite's chin. "You will, or I'll have my lads assist. And they'll be a sight rougher."

Quivering with anger, Makrov rose to his feet. Fingers fumbled at heavy buttons, and scarlet robes tumbled into the mud. Embroidered waistcoat and cotton shirt followed.

"And the rest, my lord." The woman shrugged. "Let's give Ashana a good view. Not often she's granted clear sight of one of her sister's blessed priests."

Makrov, sword-point still at his throat, fumbled with boots and britches. Melanna looked on in morbid fascination and wondered if the archimandrite would make further protest. He did not, but the gleam in his eye promised retribution.

Woollen underclothes joined the growing pile. The woman withdrew her sword. "There. That wasn't so hard, was it?"

The archimandrite shot her a look of pure poison but said nothing. Even stark naked and shivering, he clung to dignity.

The woman pointed away downhill. "Well, off you go. Steer clear of the villages. Don't want to scare the children, do we?"

The slap of sword on buttock sent the archimandrite lurching away.

Even before he was lost to sight, the laughing wolf's-heads began bundling up the discarded clothes. Leaving them to it, Melanna slipped away uphill. The night was young, and she was determined not to waste it.

Three

The city of Tressia, bastion of the north and heart of the Republic, lay cloaked beneath the gloom of night. Barnacle-crusted krai-kons stood waist-deep and motionless in the dockside's tidal waters. The evening sun, still a-glimmer through the Silverway tavern's leaded windows at the first pull, had long since slunk beneath the horizon. The vibrant bustle of day had retreated alongside. The great city was subdued, and its river wharves a haunt for dubious endeavours. It was no place for the sons and daughters of quality to seek their pleasures, and it was therefore inevitable that many did so.

Malachi Reveque stared into the brimming tankard, awash with that peculiar caution born of inebriation. Jeers, arguments and snatches of dockers' shanties burst from the fug of conversation and echoed beneath the Silverway's sunken beams. Malachi knew it would continue well into morning.

As would he, if he wasn't careful.

"I should be getting home." He strained to be heard over the hubbub. "I promised Lilyana I'd not make a night of this."

Across the table, Kasamor leaned back in his chair. Eyes widened in mock affront. "What? You'd leave me to celebrate alone?"

Rosa snorted and fixed him with a cold stare. "Thanks."

Kasamor waved an airy hand in dismissal. "I love you as a sister, but there's a bond between men that you couldn't begin to understand. Especially when that bond is tempered in battle, as was ours." Matter settled, he raised his tankard for a generous swallow.

Rosa's expression didn't flicker. "I see. When *did* you last stand your place in the line, Malachi?"

Long enough ago to know he'd no place there. Malachi winced. How had he ended up the villain? Not that it was a surprise. United, they four were the closest of friends. Divided by absence – as they were that evening by perennial lateness – and conversation turned inevitably to contest.

"I fight with words these days."

"And I fight with steel." Rosa leaned low across the table. "In fact, I recall my sword saving Lord Kiradin's hide at Tarvallion. And at Tregga's Dike."

Kasamor bristled. "And Lord Kiradin remembers *someone's* effusive thanks after that bloody business on Fellhallow's southern edge. Might it have been you, oh storied Reaper of the Ravonn?"

"Hah! My point precisely. You and I have shared a score of battlefields. Malachi hasn't so much as held a sword in ten years." She cracked a sour smile. "Tell me again how our bond is the lesser."

Knight of the Republic though Rosa was, she wielded her wits every bit as skilfully as her sword. She'd one day serve the Republic well on the Grand Council – if she could bear to forgo the green surcoat of the Essamere chapterhouse and her chamfered armour for a velvet gown. That she'd abandoned the former for the subtleties of civilian garb was a rare honour. She seemed softer without steel, but Malachi wasn't fooled. He knew just how many Hadari she'd sent into the mists. And besides, even now the sword-belt remained. No amount of reason could have persuaded her to strut about unarmed.

Kasamor would never reach council rank. He'd a tendency to speak without thinking, strong drink or no. It was part of his charm. But on this one occasion, Kasamor held his tongue and glowered at Rosa. She arched a knowing eyebrow.

Malachi stifled a grin. The lines of battle were shifting. The *kind* thing would be to deflect Rosa's ire. Then again, Kasamor's escape would only hasten Malachi's own turn as underdog. So he glugged a mouthful of ale, wiped his lips, and stoked the fires.

"You mustn't mind him," he said. "Kasamor's worried he'll not resist your charms if I leave you alone."

Joking aside, Rosa and Kasamor would have made a handsome couple. They shared hair the colour of ripened wheat, and eyes as pale and blue as the winter skies. Rosa's face was that of a divine serathi – if that serathi was given to scowling. Kasamor had a lantern jaw and heavy brow that echoed portraits of kings long dead. But they'd been friends too long. They all had. Any lingering attraction lay buried beneath a lifetime of faults and foibles witnessed at close hand.

Malachi was content with his own unremarkable looks. Even if his dark hair was already flecked with grey. A honed mind was a far more valuable tool than a handsome face, and lasted longer.

Rosa snorted. "I'd sooner kiss a goat."

Malachi grinned into his tankard.

"And why not?" mused Kasamor. "We all know you've a thing for beards."

"Just as we all know that you can't grow a beard worthy of the name."

Kasamor slumped against the chair's backrest. He clapped his hands across his chest in mock pain. "Your words . . . They're a blade in my heart."

Rosa chuckled. "It's a large target. You'll survive."

Hands still to his chest, Kasamor closed his eyes. "Not so. Even now, I hear the flutter of sable wings. Lumestra sends her handmaidens. They'll weep golden tears as they carry me off."

"I'm not sure the serathi weep tears for anyone, much less for a man." Rosa hooked an eyebrow. "Then again, you're barely a man, are you?"

Kasamor's eyes flickered open. "Is that curiosity I hear? Alas, my dear, beautiful sister-at-arms, you've missed your opportunity. I'm pledged to higher things."

With an exasperated sigh she turned to stare out across the room. "You're impossible."

"That's what I've been trying to tell you." Kasamor grew unusually sincere. "My heart belongs to another."

Rosa offered no response. Enough, Malachi decided, was enough.

"So you're still going through with it?" he asked.

"Without a flicker of hesitation." Kasamor straightened up. "My mother's mood will soften once she meets Calenne. How could it not?"

That aspiration struck Malachi as totally unfounded. A son saw much that remained hidden from acquaintances, but in this case ...

"Is your mother much given to softening?" Rosa's expression could have been carved from stone.

"On occasion. Why, I once saw her smile at Marek."

"Her steward?" Malachi tried to picture Lady Ebigail Kiradin favouring a servant with anything resembling warmth. He gave up. There were limits even to imagination. "I don't believe it."

"It's true." If Kasamor was at all offended on his mother's behalf, nothing of it showed. "He happened upon one of the indentured maids making off with the silverware. Girl looked like death by the time he was done scolding her."

"Ah." Now *that* did sound like the sort of thing to coax a smile from Lady Kiradin. "I wouldn't have thought your mother would have trusted a southwealder near the silver."

"She hasn't, not since. Stripped them all of their papers and threw them onto the streets. They'll be in Dregmeet now, hiding from the constabulary."

Malachi scowled. Indentured southwealders weren't *technically* slaves. Nonetheless, the exodus-brand on the palm meant they couldn't take paid work without papers. At best, Ebigail Kiradin had doomed her servants to a life of starvation and criminality.

"Hold on ..." Rosa grunted. "Are you drawing comparison between your betrothed and Marek, or your betrothed and a thieving servant?"

Kasamor's lip twisted. "I speak merely to my mother's occasional lightness of character."

"One smile. And you think Calenne Trelan can coax forth another?" Rosa shook her head. "You must be in love to be so blind. I'm surprised your mother hasn't disowned you."

"Disown me? Her favourite son?"

"Her *only* son," said Malachi.

Kasamor brushed the detail aside. "Some friends you are, dousing my happiness. I shan't allow it. Calenne is to be my wife, and I the happiest man in the Republic."

Malachi let the matter drop. He felt more than a little mean-spirited for needling his friend so. Whatever the complications of Calenne Trelan's southwealder heritage, Kasamor was besotted. After two betrothals ended by Hadari spears, he deserved a good marriage. And if it was one founded in genuine affection rather than in furtherance of a dynasty, then Malachi envied him.

Rosa drained her tankard. "It's my round. Another?"

Malachi stared into the remains of his ale. He should have left hours ago. Now he'd face a lecture and a polite smile undercut by disdain. Easier to face them after another drink.

"Sure."

Kasamor lurched to his feet. "Put your coin away. We celebrate in style, and at my expense. In fact ... " He paused, brow furrowed in thought.

Malachi caught Rosa's eye, but the moment of shared realisation came too late.

" ... I shall buy a drink for anyone who'll offer a toast to Calenne Trelan," Kasamor bellowed. "The jewel of the Southshires, and the brightest star in any sky!"

The hubbub gave way to a chorus of cheers. Fists and tankards hammered at tables in approval. Kasamor grinned broadly. He clambered atop his chair and drank in the adulation. Empty tankard in hand, he goaded the Silverway's clientele to greater uproar, conducting their raucous clamour as music sprung from an orchestra.

Malachi released a sigh of relief. For a moment, he'd worried that ...

"Toast your southwealder whore elsewhere."

The cheers fell away.

Kasamor froze mid-gesture. "I'm sorry, but I didn't quite catch that."

"Then I'll say it again, and clearer."

Malachi twisted in the chair, striving to identify the speaker. There, in a booth by the crooked stairs. Nearer his own thirty-five summers than Rosa and Kasamor's lesser tally. No intoxication in her face, nor in her husky voice. He'd seen her before, at council. Not in the Privy Council chamber, but attending Lord Tarev. His daughter ... but what was her name?

The woman stood. Like Rosa, she'd forgone a bare-shouldered dress for a close-fitting blouse, jerkin and trews. Practical garb for a practical woman – especially when slumming it on the dockside.

"I lost my mother and a sister at Zanya. You want to toast a Trelan, do it in the gutter where you both belong."

Kasamor jumped down and slammed his tankard onto the table. Malachi's memory snapped into place. Aske Tarev ... that was the woman's name. But not for much longer, if something wasn't done. Malachi rose a trifle more unsteadily than he'd have liked and blocked Kasamor's advance.

"Then your kin sacrificed to make the Republic whole," he told Aske. "Our divisions died with Katya Trelan. Let them remain in the past."

"Malachi Reveque, ever the conciliator," sneered Aske. "You don't speak for my family."

Kasamor growled. "And *you* owe my betrothed an apology. Must I tear it from you?"

Malachi set a hand against his chest. "Ignore her."

To his relief, Kasamor halted.

There were too many swords in the Silverway. Kasamor could only count on Rosa's in addition to his own. Judging by the stony faces at Aske's table, she had three supporters. As to the rest? Most of the clientele wouldn't risk getting caught up in a noble's brawl. Probably. But you could never be sure once the blood was up.

"Rosa?" said Kasamor.

Alone of the three, Rosa still sat in her chair. Her crossed legs and propped elbow gave the impression of a woman taking her ease. However, her eyes darted back and forth, weighing up the odds.

"This would be better discussed outside. I like this tavern. I wouldn't want to see it damaged."

Translation: Rosa didn't care for their prospects if it came to a straight fight. Malachi wasn't sure how he felt about that. The chances of walking away from a tavern brawl were much higher than a back alley duel. The latter would spare Malachi and Rosa from injury, but it might cost Kasamor his life.

"Well?" Kasamor folded his arms and levelled a stare at Aske.

There was no amusement in his voice, no trace of the boisterous suitor of earlier. His smile belonged to a wolf. Malachi shuddered. This was the side of Kasamor the Hadari saw.

Aske didn't reply at first, her watchful eyes taking their own measure of the odds. But the outcome was never really in doubt. You didn't walk away from a challenge, however coded. Not with so many witnesses to hand and reputation at stake.

"Have it your way."

Four

By unspoken accord, they settled on the alley between the Silverway's dray yard and the warehouse behind. Far enough from the roadway's firestone lanterns so as not to draw a constable's eye. Close enough that the low rush of the river weir rumbled beneath every word spoken.

Rosa halted a pace or two into the alley. She set her shoulders against the wall and shooed the others along. "Well? Get this over with."

Malachi cast a nervous eye towards the river. "You heard her. I'd rather not be caught."

Kasamor shook his head. "You're always so concerned about your reputation."

"I'm only here to stop you doing something foolish."

Kasamor offered a wry smile. "Too late. And I'm not fighting for my reputation, but Calenne's."

Might be he even believed it, Malachi decided. Pride was a complicated burden. Yet, there was a rare lightness in Kasamor's voice. Perhaps this *was* all about Calenne. Malachi only hoped the young woman was grateful for the risks taken in her name.

Malachi kept his thoughts to himself. His attention he spared for Aske's group, deeper into the alley. Three others accompanied her. Two in the crimson and black surcoats of Tarev hearthguards, and the last in plain black garb. It struck Malachi as unfair that she'd brought so many, but that was the problem with such duels. The ritual had been born on distant battlefields and carried home by soldiers on leave. There were no rules, just a loose acceptance of what was to unfold.

Kasamor clapped him on the shoulder and set off down the alleyway. On reaching the midpoint, he spread his hands wide, sword still in its sheath.

"Right! How are we doing this? Three touches, or will only blood shake an apology loose?"

Aske's only reply was a shriek of rage. Sword naked in her hand, she charged, boots thudding through refuse and horse-dung.

Malachi glanced at Rosa. She shrugged, eyes dark and thoughtful.

Kasamor stood arms outspread and sword scabbarded, seemingly frozen in place. At the last moment, he sidestepped. Aske's sword flashed past. A heartbeat later so did Aske herself, further hastened by the heel of Kasamor's boot against her rump.

"So you've no manners at all?" Kasamor asked. "Care to try again?"

Aske snarled and hurled herself into another headlong charge. It ended much the same as the first.

Kasamor drew his sword and cut at the air in sweeping circles. "Is this how your family fought at Zanya? No wonder they're not here to speak for themselves."

"Don't humiliate her, Kasamor," muttered Malachi. "It'll only make matters worse."

Aske spat. "You dare insult my family?"

Swords clashed, the blades locking. Aske twisted away. She struck again, trading high blows for a flurry of shallow cuts at Kasamor's waist. He parried them all, then thrust at Aske's belly. She stumbled back, breathing hard.

"You'll have to do better than that," mocked Kasamor. "Why, I crossed blades with Kai Saran himself less than a month ago."

Aske feinted left, then thrust right. Kasamor ignored the former and sidestepped the latter.

"All that strength," he continued, "and he couldn't land a blow. Sent him back to the border with his tail between his legs."

"Is that true?" Malachi asked Rosa, his attention still on the duel.

She snorted. "Doubt it. The Hadari are too busy worrying over their dying emperor to make trouble. I'll bet Kasamor never left his tent the whole time he was out there, much less crossed swords with the emperor's son."

The blades clashed again. Kasamor, no longer content to defend, forced Aske into a series of unsteady parries. Even to Malachi's inexperienced eye, there was a jarring difference to the two techniques. Kasamor's arcs wove beautiful flashes of moonlight in the gloomy alley. Aske's responses were jerky and uneven.

"This isn't right," Rosa muttered.

"He's better than her, that's all." Malachi shrugged. "He's better than most people."

"No," she said. "This is different. Mind and body are fighting one another."

That was the trouble with Rosa. Sometimes she needed decoding. "She's not trying to win?"

"Or maybe she's stalling." The corner of Rosa's lip twitched. "Or maybe it's something else."

Malachi looked again, but if there *was* something deeper, he lacked the eye for it. But the expectation radiating from Aske's companions struck him as misplaced. Aske had no hope of winning. The only question was how far she'd push before capitulation. Unless ...

"The others," he murmured. "They're waiting for something. This is a distraction."

Rosa frowned. "Find a patrol. I'll keep an eye on things."

Malachi opened his mouth to protest, but closed it again as he realised the sense of her suggestion. He'd be no use in a fight anyway.

Four shadows crowded the end of the alleyway, blotting out the weir behind and blocking hope of retreat.

"Too late," Malachi breathed.

Rosa pushed off the wall. Her fingers drummed on the hilt of her sword. "Get behind me." She raised her voice. "This is a private matter."

The shadows ignored her. Strides lengthened, bringing crimson and black surcoats closer, the leader outpacing his companions.

"Stand down," he bellowed, drawing his sword. "No need for you to die as well."

Rosa shook her head sadly. "Oh my lad, you've no idea how much trouble you're in."

"Suit yourself."

The leader's sword flashed out. Rosa swept it aside. Her free hand closed around his throat. Her left heel hooked behind his ankle. His back struck the dunged cobbles, a strangled cry ending in a *huff* of expelled air.

Rosa slammed down her boot and gazed sedately at a trio of hearth-guards who were a touch paler than they'd been before. "Who's next?"

Malachi tore his attention back to the duel and cupped his hands to his mouth. "Kasamor! You've been set up!"

"What?"

Kasamor glanced back over his shoulder, good humour vanished. Aske seized on his distraction. With a cry of triumph, she thrust at his spine.

Kasamor spun around. He teased Aske's blade aside and struck it from her hand. A heartbeat later he had her pinned against the warehouse wall. He had a generous handful of her expensive blouse bunched in his fingers, and his sword at her throat.

He spared a glance for her companions from the Silverway, now advancing along the alley with blades drawn. "Stay back!"

The foremost, a sallow-faced man with a stubble beard and simple black garb, shrugged. "If Lady Tarev dies, so do your friends."

Rosa reached Malachi's side. Her blade dared the remaining newcomers to push their fortune. They hung back, content to wait, or ordered to do so.

For the first time in many years, Malachi wished he'd not abandoned the art of the sword. If nothing else, he should have been carrying a weapon . . . Sure, he'd only have gotten in the way, but perhaps that was better than being *entirely* useless.

"You can't kill a councillor and two knights of the Republic," he said. "Not without consequence."

"If there were witnesses, maybe," croaked Aske.

"And it's not all of you who have to die," said the sallow man. "You can walk away."

Malachi snorted. "You'd let us leave? Witnesses?"

"It's your word against Lady Aske's. How much is your word worth, Lord Reveque? Valuable enough to make a case for murder before the Council?"

Malachi scowled. Aske's father had too much influence for any such accusation to succeed. Aske would deny involvement. The violence would be dismissed as the work of opportunistic ne'er-do-wells.

The sallow man was right. Malachi hated it, but he was right. One life or three, and no justice for anyone. He felt sick; sick, and angrier than he had in years.

Kasamor growled in frustration. Letting his sword-point dip to the cobbles, he released Aske. "Never known someone go to so much trouble to win a duel. You want to tell me why?"

Aske massaged her throat and reclaimed her sword. "You already know why. My mother was three days dying from her wounds. My sister's body was never found. We'd nothing to bury. Her voice echoes through the family vault, but I can't give her peace."

"Calenne was a child when that happened. She wasn't even at Zanya."

"Sins of the kith. Let her filthy bloodline rot in the south. It will never hold a seat on the Council."

"Sounds like my reason for dying's far nobler than yours for killing me." Kasamor chuckled, but despite his apparent mirth, a rare note of fatalism crept into his tone, betraying a decision made. For a man like Kasamor, preserving his own skin came a distant second to saving those of his friends. "You might want to think on that before you go bragging to your sister's ghost."

"Kasamor?" Rosa's eyes didn't leave her opponents' swords. "I'm not agreeing to this."

"Not your decision, Rosa," he replied. "Set down your blade."

She swore under her breath and let it fall.

"But let's be clear." Kasamor leaned close to Aske, his voice taking on a most un-Kasamoresque harshness. "You're not done hearing ghosts. I'll make whatever pact the Raven demands. My cyraeth will be back for your soul before my body's cold. It'll haunt you as only a restless spirit can. And you, my bitter little hag, will wish you'd never heard my name."

Aske flinched. Her throat bobbed.

Kasamor straightened. His sword clattered to the ground.

"Are we doing this or not? It's not polite to keep a man waiting."

A yelp sounded at the mouth of the alley. The *thud* of a falling body followed, and a choked scream close behind. Malachi's anger and shame bubbled away, replaced by giddy elation. Beside him, he felt Rosa tense as the sallow man fumbled for his sword.

Kasamor laughed and shook his head. "Decided to join us, did you?"

Even bereft of armour, Viktor Akadra cut an imposing figure in the confines of the passage. A head taller than Kasamor, nearly two taller than Malachi himself, he radiated unconcern. A hearthguard dangled like a toy from one massive fist. The fellow squalled and struggled, though Viktor seemed unaware he was even under attack. He cuffed his captive about the head and let the unconscious fellow fall atop his luckless companion. The black velvet of his cloak twitched at his heels.

"Some of us had duties."

Aske Tarev's face went ashen grey. Of course she knew of Viktor's reputation. It was a rare soul that didn't. The hero of Gathra's Field. The man who'd slain the traitor Katya Trelan. The Council's champion.

The last of Rosa's erstwhile opponents spun to face the new threat.

Rosa dived for her sword. The sallow man started forward, hearthguards at his back. Aske set her sword-point to Kasamor's belly.

"Don't even think about ... "

Malachi pushed off the wall and flung his arms about Aske's shoulders. Impact knocked the sword from her hand, and most of the breath from his body. The alley lurched. Then the strike of filthy cobbles sucked the rest of Malachi's breath away. But still he clung tight, and weathered blows from elbows and boots as she fought to break loose. For the first moment since entering the alley, he wasn't useless.

The moment passed, as all moments do – this one with an elbow to the gut that left him sucking for breath as commotion reigned about him. With a cry of triumph, Aske scrambled free on hands and knees.

Vision blurring, Malachi crawled in pursuit. He tried not to think about *what* he was crawling through. As Aske's hand closed around her sword, he sprang. The blade hissed over his head and, for the second time that night, they went down in a tangle of arms and legs. This time, Malachi ended up on top.

A hand closed about the scruff of his collar, hauling him up and away.

"Easy, councillor," said Viktor. "Her comrades have fled. She's had enough."

Malachi hadn't the breath to reply.

"Enough?" Kasamor stalked back down the alley. Of the sallow man and his two hearthguards, there was no sign. "Not nearly."

He kicked Aske's sword out of reach and hoisted her upright. "Trying to kill me? That's one thing. But threatening my friends?"

A hard shove sent Aske stumbling against the wall. Her eyes shone in defiance of Kasamor's sword at her throat. Malachi had seen that look in the Council chamber many times. She'd gambled and lost. Of course, it was a rare day when a councillor staked his or her life as she had.

"Let her go." To Malachi's surprise, the words were his.

Kasamor rounded on him, eyes ablaze. "She tried to kill you."

"And she failed." The justification rang hollow in Malachi's ears, so he strove for a better one. "Hand her over to the constabulary. She'll stand trial."

Kasamor shook his head. "You believe that?"

Thundering boots heralded Rosa's return from deeper along the alley. Cheeks flushed from exertion, she stumbled to a halt. "Lost them halfway to the Hayadra Grove. Could be anywhere by now. What did I miss?"

Viktor folded his arms and propped a shoulder against the dray yard wall. "Kasamor's about to murder Lady Tarev. Or maybe he isn't."

"You think I shouldn't?" The harshness had returned to Kasamor's voice. "Would you?"

"She'd already be dead." Malachi couldn't tell whether Viktor was joking. His friend's face seldom gave away more than he wanted, and the old scar on his left cheek lent bleak mirth to most expressions. "But we're talking about you."

"Do it, or don't," hissed Aske. "I'm not your toy. I'll not beg."

"She's right, Kas." Rosa aimed a kick at one of the unconscious hearthguards. "If we linger, someone's going to see something we'd rather they didn't."

By Malachi's reckoning, that was one vote for Aske's death, one against and ... whatever Viktor's opinion was. Did he alone see that killing Aske would only worsen matters? But Kasamor had the casting vote, and the sword, and a measure of wounded pride into the bargain. Appealing to that pride might achieve what reason would not.

"She owes you an apology," Malachi muttered.

Kasamor's head dipped. He gave a weary snort. "She does, doesn't she?"

The low rumble of Viktor's laughter echoed along the alley. Rosa rolled her eyes. Malachi eased a sigh.

Kasamor's eyes met Aske's. "So which is it to be, Lady Tarev? The apology, or the sword?"

She swallowed. "I . . . I apologise . . . "

Kasamor's sword twitched. A trickle of blood broke Aske's skin.

"'I apologise for naming Calenne Trelan a whore'," he said.

"That's how this started?" muttered Viktor.

Malachi nodded. "That's how it started."

Viktor grunted and withdrew.

"I apologise for naming Calenne Trelan a whore." Aske's defiance gave way to a glare of pure venom.

Kasamor warmed to his theme. "'And I see now that jealousy guided my tongue more than any good sense.'"

"And I see now that jealousy guided my tongue more than any good sense." Aske ground out the words from behind gritted teeth.

Kasamor leaned closer. "Now, take off your sword belt. Then you can go."

Hands fumbled at the buckle. Belt and scabbard smacked to the ground. Kasamor grinned and lowered his sword.

"My thanks, Lady Tarev, for a wonderful evening."

Face once again impassive, her shoulders set beneath a burden of fragile dignity, Aske shoved her way past Kasamor.

Viktor's hand brought her to a halt. He stooped and whispered into her ear, speaking so softly that Malachi couldn't make out the words. Then Viktor straightened, and Aske was on her way once more – if a touch more unsteady than before.

"What did you tell her?" Rosa asked.

"The price to be paid for another attempt." He shrugged. "I believe we reached an understanding."

Laughing, Kasamor reclaimed Aske's sword and scabbard and held both out to Malachi. "Here. A trophy well-won. And a reminder that you shouldn't walk the streets without one."

Malachi hesitated, then took them. The sword fitted the scabbard to perfection, and the belt sat well enough at his waist. It felt strange, like he'd stepped back into an old life – one he'd been happy to leave.

"So what happens now?"

"Now," Viktor said, "Kasamor owes me a debt. He can make payment in ale."

Maladas, 26th day of Wellmarch

The Dark is never far from our hearts. It feeds on our
pride, and on our fear. It tempts us to folly couched
in the illusion of greatness, and hatred cloaked in
devout proclamation.

from the sermons of Konor Belenzo

Five

King's Gate bustled with colour and sound. Carts rumbled to market through the maze of cramped, timber-framed townhouses, or returned to outer provinces with the fruits of trades settled. Priests strode in solemn procession, golden robes gleaming. Craftsmen, soldiers and indentured servants hastened to and fro. The lifeblood of Tressia. Malachi just wished it could all have been accomplished a shade or two *quieter*. His outward path had taken him past the Essamere muster-fields – with all the inevitable shouting and clamour that was as much a part of soldiery as spilt blood – and he'd hoped for respite at his destination.

The morning after had arrived too soon on the heels of the night before. He felt as though Lumestra's sunlight shone only for the express purpose of searing his weary eyes. The towering stones of King's Gate offered blessed shelter from that assault. Alas, they offered none at all from the commotion of the morning's traffic. He wanted nothing more than to crawl back into bed and let the morning pass. But he saw his friends little enough as it was.

"You *have* remembered the ring?" asked Malachi.

Kasamor tapped a saddlebag. "What do you take me for?"

"A man who'd lose his own sword, were it not buckled to his side."

A wry smile. "True. But there are swords to be had all over the city. There's no replacing my grandmother's ring. Its sapphires will shine all the brighter on Calenne's hand."

"I still say you shouldn't ride until your head's clear," said Malachi.

Laughing, Kasamor reached down and patted him on the shoulder.

"Nothing like the wind on your cheeks to bring clarity. Besides, there's nothing wrong with my head. Don't project your own woes onto others."

Malachi grimaced. "Be kind. If I'd wanted taking to task, I'd have stayed home."

Kasamor leaned back in the saddle and shook his head. "Another quarrel with Lilyana?"

Rosa twitched her reins. Her steed side-stepped closer, unfazed by its heavy saddlebags. "And who can blame her? Malachi's a rake. Common knowledge."

Malachi snorted at the deadpan delivery. "It wasn't Lily. Sidara met me on the stairs. You know she refused – actually flat-out refused – to let me past until I apologised for making so much noise?"

Viktor's basso laughter joined the chorus, his amusement bright contrast to the shadow of his presence. Somehow he contrived to suck in the sunlight. How he tolerated the velvet cloak on so warm a day, Malachi couldn't conceive.

"So what did you do?" said Kasamor.

"What do you think I did? I apologised. Then I sent her back to bed and staggered off to sleep."

"Some councillor you are, losing an argument with your daughter."

Malachi sniffed. "Yielding with grace is a cornerstone of politics. It's her brother I feel sorry for. I suspect she'll bully Constans fearfully."

A column of soldiery marched past, the gold-frocked priest at their rear offering mournful hymn in a reedy voice. The officer at their head clenched a fist to her chest in salute. Viktor returned the gesture until she passed beneath the half-lowered portcullis.

"I didn't have to come out here, you know," said Malachi.

"Hah!" said Kasamor. "It's the very least you can do as you shan't be attending my wedding."

"We've been over this. I can't be spared. The Council's work is endless."

"The *Grand* Council's work is endless," Rosa offered drily. "You privy councillors live a rarefied existence. Wine and splendour all around."

Malachi ground his teeth, failing as usual in his attempt not to rise to the bait. "I'd love to boot some of my workload down to that talking shop. The state of the fleet. The corn levy. Conscription levels. Clemency for undocumented southwealders. And that's *before* we even get onto the subject of the war itself . . . "

Rosa held up a hand. "Please. Enough. You're a busy man. We understand."

"We're none of us idle." Viktor's swarthy features tightened in thought. "And Kasamor should be riding, while he can."

Kasamor frowned. "What do you mean?"

"That was the third company to march out this morning. A call to arms is coming." He heaved massive shoulders in a shrug. "But if you're on the road . . . "

Malachi frowned. "I'd know if a call to arms was in the offing."

"Only if a herald found you," said Viktor. "At this hour he'll seek you at the breakfast table, or in your bed. *Not* loitering at King's Gate."

Kasamor stared back through the marketplace towards the plaza, and the looming spires of the palace. "I should stay, then. Calenne will understand."

Viktor shook his head. "The Republic has thousands of soldiers to call upon. It will manage a few days without Kasamor Kiradin. It will be a chore, but we shall endure, all the same."

"He's right," said Rosa. "There's no shame in looking to your own happiness, this once."

Kasamor threw up his hands. "Well, if the Council's champion says as much, who am I to argue?"

"You always argue," said Malachi. "About everything."

"I do not." He grinned and turned to Rosa. "Still coming along?"

"Bad enough that no one in your family will stand witness. Your friends shouldn't abandon you." She arched an eyebrow. "*And* you should have someone to watch your back. Love has you blind. The Southshires are dangerous."

"Still carrying that torch?" Kasamor gaped in mock innocence. "I told you, I've eyes only for Calenne Trelan, and she for me."

She rolled her eyes. "Shut up and ride, before I change my mind."

His face blanked, save for a mischievous gleam about his eyes. "At your order, Lady Orova."

Kasamor offered a half-bow to Malachi, and a close-fisted salute to Viktor. "Until we meet again. Please do nothing foolish while I'm gone."

Hauling on his reins, he pushed his way into the crowds. Rosa gave a sharp nod of farewell and followed. Malachi watched until they passed through the thin line of tabarded toll-keepers, then turned aside.

"He gets worse."

"Everyone does," rumbled Viktor. "We either die young and foolish, or old and stubborn. It's the order of things."

Malachi shook his head. "And which am I?"

"Treasure your family, Malachi. No one is poorer than a man who knows his wealth only when it's lost."

He scowled. What did Viktor know of his marital quarrels? "It's not that simple."

"Nothing worthwhile ever is."

The clatter of hooves saved Malachi the trouble of a reply. A young man in a herald's silver trim reined his steed to a halt. He offered a hasty bow and held out an envelope, sealed with blue wax.

"Lord Reveque." The herald straightened. His eyes widened as they settled on Viktor. "Lord Akadra. Forgive the interruption, but I bear a summons."

Malachi took the envelope and slit it open. The spidery signature confirmed what the unbroken seal had already told him. He shot a glance at Viktor.

"Seems you were right, as always."

Viktor offered a mirthless smile.

"Are you coming?" Malachi asked.

"I might as well," he replied. "Better to hear first-hand than from my father."

Malachi pocketed the envelope and flashed a grin. "You should treasure your family, Viktor."

His only reply was a flat, basilisk stare – Viktor's customary response to any defeat.

The chamber encapsulated everything Viktor hated about the Republic.

The murky memory of morning sunshine was held at bay by oak-panelled walls and filtered to rich orange and gold by stained glass. Graven likenesses of councillors past gazed down at their successors from dusty escutcheons. Their expressions ranged from grim austerity to stark disappointment. A vast map, rendered in gilded oils by some long dead artist, graced the north wall. *The Ancient and Honourable Bounds of the Kingdom of Tressia.*

Those bounds were a good measure less generous in reality than on the map. The Republic of today commanded but a fraction of the territory of the kingdom whose name it bore, stretching roughly two score leagues south and east of the city's peninsula. The distant south, beyond the rebellious domain of Eskavord and the Grelyt River, had long ago been absorbed by the quarrelling Thrakkian thanes, while the outflung east had been claimed by the Hadari Empire's rapacious spread – though this was by no means without positive aspect, as it spared Tressia direct contact with the Ithna'jîm of Athreos, who commanded the arid lands beyond the Empire's south-eastern border.

That the Republic endured at all was as much tribute to the finest navies ever to roam the Western Ocean. Unable to make landing in what remained of the Tressian shoreland, invaders had to make dangerous assault across borders fortified by the regal decree.

The kings who had made such decrees were long gone, but their legacy remained. Tradition layered upon tradition, sealed away from the vibrant city. The squabble and barter of the markets, the tramping feet of soldiery mustered from barrack and chapterhouse; the cries of street-preachers and quarrelling children – even the chime of church bells struggled to reach the austere depths of the Council palace, and risk disturbance of those gathered therein.

Gold couldn't buy a seat at this table, nor did valorous action alone admit one through the door. Even blood – while important here as in all endeavours – held no guarantee. Only the approval of those already within granted access and leave to speak. To join the old men and women who dictated the fate of untold thousands without ever truly living among them; whose patronage made or broke others at will.

Near a hundred seats lined the Grand Council chamber on the floor below. A mere nine high-backed chairs sat around the Privy Council's gilded table. One had remained unoccupied since Lord Loramir had taken it upon himself to tour the borderlands. Neither his family nor the Council expected him to return. Two seats had sat empty for a decade. They served as gravestones of the Isidor and Lamakov bloodlines.

Until the estates were settled – a resolution that served no one on the Privy Council and was therefore ignored – the Council was left with a quorum of six.

Or more accurately, five and one councillor with half a voice. Viktor's seat alone had come neither from inheritance nor unfaltering approval. It was a gift given for a victory he wished he could unmake.

"It's worse than we feared. Emperor Ceredic Saran is dead."

Little of that fear showed through Hadon Akadra's wolfish anticipation. The death of a Hadari emperor could never be entirely a bad thing, whatever complications it offered. Though well past his sixtieth year, the elder Lord Akadra still cut a powerful figure. A physique hardened in battle had softened only a little to a councillor's comfortable life. His hair remained as black as Viktor's own, save for a burnishing of grey at the temples.

Lady Marest knotted cadaverous fingers in the Sign of the Sun. "May the Raven shred his bellicose soul."

"Indeed. But it would have been better for us all if he'd clung to life a good while longer."

Viktor's father returned his gaze to the bow-legged meeting table, a flicker of disdain stifled almost as soon as it surfaced. Viktor suspected no one else had noticed, but he'd expected it. Mutual loathing of Abitha Marest was one of the few things that brought them together. The old woman clung to power as grimly as to life, and with just as little obvious benefit to others. Her silvery-white hair and frail, uncertain movements gave her the aspect of one who'd already one foot set in the mists. Then again, Viktor couldn't recall a time when she'd seemed young and vibrant. Perhaps piety *did* bring its own rewards. If an interminable, withered existence could be considered such.

"A heathen's death is always timely," Lady Marest replied primly. "Ceredic's passing is Lumestra's gift."

"Oh please, spare us your homilies. You may flatter the goddess in your own time."

Dissembling wasn't in Lady Kiradin's nature. Nor was restraint. She addressed highborn and low with equal respect, which was to say none at all – save for when she wished something in return, which was rare.

Her steel-grey hair and patrician profile perfectly matched the image of a Tressian matriarch, and if she didn't care for overt displays of faith, she nonetheless clung to tradition with a granite grip. For all that Ebigail Kiradin was Kasamor's mother, there was little to connect them. Where he was warm and generous, she was cold and calculating. It was said – though never in Lady Kiradin's earshot – that her late husband had gone gladly into the mists, for they were surely warmer than his marriage bed.

"I see no flattery in simple truth, Ebigail," replied Lady Marest.

Lady Kiradin's sneer grew somehow drier. "So we're all painfully aware."

Malachi cleared his throat. Never a tall man, he seemed smaller than ever in this auspicious company – as if he wished to shrink from sight. "Forgive me, but we're certain Ceredic's gone? Our spies have been wrong before, and the borderers have never been reliable when it comes to tidings."

"Not this time," Viktor's father replied. "We've three witnesses to his corpse getting carried into the mists. The Last Ride, they call it ... "

"Heathen nonsense," muttered Lady Marest.

Lord Akadra ignored the interruption. "And now every shadowthorn with a claim on the Imperial throne is looking to prove themselves in battle."

Viktor's lip twitched in distaste. *Shadowthorn.* An old insult, born from the myth that the Hadari had crawled forth from Fellhallow's rich, Dark-tainted soil. That they were not given life by the heavenly sisters Lumestra and Ashana, but by twisted, root-woven Jack. Too many of the older generation, prophesying a day when the Republic would be forcibly absorbed into the Empire, took shelter in strange prejudice. Viktor, though a patriot, considered himself pragmatic enough to recognise that the history between the two realms was complicated at best.

"So let them batter at one another," sniffed Lady Marest.

"I doubt they'll oblige," said Viktor's father. "We're a much more tempting target. Fifty years we held Ceredic at the border. What better way to prove worthiness of his throne than by doing what he could not?"

"This isn't conjecture, is it?"

Malachi's words echoed Viktor's own reading of the situation. His father was a pragmatist. Guesswork he derided as sloppy; chance as a fit companion only for the gambler, or the fool. For him to offer up a hypothetical future was as uncharacteristic as for him to utter a word of praise.

"I wish it were." Lord Tarev gave his beard an absent-minded tug. Viktor wondered if his dear daughter had yet informed him of her recent humiliation. "Their armies are marching on the shire lands."

"So soon?" asked Malachi.

"Ceredic's been a long time dying," Lady Kiradin said. "If only our champion had finished the job at the Ravonn six months ago. Wounds and ambition alike wouldn't have had chance to fester. If he'd died promptly, his son would be emperor and that would be that. As it is, all Ceredic's done by lingering is give a pretender the chance to gather his forces and stake his own claim."

"Nothing would have changed," said Malachi. "We'd simply have faced this same situation all the sooner."

Lady Kiradin sniffed. "We'll never know, will we?"

Viktor bit his tongue. Near three hundred soldiers had perished getting him close enough to Ceredic's bodyguard to strike him down. For their sacrifice to be so simply dismissed . . .

His temper quickened even as the room lost its warmth. The shadow in his soul uncoiled, seeking egress. Malachi shot him a concerned look. With an effort, Viktor brought his temper under control, and offered Malachi a slow nod. Lady Kiradin turned away, a sly smile at the corner of her mouth.

"How bad is it?" asked Malachi, scrambling to change the subject.

"They're marching in their thousands." Lord Tarev rose and tapped at the map. "Maggad's spears are thick on the Ravonn's eastern bank. We're expecting his blow to fall at Krasta."

"Maggad? Ceredic's warleader?"

Lord Tarev nodded. "There are banners from across the Empire in his vanguard. I'd say he's been planning this for some time. A victory against us would certainly improve his chances of claiming the emperor's crown."

Malachi frowned. "Why am I only now hearing about this?"

"The reports reached us last night, when you were . . . unavailable," said Lady Kiradin. "Or were you *not* out carousing with my son? Sober times call for sober judgements."

Viktor cleared his throat. "I was in the palace until almost midnight, reviewing proposals for the new fortifications. I heard nothing of this."

"And do you think it proper that you should learn of this before us?" asked Lady Marest. "We all appreciate your contributions, but you are not a full member of this council."

How could he forget? They found a way to remind him at every meeting. "I'd like to think the Republic's defence supersedes protocol."

"We are quite capable of managing the Republic's defence without you, Viktor," his father interjected. "At least for a few hours. The 8th and 20th regiments are already marching east. They'll be in the Marcher Lands by nightfall, and in the Eastshires two dawns after. The 12th will set out before the day's end. The chapterhouses of Essamere, Prydonis and Sartorov have pledged full support. The proctors have roused four entire cohorts of kraikons. Three days, no more, and the crossings of the Ravonn will have a wall of shields as well as stone."

Three regiments marching east, to join the four already on permanent garrison on that expanse of windswept grassland between Fellhallow's southern eaves and the northern foothills of the Greyridge Mountains. The contested borderland between the Eastshires and the Hadari Empire. It would serve, assuming Maggad didn't launch his attack before everything was in place.

"Now I do know," said Viktor, "I have a few recommendations."

His father nodded. "I'm sure you do. Let's hear them."

"Reinforce the garrisons along the northern coast. If we can spare any ships from the western fleet, send those too. Maggad isn't a fool. Holding the river does us no good if there's a landing on the coast. He'll bypass the Eastshires entirely, and we'll have Hadari loose as far west as Royal Tressia – and all without a single immortal dipping his feet in the Ravonn's waters."

Lady Kiradin snorted. "And where are these soldiers to come from?"

"The muster fields."

"They're not ready. Why, I saw one of their drills this Tzadas gone. Running behind their colours like a pack of wolves chasing a sheep. Not an ounce of discipline."

Again the disdain. Viktor supposed he should have become inured to it by now. For Lady Kiradin, soldiers were like servants, and disposed of as readily.

"Then they'll learn fast," said Viktor. "And if the Hadari do land in the north, we'll need eyes more than swords. We have leagues of coastline to watch. I'd rather the task fell to inexperienced soldiers than excitable farmers."

"I agree with Viktor," said Malachi.

"Why, of *course* you do." Lady Kiradin sat forward and steepled her fingers. "So do I. Any objections?"

Unexpected. Especially after her earlier insults. But Viktor was prepared to take his triumphs where he could find them. And Hadari loose in the shire lands were as little to Lady Kiradin's benefit as anyone else's. Much of the Kiradin wealth came from rents in the Eastshires, and dead tenants didn't pay up.

Lord Tarev shook his head. After a moment, Lady Marest did the same.

The sharp *crack* of the gavel brought the matter to a close.

Viktor's father set the hammer aside. "Then it's agreed. I trust you'll make the arrangements, Viktor?"

He nodded. "With the proper authorisation."

"You'll have it. I only pray that your fears prove unfounded."

"As do we all," said Lady Marest.

Lord Tarev shrugged. "At least Maggad doesn't have the Golden Court's full backing. Most of the other princes are waiting to see what happens next before deciding where to commit their spears."

"That'll change if Maggad starts winning," Viktor rejoined.

"If *either* of them start winning," said Tarev.

"Either of them?" Malachi straightened, forcing a pained creak from his chair's time-worn timber. "What do you mean?"

"Maggad isn't the only one with an army at his back . . . "

"This council is no place for speculation," snapped Lady Kiradin.

Lord Tarev's lip curled in irritation. "With respect, Ebigail, this is not speculation."

"Fanciful nonsense. One wayfarer catches a glimpse of an owl banner, and now they're all busy spreading stories. It's what soldiers do best, after all. Apart from dying."

Viktor focused his attention on his father. The elder Akadra had sat uncharacteristically silent throughout the exchange. Throughout the whole meeting. Whatever facts Lady Kiradin wished suppressed, *he* already knew. "I'd like to hear this *speculation*."

His father sighed. "It has been suggested – and I stress, *suggested* – that Kai Saran means to make passage of the mountains at Trelszon."

"He's after the Southshires?"

"We've no proof of that."

"There never is," growled Viktor. "Not until the dying begins. By then, it's too late."

Lady Kiradin waved a dismissive hand. "It's a distraction."

"Is it?" said Malachi. "A Saran has sat on the Imperial throne for generations. Do we believe Prince Kai will do nothing while another man steals his father's crown?"

"Who can say how a shadowthorn thinks?" said Lady Marest. "Perhaps he knows, as we do, that Maggad is doomed to humiliating defeat, and intends to distance himself from it."

"Which he'd do far better in Tregard, building his standing with the Golden Court."

"Enough." Viktor's father laid a hand on Malachi's shoulder. "Our time is too valuable to waste on guessing at Kai's motives."

"Agreed," rumbled Viktor. "I'd rather we spent it discussing how we defend the Southshires from invasion – real, or imagined."

Lady Kiradin's lips thinned to a bloodless slash. Lord Tarev turned away, his attention suddenly and irrevocably focused on the map. Viktor's father stared down at his hands. Only Lady Marest met Viktor's gaze, her wizened features twisted in a scowl of resignation.

"What they won't tell you, Viktor, is that they intend to do nothing."

"Nothing?" he growled.

Malachi shot another warning glance. This time, Viktor ignored it.

"So that's the way of it?" he demanded. "We've soldiers enough to act as their jailers, but when the real enemy threatens, there's nothing to be done?"

His father looked up from the table. When he spoke, it was in flat and level tones that Viktor knew all too well. Father and son were too much alike. Neither had a firm grasp on their temper. Neither cared to be challenged in private, much less in the company of their peers.

"I don't care for your tone, Viktor."

"And I don't care for your attitude."

The room darkened, as if a passing cloud blocked the light. Ice frosted upon the lower panes of glass. Too late, Viktor realised that his shadow had slithered free, set loose by rising frustration. He rose and braced his knuckles against the table. His shadow dissipated as he bent his will upon it and receded reluctantly into the depths. The light returned to its murky glory, its significance unremarked – if indeed any had noticed.

"Katya Trelan led the Southshires in revolt fifteen years ago. Fifteen. Years. There are boys on the muster fields who weren't born when we won the Battle of Zanya. And you're still holding a grudge? They are our people. They deserve our protection."

"They deserve nothing," said Lady Kiradin. "Zanya might be fifteen years in the past, but you know the losses we incur keeping order. You consider the southwealders our people. *They* do not."

"So they *are* our people when we wish to exploit their territory, and seize their grain? And they are *not* when they're endangered?"

She gave a curt nod. "Yes. A fine summation."

"That's not how your son would see it." Was Kasamor riding into danger even now? At Viktor's own urging?

Lady Kiradin flinched as if he'd struck her about the face. "How dare you!"

Malachi shaded his eyes and hunched his shoulders. It was as though he believed he could make himself less a part of the unfolding quarrel if he bore no witness.

"Viktor." Reason oozed from Lord Tarev's words. "The southwealders aren't your concern."

"They became my concern when you gave me Katya Trelan's seat on this council."

His father clenched a fist. "So that you might learn the principles of good governance. Not so you could make demands like a spoiled child."

"Someone should speak for the southwealders," Viktor replied flatly. "If no other can put aside the past long enough to do so, then I shall."

"What a noble soul your son has, Hadon," sneered Lady Kiradin. "Such compassion for a people he humbled, and a land he hasn't set foot in since. If you'd any feelings for the southwealders, young Viktor, you'd spend your time teaching them to behave like proper Tressians, rather than flinging insults at those whom you wish to treat you as a peer."

Viktor could smell bridges burning behind him. One did not address one's fellow councillors as he had. But it was too late. Even had he been of the mind to issue an apology, no one would have accepted it.

"Then with the Council's permission," he bit out, "I'll set foot there now. And I'll take the 2nd with me. If Saran invades, we'll hold him until reinforcements muster. If not, I'll gladly pass the time teaching the southwealders whatever you wish."

"The 2nd have duties," said his father. "As do the other regiments."

"Then I'll take recruits from the muster fields."

Lady Kiradin wagged a finger. "Ah, but we've already agreed your strategy of sending them north. I suppose there might be a handful left, but not enough to make any *real* difference."

"And if the Hadari overrun the Southshires?"

"In that unlikely circumstance, I'm sure we can count on you to conduct a vigorous defence of the Tevar Flood, and exact recompense for harms wrought." She tilted her head. Her serpentine smile widened. "After all, you are so very good at killing, aren't you?"

Viktor gazed back. Yes, he was good at killing. Better even than she knew, for he'd been careful to keep his other talents hidden. But on this battlefield, one contested with words and steeped in old prejudice? He was weaponless. Worse than that, he was alone, for even Malachi wouldn't stand with him – not now he'd lost his composure and his dignity both. In that, if in nothing else, his father was right. He had a lot to learn about Tressia's governance. How to keep his temper at council, for one.

He took a deep breath. Musty air quenched a measure of his rage. "And if I call for a vote?"

Lady Kiradin shrugged. "Why bother? You already know which way it will go."

Why bother indeed? Lady Marest *might* side with him. The Lumestran precepts she held so close were founded in forgiveness and of the shielding of the weak. And of course Malachi would offer his support. But two wasn't enough, not with his own half-vote discounted in the event of a tie.

"Then if there's no other business, I suggest we adjourn."

So saying, Viktor's father rose to his feet. Even now, Viktor noted, he wouldn't look him in the eye. He was an embarrassment. Again. It was little consolation that he felt much the same about his sire.

Six

"**A**n outrage!" bellowed Makrov. "I want the perpetrators seized!"

Josiri kept his back to the pacing archimandrite and his attention firmly on the vista beyond the window. In the middle distance, a knot of soldiery wrestled with a body atop Gallows Hill. Muddied scarlet robes – an exact match for those Makrov now wore – shone like blood in the morning sunshine. Even at that distance, straw showed at collar and cuffs.

It seemed Revekah had strayed from her instructions.

Anastacia set her empty wine glass down beside an equally empty bottle. "You mean *the Council* wants the perpetrators seized, Excellency?"

Josiri winced at the insolence of the words. *That* would hardly make matters easier.

Makrov halted his pacing. Ice crackled in his tone. "I am not only the Council's representative; I am Lumestra's herald. An assault on my person . . ."

"Perhaps your attackers were more interested in the latter than the former?" said Anastacia. "We've all heard the stories about how Lumestra's light shines out of your . . ."

Enough was enough, Josiri decided. He turned his back on the window. "Please. This helps no one."

He might as well have remained silent. Makrov's stony gaze remained locked on Anastacia, and hers on him. Her black dress, trimmed with white lace at collar and cuffs, was a perfect match for her straight-backed and cross-legged posture. The very image of a demure young woman, attending her betters. Only the slight turn at the corner of her mouth gave the impression of a cat, biding its time.

"You take a great deal of joy from this matter, demon," said Makrov. "So much, in fact, that I can't help but wonder at your involvement."

"Oh yes." With a sigh, Anastacia swung her legs up over the arm of the chair, dispelling the ladylike illusion. "I ripped myself free of these stones, tripped merrily through your enchanted wall, evaded the small army at the gates and trotted back here. All without being seen."

"My lord archimandrite," Josiri interjected. "You've suffered deplorably. I'm only glad that your assailants stopped short of injury. But I can hardly step beyond the walls to investigate, even had I the knack for doing so. And I've no doubt Governor Yanda has the matter well in hand."

Yanda didn't *look* like she had the matter well in hand. She stood beneath Katya Trelan's portrait, about as far from Makrov as possible without implying disrespect.

"Enquiries have begun," she said. "However, these weren't disgruntled villagers, my lord, but self-made outcasts. And I need not remind you that there's no shortage of hiding places out in the forests. I haven't the soldiers to roust them all. Of course, if the Council were to strengthen the garrison ... "

"The Council has greater concerns than reinforcing your failures, governor," snapped Makrov. "Wolf's-heads have family, friends. They rely on others for food, weapons and comfort. Choose a village. Make an example. Someone will talk. And as to what you can do, your grace? I expect you to denounce this assault in the strongest of terms as part of your noonday speech."

Josiri suppressed a scowl. But at least Makrov had lost interest in Anastacia. There was always the possibility, however remote, that she might have let something unfortunate slip out. It wasn't a question of loyalty, but of pride. Almost everything was.

"Are you certain that's wise?" he asked.

"This was a provocation. A deliberate humiliation. I expect you to address it as such."

This was safer ground, and a battle Josiri had prepared for. "Indeed. And the very best course of action is not to rise to the bait. I see no reason to drag your dignity through the mud."

Makrov's eyebrow curled in suspicion. "My dignity? I don't follow."

"At present, only a handful of people know of this. The patrol who found you. The outlaws themselves. Why change that? Why expose yourself to ridicule?"

"This is *not* about my pride."

Anastacia's black eyes gleamed. Josiri shot her a warning glance. For a mercy, she remained silent.

"Of course it isn't," he said. "It's about that of those you represent: the Council, and Lumestra herself. But it's your decision. I'll abide by whatever course you think proper."

Makrov folded his arms. "And the effigy on Gallows Hill?"

"A childish gesture. Ignore it."

Rare uncertainty ghosted across Makrov's brow. Josiri held his breath. This was it. The moment that would judge one of them for a fool. There was no containing Makrov's humiliation, not now. By day's end, it would have spread far and wide.

But truth mattered little when it came to pride. Josiri stared up at his mother's portrait. If there was one lesson he'd learned from her death, it was that. And Makrov had sufficient pride to swell the delusions of a dozen men. He needed only to *believe*. It was Josiri's fervent hope that he would. Otherwise his *own* pride would have consequences.

"There ... There may be some wisdom in what you say," Makrov said at last. "Perhaps it is better that your speech cleaves to broader topics."

Josiri offered a shallow bow, more to conceal a relieved smile than to offer respect. "Of course, my lord archimandrite."

Makrov's lip trembled. He radiated unhappiness, but he was trapped by his own decision. "Governor Yanda? Under the circumstances, I think it better not to feed rumour. Proceed with discretion. We shan't risk persecuting the innocent in order to expose the guilty."

Yanda's shoulders slumped a fraction of an inch. "As you wish."

A muscle twitched in Makrov's cheek. "Not I. The Council. Now, if you'll excuse me, your grace, I have prayers to lead in the town. But I'll be sure to return at noon and hear your declaration."

"I look forward to it," Josiri lied.

Yanda at his side, Makrov withdrew. Halfway to the great oaken door he spun on his heel, hands clasped behind his back. "And, your grace?

You've not forgotten my instruction about your mother's portrait? I want its ashes by sundown."

Josiri bit back a flash of anger. Like it or not, some wounds had to be borne. "I'll see that it's done."

Makrov grunted, then he and Yanda were gone. Servants swung the door closed, cutting off the sound of footsteps beyond. Anastacia's slow, deliberate handclap echoed off the walls.

"Oh, very well played."

Josiri clenched and unclenched his fists in frustration. Did she not see how close that had run? "Don't mock me. I'm not in the mood."

"Yes, your grace." She swung her legs off the arm of the chair. Dress swishing against polished flagstones, she glided gently towards him. "Whatever you say, your grace."

She gathered her skirts and bobbed a curtsey. All with that same impish inflection at the corner of her smile. Impish, and infectious. Enough so that Josiri found his own lips twitching in echo.

With an effort, he stifled the smile. "Antagonising Makrov didn't help."

Anastacia looped her hands about the back of his neck. "Of course it did. He's stuffed full of self-importance and looking for sympathy as much as justice. I nudged him, and he sailed straight into your harbour. You can thank me later, when you're in a more reasonable frame of mind."

Josiri closed his eyes and lost himself in the comfort of Anastacia's embrace – the rich, delicate scent of her. She had an answer for everything.

"You put lives at risk."

"So did you, the moment you asked Revekah for that favour."

He frowned. "That's different."

She giggled, the bright notes spilling across him like rain. Warm lips pressed to his, then withdrew. "Of course it isn't. There's no victory without risk. Taking the archimandrite down a rung or two is a victory worth savouring. It won't last. He'll seek ministration with his choir, and the serenes will smooth away his hurts . . . in one manner or another."

Josiri sighed. Some prejudices, Anastacia would never let go. Chief among them was that holy cloisters were neither so chaste nor respectable as scripture decreed. Perhaps she was right. Some very peculiar things went on behind closed doors, as he knew all too well himself.

"It's time you did more," said Anastacia.

Josiri opened his eyes and examined her expression for mockery. He found none. Anastacia was as close to earnest as she ever came.

"I meant what I said before," she went on. "That *was* very well played, but it's a small gesture. You need something larger. A flame that burns so bright no one will mistake its import."

Josiri glanced at the door, even though he knew it was closed. "I told you last night, we're not ready."

"That might be what you said, but I know your heart." A long, pale forefinger brushed Josiri's chest and tapped at his breastbone. "It's *your* readiness you doubt. And your time is running out."

He sighed. "You mean the Hadari?"

"The Hadari. Makrov's second exodus. Increased quotas from the fields. Invasion, suppression or starvation, what does it matter? Your people will still suffer. They'll still perish."

"It's not that simple."

"Oh, my poor, dear misguided heart, it's precisely that simple. History turns on simplicity. It's those who survive it who seek deeper meaning."

She had a point. Josiri didn't like it, but she had a point. "What would you have me do?"

"Symbols are important." Anastacia pulled away and stared up at Katya's portrait. "Give your people something to hate."

Maiden's Hollow lay cold and dark, even with the sun blazing above. The thick canopy of thorn-tangled branches played its part, but there was something more – something that made Revekah Halvor's skin crawl.

There were rumours, of course. There were always rumours about such places. That the ring of headless statues were not statues at all. Rather that they were flesh-and-blood dancers petrified by ancient spite, their outflung hands frozen in gay abandon and their skirts lifted by a wind long since dead. A peasant's tale, and easily dismissed as superstition ... if not for the fact that neither simarka nor kraikon could cross the dell's bounds.

Cursed or blessed, Maiden's Hollow was priceless to wolf's-heads. Revekah wondered at the cost, one levied in nightmares of black roses and scratching, crackling whispers. She couldn't have stood watch among the black trees. How others tolerated doing so, she couldn't imagine.

Revekah skirted the centre of the circle – and its toppled statue of a robed man – and descended the rain-smoothed steps to the cavern. Two men pored over a map at a rough wooden table. Other pelts screened off entrances to the warren of tunnels and caves below.

Drakos Crovan's neatly trimmed hairline and hawkish features were more suited to a courtier than an outlaw. He'd have been a sensation in the staged parades back in Tressia. The dashing young officer, striving for victory – which was what he'd been, before he'd embraced his heritage, and thrown in with the southwealders who'd been his grandparents' neighbours. Revekah didn't recognise the other man. A new recruit? Crovan had a knack for rousing the disaffected.

Crovan glanced up, a wary look in his sea-grey eyes. "Captain Halvor. Didn't expect to see you so soon."

"Might be I'd say the same. Thought you'd gone south with wayfarers on your heels."

"Changed my mind when the northwealders changed theirs." Crovan ran a hand over his two-day stubble. "Abandoned the pursuit halfway to the border. We both know why."

Revekah peered down at the map. Scribbled notes spoke to garrison estimates across the Grelyt Valley. "The Hadari?"

Crovan shared a brief glance with his companion and stabbed a finger down at the map. "That's what I'm hearing. Council are already stripping the Trelszon border forts. Border raids are one thing, but they won't hold against an army."

Revekah snorted. "They've been crumbling for decades."

She'd stood her first watch in one such fort, up at Celdon Pike. Seventeen years old and jumping at every shadow. It felt like a lifetime ago. It *was* a lifetime ago. And look at how little had changed for the Southshires …

Crovan grinned. "It's only pride keeps them manned at all. Good for us. More room to operate."

Revekah winced. "Until the Hadari come."

"Maybe even then."

Revekah lowered her creaking bones into an empty chair. "So tell me. How many did you lose?"

The grin bled from Crovan's expression. "That's none of your damn business."

"Was it worth it?"

He sat back in his chair, fingers drumming against the table top. "It's always worth it."

"And what of the dead?"

"They knew the risks."

"You had no right."

"I had every right!" Crovan slammed his fist on the table. When he spoke again it was with a voice taut as a fiddle string. "They burned Vallora yesterday, did you know that?"

"I heard."

She'd more than heard. She'd seen the column of smoke, and the monstrous silhouettes of kraikons towering over the crops. All from too far away to help.

"Fields were thick with blight, but the overseer saw only missed quotas. When old Geshra tried to explain, he was arrested. Vorn was there."

The younger man scowled. "A fight broke out. Blood spilled. Then they sent in the kraikons. Some fought. Simarka got most of those who fled. A few of us got away. Holed up in Skazit Maze."

"Not a good place to seek refuge," said Revekah.

She'd scouted the place, years back, in the hopes of using Konor Belenzo's old tunnels as a stronghold. Something about the sunken passageways had set her nerves on edge. Most of the Forbidden Places did, of course. The legacy of old magic, and the touch of gods. But Skazit was colder, somehow – worse even than the brooding treeline of Maiden's Hollow. The whispers were louder there, closer to the surface of Revekah's dreams. Shadows cast without light. But for all that, what had worried Revekah more was how the tunnels had felt like home – welcoming in a way she couldn't describe. When she'd left, she'd never looked back, and warned all who'd listen to give Skazit a wide berth. No surprise to learn some hadn't heeded her words.

Vorn rubbed at his eyes. Revekah recognised an echo of her own sleepless nights in his expression. "Didn't have much choice, not with those cursed lions at my heel."

Crovan met Revekah's gaze. "A dozen farmers dead, their families homeless, and you think I hadn't the right to act? Should I have let them drag the survivors to Cragwatch?"

"You should have asked for help," she replied. "From me. From the others. We're stronger together."

"There was no time. I scarcely had opportunity to get my people organised, let alone beg your permission."

"Really? Because I'd have had twenty of my phoenixes here within an hour." Revekah leaned forward. She'd been fairly sure before, but now she was certain. "Do you know what I think?"

"I know you're going to tell me."

"I think this was about you. Like it's always about you. About Drakos Crovan, the Wolf King, liberator of the Southshires and his reputation. Boldness is *not* the same as recklessness."

"And cowardice is too often passed off as caution," he snapped.

Revekah stifled a grimace. "I didn't come here to argue with you."

"Ha!" Crovan crooked a half-smile, his temper fading as swift as it had flared. "You always say that."

"It's always true." Enough, Revekah decided. She'd delivered her rebuke, he'd ignored it and no amount of quarrelling would change that. "Your heart's in the right place, Crovan. I'm not denying that. And you've a gift for getting folk to follow you. But reckless deeds should be our last resort, not our first."

He scowled and nodded – though Revekah knew better than to take it as agreement. "If you didn't come to argue, why are you here? To bask in my praise for humiliating the archimandrite? Don't deny that was your work. Surprised you didn't kill him."

"Makrov's more trouble dead than alive."

"Now there we *can* agree. It's an escalation we don't need. So what *do* you want?"

"I spoke to the duke last night. We're to have nothing to do with the Hadari. Whatever their business in the Southshires, they pursue it without our help."

"Oh really? And is that his opinion, or yours?"

"I'm sure he'll readily repeat it for you."

"The Hadari offer an opportunity."

"They offer nothing we can't take for ourselves."

"Wake up, Revekah!" Crovan leapt to his feet, an arm outflung towards Eskavord. "Josiri Trelan would have us wrapped in endless preparations for a day that will never arrive! He's soft where it counts."

"Not so soft that you've told him so to his face."

"What'd be the point? He'd not listen. Nobles are all the same, whether they're our own people or the Council's lackeys. He's serving a purpose. He's bringing us together. Let him be content with that." He waved a dismissive hand. "Let those of us who shoulder the real burdens make the real decisions."

"*My* decision is to let him lead. And to honour his wishes about the Hadari."

"We've more in common with the Hadari than the northwealders."

"The duke doesn't agree. He wants your promise. Which means that *I* want your promise."

"And if it isn't forthcoming?"

Revekah set her shoulders and laid her hand on her sword's hilt. "Then you and I will fall out."

Crovan chuckled and hung his head. "Old habits break hard, don't they? Look at you. Fifteen years your mistress has been dead, and you're still cracking heads in her family's name."

"It's called loyalty."

"So you say. Very well, tell the duke that I will attempt no contact with the Hadari. But tell him also that his people are growing impatient. I can't make promises for them."

"But you'll discourage *his people* from doing anything foolish?"

"For you, Captain Halvor, of course. I wouldn't want us to *fall out*."

Revekah clambered to her feet, holding his gaze the whole time. She'd no illusions about how long the promise would hold. Crovan would do as he pleased, whenever he wished.

That was the problem with the younger generation. Values were focused inward, rather than to the betterment of others. Katya would have hated Crovan. But she'd also have found a way to make him useful.

Maybe Josiri would yet do the same. Either way, there was nothing more Revekah could do.

Melanna twitched aside the wolf-pelt curtain as the footsteps faded. Crovan sat sprawled in his chair, fingers drumming against the knife-gouged table top.

"You heard?" he asked.

She nodded. "Every word."

"She's a fool, that one, chasing a dream."

"Aren't we all?"

He rose and drew nearer. A thoughtful expression tugged at his lips. "I'm not a dreamer. I believe in what I can see, what I can kill ... and what I can touch."

Crovan reached out. Melanna caught his wrist and narrowed her eyes to slits. "You forget yourself."

His grinned. "So formal, my dear princessa."

"Consider yourself fortunate. If one of my father's Immortals were here, you'd have lost that hand."

"And perhaps it would have been worth it."

Melanna squeezed his wrist until she felt the bones shift, then let his hand fall. She knew Crovan's desire stemmed as much from what she represented as an attraction to body or soul. And she hadn't fought to escape arranged marriage only to become a notch on a wolf's-head's grubby bedpost.

"And what of the promise you made?" she asked.

"I gave my word not to attempt contact. Fortunate for us all that I don't have to."

Melanna kept her face immobile. Crovan could garb his actions in whatever cloth he wished, but a lie was still a lie. Even when it served her cause. "You should not trade honour so lightly."

Crovan snorted. "Honour is a sop to conscience. It doesn't break chains or feed the hungry. It doesn't bring freedom ... "

"Or make legends?"

"Are you speaking of me, or your father?" His eyes widened in amusement. "Or yourself?"

She slapped him across the cheek, regretting the blow even before the whip-crack had faded. It spoke to a loss of control. Gave Crovan the power of satisfaction. Showed both her temperament and the inexperience of youth a little too plain. His grin reinforced the sense of failure. Still, the temptation remained to strike him again.

"Tell your father nothing has changed. When he comes, we'll be ready."

"And what of the duke?"

"He'll learn to live with his disappointments." He shrugged. "Or he won't. Either way, I'll deal with it."

Seven

For the third time, Josiri slid the opal-tipped pin through silk. For the third time, the cravat sat defiantly askew in the mirror. With a growl of irritation, he tossed the pin on the dresser.

It seemed petty to be riled so, especially with the unwanted speech looming large. But perhaps that was part of it. Anastacia's suggestion carried a good deal of risk, but it *felt* right. It felt like something his mother would have done. But what if it pushed Makrov's fragile pride beyond breaking point? How many would pay the price? There was no predicting that, not with certainty. Better to be angry at a sliver of jewellery.

"Poor brother. Bad enough your hair always looks like a windblown hay bale. Now this."

Josiri turned. The reflection in the mirror twisted to encompass the doorway and Calenne's mocking smile. She drew closer, pale skirts of a formal dress swishing about her feet. A far cry from the practical garb she preferred.

"Joining me on the balcony?" he asked, with no small surprise.

She shrugged. "I'm having second thoughts at being seen with you in public. All these years, and still you can't dress yourself. It's embarrassing."

"It's not as easy as it looks. You should try for yourself."

"And you should try lacing a corset."

Josiri shook his head in silent amusement. She'd no more laced her own corset than she'd pinned and braided her own hair. Calenne was as content to prevail upon the servants as Josiri was loath to rely upon them.

"You should have a servant do it," said Calenne.

"Some things a man has to do for himself." He reached for the pin.

"Oh, very noble. Fair sends a shiver down my spine. Why can't your demon do it?"

"Anastacia says it's beneath her."

Calenne sniffed. "I'm glad something is."

Josiri shot her an irritated glance. The recalcitrant pin, freed from his attention, pricked at his flesh. "Ah!"

In the mirror, Calenne's teeth flashed a grin. "Oh, for Lumestra's sake . . . "

She held out an expectant hand. Josiri hesitated, then capitulated. Wearing an expression entirely too triumphant for his liking, she stepped around his shoulder and set to work.

"It's not a glorious way for the Trelan line to end, is it?" said Calenne. "'The last duke stabbed himself in the throat while dressing for a crowd.' What *would* Katya say?"

"I hope she'd understand," said Josiri, his thoughts more on the speech to come than the ephemera of raiment.

"Uh-uh." Calenne unlooped the cravat, re-sited it, and set about knotting the silk anew. "Once she'd finished laughing. There. That looks better."

She stepped aside, giving Josiri an unobstructed view. The cravat was straight, the pin centred. He buttoned his waistcoat and slid on his jacket. "Who'll do this for me once you're gone?"

"You should have considered that before giving your blessing."

"I can always change my mind."

The sudden darkening of Calenne's expression told him the jest had passed her by. "Don't you dare."

He held up his hands in surrender. "I wouldn't dream of it. Plenty of cautionary tales about those who stand in the way of true love."

"Yes," said Calenne distantly. "True love. What a wonder."

The wistfulness in her tone set Josiri on guard. "You *do* want to marry Kasamor?"

She crossed to the window and stared out across the tangled gardens. "I want the marriage more than anything." She offered a lopsided shrug. "It's the man I'm indifferent to."

Josiri felt a sudden chill. "Pardon me?"

To his surprise, she laughed. "Oh, my dear brother. So perceptive, and yet so blind. It's Kasamor's name I want, not him. It's the only way I can escape this cursed family."

Frustration flooded back. Half-remembered lessons about dignity melted away.

"Does Kasamor know?"

"Of course not." She spoke without turning. "It's nothing to do with him."

"It has everything to do with him!" His anger always burned brighter when Calenne drew it forth. Even Makrov couldn't rile him so. "I won't let you do this."

"You can't stop me."

"I can tell him the truth!"

Calenne turned from the window, arms folded across her chest and fire blazing in her eyes. "Then the next time I climb the tower, I'll give myself to the Raven."

Josiri froze, overcome by the image of his sister plunging from the ruined balcony. "You wouldn't dare."

"I want my freedom, Josiri. If I can't have it one way, I'll find it another."

He willed himself to calm. If the last fifteen years had taught him anything, it was that nothing good came of butting heads with Calenne. "Kasamor deserves the truth."

"He has *his* truth. That's all most of us want. You'll only break his heart."

"And that matters to you?"

Calenne's expression softened. "More than it should. He's a good man, and he's kind. I saw as much when he first stood his turn as the Council's emissary. He's the only one who's ever treated you as an equal."

At Ascension, just last year. "You pestered me for an introduction."

"And you teased me. You were merciless."

"I was pleased. You deserve a better life than one cooped ... "

Calenne tilted her head and threw him the too-familiar "I told you so" glance.

"All right." The last of Josiri's anger seeped away into resignation. "You've made your point."

She took his hands in hers. "I promise not to make Kasamor miserable. And it's not as though arranged marriages aren't common."

"It's only an arranged marriage if both parties believe it so." Josiri rubbed at his forehead. "You could have wed years ago, if marriage was all you wanted."

"But not to a family of the first rank."

So that was it. Despite censure by the Council, the Trelan bloodline retained its status. If Calenne married beneath her station, the luckless husband would take her name. More than that, the sins of kith would cling to him as well. He'd be sealed behind the manor's wards, as much a prisoner as his bride. But by marrying Kasamor, Calenne could take his name. She'd become an adopted daughter of the Kiradin line, and censure had no claim on a Kiradin.

Josiri sighed. His mother had fled an arranged marriage for love. Now his sister conspired at a loveless marriage in order to flee. But family came first. Even before poor, love-struck Kasamor Kiradin. Who was a northerner, after all, and therefore had his own sins of the kith to bear.

"If that's what you want," he said at last, "then of course I'll support you. I'm sorry I overreacted."

She offered a half-smile. "And I'm sorry for behaving like a child. I have such dark thoughts sometimes. I swear I don't recognise myself."

"Why did you tell me?" he asked. "You must have known how I'd take it."

She pulled away. "I should tell someone, don't you think? And who else is there? You're my brother, Josiri. You're the only person who's real. The rest of the world? It's behind glass. Emissaries call on us. Servants come and they go. They all enter our lives like dreams and leave the same way."

"And you'd abandon me?"

"You could come. Kasamor would adopt you if I asked, I'm sure of it." Her voice quickened. "We'd both be free of this."

Josiri tried to picture Ebigail Kiradin's face at the news she'd be welcoming not one, but two hated Trelans into her precious family.

"I can't," he said. "This is where I belong."

"Katya wouldn't want you to live like this."

"You know that's not true. I gave our mother two promises the night she died. At Eskavord, I swore to protect you. And at Zanya, I swore to finish what she started."

Calenne's fingers brushed his cheek. "My poor, foolish brother. Katya's gone. Find a purpose of your own, while you still can."

He hadn't the heart to tell her how far that particular ship had sailed over the horizon. "And you?"

She grinned. "I shall be Lady Calenne Kiradin, adored by my husband, abhorred by my mother-in-law, and all the happier for both. But though I'll no longer be a Trelan in name, I'll always be your sister. After all, Trelans must stick together, mustn't they?"

He sighed. "Always."

The sonorous chimes of Branghall's ancient clock rang out, signalling the approach of noon. Time to address the crowds.

Josiri took to the balcony on the last stroke of noon, hands clasped to disguise their nervous tremor. Beyond the balustrade, hundreds of men, women and children stood crammed between the garden's apple trees and the low brick walls of the courtyard terrace. Rare guests to Branghall, permitted entry for this most special of occasions. There were no cheers, not that he expected any. Just a quiet, expectant murmur carried on the gentle breeze.

The temptation to change his plans returned, stronger than ever.

"You're popular today, brother," whispered Calenne.

"So it would seem."

He knew why. This was part of Makrov's triumph. Another point scored against the long dead woman who'd spurned his heart.

Makrov and Yanda waited on the balcony. A quartet of soldiers accompanied them, one of whom had a silvered buccina looped over his right shoulder. Yanda looked uncomfortable. Makrov radiated delight. He strode to greet them, diamonds glittering across his narrow crown. The polished black wood of his sceptre shone like serpent-scale in the sun.

"Your grace." The merest ghost of a smile flickered across his lips. "Your people await."

Josiri noted familiar faces in the crowd. Some had stood their turn as servants of the manor. Others had crossed his path in darker and more clandestine hours. Makrov had roused half of Eskavord, and half of the villages beyond.

Blue tabards and plate armour lined the terrace. A few soldiers bore halberds, the bas relief of Lumestra's radiant flames blazing where the backswept blade gathered to a billhook. The rest had scabbarded swords. Heavy oblong shields sat grounded at booted feet, the blazing sunburst bright upon a king's blue field. A pair of kraikons stood to the terrace's rear, flanking the knot of soldiery serving as escort to Captain Sark. The nearest was a particularly battered specimen. It bore a jagged scar where its left eye had been. Golden magic spattered and hissed from a rent in its breastplate. Its handler – a proctor with a flickering sun-stave held tight – waited close by.

"So many people," said Calenne. "I hope they're not expecting anything interesting. Josiri tends to ramble."

She extended her hand. Makrov's brow creased, then with visible effort he put aside old ghosts. Expression clearing, he stooped and pressed her fingers to his lips. "I'm certain his grace knows what is required."

"I'm sure he does," Calenne said warmly. "I'm sorry I wasn't here to greet you yesterday. I wasn't feeling altogether myself."

"Please, think nothing of it. I'm sure we'll see more of one another once you're wed. Lady Kiradin appreciates the value of spiritual advice."

To her credit, Calenne's smile didn't waver. Josiri felt a rush of admiration for his sister, who was a better actor than he'd ever be. "And won't that be something to look forward to?"

Josiri peered over the balcony's edge. The canvas-draped bundle was in position. Anastacia waited close by, her back to the balcony and her hands looped below her waist. Good.

"Could we begin?" asked Yanda. "I don't want to keep the enchantment quelled any longer than necessary."

Josiri fancied he heard real worry in her voice. Of course they'd had a proctor quell the enchantment. There weren't enough ward-brooches to admit even a fraction of the enormous crowd.

Makrov offered a thin smile. "You worry too much, governor. I doubt his grace is about to flee through the gardens . . . " The smile faded as he turned his attention to Josiri. " . . . are you, your grace?"

Josiri let his gaze linger on the undergrowth of the outer grounds. Sunlight gleamed on the bronze of a simarka's stylised fur. "I'd not make it halfway to the gate, would I?"

The smile grew frosty. "No, you wouldn't."

At Yanda's nod, the buccinator set his lips to the instrument's mouthpiece. The brash clarion swept away the murmurs of the crowd.

All morning, Josiri had wondered how he'd feel at that moment. Now he knew. To his surprise, there was no hesitation. None.

"Sons and daughters of the Southshires," he began. "Our honoured archimandrite requested I speak with you. And I'm heartened to see that so many have come to hear my words."

At his side, Makrov nodded his approval.

Josiri gripped the balustrade. He took a deep breath, savouring the scents of the garden. The duskhazel was coming into bloom, lending sweetness to the air. "At Ascension, three days hence, I offer the hand of my own dear sister to Lord Kasamor Kiradin. It's no secret to me, as I'm sure it's no secret to you, that he's not worthy of her."

Makrov stiffened, but the crowd roared with laughter. Josiri let the mirth subside before pressing on. "But I am content. Calenne is the only family I have, and she is in love. I cannot find it in me to deny her heart's wish."

Turning his back on the crowd, he offered Calenne a formal bow, one hand tucked behind his back, the other across his waist. The first cheers rang out. A little of the tension faded from Makrov's jowls. For her part, Calenne regarded Josiri with narrowed eyes, suspicious of a joke yet to be played. But Josiri had none in the offing. He simply straightened, kissed his blushing sister on the cheek, and waved for silence.

"She is the best of us." He spread his hands wide. "And haven't the Southshires always given the Republic our best? At one time, our warriors guarded its borders. It was said that one southwealder's blade was worth six from the north. And now? Now we feed their armies, their citizens, their councillors. Six? We're worth a dozen! More! That's why the Council sends so many soldiers to our lands. So they can witness our labours and see how things *should* be done."

Laughter rose anew at those words. Josiri hesitated. He knew what had to follow. But didn't know if he had the nerve.

Makrov leaned close. "Have a care, your grace," he breathed. "We don't want any unpleasantness, do we?"

"As you say, my lord archimandrite." Josiri raised his voice, addressing the crowd once more. "But we cling to the past too tightly. We neglect the challenges before us in favour of old grudges. My mother, Lumestra guard her spirit, never learned that lesson. She fought for a Southshires that never was. Many of you sympathise with her views, as I once did. Today, we stop looking to her shadow for answers."

Below, Anastacia whipped the canvas aside. The portrait of Katya Trelan stood revealed upon a bed of kindling. A brilliant, blinding flash of light and the first flames licked the oils. The last dregs of laughter died, replaced by gasps and a low, ominous rumble.

"No more divided loyalties!" shouted Josiri. "We pick a side, and we remain true to it until the fight is done! And Lumestra help those who choose the wrong cause!"

Anastacia retreated before the flames. Josiri glanced down as his mother's face blackened to ash. He clung to the balustrade so tightly his knuckles ached. Had he done the right thing? The rising growl of the crowd told him he had, but that didn't fill the emptiness in his heart, or silence the accusation of a painted stare charring to ash. It was like losing her all over again. But even in the uproar, he fancied he heard Anastacia's mirth rippling like a mountain stream.

"Katya Trelan – my mother – is dead, but we will go on! In unity! With purpose!"

"Traitor!"

A hunk of soil caromed off the balcony to Josiri's left, spattering the buccinator with dirt.

The crowd's growl blossomed into a roar. "*Traitor! Traitor! Traitor!*"

A barrage of missiles – rocks and unripe apples from the terrace orchard – whipped at the balcony. A window shattered beneath a stone. Soldiers lifted their shields to shelter Makrov. Josiri set his back to the crowd and stepped in front of Calenne. Her eyes ... He'd expected horror, or perhaps worry. Instead, they gleamed with excitement – and more than that, with understanding. For the first time, Josiri wondered just how successfully he'd kept his secrets.

"Out of my way!" Yanda shoved the buccinator aside and braced a boot against the balustrade. "Captain Sark! Bring this thrice-cursed crowd to order!"

Her words were wasted. Sark stared slack-jawed across the burgeoning riot, oblivious to all.

"Captain Sark!"

Abandoning her attempt to jolt Sark to attention, Yanda put a hand to the small of Makrov's back and propelled him towards the balcony door. Josiri ushered Calenne after them and risked a last glance across the terrace. A Tressian sergeant had rallied a knot of soldiers into a rough shield wall. Enough to keep the crowd from the remains of the bonfire, but little more. Josiri caught no sight of Anastacia, but that provoked no concern. She could take care of herself.

"*Traitor! Traitor! Traitor!*"

The chant should have hurt, but instead it awoke determination. *Give your people something to hate*, Anastacia had said. He'd done that. Let them hate him, if it gave them the strength to fight.

The first kraikon started forward in a crackle of magic. The pitch of the crowd changed from outrage to panic. He'd been wrong. The Southshires were ready. And so was he.

It was only then that Josiri realised his hands no longer shook. With a nod that was equal parts surprise and satisfaction, he passed through into the shelter of the drawing room.

"What have you done?" Makrov had to shout to be heard over the roar of the crowd. He flinched as a stone spanged off a window frame. "What have you done?"

"What you asked," said Josiri. "I burned your damn painting."

Eight

Viktor closed his eyes and blotted out the grime-tinged walls. He propped his elbows against the railing and let the suffocating air wash over him. The sharp, breath-stealing tang of molten metal. The dry heat in his lungs. The prickle of sweat. They evoked memories of childhood long past and held the cold of his shadow at bay.

Pulleys creaked. Viktor leaned out over the gantry's edge. A kraikon's towering form emerged from the seething pool.

Forging constructs was a volatile art, even for those who commanded a glint of the magic that was Lumestra's light.

The proctors who fashioned the creatures spoke of a process more instinct than rational endeavour, with Lumestra's eternal light yearning to be born anew into ephemeral form. At least, until the bronze shell was breached, and the light seeped away, leaving the metal cold and still once more. Whether that was a form of death, or no less sorrowful than a leaping flame, Viktor wasn't sure. But in the foundry, all constructs were named as diligently as all newborns, in defiance of the fact that those names were seldom used elsewhere.

Streaks of liquid bronze ran like livid wounds through a skin of older, darker metal. The figure swayed as it was borne away into the gloom. Stray magic crackled from empty eyes and arced about rattling chains. The labours of the treadwheel horses set the chainway rattling, offering up another lifeless kraikon husk to the molten pool.

Scuffed footfalls crept along the gantry to Viktor's right.

"Let me guess. You've quarrelled with your father again."

As ever, Elzar's voice held a hint of mockery.

Viktor growled, and stared down at the burbling, seething metal. "It's that obvious?"

"You're here, aren't you?"

Viktor grunted. The foundry had been his refuge since he'd been a boy. He'd been desperate, searching for a place to hide in the aftermath of his shadow's first flaring. And the foundry had ... *called* to him, in sensations he'd never been able to describe. As if his magic had been drawn to that practised within, different though it was.

Of course, the building had been cold and dark then. Dark enough to lose the vranakin footpads in the maze of hoppers, gantries and workshops. Somewhere along the line, he'd fallen asleep, and the opportunistic robbers had wearied of the chase. Hours later Viktor had woken to the hiss of steam, and Elzar's hand upon his shoulder.

Viktor had pled ignorance of the night's events, for he'd barely understood them himself. He'd been too young to know of the vranakin – the crow-brethren, as they were named in less formal language – as anything other than legend. Thieves he knew of, certainly; a starving underclass bred wickedness and desperation.

But thieves cloaked in shadow? Who walked the mist-wreathed paths of Otherworld, and offered tribute to the Raven, the God of the Dead? His mother had shielded him from these things. Perhaps too well. Or perhaps Alika Akadra had never known herself, or not believed. Otherwise, she'd never have strayed so close to where Dregmeet's sunken streets bordered the western docks – let alone do so merely to avoid returning home after the hour appointed by an impatient husband.

When tears at last ebbed, Elzar had carried Viktor home to a house ever after emptied of his mother's smile and ready laughter. There was only the memory of how she'd fought to save him from the vranakin's clutches, and the ripper's grin as the knife had opened her throat. Her body was never recovered, but such events were wholly unremarkable. Hunger was rife in Dregmeet, and not all cravings belonged to men.

The elder Akadra, too lost in the tragedy of his wife's death – a tragedy he had contributed to, in small part – had taken little interest in his son's grief, and filled his days with tutors. But at night, Viktor had slipped away to the foundry, where Elzar taught him secrets of fire and forge. Of the light that was life, and the discipline by which the proctors sought to wield it. And he spoke of other things besides . . .

Thirty years had slid by since. Long enough for Elzar Ilnarov to earn the robes of high proctor – which he never wore – and be granted comfortable chambers in the guild house on the other side of the docks – which he seldom visited. He'd changed little with advancing years. A little wirier, perhaps, but the salt-and-pepper stubble and wrinkled face still matched Viktor's earliest memory.

"I lost control today, in the Council chamber."

"Magic wants to be used," said Elzar. "Always has, always will."

"I don't *want* to use it."

And he hadn't. Not since that squalid duel with Katya Trelan. And never with the wild abandon of its first manifestation. Then, it had torn two of the crow-brethren's footpads apart. A third had clawed out his own eyes in terror. At the time, Viktor hadn't realised the billowing shadow was his own doing. He'd believed it yet another horror come to claim him. And so he'd run.

"You don't get a choice. It chose you."

"Then I wish it had chosen someone else."

"And if it had? You'd have died alongside your mother." Elzar chuckled under his breath. "Who'd play hands of jando with this lonely old man? Who'd heed his complaints about callow youngsters sent to do skilled work?"

"It's that bad?" asked Viktor.

"Tailinn has a mild glimmering of talent, and she's devoted to our work. The rest?" He snorted. "Dull brats sheltering from military commission. They can't even follow instruction. They always know best. I'm only a humble proctor. *My* opinion doesn't count."

A glimmering of talent. Elzar's usual guarded understatement – a coded admission that magic had chosen Tailinn as well. A few years younger than Viktor, she'd been as much a part of the foundry as its chainways for as long as he could recall, a keen and attentive student of the high proctor's teachings.

That Tailinn wielded magic openly meant that her gift, like Elzar's, was radiant. Only magic bright with Lumestra's gift was deemed hale, and thus permitted by religious and lawful decree. It could be bent to the creation of simarka and kraikon without shame. It gave fuel to the firestone lanterns that lit Tressia even in the deepest dark. She'd nothing to hide, and was valued for it.

Viktor's shadow was different in nature, abhorred as were all magics of uncertain provenance. And just because there'd been no burning in a decade didn't mean tinder couldn't be found. Without Elzar's lessons in control, without the honing of willpower that kept the shadow caged, Viktor would have ended his days on a witch's pyre long ago. Viktor had often wondered just how his father would react if the truth came to light.

Elzar set his back to the rail and folded his arms. "But you're not here to listen to my problems. The Southshires?"

"You've heard about that?"

He chuckled. "I hear more than most. You think the requisition of four cohorts doesn't prick up my ears? All bound for the Ravonn. Not a one headed south."

"The Council can't let go of the past."

Elzar fished a lump of clinker from his overalls and tossed it from hand to hand. Sunlight crackled in its wake. "Few can. We're all of us forged in the crucible of our yesterdays."

"I'm in no mood for philosophy."

"Then you chose a poor shoulder to cry on." Elzar grinned. "What will you do?"

"I don't know."

"Hah!" The clinker slapped into Elzar's palm and vanished into his pocket once more. "The great Viktor Akadra, rudderless on an ocean of possibility."

"The very opposite. The Council have spoken. I have no choice."

"Are you certain of that? Or have you merely blinded yourself to the alternatives?"

"What?" said Viktor. "I should storm back in there, cut them all down? Seize power?"

"Setting aside the issue of surviving the aftermath ... " Elzar cleared his throat. "You could do that? To your own father?"

Viktor stared moodily into the gloom. "There are days where I wonder if that might be for the best."

"You *are* in a bleak mood. Have *I* anything to fear?"

Viktor blinked in surprise and clasped Elzar's shoulder. "No. Never."

"Never is a long time."

"Not as long as a council meeting."

The chainway rattled to new life, bearing a fresh kraikon to the pool. The giant's chest was almost completely torn away, along with much of its right shoulder. A lattice of metal rods bound the remains together – a crude approximation of the surviving musculature.

"What happened?"

Elzar shrugged. "A section of harbour wall collapsed, took that poor lump with it. He's lost his looks for ever. Tell me, why did you accept the invitation to join the Council?"

"Why do you ask questions to which you already know the answer? Because I thought I could change things. But the Council doesn't change. The Republic doesn't change."

"And aren't you as bad, if you accede to their decision?"

"You *do* want me to kill them."

Elzar tutted. "Heavens, no. Think of the mess. But has it occurred to you that you're just as hidebound as your father?"

"Choose your next words very carefully," Viktor growled.

"I always do. One thing you and your father have in common is that deep down, you think of the Southshires as a land apart. For all your aspirations – noble as they are – you see them as conquered enemy, not estranged kin."

Viktor took a deep breath and reminded himself that Elzar was trying to help. "Not so."

"If all Tressia were overcome, and the Hadari at the gates, what would you do?"

"I'd never allow the circumstance to arise."

"Humour me." Elzar spread his hands, as if unfolding a vista. "The shire lands are charnel-fields. They overflow with the bloody ruin of our armies. You've no soldiers to call upon, and a city full of frightened citizens at your back. What do you do?"

"I offer terms. Surrender for survival."

"They're rejected." He chuckled. "Apparently, you once said something unforgivable about the Emperor's favourite pig. Your only choices are victory or death."

"Then I rally the citizens. Lead them in their own defence . . . " Viktor tailed off. Their own defence. Was it that simple? "The Council would never allow it."

"You need an army. The Council won't grant you theirs. So you need another."

"Just like that?"

"Of course not. Nothing worthwhile is ever easy."

"They won't allow it," Viktor repeated. "They're too afraid of another revolt."

"Then you need to take that fear away, or perhaps replace it."

Viktor scowled. "How?"

Elzar grinned. "That's up to you."

The coach rumbled to a halt in a crunch of gravel. Firestone lanterns cast flickering shadows across Freemont's archway. They made the stone dragon of the Kiradin escutcheon appear restless and watchful in the gloom. Beyond, ornamental trees swayed in the unseasonal wind that swept the raucous carousing of drunks up from the dockside. The wealthy could wall off their estates and have hearthguard clear the neighbouring streets, but the wind blew where it wished.

"You're certain you want to be part of this?" asked Viktor.

Malachi straightened his cravat. "We've been over this. You'll need my support. It's a good proposal. And they've no great love for me. If you're trying to spare my reputation, don't bother."

Viktor nodded, uncertain of what to say. He'd never had a knack for making friends, and so he valued those few he possessed all the higher. But expressing as much came hard. Even to those he'd known all his life. So instead, he grasped the door handle, stepped out into the night, and stalked away up the path.

It was no surprise to see a second coach on the driveway, liveried in black and its doors blazoned with a stylised silver swan. Just as predictable were the green-garbed hearthguards standing in shadow beneath the archway. In a city as crowded as Tressia, it took more than expansive grounds to guarantee privacy.

Malachi joined Viktor on the steps with wind-stung cheeks and a catch to his breathing. "There you go, leaving me behind. We don't all have a kraikon's stride."

He tugged on the laced leather of the bell-cord and rubbed gloveless hands together. A chorus of wild barks struck up in the grounds beyond.

The door eased open on greased hinges to reveal the corpulent, sharp-featured form of Lady Kiradin's steward. He wore the plain black frock coat currently in fashion for servants of the well-to-do. Combined with Marek's smooth pate and sombre demeanour, the clothes conjured the image of a bodyman, come to relieve the recently bereaved of mortal remains.

Malachi drew himself up. "Ah, Marek. Lord Reveque and Lord Akadra to see Lady Kiradin."

Marek's expression took on a wry cast at the unnecessary introduction. But protocol was protocol. "Of course, my lord. You'll do me the honour of waiting while I see if her ladyship is entertaining guests tonight?"

Of course she was, otherwise why the other coach on the driveway? But there were guests and there were *guests*. And there was more than one way to entertain.

"It's council business," said Viktor.

"I'm sure," Marek replied, the words just the proper side of respectful. "But if you could perhaps wait?"

He offered a shallow bow and vanished towards the drawing room, his footsteps lost in the carpet's thick pile. Unlike the Reveque household at Abbeyfields, where Viktor had spent much of the afternoon, there was no trace of the corn dollies or bright decorations traditional at Ascension. Doubtless Lady Kiradin believed them wasteful distractions.

"He gets worse," muttered Malachi. "But I suppose every tyrant above-stairs needs another below."

Viktor grunted and peered up at the stern portraits of Kiradins deceased. None offered resemblance to the current Lady Kiradin, who bore the name by marriage – her *second* marriage. The first had ended in disgrace when the husband had been exposed as a vranakin: loyal to the Crowmarket and its shadowy Parliament of Crows – a man steeped in the criminality that oozed from sunken Dregmeet and into the city proper. Ebigail had survived the scandal only by dint of being the first to level accusation.

Marek reappeared as silently as he'd departed. "Lady Kiradin will see you now."

Subdued lighting granted the drawing room the illusion of intimacy. A low fire crackled in the hearth, a concession to the night's unseasonal chill. Rich furnishings spoke of the legendary Kiradin wealth; the slight fading of the fabrics hinted at the thriftiness maintaining that wealth through difficult times.

Ebigail Kiradin rose from her armchair as they entered.

"Lady Kiradin." Viktor offered a deep bow, and a rather shallower one to the man who stood beside the hearth. The fellow's features were alive with suspicion. The loosened cravat and unbuttoned collar told of rare relaxation. As did the brandy glass in his hand. "Father."

Lady Kiradin reclaimed her seat. "Ever so formal, young Viktor. Is it really so difficult to address me as Ebigail?"

"I'm more comfortable with formality." It had not escaped Viktor's notice that no offer of refreshment had been made, nor had leave to sit been granted. "Especially when discussing council business."

"Yes." Her eyes tightened, as if she sought to peer directly into Viktor's thoughts and so save herself the trouble of heeding his words. "So Marek informed us. *I* firmly believe that matters for the Council should remain in council. Don't you agree, Hadon?"

Lord Akadra's heavy brows beetled. His cheek twitched in discomfort. "Viktor, what *are* you doing here? This is hardly appropriate."

Viktor allowed himself a small smile. There was joy to be taken in seeing his father ill at ease, if only for a moment. In public, he and Lady Kiradin were staunch allies. In private, they were rather more. Though what affection could possibly lie between such bloodless souls, Viktor had ever been unsure.

Equal to that mystery was the reason why marriage had never formalised the longstanding arrangement. The distance between father and son rendered such questions impossible. Kasamor opined that neither party could bear to give up their family name. Latecomer though Ebigail was to the Kiradin line, she defended it as proudly as any daughter of the blood.

Malachi cleared his throat. "In point of fact, I insisted we speak with you."

"Oh, of that I've no doubt," said Lady Kiradin. "Very well. Say what you have to say."

"It concerns the Southshires ... "

"We settled the matter this morning," said Viktor's father. "No amount of talk will turn humbled stone into fortresses, or conjure soldiers out of the air."

That last proclamation struck Viktor as particularly ironic. What else were the kraikon, if not soldiers plucked from sunlight, housed in bodies quarried from the soil? "There are soldiers already in the Southshires."

"Our garrison forces?" his father barked with disdain. "Old men, young boys and a handful of creaking constructs? Keeping the south-wealders from making trouble is about the only thing they're good for."

"I speak of the southwealders themselves."

"Hah! The Southshires haven't had an army in fifteen years."

"I don't think that's true," said Malachi. "You've seen the reports. We lose more shipments each month than the one before. Our patrols are suffering. We've even lost kraikons, though Lumestra knows how. The Southshires may lack soldiers, but make no mistake – there is an army to be had."

Lady Kiradin waved a dismissive hand. "Traitors and misfits."

"The same might be said of our forebears, Ebigail. And all those who ended Malatriant's rule."

"I see no need to bring ancient history into this, far less myth," growled Viktor's father. He swirled his glass and glanced up at Viktor from beneath thoughtful brows. "Even if I agreed with your reasoning ... Do you really think they'll follow you?"

Viktor shook his head. "No. But they'll follow the duke."

"Josiri Trelan? He's been locked in that crumbling manor for fifteen years. Why would anyone listen to him?"

"They'll listen for the same reason we've kept him locked in that crumbling manor. Because they still remember his mother. What she stood for. What I'm proposing is very simple. We offer pardon to any southwealder who takes up arms against the Hadari. We offer them the chance to be full partners in the Republic again."

Lady Kiradin spread the fingers of her right hand, seemingly lost in the examination of her nails. "Why would we do that?"

"Because whether the Hadari come or not, the Southshires are an open wound. Keeping any semblance of order costs us soldiers and resources better deployed elsewhere."

"They don't give us any choice."

"Maybe." Viktor knew it wasn't that simple. The divisions between north and south went back far further than Katya Trelan. Old hatreds and rumours of witchcraft were the least of it. "But we can offer one of our own. All I've heard in the last fifteen years is how we're better than the southwealders. Let's prove it. Let's put the past where it belongs."

Elzar had recommended he find a way to counter the Council's fears. Over the course of a long afternoon, Viktor and Malachi had agreed a broader strategy. Fear was part of it, but so was pride. Pride would suffer far less if freedom were granted to the Southshires than if it were reclaimed through insurrection. And then there was greed. A free Southshires would trade with the rest of the Republic, rather than simply having its resources requisitioned. Many of the crowns that currently spilled into the Council's coffers would instead flow into private purses.

"Katya's whelp will demand a seat on the Council," said Lady Kiradin. "*Your* seat."

Of course. Even with two of the nine sitting empty with no hope of being warmed. "I'll survive the loss."

"No doubt you will." She rapped a fist against the arm of her chair. "And who'll lead this army? Josiri Trelan?"

Viktor almost smiled at the bare-faced trap.

"We thought Governor Yanda," said Malachi. "She's familiar with the land and the local dignitaries. *And* she's loyal."

Viktor's father grunted. "She did well enough under my command."

"She did?" Even to Viktor, Malachi's surprise sounded genuine. They'd spent part of the afternoon assessing candidates too. It *had* to be someone the elder Akadra trusted, and that was a very short list. The grim reality was that few front-line soldiers made old bones, and only the best officers fought from the front. "I didn't know."

Viktor's father levied a rare note of respect. "She commanded the 10th at Tarvallion, years back. She's shrewd, and she knows her business."

He was thinking like a soldier again. For the first time since entering the room, Viktor allowed himself to hope that maybe – just maybe – his father could be convinced.

"What if the young duke doesn't cooperate?" Lady Kiradin asked icily.

Viktor's throat tightened with annoyance. Josiri was no more the "young duke" than Viktor was "young Viktor". Another of Lady Kiradin's subtle reminders of her age and wisdom. "He has much to gain. For his people, and for himself. Freedom, most of all."

"If his line was well known for wisdom, we'd have no need of this conversation."

"I'll convince him."

"The man who killed his mother? I don't envy your chances."

Annoyance thickened to anger, and with it the flickering wakefulness of Viktor's shadow. It slithered about his soul, prying at the bars of its cage. The warmth of the room shrank away. Viktor scarcely dared release a breath, for fear that others would see it frosting in the balmy air.

"Kasamor will help." Malachi offered the solution with an easy smile.

"Kasamor?"

"He'll be halfway to Eskavord by now." Malachi paused, then twisted the knife. "His coming marriage, or had you forgotten?"

"When such things slip my memory you may lay me in the ground where the dead belong."

Viktor's father sipped his brandy. "You believe Kasamor has that much influence?"

"He's marrying the duke's sister," said Malachi. "And he has spoken of taking the Trelan name. That brings influence, and a certain loyalty."

The blood drained from Lady Kiradin's cheeks. When she spoke again, it was little more than a whisper. "If my fool son had any notion of loyalty he'd not be set on this ridiculous marriage."

"He's in love."

"Love? Hah!" Strength returned to her voice, bringing fresh scorn alongside. "I'm sure Calenne Trelan is a pretty enough thing, but that doesn't excuse her bloodline. And it's not as though he's a stranger to enjoying the one without embracing the other. It's only natural that youth will have its fling, but the Republic endures on good marriages. Wouldn't you agree, Malachi?"

Malachi bore the reciprocal knife-twist stoically. "Without question."

"As well you should. Lilyana is blossoming into a fine Tressian matron. She has given you such *wonderful* children. You don't deserve her."

"As I am daily reminded, Ebigail."

"If only Kasamor saw his duty so clearly." She shook her head, her shoulders braced against weighty concerns. "Katya Trelan's brat has stolen away my son, and now you ask me to forgive her family's sins?"

"For the good of the Republic, yes," said Malachi.

"The good of the Republic? The Republic lost hundreds of loyal sons and daughters over the Southshires and its so-called Phoenix. A beacon to the shackled, indeed. It has bled dearly of lives and gold ever since. I will offer no favours – not one – to that pack of traitors and inbreds. To make that mistake once a generation is more than sufficient."

"We already have Lady Marest's support." Malachi withdrew an envelope from his inner pocket. He held it so that the others could see the rose upon the wax seal. "She believes it is time to heal old wounds."

Lady Kiradin sighed. "Then Abitha Marest is doubly a fool. Her husband's not dead, did you know that? He's sequestered in a reeve's manor a league from the border. I'm told he finds equal pleasure in the ministrations of impressionable farm-girls and the knowledge that his beloved wife believes him slain. Now *that's* a reunion I'd like to witness. Why should I care for the opinion of a blind old baggage?"

With effort that almost left him breathless, Viktor forced the shadow back into his soul. The warmth of the room returned. More than returned, for his anger had not abated.

"And Kasamor?" he demanded. "I know his mind, and his heart. If the Hadari come to Eskavord, he'll fight. What if he dies because we do nothing?"

"Then he dies." Lady Kiradin met his gaze every bit as proudly as the Tyrant Queen Malatriant must have faced Konor Belenzo on the steps of her pyre. "And I will mourn him. But I must think of his sister, and the world Sevaka will come into after my passing."

Viktor turned his gaze upon his father. "And you, Father?"

Lord Akadra stared into his brandy glass. His eyes rose briefly before settling on the tawny liquid once again. "I'm sorry, Viktor. Ebigail has the right of this."

"This isn't justice." Viktor spat the words. "If the Hadari come, thousands will die."

"And if we fight a war on two fronts, the cost will be higher still. And that levy will fall on our own people. Good, loyal citizens of the Republic. I will not chance their sacrifice for those who offered only drawn swords in exchange for our generosity and friendship."

And with that, they'd lost him to fear. Fear that mistakes sown in the past would yield a bitter harvest in the present. Or perhaps fear of the price of crossing Ebigail Kiradin. It almost didn't matter. The arithmetic hadn't changed. Lord Tarev had refused to hear them out, and Malachi's vote was not enough, even with Lady Marest's pious support. Fear was paramount. It overwhelmed greed. Extinguished pride. The only thing that conquered fear was courage, or else a grander, blacker dread.

And in that moment, Viktor knew what he had to do.

"Might I speak with you alone, Father?"

Viktor followed his father into the dining room. The remains of the evening meal had long since been cleared away, and the servants scurried to their garrets. All save for Marek, of course. He remained on station in the drawing room, in case his mistress had need of his service.

Lord Akadra set the door to and folded his arms behind his back. "Say what you have to say, Viktor. But my decision is made."

"Is it?"

Gritting his teeth, Viktor let his shadow flow free.

Darkness coiled about the elder Akadra and slammed him against the door. Viktor closed the distance before he could cry out and pressed a hand across his mouth.

"Hush, Father," he whispered. "We don't want to alarm anyone, do we? Malachi has a nervous soul."

His father's eyes bulged above pallid cheeks. Viktor kept his own face expressionless, determined not to betray the uncertainty and elation coursing through his veins. Thirty years he'd lived with the secret. Thirty years he'd been terrified of the consequences of discovery. No longer. He was free in a way he'd never imagined possible. That alone made it worthwhile.

Better yet, the shadow returned as soon as he called, sated by its brief measure of freedom. Little by little, the cold abated, until only exhilaration remained. Viktor held his father in place for another five count, then let his hand fall.

"What . . . What are you?" his father spluttered.

"You know what I am," Viktor hissed. "Or do you want another demonstration?"

Defiance fought terror in his father's eyes and came away the poorer. " . . . no."

"All those years, and you've never wondered why I survived where mother did not?" Viktor leaned closer. "Well, now you know. And so will everyone else, if you don't support our plan for the Southshires."

"You're not serious."

"Of course I am. I'm my father's son."

"I won't be able to protect you," he hissed. "They'll drag you to the pyre."

It sounded like genuine concern. Viktor had no way to judge, for he'd heard so little of it over the years.

"And if they do, that will be the end of the Akadra family. I can already hear the archimandrite's speech as he drags you from office. After all, who'll believe that you didn't know your own son was a witch?"

"I didn't know," snapped his father. "How could I know?"

"That won't save you. And you'll get no help from Lady Kiradin. She threw one husband to the mob. How do you reckon your chances?" He took a deep breath. There was no pleasure to be had in the coming words, but they could not be left unsaid. "And it won't just be you. A pity about my cousins. How old is Messela now? Sixteen? Seventeen? She deserves better. But Makrov will take no chances."

His father's lips formed a snarl, but it collapsed without a sound. "What do you want?"

"Authority to treat with Josiri Trelan. To settle the mess you made me complicit in fifteen years ago."

A little familiar steel crept back into his father's eyes. But he was trapped, and he knew it. "On one condition."

Viktor stepped away and folded his arms. "What is it?"

"That you command any forces raised, not Governor Yanda, and that you remain in the Southshires until the matter is settled." His voice thickened with disgust. "After tonight, I don't want to see your face for a good long time."

Malachi felt a swell of relief when Viktor and his father re-entered the room. Anything was better than bearing the cold silence of Ebigail Kiradin's empty stare. Doubtless, she'd sifted the possibilities as to what had transpired in the adjoining room. Just as plainly, she'd reached no happy conclusion. For himself, Malachi had no clue. He and Viktor had worn out their counterarguments. Whatever his friend was attempting, it was a mystery.

"My father and I have reached an agreement," Viktor announced. "The amnesty will proceed, but under *my* oversight."

Malachi frowned. It couldn't be that simple, could it?

Lady Kiradin jerked to her feet and levelled an angry finger at Lord Akadra. "What have you done, Hadon? Grown a backbone, have you? Or lost one?"

He met her stare with bluff dignity. "It is a private matter, Ebigail. Family. You understand."

"Family? Pfah! Yes, you're all about family when it suits you." She rounded on Viktor, eyes blazing. "And you believe I'll fall into line, I suppose?"

Viktor looped his hands behind his back. His expression remained placid as any graven serathi watching over a Lumestran chapel. "With respect, it doesn't matter one way or the other. Malachi, Lady Marest. My father. Three votes. That's all we've ever needed."

Lady Kiradin's upper lip trembled, her eyes darting from one Akadra to the other, seeking a crack in resolve. She clenched her fists so hard that her knuckles cracked, then turned to stare into the fire.

"I'll thank you all to leave my house. It's late, and this nonsense has set my head galloping." She picked up Lord Akadra's brandy glass and drained the contents in a single gulp. "You may consider yourself among the banished, Hadon."

Viktor's father scowled and withdrew into the hall. Malachi couldn't quite determine if the flash of anger in his expression was meant for his son, or his lover.

Malachi bowed. "Goodnight, Ebigail. My thanks for your time, and your hospitality."

When no reply was forthcoming, he followed in Lord Akadra's footsteps with as much haste as seemliness allowed.

"What did you do?" he asked Viktor, once they were safely in his carriage once more.

His friend sank back in his seat and closed his eyes. "I got what we wanted. That's all that matters."

Neither spoke another word that night.

Nine

The midnight chime of the guildhall bell swept across the tangled dockside slums. An hour of ravens and spirits, of housebreakers and silent blades. No hour at all for the virtuous to be abroad, nor for the wealthy to take chances in Dregmeet's shadows. But it had been a quiet night, and Apara welcomed the click of the latch and the creak of hinges. She set aside her stiletto and whetstone and waited to see what the Ash Wind had blown in from the south.

The supplicant picked her way through ruined pews. The shrine had no lantern, but shafts of silvered moonlight shining through the gaping roof left little to the imagination. Privacy was important to those who sought favours of the Crowmarket. It was certainly treasured by this woman, who held her grey hood gathered at the throat. Still, Apara had recognised her from the first. Her kind didn't come to the sunken seaward streets – not willingly. No constabulary patrols in Dregmeet. No bright lights and glittering swords to protect the wealthy. Just hunger in the shadows, and favours both begged and borrowed.

The supplicant knelt before the altar. The scuffed and graffitied stone was older than the Republic. Older than the city that had grown up around it. Older than hidden Coventaj, the Vaults and the ruins of Strazyn Abbey. Older even than the Age of Kings, or so it was said. Apara didn't know for certain, for tales changed in the telling. That was what gave them power.

"A late hour to be abroad, lady," Apara whispered.

"I couldn't sleep," the woman answered softly. "I ... I worry about my son."

"As a mother should."

"I had a dream, you see. A vivid dream."

"Sometimes a dream is just a dream, lady."

Hesitation. Second thoughts? Many had them. "He has fallen into bad company."

"And you fear he will come to harm?"

"I'm certain of it."

Apara nodded. "And your son? He is in Tressia?"

"On the road. Riding for Eskavord."

"Then you are right to worry. The roads are dangerous. Does he have no one to watch out for him?"

"One companion. A friend. She'll protect him with her life."

"But you look to the Crowmarket for certainty?"

"Yes."

Apara considered. It was an unusual request. Not in the broad scheme, but the detail ... the detail was most unusual. Eskavord lay many leagues to the south, and it would require a rare talent to cover the distance in time. And rare was expensive. "It will cost."

Gold coins spilled across the altar. "For my son, I will pay any price."

Apara bit back the urge to ask for more. The supplicant could surely afford it. "Your petition is accepted. Your son will be taken care of."

"One last favour. My son carries a ring. Its sapphires bound my mother to my father. I do not wish to lose it."

"I'm certain you shall not."

The supplicant stumbled back through the maze of rotten timber. Apara waited for the latch to click once more before claiming the offering. A bite confirmed the quality of the coin and the supplicant's desperation both.

"You heard?" she called.

Nikros unfolded himself from his perch amid the beams, his thin face bright with wicked anticipation. "I heard, dear cousin. I'll leave at once."

Ten

The wolf-howl jolted Rosa awake from dreams of battle. She reached for the sword beneath her haversack. One wolf, she didn't mind. But a pack? You heard tales about the wolves of Tevar Flood. Old stories of flesh and fur running like water into new forms.

Another howl, this time further away from the roadside dell. Or did it only seem so with comforting steel in her grasp? Peril always lessened if one had the means to face it.

Every sound, every sensation took on heightened significance. Motes and insects dancing above the fire's smouldering embers. The rustle of branches in the breeze. Dull pain in her ribs, warning too late that she'd slept atop an exposed root. The soft rumble of the horses' breath. The stutter of Kasamor's snores. Even the slow hammer of her own pulse.

A third cry split the air. Distant, this time. Pack or loner, ephemeral or myth, the creature had moved away. Rosa let go of her sword and strove for sleep. It was no good. Kasamor's arrhythmic snore juddered like the beat of a drunken parade drummer, and the anticipation of the next snorting gasp was somehow worse than the sound itself.

At last, Rosa could take no more. Abandoning all hope of reclaiming her dreams, she sat bolt upright, hugged her knees and stared across ashen embers.

"For pity's sake, Kas," she hissed. "Bad enough you wouldn't let us spend a civilised night back at Callastair. Can you not let me get a little sleep?"

The unconscious contempt of Kasamor's snore was her only reply.

But the snore was only an excuse, wasn't it? Even without it, there'd be no refuge from her own thoughts, and the dread of imminent loss. But could you lose someone who wasn't yours to begin with?

"Why am I even here?" Rosa muttered. "I should have made Viktor come instead."

But then she wouldn't have seen for herself. Wouldn't have the chance to say something – *anything* – to change Kas' mind. If she spoke at all.

It was ludicrous. She'd stood the tests of shield wall and cavalry charge without a flicker of fear. But this? Fear was all she had. Fear at what would happen if she spoke her heart's truth and Kasamor rejected her. Fear at where that course would lead if he did not. For someone who'd long made habit of keeping family and friends at a distance, success provoked as much dread as failure.

Kasamor's steed snorted and stamped. There was almost something accusing in its dark eyes.

"What are you staring at?" Rosa asked. "I know what I'm doing."

The horse turned away as far as its rope tether allowed. Rosa wasn't sure whether it did so out of huffiness, or sated curiosity.

She turned her attention back to Kasamor. He seemed younger in sleep. Less arrogant, but also less burdened.

"I don't care how sweet she is, nor how storied her line. She doesn't deserve you. There. I said it."

"Said what?" muttered Kasamor. "Some of us are trying to sleep."

Rosa's heart leapt to her throat. She forced a smile. "I promised to come smother you if you kept snoring."

Kasamor rubbed at his eyes. "I don't snore. And I'd hope the Reaper of the Ravonn might at least offer me the blade instead."

Rosa willed herself to relax. "You sounded like a cow in a sewer pipe. We had a wolf pack come close to the fire. Then you started up. One dropped dead of fright, and the rest fled."

"Some friend you are." He fidgeted with his blankets. "I never thanked you for coming with me, did I?"

"How could I stay away?"

He snorted. "Everyone else has. Even Malachi. They think I'm making a mistake. But not you. I'm glad you're here."

A voice at the back of Rosa's head urged her to tell the truth. Better to regret words spoken than unvoiced. She'd never forgive herself otherwise.

Kasamor frowned. "Still with me?"

"Of course," she replied archly. "I was thinking."

"You were away with the whispering ones. Daydreaming of birch and briar, were we?"

"And maybe I'd go if they called. Anything to get away from your snores."

"You'd make a lovely thornmaiden. Old Jack would be lucky to have you. Luring lusty young fellows into Fellhallow with your sweet serene's voice." He shrugged. "Not how I'd like to go, but I guess they die happy."

"Can you not stop prattling for a few minutes?" Rosa scowled, recognising that the edge in her voice was meant for herself, not him. "Kas, I . . . "

He held up a hand for silence, his expression thoughtful. "How long's it been misty?"

Rosa looked at their surroundings as if seeing them for the first time. There *were* skeins of mist gathering between the trees. Thin enough close up, but the road was already lost to sight. How had she not noticed? Had she been so wrapped up in her own thoughts?

"It isn't. I mean it *wasn't*."

"I believe you." Kasamor threw off his blankets and clambered to his feet. "You remember Hosgard?"

Rosa leapt to her feet, sword in hand. "I'm trying not to."

But it was hard. They'd lost half a company when the mists rolled in. Fifty souls from the garrison dragged into the mists. Those who'd survived until dawn had done so in the circle of blessed light cast by a proctor's sun-stave.

The last embers hissed out. The horses whinnied, as unsettled as their masters.

Rosa pressed back-to-back with Kasamor. "We should have spent the night in Callastair."

"I'm sorry I ever argued."

Straining her ears, she caught a new sound beyond the rustle of leaves. A chatter of scratching, croaking cries. And beneath it, a wild fluttering thrum. Bird voices and wingbeats. She raised her sword.

"What in Queen's Ashes . . . ?"

The crow-flock hit the dell in a storm front of wings and croaking voices. Rosa yelped as talons tore deep furrows in her leathers and ripped at her face and hair. Kasamor bellowed in pain.

One arm raised to shield her eyes, Rosa struck at the swirling crows. Bodies burst into darkness, the lurid green of their eyes fading into the eddying mist. Breathing came hard, each lungful sucked down through smothered lips. The air stank of things long dead.

The storm abated. The crow-things sucked away like water circling a drain and coalesced into a hooded figure. He stood on the dell's edge, garbed wholly in black and with nothing but a thin beard showing out of shadow.

Breathing hard, Rosa shared a glance with Kasamor. His blond hair was flecked with blood. Small rents on his sleeves and chest gleamed wetly. Flashes of hot, wet pain told Rosa she looked little better. But Kasamor's face possessed something hers lacked: a flicker of horrified recognition.

"Your life is over, Kasamor Kiradin." The hooded man's sonorous voice rolled across the dell. "Send your companion away, and make your peace with this world."

Kasamor's face fell. "Rosa, you need to go."

"Go?" She kept one eye on the hooded man, who for his part seemed content to wait out his ultimatum. "What is this?"

His face creased. "He's a kernclaw. He serves the Crowmarket. Leave me. I won't drag you into the mists with me."

Rosa stared at the kernclaw, and told herself that she trembled at the cold, not fear. But it was one thing to face Hadari spears, and another to stand defenceless before a witch. And the look in Kasamor's eye made it worse. She'd not seen it at Hosgard, nor at Yarismark, when the wind shook to Hadari war-horns and arrows had fallen like rain. No, Rosa had seen that bleakness only once. In the alley behind the Silverway, in the heartbeat before Viktor's arrival interrupted the duel.

Kasamor expected to die.

She reached beneath her tunic and squeezed her sun-pendant tight. The wolves had known what was coming, hadn't they? She might have noticed had she not been lost in foolish, unrequited imaginings.

Fear melted away beneath defiance. Letting go of the sun-pendant, Rosa hooked a hand around Kasamor's neck. Heedless of the blood, the regret and her myriad fears, she kissed him. She held him there as long as she dared, a moment of warmth that was all too brief, then stepped away.

"I'm not going anywhere."

Rosa turned her back on Kasamor. Sword levelled, she faced the mist-wreathed kernclaw.

"I'm a Knight of Essamere; a daughter of Orova. I do not flee, and I will not stand aside."

The kernclaw's hood came up. Teeth gleamed in shadow. Metal talons glinted.

"So be it."

Melanna crouched beside the old yew and clung tight to her bow. Her heart hammered loud enough to rattle her ribs. She glanced hither and yon, desperately seeking movement among the trees, and just as vividly hoping she wouldn't find any.

Don't stray into the mists. It was one of the few pieces of her grandfather's advice that Melanna recalled. He'd delivered it to her in earnest tones in the very heart of the Golden Court. She'd answered with all the gravity a five-year-old could muster and wondered why he'd been so insistent. Only when she was much older did she learn that the mists were a gateway to the Raven's Otherworld.

But it was one thing not to stray into the mists. It was quite another when the mists strayed onto *you*. One moment, the valley road had been swathed in a clear, balmy night. The next, it lay beneath a greenish-white shroud, the doorway to the land of spirits crooked open. A land into which her grandfather had now surely taken his Last Ride.

A thunder of wings passed by to the north. Or to what had been the north before the mists had risen. Even direction was suspect now, with flickering echoes of trees long felled crowding beneath the boughs. Past and present blurred beneath the mists.

Screams. A woman's. Then a man's.

Melanna clapped her hands to her ears. She pressed against the yew's trunk, careless of scratches earned from its stiff, spiky leaves. It wasn't her business. Nothing in the mist-wreathed land was her business. If she stayed small, stayed *quiet*, the horrors of the night would pass her by.

Except ... Wasn't that what men expected of her? Even her father, despite his protestations. That she wasn't brave enough, or strong enough, to do more than tend hearth and raise children? Never mind that her father's boldest Immortals would have blanched at the thought of entering the mists. Never mind that there were things in the mist that steel could not vanquish. Or doors that opened onto realms where no sane soul would ever willingly tread.

No. What mattered was that if she hid until the horror was past, warriors would look on her in pity. They'd acclaim it a sign that no woman could ever be worthy of the Imperial throne. After all, it would never be enough for Melanna to prove herself their equal. She had to prove herself their better.

That realisation galvanised courage. Or at least the guttering trace of what might *grow* into courage. And she was not wholly defenceless, after all. Nor wholly foolish.

Melanna unslung her bow and drew a black-fletched shaft from her thigh-quiver. With numbed fingers, she nocked the arrow.

"Ashana, guide your ephemeral daughter," she whispered. "For I fear she's about to do something rash."

But if the distant moon offered any answer, the mist swallowed it.

Melanna picked her way north along the roadside. She travelled swiftly, but not without caution. Around Tevar Flood, there were more dangers than the purely supernatural. Tressian patrols were lighter here than in the turbulent Southshires, but a chance encounter would end her life as readily as any of the Raven's minions.

She almost tripped over the woman's body. She lay face-down by a spent fire, blood glistening at the base of her back and pooling in the dirt below. A sword lay close by – the emerald on its hilt a fit match for the knight's green surcoat. Melanna swallowed, uncertain how to proceed.

The woman moaned.

Melanna scrambled away, heart in her throat.

The moan came again. The breathy agonies of the severely wounded, not the guttural cry of some grave-woken cannibal. Chiding herself for skittishness, she crept forward.

The mists billowed, revealing another body beside the fire. A man. Above him loomed a shape from Melanna's childhood nightmares. A black silhouette straight from legend. Crow-voices shrieked through the mists. The thunder of their wings grew louder and nearer.

She scrambled away as the shape reached out, metal talons hooked in beckoning. Blood ran red across his fingertips, and trickled away.

"What have we here?"

Melanna was too far gone to terror to recognise that he'd spoken in the clipped Tressian tongue. Nor did she note that a pale face lay beneath the hood, rather than a revenant's silver death-mask. Those realisations would come later. In that moment there was only the bow, the arrow and a desperate need.

Her hands shook as the arrow sped away, and the shot aimed for the man's heart took him in the shoulder. She lost his bellow of pain as the crows swept over her in a crescendo of frenzied wings. Casting the bow aside, Melanna dropped to her knees and covered her head with her hands. She offered a ceaseless, mumbling prayer to Ashana. Wingbeats buffeted her about the head and back. Talons plucked at her hair.

And then, as suddenly as it had begun, the crowstorm passed. Silence reigned.

Melanna stayed low for a long time thereafter, her hands still clasped over her head. Her breathing steadied, her heartbeat alongside. She risked an upward glance.

The killer had gone, the crows with him.

Rising on trembling feet, Melanna edged towards the second body. He lay on his back, sword still in hand. His eyes stared emptily at the sky from a face spattered the colour of his crimson robes. His throat was a bloody ruin.

"Nothing I can do for you," she breathed. "I'm sorry."

The mists were thinning. Fading into the night with the killer's departure. Had he called them into being, or had they summoned him? Melanna shook her head. It was enough that he was gone, and she was alive.

A low moan reminded Melanna that the woman still lived. She turned back . . .

A pair of large, muscular shapes appeared through the thinning mist. Recognising too late the horses for what they were, Melanna scowled away embarrassment. The beasts seemed entirely too calm for what they'd just witnessed, but who knew whether they'd seen what she had? She knelt again beside the dying woman. Shallow breaths and a slow, febrile pulse offered little promise of recovery.

Did that matter? The woman was a Tressian, a warrior and an enemy. Had they met on the battlefield, duty dictated that Melanna strike her down.

But they had not met on the battlefield, so duty had no claim. And honour? Honour decreed that Melanna offer whatever help she could. Glory in victory, fortitude in defeat, and honour always – the warrior's mantra.

Rosa danced on a carpet of autumn leaves beneath a gleaming manor house. The trees of her uncles' estate screened the sky, holding the ruddy sunset at bay with upswept arms. She clung tight to her partner as they traced the dance's spiralling steps, her nose almost touching the beak of his black-feathered domino mask.

She couldn't think where she'd been before. Nor could she recall what had possessed her to don the bare-shouldered gown whose russet skirts threatened to trip her with every step. There was only the dance, and the music's slowing beat. And a sense of belonging.

Fiddle strings fell silent. Rosa's partner arched his arm, inviting her to a pirouette. She gladly complied, and turned a graceful step. She couldn't recall his name, nor picture the face that lay hidden beneath a mask that covered all save the dark goatee.

At silent urging, she turned another pirouette, as graceful as the first. Partway round, she glimpsed something new beneath the trees. A woman, lying face down in the soil, her clothes stained crimson. Another woman knelt beside her, hands bloody as she sought to stem the flow.

Rosa turned her back on the strange tableau. Flutes fell silent as colour slipped from the sky. Her partner smiled, and they began another spiralling circuit to the lonely beat of a drum.

Melanna sank onto her haunches and busied herself with the fire. She'd staunched the bleeding and applied a handful of precious elvas tincture to the worst of the wounds. All for nothing. The woman was weak, and her breathing ever more fitful.

The fire caught. The first flames flickered skyward. The woman coughed, bright blood spilling from her lips. Melanna swore. Blood aplenty, and none where it belonged. But there was still hope. There was always hope when the moon was full.

And the moon *was* full that night. With the departure of the mist, its cold radiance filled the dell, a balm to Melanna's tired spirit. If she could see the moon, then the moon could see her.

She shucked off her quiver and dagger-belt and sat cross-legged before the fire. She'd no magic of her own, but neither did the seers upon whom her grandfather had so relied. Ashana spoke, and they listened. But Melanna at least possessed a gift – when she spoke, the goddess listened. If the goddess was so inclined.

"Blessed Ashana," she whispered. "I beseech you. I cannot save this woman. Help me do so."

There was no reply. As ever, Melanna felt foolish for expecting one.

"Blessed Ashana," she repeated. "This woman lies dying. Help me save her. Please."

"I heard you the first time," said Ashana. "And it's not *helping* if I'm to do the work."

Melanna opened her eyes. The goddess – or at least, the only aspect of the goddess she ever saw – stood on the edge of the dell, her fingers slipping through a horse's mane. She wore the form of a woman scant winters older than Melanna herself. Fair skin – paler even than a Tressian's – shone silver in the moonlight. Diamond clasps held back long blonde hair, and she wore a green dress almost as dark as the night sky.

"Goddess." Melanna hung her head.

"I've told you before about that." Ashana drew closer. The trees behind were clearly visible through a form not yet gathered to opacity. She vanished entirely where moon-shadow fell and reappeared once light returned. "An empress cannot bow and scrape."

The words contained rebuke but were framed by a wry smile. Even after all these years, Melanna had never understood why the goddess needled her so. Then again, she still wasn't clear why Ashana spoke to her at all.

"I'm not an empress," Melanna replied. "Not yet, and maybe never."

"And I seldom feel much like a goddess." A simple shrug dispelled the aura of majesty. "And I certainly never used to be, so we may consider ourselves equals, may we not?"

Melanna supposed selective equality was ever the purview of the superior. "Will you save her?"

"Why does it matter?"

"Because it's the right thing to do." She hesitated, but only the truth would serve. "If I hadn't been afraid, I would have reached her sooner. I feel responsible."

Ashana smiled. "Does it ever occur to you that you're trying too hard?"

"I know no other way godd ... lady."

The goddess cocked her head in exasperation. "What if I save this woman, and her survival prevents your father from reclaiming his throne, and thus you from inheriting it after his passing? Would you still plead for her life?"

Melanna looked from Ashana to the dying woman. "Are you telling me she will, lady?"

"I'm asking if that changes your request."

A test? Or was the question as straightforward as it appeared? Was this one stranger worth the Imperial throne? It no longer mattered. Melanna had taken the decision to save the woman the moment she'd risked the mists. Otherwise, what use was honour?

"No," she said at last, and hoped it was true. "My request stands."

The goddess shook her head. "You'll make a poor empress, but a good woman."

A cloud passed overhead. Ashana faded into darkness, only to return brighter than before.

"And what do you think, old friend? I know you're watching."

"You are sworn not to interfere."

A tall, antlered shadow gathered on the far side of the dell – a man's silhouette, given form by cloak and heavy mantle. Green eyes shone beneath a shadowed helm. The newcomer's darkness was not the blackness of death, but of angry storm clouds. It provoked no fear – only respect, and the prospect of fear if that respect went unhonoured.

"My siblings interfere," said Ashana. "Or do you think I can't smell the stink of Otherworld in this place? Dark days are returning, and I promised to keep the light shining."

"Lending magic is not the same as interference," he rumbled. "But if it is to be war, I will fight it gladly. Will you?"

Ashana folded her arms and scowled. "No. I suppose not. I'm not ready for what that will cost." Her expression brightened. "But I don't have to be, do I? After all, lending magic is *not* the same as interfering."

The antlered helm dipped in a nod. "And what of the girl?"

Ashana's gaze fell on Melanna for the first time since the newcomer's arrival. "She's ready."

Melanna opened her mouth, but her voice deserted her. More than her voice. The world had grown muffled, as by fog, or by sleep.

"She has heard more than she should," said the Huntsman.

"It doesn't matter. After all, it's only a dream, is it not? It will pass." Ashana enfolded Melanna in a translucent embrace. "I will help you mend this woman's harms, but you must afterward leave her to whatever fate brings. Your destiny is with your own kind, Melanna Saranal."

A cloud plunged the dell into darkness.

Melanna started awake beside the fire, and stared down at hands that shone silver in the moonlight.

The evening sun had faded almost to black. The dance had slowed alongside. The music had all but fallen silent. Only the double thump of the drum remained, slowed to a steady, remorseless dirge.

And still Rosa danced. Her russet dress was ragged and torn. Her muscles ached and her feet bled. But she clung to her partner through the moribund steps, and wondered where the day had gone.

The drum stopped. Her partner stepped back and offered a respectful bow. A pathway of mist stretched beneath withered trees to where the manor had once stood. He gestured towards the mist and beckoned to Rosa.

Tired beyond words, she reached for his hand one last time . . .

Silver light blazed to burn away the mists. Rosa's partner vanished in a flurry of black wings. His mask shattered as it hit the ground.

The drumbeat returned as a peal of thunder across the heavens.

Rosa lurched upright beside a crackling fire that offered no warmth. Her head spun. Her stomach heaved. And everything – *everything* – hurt.

Another spasm. She fell forward onto her knees. Trembling fingers traced the extent of dressing and bandage. Memories crashed back. The kernclaw. She'd felt his talons across her chest. In her spine. And then he'd turned away.

She should be dead. But he'd turned away. Left her to focus on . . .

Rosa stared bleary-eyed across the fire, at the low cairn beyond.

She stumbled twice in her hurry. On the third time, she fell completely. She reached the stacked stones on hands and knees. With grief-given strength, she tore them aside. Too soon, the sight she'd dreaded lay exposed beneath the boughs.

Overcome with fury colder than any she'd ever known, Rosa cradled Kasamor Kiradin's lifeless head in her hands, and screamed at the dawn until her voiced cracked apart.

Lumendas, 1st day of Radiance

Ascension

The Tyrant Queen's reign is done, but
vigilance remains.
    For just as the shadows are strongest on the
brightest of days, we are never more imperilled than
when we think ourselves safe.

from the sermons of Konor Belenzo

Eleven

They came from the north, black surcoats filthy with the dirt of the road. Near two hundred men and women marching in triple column. Horse-drawn wagons creaked and squealed behind. Revekah's heart ached at the cadence of the marching song. *The Duke of Kerval*. A tune from a life long in the past, before the raising of the phoenix banner.

"Raven's eyes." Tarn craned his neck to see over the wooded crest. "Who are this lot?"

Revekah flashed an angry glance and shoved him back down. "You want to find out the hard way? Looks like Makrov finally sent for reinforcements. Spineless worm."

But no, that didn't feel right. Two days since Josiri had burned his mother's portrait. One day of ill-feeling and violence flaring like summer flash-fires. Another of aftermath, with towns and villages under curfew.

Revekah despaired of Josiri's disrespectful act, but recognised that this was no consequence of that deed. There hadn't been time for a summons, much less for a company of Tressian soldiers to have swift-marched the long roads through Tevar Flood.

Then there was the livery. A silver swan on black. Banners not seen in the Southshires in fifteen years. And at the column's head, two men not easily forgotten. The first, a giant with a wicked scar on his cheek and a fennlander's claymore across his back. The second man, older by a few years, lacked for a right eye, and most of his left arm. Revekah remembered the day he'd lost them. After all, she'd taken both.

Viktor Akadra and Vladama Kurkas. The first the champion of the Tressian Council. The other the dishevelled captain of the Akadra hearthguard.

No, she decided, this wasn't retaliation. This was something else.

A new verse issued up from the road. The one in which the eponymous duke offered up his son to trickster Jack in exchange for an army of forest demons.

"Your hearth and home I will preserve, for an offering of kin."

Revekah breathed the words in time with the soldiers. Funny. The last time she'd sung that song, she'd not understood how anyone – even a body so desperate as the embattled Duke of Kerval – could risk everything by courting so unreliable a presence as the Lord of Fellhallow. But that reserve belonged to a younger woman. The woman she was now would have embraced mischievous Jack, merciless Tzal – maybe even cursed Malatriant, Raven take her eyes – if it brought freedom.

"Who are they?" Tarn hissed, careful this time not to expose himself above the crest.

She regarded him in silence. Like so many wolf's-heads, Tarn was young. Too young to remember Zanya, or the sacrifices of the past.

"Old ghosts." Her eyes returned to the column of soldiers.

She hoped Josiri knew what he was doing.

Josiri returned to the balcony before noon. The ashes of the portrait were long gone from the terrace, swept away at Makrov's order. His last such order before riding hard for the safety of Cragwatch. Beyond sullen Eskavord, ravens soared about fresh corpses on Gallows Hill. As much the price of insurrection as the kraikons standing silent in the streets, enforcing curfew.

Some Ascension this would be.

"Did I do right?" he asked softly.

Anastacia perched upon the balustrade. She once again wore the formal garb of a Trelan seneschal. Vapour curled from the toes of her boots as they swung back and forth. She took a last bite from her apple and tossed it away down the gardens.

"The time for that question is long behind. Now there is only what you do *next*."

"Calenne hasn't spoken to me since. She thinks I've sabotaged her wedding."

"So the gallant Lord Kiradin hasn't yet arrived?" Her tone was as dismissive as her words. "I suspect he's preparing a dashing entrance. And it wouldn't hurt Calenne to think of someone else for a change."

Josiri frowned away criticism aimed at himself as much as his sister. "As you said, I can't change the past. Now there's only what comes next."

Anastacia folded her arms. Her lip curled in thought. "Then why do you fret so?"

"Because every time I look to the future, all I see is the fire."

"Maybe that's how it should be. Maybe *you* are the Phoenix your mother sought to be." A rare moment of solemnity slipped across her face. She drew nearer, smoky eyes brimming. Her fingers entwined his, cool to the touch. "I have laid bare your soul, Josiri. You have it within you to be a great man, if you'll but let yourself."

"Or a great fool."

"That's for history to judge. History is enshrined by the triumphant. So bring triumph. For your people, and for yourself."

"And if it's not that easy?"

"Then prove yourself worthy of my affection, and of your mother's trust."

Bells rang out across Eskavord. The long-awaited end of curfew had arrived. The noonday meeting with Governor Yanda was nigh.

Anastacia's solemnity gave way to amusement. "But if you're to spend hours staring blankly at the hangman's labours, I shall bid you good morning. *Someone* needs to make sure the Ascension feast is prepared. If Calenne's angry now, how unbearable will she be if there's not a scrap of food prepared for her new husband?"

She kissed him on the cheek and stepped away, fingers slipping from his.

"Have I ever told you how much I rely on you?" he asked.

Anastacia cracked a grin. "Never enough."

"I'd tell you more, if you let me. I'd tell you I lo ... "

"No." She cut him off. "We don't use that word, remember? One way or another, the day is coming when you will leave these stones behind, and me alongside. Let's not make that parting harder."

"You think I'm so shallow?"

"I think that a duke who takes a demon for his bride is one who receives a poor end to his story."

"You're not a demon."

"So you keep telling me. But it's not your belief that sets the pyre alight."

As if to reinforce the point, her seneschal's garb rippled. It peeled outward like a blossoming rose. The petals drifted away into scattering smoke, revealing a close-fitting azure gown beneath. It glittered in the sunshine, its beauty a stark contrast to the scowl marring her expression.

"Now *if* you'll excuse me, you have guests and I have duties. We can't serve unpalatable food, and there are so *many* dishes that need tasting."

And no doubt fruits to be "checked" for proper sweetness and wines to be sampled, lest they'd gone sour. Josiri fought the urge to apologise. In their peculiar world, "sorry" was seldom more welcome than "love". The passage of time would ease the wound.

"Thank you. Please tell Governor Yanda I'll see her out here."

The clouds broke. Anastacia offered the glimmer of a smile. "Of course, your grace."

She went inside, leaving Josiri alone with his thoughts, chief among them being the resentment he felt at the coming parting. But Anastacia was right. The first of many sacrifices, no doubt, but this one cut deep. She was bound to Branghall's stones, and his destiny – good or ill – lay beyond. He could leave whenever he wished, if Anastacia opened the hallowgate for him.

The last of the chimes faded into echo. Little by little, life returned to Eskavord's streets. Hesitant townsfolk emerged in ones and twos, wary lest looming kraikons drag them away. Blue uniforms gathered in the main thoroughfares. Flesh and blood guards to replace those of metal and seething magic. Normality – or as close to it as Eskavord had – was returning.

The balcony door creaked open. "Your grace?"

Governor Yanda stood in the doorway, ward-brooch sparkling on her uniform breast, and her expression fixed in a mask of wary politeness. Two soldiers lingered close by – a rare escort, and another reminder of recent troubles.

"Governor." Josiri let bitterness bloom. "Are you proud of what your soldiers have done?"

She joined him on the balcony. "We've suffered losses of our own. A few deaths. Most were defending themselves. For those that weren't, I tender my apologies." She took a deep breath. "I can't imagine what you were thinking."

"I did what the archimandrite demanded."

"True, but I can't help but wonder about the detail."

Josiri frowned to conceal alarm. Yanda wasn't a fool. She wouldn't have lasted in her position otherwise. How much did she know? Or guess? He'd been careful in conspiracy, but there was no accounting for stolen glances, or misspoken words.

"Governor, I'm trying to be polite, but there are limits. It's one thing for Makrov to insist on pettiness. It's quite another for him to blame me for the consequences."

"Leave us."

The guards straightened at Yanda's order and retreated inside. A little of the stiffness slipped from Yanda's shoulders. Scabbard tapping against her thigh, she leaned on the balustrade and stared out across Eskavord.

"I knew your mother," she said. "Did I ever tell you?"

Josiri relaxed, but only a little. Yanda's tone warned that the conversation's end lay far distant from where it had begun. Still, he was curious.

"Not so I recall."

"I'd have been about your sister's age. Fresh from the Sartorov chapterhouse. A squire eager for the front lines. One so very resentful of playing at honour guard for a privy councillor."

"My mother?"

She nodded. "Used to walk around the city. *Nobody* of standing walks anywhere, but she did. And so did I."

"She was the same here."

"*You shouldn't force folk to look up to you*," Yanda quoted. "Only I was full of the arrogance of youth, and I *wanted* folk to look up to me. I'd earned it. I *wanted* folk to see me as something better than them. But I couldn't. Not around your mother. Second day she was in Tressia, a hospital ship came in from Northwatch, thick with wounded. There weren't enough orderlies to get them ashore to the sick-houses, so she rolled up her sleeves and pitched in. Dragged me along, too."

"I had days like that." Josiri wondered more than ever where the conversation was leading. "Chasing down lost livestock. Carting food up into the hills for old Ezrack when the snows came in."

Yanda grunted. "Sounds right. I hated her. Thought she was mad.

Then I saw her unpick a dockers' dispute where Lady Isidor and Lord Akadra spent two months without any progress. Took her an afternoon."

Josiri stifled a twitch at the mention of the hated name. "She'd a knack for that."

"It was more than that. The guildsmen trusted her. They'd seen her suffering the press of crowds instead of parting them with a carriage. They'd heard about the hospital ship ... *and* the rumours she'd stopped her arrogant honour guard handing out a beating to a pair of keelies."

"You?"

Yanda shrugged. "It's a lucky woman who's proud of all her yesterdays. Tried picking my pocket, didn't they? Point is, the guildsmen saw her more as one of their own than one of the Council. After she left, I swapped the Sartorov wolf for the hawk of the regular army."

Josiri started in surprise. A commission in one of the Republic's knightly chapters was not readily thrown aside. Whether you fought alongside your fellows or took up secondment to an officer's command in the regular army, it promised status and advancement enough to satisfy the hungriest ambition. He'd dreamed of it himself, before the War of Secession changed everything. He still recalled the recruiting poster. The crude sketch of the 'shadowthorn' emperor with his roots burrowing across the border and deep into the Republic. The call to arms for all true sons and daughters.

The Prydonis chapterhouse – that had been the dream. The gilt-edged armour and the blood-red plume. Fighting as one blade alongside an entire chapter of knights. Or leading common soldiery from beneath fluttering regimental colours as a captain. Then had come Zanya, when the blood-red plumes of Prydonis had been foremost among the Southshires' betrayers. That killed the dream, sure as stone.

"That can't have been easy."

"It wasn't, but I thought I'd do more good there. Arrogance of a different sort, I guess." She paused. "Broke my heart when your mother raised that phoenix banner. Felt like personal betrayal. I couldn't square it with the woman who'd worked so hard to bring people together."

And there it was. The arrogance so typical of the northwealders. Admiration offered, so long as you laboured towards their chosen ends.

"It's easy to preach unity when your hardest decision concerns the heraldry you wear." Josiri took a deep breath to ward off rising temper. "If you'd learned anything from my mother, you'd have stood beside her."

"You're missing the point."

"And that is?" he asked through gritted teeth.

"I spent half my adult life admiring Katya Trelan. And now? Now it takes effort not to see her as a traitor. I have to think – really *think* – to reconcile the woman I knew with the one who passed into history." Yanda's shoulder twitched in a lopsided shrug. "When I do, I can see she strove for something she felt necessary. Maybe I can even respect it. But it doesn't matter what sets you moving. It's how you end up that counts. You might want to think about that."

Away beyond the balcony, a lone rider galloped up the long approach from Eskavord. The overdue Kasamor Kiradin? Josiri hoped so. He was tired of the game his life had become. The sooner Calenne was safely married off, the better for them both. For everyone.

"Are you finished?" he asked. "Because I've a busy day. You can tell the archimandrite that you've delivered your warnings."

Yanda offered a card player's smile. The kind that served equally to conceal a bluff called, and the readying of a winning hand. For the life of him, Josiri couldn't tell which was in the offing.

"This isn't Makrov's message. It's mine. One last favour to your mother, I guess." She leaned close. Close enough that he could see the pale, hairline scar that ran from her brow to her greying chestnut fringe. "I can't imagine the pressures you're under. But the next time you want to tweak the beast's tail, have a thought for the people down in the mud."

A little tension eased from Josiri's spine. So Yanda *didn't* know his secrets. She just thought that he was an arrogant scion of an entitled bloodline. It hurt, but it was better than the alternative.

"And the beast . . . I mean, the archimandrite . . . Is he roused?"

She held his gaze, unblinking. "Damn near. But you needn't fear. He'll be here to conduct Calenne's wedding. Were I you, I'd tread carefully once it's done."

"His second exodus?" Josiri grimaced for show. With the Hadari drawing ever nearer, exodus no longer held the same threat.

"He's spoken of it. But I doubt you'll live to see it." She smiled mirthlessly. "When only one Trelan remains, the next humiliation may well be the last Makrov tolerates."

This time, Josiri had no need to pretend surprise. Somehow, he'd never considered that by removing Calenne from the family he'd be jeopardising himself. Would Makrov have the temerity to do as Yanda suggested? Hard to say, but ...

Below, the manor gate opened. The rider passed beneath the arch and cantered towards the terrace. It wasn't Calenne's errant betrothed, but a travel-stained young woman in a herald's uniform. Anastacia appeared on the terrace and took a letter from her outstretched hand.

"Something wrong?" asked Yanda.

"I don't know."

Fresh unease gnawed at Josiri. Urgent news never came directly to Branghall. It went first to Cragwatch, or to Yanda's own dwelling in the centre of town. For it to come here ... The Hadari? Josiri almost said as much. He remembered just in time that he knew nothing of the danger in the east – so far as anyone was aware.

The herald, message delivered, rode away. Moments later, the balcony door creaked, admitting Anastacia to the terrace.

"Governor."

When neither smile nor curtsey occasioned a response – or even an acknowledgement of her presence – she glided past Yanda and pressed the letter into Josiri's hand.

The envelope was scuffed from its time in the herald's saddlebags. Taking little note of the curling, spidery hand, Josiri broke the wax seal and began to read.

The writer had laid their thoughts out in distant, but polite, manner. Hardly a surprise, given the author's identity, and the subject of the missive. Only direst need could have moved Ebigail Kiradin to correspond with a southwealder. He clung to the mental image of her writing at arm's length. So much easier than engaging with the letter's content.

A deep breath helped. Steadied him for an altered fate.

Josiri folded the letter.

"Governor Yanda? Please inform his excellency that his services are no longer needed at Ascension." Josiri eyed the balcony door, little relishing what would follow. "Now if you'll excuse me, I have to inform my sister that her betrothed is dead."

Twelve

"**W**hat do you mean, you're leaving?"

Drakos Crovan remained as affectedly charming as ever, but only the deaf could have missed the undercurrent in his voice. Not quite a threat, but with threat near enough at hand. Melanna had heard that tone many times before in the Golden Court. Her father often used it in front of subordinates, as Crovan now was. A handful of other wolf's-heads looked on – the women's expressions no friendlier than the men's. And Vorn, watching her with a predator's dark eyes. That Tressian was more wolf than man.

Or perhaps she only heard the danger because Crovan stood between her and the stairway to Maiden's Hollow? Because she was alone in the face of Crovan's outrage, and Vorn's unfriendly glower?

"I've learned everything I need. It's time for me to rejoin my people."

"Oh, very convenient," said Crovan. "After you eat my food, drink my wine ... have my fellows thin the northwealder patrols at Trelszon? At no small cost in life, I might add. I thought we were allies."

"And so we remain. But my place is at my father's side, where I can properly express your friendship."

Melanna lent a little bite to those last words – a reminder that such expressions were not always positive. She hated doing it. Her father's vengeance was a useful spur to ailing manners, but harnessing it felt like failure. As if she were still a child hiding behind his robes.

It didn't help that she was still unsettled by the previous night. She recalled a dream of blood and silver, and the goddess's soft words urging her home. But like all dreams, the details slipped away the more she sought them.

Crovan nodded, the flush of anger fading from his cheeks. "I see."

"She's running," growled Vorn. "Our comforts not enough for you, princessa? If you've trouble sleeping . . . Well, reckon I can help with that."

Melanna felt her cheeks colour. A ripple of laughter echoed around the root-bound cavern. It died at the chopping motion of Crovan's hand.

"Enough. She's made her decision. We're not brigands." Crovan's gaze settled on Vorn. Its displeasure served as stark contrast to his amicable tone. "*Please* remember that."

Vorn's chair clattered as he rose. "And what guarantee do we have that the great Kai Saran will honour our agreement?"

"You have my word," said Melanna.

"Hah! This is the Southshires, princessa. Word of a noble's not worth much here. No matter how fine their promises or whose colours they wear."

A rumble of agreement issued from the onlookers, although Melanna couldn't rightly be sure which sentiment had roused it. For all the south-wealders' claims of being different to their overlords in the distant city, fascination with bloodline and heritage bore the same bitter fruit. A uniquely Tressian prejudice, and one which Melanna – who'd lived all her life in the vibrant panoply of a Golden Court whose princes hailed from across the Empire – had never understood.

"You're testing my patience. The decision is mine. And it's made." Crovan's hand rested on the pommel of his sword. "Now kindly stop embarrassing me."

Vorn gave a long, slow shake of his head. A deep chuckle spilled from his lips. He turned, whip-swift, and gathered Melanna in a bear hug. Two brisk strides, and her back was against the earthen wall.

"I say she stays. It'll help her father remember his gratitude."

"Unhand me!"

Melanna struggled in the wolf's-head's grip. But her arms were pinned close, and the nearness of the cavern wall robbed her kicks of force. Her choked-off scream of frustration provoked yet more laughter.

"Vorn! Set her down!" Crovan's sword came free of its scabbard. "I won't ask again."

The words lent fresh urgency to Melanna's fug of rage. No! She'd already invoked her father's wrath in place of her own. She'd not play the part of a helpless maiden. Her heel glanced off the wall, prelude to another momentum-less kick.

Vorn didn't even blink. His predator's leer grew crueller, tinged with fresh madness. A trick of the light made his blue eyes swirl with shadow. Melanna's breath caught in her throat to see it. Then, fear and anger coalescing in a single perfect moment of resolve, she slammed her forehead into Vorn's nose.

The howl and spray of blood came as one. His grip slackened a heartbeat after. Melanna landed with a thud and steadied herself against the wall. Head swimming drunkenly, she grabbed Vorn's collar and slammed a foot between his legs. By the time the second howl faded, he was on his knees. She had fingers wound through his hair, and a dagger at his throat.

"You want to know what my word is worth?" Savage joy made the words ragged. She took in each of the cavern's inhabitants in turn. "I promise that if any one of you ever touches me again, I'll sever whatever body part commits the offence. And I'll burn it while you watch. Am I understood?"

She trembled, as much at her own audacity as from excitement. For all her bravado, the wolf's-heads outnumbered her. One of the women was already on her feet. What price did they place on Vorn's pride?

Crovan sheathed his sword. "You're understood. Vorn was out of line. Let him go. I'll make sure he comprehends the depth of his error."

The others subsided. All save Vorn, who gazed with resentment from a bloodied face. But the shadow behind his eyes had gone. Perhaps it had never been there. A hallucination conjured in a moment of panic, and one Melanna readily dismissed as such.

"See that you do."

A tug on Vorn's hair cast him to hands and knees, where he had the good sense to remain. Stooping, Melanna reclaimed her haversack and sheathed her dagger.

"You have *my* word." Crovan offered a mirthless smile. "It's every bit as good as your own."

"I'm glad to hear it. Because you *will* hear from me again. And we'd both prefer that I speak with the voice of a friend."

It was a good exit line. One to be proud of. And one underpinned by her own strength, not her father's. Before shaking limbs could belie that purpose, Melanna strode up the worn stone stairs, and out into the afternoon sun.

Calenne stared out across the eastern valley. The breeze plucked at her hair and at her skirts. She wished it would pluck *her* from the ruined observatory and carry her far away. Nothing else would do so now. Kasamor was dead, her dreams of freedom alongside. A Trelan in a cage of glass, trapped for ever in Katya's legacy.

She wasn't proud of thinking thus. She knew it was selfishness of the highest order. But reason couldn't change the sick emptiness in her stomach. Nor could it make the tears shed for herself a bounty offered up in sorrow for a man she'd far from hated, but had certainly not loved.

Clouds parted, setting the tower awash in brilliant sunshine. Arms outstretched, Calenne edged out along one of the balcony's beams. The giddiness washed a little of her bleakness away. There was a joy to this, especially with the sun's warmth tempered by the wind. There was danger, but danger was part of what made you feel alive. And she needed that, now more than ever.

The sun dipped beneath the clouds. Calenne stared down past the inches of aged timber to the terrace far below. Servants scurried in preparation for Ascension. Was this how Lumestra saw the world? A heaving ant's nest of toil, impenetrable unless you were part of it? Did she even care about those who offered her worship?

Elda – the woman Calenne considered her true mother, for had she not raised her? – had always proclaimed Lumestra ignorant of the ephemeral world. Those who bent knee to her radiance did so like children seeking attention from an uncaring parent. But perhaps on Ascension, of all days, there was hope. Maybe the goddess would grant a boon.

Calenne turned her gaze heavenward and splayed her fingers wide. "Heavenly mother, I stand before you lost, and without purpose ... "

She tailed off, scrabbling for a prayer long unvoiced. There had been something about a land of Dark. A poet's entreaty, learned by rote as a child and long forgotten. But perhaps it didn't matter. If there was any truth to Lumestra's love, it wasn't words that sang to her, but one's heart.

"I want to be free of all this," Calenne breathed. "Show me a path. Send me a sign that this is not all my life will ever be."

As if in answer, shafts of sunlight spilled across the valley. Calenne threw back her head and basked in the warmth, her sorrows forgotten in one glorious moment of hope.

"You'd better hope she doesn't send a gust of wind."

Anastacia's caustic remark set Calenne off-balance. Out-flung arms sought equilibrium in dizzying sky. In that moment of mad panic, all she could think of were the many times she'd spoken of flinging herself from the observatory.

Balance returned with shortened breath and racing pulse. With exquisite care, she turned about on the beam, and fixed Anastacia with an unfriendly stare.

"How long have you been there?"

"Does it matter?"

The demon shrugged, her azure gown glittering like sapphire. The newfound sun had coaxed forth a smile so beatific and content that it struck Calenne breathless. It hardly seemed fair that the demon found so much pleasure in something so commonplace, while she had to fight for reprieve in a life that hated her.

"I don't like being spied on."

"A peculiar sentiment from someone pleading after a goddess's aid."

Calenne scowled to cover embarrassment. It shouldn't have mattered that Anastacia had witnessed her lapse, but it did. No one liked to be caught out for a hypocrite, especially by someone they disliked. She edged back along the beam and reached the crumbled stones of the tower. That meant being a good deal closer to the demon than she liked, but it was a day for disappointments.

"Did Josiri send you to apologise for him?"

Anastacia gathered her skirts and sat among the stones. "We haven't spoken since the letter arrived. But I heard the argument. Everyone in Eskavord heard the argument."

Calenne winced. "He called me selfish ... " And many other things besides. "Perhaps I am."

And *that* was why she avoided Anastacia's company. Her tongue was always so unguarded around the demon. She wanted to believe it an enchantment, a glamour. But it was nothing more remarkable than loneliness. In a house staffed by the transient and the elderly, she'd no one else in whom to confide. Let alone someone approaching her own age. Or who at least had the appearance of such.

Anastacia shrugged. "I understand your frustration."

"I killed him. As surely as I stuck a knife in his heart." Calenne blinked at her own sudden confession.

"Please. You're being ridiculous."

"Am I? Everything my family touches withers. Kasamor's dead because he was coming for me, and I can't tell if I pity him more than I hate him for it." She choked back an angry sob. "And you know the worst? I can't escape the feeling that if I'd at least *tried* to love him, he'd not have been taken. That his death is *my* punishment."

Anastacia's eyes widened in mirth. "Now that *is* deliciously self-absorbed."

"You think I don't know that?"

"I think you're upset, feeling guilty and used to neither. You see Branghall as a cage, but it's also a shield. It protects you from life as much as it denies you a place in it."

"That's not true!"

"Isn't it? When was the last time you went hungry? Lacked for shelter or clothing? I know you've never known grief, because no one's ever here long enough for you to grow attached to them." A sour note crept in. "No wonder you feel as you do. For all the tutors Josiri hired, for all the education you've received, you've never really learnt that the sun doesn't rise for you alone."

"You know nothing of how I'm feeling!"

Calenne hit her. Didn't even think about it. Simply balled a fist and slammed into the demon's smug, self-righteous face.

Anastacia staggered. Only hands braced against the remnant of the outer wall saved her from falling into an undignified heap. She spat a mouthful of whitish-golden blood over the wall. It hissed into vapour in the sunlight. Still sprawled, she transfixed Calenne with an icy gaze.

"As a case in point," she said, her voice as cold as her eyes. "You've never learnt not to start fights you can't win."

The stone beneath the demon's left hand split apart into a handful of rubble. Dust trickled down the tower's outer wall. A halo of golden light blazed into being about her head.

Calenne's instincts screamed at her to back away, or to fall to her knees and beg forgiveness. But the message got lost somewhere on the way to her limbs – a rabbit freezing too late after rousing a fox. She'd never seen Anastacia use magic for more than parlour tricks. The mantle of demon never suited her better than at that moment.

"I don't know how you feel?" Anastacia twisted upright and advanced. "I'm bound to this place, body and soul. And the one person who makes that bearable? One day soon, he'll leave, and I'll be alone. I know *exactly* how you feel, child."

She was close now, close enough that her halo prickled at Calenne's skin. Warm as sunshine, and inexpressibly cold. And yet somehow, the demon's words held more power than her magic.

"Josiri's found a way to escape?" The very idea awoke contradictory emotion.

Anastacia's halo faded, the fury in her expression slipping away alongside. Weariness replaced it. Weariness, tinged with surprise.

"Josiri can leave whenever he likes. I thought you'd realised." She pressed a hand to her lips to stopper a truth already poured away. "You must say nothing. Please."

With those words, two pillars of Calenne's existence fell away into wrathful flames. That Branghall wasn't the cage she'd believed it was bad enough. But that Josiri had said nothing? Indeed, that he'd repeatedly lied to her on the topic when he knew she was so desperate to leave? So much for Trelans sticking together. So much for being able to trust the only family she had left.

"No! You're lying! You have to be! If he can leave whenever he wishes, why would he stay?"

The demon hesitated. "Because his cage isn't the same as yours. The walls and the enchantment are only part of what binds him."

"And the rest?" Calenne waved her own question aside. Anger faded, replaced by a feeling of profound foolishness. "It's me, isn't it? He's protecting me."

"He knows that if he's gone, you'll have to take up his burdens."

"Then he's an idiot."

"Or he knows what you refuse to admit. That you're more your mother's daughter than you realise."

Calenne felt sick. It was too much to take in, especially on top of everything else. "So I'm both a selfish child and a noble soul all at once, is that it?"

"We're all selfish, Calenne. It's how we survive. Some of us have learned to live with the consequences." Anastacia took a deep breath. "If you wish to escape Branghall, I can show you how."

Could she really be free of it all? Calenne stared at the demon, searching for a chink in expression that would reveal the lie. But if Anastacia wove deception, she did so without loose threads to snag.

"Where would I go? What would I do?"

She hated that nagging sense of reluctance. It reaffirmed the image of a spoilt child, demanding what others had to earn.

"That's up to you," Anastacia replied. "It's a big world. Lose yourself in it. I've learnt that it's always better to do something than nothing."

"Even if it means you're following the wrong course?"

"How else will you find out where the proper course lies?"

Calenne turned her back on the demon and stared out across the eastern valley.

How else indeed?

The dappled sunlight of Maiden's Hollow was aroar with drunken laughter, fuelled by ale-stocks broached to toast Ascension. Someone had even fashioned a crude lumendoll from fallen branches and set it in the centre of the dancers' ring. A queen surveying her court. Let folk of quality toast the goddess with prayer. The old ways fired the blood better by far.

Vorn watched the merriment from the clearing's edge, but registered little. The humiliations of afternoon clung to his thoughts, and his wounds throbbed in a manner that bittered ale couldn't lull.

The broken nose was the worst, for it was a badge of shame not easily concealed. No one could see the bruise from Crovan's gut-punch. Just as no one had heard the whispered promise that the next such lesson would be delivered with a blade. Vorn didn't resent that. A leader had to lead, didn't he? And he *had* crossed a line by defying Crovan.

He just wished he could remember why.

Didn't matter now, did it? The girl had far outpaced his own transgressions and made him a fool into the bargain. If not for Crovan ...

Vorn growled and swallowed the rationalisation with another gulp from his ale skin.

Down in the hollow, pipes and fiddles raced into what would doubtless be the first of many drunken reels. Music to stir the spirit and rouse the soul. A pair of familiar figures came stomping down from the crest.

"Oho! Look who's sulking all by his lonesome," said Gregor.

"Leave it out," replied Keera. "Didn't you hear? Got beaten down by a lass half his size."

Vorn drained the last drop from the ale skin and flung it away. "I'm not in the mood."

Keera grinned, and slapped a hand against her not-insubstantial gut. "And I should listen? More meat on me than that shadowthorn princessa. You couldn't take her. What hope have you with me?"

Vorn growled and lumbered to his feet. "You fixing to find out?"

"Be nice," said Gregor. "We bring gifts."

"Yeah? Like what?"

"Like, we know which way she set off. Thought you might be interested." He shrugged. "In case you want to ... even things out."

Vorn's bruised pride rumbled at the prospect. It'd be different this time. She'd beg for forgiveness. He knew it wasn't that simple, but the temptation remained. "Crovan'll have my head."

Keera snorted. "Who'll tell him? Folk go missing in the forest all the time."

She was right. No one need ever know. And if anyone could track the high and mighty Melanna Saranal through the wilderness, it was Gregor.

Down in the hollow, the music grew wilder. The first would-be couples took their turns at the dance. On the opposite crest, Drakos Crovan joined his followers in marking time with clap of hands and stomp of heel.

Thwarted desire billowed darkly about Vorn's thoughts, reawoken by Keera's jibes. The Ash Wind take it all, anyway. Ascension was a time for indulgence. And there was little more indulgent than insults repaid and humiliation soothed.

"Show me," said Vorn.

"Are you sure this is what you want?"

Anastacia was but a hazy outline in the afternoon sunshine, little more than a ghost beneath the oak. The sight provoked an unfamiliar pang of sympathy in Calenne's heart. Whatever the demon's nature – however strained their relationship – she couldn't imagine being reduced to an echo of herself, more memory than substance.

She stared at the bower passage beneath the tree, still struggling to comprehend what she saw. How had the roots parted at Anastacia's command? She'd grown up with tales of such things, but to actually witness it for herself? How little she knew of the world.

"A fine time to ask me that. This was your idea."

The demon shrugged, the motion almost invisible as she. "Then stay."

Calenne glanced towards the house. No. She couldn't go back to a house steeped in Josiri's lies. Not with freedom so close. Katya's old travelling clothes fitted her like a second skin. A raid on the kitchens had provided food for several days, and she'd no shortage of coin. Only the sword buckled at her waist felt out of place – a burden, where her heavy haversack was not. But she could use it well enough, if pressed. One advantage of the tutors Anastacia had earlier disdained.

All that remained was to actually leave. Assuming that the demon wasn't playing a cruel joke. That was one reason to make the attempt in the afternoon, rather than waiting for night. If Anastacia *was* playing her false, better to find out sooner and cushion the disappointment. And Calenne was wise enough to recognise the folly of straying into unfamiliar territory by night.

"You'll explain to Josiri?"

The demon nodded. "When it becomes necessary."

"It shouldn't be until morning. I left word with one of the maids that he shouldn't expect me at Ascension. He won't like it, but he'll understand."

She stared again at the passage. At the insectoid shapes skittering across the exposed roots, and the gentle curl of fibrous tendrils in the shadows. The overpowering scent of damp earth clung to every breath she took, sweet and cloying with decay.

"How do I know it won't collapse?"

Anastacia shrugged. "It won't."

"Easy for you to say."

The demon sighed. "If you don't believe me – if you don't *trust* me – then stay here. Join your brother at the Ascension table and waste your prayers on a goddess who cannot hear them."

And wonder for ever at what might have been? No.

"I'm sorry," said Calenne. "I suppose I don't understand why you're helping me. I've given you no reason to offer me kindness."

Anastacia chuckled. "Perhaps that's why I'm doing it – to prove that I'm your better. Or maybe it's because the greatest gift you can offer is something you desire for yourself. Or it might be that I consider you a distraction your brother can no longer afford. Choose whichever explanation suits you best, but if you are to leave, it must be now. If one of the servants happens upon us, there will be consequences neither one of us will enjoy."

The explanation left Calenne none the wiser, but it didn't matter. It was enough that their interests coincided. There was risk, of course. But life was risk.

She took her first hesitant step.

"Tell Josiri I'm sorry."

Thirteen

It was somehow fitting, thought Malachi, how the skies wept for Kasamor Kiradin upon his homecoming.

The cobbled streets ran like rivers. Rain swept the detritus of the day into overburdened sewers. It had already driven most of the citizenry to the shelter of homes and taverns. Those who remained splashed through the streets with the hunched shoulders and hurried gait of folk wishing themselves already to their destination. They'd not soon return. Even with the sun lost behind the clouds, the bells would soon ring for Ascension.

A full company of the 7th lined the roadway. They stood at silent attention as the covered dray lurched towards the portcullis. No council edict had summoned them, but they had come all the same. A soldier's bond Malachi understood, but would never share.

Beneath the arch, a gold-robed priest led a handful of veiled serenes in hymn. The holy women looked no more pleased to be present than their master. Their black robes hung drab and dark in the hissing rain; the golden thread of hem and sleeve barely glinted. Malachi strained to hear the serenes' words. A wasted effort. It took rare voice to elevate traditional mourning-chant to beauty. These were otherwise.

Rosa walked beside the dray, one hand on the bridle. Her features were pale, her blonde hair plastered across her scalp. A forlorn cyraeth spirit come clawing its way from a shallow grave.

Ebigail Kiradin's carriage sat beneath the archway. Coachmen shivered and sought shelter beneath the ancient stones. Malachi caught no glimpse of their mistress through the veil-draped windows. He supposed even Lady Kiradin was entitled to privacy at a time such as this.

There'd be no tears, Malachi felt certain. She'd offered none in the Council chamber when the herald brought news. But then, nor had he. Public grief was frowned upon. Whether the departed was the oldest of friends or a dearest child, decorum was inviolable.

Yes, the skies wept for Kasamor Kiradin, and the skies alone.

As the dray began the final approach to the parapeted bridge, Malachi could bear it no longer. Drawing his cloak tight, he broke from cover and strode out into the rain. He was soaked through in seconds. Undeterred, he bore down on Rosa and embraced her.

The mists take decorum, anyway.

It was like hugging a statue. Cold, hard and unflinching. Malachi drew back and searched for a hint of recognition in Rosa's eyes.

"I'm so sorry." He wasn't sure why he whispered. No one would hear a thing over the rattle of rain upon cobbles. "What happened? The herald brought your letter, but it said so little."

Somehow, Rosa's expression grew bleaker. "What happened? I failed him. When he needed me, I failed him."

Malachi already regretted asking. Rosa's expression was too close a match for the one he strove to hide. Kasamor would have known what to say. He'd have made a terrible joke to lighten the mood, to force a smile. Anything.

"I'm sure you did everything you could," Malachi said.

"Where's Viktor?"

"On the road, to ..." Malachi cut himself off. That too could wait. "I've sent word, but I don't know when it'll reach him. May I walk with you the rest of the way?"

The draught horse stamped, no more comfortable in the rain than Malachi. Rosa's expression twitched with what might have been gratitude, or what might equally have been pain. She nodded.

Malachi took up station on the horse's opposite flank, and they set off anew. Soldiers fell into step behind the dray. The procession grew with every pace.

King's Gate was no longer empty when they arrived. Ebigail Kiradin stood beneath the archway, swathed in furs and head high. A Tressian matron greeting tragedy with resolve.

The blonde young woman at her side couldn't quite match the display.

Sevaka Kiradin – arrived fresh off the galleon *Triumphal* – had much to learn of the concealment of sorrows. That, or she felt Kasamor's loss more keenly. She was certainly better prepared for the weather than anyone else. The high-collared and long-skirted naval coat would have laughed off a gale's sodden bounty.

It didn't escape Malachi's notice that mother and daughter's station beneath the arch kept both dray and escort out in the deluge.

"Captain Orova," Ebigail's tone held the proper amount of warmth. "You have my thanks for bringing my son home."

"As was my duty, lady."

"Now you may set that duty aside. You've come a long way, on the hardest of roads. Others can take the burden from here."

She beckoned, and the nearest soldiers drew near.

Rosa stiffened. "Forgive me, lady, but I'd rather see this through to the end."

Ebigail frowned. "And I'd have it no other way, Roslava. But I'm told you've not slept these past two days. See out the last miles from my carriage. I'm certain Kasamor would not begrudge a grateful mother's hospitality."

Malachi couldn't help but be surprised. Generosity was expected under the circumstances, but for Ebigail to invite the rain-sodden, travel-stained Rosa into her sanctum? Then again, loss did strange things to people. It might even spur a miser to generosity.

"Respectfully, lady, it's no longer for Kasamor to begrudge or allow me anything, if it ever was." Rosa's voice crackled like ice. "He was my comrade, my ... dearest friend. I'll gladly accept whatever hospitality you offer, but first I'll see him home."

Malachi caught Ebigail's flicker of annoyance. Grieving or not, she didn't care to be gainsaid. But she nodded. And she was not done with surprises.

"I see my son was fortunate in at least *some* of his friends." She exchanged a glance with Sevaka. On receiving a small nod, she raised her voice. "Marek? We shan't need the carriage any longer."

Without another word, Ebigail took up position at Rosa's side and Sevaka at Malachi's. And so, on a rainswept evening – heralded by church bells ringing out for Ascension and surrounded by those who had loved him – Kasamor Kiradin at last came home.

Fourteen

Vorn followed the narrow boot prints, bruised vegetation and mud-died stone for five miles through Davenwood. Long enough for the evening sky to fade to black. Long enough for the last ale skin to empty, and ill-fitting boots to chafe. Gregor's abashed confession was therefore *not* warmly welcomed.

"What d'you mean, you've lost the trail?" hissed Vorn. "Never had it to begin with, more like."

"You read the signs clear as I did," Gregor growled. "And now, they've . . . stopped. It's like she's stepped off into thin air."

Vorn stared across the wooded hillside, failure joining the day's bleak harvest. Gregor was right. To all appearances, nothing larger than a fox had passed that way in hours. Nor was there any clue upon the wind. There was only the burble of water from the stream, and the hundred small sounds of the forest at night.

"She's a witch," whispered Keera. "A shadowthorn shouting prayers at the moon."

"More likely she's Raven-sworn," Gregor spat. "Drifted off into the mists."

Vorn stomped away uphill, growling to himself. Could have been back at Maiden's Hollow, full of ale and curled up with something warm and pliant. But no. Instead, he had to go harking at his pride.

Ahead, down in the hillside dell, a campfire smouldered.

Calenne drew her blankets tight and hunched closer to the flames. Thus far, freedom had brought blisters, cold bones that the fire seemed pow-erless to warm, and isolation.

She loved every minute.

Her plan was simple, forged in the afternoon as she gathered posses-sions for travel. Head east, away from Eskavord and the possibility of pursuit. Then veer south towards the forge-fires of Thrakkia, shadow-ing the roads. She'd be across the border before anyone knew she was free. No one in Thrakkia would care. The thanes were too busy fighting among themselves.

In truth, Calenne didn't know wholly what to expect from Thrakkia, based as her knowledge was on the exaggerations and hearsay of Branghall's servants. But all stories agreed that it was a more, well, bom-bastic nation than the one from which she hailed, full of colour and life. For good or ill, she could use a little of that. Flames lit in feast and cele-bration of the living, the dead and everything in between. The markets thick with treasures claimed from distant Athreos, and lands stranger still. The bright colours of unfurled sails as drakonships slipped into the open seas, making voyage of trade or war as their masters decreed. Thrakkia was dangerous, certainly, but peril had strange vigour of its own. Too much of Calenne's life was drowned in grey, overcast by a shadow whose source she couldn't see, and she'd longed to be free of it.

Even so, Calenne was aware that her plan was less than it first appeared. A starting point without definite conclusion. Food and coin wouldn't last for ever. If work of a menial sort was required, then she'd do it. Whatever it took. Education had bequeathed a skill for facts and figures, and she possessed a winning manner when roused to it. She'd work her way south and east. See realms her ancestors had never trod.

Anything was possible, if she was prepared to *do* anything.

Rustling leaves stirred Calenne from dreams of the future. She twisted, her hand closing about the short sword's grips. Left to her own devices, she'd have borne a dagger alone. Unfortunately, such weapons seldom intimidated unless they were already at the throat.

Not that the broken-nosed man looked the sort to be intimidated by anything. Scuffed travelling leathers and bruised features spoke to a dangerous life, or one marred by violent disappointment.

"Who are you?" she asked.

The man's features creased into a scowl. "It's not her."

Calenne frowned, then realised he'd not been talking to her, but to someone *behind* her. She rose, one hand on her sword, and the other on the scabbard. A thin man and a heavyset woman stood on the hillside's gentle slopes, the latter with a rusty sword drawn.

"Does it matter?" asked the woman.

Broken-nose's scowl deepened. "Guess not. Pretty little thing, aren't you?"

On balance, Calenne had preferred being ignored. "I want no trouble."

"Alone in the forest with only a scrap of metal for protection? Doesn't matter what you want." The scowl became a leer. "But we'll take care of you. If you ask nicely."

"Look at this lot," said the thin man, his tone struck with wonder.

He upended her haversack. Oil-clothed provisions scattered across the dell. Gold crowns fell like rain. The thin man fell to his knees and scrabbled in the dirt.

Calenne drew her sword and clung to it as the lifeline it had so quickly become. "That's mine! Let it alone!"

The thin man scrambled back, hands held up in surrender. "Yours? I don't think so. Duke's ransom here. Where'd you steal this lot, eh?"

Broken-nose lumbered closer, his own sword now drawn. "Don't make trouble. I've had a bad day."

Calenne spun on her heel, the point of her sword tracking towards Broken-nose. Dreams of travel had faded to nothing, blotted out by the prospect of robbery and worse. Raven take Anastacia anyway. The demon had rushed her into this. This was *her* fault. Calenne knew the thought was untrue even as it formed. Nonetheless, the spark of anger helped her stand a little taller, a little straighter.

"It can still get worse." She barely recognised her own voice, so hard and flat had she spoken.

Broken-nose flinched. "Some manners wouldn't hurt your prospects any."

"Steady, Vorn," said the woman. "Don't you recognise her?"

"What are you talking about?"

"She's the duke's sister."

Calenne's heart sank to an even lower ebb.

The thin man laughed. "You're daft. What'd she be doing out here? Locked up in Branghall, isn't she?"

"I tell you, it's her." The woman spoke soft and insistent. "I was there when they burned the painting. On the balcony, she was. Scowling like there was a bad smell under her nose. Doesn't know how good she has it. Never missed a meal, have you *my lady*? Never been rousted in the middle of the night because of some northwealder's lies?"

Fear crashed across Calenne's thoughts. Sword-given confidence faded to nothing. "Look. Take the money. Take anything you want. But leave me alone."

Broken-nose's expression brightened. "Well I never. Lumestra loves me after all, eh, Keera?"

They closed in.

Viktor mistook the first scream for a shrieker owl announcing its intent to slaughter something small, desperate and furry. It wasn't until a second split the air that he recognised the voice as a woman's.

Across the dying fire, Vladama Kurkas scowled into his tankard and began to rise. "Things haven't changed much. Fifteen years, and still a lawless bunch of cusses. Want me to take a look?"

Viktor waved him down. "No. I need to stretch my legs."

"Suits me. Bad enough spending Ascension out in the middle of nowhere without a body to cosy up to. Makes me long for the border … all those farm-lads impressed by a uniform." Kurkas set his empty tankard aside and reached for Viktor's with his good arm. "Won't be needing this, will you?"

Viktor snorted at his captain's presumption. The audacity of an old comrade. He left the tent, skirting ordered lines of sleeping soldiers and smouldering watch fires. A handful of hearthguards were awake. The thin birch-scented breeze carried the soft murmur of their conversation.

He felt wary eyes upon him, sensed the apprehension of orders soon to be issued. They were good lads and lasses all. The best. After two days of hard marching and the prospect of difficult days ahead, Viktor couldn't blame them for wanting a quiet night.

Nor did he especially want to stretch his legs, as he'd told Kurkas. But since they'd crossed into the Southshires, he'd been assailed by the lingering sense of … something. It wasn't fear, not exactly. More, it was a feeling of loss tinged with anticipation. Drink could not ease that feeling, though Raven knew he'd given it many opportunities to do so. Nor could any other form of bodily pleasure drive it out. Only activity saw it suppressed, and in the still watches of the night there was little activity to be found. Worse, his shadow revelled in the sensation.

Sentry pickets stiffened to attention at his approach.

"You heard?"

Sergeant Brass gave a sharp nod. Another veteran of Zanya, he was as glumly unenthused about a return to the Southshires as Captain Kurkas. "Off to the south, my lord. A quarter mile. No more. Was about to take a couple of the lads for a gander."

Viktor grunted. In another life, Brass had been a poacher – the scourge of the Akadra estates. Age had done little to blunt his senses. If he said a quarter mile, a quarter mile it would be.

"The watch is yours," he said. "Stay on post. I'll see for myself."

The thin man's grip tightened across Calenne's throat. Blood seeped from the cut on her brow, stinging her eyes. She blinked it away and sought her sword.

There. By the fire. Within reach, if she could get free.

Fingers closed on her wrist, dragging it up and behind her back. Black spots danced behind her eyes.

"You have her, Gregor?" asked Vorn.

"I have her. A fighter, isn't she?"

Over by the fire, Keera moaned and grasped ineffectually at her bloody shoulder. Calenne clung to the memory of her screams as the blade bit home. A bright point in a night growing steadily darker.

"Hush your noise," growled Vorn. "We've had enough caterwauling."

"Easy for you to say," Keera bit out. "It's not your arm."

"Tell you what," Calenne told her. "Give me back my sword, and I'll show him how it feels."

Vorn struck her across the face. Her reply dissolved in a blur of crimson. She spat a sticky gobbet onto the ground.

Gregor laughed. The grip on her wrist slackened. Just enough. Through the pain and the thick, metallic tang of her own blood, Calenne realised it was the best chance she'd have. She brought the heel of her left boot down on Gregor's instep, and flung herself backwards.

Calenne lost Gregor's howl of pain in the crashing, jarring thud as they slammed into the undergrowth. She drove an elbow into his face and staggered upright. Still unsteady, she fled the dell, uncaring of the branches whipping at her face or the thorns raking her clothes.

She stumbled more than ran. Her pulse raced in her ears. The footsteps behind thundered with the urgency of drumbeats. She was going to die. And yet somehow, the prospect was a distant one, as if a fate destined for another. She wished she could speak to Josiri one last time. No. This was his fault, as much as hers. What more was there to say?

She didn't see the tree in time, hidden in moon-shadow as it was. Her left shoulder struck a glancing blow, and she caromed away. She landed awkwardly on splayed hands and knees. The strike of a boot against her hip tipped her belly-up. Her head struck an exposed root. The world swam.

Calenne scrambled back on hands and haunches. Her back struck the rough, unmoving obstacle of a tree trunk. A heartbeat after, the point of Vorn's sword was at her throat. Shivering yet somehow defiant, she glared up at him. She could at least die with dignity.

"Do it," she spat. "I don't care."

"Oh no, *my lady*," said Keera, her good hand still clasped to a bloody shoulder. "First, you owe me for an arm."

Gregor limped into sight. "For starters."

The shadows surged. Gregor simply . . . vanished. A lingering scream ended in a sickening thump. A new shape bore down through the trees, blacker than the night.

"Gregor!"

Keera fumbled for her sword. She reeled away in a spray of blood and crashed into the brambles, lifeless as a side of butcher's meat.

With a garbled whimper, Vorn threw down his sword and fled.

Calenne barely saw him go. Her throat tightened as she laid eyes on the newcomer. Fear she'd thought vanquished dragged her once more into icy embrace. That butcher's sword. The black surcoat, and its blazon of the silver swan. She knew that swarthy, scarred face almost as well as she knew her own, though she'd never seen it with adult eyes.

The Black Knight. The man who'd killed her mother. He'd come for her. As she'd dreamed he would.

He reached out for her, lips framing words she did not hear. For in that moment Calenne Trelan's tortured mind cast off from the shores of the waking world and took refuge upon a sea of turbulent dreams.

Astridas, 2nd day of Radiance

Friendship is worth nothing unless tested.

    Better an enemy of unwavering purpose than an ally of uncertain faith.

                             from the sermons of Konor Belenzo

Fifteen

Calenne awoke swathed in blankets. A dull ache shadowed her thoughts. Daylight streamed through cracks in the pavilion's panels, parting gloom sweet with the scent of dew-laden canvas. She heard muffled grunts of men and women at labour beyond, and ... the clash of weapons?

The previous night flooded back. The wolf's-heads. The Black Knight.

She sat bolt upright and clutched the blankets to her thin blouse. A blouse that felt tighter about her right arm than was usual. Katya's coat and boots sat piled beside the low, slatted bed. Her scabbarded sword rested against the tent pole. Where was she?

"Good morning."

Shadows shifted on the tent's far side. The scarred face. The eyes.

She half-sprang, half-fell from the bed. Her knee jarred, but her hand closed about the sword. Before the Black Knight could close the distance, she had the blade free. Its point wove uncertainly between them.

"Get away from me!"

The shriek was fear given voice. Calenne hated its tremor.

The Black Knight arched an eyebrow and raised his hands. "You've nothing to fear."

Nothing to fear. From the man who'd slain Katya. "You expect me to believe that?"

Better. She almost sounded in control. Calenne embraced the lie, clutched it tight and willed it to be truth.

He circled closer. She sidestepped to keep the blade between them and realised too late that the motion took her further from the tent's flaps and safety.

"I *hope* you'll apply reason," he said. "I could have harmed you while you slept, had I desired. Instead, my physician tended your wounds. How *is* your arm?"

Calenne's free hand found the bandage below her right wrist, and the scabbed cut upon her brow. Neither felt as bad as they should.

The pavilion's folds parted to admit a man whose left arm ended in a knotted bundle of cloth a little above his elbow. His tunic bore both the silver swan and a captain's star.

"Bit of a racket, sah. Everything squared and set?" The newcomer's voice held the gravelly vowels of one who'd lived his formative years in the heart of Tressia. His one good eye took in the scene with wry amusement. "Begging your pardon, but I've warned you about this before. Ain't no way to meet a woman. Ain't no way to meet anybody."

"Thank you, Captain Kurkas." The Black Knight's growled reply contained a hint of humour, despite his glare. "But the matter is in hand."

Kurkas scratched at his eyepatch. His gaze didn't leave Calenne's sword. "If you say so."

"I do. Take the company on to Eskavord. Leave a dozen soldiers and one of the carts. We'll follow along, assuming our guest is well enough to travel."

"Certainly has a vigour to her. You sure you don't ... "

"That will be all, captain."

"Right you are." Kurkas bowed and beat a hasty retreat.

Calenne's captor – or should that have been rescuer? – waited in silence, hands raised in surrender to a woman little more than half his size, seemingly unworried at the tableau's inherent ridicule.

"You're going to Eskavord?" Calenne said at last, raising her voice over the noise of the departing soldiery.

"I've business with your brother." His lips shifted. Not quite a smile, but not wholly *not* a smile either. "Perhaps you'd be kind enough to introduce us? It has been some time since Josiri and I last met."

Fifteen years was indeed a long time. And yet he'd recognised her. No wonder as to why.

"My name is Viktor ... "

"Akadra." Calenne spat the word. "I know who you are. You killed my ... You killed Katya."

"So I am told," he said drily. "But you of all people should know that no truth escapes the Council's lips unsullied."

She jerked the sword-point at his chest. "What do you mean?"

"I offered your mother protection. Instead, she embraced the Raven."

Calenne glared at him. It couldn't be true ... could it? The Black Knight was a murderer. She wanted to snarl rejection, but the narrative of a lifetime's nightmares could offer no rebuttal to the soft-spoken claim. Akadra hadn't sought to convince, but to relay fact.

"You're lying." Even to her, the rejection sounded feeble.

"Why would I do so? I make no apology for those I slay, nor do I feel shame for the deed. Death, after all, is my calling and my duty."

The desire to believe him was overpowering. Why? She'd lived her whole life in fear of the Black Knight, the cruel revenant from her past. But now he was before her, the mantle didn't fit. And if that were so ...

"I always knew she was a coward," she whispered.

"No. Your mother was a brave soul." He spoke warmly, almost reverently. "In many ways, I admired her conviction. She taught me much that day. I've held the lessons close."

The compliment, delivered so close behind the accusation of suicide, served only to harden the latter's veracity in Calenne's mind. A long-held truth slid away, but another hardened to granite.

Her knuckles whitened on the sword. "She wasn't my mother!"

The commotion of voices and carts faded into the distance. Akadra fell silent, perhaps reflecting on the wisdom of confronting an agitated orphan with her parent's suicide. Or perhaps not. He didn't look the type to second-guess. Calenne envied him that.

"Must I take the weapon from you?" he rumbled. "I'd prefer you set it aside through choice. Less discomfort for us both."

Calenne suspected the discomfort he meant was hers alone. In any case, she'd no illusions of besting the Council's champion. She took a deep breath and set the sword down.

He lowered his hands, crossing them at the small of his back. "Thank you."

She regarded him sidelong, again surprised by his solemnity. Almost charming, in a grim sort of way. Not the brash, dazzling presence of the late Kasamor Kiradin, Lumestra embrace him, but a stolid certainty of manner and poise.

"Why were you watching me while I slept?"

"An exaggeration. I arrived moments before you awoke."

"I expect you're waiting to be thanked. For saving me."

Again, the not-quite smile. "Duty requires no thanks. And as to what quarrel occurred between you and Kasamor that set you fleeing into the night? I shan't pry. Some matters should remain private."

A precipice yawned beneath Calenne's feet. "You saved me because of Kasamor?"

"I saved you because you were in need." He shrugged. "That you are my friend's wife makes me all the gladder."

She could lie. Of course she could. But Akadra would discover the truth soon enough.

"Then you haven't heard?"

She felt his eyes on hers, colder than before – his expression hard where before it had offered only empathy . . . even kindness.

"Heard what?" For the first time, a hint of danger crept into Akadra's tone.

Calenne lowered her eyes from his. "Kasamor's dead. He died days ago."

Akadra's brow furrowed. A muscle jumped in his jaw. Slowly, steadily, he turned his back to her. His right hand tightened about his left wrist. He neither spoke, nor uttered any sound. Yet somehow, his presence filled the small pavilion in a way it hadn't before. Goose bumps raised across Calenne's flesh. For a moment, she thought she saw her breath frosting in what so recently had been balmy air.

"How did he die?" Akadra asked at last.

Calenne shivered away the imagined cold. *That* belonged to her nightmares, not the waking moment. "On the road. More than that, I don't know. Lady Kiradin's letter said almost nothing."

"And his companion?" His voice took on fresh urgency.

"I don't know." In all the hours she'd dwelled on the fateful news, Calenne hadn't stopped to consider if others had perished alongside. "I'm sorry. Was she important?"

"All my friends are important." He turned to face her once more.

A little of the warmth returned to his voice, but it couldn't wholly hide the darkness rippling beneath. But Calenne sensed that whatever threat it held was not levied at her. "But it's selfish of me to dwell on my own loss when yours is the greater. You have my deepest condolences, Miss Trelan."

Calenne opened her mouth to reply, but no words came. In the space of minutes, her emotions had spiralled from abject terror, to pity. Now they settled on familiar guilt. But this, at least, she could conceal.

"Thank you," she said, dully.

Akadra's eyes narrowed. "If you are not wed, you remain Trelan. You should be at Branghall."

Even now, there was no accusation in his tone, just curiosity.

She shot him as defiant a look as she could manage. "I escaped."

"The enchantment is supposed to be without flaw."

"So are many things. But they're not. You're the Council's champion. You of all people should know that."

"Indeed." A hint of a grin, as soon gone as glimpsed, flickered across his lips. "It's no concern of mine. But I must impose upon you for that introduction. Events will unfold better if your brother has reason to think kindly of me."

Calenne wondered what Akadra referred to. She decided that she didn't care. "I'm not going back to Branghall."

"I must insist." There was a hardness beneath the words, but no threat. "All I ask is that you offer witness to the small service I provided. A few kind words, if you can stir yourself to them, and no more. After that, you may go wherever you wish."

Suspicion crowded in. He couldn't mean that, could he? "Truly?"

"You have my word."

He *did* mean it. That was almost as concerning as the alternative. Calenne's world was built on a handful of ironclad certainties. That Trelans did not leave Branghall was chief among them. And yet here was Viktor Akadra, the Council's champion, offering to shatter that certainty like it was nothing. He could be lying, but what did that lie get him that he could not take by force?

And she *did* owe Josiri a farewell. Unbearable though he was, he was still her brother. Although the question remained whether he'd be as

sanguine to see her leave as the Black Knight seemingly was. She shook
the complication aside. It wasn't Josiri's choice, but hers.

As for Viktor Akadra? More than ever, it seemed the man was *not* the
monster. All those nightmares. A girl's imagining. No more real than
the hollow voice that whispered in her thoughts while she slept, or the
boggart that dwelled beneath her bed.

"I'd sooner have some warm water, soap and the privacy in which to
wash," she said. "I'm filthy, and I stink. Give me that, and you'll have
your kind words."

"I confess that I hadn't noticed," he rumbled. "But I will see what
can be done."

"Where is Calenne?"

Josiri broached the question with more force than he'd intended, but
it had been a long night, full of worry and suspicion. Even the orange-
gold of the early sun and the summerhouse's warmth couldn't dispel the
peculiar chill born of sleeplessness.

The pencil ceased its dance across the paper. Anastacia glanced up
from the desk, her black eyes empty of interest. "How should I know? Is
this why you've been wandering the grounds?"

Josiri's temper quickened. It wasn't what she said, but the way she'd
spoken. Calenne always invited an edge to Anastacia's voice. Irritation
tinged with disappointment. But not this time. Something had changed.
And he'd a sinking feeling he knew what.

"She wasn't at Ascension."

"I know. I was there, remember? Her mistake. The cooks outdid
themselves, and the wine . . ."

"Her bed's not been slept in. She's not in Grandfather's tower, and
none of the servants have seen her since yesterday."

He paused, alert for a guilty twitch. He saw only polite interest. Her
face could have been a mask, watchful and unblinking. Almost innocent,
or as close as she ever came to such. More and more, this felt like a game.
Was that why he was spinning it out? To give her a chance to prove his
suspicions wrong?

Anastacia returned to her sketch. "I've not seen her this morning either."

"But you met with her yesterday. In the grounds." Josiri strove to match her calm, collected manner. "A servant saw you."

The pencil scritched to a halt, the delicate arc of a tower's onion dome incomplete on the page. Anastacia tapped the point twice on the paper and set it aside. "Ah."

He found no satisfaction in the confession that was no confession. "You opened the hallowgate."

A hesitation. "Yes." She still didn't look up from the desk.

"How did she learn of it? What did she threaten?" He shouldn't have underestimated her. For all her faults, Calenne was as bright as the pinnacle star. It wouldn't have taken much sloppiness on his part for her to work things out. "A promise to throw herself from the tower, I suppose."

For a heartbeat, Josiri mistook the low, throaty ripple for a sob – an utterance as alien to Anastacia as tears. Then he recognised it as a chuckle.

"Threaten me? All these years, and you think a threat could move me? It was my idea."

"Your . . . ?" He took a deep breath to smother a flash of anger. It didn't work. "Do you know what you've done?"

"What she wanted. What *you* needed."

"What *I* needed?"

At last, her gaze rose from the desk. Dark eyes bore into his. "Don't play the fool, Josiri. It doesn't suit you. Or are you now to pretend that Calenne's broken wedding wouldn't have changed your plans?"

Josiri flinched. "You've sent her straight into harm's way. The northwealders are on edge. The Hadari are coming. This was no time for indulging my sister's selfish fancies!"

Anastacia's eyes pulsed. "Only your own, is that it?"

"You want to explain that?"

She rose, wreathed in golden haze as temper slackened control over her form. A small, distant part of Josiri's brain shrank back – urged the rest of him to apologise. But he held his ground and willed a trembling knee to stillness.

"Calenne's wishes have never mattered to you," said Anastacia, "not unless they mesh with yours. She wanted her freedom. I saw no reason not to grant it."

"She could die."

"So could you! At any moment. So could any of us. In the end, the Raven takes us all."

A sombre tone swelled beneath the final phrase. Taking it for a crack in resolve, Josiri pressed on. "And if the northwealders find her roaming free? Do you know what it will mean if Yanda and Makrov realise they've been played for fools?"

"Then you'd better get your revolution underway, hadn't you? I've set the shutters in place, calling for a meeting. Revekah and Crovan should be here for noon. I suggest you have something to tell them."

Josiri couldn't decide what was worse – the betrayal, or the sensation of losing control over his own life. He supposed it to be his own fault for assuming equality that plainly did not exist. For all Anastacia's professed adoration, for all the intimacy they'd shared, no bridge could span the chasm between them.

"I suppose you're pleased with yourself?" he said bitterly.

Her shoulders slumped to match softening eyes. "Oh, Josiri. What I am is tired of waiting for you to leave. I just want it over."

Her sudden sorrow almost quenched Josiri's anger. But not quite. How could he be certain this wasn't another of her games? His heart might have convinced him, were it not already heavy from her betrayal. And beneath it all, there was a spark of sullen resentment that Anastacia might be right. About Calenne. About him.

"Then I'll leave you to your sketches," he bit out, deliberately misreading her words. "I'll meet you by the oak at noon. I think it's better our paths don't cross before then, don't you?"

She stared unblinkingly, her expression unreadable. "Yes, your grace."

He nodded, recognising that the formality of her tone widened the chasm yet further.

Then he saw smoke billowing against the eastern horizon and realised he wouldn't be making the noon meeting after all – at least, not the one Anastacia intended.

Sixteen

Cracked by cold winters and patched only by the thriftiest of repairs, the north bastion shuddered with the rumbling groan of a dying mountain. Dust and rubble flooded the muddy ditch. The boneless, broken soldiers who'd once manned its ramparts lay stark against white stone-spoil.

"Get out of there, you fools!" Lieutenant Hedragg bellowed. He knew the words would never carry from the central keep to the neighbouring bastion. "It's coming down!"

Those who escaped the bastion's ruin did so only through the sacrifice of two kraikons. Uncaring of the danger, the constructs braced palms against the outer wall and steel-shod feet against the courtyard's flagstones.

Men and women took crumbling stairs three or four at a time, or leapt from the walls to uncertain fates. Then, with a dying groan of mangled rock, the upper storeys plunged. The deluge swept the last of the garrison aside and buried the selfless kraikons beneath rubble. With a yawning, groaning roar, a portion of the eastern wall gave way alongside, leaving a ragged breach as invitation to the besiegers.

Hedragg found no comfort at all in the lack of screams. No cry could have triumphed over the drumbeats. They reverberated in Hedragg's gut, jarring his bones and setting his teeth on edge. He longed for their ceasing. At the same time hoped they never did, for that meant the assault was coming.

"We can't hold them!" Even shouting, Hedragg barely heard his own words over the din.

Captain Karmonov rounded on him, teeth bared and eyes blazing. "We do not yield! Death and honour!"

Hedragg stared at her, mindful to conceal his horror from the common soldiers. Half a company lost in a single salvo, and the courtyard open to direct assault. For all that its old stones dominated the mountainside – for all that its ballistae commanded the east–west road that ran beneath its walls – Voldmarr Watch could not be held. Not with twice its three hundred blades. But Karmonov was a soldier of the old school, a veteran of victories won along the Ravonn. Death and honour. And likely both at once.

"Herald!" bellowed Karmonov.

A pasty-faced girl no more than fourteen years old threw a hasty salute. "Captain?"

"Find Sergeant Gellern. Tell him he's to hold the breach."

"Yes, ma'am."

The girl bobbed a bow and hurried away across the keep's rampart. Hedragg wondered what had brought her to Voldmarr in the first place. Likely an empty belly or a thief's brand. Half his soldiers were running from hunger or the noose.

Iridescent white flame arced high, launched from siege engines concealed where the pine-forested slopes fell away towards the border. The missiles slammed into the southern bastion. Ancient stones cracked and fell away. Ballistae crashed from their mountings. One of Voldmarr's precious remaining kraikons slid sideways as the outer walkway collapsed. It struck the courtyard's flagstones with enough force to send cracks racing like jagged spider webs.

Through it all, ballistae fired blind into the distant trees. Again the fire came, this time plunging past the ruined north bastion and the crumbling curtain wall. Gellern's hastily assembled defensive line broke apart even as it reached the gaping breach in the east wall. Wounded thrashed madly as white fire burned flesh black. Shields locked together once more, the line of flesh and steel desperate to prevail where stone had not.

To Hedragg's eyes it looked so thin. So terribly, terribly thin.

The herald returned as the bombardment faltered. She resumed her station at Karmonov's side without a word. Her eyes never left the forest.

Thick black smoke spiralled into the sky above the north bastion as fire took hold. The first gold glinted at the tree line's edge. The drums stopped.

"They're coming," Hedragg muttered.

"This is it!" Karmonov bellowed. "Make Lumestra proud! We fight to the end!"

"*To the end!*" The shout crashed back across the ramparts.

Pride emerged triumphant from Hedragg's swirling emotions. In a way, Karmonov was right. There was glory to be won and duty to be upheld. But still he couldn't shake the feeling that lives spent today were lives wasted.

The first Hadari marched up out of the trees. Formations took shape on the slopes. Silken robes and golden scales of the Emperor's Immortals advanced in steady lockstep, their shields braced against crossbow fire. The finest warriors in the Empire, come to Voldmarr Watch. Overkill in the highest degree, to Hedragg's judgement. It marked the enemy commander as impatient, or perhaps inclined to offer compliment to the doomed garrison by sending his best onto the walls. Clansmen of the Imperial heartlands pressed in behind, their garb drab and muted by comparison as they scrambled up the slope. Arrows fell like rain.

And the banners. So many banners, each bearing a warchief's heraldry. Wolf masks, snake fangs and crow brands.

Two-score banners. Two-score warchiefs. And more to come, yet hidden beneath the trees. Kai Saran had brought thousands of blades.

The drumbeats crashed back, louder than before.

A kraikon broke ranks at the northern end of Gellern's line and surged downhill. Huge legs pounding against stone, it ploughed into the Immortals. Shields buckled beneath the impact. Bodies were flung away by the killing weight of living bronze. Golden magic leapt along the blade of a longsword taller than a man. It crackled as its wielder reaped shadowthorns. A massive, brazen hand plucked a screaming Immortal aloft and wielded him as a bloody flail.

A pride of simarka crossed the rubble and tensed for the pounce. Metal clanged on metal as they struck shields, bowling Immortals away down the slope. Others darted into the newly opened gaps, raking with tooth and claw.

The Hadari formation shuddered, faltered. Cheers broke out along the walls. Fists punched the air in savage glee.

"Too soon," Hedragg muttered. "Should've held them for the charge."

Gellern had panicked, but who could blame him for that?

Horns blared. Drums boomed. The Immortals bellowed defiance and came on with quickened pace and new determination. Hammer cracked against bronze. Golden light flared. Simarka fell silent as the light left them, reverting to husks of mangled alloy. The kraikon's knee shattered, and the giant fell beneath a swarm of golden scales.

Hedragg tried to estimate the shadowthorn dead. At least a hundred, and as many more wounded.

Nowhere near enough.

The first Immortals' shields crested the ravaged east wall. Hedragg drew closer to his captain. "There's still time."

"No." For once, Karmonov's tone was bereft of anger. "It's too late. We'll feel their spears in our backs long before we reach safety. But you go. Ride to Governor Yanda. Tell her that Voldmarr Watch holds, but that it will not hold long."

And just like that, Hedragg was free of the slaughter. Free of Karmonov's hollow glory. But now the opportunity had arrived, he found he'd no stomach for it. His place was alongside his comrades – in life or death.

He took a deep breath and turned to the herald. "You heard the captain's words?"

The girl's gaze flickered from Hedragg to Karmonov and back again. "I did, sir."

"Then take my steed and see that they're delivered." Hedragg turned to Karmonov. "With your permission, I'll join the 2nd in the breach. One of us should be there."

"Granted. Death and honour, lieutenant."

He hesitated, but in the end what else was there? "Death and honour."

Seventeen

The oppressive catacomb air closed about Malachi like a fist. The serpents of sweet incense curling from the braziers lent shortness to every breath, and a rasp to every word. An interment tradition – an imitation of the mists of Otherworld. And like most traditions, Malachi could have managed quite handily without it.

"And so, we commit Kasamor Kiradin to silence, in preparation for Third Dawn, and when Lumestra leads us all once more into the light."

The priest's booming sincerity filled every crack and cranny. Confident, consoling.

"*Lumestra wake us from darkness,*" Malachi joined the congregation in the chant. "*And lead us into the light.*"

Organ music bloomed from pipes hidden by the outsize statues. They numbered hundreds, lining the aisles, silent guardians atop entombed flesh. And this was but the Kiradin reach of the catacomb. One vault among dozens.

The priest stomped the heel of his staff on tile. Once. Twice. One strike of the staff for each making of the world.

"Make the hallowed farewell," he said. "But do not mourn. For we will all be born again with the coming of the Third Dawn and walk once again with those we have lost."

The choir of veiled serenes raised their voices in hymn. The front ranks of the congregation broke from ordered rows and approached the oaken casket for the hallowed farewell. Despite the priest's words, this was a moment only for family and friends. Malachi half expected the priest's hand on his own shoulder; the slow, solemn shake of the head.

In the event, he took his place behind Rosa and began the long shuffle to the waiting casket without complication.

Rosa offered no acknowledgement. Indeed, she'd spoken fewer than a dozen words since their arrival. Her manner remained stiff and cold, and she seemed a stranger in many ways. Not least because Malachi couldn't recall when last he'd seen her exchange a uniform for a formal gown.

"Kasamor would have hated this," he murmured. "He'd have wanted a party, not a wake."

"He left detailed instructions the very first time we went into battle," she replied. "No incense, no dirge and no priests. Serenes? Serenes he didn't mind, though I shudder to think why. I told Ebigail. She ignored me."

Of course she had. Malachi cast his gaze to where the elder Lady Kiradin now parted her veil and stooped to kiss the stylised features of her son's golden death mask. Her poise, her whole manner, was of a matron striving against grief. Striving, but not overwhelmed. Her cheeks were dry of tears, and her expression as impassive. Ebigail Kiradin would love her son more in death than she ever had in life, for Tressia was built on the dead. On their deeds, and on their tombs.

Ebigail stood aside. Sevaka took her place, eyes downcast and rimmed red by clandestine tears. Shameful, perhaps, but Malachi was glad to see some genuine sorrow. The traditional kiss bestowed, Sevaka withdrew. An older man – a distant uncle – stepped forward.

"Hold."

Ebigail's pronouncement brought the line to a halt. Malachi frowned. The hallowed farewell was traditionally performed in silence, and without interruption.

"Roslava." Ebigail extended a hand, scattering kith and kin. "You should be here. Come, child. Take your place."

Malachi noted the same kindness was not extended to him, despite the greater tally of years that had bound him to Kasamor. Rosa stiffened, but made no move.

"Go," Malachi whispered, and set a hand to the small of her back. "I'll see you outside."

Ebigail took Rosa's arm and drew her towards the casket. She dipped her head to Rosa's ear, whispered briefly, and withdrew.

After brief hesitation, Rosa stooped to the casket and delivered her kiss. Her expression remained no less granite than the elder Lady Kiradin's. But Malachi had known her too long not to recognise the conflict swirling in her eyes.

Then the line shuffled forward once more, and Malachi with it. By the time he stood before the gold and black corpse, Ebigail, Rosa and Sevaka had moved on. Incense prickling at his nostrils, he stooped to kiss the golden brow.

"Goodbye, my friend," he breathed.

As was now his habit, Malachi didn't take a direct route to the surface. Where the black stone of the ancient city surrendered to granite colonnades of repurposed streets, he detoured into the unprepossessing chambers that bore the antlered crest of the Satanra family. There he stood for a time among the statues, head bowed, surrounded always by the shuddering, gnawing rumble as kraikons laboured below to open up new chambers for the never-ending bounty of dead.

He stared up at a familiar face immortalised in cold marble. "It's been a while, Father. I'm sorry for that. Seems the faster I run, the further I fall behind."

More and more, Malachi thought it important to pay homage to his parents and their kin while he still lived to do so. After all, when his last day came, he'd be interred a Reveque – such was the price of marrying into a family of the first rank. An honour, but one Malachi resented, for in his heart a Satanra he remained.

"Thought I'd find you here." Hadon Akadra stepped between the spread-winged serathi statues guarding the threshold. "Funerals have a way of stirring up memories."

Malachi regarded him warily. "True enough."

Hadon gulped from a hip flask and proffered it to Malachi. "Here. Drowns the taste of that wretched incense."

It made for a strange peace offering, but then fate had not been kind to the Akadra family. Hadon was the last and eldest of seven siblings, all of whom had been taken before their time. And then there was Viktor's mother. She'd scarcely been Malachi's age when the Raven had taken her. What was the saying? *All stood equal before the grave.*

"Thanks."

Malachi took the flask and spluttered through a pine-bark and juniper mouthful of the fiery krask spirit. The older man regarded him with stony-faced amusement.

"A poor generation we're raising if they can't hold their drink. Your wife not with you?"

"We agreed not to burden the children with the interment. They'll make hallowed farewells soon enough. Lilyana wants them to keep their innocence a while longer."

Hadon harrumphed and slipped the flask away. "What are you and Abitha up to?"

Not a peace offering then, but a prelude to interrogation. "Why should we be up to anything?"

"I'm not yet so blind that you can seal me in down here and sing sad songs, boy. You've been making the rounds, speaking to members of the Grand Council. I want to know why."

Malachi grimaced. The timing was unfortunate. Then again, it was in the nature of things that Hadon would have found out the truth sooner or later. He sifted through the possibilities. He could hedge, of course he could, but Hadon's patience ran thin at the best of times. If the older man wasn't already an enemy, that would surely make him so. Only truth would serve.

"We're exploring the possibility of peace with the Empire."

"You're what?" Hadon scowled, and his voice dropped to a level more suited to the sombre environs. "You think we should beg?"

"That's *not* what I'm proposing. The Hadari are fractured. They need chance to catch their breath as much as we do."

"That's how grovelling always starts. But that's nothing new to you, is it? Lord *Reveque*? Wouldn't be the first time you've thrown away your pride for power." He rapped his knuckles on a plinth. "If you want to abase yourself before the Hadari, you go right ahead. But you do it alone."

"And if I'm not alone?"

"Don't test me on this, boy. Not with our ancestors watching."

"I don't seek to test you, Hadon." With an effort, Malachi ignored the bluster. "But I'd remind you that peace – however brief – brings opportunities. In trade, for example."

Ruddiness faded from Hadon's expression as greed swamped outrage.

Bellicose sentiment was one thing, but Hadon Akadra loved little so much as the chink of gold in his purse. Perhaps even loved it more than he hated the Hadari.

"Trying to bribe me, Malachi?" The words held an accusation, but the tone remained thoughtful.

"I'm merely ensuring you've considered the wider possibilities."

Hadon snorted, but Malachi saw the wheels turning behind his eyes. Hadon knew, as Malachi did, that no peace between the realms ever lasted long. He lost nothing by allowing Malachi to stick his neck out, and a tidy profit to gain.

"I'll think on it. But no promises."

Brow furrowed in thought, Hadon reclaimed his flask and strode away.

Malachi waited until he was lost from sight, and let out a long, slow breath. That had gone far better than he'd expected. So much so, that he scarcely believed it. But the cat was now well and truly out of the bag.

Whatever side Hadon came down on, he'd be sure to discuss the matter with Ebigail and Lord Tarev, which meant it was now a race. Malachi stared up at his father's graven image and cursed to himself. He'd planned an afternoon loosening Rosa's tongue and sorrows through libation. Now he'd be twisting arms before others could do the same. Two steps forward, one step back. Perhaps he should have kept his mouth shut after all.

"Always my own worst enemy, Father," he muttered to the silent statue. "Always."

The alabaster trunks of the hayadra trees blazed white in the sun. Marek's father had always believed that an omen of good times to come. He'd adored the Hayadra Grove. The concentric circles of slender trees had for generations served as the site of celebration and remembrance; a meeting place for friends, colleagues and lovers alike. Where rivals settled their differences in the sight of the Goddess, just as Lumestra had made generous peace with faithless Ashana back in the mists of time.

Not that there was any such commotion within the centremost ring that day, not with a family of the first rank mourning its loss. Vigilant constables held the masses at bay, ensuring that Lady Kiradin's grief was respected. But beyond, in the outer rings where stones of the old temple still stood, the crowds remained. Most sought simple pleasures under the open sky. A few had arms uplifted and eyes closed in prayer, seeking in the holy sunlight a sign of things to come, as Marek's father had so many times.

For himself, Marek had never believed the future revealed itself so readily, within the grove, or without. For all his father's endless study of signs and portents – of pentassa cards read by gifted eyes, or the shape of the stars – it hadn't stopped him losing his head at Teldagand, had it? The Nomar family had never possessed much luck.

No, Marek believed in the evidence of his eyes, and in people, not portents. And at the moment, the evidence of his eyes told him that Lord Akadra's conversation had not gone well.

"Well?"

Lady Ebigail stepped from beneath the shade of the hayadra tree. Marek followed, careful that the parasol kept the brilliance of the noon-day sun from his mistress' fashionably pale skin.

"He and Abitha plan to sue for peace," rumbled Lord Akadra.

"They plan to humiliate us, you mean."

Even faced with ruinous news, she kept her composure. But to Marek's thinking, that was how it should have been. Some bloodlines were born to rule. One of the many reasons he served Lady Ebigail so gladly.

"Worthless, all of them, this younger generation." There was no anger in Lady Ebigail's tone, just weary disappointment. "Driven by their fears and their pleasures, and never a thought for the Republic's needs. For the duty that we bear."

"Not Viktor," Lord Akadra interjected. "Whatever his choices, he holds the Republic close to his heart."

"Really? Then why has he never married? The bloodlines are withering. The Republic needs more than merchants suffering pretensions of nobility. We've let matters slide too far."

"I'm sure our forebears believed the same of us."

"Nonsense. This is different ... " She broke off, her eyes narrowing. "Please don't tell me you've sympathy with Malachi's nonsense."

Lord Akadra winced. "I confess to seeing some small benefit to the cessation of hostilities."

Lady Kiradin sniffed. "Benefit to yourself, you mean. What use is gold if the Republic crumbles around us? But I wouldn't expect you to see that. You're weak in the middle." She drew closer. "Do you think I've forgotten how you crumpled before your beloved son?"

Lord Akadra's scowl hardened into something cold, almost fearful. "I had no choice."

"Of course you did. You simply lack the stomach to make it."

"And you know no such restraint, I suppose?"

"What a question to ask a mother at her son's graveside."

"Lady!" Marek hurried to offer an arm for support as Lady Ebigail's knees buckled. She clung to it with an iron grip as she steadied.

"Thank you, Marek. At least someone knows their duties."

"Mother? Is anything wrong?"

The day grew brighter still at Lady Sevaka's approach. Lady Ebigail was a handsome woman, no question. Marek had broken the jaw of the last man to suggest otherwise. But her daughter? She shone like the sun. When Lady Sevaka had departed for service in the navy, Marek had feared the ocean wind would wither her golden hair and turn her cheeks gaunt. But such a fate had not come to pass. Lady Sevaka remained as radiant as when a child, even in the drab grey garb of a lieutenant of sail.

"A passing weakness, my dear, nothing more. Indeed, I was discussing such with Lord Akadra, was I not?"

Lord Akadra nodded but said nothing.

Lady Sevaka's grey eyes narrowed. "There's no shame in admitting grief, Mother. And I'm sure you've been working yourself too hard. Hasn't she, Marek?"

"And we should all be grateful for that."

"Perhaps. But you must allow yourself time to grieve, Mother."

"She's right, Ebigail," said Lord Akadra. "The Republic will endure without your guidance until tomorrow."

Lady Ebigail eyed him with suspicion. "Oh, I wouldn't be so sure." She turned her attention to Sevaka once more. "You'll join me in the carriage, my dear?"

"Actually, I'd agreed to spend the afternoon with Rosa. We'd a mind to toast my brother's memory . . . once or twice."

Marek peered across the hilltop through the alabaster trunks of the hayadra trees. Lady Orova stood alone, hair and dress streaming in the wind as she stared out across the bay. A frequent guest at Freemont, but one he'd never taken a shine to. Wore her heritage too lightly, as if that made her the better for it.

"One or two toasts." Lady Ebigail smiled wryly. "And more besides, I shouldn't wonder."

"But if you need me, then of course ... "

Lady Ebigail waved a dismissive hand. "No. I won't hear of it. The young must have their rituals, and I'll not have you abandon Roslava." She nodded thoughtfully. "Yes, she was a good friend to your brother, and we should repay that in kind. Marek will take care of me. Won't you, Marek?"

"To my last breath, lady."

Lady Ebigail lowered her cheek to her daughter's kiss. "Now be off with you. But have care not to fall into too much mischief. The burden of our name falls heavier on your shoulders than ever."

"Of course, Mother."

With a brilliant smile, Lady Sevaka withdrew.

"Do you mind telling me why you've sudden interest in Captain Orova?" asked Lord Akadra. "It was only last week you deplored her for a bad influence on Kasamor."

"Yes, I do mind," snapped Lady Ebigail. She sighed. "It occurs to me that we have invested poorly in those who are to follow us."

"*A disrespectful child who shouldn't waste time grubbing around in the mud and playing at soldier.* Your words, Ebigail."

"Much has changed this past week, and it is my business where I spend my affections."

Lord Akadra scowled at the sidelong threat. "Then I'll leave you to your grief. I've much to do this afternoon."

"Don't we all?" Lady Ebigail murmured. "Don't we all."

Eighteen

The proctor bowed low, the hem of his ceremonial scarf brushing the driveway's gravel. He set aside his sun-stave and extended the velvet cushion in offering. Viktor's shadow seethed in discomfort as he plucked a ward-brooch from its velvet nest. The magic locked within hummed beneath his fingers, but it was as likely that the silvery metal – and not the enchantment – had offended his gift.

Fortunately, neither was enough to spur the shadow to full wakefulness. Just as happily, the proctor gave no sign of recognising his inner conflict. But it had always been the smallest of risks. Those who bore the gift of magic in the Council's service did so under the strictest discipline. It left them blind to much.

Viktor gave a last glance at the brooch's woven filaments and pinned it to his coat. Kurkas followed suit. Calenne did not. She regarded the proctor's leonine simarka with apprehension – a wild animal frozen in the act of bolting for safety.

"There is a problem, Miss Trelan?" asked Viktor.

"No," she replied, with tremulous defiance.

Annoyance flickered. "Is my word not enough for you?"

She hesitated, straightened and looked him dead in the eye. "No."

Kurkas chuckled. "So much for the famed Akadra charm."

Viktor sighed. If there *was* such a thing as the "famed Akadra charm", this was the first he'd heard of it. Then again, Kurkas' sense of humour was seldom bothered by fact. And the poor joke at least elicited a thin smile from Calenne.

Her manner had otherwise been cheerless and withdrawn all

morning. He'd thought it provoked by the smoke curling up from the eastern mountains. Or perhaps the bustling military presence in Eskavord as Governor Yanda set her scant forces moving. But no. This was the fearfulness of a prisoner donning shackles recently split. Understandable, but irritating.

"That brooch is your guarantee," he said. "Wear it, and this cage cannot claim you."

Calenne narrowed her eyes. She nodded at the proctor, and at the trio of hawk-tabarded soldiers who stood silently in the lodge-turned-guardhouse. "And what about them? What if they try to stop me?"

"You are under my protection. I'm sure deeper wisdom would prevail."

The proctor flinched. Calenne snatched up the remaining brooch.

"You see?" said Kurkas airily. "The famous Akadra charm. Works every time."

On the long walk up the driveway, Viktor bent his attention on the meeting to come. Whether he liked it or not, the southwealders had every reason to fear and distrust him, Josiri Trelan most of all. Perhaps Calenne's reluctance had less to do with returning to her prison, and more to do with the man who brought her beneath its walls.

The thought bothered Viktor. More than it should. But the smoke on the eastern horizon bothered him more. The Hadari were but two days' march from Eskavord, even with the poor roads of the Trelszon borderlands to slow them. Calenne Trelan's battered feelings would heal, and time was running out.

Lost to downcast introspection, Viktor scarcely realised his shadow was rising. With a scowl, he hauled it back. He glanced at Calenne. Had she noted anything untoward? He'd had one near-miss already, back when he'd learned of Kasamor's death. It was a topic he still dared not think on without further information. Kasamor would understand if need outweighed justice.

Viktor raised his eyes to the manor stairs – and the slender white-haired woman in the seneschal's uniform – and realised he'd badly misread his shadow's unease. The challenge didn't lie in the woman's manner. *That* was of a cat basking rapturously in sunshine. It lay in her very being.

"His grace, the Duke of Eskavord, is in discussion. He has no time for chance callers." Her gaze shifted to Calenne. "Even those who come slinking back to the warmth of his hearth."

Viktor noted the flash of animosity that briefly marred Calenne's features and filed it away for the future. The bulk of his attention belonged to the seneschal, and the aura of power cloaking her like woven mist. His shadow hissed and uncurled, jealous and ... fearful?

"Anastacia Psanneque, I presume," he said evenly.

Black eyes bored into his, awakening a frisson of disquiet. Not quite fear, but a sensation born of instinctive understanding that the woman before him was not so ephemeral as she appeared. He'd known Josiri and Calenne shared their confinement, but official documentation had made no reference to Anastacia's nature – whatever *that* truly was – and rumour was ever a poor guide.

"Just Anastacia. The rest is someone's little joke. One that *I* don't find amusing."

Viktor nodded. He'd never met anyone born with the name "Psanneque". It hailed from a dead language, itself sprung from half-forgotten stories – "exile", denoting one without family and without a home. It hinted at failure and darkness; the disapproval of kin, or society as a whole. At least Psanneque held more sorrow than malice. Such was not always the case.

He inclined his head. "Then Anastacia it shall be. But I must see the duke. I've travelled a long way to do so."

"Then you won't mind waiting a while longer."

Viktor's temper slipped a notch. "And if I insist?"

"I might take offence." Her aura darkened, golden light seeping into alabaster. "You wouldn't like that, for all your ... advantages."

Alien unease rippled through Viktor's thoughts. So she saw him as plainly as he saw her? A meeting of magics, open and unconcealed. The one consolation was that she seemed in no hurry to share that knowledge.

"I think I'd survive it," he said.

She smiled without warmth. "Yes. Perhaps you would."

"Hush, demon." Calenne glared up at Anastacia, fists balled. "I've had my fill of your games."

More proof, Viktor decided, that he alone was privy to Anastacia's hidden might, and its danger. Or perhaps not. Whatever else Calenne

Trelan lacked, she'd inherited her mother's forthrightness. A fine waste of potential, keeping her locked up at Branghall. A modicum of honing would have made her invaluable to the Republic.

"Please, Miss Trelan . . . " he began.

"Please, nothing," she snapped. "I've lived with this creature for half my life. In all that time, she's only played at door warden after a quarrel with my brother. Let us through, demon."

"So swiftly we change our tune." Anastacia gave a bleak laugh. With a sudden flourish, she stepped aside. "Perhaps it will please Calenne to show you the Great Hall. It could be that she is right, I am wrong, and that you are welcome. I am not in favour just now, so I will bid you the joy of discovery."

She sat again upon the steps and stared off into the distance. Calenne swept imperiously past, leaving Viktor and Kurkas to follow.

"You want to tell me what that was about?" Kurkas murmured, once the door had closed behind them.

"Who's to say?" Viktor replied. "To hear my father tell it, she's a witch locked up at the order of Makrov's predecessor."

He grunted. "I saw her eyes. But it's a rare sort of witch that crosses a priest – much less old pointy-hat himself – and goes unburned."

"Perhaps the fire wouldn't take."

"Lovely." Kurkas scratched at his eyepatch. "Witches. Headstrong noblewomen. Ain't no life for an honest soldier. I'll be glad when the Hadari march into view."

Viktor chuckled at his friend's mock-gloom. "That's a dangerous wish at this hour."

"When isn't it?"

Calenne halted before a double-leaved door flanked by armoured statues. Viktor heard muffled voices beyond. Taking the briefest of moments to collect himself, he heaved the doors inwards.

"You'll forgive me, governor, if I find your reassurances . . . "

Josiri Trelan broke off, his gaze settling on Viktor as one seeing a most unwelcome ghost. Viktor, for whom such reactions had become depressingly commonplace, clasped his hands behind his back, and offered a respectful bow.

His first glimpse of the duke in fifteen years, and the impression was not unfavourable. Josiri's wiry frame proved confinement had not tempted him to turgidity, and his eyes held a quiet watchfulness. His sister's opposite, fair where she was dark, and confident where she so far had shown only reserve.

Arzro Makrov seemed only a fraction less pleased than Josiri to see his old student. Only Governor Yanda gave a small steady nod of greeting . . . or was it satisfaction?

One ally at the table, then. One unknown, and . . .

"So it is true what they say. Misfortune seldom travels alone." Josiri rose, his voice and expression hard as granite. "You are not welcome in this house, Lord Akadra."

The echoing words would have been impressive if spoken before the hundreds the sun-dappled hall had once housed. Uttered for the benefit of the tiny war council, they struck Viktor as more petulant than powerful.

"I apologise for the intrusion, your grace, but . . . "

"Was I not clear? Leave. If you've a message, you may relay it through Governor Yanda."

Viktor bit his tongue. It was doubtful Josiri had the authority to expel him from Branghall, much less the means. A gilded prison it might have been, but a prison it remained. But none of that mattered if the duke refused to listen.

"I'm not so foolish as to have expected a warm welcome," he said. "But surely civility isn't too much to expect? After all, I've gone to some trouble to bring your sister home."

On cue, Calenne and Kurkas entered the chamber; the former guided by the latter's hand, shoulders squared and head erect. But her eyes swam with apprehension. Doubtless this was not the "introduction" she'd anticipated.

The result was everything Viktor could have wished. Josiri paled. The certainty of moments before washed away. "Calenne? What is this? What have you done to her?"

"She met with some trouble on the road. I was glad to offer assistance."

Suspicion clouded Josiri's eyes. "What sort of trouble?"

"I was attacked." Calenne scowled her embarrassment and glanced sidelong at Viktor. "He saved my life."

"Saved your life?" Makrov interrupted. "You'd no business being anywhere other than Branghall! You should have informed us she'd escaped, your grace!"

"I am not my sister's keeper," snapped Josiri.

Viktor read more evasion than truth in those words, but it hardly mattered. With Josiri disoriented, fresh battle lines opened up. The flow of the conflict was his to control.

"Captain Kurkas?"

"Sah?"

Kurkas, as was his wont when mischief abounded, let his accent blossom to drill sergeant's drawl. The bluff soldier, obeying orders. A habit Viktor had long since despaired of smothering.

"Kindly escort the archimandrite back to Eskavord."

"Escort me?" Makrov glowered at Viktor. "I've business here, and you lack authority."

Viktor had once feared that tone, so often the precursor to a birch rod's stinging chastisement. But the days of Makrov's tutelage were long past, even if his tyrannies would never be forgotten.

"Not so."

Viktor flicked aside the heavy velvet of his cloak and retrieved the first of two precious letters. The blue wax seal of the Council was as yet unbroken. He strode past Josiri and handed it to Yanda, who had thus far watched proceedings with wary interest.

"Governor Yanda. I hereby take command of the Southshires and all forces stationed within its bounds."

Yanda didn't even split the seal. "I'm glad to have you here, my lord."

"You'll return to Cragwatch and prepare a report on the readiness of our forces."

"That won't take long," she said drily. "We need all the help the Council can send."

"You'll have to make do with me for now," Viktor replied. "And two companies of my hearthguard, who've spent days on the road, without opportunity to make observance of Ascension. Which is why, Excellency, I'd be grateful if you'd return to Eskavord and lead them in prayer."

"I'll do no such thing! You will not shut me out! I speak with the Council's voice!"

"Not any longer. So far as the Southshires are concerned, I *am* the Council," Viktor rumbled. "If you wish to challenge my authority, you have only to ride north. Doubtless you will find a sympathetic ear. But until then, you will fulfil the duties of your station. Am I understood?"

Makrov scowled but had the wit to recognise both the inevitability of defeat, and the face-saving retreat on offer. "Very well, I shall bring what solace Lumestra permits."

Viktor offered a slight bow. "Thank you. Captain Kurkas won't mind if I say that he, in particular, has been troubled by wavering faith. I'm sure he'll welcome your guidance."

Captain Kurkas didn't look particularly welcoming at that moment. As Viktor retreated across the chamber, he drew near. "I'll get you for this," he whispered.

"Hush, captain, that's just your inner torment speaking."

Viktor patted Kurkas' shoulder and halted before Calenne. "You're free to go with him, if you wish. But with the Hadari on the march I'd ask you stay in Eskavord for now."

She regarded him through narrowed eyes, wary of promises revoked. "Just *ask*?"

"I promised you freedom, and you have it. However, freedom sometimes brings the burden of doing not what we wish, but what is necessary."

Calenne gave a slow nod. "I can stay with my mother. I hope so, at least. It's been a long time since we last spoke."

Viktor belatedly recalled that Calenne had been fostered and dispersed his puzzled frown before it had fully formed. "And should I need to speak with you?"

"I don't think you're welcome anywhere in Eskavord. But I'll ask Elda to forgo emptying the slops bucket over your head if you come calling." She offered a slight, lopsided smile. "I owe you that much."

"She's not going anywhere with you," growled Josiri.

Viktor rounded on him. "I thought you weren't your sister's keeper? And I am staying here. We've matters to discuss."

Josiri glowered but said nothing as Calenne and the others departed. A wise course. There was no victory for him in that moment, just as Viktor had intended. He'd come a long way in fifteen years. It could only be hoped that age had brought wisdom.

The doors swung closed.

"Alone at last," said Viktor.

That wasn't *entirely* true. He felt Anastacia's presence in the passageway beyond. He'd have laid long odds against her eavesdropping. But the room was empty of challenge, and of witness. He could speak freely – as could Josiri, if he chose. If he could see beyond the past.

Josiri stared out through the eastern window and across the town. "*Did* you save Calenne's life?"

"I had that honour, yes. Though I didn't know who she was until after."

"Then why do it?"

"Because there was no one else."

"A dangerous philosophy, Lord Akadra. It killed my mother. It may yet kill you." Josiri snorted and turned his back on the window. "Why are you here? Now, after all these years? Come to finish what you started?"

"Because of the Hadari. And to undo the damage of the past. I need your help with both."

Viktor retrieved the second letter from his pocket. Josiri broke the seal, unfolded the paper and began to read. His face remained as impassive as ever. But not his eyes.

"What is this?" He extended the letter at arm's length, as one might a pet of uncertain domestication.

"What it purports to be," Viktor replied. "Lead your people against the Hadari, and the Council will restore everything you have lost."

Josiri's expression darkened. "Bad enough that the Council have made us slaves. Now we are to be its sellswords?"

"Mercenaries fight for coin. You'd fight for your homes. For your future."

"We tried that once before, did we not?" He paused. "And this has full backing?"

"It has enough. Though it took some ... persuasion."

"*Your* persuasion?"

"As I said, I would undo the harms I have visited upon you, and upon your people."

"I cannot help you." Josiri's tone would have curdled fresh milk. "Your kind have spent years beating the spirit out of mine. You've come to a desert seeking relief from thirst."

Viktor's temper twitched. "And you insult me by taking me for a fool. Your domain is lousy with defiance. Or do you think I've not marked the tally of death and torment meted out on our soldiers? And if you, *your grace*, are not at the heart of it, then you are not your mother's son."

Josiri flung a hand towards the window, and the wall beyond. "And does my bloodline grant me the knack for passing through solid stone, unseen and unhindered by enchantment? I am a prisoner granted the illusion of agency. A man goaded to provide leadership, but who learns his lands are besieged only when the horizon is aflame! We Trelans are many things, but we are not workers of miracles."

They were the right words. The *expected* words. But more than ever, Viktor knew them to be lies. "And your sister? Is she a worker of miracles? She passed beyond the wall. She ... "

He broke off, aware that his temper was quickening. He'd come too far now to surrender to pique.

"You would have to ask Calenne."

"And I shall ... Or I would, if it mattered." Viktor plucked a ward-brooch from his pocket and set it on the windowsill. "I did not come here to trap you, Josiri, but to set you free. You, and those you choose to take with you."

Josiri's eyes flickered to the door – to where Anastacia waited out of sight. Viktor marked the nature of the glance, its longing and its regret, and drew the only conclusion he could. An interesting development. And not without its uses.

A sigh, and Josiri stared down at the brooch's tangle of silver thread-work. His eyes brimmed with suspicion and yearning. His desire for the brooch, and all it represented, was an almost physical force, matched only by the reluctance of pride. Viktor willed the former to win out. It would have been easy enough to order the enchantment quelled and the gates opened, but this? This was more than a symbol – it was freedom to be held in one's hand.

Fingers reached for the brooch, and then withdrew.

"No," said Josiri. "I cannot give you what you want."

Fury gorged on disappointment, goading forth a dangerous, brittle reply. "Reconsider."

"Or else what?" Bleak laughter swelled beneath the words. "You'll cage me? Divide my people and ship them overseas? You've no threats left to make, and your promises are worth less than nothing. I will never be your ally, Lord Akadra. Not in this, nor anything else. If I link arms with my mother's slayer, how would I face her in the mists of Otherworld?"

A chill overcame Viktor as his shadow roused. It sang in dark melody, urged him to smother Josiri's objections and bind him to the challenges to come, willing or no.

Viktor drowned in temptation. With so much at stake, would it be such a sin? One act of selfishness to smother another? He didn't question whether his shadow could be pressed to that purpose. Nor did he wonder why the certainty that it *could* had arisen. All that held him back was equal certainty that to act thus would be at odds with the atonement he desired.

"Then you are not your mother's son," he growled. "I will fight without your blessing, and without your help."

His throat tight with defeat, Viktor left the brooch where it lay and stalked from the hall.

Nineteen

This time, the lady came to the ruined chapel while the sun still graced Tressia's time-worn stones and the marketplace bustled with evening trade. A bold choice, even cloaked and veiled. It spoke to urgency. Even desperation.

Apara had mixed feelings about desperation. It brought profit, but danger too often lurked in its shadow. It brought excitement, but there was much to be said for a quiet life.

"My condolences for your son, lady," she said. "I can only guess your burdens."

The interplay of light and shadow shifted as the woman took up position beyond the wooden screen. "I shall live with my regrets. And my disappointments."

Apara winced. "Disappointments, lady?"

"I made special mention of a ring. It remains lost, where my son does not."

"I can only apologise, lady. Many things go unnoticed in the wilds." Yes, many things went unnoticed, but Kasamor Kiradin's ring had not been among them. Nikros had kept it, confident the client wouldn't make trouble. "If we can make amends . . ."

"You can. I have two further tasks. One more suited to your own skills than to your cousin's." The lady set an oilcloth bundle atop the altar. An oblong package, with a folded sheet of paper tucked beneath the string. "The note holds the location where these books are to be concealed. They must not be found without a determined search."

Apara frowned. The words were plain enough, but not the intent.

That was the problem with speaking so obliquely, but that was often the way when accepting commissions from the nobility. The ritualistic approach brought distance, as if it left the petitioner's hands unsullied by the crimes undertaken on their behalf. The rich could afford their pretensions. Apara could not.

"I don't understand," she said.

"You don't need to understand, only obey."

"Of course, lady. It shall be done. And the other task?"

"I fear for an acquaintance."

"As you feared for your son?"

A pause. "Indeed. These are dangerous times. Have your cousin stand ready."

"Of course, lady. And the payment?"

She chuckled. "Your task is your generous gift, to assuage my disappointment at the loss of the ring. Your cousin's work will attract the usual fee upon completion."

That wasn't good. Payment in arrears invited no payment at all. "But the Parliament of Crows ... "

" ... will understand my reluctance, should I make your cousin's lapse known. I would prefer it not come to that."

Apara's brow pricked with sweat. The Parliament had a reputation to uphold. She'd warned Nikros against keeping the ring.

"It shall be as you wish, lady."

"I know you won't let me down again, Apara." The lady rose. "Keep your curiosity in check. The secrets within those pages lead only to the pyre. It would break my heart if you lost your way."

The afternoon had passed in a slow but steady ramble beneath creaking tavern signs. With the sun long beneath the horizon, Rosa left the last behind. Her heart ebbed. Her shoulders were burdened by the arm of a decidedly unsteady Sevaka Kiradin.

"Jus' one last toast."

Sevaka stumbled sideways. The motion began with her arm slipping from Rosa's shoulders. It ended with her sitting in the gutter, wearing a bemused frown.

Rosa sighed and helped her upright. There had been plenty of toasts already. To Lumestra, to the Republic ... and of course, to Kasamor. To Kasamor most of all.

"One more and I'll be *carrying* you home."

"'m fine." Sevaka waved the concern away. "Jus' getting my second wind. And it's not my fault you've not kept up."

"I've matched you drink for drink."

"Oh? Then why are you still so ... so ... you know."

Rosa wondered herself. Had done for the last hour and more. Likely she was more drunk than she felt. It took her that way sometimes. It wasn't as if Sevaka made much of a witness.

"Hollow legs," she replied. "That, and all those rumours about hard-drinking naval lieutenants being nothing more than mariner's fancy."

"Hah! Prove it. One last toast. For Kasamor."

Across the river, the firestone lanterns of the Silverway gleamed invitingly. Strains of fiddle music drifted through the winds, the notes shaping the wild steps of a dance that had spilled out through the open doorway and into the street. The last place she'd drunk with Kasamor. The last place she ever would. Fitting to end things there.

"Very well," she said. "One last drink. But after that, home."

Sevaka grinned and threw an unsteady salute. "Agreed. Endala drag me to the depths if I break my vow."

"It's not sea-spirits you've to worry about, but the gutter. Because that's where I'll leave you. And I don't reckon your mother would approve of you invoking heathen gods."

"Mother? Hah! She approves of nothing! But the sea keeps us apart." Her tone grew whimsical. "It's a *good* life. Wouldn't give it up for anything. Y'should try it."

Rosa shook her head. "I like my boots on firm land, thanks."

"Pfffff! Then lead on, dryfoot."

Already regretting the decision, Rosa steered Sevaka towards the tide-worn bridge. She'd never suspected she could spend any amount of time around the younger Lady Kiradin. But as the afternoon had worn on, and liquor had chipped away at Sevaka's aristocratic mask, she found herself not in the company of hauteur, but a carefree woman whose grief was as genuine as her need to share it.

The wind picked up as they abandoned the shelter of the streets for the empty quayside. Flecked with salt-spray, it howled across the bay and whistled through the rigging of moored ships. Rosa half-led, half-dragged Sevaka past the nearest pier head, where a toiling crew laboured to batten down a forlorn-looking merchantman. With each gust of wind, firestone lamps swayed precariously in the rigging, dancing like mischievous spirits.

Even the stacks of cargo, chained down to deter would-be thieves, offered little sanctuary from the wind. Sevaka, still in a uniform fashioned for such abuse, seemed barely to notice. Rosa's panelled gown – chosen in a whim of maudlin fancy – was of no protection at all, and she shivered with every step.

And yet . . . However cold she was, however goose-marked her skin, Rosa knew it should have been worse. It was as if what she felt wasn't really cold at all, but its *memory*.

Or maybe those endless toasts lingered with her more than she believed.

"Well now, Roslava Orova. And in a dress, too. Must be seeing things."

Rosa winced at the familiar voice, colder than the wind. She turned about, staggered by the need to steer Sevaka also.

"Aske. I'm not in the mood."

Aske Tarev pushed away from the stack of chain-lashed crates. "All the better. You owe me a humiliation, you and the rest. And here you are, lumbering around like a rudderless scow. And without a sword for company. Couldn't pass that up, could I?"

Sevaka pushed clear of Rosa and squinted at Aske. "Do I know you?"

"Allow me to present Aske Tarev," said Rosa. "A bundle of pride and poor decisions."

"Ohhhh. That one. The one who couldn't beat Kas in a straight fight?" She straightened, or at least adopted a posture more vertical than diagonal. "Doesn't matter. Two against one, isn't it?"

"She's armed, and we're not."

"Ah."

Nonetheless, Rosa wasn't especially concerned. She'd seen enough of Aske's fighting style – or lack thereof – behind the Silverway. Wouldn't take much to get the sword off her. The trick would be to stop Sevaka getting hurt along the way.

"And it's not two against one." Aske put her fingers to her lips and whistled.

Two hearthguards in Tarev crimson appeared from within the maze of crates. Between dress and drinking companion, Rosa had no hope of getting clear. The merchantman was too far behind to expect help from its crew; the Silverway too far ahead. To fight was certainly to lose, but lose what?

"Let Sevaka leave . . . "

"I'm not going anywhere."

Rosa ignored the protest and pressed on. "Let her leave, and I'll stay."

Aske drew her sword. "Sins of the kith. Her brother can't pay, so she does. But I'll make you an offer. Yield, and we'll leave you here, bound and unharmed. Your clothes come with us, of course, or else there's no humiliation."

Sevaka stiffened. "And if we don't yield?"

"Same thing. Only it'll hurt more."

Rosa closed her eyes and cursed. No choice in that. No choice at all. One thing to lose your dignity – quite another to hand it over. And she'd faced worse than Aske and her good-for-nothings. What could they do to her that the kernclaw had not? What could they *take* from her that had not already been lost?

Teeth bared in a snarl, she threw herself at the nearest hearthguard. He yelped and stumbled away, blade sweeping out in a panicked arc. Rosa lowered her shoulder beneath the steel and slammed him into a crate. His sword skittered away and vanished over the quayside. Rosa drove her fist into his face. The hearthguard screamed and went limp. She hit him again, just to be sure, and let the senseless body fall.

A shriek came from somewhere behind.

Rosa clambered to her feet and spun around. Sevaka stood against a crate, one hand clasped to a bloodied forearm. Aske and the remaining hearthguard – their backs to Rosa, and the latter with an equally blood-ied nose – pressed in with swords drawn.

Kicking off impractical shoes, Rosa flung herself at Aske's back. She turned at the last moment. Rosa, in full flight, had no chance to stop. The sword-point took her low in the belly. The tearing of silk was indistinguishable from that of the flesh beneath.

Rosa gasped. Pain flooded to replace stolen breath. She clawed numbly at Aske's shoulders, glimpsed the other woman's wide-eyed horror. Then she fell, her knees cracking on cobbles.

The world blurred, its colour fading and its sounds packed tight with goose down. Aske's rictus as she backed away. The clang of her sword as it struck cobbles. Sevaka's urgent words as she fell to her knees. The wild gestures of the fleeing hearthguard. The crash of the waves against the harbourside. All impossibly far away and yet close to. All save the croak of crow-voices.

And yet Rosa felt no sadness. The Raven would take her, and she'd see Kas again, though she dreaded the explanation she'd owe.

Rosa put a trembling hand to her stomach.

There was no blood.

The world swam anew. How could there be no blood? And the pain. It wasn't … right. Like the cold of the wind, it felt like the memory of something from another time. And if there was no blood, and no pain, then she wasn't dying, was she?

What was she?

The impossible question sank beneath a surge of bleak anger. The same anger Rosa had tamped down and contained ever since Kas's death. Ever since she'd failed him. It tore through her like flame through a parched forest. Uncontainable. Undeniable. The crow-voices faded. The world regained its colour.

Rosa caught Aske within a dozen paces. Skirts tore as the two of them slammed into the cobbles, Aske below and she atop. She drew back her elbow, fist bunched.

"No! I'm sorry!" There was no arrogance in Aske's expression now. Just stark, unflinching fear.

Rosa slammed down a fist. Something gave beneath her knuckles. It felt good. So good, she did it again.

Aske shrieked.Her hands flailed to fend off the blows. She might as well have tried to hold back the tide.

"Don't! Don't! I beg you!"

Rosa struck again. All the guilt-driven rage that ritual and liquor and kind words had failed to expunge tore free in a wordless cry as her fist struck home. She lost herself in that moment. She drowned in it. Only when the scream faded did she come back to herself.

Sevaka's face, pale and more sober than it had been in hours, crowded her vision. Her hand shook Rosa's shoulder. "Rosa? Queen's Ashes! What have you done?"

The clang of constabulary bells rang out. Booted feet thundered closer. Rosa stared down through her bloodied fingers and began to shake.

A soft click, and the window fell open. Apara released her grip on the trellis and slipped inside. Boots crunched on gravel two storeys below. The soft murmur of bored conversation drifted up the mansion front and faded to nothing as she set the window to. A twitch of the drapes restored the illusion of normality.

Apara pocketed her lock picks and glanced around. If the lady's information was correct, this part of the house was unoccupied, its master away. Still, no reason to be sloppy. There were servants to consider. Hirelings took all manner of liberties when their paymaster's eyes were elsewhere. And it wasn't as if the house were entirely empty. Lights still shone in the main building and the eastern wing. Only here, in the west, did darkness reign.

She eased her way across the carpet, alert for creaking floorboards. She'd been at this since she'd been strong enough to climb a drainpipe. Since the lady had first bestowed her patronage.

Still a child, Apara hadn't questioned why she'd been chosen. She'd just been glad to be free of Dregmeet's slums, and at the prospect of regular meals. She'd always wanted a family, and the lady had given her a larger family than she'd even imagined. Hundreds of cousins, scattered across the Republic and beyond, bound by something stronger than blood.

Thirty years and more, and never once been caught. It had made her a legend among her cousins. The Silver Owl, they named her, for labours beneath sunless skies. But her once thrilling profession had become rote, even tedious. There were no real challenges. Not any longer. Part of her longed to get caught, just for the spice it would bring.

Apara shook the thought away. Now of all nights was no time to get sloppy. Not with two forbidden texts strapped to her back. Thieves got service in the clink or slaved for the navy. Witches got the pyre.

Her left eye twitching and her heart leaping at every tiny sound, Apara pressed on.

They must not easily be found without a determined search. By which Apara understood that the owner of the chambers should not discover the books, and nor should the cleaning staff or another burglar like herself. To find the books, the searcher would have to know that there was something illicit to be uncovered, and examine the chambers accordingly.

The books were a vial of poison, waiting to be broken into some poor bastard's breakfast.

Apara passed up the low bookcase. For all the joy of concealing a tree inside a forest, this particular copse was too threadbare. The top of the wardrobe and the underside of the bed were equally worthless. No aspiring heretic would stow such texts in so obvious a place. But the hearth? The hearth was perfect.

Apara shucked the oilskin bundle off her shoulders. Sitting down with her back to the fireplace, she reached up into the generous flue. Grasping fingers found the lip of the smoke shelf – just wide enough for what she had in mind.

Sure, the books *might* get accidentally burned, but not until the weather turned cold – a time still some months away. The cleanliness of the hearth cast doubt on any fire having blazed within for some time. And even if the books did burn, who was to say that they'd not been uncovered and deliberately set afire? The lady couldn't blame her for that.

Mission accomplished, Apara returned to the window and waited for another gap in patrols. Then she fled into the moonlight, leaving Swanholt – the ancestral home of the Akadra family – far behind.

Jeradas, 3rd day of Radiance

Arrogance is more dangerous than a sword.
False hope more ruinous than despair.

from the sermons of Konor Belenzo

Twenty

The encampment was already a fortress by the time Melanna took her last weary strides up the steep slope. The palisade of fresh-split pine wouldn't have deterred a true assault. Nor would the shallow ditch. That wasn't the object of the exercise. The point was to send a message: we are here, and we mean to stay.

Horsemen cantered past in a spray of mud. The leader spared her the briefest glance. Recognition? Or had he been appalled at the sight of a woman armed for war? Perhaps both. The havildar of the gate guard bowed low in a swish of silken robes.

"Greetings, *savim*. You choose a propitious time to return."

Beneath the blank death mask of his helm, he seemed genuinely pleased to see her. Such men were rare. Especially when they wore the golden scales of the Immortals – the Royal Guard.

She extended a gloved hand. The havildar stooped, took her fingers and pressed them to his lips in the age-old gesture of fealty. Loyal to the House of Saran more than to her personally, no doubt.

"It's good to be home, and to be greeted with such dignity, Havildar ... ?"

"Brannor, my princessa." He spoke without looking up. "Jastim Brannor."

"Then please, Havildar Brannor, rise. We are comrades."

After a moment's hesitation, Brannor obeyed. Without appearing to do so, Melanna took stock of the gate guards. She watched for the soon hidden flickers of surprise and disgust that a woman would claim parity with a warrior.

Even that flicker would have been enough to damn them had her aunt Saramin been present. Her mother's elder sister had never reconciled a fate that had seen her born to a gender treasured even as it was disdained for weakness. She took every opportunity to repay indignity with wrath. By contrast Aella – Melanna's younger aunt – revelled in the exertion of wiles and basked in the heady, secret power born of rank and allure. Melanna had learned from both.

Or so she told herself. Facing down Drakos Crovan was one thing. Confronting her own people was another matter.

"Perhaps you'd escort me to my father?"

"Should I not send for the lunassera?"

Saramin would have glowered. Melanna smiled. "Am I not safe in your company?"

Brannor's fingers gripped the hilt of his belted sword. "My life before yours, *savim*."

"Then we need not stir the sisterhood from meditation."

How old was Brannor? Forty winters? Fifty? A long life, filled with the screams of the dying, and the flutter of the Raven's wings. And yet the thought of being alone with her unsettled him.

Melanna breathed a silent prayer to Ashana. Her authority was slender enough. Each challenge – each denial – was a setback. But like steel, authority had to be tempered to reveal its true strength. If she hid from challenge, then the life she longed for was as good as lost.

Ashana heard her prayer. Discomfort won out over disobedience.

"As you wish, *savim*."

Melanna offered a smile just the right side of respectful, as Aella would have done. "You honour me, havildar. Lead on."

For most folk, the journey to the prince's tent would have taken an age. However, Melanna had the twin warrants of her face and the flat of Brannor's sword to clear a path.

Outriders cantered past, sallying forth to forage in the rich valleys below. Clansmen laboured to erect tents and stow possessions. And all around, the prayers and the brawls and the rich, close-harmony work songs. A hive of anarchy and raucous sound, all bent to a single overarching order.

Melanna knew every song, but they seemed incomplete without

women's voices in counterpoint. Back home, the lighter, sharper notes would have struck glorious contrast. But women were permitted more freedom back in the towns. There, noble daughters claimed vocation as merchants, advisors, priests and artists. And those of common birth joined menfolk in manual labour. A woman could carry any burden, so long as it was not a sword, and few travelled with the army.

A little beyond the vast, black consecrated folds of the tent that served as the army's temple they finally reached the palatial, fur-lined tents of his Exalted Highness, Champion of the Golden Court and Heir to the Imperial Throne, Kai Saran.

Melanna took leave of Brannor and passed inside. The Immortals within greeted her with the usual mix of curiosity and disdain. Melanna left her weapons in their care and eased aside the bear-pelt screening the inner sanctum.

A fire smouldered at the centre of the chamber. It set the air dancing with rich wood smoke, and the subtle scents of heather and jasmine. Almost enough to mask the earthy aromas of mud and stale sweat – but not quite.

Beyond the fire, crouched low over the generous, map-laden trestle, stood Melanna's father. Kos Devren, warleader of the host, was a grizzled, unhappy presence at his side, his finger stabbing down at parchment.

"We should march while we can." Devren delivered the suggestion as tersely as one could to royalty. "We have the passes. Every Tressian within a league is scrambling away west. Sitting here does nothing but rob us of advantage."

"We've been over this, old friend." Melanna's father ran a hand through his neat beard and massaged cheeks the colour of weathered teak. Even in silken robes rather than armour, he remained every inch the warrior. A full head taller than the cadaverous warleader and nearly twice as broad, he spoke softly, safe in the knowledge the words would be heeded. "We are here to invite battle, not enter it unwisely. Haste invites defeat."

"And delay gives Maggad time to seize victory in the north! If he breaches the Ravonn, he'll have your throne. You'll have the sword's kiss. And your daughter – if she's lucky – will be a bride of brief moonlight."

Melanna stiffened. Taken as a trophy, then discarded? She'd die first.

She said nothing to alert the men to her presence. Nor did Hal Drannic, her father's bodyguard, make any move to do so. Drannic wasn't much given to words, and favoured actions as the vessel of his thoughts. Only the tiniest flicker of his brow acknowledged that he'd seen her at all.

"Maggad is an old man," said Melanna's father. "His days of greatness lie squandered. He'll let caution guide him. One failure is more than he can afford."

"So why are you here?"

"Hnh." Melanna's father grinned, and rapped his knuckles on the wooden table. "In case I'm wrong, of course. And because the Golden Court sneers at complacency. Even if Maggad fails, I can expect another challenge within the year. I need a victory to cement my claim."

"Then we will give you one, *savir*." Devren's lips twisted in thought, then smoothed. Thin fingers danced across the map. "Our outriders estimate no more than a few hundred soldiers between us and Kreska. Konor Belenzo may be long dead, but his tomb and the cathedral remain places of pilgrimage. Whatever else the Tressians abandon, they'll fight for Kreska, and fight hard."

"The walls at Kreska are thick," said Melanna. "It will mean months of siege."

Devren covered his surprise with an unfriendly glance. "Six weeks, no more."

"Six weeks of dwindling supplies and blades in the night. We'd wake one dawn to find half the Republic outside our tents! And for what? A squalid brawl against warriors driven to madness by starvation? What glory is there in that?"

"With the mountain passes secured, our supply lines are clear. And with the eastern reaches abandoned, our foragers can seize whatever else we require."

Melanna stepped closer, careful not to look away. No weakness. Certainly not to a man like Devren, who'd married off his own daughters for dowry at barely respectable age. "Seize? You mean steal. My father has a mind to rule these people, warleader. Not destroy them."

"A fine goal that will not be achieved through the whimsical fancies of a girl. Even one so noble and well-meaning as yourself, *savim*."

A girl's fancies. He couldn't even acknowledge her as a woman. And as for "well-meaning" ... The phrase fair dripped with scorn. Melanna's temper rose to match warming cheeks. She fought it, recognising it to be unwise.

"I've spent six weeks here. I've walked Kreska's streets. I've spoken with its people. I don't speak with fancy, but with fact."

"You're too easily deceived." He shrugged. "It's no fault of your own. You lack judgement."

The steed of Melanna's temper threw off its harness and galloped loose. "And you lack ... "

Her father's irritated wave gestured her to silence. "Melanna. Enough."

Cheeks stinging, she obeyed. "Yes, Father."

"I will not have my daughter behave like a gutterling. Nor speak like one. Don't give me cause to regret the liberties I've allowed you."

The rebuke hurt more than Devren's insults. That, and the reminder that her life was not her own, only what her father granted. "No, Father."

Her father nodded and beckoned her over to the map. "And if not Kreska, then where?"

The answer came swiftly. "Eskavord."

"Eskavord?" Devren snorted. "How deep into their territory would you have us march?"

She ignored him, as she should have done before. "Kreska is old. It's a lair of priests who bow and scrape to Lumestra ... "

"*Astarra*. You've been too long away," muttered Devren. "Referring to the witch-goddess like one of those sun-worshipping heathens."

" ... it's not where power rests. The Southshires are governed from Eskavord. Better still, the town's walls are thin. *And* the region is infested with outlaws who dream of seeing their overlords humbled. Strike at Kreska, and you unite the Southshires against you. March on Eskavord, and the wolf's-heads will stand with us."

"And you're sure of this?"

Melanna hesitated. "There's no surety in war, Father. You taught me that. But Drakos Crovan is more honourable than he is not, and his people have much to gain in siding with us."

Her father chuckled. "Ah. The Wolf King. Here am I, unable to claim a title mine by right. Perhaps I should simply invent one to my liking."

He shook his head in voiceless amusement. "But I also taught you not to equivocate. Let's have it."

"It has come to my notice that Josiri Trelan is not the collaborator our spies believed. Indeed, he may be preparing an uprising of his own."

"And the Wolf King would choose his favour over ours."

"He says not."

"Do you believe him?"

Melanna recalled Crovan's manner as he spoke of Josiri Trelan. Not deference, not even real respect – just the echo of such. "I do, Father."

He turned back to the map, eyes sweeping from Kreska, to Eskavord and thence out to the distant western coast. As it always did when difficult decisions threatened, his right hand touched the golden locket at his throat, as if communing with the spirit of the woman whose portrait lay within. But if her mother spoke from beyond the mists, Melanna didn't hear her words.

"Warleader? I want reports on these roads . . . " His finger tapped the map three times to the north of Kreska, and once to the south. " . . . I want to know about fortifications, patrols. Whether they'll take wagons, the strength of the bridges – the usual."

Melanna could have told him all that but, wary of further disapproval, said nothing.

Her father pressed on. "And send three warbands of hunters north-east, towards Venka. They're not to bloody their spears unless challenged, and the populace are to be left unmolested. They're to make noise and draw the eye, nothing more."

The lines on Devren's face creased in concern. "My prince, you're not proposing that we act upon a girl's guesses?"

Melanna stiffened.

Her father lifted his head from the table and regarded Devren with unconcern. "No, that would be folly. I place our fate in the hands of my daughter, for whom girlhood is but a memory. I'm sure you see the difference."

Devren swallowed and nodded. "Of course, *savir*."

"Whichever banner the Wolf King howls beneath, the advantage is ours. If he fights with us, I shall embrace him as a subject, and reward his deeds. If he draws steel alongside the duke and joins his uprising, the Republic faces a war on two fronts. But we must be ready. So get me those reports."

"As you command." Devren bowed and withdrew.

"Father . . ."

An upraised hand cut her short. "Drannic? Leave us. I am quite safe from my daughter, and she from me."

Drannic's departing bow held greater respect than Devren's. When he had gone, Melanna's father gathered her up in a bruising embrace. At once, she was a child again: warm, safe – and stifled – in the presence of her sire.

"Six weeks," he breathed. "Six weeks and not a night passed by when I did not pray for you."

Melanna softened to the embrace, and at last returned it. "Ashana walked with me, Father."

"She always paid you more heed than I."

She stifled a smile. She'd been five winters old the first time the goddess had spoken to her. Proud and terrified in equal measure, she'd run straight to her father and confessed all. He'd laughed, chided her for prideful dreams and returned her to bed. He'd taken similar confessions no more seriously in the following years. Eventually, she'd stopped telling him.

He released her and stepped back. "You've done well. I'm proud of you."

Melanna's heart swelled a size larger. "Thank you, Father."

"And you had no trouble? No . . . individuals needing a visit from my icularis?"

For all the lightness in his tone, Melanna knew full well she was being invited to deliver sentence of death. The icularis – her father's "Eyes" – delivered warnings in only the starkest terms. So much like the creature of Ravenscourt she'd fought on the road to Tevar Flood.

"There was . . . one. A man of shadow and crow-feathers. I put an arrow in his shoulder."

Her father frowned in approval. "The icularis will watch for such a creature. And no others?"

Vorn's face floated up from memory. Melanna shook her head. "Nothing I couldn't handle."

"Then why do you seem so ill at ease?"

Should she tell him about the shadow behind Vorn's eyes before she'd broken his spirit? About the feeling she'd been watched most of the way to Trelszon? She couldn't have done so with Devren present, but even her father was likely to misread her fears as foolish worry.

"I'm tired, that's all."

"Or you've heard too many farmers' tales of darkness and ash."

Melanna snorted. "Certainly not. In fact, they don't even talk about what happened on their own land. It's like they don't know about the Sceadotha."

She suppressed a shudder. The long dead Sceadotha – Malatriant, as the Tressians named her – cast a long shadow, even in the warmth and light of her father's tent.

Her father scowled. "Most may not. Your grandfather always used to say that Tressians bury their past alongside their dead. I hope you've not grown afraid of the dark."

She smiled. "Not while there's a moon in the sky."

His eyes searched hers for a lie. Finding none, he shrugged. "Good. You'll let me have your reports on the roads?"

"So you knew?"

"Of course."

"Then why ... ?"

"Do I need Devren to make the same study? You'd have me force him to accept your word twice in as many minutes?"

She narrowed her eyes. "Yes."

"Devren's pride needs easing more than it requires hammering into shape."

"And what of my pride?"

"I think you've a great deal yet to learn of pride, and of leadership. Or is the prize you seek not worth a little humility?"

The prize. To one day be Empress in all the ways that mattered, not merely as a titled consort to the true ruler. Her father always spoke of it as "the prize", and Melanna hated it. Her birthright was not a spoil of war to be seized. It was an entitlement she had to fight for where generations of her forefathers had not. The mere suggestion that the throne would one day pass to her had provoked Maggad into issuing challenge.

Melanna stared down at her feet. "Only the dead have nothing to learn."

He grunted. "Good. Let me have your reports by midday, so that I've something to compare to those Devren brings me."

"You're testing me?"

"I'm testing you both. Anything else would be unwise."

Which meant the icularis would also be examining the lay of the land. Let them. She'd nothing to conceal. "I understand."

He smiled. "I know you do. And after, you'll join me at the banquet to celebrate our victories at Trelszon. I've had one of your dresses brought up from Tregard, so you can dazzle."

Melanna suppressed a frown. She could care less about dazzling a field of drunks. Especially as eyes had a tendency to wander when drink was imbibed. But there was a part to be played, and that meant silk and softness as much as steel.

"And my armour? It's time I took my place with the Immortals."

She didn't care for the silence that followed the question. Far less for the heaviness with which her father lowered himself to the fur-draped chair. "You are not to take the field with the Immortals."

"What? It's my right! My duty as your daughter!"

"Both right and duty belong to a son alone."

"We agreed!"

"No. When you left Tregard, I said I'd think on it. I have." He wouldn't meet her gaze. "You will remain with the camp, in the company of the lunassera."

"Where I can wring my tresses and await word of victory or defeat? If my father lives or dies? No!" She knew her voice carried beyond the tent. She didn't care. "Do you trust me so little around your *mighty* warriors? Is that why you'd cage me among the chaste?"

"I would have you shelter where I know you are safe!" he snapped. "You are my only child. I will not lose you to a Tressian blade!"

"You could have lost me a dozen times over these past six weeks. Why is it safe for me to wander enemy territory, but not stand the line? To fight at my father's side, as he did beside my grandfather?"

Melanna broke off, shaking with anger.

"Not all dangers are equal." Her father spoke without anger, but equally devoid of regret. "And I will not risk your life when strangers stand ready to serve me."

"And if I were instead your son?"

"A woman has no place in battle."

So that was it. It didn't matter what she did. Even her father saw her as something to be protected. Cherished, but also pitied for a weakness that owed more to perception than to truth.

"The Tressians don't believe so."

"What the Tressians believe, or do not, is of no concern to me."

Melanna took a deep, shuddering breath. Anger never prevailed upon her father, only reason. "And how am I to earn the respect of those I must lead if they never see me in battle?"

"They *will* see you. But not here, and not now." He rose and laid a hand on her shoulder. "I know you burn for this. You would not be my daughter otherwise. But now is not the time. Tradition bends unwillingly." He sighed. "And so do I. It's selfish, but I do not wish to see you scarred by war."

"Afraid I'll no longer dazzle?" she asked sourly.

He tapped her lightly on the breastbone. "War leaves its mark upon more than flesh. I don't ask you to embrace my decision, for I know you won't, but I require you to respect it. And when this campaign is done, and the throne secured, I will give you everything you wish. Even the scars."

"And if you die because I'm not there to protect you?"

And it would be more than his death, devastating though that would be. His death would be the death of Melanna's dreams. The Golden Court would never back an unblooded woman over Maggad. If her father died, the throne would go to the old warleader – as would she, were she too slow in embracing the Raven. Nothing like a marriage to cement a fickle claim. And so the line of Saran would end with a slit throat on her wedding night.

He shook his head. "What have I done to deserve a daughter who has so little faith in me? I have no plans to die, *essavim*."

The curtain at the tent's entrance swished. Melanna turned around, knowing what she'd see. No wonder Drannic had abandoned his post so readily. He'd not been dismissed, but sent to fetch her escort.

Two lunassera stood in silence before her. They were curiously alike, as were all the goddess's handmaidens. Between the silver-traced wooden half-masks that concealed all but the eyes and the olive skin of the lower jaw – and the close-fitting white robes that covered the women head to foot – there was little room for individuality.

As indeed was the point. The lunassera were perfection – as separate from desire as sea from sky. They were ephemeral daughters of the maiden goddess, as blessed in sanctity as their spiritual mother, and the pinnacle of Hadari womanhood. Melanna had once asked Ashana as to the truth of that. A soft, despairing laugh and a slow shake of the head had been the goddess's only answer.

Melanna hadn't found the courage to enquire further. She *had* thereafter wondered to whose benefit the lunassera wore such figure-hugging raiment. But she hadn't wondered long. The robes were both pedestal and cage. In that way, the lunassera were indeed the purest expression of Hadari womanhood. Admired, but seldom on their own terms.

And now, it seemed, they were to be her jailers.

"You'll have my reports by noon, my prince," said Melanna, unwilling to address her father as kin. She offered a stiff bow. "Let's hope you don't regret your decision."

Twenty-One

Dawn found Josiri where dusk had left him: staring at the silver fil-igreed ward-brooch and infused with that bewildering, jangling energy that has ever been the enemy of those who seek sleep.

All these years spent yearning to fulfil his mother's charge; to free the Southshires and its people. Some he'd spent in nights like the one just passed, worrying over consequences and detail, of lives lost, and others sacrificed. And now? Everything he'd ever wanted was his to claim.

If Akadra spoke the truth. *If* Akadra could be trusted.

Was that even a concern? Akadra had murdered his mother. Did granting her last wish even matter if it arose from her slayer's largesse? And in truth, the equality Akadra promised fell short of the freedom for which Katya Trelan had striven. Was accepting the lesser prize a betrayal all its own? Josiri glanced up at the wall, remembering too late that the portrait was ashes.

He rubbed at his face. The prickle of stubble beneath his palms served as a reminder of how long he'd sat in that chair.

Two choices lay before him. Just two. He could embrace the brooch and Akadra's offer, or he could leave his plans unaltered. Both were selfish. Both fulfilled his duty to his people. Both tempted peril. If the resistance perished, did it matter if it did so out of Josiri's misguided leadership, or from northwealder treachery? If the Southshires was freed of its bonds, was it of any consequence if that freedom sprang from Josiri's efforts, or Akadra's generosity?

Aware he was again embarking on a journey with no clear destina-tion, Josiri clambered to his feet. The chair toppled back and crashed against flagstones. A week ago, arrayed for Ascension, the great hall's grandness had been unmatched. Now the air smelt stale, and Josiri saw wilted flowers more than he did the blooms. Even the statues seemed to judge him.

He was trapped. Lost in a maze of his own fears. He needed counsel. But to whom could he turn? Not Calenne, who was no longer at Branghall. Besides, he'd lied to her too long. He'd find more well-deserved acrimony than wisdom. And as for Anastacia? The memory of their last argument was still too near.

That left Revekah, but without Anastacia to open the hallowgate, Revekah was denied him.

Josiri's gaze fell on the ward-brooch. No. That wasn't true.

After all, taking the brooch didn't mean agreeing to Akadra's terms, did it?

His fingers closed around the silver.

Calenne awoke from the first good night's sleep she'd had in years. The bed was soft, the blankets warm and the scents of the old loft room unchanged in years away. That curious combination of rose petals and wood smoke drifted up from the hearth downstairs. The fragrance of childhood. Of bedclothes clutched tight to ward off the chill of Wanetithe nights and rain rattling at the windowpane.

Calenne lay there for what seemed for ever and yet no time at all, striving to rouse memories. Fragments of light and shadow from a life lived long ago. She abandoned them reluctantly, feeling diminished for the loss, and at last emerged from beneath the covers to start the day.

Elda was busy at the kitchen hearth. "Sleep well?"

"Like a serathi on a cloud."

She snorted. "Well, I wouldn't know about that."

Calenne stifled a smile and sat at the table. Her foster-mother's icon-oclasm had changed little with the years. The past had left its mark in other ways. Black hair had faded to grey. Furrows of merriment and disappointment ran deeper than ever, her eyes haunted by private resentment. It had shocked Calenne to see her thus the previous night, but now Elda's appearance seemed natural. Time had changed them both, and not necessarily for the better. Yesterday's welcome had been ready enough, but Calenne couldn't help but wonder if it had been offered from duty, rather than affection.

Elda drew away from the hearth and slid a brimming bowl of oatmeal before her. "I'm sure you're hungry."

"Always."

A steaming mug of bark tea joined the bowl. Movement in the street outside caught Calenne's eye. A gold-robed proctor, sun-stave tapping the cobbles and two simarka trotting obediently at her heels. Calenne suppressed a shudder. She'd seldom seen the constructs up close, but distance did nothing to quell her fear of the beasts – a fear she'd never quite been able to explain. She supposed prey never could explain such fear. It was just *there*.

"Thank you for letting me stay," she said.

Elda pulled up a chair. "This is still your home. And you're still my daughter ... even if you're a deal taller than last I saw you. Fifteen years. But see how you've grown with it."

The words warmed Calenne's heart. But they also awoke an old, lingering resentment. "It didn't happen all at once. You never visited. I'd have been overjoyed to see you. I *needed* to see you. But you never came."

Elda scowled, and stared down into her tea with dark and distrustful eyes. "Those first years after Katya died ... You probably don't remember, but folk didn't come and go in Branghall as they have of late. And me? I kept expecting to end on a deportation scow, but I guess a good apothecary's hard to find."

She nudged the mug back and forth across the table top, turning the handle this way and that. Unwilling to interrupt, Calenne let her eyes drift across the nigh-endless collection of jars, pots, vials and urns that crowded the kitchen shelves. She'd vague recollections of memorising them all when a young girl, determined to learn everything Elda could teach. Now the memories were as dry and dusty as those abandoned aspirations.

"And then afterwards," said Elda at last, "when the Council's lackeys loosened up a bit ...? Well, I decided a clean break might be best for us both."

Best for Elda, in other words. "I sent you an invitation to my wedding. You never replied."

"Half of Eskavord had invitations. And near as I can tell, you're not married."

"No." Even the idea of it seemed a lifetime ago. "He died."

Elda stared at her, then reached across the table and took her hand. "My dear child. I'd no idea. What must you think of me?"

Calenne smiled, more for Elda's sake than her own. "It doesn't matter. Lumestra punished me for selfishness, and Kasamor paid the price. I have to live with that."

Elda raised an eyebrow. "And if Lumestra's in no position to judge you? If there's nothing waiting for us but the mists, and the Dark?"

"I still have to live with it, don't I?" Calenne broke off, recognising she'd spoken more archly than she'd intended. "I'm starting to wonder if that's all life is – living with your mistakes."

"Ever the earnest child. I can still see you as you were when your mother took you away. Such concern in your eyes."

Calenne remembered so little of that night. She certainly didn't recall feeling sympathy for others. Only for herself – a state in which she'd lived ever since.

Wiry fingers gripped hers tighter. "It will pass. That's why we seek triumphs – to balance our failures. Just as seeing the woman you've become eases my regret at staying away."

Calenne blinked away sudden tears. She opened her mouth to speak, but the words turned dry on her tongue. "I—"

A triplet of booming thuds shuddered the front door. A pause, enough to take a breath, and the unseen fist hammered again.

Elda offered a wry smile and clambered upright. "Another customer, no doubt. Some northwealder sergeant with a sore head from last night."

She made her way from the kitchen, leaving Calenne alone with her thoughts. How strange to have spent her adult life wanting nothing more than to escape the town, and to now be so at ease. A little freedom went a long way.

When Elda returned to the kitchen, it was not with an ailing soldier in tow, but Lord Akadra. His head struck the uneven doorframe a glancing blow. He scowled at the offending timber and rubbed his brow.

"This one wants to speak with you," said Elda coldly. "I'll be in the garden."

She retreated from sight, shoulders back and stride stiff. A door slammed soon after.

"I've had warmer welcomes," said Akadra. "On the other hand: no slops bucket."

"Elda was one of Katya's oldest friends," said Calenne. "You can't blame her for hating you. And that cloak makes you look like a hangman going door to door to drum up business."

"May I sit?"

She hesitated, enjoying the moment of power. "Why are you here, Lord Akadra?"

"Viktor."

"I'm sorry?"

"Titles are for commoners. You're a Trelan, a family of the first rank."

Calenne narrowed her eyes and sighed. "Very well, *Viktor*. You may sit."

He inclined his head. "Thank you, Miss Trelan."

"No."

Akadra – no, *Viktor* – halted halfway to his seat and frowned in puzzlement.

"If the Black Knight of my nightmares is to be Viktor, then *I* will be nothing other than Calenne."

"Of course."

The ghost of a smile touched Viktor's lips. The chair creaked as it took his weight.

Why had she insisted he address her thus? A point of pride? Or so she need not hear her hated surname? But the man before her shared so little with the Black Knight of her dreams that she couldn't discount the possibility that she *wanted* to be thought his equal.

"I didn't know," said Viktor. "About your dreams, I mean."

Calenne shrugged, already regretting revealing that part of herself. "A man drives a child from her home, he should expect to be thought a monster."

"And you think me a monster now?"

"I don't know. I think you have it within you to *be* a monster, if you wish."

He laughed, though the mirth didn't reach his eyes. "As do we all. Lumestra may have brought light to the world, but she didn't drive the Dark from our souls. It's there, waiting for when we need it, or when we're too weak to resist."

"Elda would tell you that the Dark is all we share."

"So she's not a believer?"

"No." Calenne blanched. Why had she told him that? If Makrov found out ... "I mean, she's not ... "

"I know what you meant. Or I would have done, if I'd heard. But I didn't."

"Thank you." The tension in her chest eased.

He shrugged. "In any case, it's not as though I could easily inform the archimandrite of her lapse. Captain Kurkas tells me he rode north in a fearful hurry yesterday. He might be halfway to Tressia by now."

"Good," Calenne said feelingly.

"Perhaps. He can make mischief for us in the north." He shrugged. "My actions here have left him displeased."

"Didn't I ask why you'd come here? Don't you have a war to fight?"

"The war is *why* I'm here." Discomfort flickered across his face. "I need your help. I need your advice."

So that was the way of things? "Josiri."

"Yes."

"Well, I didn't think you'd come to ask about the best way to repel the Hadari."

Another slim smile. "No. Governor Yanda has the initial phases in hand. At this point it's more an exercise in prayer than practice. Trelszon has fallen, and if Prince Saran isn't foolish enough to lay siege to Kreska, he'll be here in a matter of days."

"Can you not hold them at Charren Gorge? Oh, don't look at me like that. There are plenty of maps at Branghall."

Viktor inclined his head in unspoken apology. "We could, had we the numbers. Which is why I need Josiri to rally the Southshires to war."

Calenne glanced out the window where Elda busied herself with hanging baskets. Or at least gave that appearance. She probably heard every word.

"Survival often provides all the motivation folk need to fight."

"If it does here, they give no sign of rising to the challenge," said Viktor. "I suspect more would fight alongside the Hadari than against them."

He spoke matter-of-factly, without even the dour distaste of a man discussing inclement weather. It was worse, Calenne decided, to hear doom laid out in such plain-spoken terms, without the adornment of anger or fear.

"I wish I knew what to tell you about him," she said. "It seems to me of late that I don't know Josiri half as well as I thought."

"There must be something."

"I can count on the fingers of one hand the number of times I've changed Josiri's mind." She shrugged. "He's stubborn, he's proud, and he has no reason to trust anything you say."

"I regret that more than you can imagine, but pride is a poor coin of exchange when lives are at stake, whether it be Josiri's, or mine."

His fervency burned like smouldering flame. Calenne thought it strange that the fate of her people could matter so much to Viktor, and not to herself.

"Why is this so important to you?"

"Duty is not handed down from on high, Calenne. It comes from within."

She didn't believe him. "As simple as that?"

"As simple as that."

She *definitely* didn't believe him. But what did it cost her to help?

"Speak to the demon," she said. "Though it pains me to say so, she knows Josiri better than I and cares for him far more. If anyone can give you the keys to his trust, it is she."

Viktor rose. "Then I'll take my leave. Thank you for your insight."

She nodded silently, only now considering whether she'd spoken of more than she should.

He waited a moment longer, and then departed in a swirling of black velvet. Calenne was wondering whether or not she should have gone with him when Elda returned.

"That one's confused." The old woman set her back to the chimney and folded her arms. "Caught between what he is, and what he wants to be."

Between the monster and the man, Calenne supposed. "You heard?"

"Most of it. Do you believe him?"

Calenne decided to spare herself Elda's scorn. "Would it be so bad if the Empire conquered the Southshires?"

Elda grunted. "Katya insisted the shadowthorns lack for souls. That's why they fight so fearlessly, because they've nothing to lose to the Raven."

Calenne had heard Branghall's servants repeat the claim over the years. "Is it true?"

"'Course not. It's an excuse to keep hate burning. Otherwise we might just realise that we're more alike than not. We're all one. Just specks of Dark waiting for release ..."

"By Lumestra?" Calenne asked slyly.

"You know better than that." Elda scowled, though not unkindly. "Lumestra, Ashana – the rest of that sorry bunch. What they took from us matters more than what they gave. Tied us to the soil and set us at each other's throats. We were meant for more than this, Calenne. Katya never saw the truth of that. I do hope fifteen years at Branghall hasn't blinded you to it."

There was so much resentment in Elda's dark eyes. So much loss. Tangible almost to the point of physicality. Part of Calenne felt drawn to it, kin as it was to her own disappointments. But the rest of her sensed the danger of wallowing in a past that couldn't be changed.

"So it doesn't matter if we're conquered?"

"In the end, nothing matters. The Dark takes all." Elda chuckled to herself. "And won't that be a day full of sorry faces?"

Calenne scowled. She'd heard variants of that fatalistic declaration when a girl. Somehow, it had all seemed more comforting then. Now she just felt small. Insignificant. "You're a fine help."

"You want help, see a priest. If you want truth? You know where I am."

Viktor wasn't surprised to learn Josiri had departed Branghall. But nor did he expect that the departure marked any great change of heart. It was every bit as likely that the erstwhile duke had fled, never to be seen again. Time would tell. A little time out in the world might shake loose his sense of duty. If not? Well, another way would be sought.

But one corner of his heart was quieter than the day before. Malachi's herald had at last found him. The letter confirmed Kasamor's death, but also Rosa's survival. Viktor felt a shadow of guilt for taking more solace than grief from the letter. Better to be thankful for the living than mournful of the dead.

He entered the great hall unannounced. Anastacia stood at the eastern window, one hand pressed against the glass. Little more than drifting mist from the waist down, she stared out across the grounds. Her shoulders slumped like those of a puppet resting on its strings – a portrait of loss and longing so perfect and private that Viktor felt guilty for standing witness.

Suppressing a new frisson of wariness – kin to that he'd felt on their first meeting, and the stronger for it having been proved correct – he cleared his throat.

Anastacia's fingers slipped from the window. Her entire being ravelled back together like cotton about a spindle. The skirts of a panelled ivory dress flowed into place.

"Josiri's not here, so you can leave me in peace." The tone belied the words, and pleaded for him to stay.

"I'd hoped to speak with you."

"I'm told it's healthy to have aspirations."

"Then I'll live for ever, for I aspire to so many things."

She gave a wintery laugh. "You may not find immortality to your liking."

"A chance worth taking. Or so I'm told." Viktor looped his hands behind his back and strode closer. "I confess I know almost nothing about you."

"I'm sure the archimandrite could weary your ears with details."

"Just as I'm sure none of them would be true."

She shrugged. "I imagine so. Dear Arzro's predecessor was twice the man he is."

"Emil Karkosa? I remember him well." Still some paces away, Viktor took a seat. His eyes lingered on the cluster of empty wine bottles. "Every Lumendas without fail I'd sit in a pew no further from the pulpit than I sit from you now, and I'd listen to Karkosa preach. He'd a faith to shatter mountains in those days. But he was charitable with it. Not something one could say of Makrov."

Of course, Viktor had stopped going to church after his shadow's awakening and his mother's death – and for two very different reasons. But the rest of the tale was true enough.

"This is fascinating," said Anastacia. "But on balance, I prefer the prospect of loneliness to hearing about your blissful childhood."

Viktor ignored her. "I'm wondering what it was that you did to see yourself confined – and here of all places. And whether it had anything to do with why Karkosa spent his final years as a recluse. Even sealed himself off from his family. I'm told he'd been dead a fortnight before anyone knew. Not that anyone cared by then." He shrugged. "Too much faith can be embarrassing."

She spread her hands and dipped a curtsey. "You have me, tied and true. I slipped into his bed one night while his wife was away. No complaints at the time, of course, but he couldn't leave me alone. Followed me everywhere." She rolled her eyes. "The promises he made. The entreaties. This was my punishment for refusal."

Her halo flickered as she spoke, the golden-white tinged with red.

"If you want to shock me, you'll have to try harder." Viktor leaned forward. "Or you could accept that I see *you* as plainly as I know you see *me*, and you could tell me the truth."

Anastacia's eyes hardened. "Why should I?"

"Because Josiri's not coming back ..." Viktor didn't believe that. Though he could not claim to have ever been in love himself, he wasn't blind to it in others. Josiri would return if only because Anastacia remained. But at that moment, only Anastacia's beliefs mattered. "... and you've no one left to tell. Because who would believe me if I told anyone else? And because I won't help you cast free of these stones if I'm not certain you deserve that favour."

Her stare melted, allowing a glimpse behind the bitterness. "I told Karkosa his beloved goddess was dead."

Viktor was surprised how little the declaration stirred him. Was she still trying to shock him? Neither her gaze nor her halo twitched. If it was a lie, it was one carefully told. "And how would you know this?"

"Because there was a war, sister against sister. My angelic siblings quarrelled, with my mother and her legacy as the prize. I alone took no side. For my hesitation, I was hurled from the heavens. I heard my mother's death-scream as I fell."

"You'd have me believe you're a serathi?"

"I don't care what you believe." She extended a hand. Her fingertips blurred, drifting away into golden-white vapour. "I'm what's *left* of a serathi. The part that crawled onto the dockside in Tressia. Karkosa's proctors found me. At first, they worshipped me. I liked that. Then he begged me to tell him all I knew of his goddess. When I refused, he became more . . . persuasive. He set his provosts loose. They . . . did not worship me."

Viktor grimaced. The activities of the church's provosts were mysterious even to him. Those who drew their eye had a tendency to end in flame.

Anastacia eyed him uncertainly. "When I gave Karkosa what he wanted, he flew into a rage. I'm here because I told him the truth and he couldn't bear it."

She spun around and stared into the east once more.

If this was a lie, it was better than the first, the flat certainty all the more compelling because Anastacia made no effort to convince him. Viktor wasn't sure if he believed her, but Karkosa had believed, and the tapestry of his life had unravelled. And then he'd locked Anastacia far, far away to keep her truth hidden.

And, when it came down to it, how many explanations could there be to explain a creature like Anastacia?

"Why didn't Karkosa destroy you?"

"Do you really think anyone could?"

"Yes."

Bitter laughter returned. "You are no flatterer, Lord Akadra. As to why Karkosa acted as he did, I can offer no answers. From what you say it's too late to demand any of him. And now you too are bound to the truth that drove him mad. Let us both hope you bear it better."

"You've never told Josiri the truth about yourself, have you?"

"He has burdens enough. I've no desire to add to them."

"And what if I tell him?"

"Then your secret would remain so no longer."

Viktor's cheek twitched. "You can prove nothing."

"Nor can you."

"And nor do I wish to. We can help each other, you and I," he replied. "I need to change Josiri's mind, and I'm told you are the key to that. In turn, I'll grant your freedom. Wherever fate leads him, you can be together, if that is your wish."

The hope returned to her eyes. "A brooch will not set me free of this place."

"I'm a man of many aspirations. I can always make room for another."

The distant strike of metal on stone set Calenne's teeth on edge. It grew louder with every step, the chiming of some tortured, misshapen bell decrying her stupidity for returning to Branghall. She pressed a hand to her ward-brooch and reassured herself that this wasn't some peculiar, heartless dream.

Clang! Clang! Clang!

The worst of it was, she wasn't even sure why she'd returned. Yes, the letter had summoned her, but there was no compulsion to answer. Guilt again, she supposed. This time born of sitting idle while others strove to fulfil her family's responsibilities.

Anastacia met her at the manor gate. The demon seemed quiet, subdued.

Reason enough to be concerned.

Clang! Clang!

"Where is he?" Calenne asked.

"The chapel."

The one room Anastacia avoided like a noblewoman avoided a beggar's nest? Stranger and stranger. "Do you know why he sent for me?"

"I didn't know he had."

Calenne left the demon behind. Servants shot her questioning looks. She ignored them. What answer could she give?

Clang! Clang!

At last, she rounded the corner and passed beneath the winged serathi of the chapel's arched doorway. "Viktor!"

The Black Knight froze in the act of swinging the two-handed workman's mallet. He stood, naked to the waist and streaming with sweat, in a shallow, rough-edged pit ringed with cracked tile and broken stone. The shroud-covered altar lay perhaps six paces behind. Its statue of Lumestra regarded the sacrilege with lofty disapproval.

"Ah, Calenne." He let the hammer slide through his fingers until its haft struck the floor. "Thank you for coming."

"You appear to have dug a hole in the chapel floor."

"Not just the floor, but the foundations." He shrugged. "And no one was using it."

"And if Lumestra takes offence?"

"I'm assured she'll take no action." He spoke the words with a small smile, but the joke – if there was one – was lost on Calenne.

Viktor took advantage of the brief silence to whirl the hammer anew. *Crunch!*

Calenne flinched at the clamour. A fist-sized chunk of stone shattered to dust.

"I swear, if you do that once more, I'm going back the way I came." Had she just threatened the Black Knight? "I don't even know why I'm here."

"To repay a favour owed?"

"I did that yesterday when I spoke for you before my brother."

He set the hammer aside. "Then I suppose *I'll* owe *you* a favour."

Interested despite herself, Calenne held her ground. "For what?"

"Is there a sculptor in Eskavord? One who works with clay?"

"I imagine so ... Elda will know."

Viktor squatted. He scooped a handful of dust from the pit and trickled it carefully into a small leather pouch. He did so twice more, and tugged the drawstring closed.

"Take that to the sculptor and have him fold it into fresh clay. A lot of fresh clay." He stepped out of the pit and dropped the pouch into Calenne's hand. "And have him clear his workload for the day. He'll be well compensated."

She lifted the pouch and glowered at it. "Get one of your soldiers to do it."

"My soldiers, few as they are, have labours of their own. You do not."

Calenne grimaced. It would be nice, just once, to have a conversation where she didn't end up feeling like a spoilt child. But she supposed the key to that was not behaving like one in the first place.

"All right. For a favour yet owed."

Twenty-Two

The guest-bell chimed early at the Kiradin mansion. Earlier than respectable sorts were about their business. But Marek would never have considered himself a respectable sort. Lady Ebigail's wishes were paramount. Chief among them was that any business that presented itself before the hour of eight without benefit of the Council seal was business safely left in Marek's hands.

And if the caller disagreed? Well, then there were always the dogs. Few guests rode their fortunes hard with hounds sniffing at their heels.

It was therefore with surprise, disappointment and no small measure of horror that Marek opened the door to behold a bedraggled, torn and bandaged Lady Sevaka.

"My lady ... What has become of you?"

"Marek." Bloodshot eyes met his. "I need to speak with my mother. At once."

"I'll see if she's prepared to receive you," he said. "It is still early."

Lady Sevaka pushed past into the hallway. The stale smell of exertions past lingered behind. "We both know she's been up for hours. I need to speak with her."

Marek flinched and set the door to. He hated being caught between mother and daughter. This was how corsairs felt, chained to the harbour wall as the tide rushed in. Generally, he arranged matters so another of the staff bore the brunt. No chance of that here.

"She'll want to know what this is about."

Lady Sevaka sighed in angry resignation. "Very well, tell her ... "

"You may tell me yourself, now your caterwauling has disturbed half the household."

Lady Ebigail peered unfavourably down from the bannister. Marek winced at his implied failure but said nothing. It was not his place to answer. For a time, the only sounds were the muted *tick* of the hallway clock, birdsong from the gardens and the soft *swish* of Lady Ebigail's pleated black skirts as she descended. Marek withdrew, taking up position beside the front door.

"Been brawling again, I see," Lady Ebigail sniffed. "I keep hoping you'll learn decorum. I should never have allowed you to join the fleet. It's no life for a noblewoman."

"We were attacked," Sevaka bit out. "Rosa and I."

One eye narrowed in suspicion. "By whom? If this is another tale that begins and ends with one of your romantic misjudgements, you may save us both the trouble. I've had my fill of outraged husbands seeking recompense."

"Aske Tarev," Lady Sevaka replied. "Something about repaying one of Kasamor's insults."

"Such fragile pride, and so *much* to be fragile about. *Tell* me you gave her nothing to brag about?"

"She's dead."

Lady Ebigail didn't miss a beat. "And you'd like the body attended to before it draws notice? Tell Marek where she can be found, and he'll see to it, won't you, Marek?"

He offered a stiff bow. "Of course, lady."

How to do so with the streets already growing busy with the morning's trade, he wasn't certain. Still, he'd manage. After all, it wasn't the first time.

"Anton will miss his daughter, of course," Lady Ebigail went on. "But no one else will. No one who matters, anyway."

"I didn't kill her!" Sevaka snapped. "Rosa did. The constabulary took us soon after. They released me after Rosa confessed."

"And you abandoned her?"

"You think I wanted to? They wouldn't listen to me. They intend to bring her before council this morning."

Which meant she'd be dead by afternoon, Marek judged. Justice

with full commar
It would keep. "Y

"But I don't. I
though I never fe
I'm cursed, Mala
have to burn me.
Or whether they

Malachi shud
macabre. "You'r
are scattered . . .

Her exaspera
is sacred."

She pushed
stitches popped
Malachi, concer

"Rosa . . ."

"Don't be su

After a brief
had merely rip
Roughly half
scar the width
certain. But it

"So it's a sc

"I took this

He stared
"Impossible."

She shot h
the dress?"

She held t
ering along l

"Let me s

Rosa step
imagine wh

Malachi
speech. Gro
no doubt th

flowed all the swifter when a councillor's family had been wronged. Doubly so for a family of the first rank.

"You should have made them listen!" Ice crackled beneath Lady Ebigail's words. "You are a Kiradin, not some jumped-up dockworker with a badge. You're such a disappointment. Your brother was worth ten of you."

Lady Sevaka's face fell. "No one's disputing that."

Marek averted his gaze. He knew the chastisement sprang from love. The elder Lady Kiradin sought to shape her daughter as a sculptor shaped clay, smoothing away the unnecessary and the unlovely to reveal the hard, beautiful form beneath. But he doubted he could have spoken to his own daughter thus, had Lumestra blessed him with one.

"The Republic needs strong blood, and strong leadership," said Lady Ebigail. "It does not need callow young women who let others fight their battles and abandon them thereafter."

"Fight their own battles?" Lady Sevaka ripped back her sleeve to reveal a stained bandage. "How do you think I got this?" Her spread hand encompassed the cuts and bruises and her face, her voice growing ragged. "Or these? Do you think I came here for sympathy? For maternal concern? Lumestra knows I wouldn't expect that from you. I can't help Rosa, but I know you can."

She stopped, breathless.

The corner of Lady Ebigail's mouth twitched. She gave a sharp nod. "Then I have not entirely failed to instil you with good sense. We will see what can be done. Marek? Prepare the carriage. We leave as soon as my daughter has scraped away the gutter."

He bowed, glad that the rift between mother and daughter was, if not sealed, then at least bridged. "At once, lady."

The turnkey slammed the swollen door closed. The cell stank of salt, mould and the worst kind of filth. A green tidemark halfway up the plasterwork showed the levels to which the chamber had last flooded. Pooled water beneath Malachi's boots spoke to drains long since clogged.

He could have coped with all that. Filth could be swept away, clothes

cleaned and skir
hunched on the
knees? That test

The constabu
the once-expen:
and gutter-muc
though Rosa ha

"How is it ou
Malachi sigh
that I'm surpris
and some I do
Your uncles ha
you to trial bef

"So soon?"

"You confe:
have to confes

Rosa turnec

"Deserve i
scraped as he
barely a week

"I got caug!

Malachi sh
the confessio
And I deserv

"Why do

"Because

Malachi :
depth of Ro:

"Did Kas:

She shoo
confession."

"Don't ta

"We bot
sighed. "An

Malachi
decided ag

had cut the latter to match the former. Even in her current madness that seemed unlikely.

Especially if she weren't mad at all.

He traced his fingers along the scar. Her skin was warm to the touch, though perhaps not as warm as it should have been. And now he examined all the closer, he realised that the hairline at the scar's heart was not pinkish-red, but black.

"Does it hurt?"

"No. There should be a matching one on my back. But I can't reach there."

Malachi shook his head. This wasn't possible, was it? If Rosa had taken a wound like that mere hours ago she shouldn't even be standing. She'd be dying. She was sucking him into her grief-born madness. And he, so heartsick at the prospect of losing another friend, was letting her do so.

"You're not well, Rosa. You're imagining things."

She flicked at the flap of cloth, put one hand on her hip and held out the other. "Give me your dagger."

"I'm not carrying a dagger. I'm a councilman visiting a prisoner."

"Then give me your paper knife. You never go anywhere without it."

Malachi slipped the thin, blunted blade from his pocket and reversed it. Rosa snatched it up and brought it down on her left forearm.

"Rosa!" Malachi leapt to his feet. His shout swallowed up the wet, tearing sound.

Heavy footsteps sounded in the corridor. A fist hammered on the door. "Everything all right in there, my lord?"

No, thought Malachi. Everything was far from all right. His eyes slipped from Rosa's face to her left forearm, and he realised they were worse even than he'd thought. The wooden haft was flush with the upper side of her arm. The blunted tip projected an inch or two below. There was no blood.

Keys jangled beyond the door. "My lord?"

Malachi swallowed. "No problem here. Be about your business."

The rattle of keys fell silent. The footsteps tracked away.

"Doesn't . . . Doesn't that hurt?"

"Not as much as it should. Believe me now?"

He threw a hand against the wall to steady himself. Rosa slid the knife free of her flesh and tossed it to him. Malachi made the catch with a shudder of revulsion. A thin, glistening layer of silvery-black fluid evaporated from the blade.

"What happened to you?" he whispered.

"I told you. I'm cursed. The kernclaw cursed me."

Malachi's ears pricked up at the new information. "Kernclaw?"

"He killed Kasamor."

"No. Wait. You said that brigands killed Kasamor."

"I lied."

"Why in Lumestra's name would you do such a thing?"

"Because I was worried Kas had ties with the vranakin. I didn't want to shame his memory."

Malachi blinked. Kasamor had lived a life in the light, bright with honour. He'd not associate with thieves and murderers. "And he had magic, this kernclaw?"

She nodded. "He arrived in a storm of crow's wings. He was fast. So fast."

Malachi stared at her, familiar indecision coursing through his veins. What if Rosa had died on the road and what stood before him was some demon, or a cyraeth spirit come free of Otherworld to torment him? And if she wasn't, and he turned away when his friend needed him most?

And he'd already lost too many friends of late.

He glanced again at the paper knife. The blade was dry, and seemingly clean. "I have to go. If I'm to have any chance of getting you out of here, I need to be at council."

"I already told you, I deserve this."

"This once, I don't *care* what you think, Roslava Orova. If the Parliament of Crows had Kasamor killed, it was for a reason. Which means there's still a chance to deliver him justice, and I can't do it without you." He took a deep breath. "As to what has become of you, if there's an answer to be found we *will* find it."

He stared at her, daring her to argue. To his relief and surprise, she didn't.

"Yes, my Lord Reveque."

The sardonic tone undermined her contrite expression, but it was a start.

"I really must go," he said. "But promise me you'll make no more renditions of that charming trick with the knife? Let that part of it remain between us. Please."

"Yes, my Lord Reveque."

"Is there anything else I can do in the meantime?"

She thought for a moment and stared down at her abused dress. "My uniform. Whichever road I walk from here, I'd sooner do it as myself."

Malachi nodded. She'd not be permitted to keep it, not if she walked the gallows road. Nonetheless, it was cheering to see more of the woman he remembered shining through.

Which would make the hurt all the deeper if he failed to save her.

In the end, it took over two hours for Marek to get the Kiradin carriage underway for the Council palace – the time it took for Lady Ebigail to pronounce her daughter a fit sight for council. Even then, no amount of masking powder could entirely hide the bruises. Then had come the winding bridal procession that had blocked the streets between the Silverway River and King's Mount church. It had been a battered train of carriages – too battered for the bride to hail from a family of *true* wealth and standing – but Marek had duly brought his journey to a halt until the streets had cleared, as was tradition. Weddings, like interments, were owed respect, for each marked flourish and sacrifice in their own way. Even Lady Ebigail voiced no impatience – though the hawker who'd approached the carriage window soon thereafter received the shortest and sharpest of shrift.

By the time they finally arrived, the palace's reception rooms were a-bustle with bodies and abuzz with conversation. The noonday session was not yet underway and the lords and ladies of the Grand Council had yet to filter into the chamber. A sea of fine gowns and tailored jackets, it lapped around fluted columns and statues of worthies long vanished into the mists.

Lady Ebigail navigated a graceful path without ever slowing save to greet an acquaintance. Lady Sevaka fared less well. The sea of bodies that parted readily for the mother was less inclined to do so for the daughter. Marek remained confident that would change in time, as Lady Sevaka grew into her legacy. That was the way of things in Tressia. But for the moment, he was careful not to crowd her, lest his proximity spur unseemly haste.

"Ebigail! Ebigail, I must speak with you."

The upstart Lord Reveque emerged from the crowd. Lacking, as usual, proper respect in both tone and manner.

Lady Ebigail slowed to a halt and regarded him with restraint. "I regret it will have to wait. I have business that will not."

His face twisted in discomfort. "I . . . I need your assistance."

"Really?" She raised an eyebrow, her tone warming from annoyance to amusement. "I suppose this is worth hearing."

"Mother . . ."

"Yes, Sevaka. I haven't forgotten. Very well, Malachi. Speak your piece."

He guided her to as secluded a corner as the room allowed. After the briefest of delays and a glance at the door, Lady Sevaka followed. Marek brought up the rear and wondered why her ladyship bothered with so poor and disrespectful a fellow as Lord Reveque.

"Aske Tarev attacked Lady Roslava Orova last night." The words galloped from his lips. "Lady Orova defended herself, and Aske died."

"Shocking," Lady Ebigail replied. "The escapades of the younger generation never cease to amaze."

"*Mother.*"

Lady Ebigail raised a cautioning finger. "Kindly don't interrupt, Sevaka. This is important. The niece of a grand councillor murdering Anton's daughter? The poor man must be distraught."

Malachi scowled. "He's had his creature Horden cage Rosa like a rabid hound. Now he's whipping the Grand Council up to a hanging verdict."

"As is the man's right, surely?"

"As is a wealthy and influential man's *privilege*. Rosa was defending herself. As Kasamor defended himself against Aske a week ago."

"I hope you're not suggesting my son lowered himself to brawling."

"I was there. Aske was a heartbeat from running Kasamor through when Viktor put an end to it."

For the first time, Marek caught a flicker of surprise in Lady Ebigail's expression. "And this help you beg of me? Twisting the law? I won't do such a thing. Can you imagine the message it would send if the Privy Council opposed the common will?"

"Ebigail, please. I know we see eye-to-eye on little, but this is a matter of justice." Malachi sucked down a deep breath, his brow furrowing. "Kasamor could have killed Aske last week. He chose not to, but what would you have done if he had?"

Lady Ebigail nodded sagaciously. "You're correct, of course. Aske's death was her own doing, and it *is* only proper that everyone gets what they deserve – however tragic the circumstance. I'll see what can be done, but I'll need you to drop this nonsense of seeking a truce with the Empire. Anton will demand it, if nothing else."

By the evidence of his expression, Lord Reveque didn't like that one bit. Nonetheless, he swallowed his pride and objections both. "As you wish."

But Lady Ebigail wasn't yet done. "If this reaches the Privy Council, I cannot and will not vote with you . . . but I will speak to Anton. Perhaps I can change his mind."

Malachi's shoulders slumped. "Thank you, Ebigail. I won't forget this."

"Neither will I. Come, Sevaka."

From Lady Sevaka's restless expression, Marek judged she had a hard time holding her tongue. However, hold it she did until they entered the deserted corridor.

"I can't believe what you just did," she hissed. "Pretending ignorance, when all the time you knew. Tormenting the poor man like that. Couldn't you see he was sick with worry?"

Lady Ebigail spun on her heel. Sensing another argument, Marek hung back. There were few of Lady Ebigail's conversations to which he wasn't privy, but the illusion of distance was important.

"Consider this a lesson," said Lady Ebigail icily. "Consider this *all* a lesson. Why do you think I wanted you here, even in this sorry state? One day, when I am gone, this Republic will be yours to guide." She sighed. "It's my fault. I've indulged you. Letting you play at pirate with those moustachioed ruffians who think themselves a navy? No longer. You have much to learn and little time in which to learn it."

Lady Sevaka glared at her. "The Council leads the Republic. It will manage well enough without me."

"We shall see about that," replied her mother. "And if you've so fine an opinion of the Council's good sense, why did you show up on my doorstep this morning, begging for help?"

Lady Sevaka's eyes flared, then dropped to the worn carpet. "I'm sorry."

"Good. Because the lesson isn't over. Marek?"

Obedient as ever to his beloved mistress's command, Marek strode past and opened the oaken door to the Grand Council chamber.

With a few cobwebs and a thick layer of dust, the chamber could have been a relic of the old city. It reeked of faded history, the air thick with the breath of spent years. The stone pews were graven with creatures of myth, few of which Marek could name. The marble statue of Lumestra behind the podium bore tell-tales of discoloured stone, betraying where modern masons had lengthened the goddess's skirts and sleeves to match a more civilised age. The seascape mosaic of the floor was similarly mismatched, the roiling waves of the centre rendered in larger, newer tile than those at the edge.

Lord Tarev stood at the podium, forearms braced against the winged lectern. His lordship's face was haggard beneath the salt-and-pepper beard.

"Marek?" said Lady Ebigail. "Remain at the door. Make sure we're not disturbed."

"Yes, lady."

He allowed mother and daughter to pass, then set the door closed and turned the heavy key. As further precaution, he set his back to the timber, and kept one ear alert to footsteps in the corridor.

"Anton," said Lady Ebigail, her voice thick with effusive condolence. "I could barely believe it when I heard. Sevaka and I are so very sorry for your loss. It is no easy thing to lose a child. As I know too well."

Lord Tarev peered at her. Sevaka kept one file of pews between her and Lord Tarev, perhaps separating herself from her mother's sentiment.

"Thank you, Ebigail." His left eyelid twitched. "It is a cruel world. I pray Lumestra grants Aske peace."

"Oh, I'm certain she will."

Marek noted the dryness in Lady Ebigail's tone. Lord Tarev, he was sure, did not.

"It is some small comfort that her murderer will go to the gallows before a new dawn," said Lord Tarev.

"So soon?"

"Lady Orova has confessed the killing, and the Council shares my grief. The outcome is a foregone conclusion."

Lady Ebigail drew closer, her fingertips tracing the lectern's wingtip. "You could withdraw your support. A public expression of forgiveness, and an admission that Aske's own recklessness brought about her death."

He snorted. "Whatever her faults, Aske was my daughter. My blood."

Lady Ebigail's sympathy vanished like Lumenfade mist. "She was a woman who twice provoked a brawl. I understand Lady Orova wasn't even armed."

Lord Tarev's expression turned cold. "My daughter is dead."

"And better that way for your family's reputation." She gathered her skirts and sat at the nearest pew. "Maybe now the rumours can stay buried."

"I haven't heard any rumours." The flash of guilt in Lord Tarev's eyes told Marek otherwise. "I've nothing to hide."

Lady Ebigail offered a thin smile. "Oh, there are always secrets, aren't there, Anton? Or does your grandson know the truth? That the dead hero he believes his father was cuckolded by a wolf's-head?"

"That isn't true!"

She shrugged. "I expect you to defend Aske, of course. But a father's protective instincts are nothing to a mother's. When I learned of her attempt on Kasamor's life – not from him, of course, he was always too proud to speak of such things – I made it my business to learn more."

Lord Tarev gripped the lectern anew. "It's no secret she hated the southwealders. She saw Kasamor's marriage to Calenne Trelan as betrayal of everything our family fought for."

"She didn't hate all of them though, did she? Such a passionate child, your Aske. But she couldn't have married a southwealder. Not with her mother and sister barely cold in their graves at Zanya. Not with a fiancé pining away in Tarvallion. It's strange, isn't it, how we so often vent our frustrations on those who have the courage to act as we cannot?"

Lady Sevaka stared pointedly away. Lady Ebigail's stare didn't waver.

"None of this can be proven," Lord Tarev replied stiffly.

"No, but there are suspicious minds in this fine Republic." With a regretful sigh, Lady Ebigail rose to her feet. "As I said, such a passionate child, your Aske. And her husband. Such an honourable man to pretend the bastard was his. The Republic could have used more like him."

Lord Tarev, already haggard, paled a shade further. A note of pleading crept into his tone. "Please, Ebigail. I'd have no choice but to disinherit Jarron. He cannot be held responsible for his mother's misjudgements."

"Really?" Her face and voice held polite interest. "Not even when he is living proof? For what it's worth, I agree. But nor should Roslava Orova be punished for defending herself . . . and my own dear Sevaka." Her tone darkened. "Did you think I would forgive that?"

Lord Tarev swallowed, throat bobbing as he sought a way out of the trap. Marek had seen it more times than he could count. They always fought. And they always lost.

"You cannot ask me to choose between my daughter and my grandson."

"I'm offering you the chance to acknowledge that Aske was a wild animal and to cast her adrift as such. Or you can see *both* destroyed." Setting a hand beneath his chin, she eased it upward, forcing him to meet her gaze. "Choice has nothing to do with it."

He broke. Marek could always tell when the light slipped from their eyes. Lord Tarev pulled away. His shoulders straightened with fragile dignity.

"When the mists take you, Ebigail, I hope they bury you so deep that the light of Third Dawn never reaches you."

She cocked her head. "Is that a yes?"

With a snarl, Lord Tarev kicked the lectern. He was on the move before it crashed to the floor, striding for the exit. Receiving a nod from Lady Ebigail, Marek unlocked the door and stood aside.

Lady Ebigail righted the lectern. She smoothed a wingtip's scuffed corner with a thumb and glanced at her daughter. "You may thank me now, if you wish."

Lady Sevaka's expression – her whole being – twisted in revulsion. "I can't believe what you just did. He was your ally."

"When it suited him. But he's weak. They're all weak. That grandson of his was a weight around his neck from the day he was born, but he can't bring himself to let the brat fall by the wayside."

Lady Sevaka shook her head. "He should have let you destroy the child?"

"Of course. I'm sure it would hurt immensely, but it would only be the once, and then Anton would be free. That's the thing about pain, Sevaka. It fades. And it leaves you stronger."

"And if positions were reversed, would you cast me aside so easily?"

She sniffed. "What secrets I have are hidden where Anton will never find them. You may rely on *that*. But no. With your brother lost to us, what hopes I have reside in you, and you alone. And if *you* ever are so foolish to bear a child out of wedlock, I advise you to smother the creature or bury it deep."

Marek hadn't believed Lady Sevaka could look any more disgusted. He'd been wrong. "This is just a game to you, isn't it?"

"It is *everything* to me," her mother snapped. "Power is not a prize at the end of a race, it *is* the race. You must always be moving forward, and never fall behind. We used to understand that. Years beneath a tyrant taught us well. But the lesson has been lost, smothered by luxury and entitlement. If nothing changes, we might as well open the gates to the shadowthorns and welcome the lash and the collar. At least Malachi now owes me a favour. That should attend nicely to his ridiculous ideas of begging for peace."

"Not if I tell him that his favour bought nothing you were not already prepared to give."

Lady Ebigail snorted. "You wouldn't dare. You haven't yet learned how to be strong, which is why I must teach you. And if you cannot bear to thank me with words, you may do so with deeds."

Her daughter glowered but said nothing. She knew – as Marek knew – what was coming, for it had been the source of many arguments in past months.

"You will resign your commission with the navy, and you will come home. I shall teach you the way of guarded smiles and watchful tears. You will finally grow to be a daughter worthy of my pride and deserving of my legacy. *This* shall be your favour to me for saving Roslava's life."

Lady Sevaka's lip curled. Her shoulders shook with silent rage. "And if I don't?"

Marek wasn't fooled by the defiance. You could always tell when the last hope faded. It broke his heart to see Lady Sevaka humbled, but he knew it was for her own good.

"Must I find Anton and tell him I've had a change of heart?"

Lady Sevaka hesitated, but the outcome was never in doubt. "No, Mother. I'll . . . I will do as you ask."

"You see? You're too weak to face pain. Just like him. We'll have to see to that." Lady Ebigail left the podium and enfolded her daughter in a one-sided embrace. "In the meantime, you may carry the news to Malachi. It will do you good for him to look upon you with gratitude. *Someone* should."

Twenty-Three

Rosa hesitated only a little before entering the Reveque household at Abbeyfields. She scarcely believed she was free to do so, having been released less than an hour before. Malachi had met her at the constabulary with a pressed uniform. He'd flinched as she'd hugged him, and then insisted on waiting out in the afternoon drizzle while she changed in the carriage.

"Thank you for this," she said. "I don't know that I could have faced my uncles."

Malachi shrugged and set the door to. "For nothing. This is what friends do."

"But how did you manage all this?"

"Allow me to keep some secrets . . . and to offer you a bath. There's only so much clean clothes can do." He beckoned to a rotund, balding fellow in a grey servant's waistcoat. "See to it, would you, Braxov?"

"Already in hand, my lord. Her ladyship anticipated the need." Braxov offered Rosa a bow as low as his girth would accommodate. "It's ready as soon as you are, lady."

She offered him a reluctant smile. A free woman once more, but there was still the matter of the night's revelation – the kernclaw's curse. If that got out, no amount of manoeuvring would keep her from the pyre. If she even deserved to evade it.

"Judging by Lord Reveque's unflattering comment, I suppose I'd better . . . "

"Father!"

A dishevelled waist-high blur shot through the drawing room door. Malachi staggered as the blur wrapped itself around his midriff and beamed up at him with the earnestness unique to fools and children.

"I'm the King of Fellhallow."

The boy was filthy enough to match his claim. His face was smeared with mud, his knees were scuffed and his smock browner than it was cotton-white.

"Is that so, Constans?" Malachi's stern tones were a poor match for his smile. "Shouldn't your majesty be at his lessons?"

Constans brushed aside a mucky fringe and frowned in earnest thought. Then he did what Rosa had observed all children – and no few adults – did when confronted with an unwelcome question. Namely, he ignored it.

"Hello, Rosa."

"That's not how we greet guests in this house, is it?"

Constans frowned. "That's her name."

"And one you've not earned the right to use," his father replied. "Now, greet her properly."

The frown cleared. Constans offered a stiff, unsteady bow. "Hello, Lady Orova."

Not daring to meet Malachi's eye lest she be tempted to smile, Rosa returned the bow. "Thank you, majesty."

"Would you like to be my queen? You look like you'd belong in Fellhallow."

Malachi's smirk darkened. "Constans!"

"He's not saying anything his father didn't." Rosa squatted to reach Constans' eye level. "I'm flattered, majesty. But Fellhallow is a long way off, and I'm too tired to travel."

"He doesn't mean the *real* Fellhallow," proclaimed a new voice. "He's been playing by the river again. Hiding from Ada. She's probably still looking for him."

Sidara stood on the stairs, two steps down from the top. Her belted white dress was every bit as clean as Constans' smock was not. Straw-blonde plaits hung to the small of her back.

"Hello, Lady Orova. Hello, Father. Mother's angry with you again."

"I'm sure that's not true," Malachi replied. "And if I recall, you have lessons of your own."

"I came to greet your guest."

"And now you have done so. Please return to your lessons . . . Or must I tell your mother, and have her be as angry at you as she apparently is at me?"

Sidara pursed her lips, nodded and retreated upstairs.

"And you, young sir . . . " Malachi went on, interrupting Constans' sudden peal of laughter. " . . . are to clean your face, apologise to Ada and *return to your studies.*"

"I'd rather be fighting Hadari."

"So now you're both the King of Fellhallow, and a knight in the Tressian army, is that it? Which chapterhouse?

"Fellnore . . . " He shot a glance at Rosa. "No, Essamere."

"Well, knights of Essamere take orders, don't they, Lady Orova?"

"Without fail, Lord Reveque."

Malachi poked Constans in the chest. "And you are hereby ordered to clean yourself up, and do as you're told."

Constans scowled, but nodded. "All right."

He offered Rosa an approximation of a salute and wandered off the way he'd come. She waited until she was sure he was out of earshot before letting go the laugh that had been building inside her.

Malachi shook his head. "I'm sorry about that."

"Not at all," Rosa replied. The encounter had lifted her spirits more than she'd dared believe possible. "It seems like for ever since I saw them last. How old are they now?"

"Eight and twelve. One year each for every fifty grey hairs they've given me."

"Sidara's nearly as tall as you already."

"And thinks she's twice as clever." He scratched his head. "I've a horrible feeling she's right, but you're not to tell her."

"Wouldn't dream of it," said Rosa, deadpan. "I'm a knight. I obey orders. Especially from councillors who save my miserable neck." She turned to Braxov. "I'd better have that bath, before the water cools."

"Certainly, my lady."

She followed Braxov up two flights of stairs to a narrow door, left ajar.

Wisps of hot, sweet-scented steam curled through the gap. She reached for the door as Braxov withdrew. At the half-landing, he stood aside long enough for Lilyana Reveque to pass.

"Lady Orova?"

Lilyana drew level on the landing, a wary look in her eye. There could be no doubt from which parent Sidara had inherited her height; her mother was a good head taller than Rosa. Taken alongside a willowy frame, Lilyana had an almost ethereal aspect. Had she worn her golden hair down, instead of tightly plaited, she'd have been twin to the serathi statues so popular among the wealthy.

"It's Rosa, please. We've known each other long enough."

Lilyana offered a small, embarrassed smile. "Of course. I see so little of Malachi's friends, I'm never quite sure where I stand."

Rosa wondered if she heard the ghost of criticism. "I hope I've not put you to any trouble."

"Not in the least." This time, there was no mistaking Lilyana's warmth. "You've had many terrible experiences in so short a time. I understand your uncles are not the most . . . sympathetic of men."

Rosa shook her head. "I appal them on so many levels it's hard to tally. I'll receive more of a welcome if I let today's uproar fade before presenting myself."

"Yes, family can be . . . insistent."

Rosa winced inwardly. She knew Lilyana Reveque had wanted to give herself to the church – to serve Lumestra as a serene, rather than her family as a mother of children. But war and disgrace had thinned her family tree to sparse branches, and need had won out over desire.

"That they can," she said. "I won't be in your way long. I took leave from the border to attend Kas's wedding, and there's little of it left."

Lilyana laid a hand on her wrist. "You will stay as long as you need. I'll hear of nothing else. We're all in this life together, Rosa."

Rosa nodded her thanks, but dark thoughts awoke. Together? True enough. But alive? *That* she wasn't so sure about. At least she'd saved Sevaka from whatever disgrace Aske Tarev would have inflicted. *And* the confines of the constabulary's cells.

Sevaka . . . With everything else, she'd almost forgotten.

"Lilyana, can I ask another favour?"

"Of course."

"Could you send someone to Freemont? Sevaka Kiradin was with me last night, and I'd be happier knowing she's returned home safe."

Malachi poured a generous measure of Selanni brandy and lost himself in the patterns of reflected sunlight. A long day already, and yet scarcely past noon.

"A little early for that, don't you think?" asked Lily.

He started guiltily and turned from the window. "I've had a trying morning. I think I've earned it. Plus you're already mad at me, so where's the harm?"

She drew closer, expression unreadable. "Who says I'm mad at you?"

Experience. But experience also warned him against saying so. "Sidara."

She threw back her head and closed her eyes. "Your daughter needs to stop listening at doors."

"*My* daughter?"

"Yes, your daughter. *My* daughter is the one who studies diligently and sings so sweetly." She waved a dismissive hand. "*Your* daughter is the one who insists on bellowing those foul dockers' shanties. She's also the one who needs to stop listening at doors. Just like I need to break the habit of thinking aloud. Or believing that anything I say or do in this house goes unwatched."

Malachi set the glass aside. "So you *are* angry with me."

She shook her head and looped her arms behind his neck. "No. You always think that, and it's so seldom true."

So why did he feel like another polite lecture was headed his way? "Then why does Sidara think otherwise?"

"Because we'd agreed to spend today together, as a family. Church, then a visit to my parents and a walk along the coast, remember? You promised Constans."

He remembered. It had seemed an easy concession a week ago, but so much had changed since then. "And what was I to do? Abandon Rosa?"

"Of course not. And I wouldn't have wanted you to. But you're here so rarely. If it's not the Council, it's your friends, and if it's not your friends it's . . . " She shrugged. "There's going to come a time when you're gone,

Malachi, and I don't want our children to wonder at the kind of man their father was. I want them to know, and to know that he loved them."

The same old argument beckoned. Or perhaps not *argument*. Lily was so damn reasonable. Sometimes he wished she'd lose her temper. Shout. Throw something. That way he'd feel he could shout back. It wouldn't help, but it would silence the feeling of failure.

Thirteen years married. Five years with the burden of the Reveque seat on the Privy Council. When did he get to stop feeling like a fraud? Like a man of average aspect and wit who'd lucked into marriage to a woman who outshone him in every way? Somehow the more supportive Lily sounded, the larger failure loomed.

"I'm trying, truly I am. But there are only so many hours in the day."

"Oh Malachi, I'm not asking you to do *more*. I want you to do *better*."

The familiar request. The expected, pitying tone.

"I do well enough." He hated how defensive he sounded. "I got my way over the Southshires."

"That's not what you said last week. *Viktor did something, and I don't think I want to know what it was.* Your words, my love."

Malachi frowned. Viktor had forced his father's agreement, yes. However, it had been his own words that won the support of Abitha Marest.

"I tell you, I make a difference!"

"Do you?" She smiled wistfully. "Then why don't you tell me about the sacrifices that have driven you to brandy. Perhaps I can help."

He eyed her with suspicion. "Any time you want to take my place on the Council ... "

"You know it doesn't work like that. My father left that seat to you when he retired. I promised, you promised. I was to do nothing that would distract me from his grandchildren." The old bitterness bled into her voice. The chafing at motherhood's shackles while her husband floundered in a role she'd been born to. She sank into an armchair and waited. "So, these sacrifices ... "

Malachi took a sip of his brandy and admitted defeat. "Freeing Rosa meant asking a favour of Ebigail."

"Did she ask for anything in return?"

"The end of my proposal to negotiate with the Hadari. Not that I'd much chance of getting it through the Grand Council. Ebigail's threat-eners have already gone door-to-door."

And there was little point getting a truce through the Privy Council if there was uproar in the lower chamber. It was one thing to order an unpopular peace, and quite another to enforce it.

"Was she polite?"

"Very."

"Did she crow?"

"Hardly at all. I'm too tired for games, Lily."

She chuckled. "Little wonder, because you've been played sufficiently this morning already. I spoke with Rosa. She asked me to enquire if Sevaka Kiradin made it home safe."

Malachi frowned. "There's no need. I saw her this morning. A few bruises, but nothing . . . " Realisation crashed home with the force of a falling tree. "Oh, Queen's Ashes!"

The first genuine scowl touched her lips. "Language, Malachi."

"Sevaka was there when Aske died, which means . . . "

" . . . that Ebigail already had all the reason in the world to intervene. From what I know of Sevaka, I imagine she insisted. And you wonder why Ebigail doesn't take you seriously." Lily sighed. "She dances around you with such ease."

Malachi clapped a hand to his eyes and willed the world to go away. He hadn't known. He hadn't thought to ask, and Rosa hadn't thought to tell him. Because he'd been too focused on helping Rosa that he hadn't stopped to think. Instead, he'd galloped headlong for a solution, kidding himself that he'd done the right thing. The noble thing. What genera-tions of Reveques before him would have done.

There was special irony in having his hubris pointed out by the woman whose family name and reputation he'd invited to ridicule.

"It's not as bad as that . . . "

"No, Ebigail accounted you an idiot long ago. But that merely places you in common company with most of the Republic." Lily's cheek twitched. "But next time, it might cost you a great deal. More than that, you could have kept your promise to your son, and nothing would have changed."

Malachi downed the last of the brandy. Lily was right. Raven's Eyes, but she was right. "I'm not the only idiot in the room. You married me."

"And despite everything, I still think I chose well." Rising to her feet, she took his head in her hands and kissed him. "You're a good man, Malachi, and I love you for it. I just wish it were easier to *respect* you. You're so busy trying to prove yourself worthy of *my* family and *your* friends that you reach for more than you can grasp."

Anger. He'd have preferred anger. Anything was preferable to feeling like a beggar invited to a banquet out of charity. But he supposed Lily was right. *Better,* not *more.* He couldn't even stand up to his own wife. She towered over him even as she tried to raise him up.

"So what do I do?"

"One thing, and do it well."

"You mean, be a more present father."

Her eyes danced in approval. "Two things, then. You want this peace treaty?"

"It's too late. I've forsaken it."

"Nonsense. Ebigail lied to you, if by omission. You can lie in exchange."

The thought held some appeal, but it also sparked a frisson of fear. "That's dangerous."

But the more Malachi dwelled on the idea, the more appealing it became. So much so that he found himself standing straighter than he had before.

"So am I." Lily planted her hands on her hips and struck a pose suited to a hero of old – though not without a wry glimmer. "I am Lilyana Matilla Reveque, daughter of the first rank, and no one makes a fool of my husband . . . except for his children."

"What about the Grand Council?"

"Lumestra will guide me, and I will guide you." There was no mirth in her voice now. "You represent our family, Malachi, but you needn't do so alone."

Setting aside the last of his resentment, he kissed his wife and held her close. However fortunate she'd been in her choice, he'd been luckier still. It was just that some days it was hard to see that. *Do one thing,* she'd said, *and do it well.* Yes, it could be done. But first, he had a friend who needed help. And if Lily had made one thing clear, it was that he couldn't be trusted to manage things alone.

"Lily," he whispered. "There's something I should tell you about Rosa."

"I confess, I expected that I'd been summoned on foundry business," said Elzar. "Not ... well ... Forgive me, Lady Orova, but this lies some way outside my experience."

Rosa nodded, the familiar knot of worry gripping her stomach. Whatever else she felt or did not, her capacity for that particular emotion had no end. She'd violently rejected the idea of bringing a stranger into her confidence. But Malachi had held his ground, arguing that they'd never learn anything without risk. And so, she'd at last relented.

For all the good that had done.

Malachi leaned forward in his chair. "Please, Elzar. Viktor speaks highly of your judgement."

Elzar steepled his fingers and sank back, eyes closed. In the afternoon sunlight of the drawing room, he resembled a crag darter basking on the rocks. "There is ... something. But I must caution against repeating it."

Rosa nodded. Malachi shared a brief glance with Lilyana, who stood behind his chair looking a fraction uneasier than Rosa felt.

"It will go no further," said Lilyana.

Elzar grunted. "Oh, I don't worry for myself. But it doesn't become the nobility to go around spouting apocrypha. Not unless they mean to be prophets or martyrs."

Rosa felt her patience slip a notch. "We'll just have to restrain ourselves."

Her reward was a toothy smile. "I imagine so. This concerns Konor Belenzo, and the overthrow of the Tyrant Queen."

Lilyana folded her arms. "I served at high altar for over twenty years. I embraced the twelve mysteries and know the Books of Astarria by heart. There is nothing you can tell me about Konor Belenzo that I don't already know."

Elzar's grin broadened. "Then you know all about those who stood with him at the end."

"Belenzo faced Malatriant alone," said Lilyana. "Without Lumestra's light, he would never have triumphed."

"No. That's what scripture claims."

Malachi stirred. "It's what history records."

"And the one is built upon the other, and maybe neither of them true. Tressian history is so often fiction, and faith calls for simplicity where life is anything but. I've heard many accounts that Belenzo was but one of several who fought the Tyrant Queen."

"We shouldn't be listening to this," said Lilyana. But she made no move to leave.

"It's myth. One step removed from story. And stories have only the power you give them. It does no harm to listen." He shrugged. "Malatriant drew her power from the primal Dark that existed before the light. Could one god stand against that? Could one divine champion?"

"One did," said Lilyana flatly. "He was martyred for his courage ..."

"... but through his sacrifice, he ushered Malatriant into the Raven's embrace." Elzar nodded. "I can quote scripture too. But you're missing the point."

"Which is?" asked Malachi.

Elzar extended a hand. Golden light crackled from fingertip to fingertip. "Scripture tells that Belenzo's blessing revealed itself in his blood, for it shone with light. The same golden light that was essence to the serathi. Now, I wield Lumestra's light, but my blood is as red as yours – begging your pardon, Lady Orova – though I'll be thankful if you don't ask me to prove it."

"A point, high proctor," said Lilyana, her tone now distinctly unfriendly. "You promised a point."

He snapped his fingers. Light leapt towards the ceiling and dissipated into nothingness. "It's simply this. If Konor Belenzo bled light, can we be certain he any longer bled as ordinary folk do?"

"You're saying Rosa is as Belenzo was? Blessed by Lumestra?" asked Malachi.

"Not quite. I'm sure you'd have mentioned if she bled light. But if Lumestra's favour revealed itself in the blood, and if Belenzo had comrades similarly blessed, but by other divinities ..."

"... then I *am* cursed," said Rosa through a throat thick with despair. "The kernclaw gave me to the Raven, and he has marked me for his own. I deserve the pyre."

She took a deep breath to steady herself. It didn't help, it only made the room spin, so she closed her eyes. Her heart hammered at her ribs. Why did it labour so without blood to send coursing through her veins? Rosa could have wept, but for the shame of the tears – and out of uncertainty whether even tears were now denied her.

"What I don't understand," Sidara piped up, "is why it matters which god blessed you, so long as you wear the gift well?"

Rosa opened her eyes onto a room of comedically similar expressions. Malachi, Lilyana and Elzar twisted towards the drawing room's rear door, their lips parted, but their tongues bereft of words. Sidara stood frozen in place, fingers still on the door handle. Her face showed the first signs of understanding that she'd made an error of no small magnitude.

"Sidara! That is a wicked thing to say! Truly wicked!" Lilyana, her voice thunderous and her face flushed, jerked a hand towards the hallway. "Go to your room!"

"But, Mother, this is interesting."

"I will not tell you again!"

She grabbed the child by the arm and bundled her out of the door. Before crossing the threshold herself, Lilyana glowered at Elzar. "Thank you for your time, high proctor, and your ... opinions. But I think it would be better if you left my home."

The door slammed.

Malachi winced. "Elzar, I can only echo my wife's thanks, and apologise for her rudeness."

He waved both away and rose. "I spoke of my own volition; the fault is mine. And she's right, you know. Your daughter, I mean."

Rosa looked up to see him staring down at her.

"Though I shouldn't say so," Elzar went on, "the gods too are like stories. They may grant us power, but like Malatriant they have no power over us that we do not grant *them*. We so often claim the soul is a single, indivisible entity, when really it is three together. When we die, a part of us goes to the mists, and a part remains with the body to await Third Dawn. The gods have claim only on that third which remains. It's the only piece of ourselves we have to offer, and the only part they can take. Konor Belenzo chose to embrace Lumestra, as do I, and as does Lady Reveque. Even if the Raven has laid claim to that piece, Lady Orova, you need not embrace him unless it is your desire. What you do otherwise is your own affair."

He bowed and withdrew in a swish of golden robes. Malachi followed, leaving Rosa alone in sunlight that did nothing to warm her skin.

Twenty-Four

"Halt, 'less you want a bellyful of steel!"

Josiri hauled the horse to a standstill. Unfriendly eyes watched from the undergrowth. A thin line of wolf-fur clad men and women blocked the roadway. Swords glinted in the moonlight. Careful not to make any move that would set bowstrings humming, he drew back his hood.

"I want to speak to Drakos Crovan."

A scruffy individual pushed his way to the front of the thin blockade. He alone had yet to draw a blade. "Duke Trelan? Well, ain't this something. Thought you were trussed up at Branghall, supping from silver chalices."

Rough laughter rippled beneath the trees. Josiri, burdened by both restless soul and sleepless night – and sore from a journey made at the gallop – couldn't conceal his vexation.

"Let me through!"

The man ambled closer and spread his hands wide, playing to his audience. "Doesn't he know we're wolf's-heads? We don't take orders."

Josiri slid from his saddle. "You do today."

The man glowered at him from a face full of bruises. "Reckon so, do you?"

He went for his sword. Josiri caught his wrist.

The fellow was strong but unsteady – the sour note of ale told why. Despair gripped Josiri anew. The Southshires were invaded by both the Hadari and Viktor Akadra, and Crovan's wolf's-heads were drinking?

"Hands off!"

The drunk balled his free hand and swung. But Josiri had spent years sparring with Anastacia, and she was faster than the wolf's-head would ever be.

Tugging on the captive wrist, Josiri spun the fellow around. His boot connected with a fleshy rump, and the drunk went sprawling. The man's sword, claimed in the confusion, gleamed in Josiri's hand. He cast it into the dirt.

"I want to speak to Drakos Crovan." Time for reason. "He'll see me."

"Then he can do it with you bound and gagged!" roared the drunk. "Or do you need an arrow to make you cooperative?"

"Pack it in, Vorn!"

A familiar face appeared among the trees. Revekah.

"Stay out of this, crone!"

She sauntered towards the road, time-worn face unconcerned. "Fixing to be bested by an old woman, as well as a pampered noble? And that's without going into whatever happened to you the other night." She shrugged and nodded at Josiri. "You mustn't mind Vorn. Reckon he still hasn't learned that some maids back up the word 'no' with actions."

Vorn growled but held his tongue. The atmosphere shifted. The eyes were no friendlier than before, but Revekah's arrival had the ambushers unsettled.

Josiri bowed. "Captain Halvor."

"So formal, your grace." She flashed a mischievous smile, then rounded on Vorn. "And as for you! Who do you suppose has been feeding us word on the northwealders' intentions for years? How we learned they were moving on Vallora? Weren't for him, none of you would've gotten out."

"He's a traitor!" The objection came from the anonymity of the undergrowth. "He burned the duchess' portrait!"

"And how do you feel about that? Angry? Angry enough to fight? Good! Now put your weapons away and give his grace the escort he deserves."

Vorn at last found his tongue. "We take orders from the Wolf King, not you."

Revekah rolled her eyes. "Then let's go and see him. All of us."

He grimaced, then stalked off down the road. The other wolf's-heads hesitated, then dribbled away to a respectful distance. Watchful, but not threatening. At least for now.

Josiri let out a breath he hadn't realised he'd been holding. "Here's a thought. Why don't I cede the duchy to you? You're much better at this."

She shook her head. "No one needs to see my withered old face staring down at them from on high. What in Lumestra's name are you doing, riding about like that? Never mind what Makrov'll do if he gets word – Viktor Akadra's back in the Southshires ..."

The name soured Josiri's mood still further. "I know. It's why I've come to find Crovan."

She grunted. "Picked a hell of a time. The Wolf King's holding court to every member of the Vagabond Council he could reach."

For the first time that day, Josiri allowed himself to smile. Lumestra *was* with him. If Crovan had assembled everyone, there was still a chance to send both Akadra *and* the Hadari packing.

"Then lead the way, captain," he said. "It's time for everything to change."

"Can't be done, not in the time you want."

Bran Yorvin scratched at his greying hair and gazed at Viktor with the expression of a master craftsman well-used to holding his ground in the face of strident clients. But Viktor had spent too long around soldiers. He'd learned that what was *said* to be possible was merely the start of the bargaining process.

"I need it tonight."

"It's samite porcelain, you can't rush it. Three days, firing to cooling. Anything less, and it'll crack." Yorvin glanced at his labouring apprentices. "Look, the lads have the bulk of the commission underway, and I'll manage the rest myself. It'll be a beauty, but beauty takes time."

Viktor said nothing. Sometimes, silence was a weapon more formidable than any. Yorvin's brow twitched. Not much. Just enough to confirm Viktor's suspicions, awoken by the pieces on display. Vases and figurines finer than anything a provincial potter could fashion.

"Viktor?" Calenne stepped between them. "I agreed to help, but that doesn't extend to watching you lose your temper over the impossible."

"You've never seen me lose my temper. It's not something you forget."

She shuddered. "I'm sure. But if Master Yorvin says it can't be done . . . Not everything succumbs to council demands, or generous coin."

Yorvin cleared his throat. "I can have it finished for the day after tomorrow."

"Tonight." Viktor took Calenne by the shoulder and eased her aside. "Tonight, and I'll tell no one of your secret. Including the archimandrite."

"Hark at you." Yorvin snorted and turned away. "Keep my secrets indeed. Look around all you like, but you'll find nothing."

"Viktor . . . " said Calenne.

He ignored her. Time among soldiers had taught him how to gauge possibility. The company of councillors had taught him how to read truth in lies. "Have it your way, Master Proctor."

Yorvin froze in the act of patting down his apron. Then he shrank inwards, just a little. "I don't know what that means."

"But you *do*. There's no way the Proctor's College would let you wander off into the Southshires, which means you fled. Which means . . . "

"Viktor! Leave the man alone."

Again, he turned his gaze on Calenne. It was a stare that had shamed battle-hardened veterans into silence. Somehow, she met him measure for measure. Remarkable, considering she'd fainted at the sight of him barely two days prior. Viktor would have wagered a fair portion of his inheritance that poor Kasamor had never seen the steel at his betrothed's core.

Or perhaps he had, and that had been part of the attraction. An odd thought, but not unappealing.

"Our friend the potter is a fugitive," he said. "He has the gift of magic and should be wielding it in the foundry."

"Making more of those monsters, you mean," said Calenne.

"Kraikons and simarka are *not* monsters. They are weapons, and no more evil than a sword."

"A sword can be evil. It depends on the wielder. And constructs are wielded by council lackeys."

Her expression left Viktor in no doubt at all that the final venomous word referred to him.

"I am no one's lackey." He strove for patience. "Nor am I proposing to drag our friend back to Tressia in chains. I seek to remind him of his place in things."

"Blackmail him, you mean."

"Please," said Yorvin. "I've lived here thirty years. I have a family."

There was no resistance in him now. Just fear. Viktor felt a twinge of regret, but sometimes the breaking of a man was necessary. A gesture was needed.

He went down on one knee before the old man and bowed his head. Calenne's eyes widened in surprise, occasioning an unfamiliar glow of satisfaction. Viktor put it from his mind and focused on Yorvin.

"And I mean only to see them protected. I apologise for my directness, but the Southshires is invaded. Your work may save lives ... but only if it is completed tonight."

Yorvin frowned and glanced again across the workshop. "I don't see how. It's just a toy."

"That's my concern. Will you help me protect your family?"

"And if I don't, I suppose you'll tell Makrov about me?"

Viktor wouldn't, of course. Or at least, he didn't believe he would. After all, he and Yorvin were the same, in a way. Except if Yorvin were taken he'd be pressed to service in the foundry as an indentured crafts-man. If Makrov learnt about Viktor's shadow ... ? Well, that would end far worse, for someone. But the truth had no place in this conversation. Yorvin had to *believe*.

"I'll take you to him myself."

Viktor took no joy in the old man's crestfallen expression. Less still in Calenne's glower. The first was of no consequence ... And as for the second? If she was truly her mother's daughter, she'd understand, sooner or later.

Yorvin drew himself up. "Damn you, but I'll do it. But you'd better keep your end of the bargain."

"I'll hold my tongue, never fear."

"I didn't mean that," said Yorvin. "I'll die before I let the shad-owthorns have my family. I expect you to do the same."

That would prove the harder promise to keep. But it was also a challenge already set. "You have my word that I'll do all I can. I'm not accustomed to failure."

Calenne snorted. Yorvin nodded.

"I guess that'll have to do, Lord Akadra." He sighed. "It'll be ready for midnight. I can't do better."

Viktor nodded. "Then that must do. Have it sent to Branghall."

"Yes, my lord. And have you given thought to the other matter? I can bind the joints with steel pins, but clay doesn't flex. It'll look a mite odd with gaps showing everywhere. And that's before we've made a covering."

"Bind the gaps with leather." Viktor unclasped his velvet cloak and shrugged it free. "Use this for the rest."

Yorvin hesitated, but took the cloak anyway. "You're sure? Good cloth to waste on a toy."

"It's not a toy." Viktor shot a glance at Calenne, who was back to regarding him with suspicion. "Besides, I'm told it makes me look like an executioner. With it gone, perhaps folk will find it easier to see that I'm not."

"I'm sorry, your grace, but it can't be done."

Drakos Crovan didn't sound sorry. He delivered every word with an orator's precision as he paced about the crackling bonfire at the heart of Maiden's Hollow, addressing them not to Josiri, but to members of the Vagabond Council seated in the circle of headless dancers. Them, and the scores upon scores of wolf's-heads, rogues and outcasts on the slopes above.

Most wore the wolf-cloaks of Crovan's followers, a few the tattered phoenix of Revekah's band. The loyalties of the remainder were shown less by raiment and more by the knots they formed in the broader throng, islands of battered battle-gear and worn leather in a sea of silver fur and phoenix blue.

Josiri couldn't help but be impressed by Crovan's reach. He himself knew the burly Nikolos Korsov – merchant turned (reasonably) honest brigand – well. Nials Gavamor was as close to a friend as Josiri had outside of Revekah. But the other Vagabond Councillors? Those he knew only by reputation.

The heavyset Thrakkian twins, Anliss and Armund, stood alone. The crowds on the slopes would never have hidden them. Chainmail, plaited red hair and flame tattoos covering half of their faces – the left for Anliss, and the right for Armund – guaranteed as much. They were supposedly fleeing the wrath of a brother who'd stolen their inheritance, but who knew the truth? Thrakkian honour was complicated, and their wanderlust legendary.

The grim-featured Jesver Merrik controlled the lands to the north-east of Eskavord. Northwealders didn't enter the Kellin Valley any longer – not without a pack of simarka to flush Merrik's keen-eyed wolf's-heads from the rock-strewn fields. "Free Kellin", they called it.

Then there was Silda Drenn. Like Merrik, her reputation spoke for itself. She was a wolf's-head of the more traditional kind, little better than a bandit. Josiri knew for certain fact that Revekah would have cheerfully slit the woman's throat, save that Drenn controlled much of the land between Eskavord and Thrakkia.

Josiri rose, more aware than ever of the eyes on him. Years of preparation could turn on the next few minutes. Especially with Crovan's unexpected resistance.

"We've prepared for this moment for years. We're ready."

"To fight one enemy, not two." Crovan laced the words with polite laughter, as would a man explaining the realities of the world to a wayward child. "Trelszon is burning. How can we keep the Hadari at bay *and* throw the northwealders from our lands?"

A murmur of agreement rippled across the dell. Heads nodded around the fire, Merrik's and Korskov's included. Gavamor toyed with the simarka amulet at his neck, his lip twisting in thought. Josiri wished Anastacia were there.

"Because it's your duty, you jumped up little worm," growled Revekah.

Brief laughter overtook the murmurs, then faded. There were more wolf-cloaks than phoenix tabards among the onlookers.

"Rank buys you nothing down here beneath trees," said Crovan. "Here, we are all one in the Dark."

"We all have a duty," said Josiri.

Drenn snorted. "Duty's for soldiers. It's nothing out here. Out here, all we've got is survival."

"Not all of us." Chain rings scraped as Anliss folded her arms. "Some of us fight for honour."

"Can't eat your honour, can you, thrakker?"

Josiri marked the subtle shift in Anliss's posture, and its mirror in her brother. Quarrelling with a Thrakkian over honour seldom ended well.

"Some things are worth going hungry for," said Armund. "My sister and I cannot unmake the wrongs done us, but nor need we sit idle. Not while we've strong arms and sharp axes. Destiny is forged through deeds, not stolen like table-scraps."

"I hate arguing with Thrakkians," muttered Drenn.

"You hate being wrong," said Anliss.

"And Thrakkians love hopeless battles."

Anliss offered an unfriendly smile. "There are no hopeless battles, only warriors who have lost heart."

Drenn leapt to her feet. "Why, you ...!"

Josiri cleared his throat, interrupting her exclamation before things worsened. "Fifteen years ago I promised to finish what my mother could not. To free the Southshires from the Republic's yoke." He spoke not to the Vagabond Council, but to the crowd above. "I've spent those fifteen years preparing myself for this day – helping all of *you* prepare—"

"And we're grateful," Crovan interrupted. "Truly, your mother would be proud. Five years ago, I wouldn't have believed we'd even sit around the same fire, let alone have the numbers to challenge the northwealders. But that's just it. We've the numbers to challenge the northwealders, but no more."

"Then what?" demanded Revekah. "We hide, and hope everything works out? I'm old, I'm tired and I'm sick of living on the run!"

"So we should throw our lives away because you're dreaming of a goose-down bed?" snapped Drenn. "I don't think so."

"Your duke calls you to war! Piss on the idea of duty all you want, but Josiri is the Phoenix's son." She stabbed a finger at each of the Vagabond Council in turn, and emphasised every second or third word with an angry flourish. "You owe him fealty! Every last one of you!"

"Not me." A grin cracked beneath Armund's plaited beard. "But I'll fight. Give me an axe and firm ground, and I'll fight."

At his side, Anliss murmured her agreement. Josiri nodded his thanks, and fought to keep worry from his face. Rank had bought the twins a seat in the circle; rank, and their trading contacts in Thrakkia.

But they spoke only for themselves. By contrast, Crovan spoke with the authority of several hundred swords.

"Josiri," said the Wolf King. "The oaths I swore and the fealty I owe are to the Republic. But I turned my back on that when I saw the Southshires' suffering for myself. Duty isn't enough. Men must think for themselves. They must deal with the world before them, not one laid down by a distant council, or a dead mother's wish ... "

Revekah scowled but held her tongue.

"I know you understand this in your heart," Crovan went on. "Ask yourself what your mother would want. Katya Trelan valued the lives of her people above all things."

Onlookers rumbled approval. Josiri's gut twisted. The gathering was slipping away from him. It would have been easier if the Wolf King had been wrong, or self-aggrandising. But for all his front, that wasn't Drakos Crovan's way. They wanted the same thing, only one of them wasn't prepared to meet the cost.

"And what value is a life lived under Hadari rule?" demanded Josiri. "Or one lost in the exodus scows, or worked to exhaustion in the Outer Isles? Without freedom, life is nothing. *That* is what my mother believed, more than anything. And I will die in its pursuit, if that is the price to be paid."

Murmuring broke out in the crowd, this time almost friendly of Josiri's words. Revekah shot him a look of sly approval. Gavamor nodded.

Crovan sighed. "Josiri, the Hadari have promised us that freedom."

The onlookers fell silent. Revekah's surprise was a mirror to Josiri's own, and for that of many others. So Crovan hadn't stopped dreaming of an alliance with the Empire.

"You've spoken with the shadowthorns?" snarled Revekah. "You treacherous piece of ... "

Crovan held up a hand. "Captain Halvor, please. I was approached by Kai Saran's daughter. She offered generous terms. Prince Kai merely needs a victory to cement his claim to the throne. One victory against the northwealders. Then he'll leave us to govern ourselves."

Anliss spat. "Princes are all promises 'till they get what they want."

Josiri kept his eyes on Crovan. "Have you accepted?"

"Josiri, please. I don't want to ... "

"Answer the damn question," snapped Revekah.

Crovan shrugged. "Yes."

And with that word, the work of Josiri's adult life blazed bright and fell away into ash. "Revekah called it true. You *are* a traitor."

Crovan stepped onto the remains of the robed statue at the circle's heart and spoke with a deep, earnest conviction that might even have been genuine. "I'm a man trying to save lives, not throw them away out of soured pride."

A cloud passed over the moon and lent Crovan's fire-lit expression a hunger that hadn't been there before. A sudden shudder raised goose-flesh on Josiri's skin.

"Walk away, Josiri. For the good of everyone." There was reason in the words, but none in his tone.

"I can't do that."

"Then perhaps tell us why you're wearing a ward-brooch, and how you came by it?"

Josiri put a hand to his chest and realised too late how guilty the action looked. Crovan knew Branghall was not the cage it appeared, as did Korsov and one or two others. But to everyone else . . .

"It doesn't matter," he said. "You and I both know that."

"Do we?"

Framed by billowing soot and shafts of moon-shadow, Crovan seemed taller and grander than before – a handsome, dark-eyed presence more foreboding than flesh and blood.

"How about the fact that Viktor Akadra walks the Southshires? Or that your sister is his constant companion? How *dare* you speak to me of duty when you've made a deal with the Council!"

"I've made no deals!" shouted Josiri. "Akadra killed my mother, for pity's sake!"

Crovan stepped down from the statue. "I think you're prepared to sacrifice us all for your sister. Why else be so insistent we hurl ourselves at the Hadari? It's the swiftest way of granting the northwealders their peace!"

For the first time, Jesver Merrik looked up from the fire. "Raven's Eyes . . ."

The crowd's murmurs blossomed to a guttural, animal rumble. The irony of the situation wasn't lost on Josiri. He'd fled Branghall thinking to use Akadra's gift of freedom against him, but now . . . ? He was accused of the one thing he'd resisted his whole life. And no one would believe him. Even Revekah watched him with guarded eyes.

"That isn't true!" He already knew his words were wasted. "Nothing's changed."

"*Everything* has changed." Crovan's eyes burned into his. "Your sister is a hostage. You're afraid the Hadari will award your lands to another. And then along comes Lord Viktor Akadra, offering you a way out. I don't blame you for taking it. But I'll slit my own throat before I let you drive us into senseless battle as Malatriant once did her thralls."

The rumble rose to a throaty growl. Voices grew loud enough for Josiri to make out individual words.

Puppet. Fool. Traitor.

Yes, the Wolf King had designs on becoming the Hadari's client monarch, but Josiri read no deeper ambition in the darkly handsome face. Maybe he genuinely believed what he'd said of Josiri's so-called bargain. Maybe he'd even resisted bringing it up until he'd had to. Crovan's reputation of caring for his followers was well-proven. But in the end, it didn't matter whether a king's ambition or a protector's desire drove Drakos Crovan.

"String him up! Hang him!"

The crowd picked up on the lone voice's demand, the volume swelling as others joined the chant.

"*Hang him! Hang him! Hang him!*"

A wolf-cloaked man broke ranks. He took Revekah's fist in his throat and sprawled beside the leaping bonfire. Her sword came free, challenging others to follow his example.

The crowd surged.

"Phoenixes! To me!" roared Revekah.

Moonlight washed across the glade anew. The hillside awoke with blue tabards and drawn steel. Josiri watched, hand frozen on his sword hilt. A spectator in his own life.

"Enough!" bellowed Crovan. The intimidating majesty of moments before had faded. It left a face alive with confusion and sorrow. He seized a burning brand from the fire and climbed the toppled statue once more. "Enough!"

Uneasy quiet swept through Maiden's Hollow. Josiri, hemmed inside a ring of phoenix tabards, at last found he could move, if not speak. His mouth was too thick with failure for that.

Crovan cast the brand aside and shook his head as one waking from a dream – or a nightmare.

"Josiri. Out of regard for your mother, and all you have made possible, you have my protection until dawn." He rubbed at his brow, his eyes on Josiri but his thoughts elsewhere. "But when the sunlight comes, be far from here."

Josiri gazed on each of the Vagabond Council in turn. None save Revekah would meet his eyes. Akadra had destroyed him without even lifting a sword. In so doing he'd handed the Southshires to the Hadari.

Without another word, he strode for the circle's edge. Revekah's phoenixes marched with him. Only Revekah herself hung back.

"This isn't over, Crovan."

"No," he agreed. "It's a new beginning. For us all."

Josiri followed the path from Maiden's Hollow without conscious thought, barely aware of his escort. He was losing everything, inch by inch. First he'd driven Calenne away. Then Anastacia. And now? Now Crovan had all but stolen his birthright and his duty. Worst of all was the lingering suspicion that he'd brought it all on himself.

He'd no way of knowing how far he'd walked when Revekah fell into step alongside. One moment he was alone, and the next she was there.

"Is this true?" she asked.

"No." He snorted. "Akadra offered me a bargain, but he wanted me to lead Crovan and the others against the Hadari. In exchange, he promised to restore the Southshires' fortunes."

"You're ... " Revekah broke off and pressed on at a whisper. "You're joking."

"I'm many things, but I'm not a jester. And I'm not a traitor. I can't work with Akadra. I don't trust his promises any more than Kai Saran's."

"Good. I'm glad I don't have to cut your throat."

"Thanks," he said drily. "Why Calenne's still with Akadra, I couldn't say. Crovan might be right about her being a hostage." He'd tried not to think about it being so, for the possibility worried him greatly, but denial served nothing.

Revekah brushed a strand of silver hair back from her brow. "So, your grace. What in Queen's Ashes do we do now?"

"I don't know," said Josiri, unable to keep the bleakness from his voice any longer. For years, life had been defined by a stark choice: fight, or wait to fight another day. Now, it seemed, both choices had been stripped away. The future had become as grey and featureless as the mists of Otherworld. "I don't know."

Twenty-Five

The patrol returned after nightfall. Some walked, cradling bloody, bandaged limbs. Others were dragged on makeshift biers fashioned from broken spears and torn cloaks.

Lunassera strode down the fire-lit darkness of the hillside like ghosts. Melanna went with them but stood apart as the masked sisters went about the wounded. A touch of gloved fingers upon the brow, the warrior was borne away to physicians. The same touch on the chest – always delivered to those lost to unconsciousness, or adrift in dream-sent madness – and those men were hauled into the gloom of the sanctum tent.

Melanna sought the patrol's leader. "Havildar! What happened?"

He shuffled to a halt, so weary that his bruise-mottled face barely registered surprise at being spoken to by a woman. "Bronze giants waiting in the trees on the Kreska road. We never heard them coming. We lost hundreds."

Melanna gestured for the lunassera to lead him away. If her father saw her worrying over every last soul, it would only harden his resolve to keep her from the battle lines. She walked back to the sanctum, lost in pity for others and resentment for herself.

One warrior alone had been taken neither to physicians nor sanctum. A lunassera knelt at his side. Sweet song spilling from her lips, she closed his eyes and slid the remembrance ring from his right hand. The band of engraved silver glinted in the moonlight, then vanished into a pouch. One day, it would be returned to a family who did not yet know their loss.

The tale was scarcely less bleak in the outer sanctum. Already the cool air of the sacred tent stank of blood and misery. Dying men lined the approach to the silk-shrouded altar.

"You are troubled, *savim*." The lunassera spoke softly, her lips as expressionless as the gentle curves of her mask.

Melanna tried to gauge her age and failed. The robes left little clue to the woman beneath, beyond the athletic physique the lunassera cultivated for its physical beauty. She could have been two years younger than Melanna, or forty summers her senior.

"Do not be," the lunassera continued. "Ashana will welcome them."

"She shouldn't have to. I could have warned them. I could have *led* them." She scowled at the swelling sensation of uselessness. "I know the sounds the giants make. I know how to sift the scent of their magic from the breeze. I wouldn't have been taken by surprise."

"You must learn your place."

"I'm tired of people telling me that."

Two lunassera moved among the dying. One bore a silver pitcher, the other a goblet. At each makeshift bedside, they filled the goblet to brimming. Then they knelt, parted the man's lips, and trickled the liquid into his mouth.

Melanna wanted to look away but couldn't. Part of her felt dutybound to bear witness. One warrior to another – even if no one else accounted her thus.

"If you would serve the army, there are always the vows."

"Give myself to the lunassera?"

"To the goddess, *savim*."

Melanna shook her head. "I was made for more than prayer and solace. The goddess told me so herself."

Her lips twitched in sympathy beneath the half mask. "Did she, *savim*? Or is that merely what you wished to hear?"

"I will be empress one day, and I will pass the throne to a daughter. I can do neither from behind a lunassera's mask."

"But there is much you *can* do, *savim*. Gifts only the lunassera can give."

Across the sanctum, the dying man gave a last fitful exhalation. His attendants slid the ring from his hand, refilled the goblet, and moved on.

Melanna stifled a sigh. The lunassera meant well, but she didn't understand. She was too much a part of tradition. "I'd sooner bring death to our foes than offer dreaming mercy to our own."

"It is the goddess's desire that we do both, if called to. Our sisterhood served your grandfather's great-grandfather as bodyguard. At least, until he was wed. The new princessa did not approve of her husband living ever in the company of women."

Melanna frowned in surprise. "Lunassera do not bear swords. Women do not bear swords."

"The sword does not make the warrior." She shrugged. "And we are not women, *savim*. We are handmaidens, and it is not the same. How else could we be with the army, where no woman treads?"

Somehow, Melanna had never considered that. Her whole life, she'd accepted that lunassera accompanied armies simply because that was their role. She'd never considered *why*. Just as she'd only moments before renewed her assumption that the sisterhood prized beauty for beauty's sake.

"What is your name?"

"Sera, *savim*."

Melanna snorted. Sera meant sister in the old language. A sister in the sisterhood. Likely she'd been marked for this path from birth. A daughter given in wedlock to the goddess needed no dowry and would make no father poor. Slavery was no shame if it fuelled holy purpose.

"Why are you telling me this, Sera?"

"Because times change, and we with them. If your place is not with the lunassera, it may be that the place of the lunassera is with you."

Melanna's frown deepened as she struggled to keep pace with realigning assumptions. "And how will I know that? How will you?"

"By the goddess's gift, *savim*. You must learn your place."

You must learn your place. The second time Sera had spoken those words. On the first, Melanna had taken them as admonishment. Now, she wasn't so sure.

"You must be mad."

Viktor regarded Anastacia with as much patience as he could muster. Which, at the end of a long day, was not a very great deal.

"Far from it. You want to be free of Branghall. This makes it possible."

She stared down at the mannequin without enthusiasm. Laid on the altar of Branghall's tiny chapel – with a lantern at both head and foot, no less – it resembled the sombre engravings on the surrounding tombs more than a means of escape. Petite without seeming shrunken, slender but not willowy, it might have passed for a woman but for the immobile, deathly white "skin" of its beatific face and the dark-tanned leather of its joints.

The velvet of Viktor's old cloak had been reborn as a lace-trimmed gown perfectly fitted to the gentle curves of the porcelain body beneath. Viktor had no idea where the purple and cream hooded shawl had come from, nor the petticoats and boots. He'd simply handed over the coin and been glad to do so.

"You *must* be mad." Anastacia's dark-eyed gaze flickered to Calenne, stood to one side, beyond the lanterns' reach. "Are you part of his madness?"

"Me? I'm here because I was curious." Calenne shot Viktor a pitying glance. "And to think I used to be scared of you. One too many knocks to the head, and the Black Knight's reduced to playing with dolls."

Now she mentioned it, the mannequin was quite doll-like, but for its scale.

"It's very simple," Viktor ground out. "I can't break the enchantment, but I can cheat it. You're bound to the stones of the manor. A portion of that stone now rests within this clay. You can wear it as you would raiment. It will carry you wherever you wish, and the enchantment will never know you have strayed."

Anastacia sneered. "Trade a manor for a prison of fired clay? I don't think I'll accept."

But despite her tone, Viktor saw longing in her expression. "It's not a case of one or the other. You need only wear it . . . "

"*Her*," corrected Calenne.

Viktor pressed on, " . . . when you wish. Be yourself in Branghall, leave for a time as *her*, and then come back to yourself once more. Surely freedom is worth a little discomfort?"

Anastacia's lip twitched, but she didn't look away from the mannequin. Its wig was black where her own hair was snow-white. Somehow, its expression was both open and terrifying, and tinged with the merest hint of sorrow.

"Think of it as armour," Calenne suggested. "You won't always need it, but you'll be glad of it when you do."

Sardonic mirth bubbled up through Viktor's impatience. "So you're part of this *now*?"

"Doesn't mean you're any less mad. A change of heart, that's all. Charity." She sighed and pushed away from the wall. "I *have* been living with a demon half my life. What you're proposing is only a shade more insane."

"I'm not a demon," Anastacia bit out. Her form billowed. Fingertips and hair swelled into vapour. She swallowed and reeled herself back in. "And I don't want to be the last guest at the party."

Her despair gave Viktor no pleasure. But it propelled her in the necessary direction. Another nudge, and she'd be there. "Nor need you be."

For the first time since entering the chapel, she reached out. Her fingers traced the gold of the branch-like inlay.

"I confess, it is very beautiful. And warm to the touch. With my mother's magic." She frowned. "How is such a thing possible?"

"Its maker was gifted in more ways than one," said Viktor. "It's stronger than it appears, and lighter. He put a piece of his soul into the work, I think."

"Such is the way of all true artists," Anastacia murmured. "It must have cost you dearly."

Viktor shared a glance with Calenne. Yorvin had gaped at a final payment far in excess of that promised. Viktor hoped it soothed the old man's fears of betrayal.

"Nothing I wasn't prepared to pay."

Her head snapped up, eyes unfriendly once more. "Why?"

"Because the Southshires need Josiri, and Josiri needs you. And *you* need freedom."

"So this is a bribe? My freedom, so long as I serve as herald to your coming?"

"To do with as you wish. I only ask that you *try* to convince Josiri to good sense."

"It *is* a bribe."

He hesitated but nodded. "Yes."

To Viktor's surprise, Anastacia smiled. "Then for the first time, I feel like I understand you. But you do know I can't accomplish this alone?"

A lump formed in the pit of Viktor's stomach. "What do you mean?"

"Karkosa's enchantment. It took the efforts of a dozen proctors, but he bound me tight. It's like ... nails through my flesh, pinning me in place. Even testing the bonds is agony. I can feel the ... the ..." She glared at Calenne. "The *doll* calling to me. It's the same, but different. If I lose myself ..."

She grimaced. When her expression cleared a little of the old confidence had returned. "I need your help."

"Viktor ..." Calenne stepped into the lantern light. "What's she talking about?"

Viktor stifled a scowl. He should have sent her away. He should never have involved her as much as he had. But hindsight was fool's gold and rusted steel. If he didn't tell Calenne, Anastacia would. And then he'd have no control over how she reacted.

Anastacia laughed, though without malice. There was an almost childish joy to it, as one already privy to a secret that would only appal when revealed. "She doesn't know. How charming. But then, she has led a sheltered life."

Calenne glared at her, a brace of the demon's ribald tales surfacing from the pit of memory. "I dread to think what you mean by that. If there's to be any disrobing – if this is some northwealder's perversity – I cherish my ignorance. Just because I've spent fifteen years locked up in this house doesn't mean I don't hear rumour of what goes on among *quality* folk when the drapes are drawn and passions run amok."

Viktor held up a soothing hand. "It's not. Or at least not in the way you suggest ..."

"And what, pray, does *that* mean?"

A deep breath before the plunge. "There's a side of me that you can't see. Anastacia can. A gift like Yorvin's, but different. I keep it hidden. I have to."

He watched her closely, searching for the fear that warned of betrayal. What was he prepared to do if he saw it? He didn't know. Could he kill her? No doubt. She was a young woman half his age, untempered in battle. Her neck would snap cleanly enough. But at the same time, Viktor suspected he lacked strength of a different sort. And not just because the act would doom his attempt to win Josiri's support. He'd grown more used to Calenne's company than he could have believed.

"You're a witch." She spoke flatly, without expression.

"I'm a *man*. One who's striving to save your brother from foolishness, and your people from conquest. I will do nothing to hurt you. You have my word. But you must tell no one of this, not even Josiri."

His shadow stirred, woken from its slumbers by his fear. Viktor's skin prickled with cold as his shadow slunk to join those cast by the lanterns.

Anastacia perched on the edge of the altar, her fingers idly toying with the doll's hair. For a mercy, she held her tongue. Unfortunately, so did Calenne.

"Calenne ... " Viktor began.

"I'll tell no one, not even Josiri." She shook her head furiously, as if trying to dislodge something from her hair. "Do you believe me so shallow? I'm not swayed by labels, and certainly not those bestowed by the Council, or the church. If I'm to hate you, I'll do so on my own terms." She offered a thin smile. "And I said that you had it in you to be a monster."

Her fingers whitened at the knuckles where they hugged her elbows close. But though her expression was notably less friendly than minutes before, it fell short of the terror with which she'd first beheld him.

Viktor exhaled, and felt a burden slip from his shoulders. "You did indeed."

Anastacia's soft applause echoed around the chapel. "Oh, well done. She's grown more in two days of freedom than fifteen years of captivity. So, are we still doing this?"

"After everything it's cost to reach this point?" sighed Viktor. "Without doubt."

She spread her arms and dissipated until she was merely the echo of a woman, wreathed in vapour. A memory of what had been, and what might one day be again.

"Hurry," she breathed sharply. "I cannot bear this long."

Viktor swore to himself. He'd wanted more time, to glean from Anastacia what his role would be. And now time was lost, and preparation unthinkable. Only instinct remained.

He closed his eyes and willed his shadow to life. He gasped as it made contact with Anastacia's being, overwhelmed by the myriad emotions of a naked soul.

Fear. He'd expected fear, but not the gnawing want billowing beneath. His heart ached with the sorrow of it, even though he knew it was but a sliver of what Anastacia felt. And the light at her core ... it burned him as it did his shadow. Every breath was a struggle. Every stroke of his quickening heart a wearying toil. And yet there was beauty too – a sense of contentment so overwhelming that Viktor lost himself within it.

He awoke on the flagstones, his cheek matted in drool and Calenne's urgent hand on his shoulder.

"I was right before," she said archly, if with a note of humour. "It *was* some northwealder's perversity."

Viktor forced himself groggily up onto one elbow. "Anastacia?"

With Calenne's help, he staggered to his feet. Of Anastacia, there was no sign. The doll lay unmoving on the altar.

Failure thickened Viktor's throat. He grabbed Calenne's arm. "What did you see? Tell me!"

"Viktor, you're hurting me!"

He let go, still fighting the nausea of aftermath.

The doll sat bolt upright.

Calenne yelped then pressed a hand to her mouth in embarrassment. The doll grasped at the edge of the altar, porcelain fingers clinking against marble.

The chapel filled with a rasping, breathy sound. Had Viktor not known better, he'd have thought the doll was gasping for air. The head turned and twisted, glancing first one way and then the next. Then Anastacia's balance failed and she plunged sideways. The lantern at her feet went with her. It shattered, lengthening the shadows.

Viktor caught her at the altar's edge, but barely. He pitched her upright and swung her legs around.

[[What have you done to me?]] The desperate voice was Anastacia's, but hollow with loss and confusion. She raised a hand and flexed her fingers. Leather joints creaked and settled. [[I can't feel anything! I can barely see!]]

Her eyes, at least, remained her own – cold, dark and welling with tears.

Viktor took her hands in his. "It will take you time to adjust. You'll grow accustomed ..."

[[No!]] She ripped her hands free and braced them against the altar. Cracks crazed outwards across the marble. [[This body is cold and dead. I reject it!]]

She froze. Calenne started forward, but Viktor waved her back. Anastacia's tone worried him. They reminded him too much of a young boy, lashing blindly out at the vranakin who'd murdered his mother. There was no telling what she might do.

He lost track of how long they stood there in silence, Anastacia unmoving and Calenne an anxious presence at his shoulder. There was only his ragged pulse. This would pass. Anastacia was his only connection to Josiri. She'd gather herself. She had to.

Anastacia's head snapped upright with a low, mournful wail. She gazed at him with hatred that the immobile doll's face should not have found possible.

[[I cannot leave,]] she moaned. [[I cannot return to what I was. You've sealed me in a tomb.]]

"No!" Viktor again took her hands, speaking low and urgent. "I can make this right, I swear to you."

[[Release me!]]

She hurled him aside as if he were a child. His head cracked against a column. The world flashed bright and dark. The floor rushed upwards.

The second lantern shattered on the floor as Anastacia rose from the altar. Darkness flooded in, the moonlight of the chapel windows the only reprieve. Viktor tried to stand, to call on his shadow. Anything. Lost in a world of blurred vision and red thunder, nothing responded as it should. He slumped to hands and knees. Blood trickled down his brow and spattered on stone.

[[I never should have listened! What is there for me now?]]

Porcelain fingers clinked into fists.

A shadow stepped between them. Calenne. "Leave him be."

Anastacia raised a fist. [[Stand aside.]]

Viktor waved an urgent hand at Calenne. He nearly lost his balance doing so. "Do as she says."

Calenne hesitated, as one suddenly aware of her own actions.

Uncertainty danced across her face, perhaps in regret at an impulse that had placed her between a vengeful demon she hated, and the Black Knight she'd feared for so long. Then her expression hardened, and she folded her arms.

"No."

"I don't want her to hurt you," gasped Viktor.

"She won't." The words were hard as the mountains. "Because if she does, my brother will never forgive her."

[[And what use is Josiri to me any longer, or I to him?]]

"Touch me, and you'll never find out."

Anastacia loosed another soul-wrenching wail. Her hand fell to her side. The golden patterns of her face gleamed in the moonlight. Then she vanished into the growing darkness behind Viktor's eyes. Glass shattered somewhere distant and a cool breeze rushed in.

Viktor felt Calenne's hands beneath his arms. Her face crowded close, more worried than he'd any right to expect. With her help, he regained his feet. He stared across the chapel to the broken window and churned footprints beyond. Unfamiliar failure thickened his throat. It hurt worse than the blow to his head.

"What have I done?" he breathed.

"Blessed Ashana, I beseech you. Guide your ephemeral daughter."

Kneeling, Melanna let the intoxicating scent of incense fill her lungs. No answer came.

"Blessed Ashana, I beseech you. Guide your ephemeral daughter."

She opened her eyes into the inner sanctum's gloom. Cracks of moonlight roused the incense-fog to iridescence. All else was darkness, cold and silent. The outer sanctum was but paces away, through six veils of silk and one of cotton. It felt distant as the moon herself.

Melanna closed her eyes once more. Midnight was come and the moon in the sky. If ever there was a time for Ashana to answer, it was now.

"Blessed Ashana, I beseech you. Guide your ephemeral daughter."

"She will not come."

Melanna caught her breath upon hearing the deep voice. The familiar voice. She opened her eyes. The antlered knight stood before her. He was mantled in armour of silver scales and folds of dark cloth that glittered with the light of captive stars. Behind, swathed in iridescent fog, skeletal trees reached towards a distant moon. Of the tent, there was no sign. Autumn leaves crackled beneath Melanna's knees.

"Why won't she come? Who *are* you?"

Green eyes blazed like fire beneath the helm. "A poor Huntsman and steward to a goddess. I offer advice. Sometimes, she is pleased to take it."

Melanna bowed her head. She dared not rise. The goddess's presence was a comfort; the Huntsman was anything but.

"I wish to speak with the goddess."

"And I told you, she will not come." His tone was not unkind, but nor was it friendly.

"Why? She has never forsaken me before."

"She feels your heart quicken to the tempo of war and wishes no encouragement."

Bitterness soured Melanna's throat. "I need no encouragement, only her blessing."

"She will not give it."

"She must. War is the way of my people. We count our losses in the tally of our dead, and our victories in the bodies of the foe. If I cannot fight, the Golden Court will never accept me. The rule of Saran will die with my father."

The Huntsman drew closer. He towered over her, his cloak blotting out the moon. "She knows all this. She believes herself aloof from war. She wishes to remain so."

Bitterness blossomed into anger. "She was pleased to help my forefathers carve an empire from the anarchy of the Sceadotha's fall!"

"That was not her."

"It was Ashana! The legends all agree!"

"Ashana is but a name, and a duty to the heavens. My goddess is not the first to bear it. She will not be the last."

"That doesn't make any sense!"

"Does shared title grant shared purpose to all emperors?" Amusement rumbled beneath the words. "Or to all princessas?"

"It's not the same!" Anger drove Melanna to her feet, then faltered. The Huntsman loomed above her no less than before. If anything, he seemed a vaster presence. She stumbled back. The Huntsman's shadow travelled with her, his green eyes searing into her soul.

"No, it is not," said the Huntsman. "And nor should it be. But my mistress wishes to do things differently."

Something in his tone halted Melanna's retreat. "But you don't? You can change her mind."

He laughed like the roar of an underground river. "My mistress has endured too many lies from men seeking to control her, to adore her or to exploit her. It is the thread that binds her to you. I alone have always been honest, if not always her friend, but our shared past too often deafens her to my advice." He drew back. "But that doesn't mean I cannot help."

The mists between them cleared. A sword lay upon the leaves. Swirling silver patterns of a waxing and waning moon chased the black leather of its scabbard. Its hilt shone, even in the Huntsman's shadow.

"Here is Ashana's blessing, if you would have it," intoned the Huntsman. "When you draw that sword, no one will doubt your purpose, or your patron."

Melanna stared down at the blade. She'd never seen a weapon so beautiful. She longed to take it. Instinct warned her against doing so. "Why? Why are you doing this?"

"Because I understand war. Better it be fought by those who desire it."

"But why me? Why now?"

"Because I had a daughter once. Like you, Hélène's heart was full of fire, but she never lived long enough to set it loose. This is the thread that binds us, if you will let it. But the choice is yours. So is the glory, and so are the consequences."

The Huntsman's longing tone couldn't hide the warning in his words. Should she walk away, abandon the sword among the leaves? Part of Melanna wanted to – it trembled with memory of the tales of those drawn into divine intrigues. But was this not what she'd wanted? What she'd begged for? How would she live with herself if she walked away?

She stooped. Her hand closed around the scabbard. Darkness fell.

"*Savim?*"

Melanna awoke, still kneeling, shivering with cold and covered in sweat. She gripped the sword across her chest. The buckles of the scabbard dug into her flesh.

"*Savim?*" Sera said again. "I heard you cry out. Are you hurt?"

"No."

The chatter of Melanna's teeth subsided. Holding the scabbard, she eased back the sword's hilt until a chink of steel showed. White light filled the sanctum, driving back the darkness, and her doubts.

Sera's gloved hand flew to her mouth. She stepped back, pressing against the tent-folds for support. Melanna slid the sword home.

"Gather your sisters, Sera. There's something they must see."

Endas, 4th day of Radiance

My whole life, I have dwelled on the hour of my
death. Would I leave great works undone? My family
unprovided for? Would my name live on while my
flesh sours in the tomb?

Too late, I realise that these were the wrong
questions.

from the Last Sermon of Konor Belenzo

Twenty-Six

The mists of Krayna Dell defied the light of dawn. Revekah wasn't surprised. It was often thus in the Forbidden Places, where old magic wore thin the walls between the living realm and Otherworld. For those who didn't heed the priesthood's warnings about such places, a thousand tales counselled caution. Spirits lurked within the mists, or so it was said. Spirits, and worse. Revekah had never seen such peril for herself – nor spoken to anyone who had – but the fear remained.

Mists or no, the Forbidden Places were *different*. As if the turnings of the world held little influence on what passed within, or distant seasons lingered jealously beneath the boughs.

A time-worn statue projected from weed-choked waters. Remnants of a site of worship, cloaked in ancient power that held constructs at bay. It was also the subject of so many terrible stories that the phoenixes kept fires burning at the nearby cave mouths, just in case. Revekah rubbed her hands together to ward off the cold. Yes, too many tales. Of blood and malice, and foolish youngsters doing what foolish youngsters do. At that moment, with ethereal keening echoing through the mists, she was more inclined than ever to believe.

"I still don't see why you dragged me out here." She kept one eye on young Tarn, and another on the mists.

"Don't you hear that?" he replied.

"I hear a weeping woman. It's hardly remarkable." It was likely to become a whole lot less remarkable with armies on the march.

Tousled curls shook insistently. "Could be a woman. Could also be a prizrak, or a cyraeth."

Revekah snorted. "Ghosts, is it? Your mother filled your head with too many folktales."

"Then what happened to Tornas?"

"Tornas was a lecherous old bastard who tried things too hot and heavy with one of Gavamor's lasses. No mystery. No ghosts. And *no* cyraeth." She sighed. "I'll take a look."

"No!" Tarn hissed. "It's too dangerous!"

"Then why did you want me here?"

He stared mutely at his feet, confirming what Revekah already knew. Part of him believed that the woman was merely as she sounded and wanted her gone before she drew down a northwealder patrol. Another part – perhaps the larger part – feared she was indeed a cyraeth, the tattered hood concealing withered features and bloody fangs.

"I'll talk to her," she said firmly. "You can head back."

He twitched. "No, I'll stay."

She patted him on the shoulder. "Good lad. And if she rips me bloody, you'll be able to tell everyone you were right, won't you?"

Tarn blanched. "I ..."

"A joke, lad. Nothing'll happen to me." She thumped her chest. "Too leathery to be worth eating."

Revekah waited for a little colour to return to Tarn's cheeks before heading down the slope. Cool air sucked at her lungs and set her joints creaking. She swallowed and pressed on. It was too easy to feel the burden of lost years in the Forbidden Places, and the paucity of those ahead. She skirted the water's edge, the sorrowful sound louder in her ears with every cautious step. Mud sucked at her boots. Skeins of mist clung to her arms like grasping fingers. The sunken statue, the feathers of its sole remaining wing streaked with weed-fronds, passed away to her right.

There she was. Sitting on a rock where mud-sunk steps led away into still waters. That same mud clung to the hem of her black dress and the dangling threads of her hooded shawl. Her arms were clasped tight across a narrow chest.

Revekah sighed her relief. Otherworld take Tarn and his jumpiness.

Lost in her own private, mournful world, the woman rocked back and forth as Revekah approached. Now she was closer, Revekah noted an oddly hollow – almost metallic – note to the keening. But mist played merry hell with the ears. Wouldn't be anything more than that.

"Too nice a day for tears," she said amiably. "Want to talk about it?"

Revekah laid a hand on the woman's shoulder.

[[Don't touch me!]]

A vicelike grip closed around her wrist. The mists spun. Her back struck the water, filthy spray fountaining around her. Revekah glimpsed black eyes, swirling like smoke beneath a mask of white and gold.

Waters closed over her head.

Calenne awoke to the tramp of boots on cobbles below her window. A claggy mouth and thin purplish pre-dawn light warned of insufficient sleep. With a groan, she pulled the pillow over her head and clutched it tight to her ears.

After dressing, she headed outside. Even the thought of breakfast so early made her nauseous. She followed the marching column of blue tabards through the winding streets and out towards the east gate. The streets were otherwise deserted. Too early for most, perhaps. Or were they staying inside to avoid being drawn into whatever was afoot?

As she walked, Calenne became aware of other footfalls in the road behind. Kraikons loomed over houses in parallel streets. She knew that simarka wouldn't be far away but decided that as long as she couldn't see them, it wasn't a problem.

Beyond the gate, a desperately small army converged. A few hundred men and women gathered around campfires, playing cards or scraping whetstones across steel. Most were infantry, garbed in the familiar tabards and plate of Branghall's guards. A few-score wayfarers stood vigil on unarmoured horses at the muster's perimeter, spears aloft and their eyes on the eastern horizon. Wagons stood motionless. Draught horses champed restlessly in the chill morning air.

"Morning, missy. Come to join up, have you?"

Calenne spun around, swallowing a heart that had leapt into her throat. Captain Kurkas regarded her from the shadow of the gate with a mocking smile and customary dishevelment.

"Is that how you address your betters?" The sought-for hauteur sputtered to nothing. It was too early.

Kurkas shrugged. "My father was a soldier. My mother a crowmarketeer – in good and deep with the vranakin and their parliament, so I understand. Neither of 'em made their living doing anything you'd want to see first-hand. Makes everyone my better, but I can't spend a life bowing and scraping. Bad for the back. You sure you don't want to join up?"

"You can't be that desperate."

"Can't I?" Another column of soldiers marched through the gate. He waited until they'd passed before pressing on. "Yanda took the best of what we had two days back. Most of 'em are probably dead by now. This is whatever Lord Akadra could scrounge up west of Eskavord. Don't be fooled by the uniforms. There're more toll-keepers here than soldiers."

He spat on the roadway. Calenne cast her eye anew over the muster fields. Kurkas' dour appraisal changed little of what she saw. "They seem soldierly enough."

"Guess we'll find out, won't we? Offer's still open. Don't tell me you weren't schooled in swordplay?"

"I had duellist's lessons, and I was never that good. It's hardly preparation for battle."

Kurkas thrust his hand into a pocket and scuffed his boots against the cobbles. "No. I reckon not."

"Then why do you keep asking?"

He sighed. "Last time I was in these parts, a woman who looked a lot like you roused half the populace. The fire she put in their bellies nearly burned us all to a crisp. Cost me an arm, but right now I'd give the other for that fire to catch again."

Truth gleamed beneath the put-upon attitude, even beneath the dry humour of his tone. Kurkas expected to lose. He expected to die.

"No help's coming?"

"Not enough. Your lot don't trust us, and they're right not to. Lord Akadra reckons they'll only follow your brother. Me, I'm a firm believer in the motivational power of a pretty face."

Calenne grimaced. She'd spent a lifetime dreaming herself free of Katya's legacy. She'd not backtrack now it was finally within her grasp. The Southshires hadn't needed her the whole time she'd been a prisoner at Branghall. It'd manage without her now.

"So you're a hopeless romantic," she said. "I'd never have guessed."

"Yeah, shines through all the time. Ask anyone. Why *are* you here?"

A good question. Why was she still in Eskavord? Viktor's concerns for her safety aside, there was nothing stopping her riding for Thrakkia. She could leave whenever she wanted, so why hadn't she? Belatedly, she realised that Kurkas' concerns were a mite more focused.

"I'm looking for Viktor."

"'Course you are. Charms 'em wherever he goes."

"He does?" Calenne hated the involuntary note of alarm.

"Don't fret yourself." He grinned wolfishly. "He has a way of talking folk 'round, that's all. Why do you think I'm here in the path of Hadari spears instead of sitting safe at his father's gate? Then again, there was this one lass up by the Ravonn – a reeve's daughter, she was – went to great lengths to get his attention. The kind of carry-on you don't want the neighbours to see. Barking up the wrong tree, she was. Nothing to offer him."

"He's not interested in women?"

"Not interested in anyone, not that I've seen. No flags flying on those battlements, if you take my meaning." Kurkas straightened. "Come on, I'll take you to *Viktor*."

They threaded the muster fields towards the handful of pavilion tents. Calenne gave wide berth to the gold-robed proctors, lest they marked the presence of nearby simarka.

Now closer to the troops, she saw what Kurkas meant. Most were lads and lasses with barely sixteen years behind them. Those who remained fell on the spectrum's distant end. Men and women who'd been in their prime at Zanya, but on whom the passing years had levied a great toll. Only those in the black cloth and silver swan of the Akadra hearthguard truly resembled soldiers as Calenne imagined them. They made up perhaps a third of those assembled.

They found Viktor outside the largest tent, stripped to shirtsleeves and britches. He glowered at an unfortunate young man in a herald's tabard.

"I didn't ask *why* the Rivelan garrison isn't here," he growled. "I *ordered* you to impress the need for haste upon Lieutenant Garran. Will you do this for me, or must I do it myself?"

The herald blanched, saluted and scurried away. Viktor spun on his heel. Calenne glimpsed an expression that matched the Black Knight of her nightmares far better than the man she'd known over the last few days. As he caught sight of her, his expression cleared.

"Ah, Calenne. I was about to send for you."

Kurkas, now standing to Viktor's rear, winced.

"Send for me?" she replied icily. "Does everyone think me a soldier in the making?"

Viktor raised a hand in objection and opened his mouth to speak. Then he plainly thought better of both and let the hand fall. Kurkas grinned.

"My apologies. A poor turn of phrase. I didn't manage much sleep."

Calenne noted the circles beneath bloodshot eyes. The reason for his malaise was hardly mysterious. Even if it arose from misplaced concern.

"Can I assume that you didn't retire after escorting me home?"

He nodded. "You can indeed. Captain? I hope you're not smirking just because I can't see you."

"No, sah!" Kurkas roared. "Wouldn't dream of it!"

The grin remained firmly in place. Calenne would have told Viktor, save for her certainty that he already knew.

Viktor shook his head. "Then kindly attend to your duties. I want to be underway by evening."

"Right away, sir!" Kurkas threw Calenne a sloppy salute. He thrust his hand in his pocket and withdrew.

Viktor rubbed his brow. "I can't find her. I rode for miles, and walked for many more, but she's gone and I know not where."

"It wasn't your fault."

"Of course it was. I promised Anastacia she'd be free. Instead I changed only the nature of her prison. Better that I'd done nothing at all."

"You did what you thought was right."

"As I always do. My father claims I'm arrogant. It may be he isn't wrong." He stared past her towards Branghall. "This time my arrogance has cost another dearly."

"Out of the best intentions," said Calenne, wondering why she bothered. Anastacia was a demon, and demons deserved whatever fate delivered. But somehow she couldn't bring herself to say as much. "And intentions always matter."

"Let us hope so," said Viktor. "Because I must speak to your brother again, and now my good intentions are all I have to offer. Would you find him for me? I have wayfarers watching the roads, but a sister's instincts might prove keener than their eyes."

Calenne doubted her instincts were much use to anyone – especially where Josiri was concerned – but found herself nodding. "On one condition: get some rest, Viktor. Good intentions and arrogance are no substitute for a few hours' sleep."

He bowed. "As you wish, Lady Trelan."

She winced at the hated name, though she recognised that Viktor meant only respect. She could leave the Southshires at any time, but the Trelan name would remain with her . . .

"I'll return before noon," she said. "Successful or otherwise, I expect to find you sleeping."

Revekah came to propped against a tree; cold, weary and soaked to the skin. Mist curled around her. Memories crashed back. The weeping woman with the hollow voice. The face. Not a cyraeth, but nothing good.

She reached for her sword. Fingers closed around the grips before she remembered to be surprised it was even there. What manner of assailant left her victim armed? Then again, what manner of assailant saved their victim from drowning, as hers had?

[[I apologise for how I reacted.]]

Revekah's heart skipped a beat. Her eyes scoured the mists. There. Waist-deep in the pool, her back to Revekah once again, as if communing with the lonely statue at the water's heart.

[[I am not at my best.]] She flexed gloved fingers, then clenched the fist and let it fall. [[You surprised me.]]

There was something familiar about the voice. Revekah let her sword fall. "Do I know you?"

[[You know who I *was*. I don't know who I *am*.]]

"Anastacia?" Revekah clambered to her feet, wincing as damp clothing found dry flesh. "Is that you?"

[[What's left of me. No matter how much is stripped away, there's always more to lose.]]

Anastacia turned. Hesitant fingers brushed the shawl from her brow.

She peeled away her glove and set pale white fingers to her cheek. They didn't flex as they should, and met her "skin" with a soft, scraping glink. Revekah stifled a gasp.

[[This is who I am now.]] Self-pity swelled beneath the words.

Revekah shook her head, uncertain how to respond. So many questions. "What happened to Tarn? The lad who was with me?"

[[He ran as soon as I saw him. I didn't mean to scare him.]] She paused. [[No. That's a lie. I did. I very much wanted to scare him.]]

"Wouldn't have taken much." Revekah circled towards her, alert for danger. "Big one for stories, is Tarn. You've given him one to treasure, but . . . I thought you couldn't leave Branghall?"

Anastacia faced the statue once more. [[They worshipped me here, long ago. No service was too great, no offering too generous. That adoration sated my every whim. Your realm is so much more . . . immediate . . . than my home. The notes sweeter, the flavours sharper. My mother thought me wicked. Selfish. She told me I'd come to a poor end. She was right.]]

Revekah frowned at the evasion, the details of which she poorly understood. She took a faltering step closer. She'd never truly known what to make of Anastacia, save that she lay some way short of both the demonhood Calenne ascribed and the perfection Josiri perceived. She shot a glance at the statue in the pool, raised long ago in a serathi's likeness, and considered that she might well have been wrong on both counts.

"What happened to you?"

[[A deceiver slithered into my cage. He offered freedom, as I once offered to cure the sick and quicken life within the barren. Like my promises, his were worthless. I am free, but trapped within this . . . this . . .]]

The words choked off in a scream. Anastacia slammed her fist into the statue. Dust exploded into the mists. Thick spider-web cracks jagged out across the slime-ridden stone.

Revekah stepped back, her hand once again at her sword. Tarn had been right about leaving well alone. Soon as she'd stepped into Krayna Dell, she'd left the real world behind. This was the stuff of folktale and drunken imagining.

"The deceiver. Does he have a name?"

[[Akadra.]] She spat the word. [[Viktor Akadra.]]

Revekah nodded, relieved that there was to be no further intrusion of myth. There was, after all, already a superfluity to hand.

"A busy bugger, that one," she said. "Calenne's trailing him like a lost kitten. Josiri's knotted up with frustration because most folk think Akadra's bought his loyalty. And then there's you."

[[Josiri?]] Pity fell away into concern. The new tone was no better a fit. [[How is he?]]

"Raging inside and out. Looks like you must know something about that."

[[Whatever pain he feels is nothing to mine.]]

Now *that* sounded like Anastacia. "I don't know. I rode back with him from Maiden's Hollow. Reckon the only thing kept him from screaming is pride. He doesn't know where to turn. But don't take my word for it. He's at Branghall. See for yourself."

Anastacia hung her head. [[I can't. Look at me. We were barely the same before. Now . . . Now, I can offer no respite. I feel neither the chill of the mist nor the warmth of the sun. Not the fall of a hand on my shoulder or fingers on my cheek. My embrace would as likely crush him as bring comfort. Why would he want me now?]]

"Because he loves you. Never understood why, but he does."

Anastacia stiffened. [[And what use is that now? To him or to me?]]

"Nothing? Everything? But you'll not find answers skulking out here in the mists."

[[Maybe I don't want answers. Maybe I want the Raven to take me away.]]

Irritation burned away the last lingering fear. "Then you're a fool. I buried my son fifteen years back. My husband, two years prior. I'd give anything for another day with them. Another hour, even. And that's whether or not they could feel the warmth of my hand. *Or* if they were clad in white and gold, like a mummer dressed up for Reaptithe carnival."

Anastacia turned. Baleful black eyes blazed within her perfect, beautiful face. [[You *dare* match your loss to mine?]]

Revekah held her ground. "No. Because however much you reckon you've lost – and I'm not saying it's nothing – you're still *here*, and you still *feel*. Folk who feel nothing don't weep for their loss, not even when they think no one's watching."

She received no reply save for that ominous, unblinking stare. All told, Revekah preferred the old Anastacia to whatever she had become. Whatever Akadra had made her.

"All I know is that you're a big part of what's kept Josiri sane these past years. He could use a little of that now. So could you. Find Josiri. Let him decide. I don't pretend to know what you were, or what you are now. But we're stronger with those we care for than without them. Every last one of us."

The perfect brow tilted, curiously birdlike in gesture. [[You're trying to be kind. But you do not understand.]]

She chuckled. "Lassie, I'm an old woman. Time's treated me better than most. But if you think these old bones offer up more than a fraction of what they used to, then you're as big a fool as ever I met. Should have packed all this in years ago, 'cept *some* folk think there might be a bit of wisdom rattling around my head. But you do what you want. I can't stop you."

[[No,]] said Anastacia. [[You can't.]]

She held the stare for what seemed for ever. Long enough for Revekah to wonder if Anastacia was considering hurling her back into the pool. Then without another word, the shawl came up anew. Water streaming from her clothes, Anastacia stalked away into the mists.

Cold, wet and fighting an odd mix of anger and ennui, Revekah let her go. Fifteen years. Fifteen years she'd watched and waited, helping Josiri become the man Katya would have wanted – the leader the Southshires needed. It was all coming apart, and one man lay at the heart of it all.

Viktor Akadra. She couldn't stop Anastacia doing as she wished, but she could sure as sunrise put an end to him.

Newfound determination burning away the chill of sodden clothes, Revekah went in search of Tarn.

Calenne returned to the muster fields an hour before noon. Viktor emerged from his tent in full plate armour and surcoat, the great fennlander's claymore strapped in place across his back.

"You promised to get some rest."

"Your expectation is not my promise," he replied, with only a hint of mockery. "For what it's worth, I *did* sleep for several hours after you left."

Calenne crossed her arms, uncertain if she believed him. "And if I asked Captain Kurkas?"

"He'd offer whatever reply granted him the quietest life. But it *is* the truth. My good intentions and arrogance both now have their second wind." He hooked an eyebrow, the motion tugging on his scar. "Did you find him?"

She nodded. "You're wasting your time. He won't listen."

In point of fact, Josiri had been halfway into a bottle when she'd left him. She hadn't asked why. She hadn't dared, for fear of the topic turning to Anastacia. And if that happened, everything would bubble to the surface – Josiri's deceptions about their captivity at the fore.

More and more, Calenne wondered just how much she'd known of her brother had been the truth, concealed too long from the woman she was by the blinkered assumptions of the girl she'd once been. Her world had changed so much since she'd left Branghall. The brother she'd trusted stood revealed as a liar, and the man she'd feared was nobler than she could have believed. Trying to unpick it all only left her angry. Until that faded, Josiri was better off avoided. Selfish, perhaps, but wasn't she entitled to be so, if only for a little while?

Viktor nodded. "I have to try. Without Josiri – without at least his backing – we'll be hard-pressed in the days to come. The Raven will feast well."

"Then leave us. Take your hearthguards, and that insolent captain of yours, and march home."

"I cannot."

"Why?" Calenne hadn't known the frustration she harboured until the demand tore free. "If my brother won't stand up – if my people won't fight – why should you die in our defence?"

Viktor drew closer. A wry smile touched his lips. "All this concern. Would you truly weep if the Black Knight met his end?"

"I have no tears for the Black Knight," said Calenne. "But for Viktor Akadra, I might manage a few."

She glared at him, daring him to read more into a confession she barely understood herself. Was it because Viktor expected more of her than Josiri ever had? That he challenged her to be better?

He took her hands in his. "I'm a soldier. My duty is to fight for those who cannot. To stand the line when no one else will. Your mother understood that."

"My mother ..." Calenne chased the word from her thoughts. "*Katya* is dead."

"Her people are not. I have a duty to them. So does your brother, even if he finds the price too painful."

"Is it duty? Or is it pride?"

Calenne pulled free and turned away, overcome by contradictory emotion. Josiri had a duty. So did she. Viktor hadn't spoken the words, but he must have thought them. Looking out across the muster field, she felt that duty more keenly than ever. Instead of flesh and blood soldiers, she saw grinning skeletons, caked in mud from upturned graves.

It had been easier at Branghall, when folk had been distant names and faces seldom seen. When Viktor Akadra had been the murderous Black Knight at the head of an anonymous, oppressive horde. But what good did it do if she hurled herself into this madness? She'd spent her life fleeing her mother's ... *Katya's* ... poisonous legacy. If she gave that up, if she abandoned her dreams of untetherment, she might as well be dead.

Viktor's hand rested on her shoulder. She shook it away.

"Josiri is back at Branghall," she snapped. "It's the only home he knows, and he lacks the courage to seek another. I wish you the joy of getting him to listen. He's certainly never paid me any heed. Not that anyone ever does."

"Calenne, wait!"

She strode away without reply, and without a backward glance. But though she left Viktor behind, the conflicts he'd awoken remained with her at every step.

Twenty-Seven

The door slammed back with a boom that echoed to the rafters. A cold draught swirled wilted flower petals from the flagstones. Josiri glanced tiredly up from the table. He'd hoped wine's embrace might make Branghall seem less empty, and his life less the punchline to a poor joke. It had only pushed the world behind filthy glass and left him a prisoner with his scalded pride.

"Josiri Trelan! It is past time we had words!"

Viktor Akadra bore down, his shoulders set and his face impassive. Fully armoured and surcoated from neck to boots, he was the spit of Josiri's memories of that long-ago Ascension night.

Josiri reached for his glass. "I've said all I care to."

"Then listen."

Gripping the heavy oaken timbers in gauntleted hands, Akadra heaved the table first onto one end, and then tipped it aside. Bottles shattered on flagstones.

Josiri leapt to unsteady feet and swung a fist at Akadra's face. Into that blow he poured every drop of self-loathing for driving Calenne away. Every ounce of disappointment that Anastacia was gone. Every scrap of worthlessness for having been so easily supplanted by Drakos Crovan.

It flailed to nothing in empty air.

Josiri had a drunken heartbeat to contemplate fresh failure. A hammer-blow struck his ribs. He doubled over, gasping. A heavy hand clamped about his collar and dragged the world sideways.

"Unhand me!"

Akadra dragged him backwards across the hall. Josiri battered at the

Black Knight's forearm and dug his heels against flagstones. He might as well have struck stone or sought purchase on Wintertide ice.

"Unhand me! Guards! Guards!"

Akadra ignored him. No guards came. Of course not. Their allegiance had never been his. Reaching the window, Akadra yanked Josiri to his feet and crushed his cheek against the glass.

"Do you see that?" demanded Akadra. "Do you?"

The streets of Eskavord fell away below. Through the twin filters of inebriation and glass, Josiri made out the pitiful army on the muster field.

"Five hundred souls, no more," Akadra bit out. "I've others waiting on the Kreska road. But Kai Saran has at least six thousand. Six thousand veterans of the border wars, and I have an army of children and old men! It's not enough."

He released his grip. Josiri wriggled free.

"Then leave!" he growled. "Run away north and leave us be!"

"Your sister gave the same advice. I'm glad to see you've *something* in common."

"And what's that supposed to mean?"

"That *she* has fire," sneered Akadra. "*You're* a spoilt child clinging to a worthless throne."

The words hit home with the force of Viktor's fist. "Why do you care?"

"Because I've no other recourse. I can save your lands, your subjects. But I need your help."

Josiri laughed. "I've no help to give! I played the part of puppet too well. The 'allies' you'd have me deliver despise me for your catspaw!"

"And you yielded to their distrust." Akadra snorted. "You are your mother's son, even to the end."

Anger solidified to cold fury. Akadra didn't see the punch coming. His head snapped aside. He steadied himself against the window frame.

"You don't get to speak of her," snarled Josiri. "Not here."

He struck Akadra again. The giant staggered. Blood showed at the corner of his mouth. He wiped it away. "What will you do otherwise? Plunge a knife into your heart, as she did?"

His words caught Josiri short. "That's not how it happened! You murdered her!"

"With Lumestra as my witness, I did not. I offered her protection. But dying for a lost cause is easy. Living for one, with all the disappointments and hardships it brings? She hadn't the stomach." Akadra straightened and looked him up and down. "You've learnt her lessons well. I hope she's proud."

Again, Josiri swung. Akadra's open palm took him across the face before the blow landed. Teeth rattled in Josiri's jaw, and he dropped to one knee. Akadra's hand clamped around his throat. His skin prickled with sudden cold. The windows darkened and the room passed into shadow.

"I sought to be your friend," growled Akadra, "to mend the wounds between us for the good of your people. I no longer have that luxury. You will give me all that you have, or I will take it from you."

Josiri clawed at the hand around his throat.

"You already have," he gasped. "Where is Anastacia? What have you done to her?"

Akadra lurched back, his hand falling from Josiri's throat. The darkness cleared, and warmth returned to the room.

"I gave her freedom, as I did you," he said, his words stilted. "What she has done with it is no matter for me."

Josiri strove for breath and wondered at Akadra's defensive tone. Something had shifted, but he knew not what or why. Nor could he shake the presence of a yawning precipice.

"If that's true, then thank you," he gasped. "She deserves better than to be trapped in Branghall."

Akadra sat on the windowsill and wiped a fresh rivulet of blood from his lips. He looked every bit as weary as Josiri felt.

"That's for her to judge. But of your mother, I do not lie. I would have saved her. She wouldn't allow it. Then my father used my 'victory' to further my position, and the truth slipped away." He straightened. "Out of respect for her, I ask you one more time. Join with me. Let us be as brothers. Let us save your people."

Josiri sank back, mired in a sea of regrets and lost opportunities. If he'd accepted Akadra's offer on the first day, he could have presented it as a victory. Maybe even wrested the Vagabond Council from Crovan's influence. But it was too late. And there was still that wall between them, mortared in old blood. Even if Akadra spoke the truth about his mother's death, the thought of scaling that wall hurt like losing her all over again.

"What you ask, I cannot give."

Akadra rose. There was no trace of his earlier fury, nor even disappointment. Just the flat, grey bleakness of a winter sky, forlorn of life and hope.

"Then you and I have something in common," he said. "Today, we both had opportunity to alter how the future unfolds. We neither of us had the strength for what had to be done. Let us hope we can live with the consequences."

He stalked from the great hall, leaving Josiri to dwell on decisions past. And on what opportunity Viktor had lacked the strength to seize.

Viktor's return trip across Eskavord passed in a blur of seething anger and might-have-beens. So much hung on Josiri's cooperation. Still the duke had refused to see reason. Too much pride. The curse of the Trelans.

But was he himself any less complicit? Viktor knew his shadow could have bent Josiri to his will, had he possessed the courage to set it free. And it *had* wanted to slip its leash – wanted it so badly he could still feel its frustration at being denied. But he couldn't have risked it, not after his failure with Anastacia. He'd been so certain of that, too, and now another – a daughter of Lumestra, no less – paid the price for his hubris.

Viktor told himself the situations were different. Anastacia had at least offered help. Josiri had wallowed in anger and self-pity. He deserved neither respect, nor regard for his well-being. The claim rang hollow. Josiri may have struck the first blow, but Viktor had provided all the provocation he'd ever have needed. Calenne had been correct. He should have slept. And because he'd been too proud to take her advice, only a fool's hope remained.

Vladama Kurkas met him at eastern gate, his usual carelessness in wary abeyance.

"His grace see the wisdom of things, my lord?"

"His grace did not," said Viktor, "so we proceed as planned. Get everyone ready to march."

"I'll see to it." Kurkas made a doomed attempt to straighten his battered uniform. "Always knew this blessed province would be the death of me. But you never know ... something might turn up."

He struck out across the muster field, orders already booming from his lips. Viktor watched him go. A shame Josiri Trelan didn't have a tenth of Kurkas' courage. If only Viktor Akadra had half his wariness for lost causes.

And lost causes weighed on Viktor's mind as he parted the flaps of his tent. He'd burned so many bridges back in Tressia to come this far – with his father, most of all. To go back without a victory to show for it was impossible. There was only the road ahead. A road that might see him, and all those who trusted him – Kurkas among them – buried in the same pit.

It spoke to Viktor's distraction that it wasn't until he was fully inside the tent that he realised he wasn't alone.

"Calenne?"

She sat opposite the entrance but rose as he spoke. The dress was darker than the one she'd worn that morning, closer-fitting and recently pressed. Her black hair, then free of comb or band, was bound in tight plaits and trimmed with king's blue ribbons. The formality of her appearance made her seem older. Yet it somehow highlighted the gulf of years that lay between them.

"I never loved Kasamor Kiradin." She met his gaze as she spoke, a slight tremor beneath the words. "It's important you understand that. I'm not proud of it, for I know how he thought of me."

Viktor frowned. The words themselves were no surprise, for she'd grieved little in his company, but the timing . . . "Calenne. What is this?"

"Let me finish." Seeing how her hands worked against one another, she hid them behind her back. "I let Kasamor see his love reflected because I wanted to be free of this place, and of my mother's legend. If I hadn't, he might still be alive."

Poor Kasamor. A good soldier, but a poor judge of a woman's heart. Perhaps it was better he'd never know. "You are not responsible for Kasamor's actions."

"But I am responsible for my own. I'm not a fool, Viktor. I know my brother. I know he refused you. And I know the consequences of that refusal."

Viktor's pulse quickened with new hope. "Then do what he will not."

She shook her head. "I cannot live my life as Katya Trelan's daughter. I can't. She'd smother me, or else devour me from within until Calenne was gone, and only an echo of a stranger remained. That's what you ask, and I cannot give it to you."

Bitterness crowded Viktor's throat as hope turned ashen. "I've no time for games, Calenne. Speak your piece and be on your way."

"I didn't love Kasamor. I didn't even respect him, as I have come to respect you. But he was prepared to welcome me into his family, and thus free me of mine." She took a deep breath. The last tremor vanished from her voice. "I do not love you. What you think of me I can only guess, though I find myself hoping my guesses are not wide of the mark. Whatever we are – whatever is between us – it's not love. At least, not yet. But if you bind me to your family, I will play the part of Katya Trelan's daughter until the bells chime to mark our wedding."

Objections buzzed about Viktor's head like flies. They slipped through his fingers even as he reached for them. He swore he heard Kurkas' riotous laughter, for he suspected the captain had seen this coming just as plainly as he had not.

Was it such a terrible idea? Viktor, disdaining the nonsense of courtship and more at home on a battlefield than among polite company, had long ago resigned himself to a marriage of convenience. After all, the continuation of the family name too was duty. It was an overdue prospect that grew nearer with every greying hair.

Why then did he feel so ill at ease? It wasn't because the utilitarian proposal offended him. Indeed, he'd a certain stark admiration for Calenne's cleverness. Pride and duty. This satisfied all, and for them both.

Was it then the disparity in their ages? But again, a fifteen-year span was hardly unusual. Especially when marriage between families of the upper rank was wielded as a tool of alliance more than love.

No, Viktor decided, it was more that Calenne's forthrightness had taken him off-guard. It was not in his nature to react well to surprise. But still, he couldn't shake the feeling that a portion of his reserve was grounded in the inexplicable feeling of having crossed a finish line while having been cheated of the race.

"You don't know what you're asking," he said.

"But I do. If it is within my power to deliver you an army as dowry, then I shall do so. But after the battle is done, win or lose, I will be a Trelan no longer." She gazed up at him with a smile more knowing than nervous. "Well, Lord Akadra? How do you answer?"

Twenty-Eight

"Father, I'm bored."

Constans' pronouncement startled a handful of doves from the church steps, scattering them to flight across a marketplace still hung with the wreaths and garlands woven for Ascension. Malachi's enthusiasm for an afternoon with his son scattered alongside. With every step, the nagging sensation that he should have been doing something – *anything* – else grew stronger. Which at least gave him *something* in common with Constans. The boy had been no more impressed by the statues in the church than the changing of the guard. Worse, the boy had twice wandered off into the crowds, ever-curious about the brightly painted roamer wagons of the travelling fair, and seemingly oblivious to his father's galloping heart.

A procession of serenes ascended the church steps, bearing candles and birch offerings for the evening service. Malachi put a hand to his son's shoulder and steered him away.

"More or less bored than if you were at your lessons?" he asked.

Constans cocked his head, considering the weighty proposition. "Less. But my lessons don't last long. Ada isn't very good at hide-and-seek."

Which meant that his son spent more time fleeing responsibilities than fulfilling them. Malachi supposed he should have scolded the boy, but felt oddly proud. Were his own life any proof, there'd be years of duty and rote ahead of Constans. Perhaps the boy should run free while he could.

Lily would *not* approve.

"So what *would* you like to do?"

Constans stared out across the bustling street. Beyond the striped canopies of the marketplace – beyond the close-set, crooked townhouses – the greensward and breeze-harried branches of the Hayadra Grove shone in the sunshine. "Climb a hayadra tree."

Malachi blinked away his surprise, then rallied. "You do that, and the serenes will lock you away without food or water for three days. The white trees are sacred, and not for climbing."

Constans harrumphed. "Mother would never allow it."

"You've much to learn about your mother, young man. She tended those trees when she was your age. If you so much as scuff an inch of bark, we'll both of us be in deep trouble."

"Perhaps we could just take a look?"

Malachi had no doubt that once in the holy grove, his son would escape his guardianship as easily as he did Ada's. Soon after, there would be a shout, a triumphant wave, and a proud child among the branches.

What Lumestra would think was anyone's guess. Nor her heavenly sister, from whom the trees had been a peace offering. But Lily? That reaction was easily judged.

"I don't think so, Constans."

"You asked what *I* wanted to do. It's not ... " He broke off as a shadow fell across him.

"So strident a tone, young Master Reveque." Makrov emerged from the market's throng. His plummy tones walked the line between chastisement and kindness – a wise proctor handing down advice to a soul in torment. "You should have more respect for your father."

Constans lapsed into downcast silence. Makrov offered Malachi a stiff bow.

"My Lord Reveque. It feels like for ever since we last spoke."

Malachi smiled without pleasure. "I thought you were in the Southshires, excellency."

"Lumestra called me home on sable wings." He lowered his voice. "The Goddess believes I can serve better as a witness to Council than to war."

"Is that so?"

Malachi felt little surprise at the revelation. Most priests stood a turn on the border, offering spiritual succour to the garrisons along the Ravonn. To his knowledge, Makrov had never willingly come within a league of a Hadari – save for the occasional prisoners paraded through the streets.

"There are ... developments in the Southshires that she finds most concerning, my lord. Viktor Akadra has set the Trelans loose. He has spoken of restoring them to Council!"

"I take it you don't approve?" asked Malachi.

"Did I not say so?" Irritation crept into Makrov's voice. "I cannot believe the Council ... "

"Viktor has the Council's full support."

Makrov's eyes narrowed. "I see. So you are as responsible for this lamentable state as he?"

"I'm proud to be so. The shadowthorns must be contained, by any means."

Makrov's jaw tightened. "A lax view, Lord Reveque, and one we all may yet regret."

He waddled away up the steps and into the church. Malachi took no small satisfaction from a rolling, lurching gait that spoke to too many leagues travelled on horseback in too short a time. An irritation well-paired with its victim.

"Father, what's a shadowthorn?"

Malachi cursed silently. "It's a word that your mother should on no account hear you use, nor learn that I've been using. Do you understand?"

Constans grinned, but only briefly. "Yes, Father."

A bribe was called for, Malachi decided. "How would you like to see the foundry?"

Constans had ambled and dragged his heels all afternoon. Now he was a blur of excited activity and wide-eyed wonder among sparking magic and rivers of sun-bright ore.

Malachi, who could hardly breathe in the smoke-bittered air of the observation gantries, was as grateful for having finally hit upon something to hold his son's interest. He was also increasingly concerned at what Lily would say at his having brought him there. Still, some rules were made to be broken. And Constans had respected the dangers ... so far.

"Thank you for this, Elzar."

The old man heaved his shoulders. "It's good to see the young taking interest. Too many boys his age think only of battle. They don't consider how its tools are made. A knight is more than his sword, yes. But the sword *helps*."

"Kraikons are a little more complicated than swords."

Another shrug. "I'm a proctor. You should expect metaphor. It's why so few of us marry. Hard to find someone who'll tolerate tangential replies."

Far below, rattling chains lowered a glowing metal skeleton into a cooling vat. The hiss of steam almost drowned out Constans' awed sigh, but only almost.

"If I'd an army of kraikons," said the boy, "I'd conquer Fellhallow and wipe the Empire off the map."

"I thought you were the King of Fellhallow?" asked Malachi.

"That was *yesterday*." The boy spoke as one addressing a halfwit. "Today, I am Constans Reveque, Saviour of the Republic."

Elzar chuckled. "And we shall be very glad to have you as such. But perhaps I might have a moment alone with your father?" He beckoned down the gantry to a young woman in apprentice's robes, her tight curls the same rich red as the slow-flowing bronze. "Tailinn will look after you. She was about to name the new forging of simarka. You could help."

"They have *names*?"

He nodded sagely. "Of course."

Constans rounded on Malachi, eyes agleam. "May I, Father?"

"You may." Malachi hesitated. "But only if you do exactly as Tailinn tells you."

Tailinn's freckles twitched in mirth. "He'll be safe with me, my lord."

"Ah, but will you be safe with him?"

She inclined her head and led Constans away.

"He's a fine boy," said Elzar. "You should be proud."

Malachi grunted, not wanting to admit how little he had to do with his son's raising, or his character. Besides, he'd been a politician too long not to hear an ambush coming. Elzar wanted something. "What you said last night, about expecting to talk about foundry business . . . ?"

"Ah. I grow transparent in my old age."

"Don't apologise. In many ways, it's a relief," Malachi replied. "What can the Council do for you, high proctor?"

Elzar glanced back and forth along the gantry. "Someone is stealing kraikons."

Malachi didn't respond at first. He scrutinised Elzar's expression for a clue to what seemed a poor joke. The dull backwash from the molten metal revealed nothing but shadow and sober concern.

"One or two go missing every year," he said. "The metal's valuable, and not every proctor is as noble as yourself . . . "

"To my certain knowledge, we've lost a dozen this past year," said Elzar. "And a similar number the year before. That's a sizeable portion of our output. They leave here, bound for border garrisons or the Outer Isles – at least, that's what the records show – but they aren't reaching their destinations."

"Why haven't you reported this before?"

"I have. Many times. That you remain – begging your pardon – ignorant of the situation tells me a great deal. I shouldn't even be telling you this now. Protocol is very clear. But someone should know."

"You think it's the Crowmarket?"

"No one else has the resources to do this so quietly." Elzar shook his head. "The sheer amount of bribery and blackmail it must take. Whether at warehouse, fleet or convoy, that's a lot of eyes that need to be looking the other way. More than ever, I'm glad we don't wake them until they reach their destination."

Malachi grimaced. "So long as no one in the Crowmarket has learned the knack."

"We'd notice if they had. Not that a kraikon meshes well with the Crowmarket's activities. They have a way of drawing notice."

"It *is* hard to imagine one shinning up a drainpipe or slitting a purse," Malachi allowed. "I'll order the constabulary to sweep the dockside. Most of the stolen kraikons will likely have been melted down or gone into Dregmeet, but we might recover one or two. At worst, it'll send a message."

Elzar nodded, a wary look in his eye. "And if anyone asks what prompted this action?"

"I'm a privy councillor. We're known for our whimsy." He shrugged.

"To be honest, Elzar, the reputation I'm getting with my peers they'll see nothing more than upstart meddling. None of this will come back on you."

"My thanks, my lord."

"For what? I haven't heard anything. Now, let's find that son of mine before he falls into a cooling tank."

As it transpired, Constans had engineered no dreadful fate and waited with Tailinn in one of the brick-lined storage vaults. Rank after rank of simarka sat on their haunches in silent contemplation, forelegs straight and tails curled about bunched feet.

"That one's Thekas," said Constans. "And these are Jaspyr, Fredrik, Ozcor, Parzlai, Londo and Shade."

Malachi followed his enthusiastic gestures but couldn't tell the seven apart. Nor indeed could he do so from the dozen or so other simarka in the chamber.

"Good names," said Elzar. "They'll bear them well."

Constans nodded thoughtfully. "I'd like a pet cat, Father."

"I'm not sure your mother would approve," said Malachi. "Nor will she be pleased if we're late for dinner. Say your farewells."

Rosa rang the bell at Freemont with no small apprehension. In all the years she and Kasamor had been friends, Lady Kiradin had spoken to her only out of politeness. Never – so far as Rosa knew – from friendliness, except where demanded by tradition, as at the funeral.

But the invitation had come to Abbeyfields, and so now Rosa waited while hounds barked at the bell's chime. Lilyana had all but chased her out of the door, insisting she not hide away. Easy for her to say. Lilyana wasn't cursed. Even if she were, Rosa suspected her faith would scarcely have buckled.

The door opened. Marek offered a stiff bow and ushered her inside.

"Good afternoon, Lady Orova. Lady Kiradin will be with you shortly."

Rosa nodded, somewhat relieved at the delay. "Of course. Council business must come first."

In the event, Rosa was left waiting scarcely a few seconds before Marek reappeared. He ushered her into a generously appointed sitting room at the mansion's rear. The granite mantelpiece dominated a chamber of soft, tastefully upholstered armchairs. The gentle curves of the plaster cornice complemented perfectly the soft waves of the carpet's weave.

"Roslava." Ebigail rose in greeting, her arms extended in the formal greeting-clasp. "I'm glad you could make it. It's not often I've cause to entertain a hero of the Republic. What is it they call you?"

Rosa winced. "The Reaper of the Ravonn. It's a foolish name."

"But one that speaks to heroism, I'm sure."

Rosa took her host's hands – palms down, as was customary for a guest – only to be surprised when the older woman leaned in to kiss her cheek. Either she'd misjudged Ebigail for a good many years, or she was now making an effort to compensate for earlier chilly receptions. She wasn't sure what to believe – or even whether or not she *wanted* to believe.

"I was pleased to come. I haven't spoken to Sevaka since . . . the day of the funeral. Malachi assures me she's well, but it's not the same as seeing for yourself."

Ebigail gestured for her to sit. "I'm afraid my daughter will not be joining us. Her departure from the navy requires a certain amount of tedious protocol."

"She's resigning her commission?" This time, Rosa couldn't keep the surprise from her voice. "I thought the life suited her."

"It did," Ebigail replied. "Perhaps a little too well. We decided it was time she came home."

Rosa nodded her understanding. With Kasamor gone, Sevaka had Kiradin duties to uphold. Ebigail would insist.

"You will accept my word that Sevaka is in good health and spirits?" asked Ebigail.

"Of course."

"Then you must also accept my thanks for delivering her from harm. It occurs to me that you have been a better friend to my family than I have deserved. It saddens me that I never thought to chide Kasamor for his blindness. Who can say how things might have worked out otherwise?"

Rosa blinked. "I'm sorry?"

"A mother sees much that is hidden from her son. I can only imagine the burden you've borne. When Kasamor's father died – traitor though he was – it was days before I could face the world."

Rosa closed her eyes. It made the renewed swirl of loss and resentment easier to bear. "There's no replacing him."

"No," said Ebigail. "Kasamor was a man alone, as his father before him. Would you care for tea?"

"Very much."

Ebigail tugged a bell-cord and seated herself opposite Rosa. Moments later, Marek bore refreshments into the room and left as silently as he had arrived. Ebigail poured, filling both butterfly-handled cups to the brim, and the room with the scent of bark and jasmine.

"If you don't mind me saying, it's a shame to see you in uniform again," said Ebigail. "That dress suited you. Even a soldier should embrace her softer side."

Rosa noted that no amount of lace and silk had ever made Ebigail Kiradin appear "soft". Even now, with grief still near and making an effort to friendliness, she'd edges that could slice steel. As indeed did Rosa herself. Strange to find that they had something in common beyond Kasamor.

"I'm due to ride for the border the day after tomorrow," she said instead.

"My dear, I won't hear of it. You're in the 7th, aren't you? Under Lord Karev's command?"

"I have that honour."

"He's a friend. I'll send word that you'll be staying in the city for a time."

"I can't ask you to do that!"

"You're not." She wagged a cautioning finger. "I'll accept no protests. You said you wished to see Sevaka for yourself; this will give you opportunity. And it will give you a chance to put recent events behind you. A burdened soul is an unfit companion for a dangerous road."

Rosa grimaced, but saw some appeal in Ebigail's suggestion. With all that had happened since Kasamor's death, her thoughts and emotions were awhirl. Returning to the 7th without him would stir everything up anew. Maybe it was better to let things settle.

"Thank you."

"There has to be some small benefit to serving on the Privy Council." Ebigail took a sip of tea and flashed a small, conspiratorial smile. "What use is influence if it cannot serve one's friends? It pains me that I must ask a favour in return."

"What sort of favour?"

"I would know the truth about my son's death. Not the version you told the constabulary."

Cold fingers brushed Rosa's back. "There's nothing more to tell."

"Then why were there marks of witchery on his body?"

The fingers closed tight about her lungs. "I don't know what you mean."

The cup was set aside, and the old Ebigail Kiradin – the one whose stare could level mountains – returned. "I know what I saw. And I want to know why I saw them. This was no ordinary brigand, was it?"

The stare won out. Rosa stared down at her tea as her resistance crumbled. "Kas called him a kernclaw. An assassin for the Crowmarket."

Ebigail loosed a wretched sigh. "So it's true. I'd hoped he was wrong. Why didn't I believe him?"

Rosa glanced up. "Didn't believe him about what?"

"It's better you don't know."

"I can't accept that."

A wintery smile. "No, that *was* foolish of me, wasn't it?"

Rosa knew better than that. Grieving or not, the thought of Ebigail speaking out of turn – much less letting something slip by mistake – was the stuff of fancy. Everything she did and said was to a purpose, even now. But that didn't mean that purpose was to be distrusted. Kas linked them in death. "Tell me. Please."

"On one condition: that my words do not leave this room. They do not reach the ears of your friends, and most certainly not Sevaka's. I will not have them endangered."

"You have my word as a Knight of Essamere."

For a long moment, Rosa wasn't certain the pledge would be enough. Then the older woman nodded.

"Last week, before he died, Kasamor came to me with . . . suspicions . . . They concerned a senior member of the Grand Council. Someone in whom the Republic has invested much of its trust. Allegations of bribery and blackmail. Of influence squandered and sold in the name of the Crowmarket. Of constructs stolen from the foundry to who knows what purpose." She shook her head. "Even now, with everything that has happened, I find it so difficult to believe."

"Who? Who did Kasamor name?"

"Are you certain you wish to know?"

Know the name of the traitor who'd wanted her beloved dead? "More than anything."

"Viktor. It was Viktor Akadra."

Rosa swallowed to clear a sudden tightness in her throat. "No! That's impossible. You must be mistaken."

"These are not my words, child. They are Kasamor's. Viktor approached him several months ago. He wanted to know if Kasamor retained any of his father's contacts within the Crowmarket. Of course, Kasamor didn't. He told Viktor as much, and warned him off getting involved with those scum." She sighed. "Viktor prevailed upon their friendship, and begged he reveal nothing. It was only when Kasamor discovered the extent of Viktor's corruption that he broke his confidence. If only he'd done so sooner!"

"Kasamor would have told me!"

But even as she spoke, doubt trickled beneath the words. Kasamor *had* said something to her about the vranakin, hadn't he? He'd known the kernclaw for what it was, and what its arrival denoted. And his manner in the moments before his death ... like he'd expected it.

"I can only assume he sought to protect you," said Ebigail.

"But Viktor? He's the best of us! Kasamor must have been mistaken." Rosa clung to the words, drawing strength from them. "Viktor's my friend."

"And he was Kasamor's too, for all the good that did him. How well do you truly know him?"

Rosa glowered at her. She'd known Viktor nearly a decade, ever since she'd been a lowly squire and he the commander of the 7th. In all that time, she'd learned few intimacies. Yes, she counted him among her closest friends, but Viktor had always stood apart, his life shrouded from her sight. No. Viktor had saved Kas, hadn't he? From Aske Tarev's soured pride. Why do that, only to kill him later? Because he'd known Aske wouldn't have finished things? Because he wanted to be sure?

Or had something changed? She hated that she even considered the possibility.

"No," she said. "I don't believe it."

"Kasamor did," said Ebigail. "He told me he had proof. And where is Kasamor now?"

More doubt trickled in, cold and insidious. Kas. She'd failed him on the road. Could she fail him now? "Why are you telling me this?"

"Because you demanded I do so."

Rosa closed her eyes. She had, hadn't she? "What is to happen?"

Ebigail grimaced and set her cup and saucer aside. "I don't know. Not for certain. I cannot let this matter rest, but whatever proof Kasamor had is lost. Poor Hadon will not readily believe unfounded claims."

Queen's Ashes, could it be true? Rosa exhaled. Yes, Viktor was her friend and Ebigail a creature of uncertain motive. But there were duties beyond friendship. To the Council. To the precepts of Essamere. And to Kasamor most of all. If there were truth to be found, it was for her to seek it out. However painful the answers.

"What would you have me do?"

Ebigail's eyes widened. "Nothing! My dear child, until you told me of the kernclaw, all I had were suspicions and a mother's regrets. My thoughts are a maelstrom. When they've settled I can perhaps find some way through this thicket of tears. Until then, you must promise me you'll do nothing foolish. Viktor may be in the Southshires, but the vranakin are everywhere. One hint – one whisper – could be enough to doom you."

Rosa flexed her fingers and stared down at her forearm. The wound from Malachi's paper knife had left no scar and was hidden by her sleeve. It served as a reminder nonetheless.

"Let them come. I'm hard to kill."

She glanced up. Ebigail's face was twisted with an emotion she'd never seen before.

Fear. For her? How things had changed. Determination burned away confusion, leaving purpose in its stead.

"I promise you, I'll do nothing foolish. But if Viktor is responsible for Kasamor's death . . . " She jerked to her feet and offered Ebigail a formal bow. "My thanks for the tea and your kindness both, Lady Kiradin. I'll keep your warnings close to my heart."

Ebigail rose and embraced her. "See that you do. I do not want to lose you as I lost my son."

Marek set the front door to.

"Is she gone?" Lady Ebigail asked from further down the hall.

"Yes, lady."

"And you're certain she didn't see Tailinn depart?"

Marek bristled. As if he'd let a foundry proctor use the front door frequented by guests of quality. "Quite certain, lady."

She nodded her contentment, her thoughts plainly far afield. "Good. It would be a shame for so timely a convergence to be spoiled by untimely departure."

By contrast, Lady Sevaka's expression was full of storm clouds. "Kasamor would hate you for using Rosa like this."

"If your brother had any wits worth respecting, he'd have married her long ago and we'd none of us be in this situation. He was fool enough to get himself killed, but he serves his family still. And so will Roslava. Young Viktor will bring this Republic low. He must be removed, but I cannot be seen to act in this – my dislike is too well known. Those who would disbelieve an accusation from me will experience no such reluctance should it come from one known to be his friend, and a hero of the Republic, no less. Yes. She'll do very well indeed."

"What if Viktor's innocent?"

"I'm sure he is." Lady Ebigail's lip twitched. "But if the accusation doesn't stick, I'm sure I'll find something else that will."

The daughter glanced away. "And Kasamor? Don't you care who ordered his death?"

"I doubt the truth will ever come out. Your brother had a gift for cultivating enemies, and you know how this city of ours can be. However, I see no sense in letting events, however regrettable, go to waste."

Lady Sevaka folded her arms tight across her chest, the action part self-comfort and part shield. "There are times when I weep to know that you are my mother."

Lady Ebigail closed the distance with a single stride. She seized her daughter by the chin and forced her head back against the wall. "Yes, your tears ever come easily, don't they? Especially when they flow for you, and you alone."

Marek looked away, unable to bear witness to the acrimony between his beloved mistresses.

"If my methods appal you so, follow her!" snapped Lady Ebigail. "Follow and confess all! But know it's not just my future you throw away, but yours too. Now is not the time for weakness."

"No," said Sevaka. "It's a time for strength. But as you said, Kasamor was worth ten of me. I've everything *but* strength. Just as you've always wanted."

Lady Ebigail released her grip and stroked her daughter's cheek. "I know this is hard, but it will all be worth it in the end. For us, and for the Republic. You need only have faith."

Twenty-Nine

The second Hadari assault died much the same as the first. The jutting faces of the gorge funnelled them along the narrow roadway, straight into a wall of Tressian shields. Kraikons anchored the line at either end and stiffened resolve across its centre. Magic crackled as they swept the shadowthorns into the Raven's embrace.

Heavy cavalry could have broken that wall, with lances striking at the gallop. But no horse could maintain momentum across the steep and broken ground for that one unstoppable punch. Swift-hooved outriders could have skirted the flanks, but the gorge's sides were too steep and too thickly forested.

And so the shadowthorn infantry died in the valley. They turned the waters of the Greshmar red with blood, and gold with lifeless armour. Steel clashed. Men and women spat and swore as shield ground against shield. Then the drums fell silent, and horns bellowed for the retreat. The Hadari fled, leaving a tidemark of dead.

Captain Sark cheered with his soldiers. He shared their exhilaration as he had shared their striving. Or nearly so. An officer led. He didn't brawl in the mud with the common ranks. He'd witnessed both assaults in the company of his Prydonis castellans – the only heavy knights in his sparse command.

The last of the Hadari banners went back. Sark swept his unblooded sword skyward so Lumestra would better see the victory he had wrought.

"Release the simarka!"

Shields parted. Bronze lions loped away and bowled fleeing men to the ground. A handful of shadowthorns fought, facing death with the bravado of the doomed. One even split a simarka's brow with a desperate stroke of his war hammer. He perished even as golden magic arced free, borne away by another of the lions as he readied another blow. The simarka pounced anew, maws bloody.

"Call them back!" Sark cried. "Their work's done."

The simarka halted as if at a thrown lever and prowled back down the hill. Survivors scrambled for the safety of the crest.

"Fine work, my lads and lasses," Sark bellowed. "No shadowthorn's a match for Tressian steel!"

Two-score weary voices joined his cheer. Silence reigned elsewhere, broken only by the moans of the wounded.

"They'll come again! We'll send them all into the mists before they're done!"

Again, murmur-broken silence was his only reply. Fine. Let them be as sullen as they wished, so long as they fought. And Queen's Ashes, they fought well. No finer soldier than a Tressian. The gorge could be held through Third Dawn, if need be.

The able-bodied dragged wounded comrades away to the physicians. The dead were hauled to the gorge-side, the ceremony halted only long enough for their quivers to be rifled for precious quarrels, and pockets emptied of coin.

Sark gulped from his water skin and eyed the sun. Evening was drawing in. Would the Hadari come again? Or would they recognise their folly? A novice of war fresh from the chapterhouses could have held that road with a hundred men. Sark still had more than two hundred and fifty blades who could stand the line. The Hadari had lost near twice that number since day's dawning. A heroic trade, all told. Not bad for a younger son of a lesser bloodline.

Lesser for the moment. Victory elevated a man.

Screams rang out from the north-eastern heights where the running battle between Sark's pavissionaires and shadowthorn huntsmen yet raged.

An enquiring glance sought the turtle-like silhouettes of the former among the trees by the heavy steel-rimmed shields on their backs. The nearest pavissionaire turned, setting the faded lion-insignia of his shield to the foe as he reloaded his crossbow. Timber splintered beneath an arrow's strike. The pavissionaire staggered and lurched about. A second arrow took him in the throat before he could loose a shot.

"Sergeant?" Sark beckoned to Sergeant Kalvet. "Take a dozen men and three simarka. I want the slope cleared before the next attack."

"Yes, sir." Kalvet threw an unhappy salute and strode away. Hooves clattered on the road behind, marking the arrival of a young woman with a herald's eagle at her collar. She was filthy with the dirt of the road, and her uniform damp with sweat. Not a good look for a soldier, to Sark's way of thinking.

"Captain Sark, sir?" She threw a weary salute. "I've a message from Governor Yanda."

"Very well, let's have it." He held out his hand. The herald made no move to present the expected envelope. "Well, where is it?"

The herald drew back in her saddle, eyes wary. "The rest of the army has withdrawn to Kreska. She requests you begin your retreat."

Sark frowned. Any missive of worth was delivered by letter, not a herald's uncertain memory. As for the implied criticism ...

"We have the shadowthorns at a disadvantage. One I do not intend to yield."

The herald's gaze took in the wounded. "The Governor was insistent. *Very* insistent."

"Now look here, Herald ... ?"

"Morvinna, sir."

" ... Herald Morvinna. If we break cover, the shadowthorns will run us down."

"The Governor has two companies of wayfarers ready to cover your retreat."

"Then she can send them to bolster our line. I can end this. Send the whole damned lot of them running back to the border!"

Drumbeats crashed back. The shield wall tensed. Taut gazes scoured the empty, arrow-studded slope searching for the first banner, the first spear tip.

"Deliver my words, Morvinna, or join the line." Sark swept his sword down and shouted to be heard over the din. "Stand firm, lads and lasses! Third time's the charm!"

The line rippled. The second and third ranks braced against a new swarm of arrows.

None came.

A banner-pole broke the crest. A silken flag followed, the silver moon at its centre shining even at a distance. A woman in emerald robes and delicate golden scale bore it aloft from the back of a caparisoned rowan horse. Sark was more used to the sight of cataphracts. Tall, broad-shouldered men in heavy scale, their horses as armoured as they.

"It's a woman," muttered Morvinna.

"Shadowthorn slatterns don't fight," said Sark. "Unless it's over coin changing hands."

More figures appeared on the crest. More *women*. Close-fitting white robes and half-masks, and not a sword between them. Sark wracked his brain for lessons long-forgotten. Holy women, weren't they? Lunassera. Like serenes, but immodest in their mode of dress. Just as Ashana, the goddess they worshipped, was less modest in all manners than radiant Lumestra.

The banner-woman's horse began its descent. The others followed behind like mourners behind a funeral procession. Song drifted into the gorge. The words were sharp-accented and heathen. The notes bound to close-harmonies that were mournful, and yet somehow thick with joy.

"The men are too scared to face us," Sark crowed. "So they've sent their wives and daughters."

If the shadowthorns thought he shared their quaint belief in the sanctity of womanhood, they were destined for an unwelcome surprise.

"Down shields!" he roared. "Take aim!"

Heavy crossbows readied in the rear ranks and were set upon the shoulders of those in front. Sark eyed the oncoming lunassera. They were right on the edge of killing range, but a little blood would cool their ardour. And there'd been plenty of time to reload.

"Loose!"

Triggers slapped against stocks. Death hissed through the air.

No lunassera fell. If any staggered, Sark did not see it.

"Reload!"

Still the women came on. Not at a run, but at that same, purposeful walk. The crest behind filled with the emerald robes and golden scale of shadowthorn warriors. Not in formation, but in the manner of an expectant crowd. Sark's unease fanned to fear.

"Loose!" The word almost caught in his throat.

Again, the air filled with quarrels. Again, they passed through the lunassera like wind through a meadow.

The banner-woman hauled her horse to a halt. She let the reins fall to her saddle. Her hand found the grips of her sword.

"Reload!" bellowed Sark. "Release the simarka!"

The nearest proctor jerked about, his golden scarf trailing. "Captain, I don't think ... "

"Do it! Bring them down!"

Shields parted. Bronze blurs sprang away up the hillside, gaining speed as they closed. And then they simply ... stopped. As one, the simarka downed haunches and sat amid the carnage of the roadway.

Morvinna touched her brow in the sign of the sun. "They can't see them."

Sark spurred his horse towards the proctor who'd voiced objection. Leaning low in the saddle, he seized the man by his collar and dragged him off his feet.

"What are they doing?" he bellowed. "Have them tear those holy drabs apart!"

The proctor cuffed at Sark's wrist. "They can't. You said it yourself! They're holy! Blessed by Ashana!"

Like the Forbidden Places were blessed by Ashana, or by Jack, or by another of Lumestra's cursed siblings. And if the simarka couldn't see the lunassera, neither could the kraikons.

"Loose! Loose, damn you all!"

Crossbows rattled a third time, shooting far over the heads of the frozen simarka. This time the rank of women shuddered and left bodies behind on the slope.

The banner-woman drew her sword. Moonlight spiralled skywards as a perfect white flame. "Ashanael Brigantim!"

"*Ashanael Brigantim!*" sang the lunassera. The words spilled from the rhythm of their bleak, beautiful hymn with the inevitability of moonrise.

As one, they charged.

"Loose!" bellowed Sark. "Loose!"

Too late, he realised that not all in the shield wall had reloaded. What should have been a rush of quarrels sounded as a ragged stutter. A volley that should have sucked the heart from the charge felled barely a dozen lunassera. The rear ranks of the shield wall, whose halberds should have been levelled to greet the charge, were still tangled in the business of reload.

"Shields! Brace!"

Even then, Sark knew it was too late.

The banner-woman crashed against the front rank. Her sword hacked down. White fire surged. A shield struck the roadway, smote in two. Its bearer reeled, his face masked in blood. A halberd thrust from the second rank. The woman twisted past the heavy blade. Her counterblow split the halberdier's helm. Still keening her battle hymn, she spurred into the gap.

The lunassera came after. Their hands were no longer empty, but clutched spears of angular, silver light, like shards of splintered glass, or the spirits of smelted weapons. Shields shuddered. Blinded soldiers cried out as the shard-spears cheated shield rims to draw blood behind.

One lunassera leapt impossibly high, her skyward climb hastened by the locked hands braced beneath her bare feet. She descended with spear braced and landed in the third rank. A scream sounded. Silver flashed. Blood spattered blue tabards. The space around her bloomed as soldiers shrank away. Another lunassera dropped into the clearing. And another.

Sark watched it all frozen in his saddle. Unable to speak. Barely able to think. This couldn't be happening. His perfect battle. His victory. Swept away by shadowthorn witches come singing out of myth. It wasn't fair. It wasn't right.

The shield wall crumpled, battered from the front and eaten away from within. Kraikons looked on, silent and unmoving, deaf to their proctors' desperate commands. Sark was dimly aware of thundering hooves as the Prydonis castellans charged to bolster the line.

They were an age too late. Desperate men and women streamed back along the road, past the immobile kraikons. Lunassera came with them, steps graceful as a dancer's. Each spear-thrust placed not with a warrior's frenzy, but an artist's grace.

But he couldn't tear his eyes from the banner-woman and her burden.

Sark had learned from the finest tutors coin could buy. He'd won tourneys of the sword, and always from horseback. He knew, with the certainty of stone, that there was no finer student of that particular art than he. He recognised with equal surety that the banner-woman was a novice, borne to victory through wild abandon more than skill.

Though sheeted with blood, the silk banner glimmered with brilliant light that echoed the sword's darting flame. Beautiful. Perfect. Too perfect. A witch's talisman, drawing favour from a heathen goddess.

Determination kindling fire in his blood, Sark spurred forward. His sword, previously so heavy in his hand, deflected a spear blow and swept a lunassera from her feet.

Fleeing soldiers blocked his path. He struck them aside with the flat of his sword. A soldier sprawled face-first on the road, a spear in his spine. Sark rode on through a gorge filling with the dead and dying, haunted by bleak song. And there ahead of him was the banner and the flaming sword.

"Witch!"

He bellowed the word, drawing on hatred learned at high altar. Ashana the Traitor. Ashana the Jealous Sister. Corrupter of Light. He rowelled his steed and levelled his sword. Even the greatest battles ended in a single stroke.

The banner-woman turned. The blow meant to split her skull glanced off the golden circlet about her brow. She flinched in the saddle, the banner drooping. The keening ceased.

Sensing victory, Sark lunged.

White fire checked his steel. Heart pounding, Sark back-cut at her throat.

Again fire blazed between them, the incandescent blade rigid and immoveable. Beyond, dark eyes stared unblinking from a still face. Sark's fervour melted away. No more the avenging hand of Lumestra, no more the valiant knight. He felt scarcely even a man, but an ant staring up in terror at a boot's descent. He knew the truth of himself. A failure, a braggart and a bully. A man who in his arrogance had doomed those who took his orders.

But worst of all was that the woman knew all that. He was nothing to her. When night fell, he'd be one face among a roster of dead. Another victim of a moon-sent witch.

Weeping with anger and fear, Sark ripped back his sword and swung anew.

Fire rushed to greet him.

The last hoof-beats faded, and the gorge shook with song. Not the madrigal whose unfamiliar verses had sprung full-formed from Melanna's lips as she'd ridden to battle. This was the cruder bombast of a warrior's victory. Hammers rang out a pulsing rhythm as they broke apart paralysed constructs and banished the crackling magic within.

Melanna stood apart from the menfolk. Not one of their number had dared approach her. Her head still ringing from the sword-blow that had nearly ended her life, she drank in the cruel, merciless beauty she had wrought.

The gorge was choked with dead, both Hadari and Tressian. The former were already stacked for the midnight pyres. The latter would keep until later – and if the vermin ate their fill before then? Such were the fortunes of war. But these were not the bodies that grieved Melanna the most. Many lunassera would whisper no more prayers to Ashana. Nor could they usher the gravely wounded to her embrace, for they were now at her side themselves. Slain because they'd followed her into battle.

And that last man she'd killed. Less a man at the end, and more a frightened boy.

Was this how all warriors felt after a battle won? How did they stand it?

But if the sight was heart-wrenching, the smell was worse. The thick, rich tang of blood clung to her.

"*Savim!* You are wounded."

Sera drew closer, the grace of her movements lent sharpness by her bloodstained robes. Melanna heard concern in her voice – her expression, as ever, lay hidden beneath a silvered mask.

She touched a hand to her brow. The fingers came away red. She'd come even closer to death than she'd believed. But the goddess had preserved her. Or had she? What if the goddess had forsaken her for marching to war in her name? What if it was just good fortune? What if it ran out?

"I'll live. I'm sorry about your sisters."

Sera's lips twitched. "They died for the goddess, *savim*. We will pray for them. We will weep. And we will be the stronger for their sacrifice."

Melanna's stomach churned. But they hadn't died in the goddess's service, had they? They'd died for her. The thought shook her to her core. What made it worse was that she knew she'd let it be so again, and without hesitation. After all, that was an emperor's burden.

Sera brushed a hand to Melanna's cheek. "You have taken a first step today, Ashanal. Now your father will know your true worth, as he will know the worth of the lunassera."

Ashanal. Daughter of Ashana. A poetic name of which Melanna felt unworthy. And as for her father ... She dreaded the conversation to come almost as much as she longed for it. Was that now her life? Truths held in opposition?

"*Savim*." An older man in Immortal's scale and a warleader's midnight silks splashed through the Greshmar's shallow waters. The impassive mask of his helm stood stark contrast to the vigour of his tone. Head bowed in respect, he dropped to one knee. "You have my thanks for the victory. And for avenging my son, who fell in the first charge."

Melanna nodded stiffly. "He served Empire and Goddess well, warleader. As does his father."

The Immortal's armour shifted as his chest swelled. In pride, or in grief? Probably a little of both. "It is my honour, *savim*. Please ... when the pyres are lit, will you lead the prayers, to guide my son on his Last Ride?"

Melanna hesitated. The rites were the business of priests, not princessas. But Sera offered a surreptitious nod, and she found herself echoing it.

"If that is your wish." She took a deep breath. "But rise. I will not have you shy from me."

Haltingly, he obeyed. "Yes, *savim*."

"Ashanal," corrected Sera, a warning edge in her voice.

The Immortal nodded. "Ashanal ... And there is one more thing."

"And that is?" asked Melanna.

"We have prisoners," he replied. "Enough to slow us down and too many to set loose to fight again. What is your order?"

Her order? Melanna stared down the gorge to a knot of bloodied and miserable Tressians ringed by spears and watchful eyes. She knew the decision the warleader sought. Too many had died that day for clemency. The warleader's son, and those who had fallen at his side could not ride into Otherworld without companions. Better it be those who had brought about his death than his surviving kinsmen.

And yet, it was one thing to kill in battle. Quite another to order the deaths of the defenceless. To enter the mists was death, whether you did so through failing mortality, or because magic opened the door and duty bore you through. She couldn't do it. She *wouldn't*.

She had to.

For a heartbeat, Melanna thought she saw the Huntsman watching her from among the trees. She thought she heard his voice. *This is what you desired. And now you must make it your own.*

She couldn't show weakness. Not now. The history of the Empire was a history written in blood. If she was not prepared to author that tale . . .

"Put them to death," she said. "All of them."

Thirty

A crisp, strident blare of buccinas awoke Josiri from wine-sodden dreams. Wincing at the bright evening sun, he edged to the window and stared down at Eskavord.

Beyond Branghall's wall, a crowd gathered outside the reeve's manor. The marketplace was full. Not of soldiers – though soldiers stood on the periphery – but of ordinary folk. *Properly* full, from the lychfields of the church to the walled bank of the river. A double-line of blue council tabards stood at silent attention beneath the manor's balcony. Josiri frowned. There hadn't been a reeve in Eskavord since his mother's death, and Governor Yanda had never been one for speeches. Akadra. It had to be Akadra. Not content with all he'd taken, he now eyed Eskavord. How long before he sought the dukedom alongside?

"Bastard's welcome to it." As he spoke, Josiri knew the words a lie.

Even through the haze of alcohol and self-pity, a part of him yearned to go down there. But only a small part, tamped down and wearied. The rest reached for another bottle.

"Sorry about that." Revekah pulled on the "borrowed" helmet. "You'll sleep it off."

The Tressian soldier – now bound, gagged and wedged firmly behind the stable's stalls – said nothing. Revekah fought a twang of distaste. The lad looked so young. Everyone did, the older you got. Despite the lad's occupation – despite the creak in her bones – Revekah felt as much a bully as she had at her first meeting with Katya Trelan.

She still remembered that night, clear as Selanni crystal. She'd caught the privileged little snot sneaking about town at an unrespectable hour. The rest of the patrol had egged her on to throw the girl a scare. Barely of serving age herself, Revekah had acceded and dragged the eight-year-old back through the streets to the jail.

Katya hadn't wept, hadn't wailed. But the look in her eyes ... Well, that was where you saw truth, in the eyes. Front couldn't hide it, nor pride conceal it. It wasn't until years later, when Kevor Trelan left for Council, never to return, that Revekah marked that same desperate worry in the eyes of the woman who'd since become her dearest friend.

Funny how things changed. And how much stayed the same.

Revekah straightened her sword-belt. Close enough to pass muster. With a last tug on the tabard she left the dung-laden confines of the stables behind for the crowded streets. Soldiers hurried east. Everyone else headed west towards the marketplace.

Revekah joined the former, taking care to put snap in her step. One of the first lessons she'd learned back in the day: look like you belonged, and you could go wherever you liked. So it proved. No one challenged her as she trod the cobbled road straight through East Gate and out onto the muster field.

The black pavilion couldn't have more obviously belonged to nobility without squires standing at attention with wine and roast swan. Unguarded, which was all for the best. Getting in and out would be tricky enough without enemies close at hand.

Careful to maintain her steady "I belong here" pace, Revekah slipped inside. As her eyes adjusted to the gloom, she felt a pang of disappointment. The interior was almost frugal. A blanket-strewn cot, a trestle table, two folding chairs and a pair of haversacks. Hardly the decadent vista she'd expected.

And no Akadra – although that had been a slim hope. Still, that was how life went. Hurry up, do nothing and wait. The owner would return before his army marched.

And then she'd kill him. For Josiri. For Anastacia. And for Katya. For Katya, most of all.

"Time to prove your patience, old girl," she breathed. Soft, heavy footfalls thumped beyond canvas. Revekah stiffened and reached for her dagger. "Or maybe not."

The tent folds parted.

"Forgive the intrusion, my lord, but a herald's . . . " Kurkas let the flaps fall closed. "What do we have here?"

Revekah winced. Of all the men to cross her path, it *had* to be Kurkas. If he recognised her . . .

She threw a salute. "Was looking for his lordship, sir. A message from the duke."

Kurkas nodded. "What it is to be popular . . . No one ever teach you it's poor manners to enter an officer's tent without invitation?"

She swore silently. "The duke said it was important, sir."

Kurkas snorted. "I'm certain he did. Go on, give me your message and be on your way."

"The duke said it was for Lord Akadra only."

Kurkas crooked the brow above his eyepatch and rolled his remaining eye. "I shall be the soul of discretion. Let's have it!"

"As you wish."

Revekah sprang. Seizing a handful of Kurkas' tunic, she hooked a heel behind his boot. She bore him to the ground, knees astride his chest. Her forearm slammed against his throat, choking off his cry of alarm. The oiled dagger slid free and arced down.

Kurkas' forearm slammed into hers. The dagger shuddered to a stop an inch from his throat.

"Changed my mind," he gasped. "Reckon this is a message best left for his lordship."

Revekah grunted and ripped the dagger back for another blow.

Kurkas bucked beneath her. His hand closed around her throat.

Starlight exploded behind Revekah's eyes as his forehead slammed into hers. A heavy shove sent her backwards. Blinking furiously, nausea crowding her throat, she staggered to her feet.

Kurkas reeled unsteadily upright. He blinked away a trickle of blood, the gesture disturbing his tangle of greying hair. "Yeah. Never doing that again."

"You're right about that."

Revekah let the dagger fall and ripped her sword free. Kurkas' shoulder took her in the chest. He crushed her against the tent's heavy central pole before she'd time to swing. His fingers hooked beneath her helm and dragged it away. A beady eye stared out from an unshaven face.

"Thought I recognised that voice. Captain Halvor, eh? Years ain't been kind."

"You're one to talk," spat Revekah.

"Years alone didn't take my arm, nor my eye. Which reminds me, you still owe me for both."

"Then you can add this to my debt!"

Revekah brought her knee up between his legs. Kurkas yelped and sank away.

"Well played," he gasped.

Revekah lunged.

"You're certain of this? I'll not think less of you for changing your mind."

Calenne sighed with exasperation. "How many times must you ask that question?"

Viktor shot her a sidelong glance as they left the quartermaster's tent. Her travelling clothes topped with borrowed breastplate, sword and a rich king's-blue cloak, Calenne looked every inch her mother's daughter.

"At least once a day."

"I'm giving you my hand, Viktor. Not my soul."

"That's not the part that concerns me." The wedding, and all the complications it awakened, were a problem for another day. A day that might never come.

Her forehead wrinkled, then smoothed. "I know. I'm not a fool. I'm prepared for the risk. At least ... " She paused, her lip twisting as if chewing on bitter fruit. "At least I'll have done *something* for someone other than myself."

Would she say that if she'd lost as many comrades as he? If she knew not only the cost, but the tally of blood and fear in which the reckoning would be levied? Viktor wasn't sure. Then again, who was he to judge? Guilt and duty differed only in the timing. Perhaps he only embraced one to avoid the other? And in the end, what did it matter if the gathering war claimed Calenne alongside the hundreds it would surely take before it was done? To the world, almost nothing. But to Viktor himself?

Perhaps it wasn't her commitment he questioned, but his own.

Lost on a sea of troubled thought, he let most of the distance to his tent fall away before speaking. "Your mother would be proud."

Calenne snorted. "My whole life, I've been surrounded by people certain that Katya's voice carried to them from beyond the pyre. But this time? Maybe you're right."

Viktor nodded. "I'm certain . . . "

A dozen paces ahead, the tent shuddered. A man's cry of pain split the air.

Viktor covered the distance at a flat run and ripped the tent-folds aside. He took in the prone, bloody Kurkas; the white-haired woman with a naked sword. She spun towards him, face contorting with anger.

His shadow erupted, a torrent of icy darkness that flooded the space between them. The woman screamed as it gathered her up. It twisted the sword from her grip, wended about her limbs like hissing snakes, then hoisted her a foot above the ground.

"Who are you?" he demanded. "What is the meaning of this?"

Even through his anger, Viktor recognised the pointlessness of the first question and the stark obviousness of the second. More than that, he felt the first uneasy glimmer at how suddenly and completely the shadow had burst free, and without conscious command. Elzar had been right. It wanted to be used.

The woman gasped as the shadow-coils constricted. "You'll have nothing from me."

"Viktor!"

Thin fingers closed around his arm – a reminder that Calenne would see what came next. Drawing down a deep breath, he checked the shadow's contraction. "I want answers!"

Kurkas staggered to his feet. "Said she had a message for you, sir. From the duke. Seemed said message took the form of a beating and a ripper's grin."

Relief that Kurkas yet lived eased Viktor's temper another notch. He dragged the shadow back deep. The woman crumpled to a heap. "Do you need a physician, captain?"

"Me, sir?" Kurkas swayed. "Made the error of head-butting a helmet. She's still a fighter, after all these years."

The comment made Viktor look closer. As his anger fell to a dull ebb, he put a name to the face. "Revekah Halvor. You're a notorious woman. Did Josiri truly send you to slit my throat?"

He didn't believe so. The Josiri he'd seen would never have the courage to order an assassination.

"I came here to kill you *for* him," she snarled. "For what you intend for the Southshires. *And* for what you did to Anastacia."

Viktor's conscience seethed anew. "I intend nothing for the Southshires but the best of fortunes."

"It's true, Revekah," said Calenne. "I've seen the warrants. Viktor will set you free of the Council. Would have done already if my idiot brother hadn't refused him."

Her scowl deepened. "So you *are* with him. I weep for your mother's loss."

"Then stop! While you and Josiri carry on like frightened brats, Viktor's trying to save us!"

"And Anastacia?"

"A mistake," said Viktor. "One I'll gladly undo, if I can."

Kurkas cleared his throat. "Permission to take this harridan outside and give her a good hanging, sir? Takes the fight out of a body, a nice bit of rope about the neck."

The fingers on his arm tightened. "Viktor . . . She was Katya's dearest friend. You can't."

He shook Calenne aside. "She's an outlaw, and by her own confession came to murder me."

He crouched and stared into Revekah's eyes. She gazed back without fear.

"And you're northwealder scum," she said, "and a witch into the bargain. I won't beg clemency from the likes of you."

Viktor nodded, and straightened. "Captain?"

"Sah?"

"Escort Captain Halvor from the camp. We'll keep her weapons to prevent any further . . . rash behaviour on the way."

"Sorry sir, sounded like you said . . . "

"Then you heard me right. See to it. At once."

Revekah regarded him through half-lidded eyes. "Why?"

"Because I kill only if called to." He offered his hand. "There will be death enough in the days to come. I intend to fight for your home, and I am woefully outmatched. You can help, or you can live with the aftermath. But choose swiftly."

She struck his hand aside and clambered stiffly to her feet.

Viktor nodded. He understood Halvor's enmity, even if he could not respect it. But he didn't have to reciprocate. He only hoped he'd not regret his mercy.

"Captain Kurkas? Kindly see her out. And captain? I'd deem it a favour if nothing you witnessed here today became the stuff of campfire rumour."

Kurkas threw a salute. "Sah! What's one more secret between friends?"

Josiri ignored the first two cheers. By the time the easterly wind carried a third to Branghall's walls, curiosity overcame reluctance. He took to the balcony.

And on the balcony of the reeve's manor, one hand braced against the wooden handrail, and the other bunched in a fist and raised aloft, stood Calenne.

Calenne?

Josiri barely recognised her at first. Never in his life had he seen her in armour. It suited her. But how could it not? Their mother had never looked more herself than when arrayed for battle.

"You all know what has befallen." Calenne's windblown words crackled at the edges as words so often did with force behind them. "The Hadari have crossed the mountains. Our borderlands are burning."

There were no cheers now, nor any murmurs that reached Josiri's ears. They listened to her more raptly than they ever had him. Then again, what had he ever fed them, save platitudes? He'd tried to serve two masters, and in the striving disappointed both.

"My mother, Katya Trelan, was the Phoenix," shouted Calenne. "She died fighting those who sought to steal our lands. Now we are invaded once more. And it is in the nature of phoenixes to be reborn!"

A murmur broke out among the crowd. Josiri's knuckles whitened on the balcony balustrade.

"For the sake of your families, you followed my mother." All of a sudden, Calenne's gaze lifted from the marketplace. Josiri knew with certainty that she stared at him as unblinkingly as he at her. "For their sake again, I ask you to follow me!"

Josiri felt sick. Calenne in battle? It was everything he'd striven to prevent. One more failure to add to the list. He didn't have to ask who'd filled her head with such nonsense. Not with Viktor Akadra standing at her shoulder like some malignant shadow.

The crowd cheered. They cheered for her as they never had for him.

"We will be free of the Hadari," shouted Calenne. "And equals in the Republic once more. I have asked Lord Viktor Akadra, the Council's champion, to join his future to mine. Our families will stand united. The line of Trelan is rising, and the Southshires with it. At long last, we have the power to unmake injustices of the past, and we shall all of us have the future we long for!"

Josiri barely heard the cheers. He scarcely saw Akadra sink to one knee before Calenne. They intended to marry? Every time Josiri believed things could get no worse, they conspired to do so. But how could he stop her?

Muffled cheers rang out again as he entered the great hall. Self-pity boiled away into anger. His hands closed about a chair's backrest. A wordless, heartsick cry ripping free of his lips, he flung the chair across the chamber. It shattered against flagstones beside the ruin of the upended table. With a choked snarl, Josiri sank to the floor and stared at the empty space where his mother's portrait had so recently hung.

"I've failed you," he muttered. "I've failed everyone."

She offered no answer, as he knew she could not. In any case, he knew it wasn't her voice he longed to hear, but Anastacia's.

He was still there when the cheers at last faded and the church bells rang for seven. The doors to the great hall parted to admit Revekah Halvor.

"I take it you've heard?"

"All of it." He paused, a new thought breaking to the surface. "How did you get in here?"

"Took a brooch and walked."

"The guards didn't stop you?"

She shrugged. "There aren't any. Akadra's co-opted them into his army."

"His army? A few hundred souls cowering in the shadow of kraikons."

"He'll have more soon enough. Your sister lit quite the fire. Might even shake a group or two out of the Wolf King's shadow."

Another reminder of failure. "Like I should have, you mean?"

"I didn't say that."

"But you meant it."

She sat beside him and rested her forearms on crooked knees. "I spoke to Calenne today. She told me you and I were carrying on like spoilt brats."

"She said that?"

"That's the gist." Revekah sighed. "What if she's right?"

"She isn't."

Josiri gritted his teeth. He wanted to shout, to scream. To rant about the unfairness of it all. But it wouldn't come. The aftermath of anger left emptiness stretching from toenails to fingertips and was never stronger than about his heart.

"I think ... " Revekah hesitated. "I think she might be. Why didn't you discuss Akadra's offer with me?"

"Why would I?"

The last of the warmth slipped from her voice. "Oh, is that how it is?"

"You think I should bother you with the lies of my mother's killer?" He shook his head, more to convince himself than her. "I'm ... "

"Lumestra help me! If the next words out of your mouth are to be 'I'm the duke, it was my decision', then I suggest you stay silent."

Despite a tone that could have shattered steel – despite even his own mood – Josiri smiled. "You've not spoken to me like that for a very long time."

"I haven't needed to. If I'd known about Akadra's offer, we might have been able to make a stronger case before Crovan and the others. Or maybe ... ?"

"I should have accepted? No."

"In the long run, what's the difference?"

"Not everyone will believe Calenne. Not everyone will follow her."

"Maybe not. But I do, and I will. I spoke with Akadra earlier today ... "

Josiri leapt to his feet. Things always *did* get worse. "What?"

"Wasn't by choice. Point of fact, I went there to murder him. Made a proper botch of it, too. He could've killed me. Should've. Instead, he lectured me." She rose, her eyes meeting Josiri's. He had the sense that she did so not to make a point, but because she was looking for something. "Your mother always wanted what's best for folks. Somewhere along the line, I've lost sight of that."

"Have you forgotten what he did? To my mother? To her dream?"

"I'm forgetting nothing. There's not a day goes by when I don't miss Katya. But it doesn't matter what Akadra did in the past, not if he's prepared to fight for us today. I'm going to stand with him. I'd like you to come with me."

He didn't believe her. He couldn't. Calenne, he almost understood. Especially with the prospect of escaping the family name. But Revekah? He stared up at the bare wall. It was strange. He couldn't even picture the portrait in his mind's eye any longer. Now, whenever he tried, he saw only Calenne.

"Then you're betraying her too," he said softly.

The stinging slap rocked Josiri back on his heels.

"How dare you. Katya was my friend. My sister. I fought for her. I'd have died for her. I'd have fought for her son, had he risen to it. I'll sure as Queen's Ashes not abandon her daughter." She shook her head. "You're a selfish, prideful ass. Katya would be ashamed."

She spat on the floor and strode away, leaving Josiri in accusing silence.

Thirty-One

Sevaka arrived at the Silverway as the bells rang for nine. Rosa barely recognised her. Vigorous strides practised on rolling decks had fallen away into uncertain, almost hesitant paces that barely twitched her grey skirts.

"Sevaka," Rosa stood and embraced the other woman. "Thank you for coming."

She offered a distant smile. "I'm sorry I wasn't home when you called. A busy day."

So it was a dour mood to match a dour dress? "I heard you've resigned your commission."

"Times change. Mother reminded me of broader duties."

They sat, and Rosa poured Sevaka a glass of wine from the chipped bottle. She'd not yet brought herself to touch her own glass.

"How are you feeling?" she asked.

"Like I've been dashed against the rocks at Scyllarest." Sevaka sipped her wine. "You?"

"You might say that this week's been a hell of a year."

"I like that." Sevaka raised her glass in toast. "A hell of a year. May our enemies have it worse in the week to come."

Rosa clinked her glass to Sevaka's. After the merest hesitation, she took a sip. It didn't much taste of anything. Then again, nothing did any longer.

"You have enemies?"

"I'm a Kiradin," said Sevaka. "Of course I have enemies. And I'm sure to inherit more from my mother."

"Such is life in the nobility."

Well, not for everyone. Rosa couldn't imagine her uncles having much in the way of grudges awaiting settlement. They lacked the ambition to cultivate any.

A drunken roar and clash of tankards erupted from a nearby table. Sevaka leaned back and stared up at the cross-hatched timber beams. "What about you? Enemies, I mean?"

Rosa scowled. "A few. And maybe one I never knew I had."

"I hope you're not talking about me."

Rosa took the childlike bleakness for affectation, so ill did it sit with the woman she'd drunk with so recently. "No. But I wanted to ask your advice."

"I'm not sure what my advice is worth. You'd be better asking Malachi."

Rosa shook her head. She'd considered that. "I can't. I need a different perspective. Malachi's too much the politician."

"Well, that's one thing of which I've never been accused. Tell me."

Rosa took another sip. She'd rehearsed this conversation in her head, but now it was upon her ... ?

"A fellow knight ... " She couldn't bring herself to use the word "friend". She told herself it was because that would too easily give Viktor's identity away. " ... stands accused of conspiring with the Crowmarket."

Sevaka gulped down a mouthful of wine and scraped her chair closer to the narrow table. "Do you trust the source?"

"The source is your mother."

The corner of her mouth twitched. "My question stands."

"Should I?"

Another gulp. Sevaka glowered at the empty glass and refilled it from the bottle. "My mother hears many things. More than I'd like. If she brought this to you, she must have had reason."

"I don't doubt that."

"Don't be coy. There's nothing you can say in my mother's absence that I haven't said to her face. Often at pitch and volume."

"You're not close, then?"

"Close? My brother was the only thing that mattered to her, as she has taken great pains to remind me. Everything else ... " She shook her head. "So on the one hand, you have the honour of your comrade, and the possibility that my mother is lying, or mistaken. On the other, you have honourless – and I'm guessing – criminal endeavour by said comrade."

Rosa nodded. "Pretty much."

"Have you considered walking away?"

"I can't!" She winced, having all but shouted the words. Fortunately no one had taken obvious interest. Bellowed denials were common currency in the Silverway. "I have a duty."

Honour and duty. Ever a complicated mix. She'd sworn to Ebigail that she'd not repeat the allegations to Sevaka, and this discussion edged close to breaking that promise. Why had she sought her counsel anyway? She barely knew the woman. But if Viktor *was* guilty, there was every possibility Malachi was compromised. Lilyana too. Who did that leave? No one her own age. At least, no one nearer than the border.

"Even so . . . " Sevaka toyed with her glass, eyes on its contents rather than on Rosa. "This comrade . . . he's well-connected?"

Rosa hesitated, but that alone would hardly give Viktor away. "He is."

"Then this will end with you trapped between my family and his. Are you prepared for that?"

She'd not thought of it that way. But Kas wouldn't have hesitated. "If there's guilt, yes."

"Then you need proof. Something more substantial than my mother's word."

Would it change anything if she knew the accusation came from Kas? Or had supposedly done so? "And if there's no proof?"

"Then my mother must be mistaken. And we can none of us be blamed for that."

Sevaka leaned back in her chair. Her manner was that of a duellist having delivered a deathblow, now content to wait out her opponent's last breath. And yet there was an intensity to her gaze . . . almost an eagerness. Such a pity she couldn't be told more, for Rosa had an inkling she'd make a capable ally.

"You're right. I need proof." Rosa stood, seized of fresh determination. "Thank you."

"So you've used me up, and now you're to abandon me on the

dockside?" Sevaka asked without rising. "You dragged me down here, you can at least share another drink or two. We never finished our toasts ... and I'm in no hurry to return to Freemont."

The need in her voice chimed kinship in Rosa's soul. There was little she could do at that hour save dwell on her next move. And unless she was prepared to aimlessly walk the city streets, she'd do so amid the lights and laughter of Abbeyfields. She couldn't face that. Alone in a crowd was alone in a crowd, whether you were a solitary drunk at a tavern table, or a guest in a family home.

"All right," she said. "But no politics, no intrigue and no brawling."

Sevaka beamed. "Agreed!"

She emptied her glass and called for another bottle.

"The situation is intolerable!" insisted Makrov. "I demand the Council take action!"

The archimandrite stood with his back to the window and the moonlit gardens, his scarlet robes ominous in the gloom. Outspread arms and rigid posture drew forth Marek's childhood memories of fiery sermons delivered from high pulpit. Expected in the solemn confines of a church, but wholly unfit for Lady Ebigail's drawing room.

Possibly the archimandrite knew no other way of making address. More likely he was too angry for appropriate behaviour.

"Demand, archimandrite? Lord Akadra and I are not children. Nor are we penitents seeking absolution. Kindly refrain from addressing us as such." Lady Ebigail returned her attention to her teacup, leaving her guest in the throes of speechless apoplexy.

Makrov glanced at Lord Akadra, reclining in the chair to Lady Ebigail's right and received a weary wave of the hand. "Sit *down*, Arzro. No one disputes your intentions, but as Ebigail says, we should manage a little decorum."

Makrov havered, grimaced, and finally lowered himself into a chair.

"Better." Lady Ebigail set aside her teacup and at last looked up at Makrov. "But I feel you may be overstating the situation, Àrzro."

"Overstating?" Makrov bit out. "Hadon's son mocks everything I've worked for! And with the Council's backing!"

"With the Council's *reluctant* backing," said Lady Ebigail. "The

Southshires have always been ... problematic. I think it's something about the soil. It grows rebellion as readily as crops."

"Then you agree nothing good comes of letting them off the leash?"

"Oh, of course. It has been my guiding light that orderliness arises from strength. Better a Republic unhappy at the boot on its throat than one lost to anarchy. If we cannot keep the darkness of the soul in check, we must trammel the flesh with steel and the mind with law."

"You're talking about tyranny," objected Lord Akadra. "It goes against everything the Republic was founded upon."

"The Republic was *founded* on tyranny, or have you become so addled with advancing years that you pay the Grand Council any heed? A crowd is no cleverer than the meanest dolt in its midst. No. Strong leadership is key."

"And you believe that Viktor can restore order to the Southshires?" Makrov threw a glance at Lord Akadra. "He was always a capable student, but altogether too ... forthright."

Lord Akadra snorted. "You mean 'rebellious'. We shall have to hope that he will rise to the occasion, and not pile kindling on a rising flame."

"Or a phoenix?" said Makrov. "You'll forgive me if that's not enough. Katya Trelan tore this Republic in two ... "

"Always this fascination with Katya Trelan, Arzro." Lady Ebigail shook her head in weary disdain. "It's not good to harbour obsession. Remember your predecessor. Years fretting over the lost sermons of Konor Belenzo sent poor Karkosa out of his wits."

"Emil was a righteous soul," Makrov said stiffly.

"An addled one," rumbled Lord Akadra. "He saw Malatriant's spirit in every shadow."

Lady Ebigail chuckled to herself. "You remember how he prayed for Lumestra to send a serathi to shield him from the Dark? Madness."

Makrov's jowls tightened in irritation. "Be that as it may, Katya Trelan's son ... "

Lady Ebigail arched a perfect eyebrow. "Did I misread your reports, Arzro? You led me to believe that Josiri was a model puppet, eager to do as the Council instructed."

He shifted in his chair. "I ... regret that I may have been mistaken."

"*Well.* That is unfortunate. Your assurances as to Josiri's good character went a long way to easing our minds when permitting Viktor's ... escapade. Isn't that right, Hadon?"

"Absolutely." Lord Akadra uttered the lie deadpan. "You see how this is a situation of your own making, Arzro?"

"I have made penance for my misjudgements," said Makrov stiffly. "But the fact remains that the situation must be rectified. Lumestra demands it."

"Oh don't go *on* so," snapped Lady Ebigail. "You'll burst something important, and that rug has been in my family for five generations. Lumestra demands nothing. The voice echoing about that thick skull of yours is your own pride, no more, no less. First the mother makes a fool of you, and then the son."

To Marek's surprise, the archimandrite didn't back down. "And what of order? What of anarchy? Those who are unprepared for necessary deeds are soon replaced by those who are."

Lord Akadra leaned forward, his features stony. "Is that a threat, Arzro?"

"Not one of my making. That son of yours ... "

"Enough!" Lady Ebigail stood abruptly, her beauty stern in the glow of firestone lanterns. "This bickering gets us nowhere. There is opportunity here, if we have but the wit to seek it."

Lord Akadra's unblinking gaze didn't waver from Makrov. "We're listening, Ebigail."

"There is, at heart, very little wrong with the common folk of the Southshires. True, they are lazy and tend towards the dull-witted, but they need only a firm hand at the tiller. Alas, simple folk are easily led astray. By troublemakers we have singularly failed to capture, much less eliminate."

"It's not the fault of our soldiers," said Lord Akadra. "There are too many Forbidden Places in the Southshires. Without kraikons ... "

"But if your son is successful, the scoundrels will no longer be in hiding. They'll be ours for the taking."

Lord Akadra grimaced. "The Council promised clemency. Viktor bears documentation with our signatures, and our seal."

Makrov snorted. "Promises to traitors have no validity. There will be few tears shed at Council, save by the likes of Lord Reveque. But we don't have the soldiers."

"We won't need many," said Lady Ebigail. "One regiment would do. We'll wait for this Hadari nonsense to run its course. I've no doubt Viktor will have his triumph – he *is* singularly determined – but even triumph will leave the dissidents weary and vulnerable. We'll take the ringleaders, Josiri Trelan included, before they even know their danger. The common folk will fall into line. They did fifteen years ago."

"Much good it did us in the long run."

"History is a bloodstain," sniffed Lady Ebigail. "One that must be re-inked ere it fades from memory."

"We don't have a regiment," said Lord Akadra. "They're committed to reinforcing the border."

"We have a few companies of the 7th, and the 12th are only a day away – they're nearer the Southshires than we are. There was some confusion surrounding their orders and they made a late march." Lady Ebigail offered a thin smile. "And we hardly need them on the border any longer. I understand Warleader Maggad woefully underestimated the task ahead of him and was bloodied accordingly. The Ravonn will hold."

Makrov rubbed his chin and nodded. "And if the Hadari take the Southshires?"

"Then the 12th will fight to reverse the situation." A note of sorrow crept into her voice. "And to avenge those poor, patriotic souls who perished for the good of the Republic."

Lord Akadra gripped the arm of his chair. "Raven's Eyes, Ebigail. That's my son you're talking about!"

"A parent can make no greater sacrifice than their child." She shrugged. "Viktor's a survivor. I don't imagine the Hadari will end his tale."

"And the Council," said Makrov. "They will support this ... endeavour?"

"Anton will stand with us," she replied. "He would have been here, but had to bury that fool of a daughter. Loss will make him ... tractable. We'll have his support."

"You won't have mine," growled Lord Akadra. "Do you forget, Ebigail? Viktor has my full backing. And I don't fancy your chances of getting Abitha or Malachi to agree with this betrayal. Yes, betrayal, for that's what it is."

"I forget nothing. And you assume that I don't know *why* you voted with Viktor."

Lord Akadra blanched. "You don't know what you're talking about."

She turned on him. "I'm delighted to hear it. And shall feel comfortable giving the matter free rein the next time I'm present at the Grand Council."

Marek was no stranger to watching Lady Ebigail dismantle resistance. But even by her standards, she'd performed a masterpiece on Lord Akadra, whose face fell. Marek didn't know the secret to which she alluded, nor did he know if Lady Ebigail even knew the truth of the matter. But it was clear that Lord Akadra, who had spent more recent nights in her bed than his own, now understood how little influence those intimacies granted in other endeavours.

Makrov looked on with sly interest. Curiosity vied with grim delight for command of his expression.

"Ebigail ... " Lord Akadra swallowed. "What of Viktor? If he ... "

"Viktor will fall into line, as my own dear Sevaka is falling into line. We've been too lax with our children, Hadon. We've given them freedom without wisdom. Clipping their wings will serve them every bit as well as it serves the Republic."

Lord Akadra nodded and hung his head. "And Malachi? Abitha?"

"Will make the usual fuss and display. But the vote is the vote. Dear Arzro will have the 12th, the hangman will have Josiri Trelan. The Republic will have the unity of a single voice once more."

Eyes shining with delight, Makrov pushed off from his chair and offered her a deep bow. "Lumestra thanks you, my lady."

"I need no thanks," said Lady Ebigail serenely. "I do merely what this great Republic of ours demands."

Rosa jolted bolt-upright, heart pounding and fingers grasping at a sword that wasn't there. A dozen hurried breaths rasped through her lungs before she realised that the gloom was not so unrecognisable as she'd feared. It was merely unfamiliar. The Abbeyfields guest chamber. Lit in soft, dappled greys by strands of moonlight that cheated the drapes.

Then she heard it. The soft, whispering creak of a floorboard yielding beneath carpet. A noise that was barely a noise at all. Once heard, it was unmistakeable. Too heavy for a sneaking child. Too furtive to be anyone with honest business in mind. Expression hardening to match a suddenly flint-edged heart, Rosa bunched her borrowed cotton nightgown about her knees, and ghosted from the room.

Barefoot, she crossed the landing and descended to the first floor. She heard no more footfalls, but a gentle draught brought further warning that something was amiss. The front door hung ajar.

Gooseflesh no longer anything to do with the cold-that-was-not-cold, Rosa crept down the final flight. She peered outside. Two shapes lay huddled at the foot of the sandstone steps. Glass from the shattered lantern lay scattered about them. The hearthguards' throats were open to the sky, torn in the bloody fashion that Rosa remembered so well. The talons of the kernclaw.

She crouched beside the nearest, careless of the blood soiling her gown. Had the kernclaw come to finish what he'd started that night on the Tevar Flood? No. He couldn't have come for her, or she'd be dead already, throat slit while in the grip of the first true sleep she'd had since that awful night.

And if he wasn't there for her . . . ?

Rosa slid the hearthguard's sword free of its sheath – that it needed to be drawn at all spoke to the suddenness of his death – and turned back towards the door.

. . . and found herself staring into a young, worried face and golden tresses lit by a hand-lantern's light.

"Sidara?" Rosa stepped aside, blocking the girl's view of the bodies with her own.

"Something woke me." Sidara tilted her head, trying to see out onto the steps. She too was barefoot, and wore a nightgown a good three sizes too large. "Are they dead?"

Rosa pursed her lips. "Yes. Someone's in the house. Someone who shouldn't be. I need you to go back to your room and hide."

Sidara took the news with remarkable aplomb. Though a furrowed brow betrayed her worry, it fell some way short of fear. "Why? What are you going to do?"

"I'm a Knight of Essamere. I'm going to find him and stop him."

If I can. She recalled the kernclaw's speed. The agony of his claws. And

Kas' scream ripping through her own red haze of agony. She gripped the sword tight.

"I'm going to stop him," she said, firmer this time.

"Promise?"

"Yes."

"Good." Sidara's face rippled with competing emotions. "I'd rather stay with you."

Rosa decided she'd be happier if the girl was with her, rather than wandering alone with a murderer loose in the house. "All right. But stay behind me, and put that lantern out."

Sidara nodded mutely and set the lantern down. Its white light flickered to nothing. Rosa pinched her eyes shut and willed her night vision to return.

"Which way to your parents' room?" she breathed.

Already moving, Sidara pointed towards the west wing. "This way."

She jerked to a halt as Rosa seized her wrist.

"Me first, remember?"

The girl nodded and slunk back. Her fingers found Rosa's free hand and squeezed it tight.

The jarring crash of furniture and a woman's scream sounded only a heartbeat apart.

"Mother!"

Sidara ran for the stairs. Rosa overtook her before the first landing. Moments after that, she stood in an open doorway. A torn curtain hung limp. Lilyana lay sprawled before the window, a dresser overturned at her side. Blood masked her face, but she was still breathing.

"Stay away from my wife!"

Malachi stood between Lilyana and a man-shaped shadow. His nightclothes were in disarray. His sword-point dipped and wove. Rosa saw more fear in his eyes than fury.

"I'm not here for her."

The kernclaw's voice was a rumbling echo. Harsh bird-cries sounded beneath, scratching at Rosa's ears and hollowing out her heart. Her legs shook. She was in the Reveque mansion no longer, nor even in Tressia, but lost among the trees of the Tevar Flood. Unable to breathe. Unable even to think.

"You've been poking around in Crowmarket business, Lord Reveque," said the kernclaw. "Make no fight, and your line will outlive you. Fight me, and they ... "

Rosa lunged. She hadn't known she meant to attack until she was already in motion. The woman might have been crippled with fear, but the knight knew her duty.

The shadow parted in a storm of feathers, and her blade kissed only empty air. Rosa back-swung, chasing the wisps of darkness. They danced ever ahead, reforming only when out of reach.

Steel talons raked her wrist. She cried out, her sword falling from nerveless fingers.

"Rosa!" Malachi's blade hacked down. The shadow pulsed, hurling him away.

Talons closed tight about Rosa's throat. The blades sliced at her skin. The kernclaw's weight drove Rosa to her knees. The kernclaw bent low over her, eyes dark and thoughtful beneath the hood. On the fourth finger, inches back from the blade, sapphires glinted on a golden ring.

"Didn't I kill you already?"

She tried to speak. No breath came. Darkness blotched the corners of her vision. Her right wrist blazed with fire. She grabbed at the kernclaw with her left hand. His form parted beneath hooked fingers, dribbling away like smoke.

"No matter." The shadow heaved a shrug. "A mistake easily mended."

Bright pain flared in Rosa's throat to match the ripping, tearing sound. Gasping for breath that wouldn't come, she fell. Darkness took her before she hit the floor.

It bled away in a series of rapid, desperate tugs at her shoulder. Muffled words assailed her ears. Shadows burned bright, resolving into white and gold.

"Aunt Rosa!" Sidara's words broke across Rosa's thoughts like waves on the shore. "You can't be dead. You can't bleed. I heard you say it. You can't bleed, so you can't die!"

But I am dying, she whispered without words. *I can't breathe.*

The world turned grey and cold. Shadows coalesced at Rosa's side. A tall, thin fellow peered out from beneath a feathered domino mask. She'd seen him before but couldn't place where. He crouched beside her, a gloved hand extended. Tendrils of greenish-white mist brushed at Rosa's skin.

"Are you ready to come with me now?" he asked.

Something dark and heavy hit the floor behind Sidara. A sword shone as it skidded away. A man's cry of pain split the air.

"Leave them to it," breathed the masked fellow. His fingers brushed her cheek. Soft. Caring. "Take my hand."

"Aunt Rosa! Please! He's going to kill Father." Sidara's tug on Rosa's shoulder grew more insistent. She stared right through the masked fellow without reaction. "You said you'd stop him. You promised."

Promised. The word quickened Rosa's soul. There was no pain in her throat now, just wet, icy heaviness. Starved lungs spasmed, forcing a baying, hollow croak. It hurt. Lumestra, how it hurt. She didn't care.

She could breathe again. She could *breathe*.

And she had a promise to keep.

The masked fellow hung his head. With a sigh, he faded from sight and memory. The mists went with him.

Rosa grasped at the bedpost for support and clambered upright on trembling legs.

Three paces away, a squirming Malachi lay facedown on the floor. The kernclaw had a knee braced against the small of his back, and the fingers of one hand wound through his hair. Some whisper of movement must have warned him, for he turned, eyes widening in pleasing alarm.

"Raven's Eyes, what *are* you?"

Rosa barely had time to register the irony before she was on him. The kernclaw's cloak screeched and scattered. Her hands closed around his throat.

Talons ripped at her forearms as she dragged the kernclaw clear of Malachi. It hurt, but that hurt was nothing compared to the dredging, raking breath of moments before. She ignored it and slammed him against the wall. A vase shuddered from a shelf and shattered at her feet.

"Let me go! Release me!"

The kernclaw's nose crumpled beneath Rosa's forehead. His fearful demand vanished in a screech of pain. Blood gushed over her nightdress. He sagged. She let him fall.

Instead of hitting the floor, he lunged. Talons ripped clean through her nightgown, deep into the flesh beneath. But pain was nothing to a knight's promise. Rosa bore him to the ground once more, kicking and punching in blind, desperate flurry.

Her hand closed around the grips of a sword. Hers or Malachi's, she didn't know. She hacked down. The world turned red. The kernclaw howled. A severed hand thudded onto ruined carpet. The sapphire ring's brilliance drowned in blood. Bird voices screeched and wailed, the beating of spectral wings like thunder in Rosa's ears.

Then the bedroom's leaded window burst outwards in a glittering spray, and the kernclaw was gone into moon-shadow. The night air rushed in, setting the ruined curtains dancing. Beside Rosa, Malachi groaned.

Sidara cried with relief and rushed over. But it was not her father she embraced, nor even her prone mother. Careless of the blood, she threw her arms about Rosa and muttered incoherent thanks through tears of relief.

Suddenly weary, Rosa let the sword drop. She held the child tight and drank in the sweetest air she'd ever tasted.

Maladas, 5th day of Radiance

The irony of order is that it foments indiscipline.
    In seeking to control all we survey, we
invite anarchy.

from the sermons of Konor Belenzo

Thirty-Two

His Imperial Majesty Prince Kai Saran of the Hadari Empire rode into Charren Gorge an hour after dawn. Owl-banners of green silk heralded his coming. A bodyguard of cataphracts cantered at his back. Marching songs melded with the clatter of hooves; barked orders with the groaning of oxen.

Melanna watched from a rocky spire, lost in memories of yesterday. Her father's long absences on campaign against Thrakkians, Tressians and Ithna'jîm. The embraces of his eventual return. The roughness of scale armour dulled by the bear-pelt cloak. She'd always longed for his arms to enfold her. It meant another day passed without a downcast messenger's arrival. Without empty homilies and the silver ring that meant her father had fallen in battle.

Suppressing a shiver that had nothing to do with the stiff breeze, Melanna drew her cloak tight, and went down to greet him.

The column halted. In its way, the line of horsemen was no less terrifying than the shield wall of the day before. Melanna drew on that memory, let the echo of victory quicken her courage. Her boots struck purposeful rhythm on the stones. Awe billowed around her as she advanced. The Immortals of her father's guard regarded her with uncertain – almost fearful – eyes. A backward glance revealed why.

Melanna was no longer alone. Lunassera emerged from among the rocks, ghostlike and silent. Melanna felt a comforting hand brush her shoulder, and knew Sera stood at their forefront.

"Father."

She offered a warrior's bow in place of a curtsey. When she

straightened, it was into the full force of a disapproving gaze. Eyes glowered beneath a furrowed brow. The laughter lines about his mouth set in stern appraisal.

"You look like my daughter," he said. "You even sound like her. But my daughter would never shame me as you have."

Melanna's cheek twitched in irritation. If her father meant that – if he truly *believed* those words – then he'd paid little attention these past few years.

"I won this victory for you, my prince," she said instead. "As is a firstborn's duty."

"As is the duty of a firstborn *son*."

Kos Devren stirred at her father's side. Bony fingers tugged thoughtfully at a thin beard. "And I doubt if this victory was truly yours."

Melanna's father shot him a warning glance. Her spirits lifted. At least he believed her. Or at least was not ready to countenance criticism. Hal Drannic, seated to her father's left, spoke no word. His face was an impassive mask.

"Whatever the truth," rumbled Melanna's father, "you had no place here. You have no business wearing that armour, nor bearing that sword. You will surrender it to me."

She gripped the hilt. Surrender the goddess-given sword? "I will do no such thing."

A twitch of the reins, and her father trotted closer. He leaned low in the saddle. Hurt welling in his eyes, he spoke too softly for anyone else to hear.

"*Essavim*, if you hold any love for me in your heart, end this game." He straightened, his voice raised to proclamation. "Give me the sword."

Melanna let her hand fall from the hilt. "It is not mine to give. It is of the goddess. As my purpose is of the goddess."

Devren snorted. "Are we supposed to be impressed? We're not impressionable handmaidens."

Melanna ripped the sword from its scabbard and held it aloft. White flame blazed free. Gasps broke out among the Immortals' ranks. Some incredulous, most undercut with fear.

"Protect the prince!"

Drannic, curved swords already in hand, spurred between would-be emperor and wayward daughter. Immortals broke ranks to join him, their own blades scraping free.

Sera darted past Melanna's shoulder. A silver shard-spear glinted to life in her hands. She was not alone. Lunassera formed a wall of braced spears between Melanna and her father's escort.

"I am not deluded!" Melanna shouted. "I am not a liar! I am Ashanal. I am chosen. I fight for my father, whether he accepts it or not. And I will bring him victory in the goddess's name!"

She sheathed the sword. Alone of his escort, her father showed no fear – and for a wonder, no disappointment.

Melanna set a hand on Sera's shoulder and nodded. The lunassera withdrew. Melanna stood alone before the drawn swords of her father's escort. The last of her fear had gone. Reluctance was but a memory. The path ahead was clear as moonlight on open water.

Kneeling, she unlooped her sword belt and held it extended. "If you believe yourself worthier of this sword than I, then take it, Father. But it will serve you no better."

Moments creaked past. Melanna fought the tremor in her arms and the urge to break eye contact with her father. Only two roads led away from this point, and the route not taken would remain for ever closed. Drannic leaned back in his saddle. His lips moved silently at his master's ear.

Melanna's father nodded. "I will speak with my daughter. Alone."

Immortals sheathed their swords and withdrew. Devren went with them, his eyes hooded and unfriendly. Drannic went last of all. Before he turned, his left eyelid fluttered in a surreptitious wink. The lunassera had already bled away into the rocks. For better or for worse, Melanna and her father were alone. Or as alone as could be with wary eyes watching from either end of the roadway.

Melanna's father remained silent and motionless. She gritted her teeth and kept the sword level, determined not to cede even so petty a victory. At last, he swung down from the saddle. His fingers brushed the scabbard's leather.

"Keep it."

"Thank you, my prince." Stifling a sigh of relief, Melanna eased the sword to the ground. "May I stand?"

"Always. But I remain furious with you." His hand drew her upright. She sought truth in his expression, to no avail. Her father seldom showed his feelings unless he wished to. "Drannic thinks I should indulge you. Devren believes I should send you home."

"And how would you do that?" asked Melanna sourly. "I surely cannot be trusted among your soldiers ..."

" ... and you can be trusted around the lunassera even less, I know." He stared out across the valley. "Why do they follow you?"

"Because I am Ashanal." It didn't matter how much she used it, still the title felt unearned.

"And is the daughter of the goddess still the daughter of her father?" His tone hardened. "Or do you seek to supplant me? The lure of a crown burns brighter than the strongest love."

"Not brighter than mine," she said, willing him to believe. "I have never wanted anything more than to be your heir, as a son would be your heir. That is the goddess's wish also."

That, at least, was the truth. Or had been.

He nodded slowly. "Then I can protect you no longer. But I will not humiliate you, as you have me. If it is your wish to fight, then so be it. Tradition has no sway over the Divine, nor those they choose as kin. I will remind my warchiefs."

Melanna shuddered with relief. Her shoulders straightened as her father's words lifted the burdens on her soul. She stepped forward to accept the coming embrace. "Thank you."

The embrace never came. Instead, her father hauled himself back into the saddle. "Thank me by surviving. I'd rather the embarrassment of a daughter who thinks herself a son, than the sorrow of her death."

He rode away, leaving Melanna with his acceptance renewed, but robbed of something harder to define.

"This isn't what we agreed," said Crovan.

Jesver Merrik halted on the edge of Maiden's Hollow. As ever, he looked the weather-worn poacher more than he did the Terror of Kellin Valley. His fifty or so companions were no better, swathed in ragged leather and torn wool-cloth. But their weapons were sharp. They'd spent the better part of the morning honing the blades.

Merrik shrugged, dislodging his haversack. "A week back, I agreed to fight. Then I agreed not to. Now I'm back to where I started."

Crovan rubbed his forehead, searching for the words to carry the day. "The Hadari bring us freedom. Do you want to live beneath the Council's boot the rest of your life?"

He snorted. "I've never lived under the Council's boot. And I'll sure as Queen's Ashes not live under shadowthorn rule. Should've said so when the duke was here. I'd rather fight for my freedom than hope for it."

Crovan didn't have to ask what had spurred Merrik's change of heart. New arrivals at Maiden's Hollow had spoken of nothing else.

"The Phoenix is a myth," he said. "Nothing more."

Merrik ambled closer, his friendly tone laced with a hint of danger. "See? That's why you'll never belong here, northwealder. You can talk like us. You can pretend to share our cause. You can even mucky your blade, when called to it. But you're still an outlander."

The words stung after everything he'd done for the Southshires. The career he'd thrown away. The bridges he'd burned. The disinheritance from a family who sought to hide roots buried deep in Eskavord. He felt something cold beneath his palm. The pommel of his old army sword. Crovan didn't recall putting his hand there. Come to that, he hadn't worn the blade since gathering the Vagabond Council. So much easier to preach non-involvement without a weapon slapping your thigh. Why had he belted the thing on that morning?

Maybe it was for the best. Merrik was close. He suspected nothing. A show of strength, inked in blood for the rest of the Vagabond Council to see. They'd fall into line. Some might even thank him. Crovan blinked the thought away, appalled. That wasn't who he was.

"Calenne Trelan is a child. She'll get you all killed."

"Then we'll see our families again, won't we?" said Merrik. "When you stop running long enough for the Raven to take you, seek me out in Otherworld. You can tell me *all* about how much better you lived your life while I was gone."

Merrik stomped away up the hill, his followers falling into step alongside.

"I'm not a coward," Crovan muttered. The words were not the balm to his stinging pride he'd hoped. "I'm not."

"Let him go." Vorn folded his arms and sank against a tree. "Merrik has what? Fifty blades? Seventy? Not enough to change anything."

"But it's not just seventy blades, is it?" Crovan snapped. "The twins left last night. Korsov at first light. I'm losing them."

"Not for long," said Vorn. "I hear our Hadari friends'll be at Eskavord come morning. Wind's blowing for battle."

In his mind's eye, Crovan saw the lowland approaches to Eskavord. Good, firm ground enfolded by the spreading eaves of Davenwood.

"Akadra won't let them get that far. He can't."

"Like I said, they'll not be gone long. First clash of shields and they'll come running back, begging for protection. What does Akadra have? A thousand blades?"

"More. If what I'm hearing is true, half of Eskavord's villages turned out for him. Others too."

Vorn snorted. "Old men who've not touched a sword in fifteen years? Unblooded youths? Calenne Trelan had better be the Phoenix of legend if she wants to stomp the Hadari with that."

"There's another thousand in Kreska."

"Fine, call it three thousand. Call it four, if you like. You heard Kerril's report. The Hadari have at least six."

Crovan nodded. Numbers weren't everything, but they helped. Between his own wolf's-heads and those loyal to Gavamor and Silda Drenn, he'd nearly a thousand blades of his own. Enough to narrow the gap. Maybe even bring the victory the Southshires needed.

Struck by sudden weariness, he glanced away through the trees. No matter Vorn's words, he felt an abiding loss. No, *he* felt lost. More than he had since that night after his patrol had been ambushed by south-wealders, when he'd been trapped in Skazit Maze, with only his thoughts and a broken leg for company.

He should have died with his patrol that night. Would have done, if only the ground hadn't swallowed him up into the root-breached tunnels beneath Davenwood. Call it fever, call it enlightenment, but he'd experienced revelation in the darkness. He realised he'd more sympathy for his estranged southwealder kin than loyalty to his superiors. Rescue came at noon the next day, hours too late to change the course of Crovan's deliberations. He deserted the army as soon as he'd healed, and never looked back. Not until now.

"What if I'm wrong?"

The question was a mistake. The words sounded foolish when spoken aloud.

"You ain't," said Vorn. "Calenne Trelan's not the Phoenix. She's a frightened girl, cowering behind Akadra. Others want to gamble on her, more fool them."

Crovan wondered at the vehemence Vorn expressed for a woman he'd never met. He shrugged the thought away. After all, he was right. Drakos Crovan, the Wolf King, could save only the willing. If some allies perished to prove him right, then that was a price worth paying to save those who remained.

Calenne awoke from rich, shadow-laced dreams into the stuffy, greyish light of Viktor's tent. As she pulled on Katya's old leathers, she peered blearily at the high-backed chair. Viktor had insisted it would serve him perfectly well as a bed. Judging by the stack of neatly folded blankets, it had not done so.

She struck out for the open air. As she did, she spared a glance for her armour and cloak, but decided against them. The armour fitted well enough, but it was still a costume for a part she didn't relish playing. It could wait.

She emerged onto a hillside dotted with tents and smouldering campfires. She was surrounded by the king's blue uniforms and the patchwork raiment of citizenry roused to the fight.

To the north, the eaves of Davenwood – little more than shadows against darkness when Viktor had ended last night's march – rippled in waves of brilliant green beneath the morning sun. And beyond that, smoke gathered against the clouds, a grim reminder of why she was there.

The scale of it took her breath away. The crowds in Eskavord had been intimidating enough. The sight of the swelling army made her giddy – not least because so many of them were there because of *her*. Which meant a great many of them would *die* because of her. As humbling – as horrifying – as that thought was, it was somehow exciting. Was this how her mother had felt before Zanya?

Belatedly, Calenne realised her slip. But there, amid the gathering ranks, it was hard not to feel kinship with the woman whose mantle she reluctantly wore.

"Sleep well?" Even without his cloak, Viktor was a towering shadow in the glorious day.

She nodded. "Better than I should. And you? I know you didn't come back to the tent."

"I slept by the fire. I thought you'd appreciate the privacy."

Calenne laughed. Not at the kindness shown, for she knew the demands others might have made in Viktor's position, but at the sombre, inevitable way in which he voiced it.

"We're to be married, Viktor. If you snore like a bull, better I learn that now."

He smiled, though she had the impression he did so to humour her, rather than out of mirth.

"What is it?"

He looped his arms behind his back. "Hadari outriders have been sighted west of Kreska. The bulk of their army won't be far behind. I'd hoped to link up with Yanda's forces before forcing battle. It seems we aren't to be given that luxury." He hesitated. "I think you should return to Eskavord."

"And you?"

"I have a war to fight."

It wasn't the first time Viktor had expressed that sentiment. It *was* the first time he'd done so with a note of ... not defeatism ... but certainly bitter concern.

Calenne didn't have to wonder why. She'd listened in as Viktor had discussed the night's wayfarers' reports. Even with the influx of south-wealders drawn to the Phoenix's promise of freedom, they could scarce afford to be cut off from Yanda's army.

The invitation was obvious. Run away. Be safe. A week prior, she'd have done so without hesitation. But so much had changed in that week. Strange how the further she tried to run from her mother's legacy, the closer she felt to a woman she'd hated so long. Or perhaps it wasn't Katya Trelan she felt closer to at all, but the man who'd haunted her nightmares for fifteen years. Either way, she couldn't leave. Not even if it cost her life to remain.

She folded her arms. "I'm staying. You're not the only one with responsibility here."

A heartbeat flickered past. Viktor nodded. "As you wish."

Thirty-Three

Grey robes shifted in the dark. Cold green eyes gleamed beneath ragged woollen hoods. In her haste to stand, Apara fell from the creaking chair. Her knees cracked against stone. Her breath fogged the air.

"Where is he, cousin?"

Apara couldn't tell which of the three had spoken. The words came as a raw whisper, more like a crow's croak than a voice. She'd only been in an elder cousin's presence once before. When she'd been granted dominion over the chapel and its hidden trade. That had been one alone; stern, but kindly. As kin should be when a cousin had proved herself worthy. This had an altogether different feel. Cold. *Angry.*

"In the ... the ... cellar," she stuttered.

"Show us."

A different voice. A woman's. And not a request.

Apara took the firestone lantern from its hook, shook it to life, and descended the stairs. The lantern helped a little, but not nearly enough. The elder cousins drank in the firestone's glow as they had the moonlight from the windows. Still, enough remained to guide her through the maze of crates and barrels "liberated" from unwary merchants.

At the centre of the room, Nikros stirred on a filthy bed. Blood crusted his bandaged stump and stained the sheets beneath.

"Apara?" He stared up at her with bloodshot eyes. "What ...?"

Shadows heaved. Apara's hair danced in their wake. The elder cousins loomed over the bed, vaporous against the lantern's light.

"You have failed us, cousin."

Apara offered no reply. The words were not meant for her. And she was glad beyond expression.

"I know," croaked Nikros.

He swung upright, boots hanging over the side of the bed. His good arm cradled the bandaged one. There was no trace of his customary Raven-may-care swagger. Apara knew it wasn't pain that held it at bay. They'd never been close, he and she – distant as cousins could be, at times – but in that moment she pitied him.

"I know," he repeated, his eyes furtive and desperate. "I'll make amends. Anything the Parliament demands."

"What is our first law?" asked one voice.

Nikros' eyes went wide. A sob escaped his lips. "No! I beg you!"

"What is our first law?" asked another.

"That . . . " His breathing slowed. "That the light creates us; it does not reveal our purpose."

"Then why does the city hum with rumour?" asked one.

"Why do we hear whispers of a kernclaw's public failure?" asked another.

"It wasn't my fault! I tore her throat out. She should . . . She shouldn't have been there! She should . . . she should have died at Tevar Flood."

A sharp, breathy intake echoed around the room. The shadows pulsed. Green eyes met in silent communion. The name wasn't lost on Apara. Tevar Flood. Where the lady's son had perished. The son alone, as it now transpired.

"Then you are twice the failure."

The last resistance bled from Nikros' face. Resistance fed upon hope, and there was none in that filthy cellar. Everyone *knew* the Crowmarket existed, of course. The first law was ritual more than truth. But knowledge was one thing; proof another. Nikros' blunder had left at least four witnesses.

Apara knew what was coming. She backed away. Her heel caught on the stair.

Green eyes blazed in her direction. "Cousin. Stay."

She froze, heart in her throat.

One shadow broke from the others and approached the rear wall.

Gloved fingers brushed filthy brick. A high archway took shape, hissing white-green vapour rushed to fill the bounds within.

The remaining elder cousins seized Nikros by the arms.

"No," he moaned. "Please . . . "

They dragged him away towards the luminous arch. He reached out with his good hand.

"Apara! Please."

She watched, rooted to the spot, unable to make a sound.

"Do not beg," said one.

"Your bargain has come due," said another.

"You belong to the mists," said the third.

The elder cousin by the arch finished his labour. Brickwork fell away. Mist trickled across the floor. It curled about Apara's ankles and billowed upwards to her knees.

Beyond the arch, dark walls mirrored the cellar. The distant chamber lay bare save for broken statues of black stone, and a lone, ornate tomb where the bed should have sat. Behind the tumbled ruin of stairs and a collapsed wall, buildings towered away into the mist. Otherworld was for ever an echo of the living realm, or so the priests preached. Apara had hoped never to see it with waking eyes.

Beside the tomb, his back propped against stone, stood a tall, thin man in a beaked and black-feathered domino mask. A neatly trimmed beard showed beneath the mask. Pale skin at the neck and cuffs of his severe black suit.

Apara's throat tightened. She wanted to run, but to do so was to make matters worse. So she bowed her head, closed her eyes and begged not to be noticed.

"Well?" The Raven sounded impatient and amused all at once. A father disappointed in his children's inevitable flaws. "What have you brought me?"

"A failure," said one.

"He is kin no longer," said another. "You may take from him all that he owes."

Nikros sobbed. Apara glanced up. He lay sprawled in the mist beyond the gate, bloody stump clutched to his chest.

The Raven squatted and shook his head in lament. "Pray, don't bawl so. I'm not the one who brought you here, am I?" He offered a languid sigh. "No one ever wants to pay the price."

It seemed to Apara that his eyes were not on Nikros in that moment, but the three elder cousins. They shrank away from the arch, heads bowed.

The Raven rose. Nikros stood with him. His sobbing fell silent. His motions were stiff as a man transfixed. He turned, offered one last, lingering glance through the arch. Then he was gone, lost in a storm of ebony feathers that bled through the mist like smoke.

Apara clapped a hand to her mouth, too slow to smother a horrified gasp.

The Raven's expressionless gaze met hers. "She is his replacement?"

"Yes," said one.

"She is a faithful cousin," said another. "She will not disappoint."

The Raven sighed again. "They all say that."

He stepped through the arch. Though he was but one shadow among many, his presence filled the cellar. Even the air tasted different, like dust undisturbed for ten thousand turnings of the world. Apara fought for breath that wouldn't come.

"Please," she gasped. "I'm a thief, not a ripper. I steal . . . "

The words died on her tongue as the Raven took her nerveless hand and pressed it to his lips.

"I understand." He spoke with cold charm, and a hint of . . . regret? "But your cousins wish you to be both. Family are *nothing* but trouble. Even when they're not really family at all."

The firestone lantern flickered and went out.

Ellren stared up at the double doors, too lost in apprehension to appreciate the swirling thorns and vibrant roses depicted on its panels. Every servant in Silvane House knew you didn't disturb Lord Tarev in his chamber. Maids had been cast out for less.

Though a city-girl by birth, Ellren's parents were southwealders, and she'd borne the rose-brand since her fifth year. If she trespassed she'd end in Dregmeet, her papers burned.

But lots had been drawn, and she'd lost.

With trembling hand, Ellren knocked on the door. "Lord Tarev?"

She braced for the bellow; the rush of footsteps and the stinging flat of his lordship's hand. None of those things came. Silence, broken by birdsong from the gardens, was the only reply.

"Your lordship?"

She took a deep breath, turned the handle, and stepped inside.

The chamber lay thick beneath ruddy gloom, the light of the morning given hue by the heavy crimson curtains. Scents lay heavy on the still air. Ash, liquor and something else, thick and rich beneath.

The four-poster bed hadn't been slept in. Indeed, Ellren could have believed herself the only person to have trod the carpet since the previous morning, but for the empty brandy bottle lying sidelong on the dresser. That, and the previous night's ashes in the grate.

"Lord Tarev?" she whispered, as afraid of going unnoticed as she was of discovery. You heard stories about the nobility. Well, not Lord Tarev, who'd by all accounts led a strictured life even before his wife's death at Zanya. But it was never too late for new interests to take root.

"Lord Tarev? It's Ellren." She skirted the bed and stepped through the door to the adjoining study. "Master Gosrig was wondering . . . "

She shuddered to a halt, fist jammed in her mouth to stifle a scream.

Lord Tarev lay slumped across his desk. His sleeves were rolled to the elbow, his wrists bloody and his eyes staring sightlessly towards the door. A thin-stemmed glass lay on the desk. Blood pooled around it and across the trifold portrait clasped between pale fingers.

Ellren sucked in a breath. A mistake. The sour, coppery smell of cooled blood – all but undetectable in the bedroom, but suffocating here – struck the back of her throat. She clutched at the wall for support, fighting a rebellious gorge.

"Master Gosrig! Master Gosrig! Come quickly!"

Even as she shouted, she wasn't sure why she bothered. Lord Tarev had no need of haste. Not any longer.

Malachi found Rosa in gardens grey and troubled as his mood. A pebble left her hand, shot across the river's rushing waters and cracked against the sheer cliff of the opposing bank. Beyond, the crumbling arches of Strazyn Abbey loomed large – another reminder that all things passed, in time.

"Don't let Lily catch you. Constans doesn't need the encouragement." He tried to muster a chuckle, but it wouldn't come. "How are you?"

Rosa turned from the waters and smoothed the folds of her surcoat. "Better than I should be."

Malachi winced. Between panic and darkness, he recalled only a little of the kernclaw's attack. But the image of Rosa lying motionless on the floor, her nightgown shredded and her throat torn out? The stuff of nightmares to come. More than ever, he struggled to comprehend what his friend was going through.

"What about you?" she asked.

He touched a hand to his bruised cheek. "I'll live. It's done nothing for my looks, and less for my mood ... but there was no saving at least one of those." He paused. Words seemed so inadequate at times like these. "I owe you my life ... my family's lives."

The smile wasn't much, just a small crook of the lips. "You owe me nothing. In a way, I'm grateful to the kernclaw. I've been direction-less since Kas died. I'd forgotten my purpose. My duty. He gave that back to me."

Malachi laughed, though its tug at bruised ribs made him wince. "Next time, perhaps don't involve me in your quest for enlightenment?"

Now there was nothing half-hearted about Rosa's smile, nor her soft laughter. "And Lilyana? The children?"

"Lily has a bump on the back of her head the size of an egg. Constans slept through the whole thing." Malachi shook his head in wonder. "Sidara ... Sidara declared this morning that she wants to go to the chapterhouse as soon as she's of age. You made quite an impression."

"Lilyana can't be pleased."

"She isn't, but she's keeping her distaste hidden." He twisted away to hide a blush of pleasure. "Wouldn't let the physicians touch my wounds either. Insisted that she and Sidara do everything, and they did their work well. I think my daughter has a talent for this. I've no other cause to feel as hale as I do."

Rosa offered a wry smile. "So you're well enough to spar?"

"I'm never *that* well. And Lily would *not* approve."

"I think perhaps that she loves you, however little you notice it at times."

"I've not done well by them of late. By anyone. Last night brought that home to me, quite literally so."

Rosa grunted. "They do say we are only truly ourselves in moments of crisis. It's why old soldiers can't put down the sword. It means setting down a piece of themselves alongside."

"And you? What did you learn of yourself?"

She flexed her fingers, holding them in a fist before spreading them wide as Lumestra's rays. "That I'm still Roslava Orova, Knight of Essamere and Reaper of the Ravonn – though Lumestra knows I hate that nickname. Elzar was right. This *is* a gift. I'm stronger than I used to be, Malachi. Faster, too. And that's to say nothing of ... " Her voice snagged on the next word. " ... of the rest. I can put that to use."

Malachi frowned, his mood soured by wariness. "You must be careful. If others learn how you are ... The church's provosts won't care for what you've done, only what you are."

"You worry too much, old friend."

Just as she worried too little. Malachi decided not to spoil the moment with argument.

"Tell me," Rosa went on. "What did the kernclaw mean about you interfering in Crowmarket business?"

He cursed. He'd hoped she'd not caught that. But he couldn't lie to her. Not after all she'd done last night. And she *was* better placed to survive any consequences than he.

"Someone's stealing kraikons from the foundry – melting them down for their metal. Late yesterday, I ordered the constabulary to make a sweep of the dockside. I didn't expect they'd find anything, but reckoned it'd at least make the Crowmarket more circumspect."

She gave a slow, thoughtful nod. "And this was their response?"

"What else could it be?"

Rosa turned away without speaking.

"Rosa? What is it?"

"Nothing. Or at least nothing I can prove." She sighed. "I don't even know that I believe it myself. You don't need my confusion muddying your own concerns."

So her dour mood wasn't about last night, or not entirely. "Tell me. I can help."

"As you helped last night?" She straightened, a scowl haunting her features. "Sorry. That wasn't fair. If I find proof, I'll speak of it."

Malachi frowned, but Rosa hadn't put enough of her riddle on display for him to unpick. "I don't understand."

"Good." She faced him, her eyes hard. "I have to go. Promise me you'll stay safe."

"I'll be nothing but. Lily has borrowed hearthguards from half the family. The estate will be thick with uniforms until her worries fade. I am to go nowhere without at least four blades at my side."

"Except here, with me."

"Lily believes you're worth a good sight more than four blades." He laid a hand on her shoulder. "But that doesn't mean I don't worry for you. Whatever it is you intend, stay safe. And remember that I'm here, should you need me. Or rather, I'll be at council."

"Are you sure that's a good idea?"

"The vranakin are bold, but they'll not trouble me in broad daylight, and certainly not while in session at the palace. Though I've often wished they would."

"That's not funny, Malachi."

"No, I suppose not." He sighed. "In any case, I've work to do. I'd no chance to tell you last night, but Ebigail's sunk us even deeper into the mire. She's forced through a decree to round up any poor southwealder bastard who accepts Viktor's offer of clemency. She says it's only so that their innocence can be proven at trial ... "

"But you don't believe her?"

He recalled the glee on Ebigail's face when she'd aired the proposal. "Not when she's sent Makrov and a whole regiment south to ensure their 'cooperation'."

"I thought there weren't any troops to spare?"

"Ebigail can always find soldiers when it suits her." He scratched at his scalp, glad the sudden itch had manifested away from the bruises. "I thought Viktor had won his father over, but the vote was the same old battle lines. I have to find a way to undo it, though I don't know how."

"I can talk to Ebigail, if you'd like?" said Rosa.

What could Rosa achieve that he could not? All she'd earn was enemies she didn't deserve. "No. I can unpick this. Viktor found a way to change his father's mind. So can I."

"Yes. How *did* he do that? You never said."

"I never said because I don't know. It's Viktor. You know how he is. I think he likes to cultivate an air of mystery."

Rosa grunted noncommittally, a shadow flickering across her face. Malachi took it for concern and offered a reassuring smile. "Don't worry about me. I'll be fine."

Her lip twitched, but the darkness remained. "Let's hope so."

"He's what?" demanded Ebigail.

Somehow – and Malachi didn't know how – Captain Horden kept his composure. "Dead, lady. Maid found him this morning. Embraced the Raven, by the look. Gaping wrists, skinful of brandy and surrounded by the painted smile of wife and daughters. Worse ways to go."

Hadon Akadra drummed his fingers on the meeting table. "You speak of a member of this Council. Show some respect!"

"Yes, sir. Sorry, sir."

Malachi tore his gaze from the Council chamber's grandiose map. Somehow it had been easier to focus on that than Horden. He'd not miss Tarev, but nor could he bring himself to revel in the man's death. And then there was the timing of it all – a coincidence to which every flash of pain in his ribs drew closer attention.

"You're certain he took his own life?"

"Nothing's certain, my lord, but if the maid knows more than she's telling, she'll talk."

Hadon scowled. "I thought you said he embraced the Raven."

"The maid's a southwealder," said Horden. "Can't be too careful."

"Ah."

Abitha Marest rapped her walking stick on the table. "She's to be well-treated unless you have proof of foul play. Do you understand me, captain?"

"Of course, lady. Everyone gets fair treatment in my cells ... " He shot a sidelong glance at Malachi. " ... unless the Council requests otherwise."

Malachi couldn't find the energy to offer rebuke. Truth was, he and

Ebigail both had twisted justice to get Rosa out of Horden's jail. Now Tarev was dead. And on the day following his last surviving daughter's funeral, no less. Even Horden's limited intellect could piece that one together.

Ebigail sank into her chair. Malachi could swear she'd gained more white hairs among the grey since Horden had knocked on the door. "Thank you, captain. Keep us informed. I'll offer our condolences to the grandson. We'll make a formal announcement later today."

"Yes, lady."

Horden withdrew. The heavy doors slammed behind him.

"A black day for our Republic," said Ebigail. "One councillor dead at his own hand, and another assaulted in his home."

Hadon grunted. "The latter, at least, we can do something about. The Crowmarket must be humbled. Only a fool would think it possible to be rid of them entirely, but they've become too bold."

"And with good reason," said Abitha. "Half the constabulary line their pockets with bribes. The other half are terrified."

"Then we won't use the constabulary," said Malachi, "but our own hearthguards. Inspect every wagon and merchantman entering the city. Roust not just the docks, but the Dregmeet slums."

Hadon laughed. "You're a new man this morning. A blow or two to the head might have done you some good. Tell you what, I'll see to it myself. I can't spare more than a hundred – Viktor's taken half of my lot off on his foolish crusade. But if we can round up another four or five, I promise you I'll drive the vranakin back underground within the week."

"I pray Lumestra you're right," said Abitha, her eyes raised heavenward.

Ebigail nodded. "I don't think we need put this to a formal vote."

Malachi shook his head – as much at the rare display of unity as in agreement. Despite Hadon's confidence, he doubted much lasting impact would be had. But it was a start.

Little by little, he became aware of a soft, musical murmur, little louder than a whisper. Abitha sat with eyes closed, her fingers locked and her elbows braced on the table. Her lips worked feverishly. Now he listened closer, Malachi made out a few of the words. A prayer for the dead.

"Must you sully our ears with that nonsense?" snapped Ebigail. "You'd have done better to pray while dear Anton was alive."

Abitha's eyes flickered open. "But I didn't, and now it's too late. A lament is all I can offer."

"Still, you'll oblige us by doing so in your own time."

"As it happens, I just finished."

The women fell silent, each wearing a victorious expression.

Hadon cleared his throat. "I suppose we'd better make preparations for this grandson to take Anton's seat. What's his name, again?"

"It hardly matters," said Ebigail. "The boy's not of the blood. Dear Anton tried to keep it quiet, but I've no doubt it'll come out now. There's no loyalty among the nobility. Not any more."

She paused, inviting the suggestion of scandal to blossom in the shocked silence.

Despairing at the tawdriness of gossip, Malachi hurried to move the conversation on. "So what happens to his seat?"

"There's a cousin, I believe. On Selann. It will doubtless take time for word to reach her."

Malachi filed away the information and resolved to find out more. Anton's death shifted council arithmetic yet again, but only into stalemate and not enough to overturn Ebigail's machinations regarding the embattled southwealders. Viktor's vote could have done so, but Viktor was leagues away. He might even be dead. But there was some hope. If Makrov brought the southwealder leaders north before the seat was filled, Viktor would come with them. A new vote could be called and won.

He rubbed his chin thoughtfully. It might even be for the best if Anton's successor didn't arrive for some time. Perhaps Braxov could help with that – the steward had family in the Outer Isles. It wouldn't take much. A small, harmless delay might make all the difference.

It wasn't perfect, it wasn't honourable, and it would likely cause more suffering before all was done. But perfection had ever been lacking in the Republic. If Ebigail was for ever outdancing him, as Lily had so forcefully said, perhaps it was time he learned some new steps of his own.

Malachi rose, wincing as bruises reknitted into new and exciting configurations. "Then with your permission, I'll return to my family. I haven't seen them as much as I should – as recent events have reminded me."

"Yes, of course." Ebigail's brow knotted in concern. "Please offer my sympathies to your wife. The Republic is fortunate that you're both still with us."

To Marek's understanding, the side table had been in the Kiradin family for at least four generations. A pinnacle of its creator's art, the graceful, flowing curves of its legs combined masterfully with the slivers of semi-precious stones to grant the work a dazzling, iridescent quality. It was not only a treasured heirloom. It was irreplaceable. But when flung at a wall it shattered with much the same scraping crack as any slum-dweller's table would have.

"Idiots!" shouted Lady Ebigail. "I'm surrounded by idiots!"

She aimed a kick at a forlorn table-leg. It skittered across the carpet, slid past Lady Sevaka and bounced off a chair.

"I've always known that." Lady Sevaka's tone held a certain dry satisfaction. "But you'll have to narrow the selection if I'm to feel any sympathy."

"That fool kernclaw for one!"

Satisfaction slid into horror. "So now you're dealing with the Crowmarket? Is nothing beneath you?"

"Very little is beneath the powerful, when the need is there."

"And the fact that someone had them kill Kasamor doesn't matter? Have you no feelings? I know you don't think much of me, but you loved my brother."

"It won't have been anything personal on their part. Just one more commission. I doubt it was even the same kernclaw, and I see no reason not to put them to good use over something that cannot be altered, whatever we might wish." Lady Ebigail waved a dismissive hand. "Malachi's death would have kept the Council under my control until well after this business with the Southshires is done. Long enough for everything else to fall into place. Instead, he's still scheming. Worse, that feckless coward Anton's slit his wrists over his harlot daughter." She spun around, eyes ablaze. "Well if he thinks her bastard's getting a chair at my table, he's very much mistaken."

"Why does it matter?"

"*Why does it matter?* You're as bad as the rest."

"I've always known that, too. Perhaps I'd be less useless if I understood the game you're playing."

"The game?" Lady Ebigail's voice dropped to a dangerous whisper. "Malachi Reveque aims to drag the Republic into soft-bellied anarchy, and you think this is a game?"

"When did you become obsessed with Malachi?"

"When he grew a spine. If only my daughter would do the same."

"Then have the kernclaw make a second attempt."

"The Crowmarket won't risk another failure. They've a lot of pride for a den of thieves."

Lady Sevaka shrugged. "Then I don't know what to suggest. Now if you'll excuse me . . ."

"And where are you going this night," asked Lady Ebigail. "Another dalliance, I suppose?"

Her daughter halted, her hand on the door. "As it happens, Rosa asked for my help."

"Oh, so you're *friends* now, are you?"

Her back still to her mother, Lady Sevaka's expression soured. A bleakness settled in Marek's heart to see it. She'd smiled so little since coming home.

"That's what she thinks. That's what you wanted, *isn't* it?"

"Yes. See that you remain mindful of how things really are."

"How could I forget?"

The door slammed. Lady Ebigail stared in silence for a long moment. Then she collapsed in an armchair, palm braced against her brow. "Never have children, Marek."

"No, lady."

"Only those you cannot claim have any worth, and the rest . . ." She leaned forward, her expression clearing and dry enthusiasm crowding her tone. "But Sevaka was right, wasn't she? I *have* allowed my gaze to wander. Malachi is only part of the problem. But I cannot leave the house. After last night's failure, that would draw too much notice. I must be seen to cower behind my guards."

Her head snapped up. Marek straightened as her gaze touched on him. "Lady?"

"I need you to deliver a message."

Thirty-Four

Sunlight shone down on the Southshires. The *free* Southshires. Victory had been a long time coming, its cost measured in widows and orphans. But this one glorious moment – the hour of the Council's long awaited surrender . . . ? Josiri was determined to enjoy it. It was a new dawn.

"Are you coming, brother?" Calenne stood at the balcony doorway, her gloved hand extended. "It's time."

He nodded. "Past time and true."

"Mother would be proud. *I* am proud."

"We both are." Anastacia's impish smile belied her statement. "Enough stalling. Your people are waiting."

Josiri frowned. A crowd gathered below. Men, women and children, waiting for his word. Problem was, he was certain they hadn't been there before.

"I don't understand . . . "

Calenne led him to the balcony's edge. Her sapphire eyes turned dark. Jagged black lines crept across her cheeks. "Say a few words, that's all. After all, you led us here."

Josiri stared out across the terrace. Lifeless eyes shifted in sockets of withered flesh and rose to meet his. A field of corpses in ragged clothes. Behind them, Eskavord burned against a darkening sky. The first wisps of green-white mist curled across withered grass.

He gagged. The world spun beneath his feet. Gloved hands caught his, holding him upright.

"You cannot leave, brother." Beneath Calenne's funeral veil, maggots burrowed free of scorched and blistered flesh. "You belong with us. We will all be one in the Dark."

He screamed and pulled away. Brittle fingers snapped and fell into the dust.

"Josiri?" Anastacia's voice came everywhere at once, and yet nowhere. "Josiri?"

"Go away!" he bellowed. "Leave me alone!"

He spun about, lost his balance and fell into the mists.

Josiri opened his eyes into morning sunlight. The cold stone was rough under his left temple. Sourness crowded the back of his mouth. The pounding in his head matched the sullen thump of his heart.

[[This is *not* the reunion I envisaged.]]

"Anastacia?"

He rolled over. Anastacia stood at the balcony's edge, her back to him and hands crossed lightly at her waist. The hooded shawl and black velvet dress seemed too humble for her tastes. Beyond, the roofs and spires of Eskavord revelled in Lumestra's light.

"Where have you been?" he croaked. He unsteadily hoisted himself to a sitting position. "I was worried."

[[Were you?]] Her voice wasn't right, though he couldn't say why. [[I've been beyond the wall.]]

"What? How?"

[[Akadra made it possible.]]

"That's not an answer."

So it *had* been Akadra's doing. Just another means of tormenting him. Of isolating him. But it had failed. Or had it? Anastacia didn't sound herself, and it was more than the catch in her voice.

"But you're back?" He hated how pathetic the question sounded.

[[I don't know. It's not wholly my choice.]]

Slowly, with one hand pressed against the manor wall, Josiri rose to his feet. He was used to Anastacia's evasions, so why did this one send a shiver down his spine?

"Whose choice is it?"

Her head dipped. [[Freedom came with a price, extracted from us both.]]

He shook his head and cursed softly as the motion set the world spinning. "I don't understand."

[[You will.]]

She turned, fingers brushing the hood from her brow. Dark eyes swirled in a face of smooth, white porcelain chased with gold and framed by black tresses.

Josiri's heart leapt into his throat. His shaking fingers clutched at the wall. He felt sick, as if all the festering ills of the past days had settled deep within his gut, and now sought to spill free.

"That's ... That's not a mask, is it?"

[[No.]]

An eternity passed as he struggled to find his voice. Another crawled by while he sought words beyond his straining grasp. He felt smothered by ice, the warmth sucked from his bones even as his lungs cracked.

"How?" He gasped the word from a raw throat. "How did Akadra do this?"

Anastasia's gloved fingers clinked against her face. [[He made this body. He promised it would carry me beyond the walls, and it has. But it is also my prison. I cannot leave, and the world is dust, for all the sensation it offers.]]

"No!" Josiri ground the heels of his hands into his eyes. "This isn't real! What you're talking about ... it's not possible."

[[You know I was never flesh as you are flesh ... and many things are possible with magic that are otherwise not.]]

"Magic? *Your* magic?"

[[And his. I thought together ...]] A hint of panic touched her voice. [[This was a mistake. I shouldn't have come.]]

The note of dismay, of loss, finally cracked a chink in the ice around him. Josiri's hands slipped from his face and looked again at the horror Akadra had wrought. The *thing* he had made of the beautiful, effervescent creature with whom he had shared so many years.

Ice melted before a raging flame.

"I'll kill him!"

A gloved hand closed around his arm, the grip tighter than it had any right to be.

[[No! If I'd wanted that, he'd be dead already. And I did want it, for a time. I have wanted so many things this past day. I have dreamed forth enough woe on others to drown an ocean. But in the end, I have one need alone. Even if he can no longer bear to look upon what I've become.]]

Josiri caught the fearful expectation in her voice. That was what she'd meant about it not being her choice whether or not she remained. If he asked – if he even spoke the wrong words or let his revulsion show – she'd leave. And then there was the unspoken question. How did he answer? How could he?

Easier to focus on hate. "Akadra must pay."

[[He made an honest mistake. I compounded it through greed. Revenge offers no solace. Only . . .]] The grip on his arm slackened. She turned away. [[I have used my life poorly. I have sought only gratification. I have not stood beside those I loved when I should, and I have not fought when it was my time to do so.]]

"Anastacia . . ."

[[Let me finish. I once said you had it in you to be a great man.]] She held out her hands and stared bitterly at them. [[In seeking to spur you to that greatness, have I poisoned you with my own selfishness? If that is so, then whatever becomes of *us*, I beg you: be better than *me*.]]

Whatever becomes of us. Josiri knew what she wanted to hear, but didn't know if he could utter the words. And what did that say of him? Of the love he'd sought so many times to profess? Was it truly as shallow as the skin she'd worn? Was *he* so shallow, for his feelings to sour when lissom flesh was replaced by clay? Surely Anastacia was no less real, her being no less an illusion?

But it *was* different. She was different. And so would they be, if his touch was no longer comfort to her, or hers to him. If Akadra had desired to drive them apart – to remind Josiri of the gulf separating his ephemeral yearnings from Anastacia's deathless being – he could have found no better way. And yet she, who recalled every mouth of soured wine, every unseasonal chill and every last slight – bore him no ill will?

This was too much to bear. It would have been too much if he'd been well-rested, and no aftermath of drink taken fogging his thoughts. But this wasn't about him, was it? If he felt thus, how must Anastacia feel, trapped in a body not her own? Numb to the sensations in which she'd revelled.

Calenne. Revekah. Even Crovan, after a fashion. He'd pushed them all away, and in the process lost pieces of his own being. If he rejected Anastacia also – now, when she needed him most, what remained of Josiri Trelan save his name?

And he needed her too. Now, more than ever.

"Anastacia?"

He laid a hand on her shoulder. After a moment's resistance, she turned about, eyes brimming with wary expectation. Strange how they were more expressive now they were trapped within an immobile face. Josiri raised a faltering hand and cupped her cheek.

Warm. The porcelain was warm beneath his fingers. He hadn't expected that.

He drew her into an embrace. "Stay. Please."

Calenne hauled her horse to a standstill. She stared out past the hastily raised redoubt and towards the forest of silken banners. The first Hadari outriders had entered the plain in late morning. The first infantry by early afternoon. Their tents spilled across the fields like a stain. Two farms had already fallen within the spreading cordon. Kai Saran's owl-banner flew free above. Crackling flames framed a third. Despite her eagerness to leave, Calenne couldn't bear the thought of Branghall burning thus.

"There are so many," she breathed.

Viktor wheeled his horse back around to join her. "And more to come."

More to come. It seemed impossible. But then, she'd no experience of war. No experience of so many things. "Is there any chance at all?"

He grunted. "If luck is with us."

"I thought soldiers didn't believe in luck."

"I'll believe in anything that brings victory."

She chuckled, more to hold back the feeling of despair than from any humour. "So you'll be praying tonight?"

He gave a wry shake of the head. "*Almost* anything."

She wanted to look away, but there was something hypnotic about the sun-glimmered green of the Hadari banners. So much more vibrant than the stark king's blue standards of the Tressian companies. And they were a world away from the patchwork militia. Most were Eskavord's citizens, but some had come from as far afield as the coast, or the Tevar Flood. Drawn by the promise of the Phoenix.

The promise that would get them killed.

"It's not too late," murmured Viktor. "You don't have to be here."

She shook her head. "There's no place else I belong. Not now. Can we win?"

"Yes."

She searched for the tick or flinch that would betray the lie. "You wouldn't deceive me on this, would you, Lord Akadra?"

"Not on this, nor anything else, Lady Trelan. I'd not dare."

Try as she might, Calenne sensed no lie in his words. "Then how can we win, when the numbers lie so heavy in their favour?"

"Because I do not intend to lose."

The simple arrogance ripped wild laughter from her lips. "And the weight of history turns on your wishes?"

He shook his head. "History is the sum of our deeds and our failures. How many men and women long for a chance to make a difference? How many act upon that chance when the moment comes? Those moments are Lumestra's greatest gift. I will seize all that present themselves. If others do the same, victory will be ours."

"And how will I know when my moment arrives?"

"I've no advice to give you. Not in this."

She smiled. "Then I suppose I'll have to trust my instincts."

"In the end, our instinct is all we have. That, and our duty."

The icularis arrived in Maiden's Hollow as the sun made a majestic descent beneath the western hills. The Hadari emissaries made no attempt to conceal their black, dag-necked silken robes, nor the sallow features so common to their kind. The gathered wolf's-heads parted warily, clearing a path to Drakos Crovan.

"We seek the Wolf King," intoned the tallest icularis.

Crovan shared a glance with Gavamor and Drenn – the only members of the Vagabond Council still loyal – and offered a shallow bow, his own expression no less wary than those of the icularis. "You have found him."

The icularis returned the bow. The three were curiously alike, with stiff-necked manner and watchful eyes. "We thank you for your hospitality," replied the tallest. "Such as it has been."

Crovan caught the sidelong gaze at the escort who had brought the icularis into the hollow. An escort now laden with belted swords, recurved short bows and bristling quivers.

He waved. "Return their weapons."

The wolf's-heads did as bidden and the icularis lost themselves in the process of rearmament. When they had done, their leader offered a nod. "My thanks."

Crovan shrugged. "My folk have learned to take precautions."

"As is understandable." The icularis waved the apology aside. "My name is Haldrane. I carry warmest greetings from his majesty, Kai Saran."

"And I'm pleased to receive—"

"Greetings, and instruction."

Crovan bristled. "If he has a request, I'll be happy to entertain it."

A wolfish smile touched Haldrane's lip. "Very well. His majesty expects to bring battle upon your oppressors at the first light of dawn. And he *requests* your every support."

"Of course." He turned to Vorn, who stood silent in the dappled shadow of a dancer's statue. "Fetch Kerril."

Vorn nodded and slunk away.

"Kerril has many spies in the Tressian ranks," Crovan went on. "He'll share all he has learned."

Haldrane's teeth gleamed. "Ah. You misunderstand. His majesty does not come to you seeking stories, or rumour, but blades."

Gavamor shared an uneasy glance with Silda Drenn. "You want us to fight with you?"

"That is his majesty's *request*."

"Can the mighty Hadari Empire not manage the Republic's leavings?" asked Drenn.

"Silda!" snapped Crovan. "I apologise for her tone . . . but she deserves an answer."

"The Hadari Empire is capable of many things. This request concerns not our need, but yours."

"I don't understand."

"We are not bringers of charity, or breakers of chains. We stand with those who stand with us. A seat at the Golden Court is earned, not given."

Haldrane's tone remained respectful, even friendly. Even so, Crovan didn't miss the threat in his eyes. Anliss had been right. Princes were all promises until they had what they desired. "What if we refuse?"

"His majesty is a forgiving soul. I am not." Silk whispered as Haldrane stepped closer. "Were you to betray his trust, my recommendation would be to raze every cot and field between here and the border. To sow every scrap of soil with salt."

Drenn leapt to her feet, her sword scraping from its scabbard. "Might find that hard without a head!"

Uproar overtook the hollow as a hundred voices vied for dominance. Steel glinted as Drenn's followers readied blades or set arrows to bowstrings.

The icularis made no move to draw their own weapons. Haldrane's gaze bored into Crovan throughout, oblivious to the commotion.

"Were I not to return ... " A raised voice was his only concession to the clamour. " ... then the burden of advice would fall upon another. His counsel would be no different. He might even levy a heavier coin for the discourtesy of my murder. Your children, perhaps. I'm sure, in time, they would embrace the loyalty you reject."

Crovan gritted his teeth. "You ask us to fight our countrymen."

"You have fought them for years on end," Haldrane snapped. "You make distinction among your own kind only when it pleases you. Or does the Wolf King not remember his time under arms in the Council's service? Does he believe we have not noted his haemorrhaging support? You promised us unity, *majesty*."

Crovan saw now that this had always been the shadowthorns' intent. It wasn't what he wanted – what he'd planned for. Perhaps he *should* have let Josiri have his way. "Do you have any further *requests*?"

Haldrane spread his hands, his manner suddenly that of a supplicant, not an extortionist. "You need offer no answer today. By your actions on the field we shall know your heart."

The icularis strode out of the hollow. No one moved to stop them.

All stood transfixed. Only when the last whisper of black robes had vanished into the trees did Silda Drenn throw down her sword with a cry of disgust.

"Raven's Eyes, Crovan! You a wolf or a scared pup?"

"And you've a better idea, I suppose?" Crovan growled.

"I won't do it." Gavamor toyed with the lion amulet about his neck. "I've no love for the northwealders, but I won't fight Halvor, Merrik and the rest. They're our people, for Lumestra's sake!"

Crovan closed his eyes. Answers came easier in the dark. Perhaps this one would also. There it was. The truth the light had hidden. That Gavamor, Drenn and the others were weak. More scared than he. That's why he led, and they followed. He need only stay strong a while longer. After all, everything would change at dawn.

He let the confidence of the dark fill him. Embraced the solace it offered as he had when facing down Josiri in this very place. The solace of that long night in the gloom of Skazit Maze.

"You *will* fight them!" He spread his arms and turned a slow circle so that none could miss the determination in his face. "You'll all fight them! Otherwise we'll be left with nothing. A sacrifice must be made."

"But our own kind." Gavamor spat into the dirt. "These are our friends. Even our family."

"They chose their path. Or do you propose we fight *with* Viktor Akadra, as Josiri wanted? The man who slew our beloved Phoenix? Who now defiles her memory just as he surely does her daughter? If we want to be free of the Council, this is the only way. If I'm wrong, then you need only strike me down. Another can make the choice."

Crovan let his arms drop. His gaze fell on Gavamor and on Drenn. On their lieutenants and his. All looked away.

"That's what I thought. Gather everyone you can. Everything changes, come the dawn."

Despite his earlier words, Viktor felt no great hope for the coming dawn. He'd no fear of the battle itself, save that which only fools lacked once beneath its shadow.

Nor did the disparity in troops alone cause him concern, for he'd many times achieved more with far less. But as he gazed around the campfire at the captains under his command, he felt the unevenness of the coming battle more than ever. Too many old faces, and too many young ones. Some in familiar uniform, others in little more than rags.

Some he knew. Tavor Lavirn of the Knights of Essamere. A competent commander by reputation, but Viktor would have given anything to have Roslava Orova at his side – or Kasamor Kiradin, returned from death to crack a joke and make light of the slaughter to come.

Lieutenant Dregar, who'd rescued a half-company from being trapped inside Kreska. And Revekah Halvor, of course. Her eyes had lost little hostility, but she'd not yet tried to stick a knife in his craw, so there was that.

Others, Viktor recognised from reputation alone. Jesver Merrik, the Terror of Kellin Valley. A fair price to be claimed for his head alone, and more for his men. Captain Kalla Masnar, who until two days earlier had served as military reeve at the inland port at Ardva. She'd brought near on two hundred blades with her – a motley mix of sailors, pavissionaires and tail-coated marines. An adventure-seeker, or a loyal soldier? Viktor supposed he'd find out.

But still, there were too many he didn't recognise at all – the Thrakkian twins among them. And too many who were prone to argument more than action.

"Raven's Eyes!" bellowed Kurkas. "Will you close your bloody mouths and listen?"

The din ebbed, though slower than Viktor would have liked.

"Thank you, captain."

"A pleasure, sir."

Viktor waited a moment before pressing on. His shadow, never at its most diffident when presented with conflict, coiled eagerly about his heart, longing to be set free.

"As I was saying, we cannot afford to be scattered. If we fight together, we win. If not ... Then we'll all feel foolish when called to account by the Raven, won't we?"

Laughter rippled about the fireside. No one laughed easier than a body fearing death.

"They want Eskavord. The only way is through us. This is about pride. Prince Saran needs to prove himself. He'll come, we'll hold him. And if they don't break apart on our shields, they'll scatter when Governor Yanda marches from Kreska."

He'd no idea if that was true, or even possible. But better a fool's hope than a savant's despair. Even a sliver of daylight made a difference in the dark.

"Where do you want my phoenixes?" asked Halvor.

Viktor tapped at the diagram he'd scraped in the ash with a stick and indicated the positions of the two hastily erected palisade mounds, one to the north of the battlefield and the other to the south. The Katya and Kevor redoubts, named for the duke and duchess of old. Thin defences intended as fortifications from which the army's few pavissionaires would fire.

"The centre. Between the redoubts. I'll be there with my own Phoenix ... " He shared a glance with Calenne, who sat opposite. " ... and the bulk of our new recruits. We've a few old soldiers among them, but I can think of no one better to make certain their efforts are wisely spent."

Halvor nodded. "Don't worry. My lads and lasses know what we're fighting for. We'll let old business lie until we've the luxury of ... conversation."

More laughter sounded, not all of it friendly. Viktor nodded. "Good enough. Kurkas?"

"Sah!"

"You'll have the southern flank. Take the hearthguard, and what we have of the 14th."

Kurkas frowned, as Viktor had known he would. "All things being equal, I'd rather be at your side. Won't hear the last of it if you catch a shadowthorn spear in the throat."

"And I need a steady hand and seasoned soldiers to the south. I promise not to embarrass you by dying foolishly."

The frown smoothed away. "Appreciate that, sir. Let me know if you change your mind."

"You'll be the first to hear. Captain Masnar, you'll have the north. Ground's too broken there for shield walls or cataphracts. It'll be bloody. Master Merrik, I imagine you'll find it to your liking."

"Do you indeed?" Merrik drawled. "We'll see."

"Splitting us up?" asked Halvor. "Worried we can't be trusted together?"

"If I thought that, you'd not be here. Lord Lavirn? You have the reserve, and what little cavalry we have. We haven't the knights to match them on the charge, so you're a counterblow unless I send word otherwise."

The list went on. Viktor took care to acknowledge each of the captains about the fire. To spare them a word and remind them of their purpose. Too soon, it was done – a reminder of how thin the lines would be come the morrow.

"If there are any more questions, now's the time."

"No questions, Lord Akadra," said Calenne. "But I'd like to say something."

He dipped his head. "Of course."

Her eyelids flickered, but so briefly that Viktor was certain everyone else missed her hesitation. Then she stood, her armour bright orange in the firelight as the folds of her cloak fell open.

"Fifteen years ago, my mother made the legend of the Phoenix into a symbol of hope. I won't pretend that we're all here for the same reason." Her voice quickened as she spoke, as it had in the marketplace the day before. "Some of us are fighting for family. Others for duty, or out of pride. And I suspect more than a few because of coin."

Kurkas' soft chuckle faded as Viktor's gaze fell on him. Viktor knew, as he hoped the others did not, how desperately nervous Calenne had been of this speech. She'd fretted over every word and phrase. Viktor had offered to take the burden instead. She'd refused. The Phoenix had brought them together. It was her voice they needed to hear.

"I don't know what comes after tomorrow," Calenne pressed on. "Lord Akadra believes that we can put our unhappy history behind us. That northwealders and south can consider themselves kin once more. I don't know that I agree. But it doesn't matter, because we *are* kin, if only for tomorrow. If only because we share an enemy who neither of us can defeat alone. Beyond that, we'll see. But first, we have to win."

Halvor closed her eyes, lost in treasured memory. Calenne drew her sword. She'd chosen the blade with care, and with the benefit of Viktor's advice. It was lighter and slenderer than most, to suit an arm untempered by battle. It shone like silver beneath the moon, and the stylised golden wings of its hilt blazed like fire.

"I have put old wounds behind me. Whether you fight for family, for duty, for pride – or even for coin – I ask you all to do the same. And when Kai Saran is dead, and his army scattered? Maybe that kinship will last."

She reversed the sword – holding it by the blade as Viktor had tutored her – and extended the pommel above the dying fire in salute. The old salute that predated Konor Belenzo. That came even before the kings of old from whose line Malatriant had sprung. An offering of service. Of protection. A soldier's duty, and a noble's responsibility.

Rising, he drew his longsword to mirror Calenne's and set its pommel touching hers. The blade felt tiny in his hands, but it would have made poor theatre to accidentally decapitate one of the captains with his claymore.

Halvor followed suit. The wobble to her lip told Viktor he had chosen well. Some traditions were stronger than steel. Kurkas' battered sword joined the circle. Then Lavirn's. Then Masnar's. Then the hooked blades of the twins' axes. On and on, until a ring of unbroken steel topped the flame.

Viktor met Calenne's gaze once more. The nervousness was still there, but pride held it at bay. She even managed a smile.

"Lumestra shine for us all," she said.

Thirty-Five

The constabulary patrol clomped on, their rhythm tightening as they passed Swanholt. Rosa pressed deeper into the alley's shadows and stifled a smile. Folk always raised their efforts around an Akadra. Especially Viktor. Why, back at their first meeting – she a squire fresh from the chapterhouse of Essamere, and he the commander of the 7th – there had been ... *something* ... about him that had made her want to do better. To *be* better.

Though it hurt to recall, she'd been a terrible officer. Too sure of herself. Too ready to scorn advice. And then there had been that dreadful day out past the village of Rackan. A dozen dead – the sergeant who'd warned her of the ambush among them. Others had wanted to send her back to the chapterhouse. Viktor alone had argued for her. What she'd made of herself since, she owed to him.

And now she was about to betray him.

"Didn't think you were the type for an illicit alleyway rendezvous." Sevaka's breath brushed warm against her neck. "But I'm not *wholly* against the idea."

Rosa winced. Too lost in thought to hear her coming? That didn't bode well for the night's labours. "Didn't know the navy taught sneaking about."

She sniffed. "We're not all club-footed webbies. Learned this in the city, flitting from bedchamber to bedchamber."

"I'm sure I don't want to know."

"*I'm* sure I'm not going to tell you." She folded her arms. "Well? What's all this about?"

Rosa hesitated, but the time for doubts was long in the past. "I was thinking about what you said. About proof."

"*Okay . . .* " She stared past Rosa's shoulder to Swanholt. "Your 'fellow knight' with feathered wings? You meant *Viktor*?"

"Yes."

Sevaka massaged her brow. "And the proof. This is happening now."

"Viktor's still away in the Southshires. His father's . . . "

"His father's at Freemont. I know."

" . . . so the house is as empty as it's likely to get."

"Empty? You call a dozen servants and fifty hearthguards empty?"

Rosa folded her arms. "Does Hadon strike you as the sort that gives his staff free run of the mansion while he's away?"

"Not now you mention it." Sevaka shrugged her defeat and looked Rosa up and down. "That's why you're dressed up like a vranakin?"

"If I get caught, it needs to be about me, and only me. I won't drag my chapterhouse into dishonour."

"But you'll drag me along?" Sevaka asked deadpan. "Should I be flattered?"

"You're not coming inside. You're the feint . . . the distraction."

"I know what feint means, thank you very much." Her eyes narrowed. "How am I being distracting, exactly?"

"See that?" Rosa pointed towards Swanholt's darkened west wing. "Those are Viktor's rooms. He and his father don't care for each other's company."

"I *had* heard."

"This is the closest point of approach through the grounds. I can handle the wall . . . "

"A six-foot wall topped by a four-foot railing? I don't like your chances. 'less you've a pair of wings yourself."

Rosa scowled. The last thing she wanted was a discussion about why she felt confident of an impossible jump. "Like I said, I can handle the wall, I'd like the patrols looking the other way. That's where you come in. Head around the far side, make a bit of noise."

"Like *what*, exactly?"

She shook her head in exasperation. "I don't know. Sing Deverett's *Requiem* for all I care. Bellow a shanty and throw rocks at the railing. Don't tell me you never did something like this as a child?"

"You're mad."

Rosa had to give her that one. Breaking into the home of a dear friend because of hearsay. But it wasn't hearsay, was it? It was Kas' word, delivered by a grieving mother to whom he'd been the only source of joy. And now Kas was dead. If she found nothing, she'd live with the stain on her honour for the hope it offered that Kas had been mistaken about Viktor, or that Ebigail had misrepresented his words for reasons of her own. But if she uncovered anything that even hinted at a connection with the vranakin ...

She fished the ring from her pocket and held it out. "Do you recognise this?"

Sevaka's eyes narrowed to slits. "My grandmother's ring. Where did you get it?"

"I was with Malachi during last night's attack. I took it from the kernclaw's hand ... after I severed it."

Sevaka's brow knitted in suspicion. "And where did *he* get it?"

"When he killed Kasamor."

"No." Her face, already pale in the shadows, lost the last of its colour. She gagged, and grasped at the wall for support. "No. No. No. You must be mistaken. You *must.*"

"I'm not. I was there. It was the same man. He remembered me – and I'll never forget him."

Sevaka twisted away, her face contorted in anguish. A part of Rosa wondered why the revelation had hit her so hard. But then she recalled Ebigail's insistence she not involve Sevaka. Perhaps the sister simply lacked the brother's strength, though Rosa couldn't find it in her heart to disdain her for it. Some losses should never be easily borne.

"You think Viktor ordered *both* deaths?" said Sevaka.

Her incredulity brought swirling emotions to the surface once more. But that was the thing about Viktor, wasn't it? He left an impression. He made you believe in him. Rosa wondered briefly how Sevaka knew him, but it would have been more remarkable had she not, given their parents' close association.

"I also thought him above such things," she replied. "But the more time passes, the more I wonder."

"Very little is beneath the powerful, when the need is there." Sevaka spoke softly. "Especially when status and pride are at stake. No, this is a mistake. A horrible mistake. It has to be."

Her insistent words wrestled with an unpleasant truth. Her eyes mirrored Rosa's own heartsick mood.

Rosa laid a hand on her arm. "No more arguments. I have to do this."

Sevaka's head snapped about, eyes red-ringed. "No. You don't. Go home."

Rosa shook her head. "I can't. I've thought about this all day. The ring proves the connection between Kas' death and the attempt on Malachi's life. It doesn't prove Viktor gave the order ... "

"No." Sevaka spoke in barely a whisper. "No, it doesn't. Rosa ... What if it wasn't Viktor?"

"I still have to look. I have to know for certain."

"If I ever doubted how much you loved my brother, I do so no longer. Walk away. Please."

"This was your idea."

"Don't remind me."

"So you won't help?"

Sevaka took a deep breath. A little colour returned to her cheeks. "No. I'll help. Because if I don't, and you're caught ... and with all the fun *that* entails ... I don't know how I'll live with that." She sighed. "And because you asked. Everyone else *demands*."

Apara drew the cloak of ravens close about her body and stepped off the rooftop. The wind swept her away. Cobbles blurred far beneath her feet. Then the iron-tipped stone and trees of the mansion's boundary wall. She could have touched the sky, save for the clouds. She was above everything. A god among ephemerals.

So why did she feel so wretched?

The cloak shifted as Apara descended, its manifold voices croaking their delight. Still consumed by the giddiness of flight, she landed heavily. Knees buckled and her boots gouged the sod. The ravens croaked one last time, and dispersed, and the cloak was simple wool-cloth again. But the cold remained. Apara suspected she'd never be free of it.

Voices broke the cool air. Apara's pulse quickened. Crouching low, she stared off through the trees at the firestone-lit paths leading to the mansion's drive. She marked at least a dozen uniforms in the gloom. Another consequence of Nikros' failure.

Still, the lady had been insistent, and the consequences of failure unthinkable.

Keeping close to the trees, Apara wended her way to the mansion's rear. Twice, she fell prone as a patrol drew near. Twice, the hearthguards tromped on along the gravel without backward glance.

She could have used the cloak again, of course. But she didn't like the way it whispered in her thoughts. Nor the creeping sensation that not all those thoughts were her own. She still heard the Raven's dour, sardonic voice. His promise of further "gifts" if she proved herself mistress of those already given. Apara didn't want the ones she had.

At last, the raised terrace came into sight, its vine-wreathed trellises concealing what passed within. Apara let the nearest patrol amble deeper into the darkness and eased the latch clear.

No firestone lanterns blazed beyond the gate. There was only the gentle glow of moonlight, and the soft murmur of water trickling away into the pond. Apara took a deep breath. The cool, moist air drove back the raven-cloak's chill . . .

"I asked to meet with your cousin, not you."

The lady emerged from the shadow of a rose bower, her expression the familiar mask of disappointment and watchfulness. Apara could have sworn she'd been alone but was not surprised to discover otherwise. A lady who knew as much of the Crowmarket as this one did likely had many hidden talents.

"My cousin now serves the Raven in Otherworld," Apara replied. She drew back her hood. "Whatever business you had with him, is now with me."

The lady's eyes widened in surprise. Then the stony expression recovered itself. "I see. The Parliament were ever wasteful. Too much pride, and not enough heart. Was this your choice?"

Apara stared down at her moon-cast reflection in the pond. At the single white streak of hair that marred the black. "My cousins chose for me."

"I'm sure it's not what your mother would have wanted." Was that a note of pity in the lady's voice? "But I'm also sure you'll acquit yourself with excellence. You always have."

Apara hung her head to hide her woeful expression. "Yes, lady."

She'd loved the thief's art since her earliest days. The game was played for high stakes, but it was a game nonetheless, and put only her own life at risk. She'd broken bones and left bruises, of course. That was a cost the game sometimes demanded. But murder? That wasn't a game, no matter how much her younger cousins might brag. You were changed by every dying breath.

The lady's lips parted, then closed again as if she'd thought better of words she'd intended to speak. "As it happens, the task will benefit from your skills. We cannot afford another blundering display. This must be quiet, precise and elegant. Am I understood?"

Apara hesitated. She could refuse the commission – flee far from Tressia and the lady's reach. But flight would solve nothing. Her life was now forfeit. Only the deaths of others could keep her from the Raven's grasp.

"You are, lady," she said at last. "What must I do?"

"Stay back! I mean it!"

Even knowing *something* was coming, Rosa had to fight the instinct to investigate. The words had just the right pitch of terror, of pleading. Never mind the navy, Sevaka had missed her turn on the stage.

Or she had a surfeit of raw emotion to excise. Rosa knew how that went.

"No! Lumestra! I ... " The scream trailed off into a jagged, stuttering sob.

Shouts rose to fill the silence – within the Swanholt wall, and beyond it. Running feet came close behind.

Rosa pulled her half-mask into place, counted to three, and broke cover for the iron-topped wall. Three paces distant, she hurled herself into the air. Fingers strained for the railing's crossbar. She'd just enough time to reconsider the wisdom of her actions before her fingers brushed the gilded metal. A sharp tug, a soft scuff of boot against stone, and she was over the spikes and in among the trees.

She lingered at the foot of the wall, eyes adjusting to the gloom-laden grounds. Commotion echoed from the east. The clamour of bells rose above voices as pursuit quickened.

"I hope you're running, Sevaka," Rosa breathed.

She shook her head. She couldn't worry about that now. The Swanholt hearthguards wouldn't trouble themselves with affray beyond their walls. Even now, those lured away would be returning.

She broke cover for the west wing, and the servant's door hidden behind the terrace. What she hadn't known was that the door would be guarded. But the guard clung too close to the lantern-post and its comforting circle of light. He was blind to everything beyond. By the time he saw Rosa coming, he was within reach.

Her fist struck home. The cry of alarm dissipated alongside its utterer's wits. Rosa caught him as he fell. Pausing only to slip his keys from his belt, she dragged him into the shadow of the terrace wall and made her way inside.

No one challenged her as she made her way to the upper floor. Rosa hoped the guard remembered only the mask. One stint in the constabulary cells was sufficient. Either way, time was short. Another alarm would soon be raised.

Rosa's search of Viktor's chambers was efficient as it was fuelled by belief that there was no one to note her ransack. She upended drawers and emptied cupboards. She opened the curtains a crack to read correspondence beneath moonlight, and tipped mattress and cushions aside. Each tick of the grandfather clock drove her to greater recklessness.

Clothes and trinkets. Mementoes of past battles. The assorted ephemera of a man with an eye for curiosities, and the wealth to indulge it. Letters revealed nothing but friendships sustained by penmanship, or favours sought by nobles. But of the Crowmarket, there was nothing. Not even the merest trace. No correspondence. No tally of goods. No coded papers. No suggestion of influence peddled to the Parliament's benefit.

Rosa screamed silently and set the last of the letters aside. She'd been a fool. There'd never been anything to find. Either Kas had been wrong... or Viktor was too canny to keep anything incriminating so close to hand. There she stood, in the scattered remnants of his possessions, and he'd needed to take only the simplest of precautions to protect himself. Queen's Ashes, but he'd surely have burned any...

The fire. There might be some trace.

Rosa knelt at the grate, but the fire had seen no use in recent weeks.

The fragments of charred but readable paper retreated back into her imagination.

She sank onto her haunches and stared at the firebox.

And she saw the fold of oilcloth, black against dark stone.

Questing fingers traced the material back to its source: a heavy bundle on the smoke shelf. She tugged it free. Spluttering as the soot clogged her throat, Rosa peeled back the cloth. Two leather-bound books, their spines cracked with age, stood revealed in the gloom. Her heart leapt. Was this what she'd searched for all this time? She didn't know whether to cheer or to weep.

With trembling fingers, she eased back the cover of the first. Silver letters shone upon a jet-black page. No, Rosa realised. This wasn't what she'd sought. This was much worse.

The bells chimed for midnight by the time Apara stood before the clifftop mansion. Jagged walls and paths that jutted into nowhere spoke to the sea's timeless hunger. For now, Windchine mansion remained hale – even if its position grew more tenuous with each passing year.

A practical owner might have buttressed the cliffs, or else rebuilt the imposing towers further inland. No such precaution had been taken. The only stonework were remnants of burial alcoves, jutting from the wind-swept grass – outriggers of the sepulchres that riddled Tressia's bedrock.

Apara wondered how many caskets the waves had swallowed. What had become of their occupants? Would Lumestra know to seek the faithful amid the waves as well as in stone's cold embrace? Would those souls for ever wander the paths of Otherworld, never seeing their loved ones come the light of Third Dawn?

She wondered also why it bothered her so, for her blood family had forgotten her, and she them. The Crowmarket were now her only kin.

The raven-cloak saw Apara safe past the thin patrols. Each use came easier, the giddiness ever lesser than before. She passed within reach of one guard with him never the wiser. She could have slit his throat without ever leaving the shadow. The thought excited almost as much as it appalled. She wondered whether the notion had even been her own, or one dreamed up by the cloak?

Another shadowed embrace, and she alighted upon a balcony. A scrape of lock-picks, and she was inside. She trod chambers drowned in dust sheets, and where faded paint marked the extent of portraits removed. The house was as much a tomb as the shattered mausolea lining the cliff face below. It was sad, threatening and eerie all at once.

The chapel. The lady had said to seek the chapel.

Apara slipped out into the hallway. A measure of light and life crept up the central stair to greet her. She turned aside from the rich furnishings of the entrance hall and began the ascent to the upper floors.

The chapel nestled at the eastern end of the uppermost floor. Such was often the way. If one were to make dawn observance to Lumestra, better to do so in such a way as to lift your prayers above those of the common people. Even omniscience needed a helping hand. Gentle song crept along the passageway. One voice alone. An old voice.

Apara slipped her stiletto from her belt and eased open the chapel door. The light within reflected off the door's stained-glass panels. Fragments of orange-white light danced along the wall. Not the light of firestone lanterns, but the flickering flames of votive candles set along the altar's rim.

The chapel itself was all but empty. A lone figure knelt before an altar laden with dry, withered scrolls. A nightgown pooled about her knees, and her hands were clasped in prayer. The song ceased.

"So you've come," said Lady Marest. "I knew you would."

Apara froze, expecting at any moment to hear the ringing of bells and shouts of alarm. But she heard nothing. She eased the door closed. "You couldn't. I didn't know myself until an hour ago."

"Oh, I didn't mean you specifically, young lady. But someone *like* you." A thin chuckle echoed around the room. "In a way, I'm surprised it's taken this long. Have you harmed my servants? My hearthguards?"

"No. I'd no need."

"I'm grateful. They've served me well. I suppose Ebigail sent you?"

Apara drew closer over chequerboard tiles. The stiletto hung heavy in her hand. *Quiet, precise and elegant.* By the lady's instructions, she'd hoped that meant Lady Marest could be taken unawares, or even asleep. That would have been easier.

"I cannot say."

Her withered legs shaking with effort, Lady Marest rose. She had no weapon. Her lined face held neither hatred nor fear. There was only calm. Her serenity was a close match for the serathi caryatids whose wings supported the chapel's roof.

"Oh come," said the old woman. "You're here to kill me. Do me this small courtesy. I won't fight. I won't make a fuss. You'll find my soul slips free with ease. Did Ebigail send you?"

Apara took a half-step back. The old woman's calm was terrifying, in its way. "Yes."

Lady Marest hung her head. "I thought so. Hadon, Malachi, everyone else . . . she has them so entangled in games of status and pride that they don't see the web she's weaving. But I do. I am not a fool, young lady . . ."

"I'm not a young anything. Not for years."

"These things are relative." She shook her head. "When you reach my age, when friends and family have gone to dust, everyone seems young. But kindly don't interrupt. I'm not a fool, though many think me foolish. I've had one foot in the mists for years and am not easily blinded by pride. Ebigail believes herself a growing shadow that will eclipse us all. But even a shadow has no purchase in the Dark. Your patron knows that better than any."

Apara shook her head. She wanted to discount the old woman's words as babble. However, her proud demeanour demanded otherwise. And she *definitely* didn't want to be reminded that the Raven had his talons deep in her soul.

"I'm in no mood for a sermon."

"I imagine not. But the Dark always returns. It whispers in our souls. It gorges on our quarrels. And it breaks us apart so that tyranny can flourish – until there is no voice save its own. Konor Belenzo knew that, but the first council hid the truth. They thought it enough to bury Malatriant and forget her. Make her physical fact into deepest myth. Arrogance."

Perhaps she was mad, thought Apara. But if so, it was a quiet madness borne by many whose faith outshone their reason. "You're fortunate I've come. The church's provosts would burn you as a heretic for those words."

Lady Marest ran a hand along the nearest scroll. "Not my words. Belenzo's. It took Karkosa and I a lifetime to find them all. Longer to understand their meaning. So many lessons we should have heeded. Now it's too late."

Apara frowned. If the scrolls truly contained the last sermons of Konor Belenzo, they'd be worth a fortune. As she started forward, Lady Marest toppled a candle. Fire crackled across dry brittle paper.

"No!" Apara cried out. "Why did you do that?"

"Because we deserve what's coming. We deserve *her*." A tear glistened on her cheek. "I've heard Malatriant's voice in my dreams so often in recent days. And Lumestra is no longer here to save us."

She *was* mad, Apara decided. A wandering mind lost in a world of prophecy and scripture. "I thought Lumestra was eternal."

"Only the Dark lasts for ever," said Lady Marest. "And I've no desire to feel it settle in my heart. I'd go to the Raven with my soul still radiant with a reflection of Lumestra's light ... So you see how in serving one, you serve us both?"

Apara did. Whatever reward the addled noblewoman sought, she'd wit enough to realise that it would be denied her if she embraced the Raven. She needed another to end her life. So why then did the burden of the coming murder not lessen? "I do."

"Will you give me this gift?"

Apara hesitated, but what else could she say? "Yes."

Lady Marest gave a shuddering breath. Her expression lit up with joy pure as the brightest sunlight. Her smile didn't so much as flicker as Apara slid the stiletto between her ribs.

The kitchen door creaked. Marek stared blearily at the remnants of his evening meal. It had been a long day, and he wasn't getting any younger. Didn't mean he couldn't exercise his frustrations on whichever of his subjects had disturbed a rare moment of quiet. One of the footmen, no doubt, sneaking in for leftovers while he thought his betters asleep.

His chair scraped against tile as he stood. "Quit your sneaking around. You want to feel the flat of my belt?"

The door fell closed, revealing not the expected footman, but Lady Sevaka. Or someone who bore a passing resemblance to Lady Sevaka. In all his years, Marek had never seen her eyes so hard or her skin so pale.

"Marek?" she said, her voice taut as a steel bar. "What has my mother done?"

Tzadas, 6th day of Radiance

We speak of the Dark as a living being. It is far more – but also far less. Even that splinter that survived Lumestra's wrath has the power to reshape the world, but it can only act through our flesh and our souls.

Why else would it shape others to its service?

from the sermons of Konor Belenzo

Thirty-Six

The sun did not so much rise as slink from beneath the horizon, casting reluctant light on the distant imperial battle lines. The green silks and golden scale of the Immortals. The dark robes and leathers of shieldsmen and outriders. And to the west, no distance at all across the valley's wheat-fields, the king's blue tabards among golden crops. Outnumbered. Doomed. Drakos Crovan suspected Lumestra wanted no part of what the day would bring. Nor did he.

"Having second thoughts?" asked Silda Drenn.

"Second, and third, and fourth," Crovan replied. "Trastorov once wrote that we delight in breaking oaths. The ultimate freedom."

She spat. "There's a reason they burned Trastorov. Bugger was a witch."

"Three factions muster below. I've given my oath to each, at different times. I've broken one already. By dusk, I'll have broken at least one more."

"Then rejoice," she replied. "For you're about to be freer than ever."

Crovan shook his head angrily. On the field below, Tressian shields formed up beneath towering kraikons. There'd be simarka too, prowling the wheat. "I haven't felt free since I came home. I never wanted any of . . . this."

"Then what do you want?"

A good question. He'd wanted to fight injustice. Once, he'd had a plan. Now . . . Now he wasn't sure how he'd even got here, or where he was going. The path ahead was steep, but the path behind was shrouded in the mist of inconstant memory, and a dark voice tempting him to ruin. How could a life change so much without conscious choice?

"To live out my days with a clear conscience," Crovan replied.

"Can't be done. Better to embrace it."

Maybe Drenn was right. A few paces more; the slope would lessen and the mists would part. He'd feel the sun on his face, instead of the chill in his bones.

Drawing himself up, Crovan turned his back on the quickening battle. "We'll let the Hadari take the brunt. We may have to fight at their side, but I'll embrace the Raven before I let our people win Saran's war."

Drenn nodded and slipped away through the trees.

The phoenix re-buckled and re-sited her sword belt three times before Viktor passed her. Her neighbour in the shield wall scraped a whetstone across a dagger already sharpened to a razor's kiss. Hands pressed to lockets, sun pendants and wedding rings. Talismans all on a bleak day where even the wind seemed stale and unwilling.

Viktor understood the rituals, but he'd none of his own. You fought, maybe you died. In the aftermath you remembered friend and foe. Until then, there was only the killing.

The twin banners of their centre twitched fitfully in the breeze. The swan banner was one of two Viktor had brought from Tressia. The second streamed to the south, above the walls of Blackridge Farm. The phoenix seemed drab by comparison. But miracles couldn't be expected from a refashioned tabard.

Revekah and Calenne waited beneath, the former on foot and the latter astride a steed. Their conversation fell silent as Viktor approached. Revekah offered a sharp nod and strode away south to the company of her phoenixes.

"She doesn't care for me," rumbled Viktor.

"She's spent fifteen years hating you," said Calenne. "That doesn't pass overnight."

"It did for you."

"That's different. I didn't hate you – I hated the nightmare I made of you. It's not the same."

He grunted. "So long as she stands the line."

Calenne's wry smile did little to hide her nervousness. "She's also spent the last fifteen years fighting a lost cause. Today's no different."

Viktor stared out across the gently swaying wheat. Hadari spear points gleamed in the wan light. Emerald pennants twitched in the wind. If only there'd been more time to prepare. Alas, fate mocked intent. You could divert the river's course, but not cease its flow.

A babble of whispers interrupted his thoughts. A towering, hunch-shouldered form lumbered into sight across the field. Thrice the size of a horse, its leathery, wrinkled flanks and stocky legs were almost hidden beneath a caparison of scale and silk. The beast's head hung low between its shoulders. A thick horn curved upward from its broad snout. A chariot rumbled into view, drawn thus by a thick yoke across the beast's neck.

"What *is* that?" breathed Calenne.

"A grunda," Viktor replied. "They roam the Empire's eastern plains. It'll crash clean through our lines if we give it the chance." He raised his voice. "Crossbows will bring it down. If they don't, kraikons will."

Or one of the ballistae hurriedly dragged from Cragwatch, he added silently. They'd four of the machines, two each in the Katya and Kevor redoubts. The kraikons would need the help. Viktor glimpsed heavy-handled war hammers among the Immortals' spears. A strong man working a war hammer's tail-spike could prise the armour apart and set the magic loose. No magic, no kraikon ... and no hope.

"We hold the line," he said. "They'll tire themselves out. Happens all the time on the border."

Grey heads nodded. Old soldiers from Zanya and the years before. They gave him hope. Experience. Calm. Discipline. These counted for more than youthful vigour.

Viktor raised a fist. "Shields to the fore!"

The line rippled. Shields the height of a tall child slammed into place, forming an unbroken king's blue line. Short swords slipped from scabbards. Halberds, too cumbersome for the front rank, were readied in the second and third. Viktor would have liked a fourth, but their numbers were too sparse. Already, the back ranks held more militia than he'd have liked. Steel didn't make a soldier.

Calenne's horse champed restlessly. "Is it me," she asked, "or are you enjoying yourself?"

"What makes you say so?" Viktor replied.

"You seem less ... I don't know ... conflicted."

"I prefer battle's simplicity," he admitted. "I'd sooner face a man with a sword in his hand than talk him out of its wielding."

"So much for Viktor Akadra the silver-tongued charmer."

"Who says I'm that?"

"Captain Kurkas, for one."

"Captain Kurkas talks too much." Viktor scowled in rare embarrassment. Talkative or no, he wished Kurkas were at his side. But there was too much at stake, and he needed a trusted voice to the south. If only he'd as much confidence in Masnar and her rabble in the broken ground to the north. "I wish you'd fight on foot."

Calenne arched an eyebrow at the artless change of topic. "A fine sentiment from a man who refuses a shield."

"A shield slows me down."

"And relying on my own feet slows *me* down. We've been over this."

"The horse makes you a target."

"It makes me a symbol. We both know I'm no soldier. If I've any value, it's when folk can see me – when they see my mother, if they're so inclined. They can't do that if I'm lost among the wheat. Not even if I jump up and down ... which wouldn't be very dignified."

He chuckled at the image of her bobbing up and down like a child on a teeter-tilt. Southwealders shot him startled glances. It seemed mirth was an unfit companion for the legend of Akadra the Phoenix-Slayer. Akadra the Monster.

Good.

"Honestly, Viktor," said Calenne. "You needn't worry. I shall do nothing needless."

He nodded, painfully aware she was there only because of his actions. At his insistence, the proctors had assigned a full dozen simarka to her defence. They couldn't shield her from arrows, but anything else ...?

"I suppose that will have to do."

"Ever the gallant." She tugged a length of blue ribbon from her plaits and pressed it into his hand. "Here."

"What's this?"

"A token of my favour to remind you why you're fighting. That's the done thing, isn't it?"

He wound the material through his fingers. "I've duty for that."

"Duty." She growled the word in gruff imitation. "To the Republic, I suppose?"

"I *am* the Council's champion."

"And today you're mine also."

Viktor glanced at the ribbon, and then at Calenne. He marked the tightness about her eyes. The slight, erratic twitch of her lower lip. Had a scryer foretold their friendship in a hand of pentassa cards, he'd have laughed. But friendship there was, nonetheless ... and perhaps a glimpse of ...

They both had something more to lose this day.

He shrugged his claymore from his shoulders and knotted the ribbon about the pommel. "Strange. Seems heavier now. And too pretty a gift for a monster."

"I thought you weren't a monster?"

"I am today. We must all be as monstrous as events demand."

"Then go, be a monster. Just remember that the man owes me a ribbon."

The thunder of drums split the sky. Away beyond the sea of wheat, the golden line swelled.

Viktor pushed his way to the centre of the front line. The wind picked up. The twin banners ripped and snapped, their emblems clear for the first time since dawn. The swan and the phoenix. Together. How things had changed.

"Weapons up!" bellowed Viktor. "And may Lumestra's light shine for us all!"

The drums crashed in crescendo then faded. Havildars' swords gleamed along the length of the line.

"Loose!"

Arrows hissed away. Melanna knew those that didn't fall short would more likely find shields than flesh. But ritual was ritual. Three volleys. Tradition. Once for the goddess, once for the Emperor ... and once for his heir.

At least, so long as that heir was a son.

The drum-roll crashed back, louder than before. Melanna walked her horse along the cataphracts' front rank. Spears dipped to her touch, to the blessing of the Ashanal. She acceded with reluctance, and Sera's silent urging. Was she not the goddess's chosen? Even if the goddess almost certainly did not approve of what she'd done?

The handmaiden rode a little behind. Her steed was more moonlight and shadow than flesh and bone. Its single pale horn glinted with the same light as its rider's shard-spear. It bore neither harness nor saddle. Melanna knew of the chandirin from a hundred tales. She'd believed them myth until the herd had arrived with the moonrise. From the eyes widening behind the Immortals' close-fitting helms, so had many others.

The drums broke off. Arrows blackened the skies for a second time.

At last, she reached her father. Sturdy parentage and a life of battle had gifted Kai Saran with a powerful, barrel-chested physique. One Melanna was glad not to have inherited. Mantled in cloak, crested helm and emerald-studded armour, he looked nothing less than a god – a brother to cold Ashana and radiant Lumestra. The high-browed visage sculpted into the helm's visor and cheek-pieces only accentuated the comparison.

Melanna spurred past Hal Drannic's black-cloaked frame and Kos Devren's unyielding scowl. Close enough to make herself heard over the clamour of the drums. Sera hung back, her chandirin flicking a restless tail.

"Father."

He stared rigidly ahead across the wheat. "Daughter. Have you come to steal the honour of the first charge?"

"Of course not," Melanna replied softly. "All I have ever sought is to serve you, as your firstborn should."

"And if I command you leave the field, as a *daughter* should ... Will you do so?"

Still he wouldn't look at her. Was she such a disappointment that he could barely acknowledge her presence, let alone her desires? Now, on the eve of a battle that might separate them for ever? Melanna's throat thickened.

"No." She strove for a balance between respect and firmity. "Because I *am* your daughter. I am a Saran. If you ask me not to prove my worthiness even as you do the same ... then I cannot obey."

Still he stared away. "Then take your disobedience north. Harness it to victory. The warchiefs expect you ... Ashanal."

The drums faded. A third hiss of arrows cleaved the grey morning. Melanna caught her breath. The heir's salute. For all his rigid manner, for all his stern tone, her father had just decreed that his daughter was the equal of a son. Her heart swelled, its burdens forgotten.

"I shall make you proud, Father."

His hand slipped from the pommel and gripped hers. "You already have, *essavim*."

The ridged metal of his gauntlet dug into Melanna's flesh. She didn't care.

"Now go," he said. "You have duties to fulfil. For your goddess, and for your emperor."

After an eternity beneath the boughs of Davenwood, the trees fell away. Josiri hauled his steed to a standstill, awed and terrified at the spectacle below.

At that distance, warriors were no more than ants marching to a purpose. Walls of spears, fronted by bright colours and stark emblems. A golden wedge of cavalry at the centre, and another of silver and white to the north. The lumbering, implacable tread of grunda wagons. And everywhere, the foreboding promise of the drums.

Josiri beheld it all and regretted his hasty departure from Branghall without taking down his uncle's armour from its plinth. One more regret to join all the others from recent days.

[[We're too late.]] Anastacia tightened her grip around Josiri's waist.

His gaze drifted to the Tressian lines. The thin, truncated Tressian lines that waxed thickest between two uneven palisades. At the northern end, amid the broken ground of the Davenwood Heights, there were no lines to speak of, just clusters of warriors among the rocks. Hopeless. It looked hopeless.

And Calenne was in the thick of it. Because of him.

"No," he said firmly, as much to convince himself as Anastacia. "We're not. If I can make Crovan see sense ... "

But it wasn't that easy, was it? Convincing Crovan didn't guarantee victory. It merely shifted the odds. But what else was there?

[[And if you can't?]]

The drums quickened. Golden cavalry dipped spears and rowelled their horses to the charge. Horns rang out. A ballista shot from the nearer bastion ploughed a bloody furrow in the shadowthorn lines. Arrows arced high and shivered against shields.

A chill gripped Josiri's gut. He welcomed it. Better fear than the anger and self-loathing of late. For the first time in days, he felt like himself.

"Then I'm going down there anyway," he said. "Alone, if I must."

Thirty-Seven

The cataphract charge held no subtlety, apt for those who took to the field in armour that shone like the sun. Instead, Kai Saran gathered his finest warriors like a thunderbolt and hurled them across the field.

"Hold the line!" Viktor bellowed above the rising drums. Veterans of Zanya echoed his words. Timber and metal rattled as the line closed up. "If the shields hold, we live!"

He thrust the point of his claymore into the ground and glanced along the line of trampled wheat. There'd been a simple truth to his words. With the line anchored north and south by the redoubts – and further reinforced by kraikons, no less – it could not be outflanked, only breached.

And it would be. There were too many whispered prayers and furtive eyes among the militia. Viktor had seen that same doubt countless times on the border. Recruits saw only the gilded glory of the Hadari armour. Never the vulnerable flesh beneath.

"My lord ... You need a shield. Begging your pardon, but the buggers'll ride you down."

Calmly, deliberately, Viktor set his back to the onrushing Hadari. The speaker was a weather-beaten man in a sea-grey tabard not seen in the Southshires for fifteen years.

"What's your name?"

Eyes narrowed beneath salt-and-pepper brows. "Zhastov. Corporal Zhastov, used to be."

The hoof-beats quickened in tempo and volume. Viktor ignored them. "Were you at Zanya?"

"I was."

"You see me use a shield there?"

" . . . no, my lord."

"Who won that battle?"

Zhastov's lip curled in the echo of a snarl. "You did, my lord."

Viktor nodded. He blotted out the sound of the approaching cataphracts. Instead, he gauged their closeness by the horrified expressions of the southwealder militia. Behind, he glimpsed Calenne beneath the twin banners. Their eyes met. Hers tightened in concern.

Time for a little bombast.

"And do you know why?" He roared, addressing every man and woman within earshot. "Because I am Lord Viktor Akadra! While the Republic stands, so do I! And so do you! You hold this line, and we'll claim victory together! Now give me a damn cheer! Let the shadowthorns know they're riding to their deaths!"

They gave him a damn cheer.

It echoed across the plain, vying for dominion with the thunder of the charge. The fire of defiance caught and blood roused to the boil.

"But you're right, corporal." Viktor laid a hand on his claymore's pommel and toyed with the trailing end of Calenne's ribbon. She'd never forgive him for this. "I've no place on the line without a shield. So close up."

A frown. "Beg pardon, my lord?"

"Close up!" snapped Viktor. "Must I repeat myself?"

A woman in the second rank shuffled forward. Her shield thudded into place alongside Zhastov's. The rippling, churning rumble of hooves reached a crescendo. The shadow seethed within Viktor's soul, sensing it would soon be loosed.

He counted to three. And then to another three, until the clamour of hooves drowned out all else save his thoughts. Then, with a cheer of his own, he wrenched the claymore from the ground and faced the golden thunderbolt.

Kurkas had a perfect view of the battle from atop the barn's tiles. Not so much as a single shadowthorn had strayed south of the Kevor redoubt, though he knew that wouldn't last. Or he *hoped* so, anyway. Danger ranked low amid his concerns. Boredom perched right at the very top.

He whistled through his teeth and stared down at Blackridge Farm's uneven courtyard. Timber-framed buildings and a low stone wall didn't make for much of a bastion. But it beat raven feathers out of standing in the open. And if some aspiring shadowthorn had a mind to slip between the farm and its neighbouring redoubt? Well, Kurkas had fifty pavissionaires of the 14th who'd make them sorry for the attempt, and two hundred Swanholt hearthguard to back them up. He'd have preferred to be in the centre, but understood that his position on the flank betrayed Lord Akadra's unspoken nervousness about the battle to come. The hearthguard could be trusted to stand to the last, and the centre would hold longer if inexperienced soldiers weren't worried over endangered flanks.

Quarrels and ballista-shot raked the killing ground. Golden corpses littered the cataphracts' wake. There was even a dead grunda, its caparisoned hide peppered with bolts. Kurkas reckoned that was just as well. Though not a squeamish man, he'd no enthusiasm for seeing what happened when an enraged grunda struck a shield wall.

The Hadari charge gathered speed. Kurkas shook his head at the lone dark figure standing in the teeth of the charge. "Daft grandstanding bastard. Always have to do it showy, don't you?"

"What was that, captain?" asked a nervous-looking Major Keldrov.

"Never you mind."

He'd marked Keldrov out as a pampered brat from the first moment. So far, she'd done nothing to dispel the idea. He suspected she was every bit as unimpressed by him. No "real" soldier liked taking orders from one she outranked. Especially not a tattered ruffian who'd left too many parts and pieces on old battlefields.

"What in Lumestra's name is he doing?" breathed Keldrov, her wide-eyed gaze directed north.

"What he always does," Kurkas sighed. "Making the rest of us look useless."

"But ... he'll be killed."

"Will he though?" Kurkas grinned. "Care to make a wager of it?"

She hesitated. "No."

So much for easy coin. "Then get yourself down to the courtyard. Make sure we're ready."

"Are we moving out?"

He snorted. "Blessed Lumestra, no. You think I want to go traipsing all the way up there to die? Our turn will come soon enough."

An arrow skittered off a tile at Kurkas' feet. Others thudded into the gable wall. He fell prone, feet skidding as he grabbed at the moss-caked ridgeline. Keldrov collapsed beside him. A tile shattered beneath her hip and fell into the barn. Dark shapes flitted through the woods to the south-east.

"Look alive!" Kurkas bellowed down at the courtyard. "We've shadowthorns in the trees! And someone wake that dozy proctor! We've sport for the simarka!"

Even as Kurkas slid towards the ladder, dark trails appeared in the crops. A dozen unseen simarka converged on the tree line.

The cataphract dug back his spurs and dipped his spear. Viktor's shadow slithered free without urging, unseen in the murk of morning. The cavalryman shrieked as it smothered the light in his eyes. He clawed uselessly at his face, the spear falling from his hand.

Then Viktor was moving. The point of his claymore thrust up through the cataphract's exposed belly scales. Blade scraped against bone. Weight shifted. The lifeless body toppled from the saddle. Viktor ripped the claymore free. Its bloody arc split the shaft of another spear.

Cataphracts thundered past in a spray of trampled wheat and churned sod. Soil spattered Viktor's armour. Simarka sprang from the crops, tearing riders from their saddles. Screams and the crash of shields rent the air. A kraikon swept three cataphracts from their saddles in a single swipe. A grunda ploughed headlong into its armoured bulk with a booming, clanging thud. The construct toppled. Lightning arced from its ravaged chest and crackled about armour and spear-tip.

Viktor had eyes only for the emerald-studded armour of the would-be emperor. He'd be there. No man who sought to rule the Golden Court could leave the first assault to another's command.

A guttural shout sounded. A cataphract galloped in, spear levelled at Viktor's belly.

The shadow took him without a sound. The man jerked backwards out of his saddle as if a hangman's noose had closed about his neck.

The horse thundered on. Its rider spun into the path of yet another cataphract. The steed came crashing down in a flurry of limbs. The newly come cataphract rose from the ruin, sword scraping from his scabbard.

Viktor's first whirling stroke swept the lesser blade aside. The second struck the shadowthorn's head from his shoulders.

High on the sparsely wooded slope, Melanna saw the first charge strike home. Her father had blooded his sword. She was now free to do the same.

"The men are ready," announced Warleader Aedrun. "They await only your command. *I* await only your command."

His voice held the same reverence as it had after Charren Gorge, when he'd asked her to lead the ritual of his son's Last Ride. His wasn't the only familiar face among the gathered shields. Most were survivors of that unhappy skirmish.

Melanna shared a glance with Sera. The handmaiden's chandirin was as sure-footed as a goat on the uneven slope, and the improvised altar-cloth banner sat furled in her hand. The lunassera nodded. Melanna took her thoughts as a mirror of her own. The moment was come. She, though a mere princessa, had an army of her own to command and duty to meet.

Rising tall in her stirrups, she stared at the coiling serpent that was the northern end of the Tressian line. Two hundred ragged souls and barely a score of shields. Not that shields offered unswerving advantage on the hillside. The ground was too broken to support a sturdy line. Moreover, the cleft- and stream-riddled slopes were fertile fields for ambush. And there would be ambush aplenty. Melanna knew the drab leathers of Jesver Merrik's Free Kellin band from her time in Maiden's Hollow.

Still, she had near five hundred warriors, and her fifty lunassera could have taken the slope without them. But there were rituals of battle that even an Ashanal was wise to follow.

"Warleader, the honour of the first charge is yours."

Aedrun squared proud shoulders. "As you command, Ashanal."

The shuddering ground. The rumble of galloping hooves. The chill of fear and the fire of defiance mingling in the blood. The oppressive, claustrophobic closeness of comrades. The hardness of the sword-hilt Revekah knew she gripped too tight. The sawing, chafing pressure about her left forearm from the shield-slings.

The final hours of Zanya crashed back; unstoppable, implacable.

That too had been unwinnable. Didn't mean you didn't fight.

"Brace!" bellowed Revekah. "Brace!"

She leaned into her shield, felt the press of bodies at her back. A whimper. A prayer. A curse to shiver the soul. To her right, Tarn closed his eyes, his lips moving wordlessly. Revekah thought only of Katya, and what her long dead friend would ask of her this day.

The cataphracts struck the line. Screams rang out from men and horses. A spear shattered against Revekah's shield. Her boots skidded on trampled crops. The press of bodies held her upright.

Above her, a faceless cataphract abandoned the wreckage of his spear and drew his sword. Revekah bent her knees and scraped her shield higher against its neighbours. The cataphract's sword clanged off the steel rim. A heavy spear took him in the throat. Blood rushed golden armour red, and he slid from the saddle with a gurgling cry.

Another took his place, but the charge's impetus had passed. With it went the cataphracts' chief advantage. The shadowthorn's hooked spear hissed over Revekah's head. A choking scream sounded behind.

The spear did not withdraw. The cataphract lurched forward as unseen hands hauled on the shaft. He released his grip too late and fell against Revekah's shield. She thrust.

A scream. A wet, rasping breath. The weight on her shield vanished.

A horn rang out. Cheers rippled along the line. Revekah blinked sweat from her eyes. The space to her front filled with riderless horses. She felt, more than saw, the phoenix-line start forward.

"Hold!" she roared. "Hold! See to the wounded! They'll be back!"

Moans of the dead and dying overtook retreating hoof-beats. The press of bodies thinned. Injured comrades were dragged back to the physicians. Whimpers danced on the air as Hadari throats were cut, speeding them to whatever reward Ashana offered.

A dry cough overtook a parched throat. Revekah hawked, spat and reached gratefully for Tarn's proffered canteen. The lad was pale, and no wonder. It was one thing to launch an ambush from the shelter of the trees. Even to scramble away into the night after a raid gone wrong. Standing the line was different.

She returned the canteen. "You all right?"

He nodded a mite too hastily. "I think so."

"First time's the worst. Keep your shield locked, and don't strike unless you mean to kill."

He clamped his lips. His head bobbed. "I won't let you down."

Revekah glanced north, to the banners flying free between the redoubts. "Not me, lad. The Phoenix."

A nervous grin. "I thought we were all phoenixes."

"That we are. So let's make her proud, shall we?"

Horns came again. Drums quickened to match the thunder of hooves.

"Shields up!" Revekah bellowed. "They're coming back for more. Let's not disappoint!"

Melanna heard the winding of the horns. She knew its meaning even before her father's charge fell back in disarray.

He'd struck deep. Broken bodies lay scattered across a bloodied field. But it wasn't enough. The twin banners still flew.

Sera drew level. "The battle goes well."

Melanna supposed she was right, but there was too much bloody gold amid the wheat. Too many fathers and sons who'd return home only as treasured rings and honoured memories. She only hoped her own sire was not among them.

"There's no victory if my father falls."

"Then go to him." Sera gestured at the lunassera and chandirin scattered through the rocks. "We will follow wherever you lead, Ashanal."

"No." She shook her head. "I've been given a task. I will see it done."

A clash of steel rang out across the slope, followed by a sharp scream. Aedrun's ragged line of shields shrank inwards. A band of leather-clad figures ran headlong for the Tressian lines, pausing only to trade arrows with longbowmen scattered throughout Aedrun's line.

Melanna scowled in frustration. "This is going too slowly."

"Then set a new pace, Ashanal," said Sera. "If men cannot carry the day, then women must."

*

Viktor welcomed the fire in his limbs, the rising sweat that spoke to labours well-pursued. So much better than arguing. So much more direct. And directness had been the order of the day. If ever he'd doubted that Kai Saran sought spectacle in victory, he did not do so now.

The militia line had buckled, but it had held, if at terrible cost. Too many of the dead wore blue tabards. The old soldiers upon whom he'd relied to hold the line together. They'd not disappointed him, and they'd paid a heavy price.

The horns sounded again. The Hadari were returning. The line wasn't ready.

They needed time.

"Lady Trelan!" he shouted. "Re-form the line!"

"Why? Where are you going?"

He caught the tinge of dread. "I have business with the Hadari!"

Offering a low bow, he rested the flat of his claymore against his shoulder and strode across the tideline of dead.

"Raven's Eyes! What is he doing?"

Calenne watched Viktor go, scarcely able to believe her eyes. He was already two-score paces from the shield wall. Much further, and a galloping cataphract would run him down long before he'd hope of reaching safety.

"He's offering a challenge," Armund af Garna rumbled from the level of her booted knee. "It's a canny move. Saran's prized Immortals just bounced off a wall of farmers. His pride's got to be hurting."

She stared down at the rust-haired Thrakkian. Like his sister, he'd not left her side since Viktor had joined the line. Another subtle attempt at keeping her safe. But gruff as the twins were, she was grateful for their presence. Calenne knew enough of Thrakkian honour to know it for a tangle of incomprehensible and contradictory rules. But Thrakkian loyalty, once given, was unbreakable.

"You mean the prince might actually *fight* Viktor?"

"Doubt it." Anliss set her axe spinning about its haft like a wheel on its axle. The intricate knot-work of wood and metal blurred. "Saran'll send a champion. Hadari carp about honour, but they don't really understand it. It's one thing to fight for someone else, it's another to let someone else fight for *you*."

"As I'm letting Viktor fight for me?"

Armund laughed and slapped his generous belly. Chainmail jostled the ridged leather of his breastplate. "From the look on your face, you didn't ask him to."

"And you're Tressian," said Anliss dourly. "No one expects honour from you."

Calenne bristled. She'd nothing to prove. But the fluttering phoenix-banner – her mother's symbol – made lie of her unspoken claim.

What if Viktor lost? If he died? The army would look to her for guidance. More than ever, Calenne knew she'd none to give. Horrible as that realisation was, it was nothing to the sick emptiness at the prospect of Viktor's death.

With an effort, she pulled herself back from the brink of panic. That wasn't how the Phoenix comported herself, nor a lady – whether she bore the name Akadra or Trelan. "What can I do?"

"What his lordship asks," said Armund. "Get the line into shape. Win or lose, they'll be coming back."

Viktor halted two hundred paces distant of the Hadari shield wall. He thrust his claymore into the ground and folded his arms. He offered no words. He'd done this enough to know none were necessary.

Sure enough, the line parted. A black-cloaked Immortal rode clear. He cantered closer, his face hidden beneath a crested helm.

Viktor's shadow seethed in eagerness. He sucked down a deep breath and dragged the recalcitrant magic into his soul. Too many eyes were on him. It was one thing to set the shadow loose in the chaos of battle, and another entirely to do so on an open field.

He made no move to approach the oncoming rider. Every passing moment increased Calenne's chances of bringing order to the buckled line. He didn't dare look behind, for fear that his motive would stand revealed. Instead, he spared a glance to the south, where black uniforms fought for the shallow rampart of the farmhouse walls, and to the north where white flame burned bright among the trees. Distractions, both. This battle had begun with the Phoenix. It would end with her.

The black-cloaked Immortal dropped from his saddle. Leaving his twin swords in their scabbards, he offered a deep bow. Viktor grunted.

Strange how you could meet politely with an enemy even as you planned his death. Maybe war was like politics after all.

"Lord Akadra. Hard to believe we've not met before."

Like most Hadari of Viktor's acquaintance, the man's Tressian was oddly accented, but otherwise fluent. He'd often wondered at the curiosity of learning an enemy's tongue, but never enough to adopt anything of the shadowthorns' fluid speech. Screams sounded much the same in any language.

"And you are?"

"Hal Drannic. Son of Harvald Drannic, and champion to his glorious majesty Kai Saran."

"His majesty isn't glorious enough to fight his own challenges?"

"Only when the opponent is worthy."

"Worthy enough to fight his majesty's champion."

"Someone has to sweep filth from the doorstep."

The last was spoken without rancour. Drannic was playing a role. Much like Viktor himself. A loyal servant to the crown prince. War killed more good men than bad.

Viktor scraped his claymore clear of the soil. Under cover of the motion, he glanced over his shoulder. A row of unbroken shields stared back. Good. No reason for further delay.

He brought the claymore up in a two-handed high guard, the blade angled downward. "Sweep away."

Drannic's swords whispered free of their scabbards.

Viktor circled right. Drannic matched the motion and extended his right-hand blade. A tempting target. Sweep that sword aside and take the champion's heart before the other could land. Viktor knew it for a trap. Instead, he kept moving and waited for his foe to make a mistake.

Drannic sprang. The confinement of his golden helm muffled his battle cry. His right-hand sword hacked at Viktor's head. Viktor checked the blow with a banshee screech of scraping steel. Even as his right was struck wide, Drannic's left sword speared for Viktor's belly.

Viktor pivoted on his heel. The disembowelling blow tore his surcoat's rich cloth and glanced off his breastplate.

For a heartbeat, he was off-balance. A heartbeat was a lifetime to someone like Drannic. The champion's blades, always in motion, wove a gleaming web of steel. Viktor parried the first blow and evaded the second. The third slipped past his guard. It cheated the join between the upper and lower plates about Viktor's forearm.

Flame coursed through Viktor's arm. Bright blood welled up between armour plates. His shadow hissed, pulling free as pain sundered his concentration. Flame flickered and died beneath a torrent of cold. Viktor's breath steamed in the balmy air.

He stumbled back, his attention divided between the darting blades and the shadow's bid for freedom. He parried one blow mere inches from his brow. He ducked another. A ragged cheer broke out from the Hadari ranks at the prospect of their champion's victory.

All the while, the shadow fought Viktor's grasp. He wrestled the overwhelming temptation to set it free – to end the duel in an eye-blink. But he knew the folly of that course. He squeezed the shadow tight and forced it down.

The cold faded. The pain in his arm returned. Viktor welcomed it. He embraced his rising anger at the Hadari cheer. At himself for presenting weakness for Drannic to exploit. The claymore clove the air, driven on by a roar.

Drannic's swords came up to block, blades crossed to trap the claymore. The left buckled. The right shattered with a dull crack, its upper portion falling into the dirt.

For the first time, he backed away.

Viktor pursued. The claymore battered Drannic's remaining sword aside. Armour turned aside the stump of the other. Not so Drannic's golden scales and Viktor's claymore.

The blade's point took the Hadari champion in the chest. Driven home by anger as much as momentum, it pierced the armoured scales. Drannic froze, transfixed by the colossal sword that was now his only support. A choked, bubbling gasp issued from beneath the helm. Swords fell from twitching hands.

The Hadari cheer died. Away to Viktor's left, another rose to take its place – wild, almost disbelieving. A disbelief Viktor shared. Not because he'd won the duel, but because the people of the Southshires – wolf's-heads, malcontents and rebels all – cheered *him*. The Phoenix-Slayer.

Blood dribbling from his forearm, Viktor twisted the blade. Drannic's body slipped free. Using the claymore as a crutch, Viktor stooped beside the corpse.

"May you find whatever reward you deserve," he muttered.

His free hand closed around the grips of Drannic's unbroken blade. Rising, he held it aloft as a trophy. Immediately – impossibly – the Tressian cheer redoubled.

Viktor shook his head in wonder and cast the purloined sword aside. With one last glance at the impassive line of Immortals, he set Drannic's horse to flight with a slap to its haunch.

He didn't run. Didn't look back. With every step, he challenged Kai Saran to break convention by loosing his cavalry to vengeance.

But the crown prince had no stomach for treachery that day. King's blue shields parted. Viktor rejoined the exultant company of men and women who a week before would have cheered his death.

Calenne alone offered no word of congratulation. She merely slid from her saddle and held him tight with a strength Viktor had not known she possessed.

Across the trampled field, the drums sounded.

Thirty-Eight

Caparisoned hide bristling with spent quarrels, the grunda struck the shield wall a dozen paces to Viktor's north. Shields shattered. Bodies cartwheeled away. Screams rent the air. Then the next wave of the lopsided charge slammed home, and Viktor had eyes only for the battle to his front.

Driven by the clamour of drums, the Hadari shield wall came on without hesitation. Willow-bound shields crashed home. Beast-icons daubed on taut leather fields seemed almost to leap forth alongside spear, sword and axe.

Viktor fought from the second rank, his overhand stance bolstered by his left hand tight around the claymore's foregrip. He stabbed the blade low over the Hadari shield-rims. Hard, heavy work.

Halberds angled to catch a shield's rim and drag it low enough to expose the warrior behind. Others stabbed through the gaps with the wicked point at the tip, rather than the heavy blade.

A Hadari screamed and slumped against the line of king's blue. Then he was gone, replaced by another. Viktor's blade took his throat.

Viktor didn't cheer the death. Eyes stinging with sweat, he saved every breath for the strength it lent weary arms and a flagging heart. There was only the press of bodies. The dead and the dying trampled underfoot. And the determination to outlast the foe.

The woman to Viktor's front fell, her head hacked half away. Viktor set his shoulder to the dead woman's shield and grabbed the loops – her place in the line was now his.

Each impact on the shield set dark fire coursing along his wounded arm. His shadow clawed at the cage he'd made for it, seeking escape – seeking licence. Viktor kept a tight grip on both and lost himself in the wordless fury of desperate warriors.

The Hadari convulsed. The pressure on Viktor's shield lessened. A primal bellow from the Hadari lines grew in pitch as alarm set in.

The enemy shield wall disintegrated. Harried by sporadic fire from the flanking redoubts, the survivors fled. Tireless simarka pounced in pursuit. Viktor felt no guilt for the slaughter, only relief that the line had held. Guilt would come tomorrow, if he survived to see it.

"You, lad. Take my place."

Viktor unslung his borrowed shield and thrust it into the young man's hands. Drawing back from the line, he stared to the north. There, the line was badly bowed from the grunda's impact. The creature's corpse lay where it had fallen, a hill of steaming flesh among the shields. Sergeants' voices rang out. The line flowed forward, past the leathery corpse to reform on the far side.

Viktor glanced away behind the lines, searching fruitlessly for Calenne. He noted the twin banners flying proud above the thin brotherhood of knights of Captain Lavirn's reserve.

Horns rang out anew. To the east, golden scale gleamed.

The Immortals were coming again.

The bearded Hadari bellowed his last and toppled backwards off the low wall. Kurkas braced a weary shoulder against stone. Arrows whistled overhead. They clattered off stone or thunked into shields. Whimpers and screams marked where they found flesh.

"Seek cover!" bellowed Kurkas.

All along the wall, soldiers hastened to obey. Some sharpened blades blunted in the fight. Others drank from water skins or canteens and wolfed down scraps of food. The wounded hobbled to the comparative safety of the barn.

Kurkas laid his sword aside and popped a metal flask free of its belt-cradle. He closed his eyes in silent rapture. When he opened them, Major Keldrov stood a pace back from the wall. She stared out across the field, the left side of her uniform drenched in a Hadari axeman's blood. He'd seen the strike – as precise a blow as any tutor could have taught.

"When I said, 'take cover'," he said, "that meant you too, major."

A low chuckle rumbled up and down the wall. Keldrov flinched as if waking from a dream and dropped to her haunches.

"Yes. Sorry."

"First time on the field?"

"Used to run the stores at Northgard. Posted here three weeks ago."

A scream sounded away towards the courtyard gate. Someone hadn't found cover quickly enough. Kurkas proffered his flask.

Keldrov took a sip and grimaced. "That's not water."

He snatched the flask back. "Of course not. Who wants water at a time like this? It's Selanni brandy. The good stuff."

"The good stuff? Reckon it'd strip the rust off a sword."

Another ripple of laughter. This time directed more at Kurkas than her. He gave a half-shouldered shrug. "So it's versatile. Nothing wrong with that."

She bobbed up and down, restless.

"Something wrong?" he asked.

She scowled. "Don't like being penned in. I feel trapped."

He nodded. Too much of soldiering was spent in dull anticipation of bloody excitement. "You want some advice, Keldrov?"

"Do I get a choice?"

Kurkas laughed. "You're learning. And if you want to go on learning, you'll never pass up good walls when you get the opportunity."

"And these are good walls?"

Kurkas thumped the brick at his shoulder. A chunk of plaster fell away. Dust spattered his black uniform grey.

"Lumestra, no. But they're a damn sight better than sitting out in the open field, waiting for some bloody great horse to trample you flat."

Her lip twitched. Not in a smile, but near enough. "I wouldn't want that."

"I imagine not." Kurkas shot a look over the wall. Still nothing. "*Anyway* ... it could be worse. We could be stuck in the redoubts. No bloody room to breathe in there. This is luxury. Worth fighting for."

"If you say so."

"That's the spirit."

He peered up over the wall. To the north-east, a fresh line of Hadari shields formed. The banner of the spread-winged owl rippled and snapped above their heads. Emerald-encrusted armour glinted.

"His lordship's getting a visit from the prince. Which means we'll have friends before too much longer. See if you can scrounge me up some food, would you? I'm starving."

A crash of drums. A blare of horns. The distant line of Immortals started forward, shields raised high against incoming shot. Golden armour glinted beneath the owl banner and a forest of fluttering spear-pennants. The emperor's chosen were coming.

No one spoke. Likely they were contemplating the Immortals' unflinching advance through the hail of quarrels. How the oncoming wall of spears and golden shields was at least twice as deep as their own. Viktor felt their fear – could practically taste it. But he did not share it. Kai Saran was coming, and Kai Saran could be slain. His ambition had brought the Hadari to the killing field. His death would drive them from it.

A ballista shot struck a bloody smear in the outer face of the Immortals' line. Living warriors flowed to replace the dead.

Silence dissolved beneath whispered prayers. Viktor gritted his teeth. He couldn't allow the fear to take root. And take root it would, if they did nothing but wait for the lines to clash. His ragtag army had given a grand account of themselves. It wouldn't be enough. Not if they lost heart.

He pushed through to the front line and set his back to the oncoming foe.

"I've had my fill of waiting!" Horns blared. Viktor let their brazen notes crash away before pressing on. "The would-be emperor's coming for us! We kill him, and this is over! I'm going to end this. I'll go alone if I have to, but if you want to be free, you'll follow."

He glimpsed wary nods as the first glimmerings of courage renewed.

Viktor held his claymore aloft. "For the Republic. For the Southshires."

"For the Phoenix!"

The lone voice belonged to Revekah Halvor. Away to the south, she too broke the line and regarded her soldiers with disfavour.

"What?" she bellowed. "You all going to let this pampered north-wealder show us up?"

Viktor scowled the insult away.

"You'll let that gilded princeling take your land?" Captain Halvor's voice cracked. "Your sons and daughters? Or are you going to give Lumestra a battle worth watching?"

It seemed the goddess heard her words, for the clouds broke. Sunlight blazed across the croplands. Across the dead and wounded. Across swords and halberds hoisted high with renewed strength. Voices roared as one.

"For the Phoenix!"

Halvor cheered with them. Her gaze met Viktor's. Her left eye twitched in what might have been a wink. Kraikons started forward, their stride outpacing flesh-and-blood comrades.

The sun warming his face, Viktor set out across the field, leaving the redoubts behind. The tramp of feet behind told him he was not alone.

The crackle of white flame swallowed the Tressian's scream. Melanna scraped the sword back and spurred forward over the rocky ground. Her horse slammed into a knot of Tressian warriors. One went sprawling. Another perished as fire slid between his ribs.

"Ashanael Brigantim!" Aedrun's bellow sent his men splashing through the rushing stream.

The ragtag enemy line broke. Dark figures slipped through the rocks towards the eaves of Davenwood.

Melanna's blood blazed bright. She ignored the wearying ache in her left shoulder and hoisted the moon-banner high into the new-come sunshine.

"Drive them back! For the goddess!"

Her voice faltered as she glanced back eastward. At the bodies strewn across gulley and crag. At where the waters ran red. The white of the lunassera. The gold of Aedrun's Immortals. The mismatched garb of the enemy dead.

Lunassera and Immortals flooded past in pursuit. Melanna let the banner drop and stared down at a sword-arm bloodied to the elbow. She'd no recollection of how many she'd slain. There was just the blur of fire, and the perfect jubilation that set her blood atremble. The same feeling as had overtaken her at Charren Gorge. The one that had set her soul coursing with incomparable joy ... and whose ebb had left her empty and soul-sick.

She wasn't ready to feel that way again. Not yet. Blood could fill that void – at least for a time.

The wind changed, and carried with it a rumbling, wordless battle cry. Not in her own tongue, but in dull, artless Tressian voices. Away to the south, past the hilly flanks and the nearer of the palisaded redoubts, the enemy marched into an arrow-darkened sky. At their head came a terrible, clawed shadow whose wings touched the sky.

"Ashana preserve us." Her blood cooled with the words.

"*Savim?*" Aedrun halted and stared up at her with obvious concern. His helmet was gone, his brow swollen and bloody above his right eye, but he stood tall. "What troubles you? The Tressians are desperate. Your father's guard will make swift work of them."

"But the shadow! Do you not see it? There – at the head of their advance."

Aedrun frowned. "I see a man, Ashanal. A brave man who'll earn a good death."

Now Melanna looked – *really* looked – she made out a man's form. But the shadow remained. Alive. Thrashing like strands of hungry mist. How could Aedrun not see it?

"He is a scion of the Dark."

Melanna jumped at the suddenness of the words. So Sera saw it too?

"Like the Sceadotha?" Aedrun cast his eyes skyward in horror and traced the arc of the crescent moon across his chest.

The name sent ice rushing through Melanna's veins. The Sceadotha. Malatriant. The Tyrant Queen.

The blood-spattered folds of Sera's robes shifted as she nodded. Her chandirin stood motionless as a statue. "An echo only. But an echo is enough."

A pair of kraikons broke free of the Tressian lines. Massive feet pounding the well-trampled soil, they lumbered headlong into the wall of golden shields. Fleet-legged lions loped in their wake. The line crumbled. Pennants dipped as bodies flew wide. Golden light crackled, bright against the shadow that came behind.

"This is your moment, Ashanal," said Sera. "You bear the goddess's flame. Drive back the shadow before it claims your father. The goddess is with you. *We* are with you."

But the goddess had rejected her. The Huntsman had granted her the power she wielded. What if his favour alone wasn't enough?

She swallowed. She'd thought her fear of battle conquered. But that was of ephemeral foes. If the teachings of her youth were anything to go by, the man-of-shadow was far different. But a leader had to lead, did she not? And was it not the duty of an empress to perceive threats others missed? To perceive them, and to bring about their obliteration?

Below, the Tressian line quickened pace.

"Warleader Aedrun . . . " Melanna heard the tremble in her voice. She gripped the moon-banner's pole tight. "The heights are yours. I have business on the field below."

He bowed. "As you command, Ashanal. Goddess ride with you."

As Viktor had gambled, the kraikon charge succeeded where the Immortals had failed: it broke a line of shields. The Immortals responded with stoic precision. Golden shields crashed together, trapping the bronze giants within the formation and their flesh-and-blood masters without. War hammers crashed. Heavy spikes prised apart armoured plates to dissipate the magic within.

Viktor's lowered shoulder struck the closing join between two shields. The impact jarred every bone in his body, but then he was through, and the claymore death in his hands. It flashed like bloodied silver, widening the corridor of the kraikons' wake.

Southwealders flooded in behind. The air filled with screams and the scrape of metal on metal. Viktor's shadow snarled to be free. He kept it caged, tamped deep in his soul, and strode on into the slaughter. Each stab and thrust of his sword brought him closer to the owl-banner and to his prey.

Viktor caught a war hammer's haft across his claymore's hilt and its wielder by the cloak. A twist, a heave, and the attacker was behind him, hurled to the mob following in his wake.

Two more Immortals pressed in. Too close to swing his claymore, Viktor backed away. Another kraikon, come late to the charge, battered its way through the formation. The first Immortal vanished screaming beneath its steel-shod feet. The second dived clear and found Viktor's sword at his throat. A cut. A gurgle. Viktor strode on into the battle's din, the screams of his victims herald to his coming.

"Saran!"

The Hadari prince spun about. His sword arced to block the claymore's strike.

Viktor grunted and leaned into the blade. Saran twisted aside. Claymore skittered across an armoured sleeve. A golden buckler slammed into Viktor's upper arm. He staggered back, scrambling for footing among the corpses. He'd forgotten the man's strength.

"Nowhere to run this time, *my prince*," he snarled.

Saran bellowed in the Hadari tongue and closed the gap.

A swipe of the shield drove Viktor's claymore aside. A thrust of his sword stopped short of disembowelment only because Viktor twisted away.

Viktor drove his elbow into the sculpted helm. His vambrace clanged against gilded steel. Emeralds scattered. Saran stepped drunkenly back, arms wide. Viktor pressed forward. The claymore blurred as it sought Saran's head.

The golden buckler blocked the first blow. It split under the second. Saran hurled it away. Viktor ducked too slowly. The heavy rim gashed his brow. His shadow screamed for release. Dark spots danced behind his eyes. When they cleared, Saran was on him once more. With a shriek of tortured metal, the sword-point punched clean through Viktor's lower breastplate.

Hot, searing fire crackled through his veins. A bellow of pain choked off as Saran's free hand closed around his throat and forced him to his knees.

The prince grunted and twisted his sword free. "My thanks, Lord Akadra, for your head," he said, the words rendered all the more mocking by his hallowsider's accent. "It will make quite the gift for the Golden Court."

The sword came about. Teeth gleamed beneath the battered helm. Viktor's shadow screamed to be freed.

With death the only alternative, he complied.

Saran grunted as the shadow flooded beneath his eyes. His fingers slipped from Viktor's throat and he staggered back, lurching as if caught in the teeth of a gale.

Roaring to numb the pain, Viktor rose up and smote him in the face.

Saran's heel caught on a body. He fell backwards, helmet and sword shuddering free as he hit the ground.

Gritting his teeth against the pain, Viktor reclaimed his claymore. He set the point against the prince's chest.

"*Your* head will burn with the rest of you," he said. "We're not barbarians."

"No," spat Saran. "You're a monster, a herald of the Dark."

"Only today," said Viktor wearily. "Tomorrow, I'll be a man once more."

He tightened his grip on the blade, bracing for the thrust that would take the prince's life.

The northern skies exploded in fire and song.

Thirty-Nine

"*A shanael Brigantim!*"

The battle cry rose out of song, its harsh notes riding high over steel and strife.

And everything changed.

Revekah vied shield-to-shield with an Immortal half her age. She felt the man's desperate blows grow strong as confidence returned. She saw a kraikon seize to a sudden, impossible halt.

Then came the pale-witches. Horned steeds darted nimbly through the melee. Moonlight spears gleamed in their hands. Each slash or stab was answered by a scream and a spray of blood. And then the newcomers were behind the line of shields. The slaughter began.

"Raven's Eyes!"

Revekah rammed her shoulder against her shield. Her thrust bit through scale and flesh, and she kicked the body away.

Tarn ran past, his eyes wide with terror and his shield abandoned. Revekah dragged him to a halt. "Pull yourself together, lad!"

"What for?" he demanded. "It's lost!"

Militia shoved and clawed at one another in their hurry to flee.

"Shield ring!" Revekah bellowed. "Shield ring!"

A handful of voices took up the cry. Most kept running. Some westward to the distant shelter of the redoubts. Others fled south, and the hoped-for safety of the trees. Of Akadra, Revekah saw no sign. A battle in the balance only moments before had blossomed to bitter defeat.

Revekah stared bleakly at the handful of faces who'd heeded her cry. First Zanya. Now this. It was all happening again, and she was helpless to prevent it. The witches were everywhere. The Immortals came forward anew.

To stay was to die.

"Go!" she shoved Tarn. "All of you! Get out of here!"

With heavy heart, Revekah joined the rout.

Warned by his shadow's scream, Viktor threw himself aside. White fire cleaved the space he'd occupied a heartbeat before. It whirled about, driving him back from Saran's prone form.

"You will not take my father!"

Desperation tinged the woman's voice. Determination gave her blows shattering force. Viktor's claymore shuddered beneath each parry. His shadow curled deep in his soul, away from the blinding flame.

She spurred close. Viktor struck her lunge aside. Sparks flared. Molten metal splashed at his skin and hissed against his surcoat.

An Immortal rushed at him, sword swinging. Viktor hurled the man into the horsewoman's path. The rowan horse vaulted the flailing unfortunate and the white fire surged for Viktor's throat once more.

Again he parried, eyes slitted against the hissing, sparking metal. The woman's sword scraped free and she passed away behind, carried clear by the momentum of her charge.

Viktor pinched his eyes shut. He clasped a hand to his head to block his shadow's scream. The shriek reverberated through his skull. He could no longer tell where the shadow's pain ended and his began. He'd never known it react thus. His whole life it had been wilful, predatory. Terror was new.

His shoulder struck unyielding metal – a kraikon, its colossal sword frozen in arcing descent. Viktor set a hand against the kraikon's leg and steadied himself.

"Ashanael Brigantim!"

Hooves gouged dirt. The woman came again, fire billowing before her and the moon-banner streaming behind.

Viktor threw himself aside. The blazing sword bit deep into bronze with a tortured, squealing hiss. Molten metal oozed from the wound. Wheat-stalks blazed at Viktor's feet.

The falling kraikon blotted out the sun.

*

A cold fist closed around Calenne's heart. She felt a stranger in her own skin, trapped in a waking nightmare. And as had ever been the case, the Black Knight was at the heart of her fears ... Though this time for very different reasons.

A twitch of reins sent her horse trotting forward past the nervous block of infantry of the tiny reserve. She reached the serried ranks of the Knights Essamere, resplendent in hunter's green. Captain Tavor Lavirn alone had his visor up. His eyes bore a worry as great as her own.

In the distance, the leading outriders caught up to the fleeing militia. Spears thrust. Calenne swallowed hard and glanced away.

"We have to help them."

Lavirn shook his head. "We can't."

She flung a hand across the waiting ranks. "Do I imagine this host of knights at our back?"

"What host? I have fifty lances, no more." His expression darkened. "It's not enough. Their outriders alone outnumber us, and what infantry we have cannot keep pace."

"So we abandon them?"

"There's no choice."

"I don't agree."

"With respect, *Lady* Trelan, it doesn't matter. The command is mine. The responsibility is mine. Whatever regard you command in the Southshires – even with Lord Akadra? It doesn't matter. You've no authority over a Knight of Essamere."

"And what *does* this Knight of Essamere intend?" she bit out. "To cower beneath the redoubts?"

"Not cower." Lavirn spoke with strained patience. "We'll ride out to cover any who get this far. When the pursuit's fury is spent, maybe we can forge a ceasefire, recover the wounded. But I won't risk what strength we have over a few ... "

He broke off too late, the scowl confirming Calenne's rising suspicions.

"A few what?" she demanded. "A few southwealders?"

Lavirn's scowl deepened. "That's not how I meant it."

Calenne stared across the field. At the hundreds of her countrymen and women in desperate flight. "No. What you *meant* was that if they were northwealders – if they were your brothers and sisters of Essamere – you'd already have ridden out."

Lavirn drew himself up in his saddle. "I'll not sacrifice lives to rescue a prize beyond our grasp. Most certainly not at the demand of a cosseted child."

The insult challenged Calenne's inexperience. It stung for the truth locked deep within.

"I'm talking about *saving* lives," snapped Calenne. "Lord Akadra would agree with me."

"Lord Akadra is likely dead." Lavirn spoke too quiet for the words to carry. "And with him all assurances as to your future. You are Calenne Trelan, daughter to the greatest traitor of a generation. Should you prove difficult, I'd be well within my authority to have you locked up … or executed."

Calenne's rising anger dissipated like a shadow before the sun. She strove for a rebuttal, but the words fell ashen on her tongue.

For the first time since agreeing to bear her mother's mantle, she felt alone. No Viktor. No Josiri. She'd have been glad even to see Anastacia. The demon would have known the words to put Captain Lavirn in his place.

"The field is lost," said Lavirn. "You're free to leave. I'll give you an escort back to Branghall. But you will not interfere with my command."

Even now, there was no triumph in his voice. No joy. There was even a note of pleading. A reasonable man faced with events beyond his ability. But even reasonable men lashed out when their meagre authority was threatened.

"I'm staying," growled Calenne. "And if Viktor lives, he'll hear of our conversation, and your threats."

She hauled on her reins and rode away, seething with fear and impotent rage. And not just at Captain Lavirn, for in that last moment she'd invoked Viktor's name, not her own. Proof that she was the spoilt, whimsical child Lavirn thought her. She wasn't a soldier. She knew that. But it didn't alter the burning, irrevocable belief that Lavirn was wrong to do nothing.

And if Viktor *was* dead? She didn't know how to process *that* tangle of emotions.

Calenne brought the horse to a halt in the shadow of the Katya Redoubt. High above her head, pavissionaires lined the crude rampart. Crossbows sat levelled but silent, waiting for the order to loose.

She stared out across the battlefield, unable to look away as Hadari spears overtook fleeing militia. Lost in the distant screams and the churn of hooves, she barely noticed the Thrakkian twins draw their horses up to either side.

"Take it that didn't go well?" said Armund.

"It did not." She made no attempt to keep bitterness hidden. "In the opinion of the high and mighty Knight-Captain of Essamere, my options are as follows. Flee to Branghall. Stay quiet as a dutiful figurehead should. Or face execution. He accused me of being a child. And he's right. I've been trapped behind glass for so long. What do I know of the world, or of battle?"

Anliss spat. "Bugger's scared."

"Likely the case," her brother agreed. He unstoppered a water skin and took a swig. No. Not a *water* skin, not if the bitter scent were to be believed. "No offence, lady, but you Tressians set too much stock in personal glory, and not enough in the greater good."

Anliss nodded. "It's the one thing you and the Hadari have in common. It's not enough to know that songs'll be written of your deeds. You want to hear them too."

"And I suppose it's different for Thrakkians, is it?" In her frustration Calenne forgot that either twin could have snapped her in half without effort.

"Only a fool speaks for all." Armund thumped his substantial chest. "But for myself? I'd like to drag Ardothan off our father's throne and cut off his head. It's the only thing to do with serpents. But if I can't have that? I mean my life to amount to something, and my death to amount to more. There'll be songs, even if I don't get to hear them this side of Astor's forge and the halls of Skanandra. *Brenæ af Brenæ, yr Væga af væga.*"

"Fire from fire, and death from death?" Anliss glared at him. "You won't hear a word in Skanandra. You'll be drunk."

He laughed. "And you won't?"

Calenne shook her head, unable to contain a smile. The Thrakkian afterlife appealed more than cold bones in the ground until the light of

Third Dawn. Better an eternal revel among friends and family, glimpsing the world through mirrors and forge-fires. Even if you'd no family left to celebrate. Even if your legacy – such as it was – had soured to failure.

"Who's Ardothan?" she asked.

"Our brother," said Anliss, "and more's the pity. He has his lies, his army and *our* throne. The Wolf King promised to help us set things right, though I imagine he's changed his mind now. Family. No greater curse ever sprung from the flame."

"Oh, thank you, dear sister," said Armund.

"I know what you mean," said Calenne. "I've spent my life hating my mother. And here I am, repeating her mistakes. I don't even know how I came to be here. I look at who I was even a month ago, and I don't recognise her. And I doubt she'd recognise me."

She wondered why she shared so much of herself. Truth was, however intimidating she found them, the twins were the friendliest faces in a sea of strangers. They were also the only souls to whom the name Katya Trelan meant little.

Anliss grunted. "It's only a mistake if naught good comes of it. We're all born from the sparks of Astor's forge. He never meant for us to bob heads and bend knees to sun and moon, as you lot do. But do you hear me complaining? Without the straying, we'd have no one to fight but ourselves, and where's the joy in that?"

Calenne gripped her saddle's pommel. "Viktor told me that the secret to making a difference lies in recognising the moment for what it is, and seizing it. But what if that moment never comes?"

Armund gave a low, rumbling chuckle. "Just like a Tressian."

Anliss set her axe across her shoulders. "A warrior makes her own chances. She doesn't wait for them."

"I'm not a warrior. I'm not a soldier. This . . . " Calenne ran her fingers across her breastplate. "This is a costume. It's a lie."

"Then make it the truth."

Calenne snorted. "Just like that?"

"Why not?" Armund tugged at his plaited beard. "No one else can do it for you. I hear tell that your mother fled when the battle was lost. Who knows what might have happened had she stayed? If she'd forged opportunity?"

Calenne stared back at the gathered ranks of knights. At the phoenix banner that was hers by right of birth, and at the swan that was hers by bond of betrothal. Hers. Not the Republic's. Not the Council's. And most certainly not Tavor Lavirn's.

Hers.

When the Hadari came again for Blackridge Farm, they did so not from the forest, but from the open plains to the south-east. A line of shields spilled up the slope, spanning the dusty wain track and its low walls.

"Looks like mischief to me," said Kurkas.

"How so?" Keldrov frowned her confusion.

He took a final bite from the apple and tossed the core over the crumbling wall. It bounced once in the muddy dust and came to rest beside a wide-eyed corpse. One of many serving as a secondary rampart of flesh at the wall's foot.

"Tell the pavissionaires to hold their fire."

"But, if we ... "

"Just ...!" Kurkas broke off. With heroic effort, he choked back the worry and frustration awoken by the collapse of Akadra's line. "Just do it, major. Pouches are light enough as it is. We can't be wasting shot on shields."

Keldrov nodded and scurried away. Kurkas swore to himself and stared north. To the flood of fugitives streaming away from leaping white flame. He liked none of what he saw, least of all the motionless, frozen kraikons. The Raven only knew what had made them react so. If nothing else, it meant he couldn't rely on the pair attached to his own beleaguered garrison.

"You daft bastard," he muttered. "If you've gone and got yourself killed ...? If you've left me in charge of this mess ...?"

The thought of Akadra being gone? Unthinkable. The man had the Lord of Fellhallow's own luck. Kurkas scratched at his eyepatch. But luck ran out, didn't it? And battle seldom went the way you expected. He couldn't even find solace in the thought that Revekah Halvor was likely already dead on the field. Serve the harridan right.

"Grunda!"

Yesterday's battles scattered at the sentry's bellow. Hand steadied against the barn, Kurkas vaulted onto the wall and stared southwards. Lumbering beasts crested the rise. One on the road, another to either side. Each pulled a heavy wagon whose axles shrieked like souls in torment.

"Doesn't this keep getting better and better?" Kurkas let his voice blossom to a roar. "Crossbows to the southern wall! Bring those grey bastards down! Sergeant Brass! I want your company at the gate! And someone wake up Proctor Gillart!"

The courtyard filled with running feet and the bellow of repeated orders. Kurkas jumped down from the wall. He missed his footing, righted himself, and found a very much awake Gillart staring at him with disdain.

"You had a request?"

What was it with proctors and their delicate pride? Fussy as a serene in a barracks. "I want our kraikons at the gate, braced and ready."

"They can't stop a charging grunda!" Gillart couldn't have looked more appalled if he'd been asked to set his infant child in the grundas' path. "They'll be crushed."

"They stand a damn sight more of a chance than the rest of us." Kurkas grabbed a handful of the proctor's golden robes and shoved him towards the gate. "Bloody do it, or I'll have you staked down in their stead."

Gillart scurried away towards the nearest kraikon. Kurkas shook his head. "Raven's Eyes! Major Keldrov! I want those brutes in the dust! Now!"

The rush and clack of crossbows hastened as Kurkas made his way to the gate. His fingers itched with inactivity. He longed to snatch up a crossbow and join the volleys himself, but while a one-armed man could load and shoot – just about – he'd been a terrible shot long before he'd lost his eye.

Arrows hissed out from behind the approaching shields. A pavission-aire to Kurkas' left collapsed without a sound, a black shaft buried in her throat. Another pitched from the stable roof with a thin cry.

"Hearthguard! Get your bloody shields up!" roared Kurkas.

Swan-painted shields hitched up another inch along wall and rooftop. Dust sprayed as a kraikon thrust its great sword deep into the packed mud behind the gateway. Then it stooped and set shoulder to the timbers. The second joined it as Kurkas took his place on the wall.

The rightmost grunda gave a mournful, hooting bellow and reared up in sudden spasm. The wagon's timber spars shattered like matchsticks. The beast pitched sideways, crushing a handful of luckless Hadari. Kurkas cheered with the rest of his soldiers.

"That's one!" he bellowed. "Now bring the others down!"

Ahead, the wall of shields parted. The Hadari shrank away, and the grundas picked up speed. The ground shook. Kurkas' teeth rattled in their sockets.

"Come on, you worthless bastards! Bring them down! Now!"

Another volley hissed out. The leftmost grunda stumbled but lumbered on. The creak of the accompanying wagon was almost as loud as the thunder of its three-toed feet. Kurkas couldn't tear his eyes away from the beast. It was coming straight for him. It cared nothing for the wall and the braced shields in its path.

The first treacherous voice of dismay whispered in Kurkas' ear. He shouted all the louder to drive it out. "Brace yourselves my lads and lasses! Brace ...!"

The wall exploded in a shower of dust and fragmented stone. A hearthguard vanished beneath a filthy slab the size of a tomb's lid. Another died beneath the grunda's lumbering feet. Kurkas sprawled to his left, thrust clear by the hearthguard to his right. She died in his place, impaled on the massive, curved horn.

The grunda slumped glassy-eyed atop the broken wall, its last strength oozing from its sides.

Kurkas scrambled to his feet. He hawked to clear the dust from his throat. "Hearthguard! To me!"

The line reformed as the Hadari shieldsmen struck the breach. Kurkas parried a spear thrust and lunged to kill his attacker. The space beyond the dead grunda was thick with foes. War horns blared as the Hadari sensed victory. Kurkas leapt onto the ruins of the wall. A sword-thrust took one Hadari in the face. His boot lashed out to send another backwards onto his comrades' spears.

"This is my bloody farm! Find your own!"

The third grunda struck the gate in a cacophony of breaking timber and mangled bronze. Golden light crackled outwards. A massive, invisible hand hurled Kurkas from the shattered wall.

Armund struck at full gallop. His mailed fist smacked around the phoenix banner's shaft. Its knightly bearer, faced with the choice of being dragged from his saddle or relinquishing his grip, wisely chose the latter.

The second banner-bearer sought a middle-ground and spurred his horse to motion in a vain attempt to keep pace with Anliss's steed. The Thrakkian crooked her elbow and reeled him in. Releasing the reins, she slammed a bunched fist into the knight's visored face. Stunned, he slumped across his saddle's pommel and the swan banner came free. Voice raised in a melodic, triumphant cry, Anliss hauled her steed to a halt at the head of Lavirn's knights. She fell into place on Calenne's right-hand side, mirroring her brother's position on the left.

Knights pressed forward, voices raised in outrage.

"What is the meaning of this?" spluttered Lavirn.

He let his lance fall and thrust back his spurs. His sword gleamed in the sun.

Calenne held her ground, surprised at her calm. No room for second thoughts now. Nor fear. There was only the path ahead. The opportunity she'd chosen to forge. Her slender blade felt insignificant before the killing weight of Lavirn's broadsword. Nonetheless, its threat was enough to check him. *That* fuelled her confidence even further.

"You know what I intend," she said, striving for the tone that had come so easily at the fireside the night before. "I'm going to help my people."

"The three of you?" He snorted. "You're throwing your lives away."

"That depends."

"On what?"

"On whether the Knights Essamere are prepared to be known as cowards. Cowards who hung back while a cosseted child and a pair of drunken Thrakkians ... "

"Oi!" shouted Armund.

Anliss grinned. "Fair. Very fair."

" ... shamed them all!"

Calenne swept her gaze across the assembled ranks. She glimpsed no eyes beneath the slitted visors, but that didn't matter. It wasn't about what she saw of their mood, but what *they* beheld of her.

"You can do as you wish." Her voice quickened with confidence. With surety. "Stay. Run. Fight. I don't care. My people – *our* people – are dying. If I can save even one, then I'll face the Raven content. How will you live? Choose, and choose quickly!"

Without waiting for a reply, she urged her steed to the gallop.

Forty

No one challenged Josiri's descent into Maiden's Hollow. Those few wolf's-heads who paid heed did so with hooded and disinterested eyes before turning their attention back to campfires and conversation. A far cry from past accusations of *traitor*.

The air beneath the trees lay thick with sullen expectation. Peculiar, given Crovan's fervent disavowal of battle. Perhaps it was the drums. The screams. The discordant clash of blades. Perhaps they reverberated through the wolf's-heads' souls as accusingly as they did Josiri's own.

He walked his horse to a standstill at the dell's heart. Anastacia, her face in shadow beneath the shawl's hood, shuddered at the statues.

"What is it?" he asked.

[[Old memories,]] she muttered. [[Family squabbles.]]

Divine squabbles, in other words. Josiri still couldn't quite believe what Anastacia had at last told him of her past. Nor did he *dis*believe it. Of all her tales, this fitted far better than the rest. Or did he simply prefer to think of Anastacia as a serathi, rather than the demon Calenne named her?

Calenne. She could already be dead.

"Josiri?" Gavamor appeared at the stairway. Restless eyes and haggard expression lent urgency to unease. "Why are you here?"

"Same as before, Nials," said Josiri. "Trying to prevent a terrible mistake."

Gavamor swallowed. "You don't know how much of a mistake. Crovan's . . ."

"Crovan is capable of speaking for himself."

The Wolf King stepped from the shelter of the trees. Silda Drenn came with him, an arrow nocked but the bow undrawn. Others appeared against the grey skyline. The mismatched leathers of Drenn's brigands. The wolf-pelts of Crovan's loyalists.

"I told you my protection had limits," Crovan said wearily. "You shouldn't have returned."

"How could I not?" Josiri tried to forget how close he'd come to doing just that. He spread his arms to encompass the distant sounds of battle. "Our people are dying. Our *friends* are dying! Our families!"

Agreement swept the glade. Drenn's sidelong glance at Crovan told a tale all its own.

Crovan batted the accusation aside. "They made their choice."

Gavamor sat on the edge of a dancer's plinth. His head hung almost to his knees. His weathered fingers toyed with the amulet about his neck. "Why don't you tell him the rest, Crovan?"

His tone sent ice rushing through Josiri's veins. Shrugging off Anastacia's restraining hand, he approached Crovan. "Tell me what?"

Crovan brushed back his silvered wolf-pelt and laid a hand on his sword. Puzzle-pieces locked into position behind Josiri's eyes. Crovan wore armour beneath his cloak. The wolf's-heads were geared for battle. But they'd no intention of fighting? Or at least no intention of fighting the *Hadari* ...

The day lost the last of its warmth. Revulsion crowded Josiri's throat. He closed his eyes and waited for the anger to come. It never emerged from the black, choking cloud of despair.

"And you called me a traitor."

Crovan jabbed a finger. "I won't be judged by you! I've given everything to this cause! While you sat safe and cosy in Branghall, I suffered for our people. I bled for them! The blood in your veins counts for nothing – only the blood you've shed!"

"This isn't about my pride. Or yours. It's about freeing the Southshires."

"Yes, it is," Crovan replied. "If we don't side with the Hadari, they'll leave this place a blasted wasteland and take the children for slaves. Is that what you want?"

Now the anger came. Josiri clenched his fists and strove to control it. Unfocused anger had almost destroyed him this past week. He couldn't give in to it now. "You know it isn't."

"We have to earn the Empire's support." Crovan's tone grew pleading. "We need only show willingness to fight. Might be we can even bring a little mercy along the way."

Anastacia snorted. [[Killing the wounded to spare their accusations?]]

Gavamor's head sank lower. Drenn scowled. Crovan stared at Anastacia, his expression caught between suspicion and resentment.

Josiri shook his head. "And what happens next time?"

Crovan frowned. "Next time?"

"When taxes go unpaid." Josiri let his voice carry through the trees. "When there's trouble on the Ithna'jîm border, and the emperor wants to shed *your* blood in *his* wars. What then, but more threats to keep you in line?"

Agreement rippled beneath the trees, louder than before.

"And what do you offer?" demanded Crovan.

Josiri strode closer until he stood nose to nose with the would-be Wolf King. "I offer nothing. I promise nothing. This is simply how it's going to be. The Southshires need us. Our comrades need us. We're not going to let them down."

Crovan laughed. Not with mockery, but with the bitter tone of a man who saw a tragic joke while all about him remained blind. "And if I refuse?"

"I'm not talking to you, Drakos."

The Wolf King's lips hooked into a snarl. "Fine. Drenn? Lock his grace up. He'll go to the Hadari. *That* should save a few lives."

She showed no sign of moving. Expressionless for a moment, her lips curled slowly into a scowl. "He's right, Crovan. We give Haldrane what he wants, we'll never be free."

Crovan pressed a hand to his head. "And you, Nials?"

Gavamor rose, quiet determination in his eyes. "Reckon I'm with them."

"I didn't want this." Crovan shook his head. "I didn't."

He struck the longbow from Drenn's hand and pinned her against a tree. Cries rang out around the hollow as wolves and brigands went for their swords. Josiri started forward. He checked his advance as steel gleamed in Crovan's hand.

"I'll gut you for this, Drakos," hissed Drenn.

"You'll thank me." A faraway look entered his eyes. "This is all for the best, so tell your scoundrels to *put their weapons down*. And as for you, *your grace*, you'll go quietly into confinement, or Vorn will slit your lady-friend's throat."

Josiri turned. Vorn stood behind Anastacia, an arm across her throat and a dagger ready in his hand. She stood perfectly, unflinchingly still.

Could steel even *hurt* Anastacia? Josiri wished he'd thought to ask. She didn't *look* fearful, but the transformation had only made her mood harder to read. "Are you all right, love?"

[[I don't know,]] said Anastacia. [[I've a great deal of repressed anger. I'm worried I might hurt someone.]]

"Enough jokes!" snapped Crovan.

"I don't think she's joking," said Josiri.

He cast an eye around the hollow and saw more worried faces than eager ones.

"Let Silda go, Crovan."

"You made this necessary, not me!"

"Maybe that's true. But what happens next is on you."

"You're right," said Crovan, his eyes dark. "Vorn! Kill her!"

Revekah closed her ears to the pale-witches' eerie hymn. To the distant hoof-beats. To the screams that marked a race run to a bloody end. She knew she should have died long ago, cut down from behind. But if the bloody aftermath of Zanya had taught her anything, it was that you couldn't dwell on that. You ran until you were safe, or you were dead.

New notes rose out of the slaughter: crisp, strident and clear. Revekah had lived fifteen years in fear of that sound. The fanfare of buccinas rousing knights to the charge. Now it was the sweetest of music. At last, she understood why she'd lived to flee so far.

The Knights of Essamere were charging.

Cloaks and plumes streaming in the wind, they galloped past the fleeing militia to the north. Swords glinted in the sun. Lances bit home. The leading edge of the Hadari pursuit disintegrated.

Revekah glimpsed Calenne among the knights, sword brandished high. In that moment the daughter was truly the mother reborn.

Cataphracts spurred forward from the east. A second wave responding to Calenne's charge. Further north, pale-witches' flickering steeds danced from the broken ground to join the counter-assault ... And with them, a woman on a rowan horse, a moon-banner snapping behind her.

"Captain!" A breathless Tarn shook her by the shoulder. "We have to keep moving!"

"Go," Revekah said, her lungs still heaving. "I'm right behind you."

She looked northward once more, searching for Calenne in the melee. She saw only a mass of striving bodies, half-hidden in clouds of hoof-kicked dust.

"I'm sorry, Katya."

Tarn screamed, a pale-witch's spear in his back. The light fled his youthful eyes even as Revekah caught him. The killer galloped past in a rippling thump of hooves. She wheeled about, her steed sidestepping daintily.

Revekah let Tarn's body drop. Cold fury boiled up from the pit of her stomach. She cursed Akadra for his gamble and herself for embracing it. But she cursed the pale-witch most of all.

The killer watched from atop her steed, in no hurry to finish what she'd begun.

"What're you waiting for?" shouted Revekah. "Scared of an old woman?"

The witch spurred forward. The moonlight spear flashed. Revekah's shield disintegrated like rotting parchment. The blade stabbed deep into her shoulder.

Revekah screamed and threw herself clear of the thundering hooves.

The witch's steed came about. Revekah rode anger through the pain. She ducked beneath the flashing spear and swung hard at the beast's mouth. Flesh parted in wisps of light and shadow. But the steed's shoulder was tangible enough. The glancing blow knocked Revekah from her feet and her sword from numbed fingers.

A name from childhood tales flooded back. *Chandirin.* Ashana's moon-coursers. Invulnerable to harm save beneath starlight.

The hoof-beats began anew. Revekah stared down into Tarn's sightless eyes.

How did you fight that?

You couldn't.

Calenne parried the first spear and jerked sharply in her saddle to avoid the second. What in Lumestra's name had she been thinking? She'd no place among the rush of hooves and the crash of steel.

Chest heaving in near panic, she checked a sword-thrust. The Hadari leaned into the blow, and the blade scraped down to her hilt. Calenne held firm. Her eyes came within two spans of her enemy's sallow, thinly bearded face. Their horses circled. She felt the slow, inexorable retreat of her sword. She wasn't strong enough to check him. He'd force her sword wide, and then . . .

Calenne angled her sword. The outrider's blade, the weight of its master still behind it, skittered away. The Hadari fell across his horse's neck. Shouting with all the fear and frustration of preceding moments, Calenne thrust.

A dull tearing sound marked her thrust's passage through the man's leather breastplate; a choked *pah* of expelled air and a welter of blood as it slid between his ribs. The outrider fell from his saddle with a gurgling cry, his dying weight almost dragging Calenne's sword from her hand.

She urged her horse clear, eyes fixed on the bloody blade. Fear dissipated into excitement, and revulsion at having taken a life. She'd known she might have to before the day was done, but in the moment of the deed . . .

She snapped from her reverie at a bellow. An outrider galloped from the north, gore-slicked spear braced in the crook of his elbow.

Calenne hauled on her reins to face the charge. She knew even then that she'd no time to parry. Life or death now lay in the gift of a shield she barely knew how to use.

A blur of black and silver shot in from Calenne's left. Wild, rough laughter streamed in its wake. The steel-shod butt of the swan banner, levelled like a lance, struck the outrider in the chest. His horse went one way and he the other.

Anliss' steed circled about. Her long-handled axe swung a lazy arc. The dismounted outrider lost his head before he reached his knees. Then the two women were alone in a ring of dead and dying and the surviving Hadari retreating eastward in a cloud of dust.

Anliss grinned. "No room for conscience here, lady."

Calenne stared at the stocky woman. She realised for the first time that Anliss used no reins to control her horse, but the goading of her knees. "It's that obvious?"

"First time's always a shock."

Armund drew up alongside. His chainmail was a mass of twisted rings at the left shoulder. His face was bloodied. He grinned. Like his sister, he disdained the need for reins. "No fears. It gets easier."

Calenne stared across the bloodied field. At the motionless bodies, and those who wailed for aid. "I hope not."

"Then cast your eyes behind, not ahead," said Anliss.

Calenne did as bidden. To the west, the trampled expanse between the redoubts was alive with fleeing militia. Men and women who'd now be dead but for her actions. Death served many purposes. Sometimes it served life.

"We should rejoin the others," she said.

But the Knights Essamere were already on the move. Their scattered formation reformed and spurred east. A motley array of cataphracts and white-robed women cantered to meet them, the latter mounted on horned steeds of light and shadow. And at their head, the moon-banner and the blaze of white flame that had wrought Viktor's doom.

"I don't like the looks of that," Armund muttered.

"Surprised Lavirn's not turned tail," said Anliss.

"He can't. They'll run him down. It's head on or nothing." He spat on the ground. "And when he's gone, the cataphracts will finish what these buggers started."

Calenne stared again at their foe. This was no longer mere battle. This was magic, and legend and all manner of things she didn't come close to understanding. But it was also painfully simple. She couldn't turn back. She'd made her moment. She had to seize it. She'd finish what Viktor had started.

Melanna rose up in her stirrups, moon-banner held high. "Ashanael Brigantim!"

She urged her horse to the charge. It leapt the narrow gorge without slowing and galloped down the hillside to the open plain. The uneven silhouette of Blackridge Farm loomed away to the south-west. Its swan-banner fell, replaced by Kos Devren's serpent.

Melanna's blood raced with the thrill of it all. She'd claimed the heights and broken the centre. The redoubts yet stood, islands in a sea of spears. *Her* spears. And beyond, not even an hour's ride distant, the prize of Eskavord.

In all the years a Saran had ruled the Empire, a woman hadn't led as she now led. Hadn't inked her right to rule in the blood of her foes. The thought quickened her blood to fire. She felt no fear at the onset of the galloping knights. Was she not a Saran, blessed by the divine and destined to rule? The goddess would not let her die.

"Ashanael Brigantim!"

"Ashanal! Melanna Ashanal!" The bellowed reply echoed up and around her, voiced from two hundred throats and more. The song of the lunassera rose beneath. *"Melanna Ashanal Brigantim!"*

Melanna's heart swelled. She was their warleader. Their battle cry. They begged her for victory.

But her fire dimmed as a new realisation struck home. They begged *her* for victory, not Ashana. She'd supplanted the goddess in their prayers. A goddess whose favour she'd falsely claimed.

Then the knights were but a spear's-length away, and there was no time for doubts.

Melanna swerved her steed to avoid a lance-point and swept a vicious back-cut at the wielder's head. Metal spat and seethed. A scream. A brief scent of seared flesh rose above the blood and sweat, and then the dying man was behind her.

"Ashanael Brigantim!"

"Melanna Ashanal!" roared the reply. *"Brigantim! Brigantim!"*

Choking back fresh unease, Melanna lost herself in the red fury of battle. There was only the fire in her hand, and the foe, and the one to be borne against the other.

She spurred towards the twin banners – the silver swan and the phoenix. Two Thrakkians, and a Tressian woman little older than herself.

White fire bit into chainmail, and the swan toppled with its bearer. Red hair splayed from beneath the woman's helm as she struck the ground. Sightless eyes stared into the bright sun.

"Anliss!" The second Thrakkian howled and dug back his heels. "*Brenæ væga tikyr!*"

Melanna sent fire billowing into his face. His bellow rose in pitch, rage diluted by pain. His whirling axe split the moon-banner's shaft and chimed Melanna's armoured circlet like a hammer striking a bell. The world lurched. Black fog drowned her vision.

When it cleared, Melanna found herself on her knees beside the woman she'd slain. The second Thrakkian was gone, swept away by a tide of vengeful lunassera. His axe lay on the ground beside her, its haft split.

She clambered to her feet.

"Die, witch!"

Pain flared across her cheek. Steel shone like sunlight as the Tressian woman wheeled about. Melanna let the remnants of the moon-banner fall. She strove for balance on a field pitching beneath her feet.

The woman came about. Melanna's vision cleared. She noted the slenderness of the Tressian's sword. The poor fit of her armour. The pallor of skin from a life lived indoors. Was this Calenne Trelan? She'd heard Crovan speak of her as unfledged and flighty. Neither word suited the cold-eyed woman who dipped her sword to the kill.

Then again, Melanna knew the transformative power of bloodshed better than any.

The ground quivered. The slender sword thrust at Melanna's throat. Numbed reflexes scraped a desperate parry. Knees buckled.

Was this the price of her hubris? The thought drove Melanna to unsteady feet as Calenne bore down a second time. Warm, sticky blood pooled at her collar. It trickled beneath armour to slick her chest and armpit. Her sword had grown too heavy for one hand alone, so she gripped it tight with both.

As the slender sword came forward again, Melanna struck at Calenne's steed.

White flame roared. The horse screamed in sudden terror and shied up. Melanna flung herself back from the flailing hooves. Calenne's cry of panic drowned Melanna's own. Sword abandoned, she grabbed for the saddle's pommel. Then the panicked horse fled, bearing her away towards the forest.

Melanna staggered drunkenly upright. She prayed to the goddess she'd disobeyed that no Tressian would come to finish what the Thrakkian had begun. She felt the whisper of movement at her shoulder and reeled about, her sword barely rising from its downward slant.

Sera, her white robes stained crimson by the day's labours, reached down for her. "Come, Ashanal. Your time on this field is done."

Melanna's gullet soured with failure. But she knew that to stay was to die, or invite capture and all its myriad horrors. As a pair of Tressian knights at last thundered towards her, she seized Sera's hand.

The chandirin came at a gallop, snout lowered and silvered horn aimed at Revekah's chest. The pale-witch's shard-spear hung loose in her hand, the rider content for her steed to deliver the deathblow.

Revekah rose on creaking limbs, the burden of years heavier in that moment than for many long days. But alongside that burden came experience. The knowledge that no battle was ever lost until you lacked the strength to fight.

She'd not yielded fifteen years before. She'd not do so now.

She let the chandirin come, counting down the moments of its approach. With the creature six paces distant, Revekah stooped. Her hands closed around a fallen spear. She drove the butt into the ground and planted a boot behind.

The point, angled sharply upward, pierced the dancing shadow of the chandirin's chest. The creature hurtled on, unaware it had suffered a wound that would have slain an ephemeral steed. The spear-point burst clear of its back and skewered its rider through her heart.

The pale-witch slumped. The chandirin gave a shrill, echoing whinny and reared up. Revekah fell, the spear released in an instinctive attempt to ward off flailing hooves.

She struck the ground at the same time as the pale-witch. Of the chandirin, no sign remained save a dissipating haze.

Revekah rose on trembling legs and grabbed her sword.

Her gaze fell on the dead pale-witch, on robes already awash in crimson. The half-mask had come free in her fall. A dark, young face stared sightlessly out from beneath the hooded robe. Sixteen years old. If that. But then Tarn had been all of what? Nineteen?

Feeling older than ever, Revekah stared across a battlefield of which she no longer felt a part. The centre was a ragged mess of corpses and stray horses; the space between the redoubts choked with panicked men and women. To the west, the walls of the crumbling farm swarmed with Hadari. Kurkas' swan banner was nowhere to be seen. Gold glinted on the northern heights. The ruin of kraikons smouldered where Akadra's shield wall had died. And the owl-banner of Kai Saran still flew.

Clutching her shoulder, she stumbled south towards the forest. One foot in front of the other beneath Lumestra's unremitting gaze. The dull, throbbing pain of her wound grew with every lurching step. Her vision swam. But still Revekah forged on across the corpse-haunted plain.

She barely made it beneath the eaves before darkness took her.

Vorn spun through the air, arms and legs thrashing. He struck one of the stone dancers with a fleshy thud and lay still, his head lolling awkwardly.

Anastacia stood motionless in the circle. She held the blade of Vorn's dagger between finger and thumb. Her shawl's hood lay flat across her shoulders. Black smoke curled up from porcelain eye sockets.

"What ... What are you?"

Crovan stared at her, his eyes wide and his face suddenly pale. Drenn, her own expression only fractionally less shocked, ceased struggling against his grip.

They weren't alone. Anastacia had the attention of everyone in Maiden's Hollow. Not that she seemed pleased. Sloped shoulders and tilted head conveyed the sneer her frozen lips could not express.

[[Maybe I'm the one who turned these fools ...]] She flicked the nearest dancer. The clink of stone on stone was unmistakeable. [[... into statues. *They* chose the wrong side. How about the rest of you?]]

"Shoot her!" snapped Crovan, his voice still strained by disbelief. "Someone ..."

Josiri's shoulder took him in the gut. The dell exploded with vying voices as they fell.

Josiri blotted it out, concentrated on Crovan. He struck the other man in the face, felt something give under his hand. Crovan thrashed, sending them rolling away into the briars. Shards of daylight spiralled above. Brambles tugged at Josiri's clothes. A tree-root cracked against his spine. And then Crovan was astride him, face bloodied. Madness gleamed in his eyes, and a dagger in his hand.

"Shouldn't have come back, Josiri."

A blur of motion. A hollow thud and gasped exhalation. Crovan and Gavamor rolled away, the older man pounding at the younger with a vigour Josiri hadn't suspected he'd possessed.

Drenn leaned over, blotting out branch-webbed sky. Her hand reached for Josiri's. "Can't lie there all day, your grace."

Josiri clasped her hand and lurched upright. A few paces distant, Gavamor had Crovan pinned amid the thorns, a knife at his throat.

On the slopes, Crovan's and Drenn's followers regarded each other with uneasy eyes and drawn blades.

Calenne's steed crashed into the forest, resisting her every attempt to bring it under control. She alternated between sawing madly on its reins and clinging on for dear life. Uneven ground and the press of undergrowth transformed headlong flight into jolting, jarring torment.

At last, she could hold on no longer. The reins ripped from her hands, and she crashed into the underbrush. The hillside claimed her. She rolled over and over, the world a blur of light, muted colour and skinned knees. Branches tore her skin. Ravens cawed and took wing, disturbed from their roosts.

Her back struck something solid. With a heartfelt groan, she propped herself upright. Her whole body felt like one vast bruise.

"The Trelan luck's holding true to form," she muttered.

Then she remembered that Anliss was dead – Armund too, most likely – and felt ashamed. The Trelan luck had kept her alive. She should be thankful for that.

Hadari voices sounded beyond the ridge. Calenne pressed close to the statue that had broken her fall. She cursed her missing sword and shield, lost in the hillside descent. She counted to ten before standing. She clutched herself tight and wondered why she shivered so. It was only natural for it to be cool beneath the trees, even when the sun blazed beyond. But this . . . ? This was different.

She took a step away from the statue. Ice crunched beneath her boot, plunging her foot into the stream. She pressed a wrist to her mouth too late. Her yelp of surprise echoed up, deafeningly loud to her own ears. There were no cries of discovery, nor even the straining wings of panicked birds. Everything remained quiet and still. Even the ongoing roar of battle sounded like something raging on distant fields, rather than less than a mile away.

She caught her breath and took another step, this time onto the rocky stream-bank. Remnants of fluted columns and walls reached back through the brambles to a cave mouth buried in the hillside. And as for the statue itself . . .

It had once been a woman of stately build with a preference for figure-hugging dresses. The head was long gone and the body so overgrown with white-flowering briar that she could make no guess as to identity. Lumestra? Ashana? Some other divine presence?

There was something about the statue – headless and enswathed though it was – that seemed familiar. It called to her. She felt . . . She felt like she had the night Viktor used his magic on Anastacia. As if there was another skin beneath the one that puckered in the cold. It wasn't unpleasant. It wasn't *anything*. It simply . . . was.

Breath misting the air, she reached out. A raven alighted on the ruin of the marble shoulder with an indignant caw. Calenne snatched back her hand and glared at the bird. It peered back, glassy eyes curious but unconcerned.

"Do I have the pleasure of greeting Calenne Trelan?"

Calenne spun around. Fingers tightened about a missing sword. A black-robed, swarthy Hadari stood a dozen paces away. His arms were folded, though she'd no doubt he could draw his weapons soon enough if called.

"I don't know that name." Calenne edged away upstream.

He shook his head. "Please. A phoenix should not conceal her light. Especially when it might yet save her followers. My name is Haldrane. I have the honour to serve his majesty Kai Saran. I offer you his . . . hospitality."

"Really." Calenne offered the reply in a flat, level tone. "I'll have to refuse."

She feinted left. When Haldrane drew a sword and moved to intercept, she turned heel and ran headlong for the dell's far slope. Black cloaks appeared among the trees.

With no other choice remaining, Calenne drove hard for the cave. She charged across the threshold and into the gloom, risking uncertain footing and injury in her bid to escape. Alas, the hoped-for warren of tunnels didn't materialise. Only bare rock walls, and a floor eaten away by the long centuries of the stream's passage.

"I admire your spirit, Lady Trelan, but this serves no purpose."

Calenne turned. Haldrane and two of his companions stood silhouetted against the cave mouth.

He made no attempt to advance. Waiting for his eyes to adjust to the gloom, or wary of a trap? Biting back a snarl of frustration, Calenne examined the cave once more.

She'd been wrong. There *was* another opening deeper in. Wide enough to climb through, and better than nothing. She'd take uncertain darkness over the certainty of capture.

She scrambled back into the darkness, pebbles skittering away from her boots. Behind her, Haldrane issued a snapped command to his companions. Footfalls echoed out.

Rock lurched beneath Calenne's feet. Stones splashed into the streambed. Others cracked away into the darkness. She picked up her pace, clutching at stalagmites for purchase.

A hand closed around hers. Spinning around, she yanked free. Balance lost, Calenne went to brace feet against stone, only to find there was none to be had.

With a last startled cry, she fell into darkness.

Silence reigned. Anastacia rearranged her shawl across her shoulders. She plucked free a quarrel that had snagged amid the weave.

Josiri felt as though he were back atop the shifting stones of Branghall's observatory. One false move, and there'd be no recovering from the fall. Crovan's reluctance to fight the invaders he deemed selfishness in disguise: ambition, clouding conscience. For the rest? Even those in wolf-garb? Fear. Uncertainty. Maybe even disappointment. He could work with those.

"I don't want to fight alongside Akadra," he said. "I hate everything he represents. Were this a just world, we wouldn't need him. But it isn't, and we do."

No one spoke. Sword-points remained undipped. Josiri took a deep breath and pressed on.

"You want to stay here and fight one another? I can't stop you. I can't promise anything will change if you come with me. I can't promise that we'll finally have the freedom we deserve. All I can offer is a chance to make a difference. How will you look back on this day, knowing you let that chance slip by?"

Nervous glances were exchanged. Swords sheathed. The silence remained, but held the first glimmer of determination. Of hope.

A low, bitter chuckle split the air.

"You're all going to die," said Crovan.

Josiri nodded at Gavamor. The older man scowled, but rose to his feet, setting Crovan loose.

"It's a risk," said Josiri. "But one worth taking. You can still be part of it."

Crovan sneered and clambered upright. "A duke's generosity?"

Josiri shook his head, wondering what had happened to the man. Crovan had always been opinionated and ambitious, but somewhere along the line those traits had soured. He knew better than anyone that disappointment was sometimes the hardest burden.

"The promise of a comrade." He extended his hand. "You've been part of this fight in a manner forbidden to me. Be part of it again now."

Crovan stared off into the distance, then gave a reluctant nod. "It seems I've no other option."

His right hand closed around Josiri's. The thoughtful expression melted into a snarl and his eyes darkened in sudden malice. His hand jerked. Josiri, off-balance, stumbled forward. Crovan's left hand came about, the dagger's blade angled upwards.

[[Josiri!]]

Josiri caught Crovan's wrist. Bracing his feet in the soil, he tried to pull free. He succeeded only in drawing them together at greater speed. The two men collided in a macabre embrace. The ridged metal of Crovan's armour dug into Josiri's belly. Crovan shuddered. When his lips parted, the laughter was little more than a ragged gasp.

"Congratulations, your grace." Flecks of blood spattered Josiri's face. They felt cold as ice. "You've killed the first of those you once called friends. How many will follow?"

His grip slackened. Josiri released his own. The shadow passed from Crovan's eyes and he fell back into the dell, the dagger lodged deep beneath his breastbone.

Pain woke Calenne into darkness. Hot, sharp and urgent, it ran the length of her right forearm and spiked when she tried to flex her fingers. Once again, the Trelan luck had failed her. Or perhaps not. Judging by the huddled and motionless form of the Hadari at her side, she was fortunate to have fetched only a broken wrist. Give or take a handful of other knocks and bruises.

Calenne lurched into a hunched sitting position. A new, violent throb made itself known at the base of her skull. At least there was no sign of Haldrane and his men – no *living* sign. Likely they'd taken her for dead and lost interest. Hissing away a whimper, she breathed in the chill, damp air and took stock.

A wisp of pale light shone high above. Thirty feet, at least. More. Too high to climb even without a broken wrist, given the smooth black stone that lined the collapsed passageway.

Even without that tormenting light, it wouldn't have been completely dark. There was a strange, luminescent quality to the black stone. No, that wasn't right. Somehow, it contrived to be darker than everything else. As if it drank in the shadow, rather than emitted light.

Calenne made out an exit a short distance behind her. If there'd once been another, the collapse that had shattered the ceiling had swallowed it up. A trickle of water running down the walls and vanishing between cracks in the stone proclaimed the stream as not entirely blameless.

But one exit was enough – or so Calenne hoped. She had to be in Skazit Maze – Konor Belenzo's old warren of tunnels from the days of a much older struggle. The tunnels ran for miles – or so rumour said – which meant there were other exits, just waiting to be found. At least one passage was rumoured to come up in Eskavord – inside the churchyard no less.

"I'm *not* trapped," she said firmly. Hearing the words helped. She almost believed them.

Rising to her knees, she unbuckled her breastplate and let it fall. Achieving it one-handed drove Calenne almost to distraction. She forged on through the pain, and greaves and vambraces followed. The dead Hadari's dagger-sheath made an acceptable splint for her broken wrist. The belt and strips torn from his cloak served as adequate bindings. By the time she was done, she was sheeted in sweat.

But she was alive and she could walk. It would do.

Tucking the Hadari dagger into her belt, Calenne inched her way into the darkness.

Forty-One

"Useless, deadweight southwealder. Beats me how a stick like you can be so damned heavy."

The bitter mumble pierced thick, black clouds. A tug on Revekah's collar shot a spike of pain through her shoulder – her *bound* shoulder. It jarred her the rest of the way to wakefulness. Undergrowth tore at her arms and legs.

A birch tree lurched past. She grabbed for it and twisted against the hand at her collar. A guttural curse sounded. The weight on her collar vanished, and Revekah rolled free. Hand closing on a fallen branch, she rolled to her feet and swung.

She froze mid-blow. "Kurkas?"

He sank against the nearest tree and glanced furtively about. "Not so loud. This forest's swarming with i, *iculars*."

"Icularis?" She couldn't place the word.

"Saran's emissaries. Not the kind of folks you want to be beholden to."

She let the branch fall. "Weren't you at Blackridge?"

His expression soured. "Blackridge is gone. Bunch of the lads and lasses made it back to the Kevor redoubt. Not enough."

"But not you?"

"Got cut off, didn't I? Times like that, you find whatever hidey-hole presents itself." He rubbed a filthy brow. "Shadowthorns were so intent on the pursuit that I slipped away. Thought I'd stand a better chance in here. Tripped – and I mean *tripped* – over you not long after. Couldn't exactly leave you there for the Hadari, now could I?"

Revekah grunted. She'd heard variations on Kurkas' tale over the years, most often from deserters justifying cowardice. Nonetheless, she couldn't imagine the one-armed northwealder giving up so easily. If easily was the word. His black uniform was torn and bloodied. And deserters weren't known for their kindnesses.

And did it matter if Kurkas had fled? *She'd* fled.

Belatedly, she realised how quiet it was. If battle still raged, it did so a long way off. The sun, barely visible through the forest canopy, was lower than she'd expected. Much lower. She'd been out for hours.

"How bad is it?"

Kurkas' lip curled, and his eye fell. "Bad. Lord Akadra, Lady Trelan? Reckon they're dead or taken."

Revekah hung her head, her breath stolen by the feeling of utter failure.

"Last I saw, there was still fighting off to the north," he said. "The redoubts are holding, but they'll crumble as soon as Saran sends in his Immortals. Might not even do that. Bugger's got catapults. No sense wasting lives to prove a point."

"Why not?" asked Revekah. "We did."

"Fortunes of war." Kurkas held up the remnant of his left arm. "Some you win, others you lose."

She glared at him. "Easy for you to say. You'd nothing at stake."

"Yeah, you keep saying that if it makes you feel better. I lost a lot of lads and lasses back at Blackridge. And Lord Akadra? I'd have died for him. Still might, before I'm done."

With those words, Revekah was back in the rain of Zanya as the silver swan broke apart Katya Trelan's dreams. "Why?"

He shrugged. "Because he'd do the same for me. The best kind of loyalty goes both ways. You used to be a soldier. You should know that."

Used to be? The gall of the man. "I want to see for myself."

"I don't advise that."

"Did I ask for advice?"

"All part of the service. Physician, beast of burden, sage counsel ... "

"Physician? For all I know, my arm'll rot and drop off!"

"At which point you'll only owe me an eye, won't you?" Kurkas growled. "Ungrateful besom. Would it kill you to offer a word of thanks?"

She glowered at him. "*Thank* you. Better?"

To Revekah's surprise, he cracked a smile. "Much. You'll want this."

He fumbled with his sword belt. One of two, overlaid so close that Revekah had missed that detail. Tugging it free, he tossed the sword to her.

"If you're determined to lurch back into the fire, might as well do it armed."

Revekah stared at him, suspicious once more. "You don't have to come."

"You're right, but I'd planned on heading back once I'd stashed your useless lump somewhere safe." He grinned infuriatingly. "Together again, eh?"

Calenne couldn't be sure she wasn't wandering in circles. The chambers would have looked similar even with a firestone lantern to hand. With only the strange, anti-luminescence to guide her, she'd no chance. But she pressed on, striving to ignore a wrist that throbbed with every step, and a throat burning from lack of water.

Without the certainty that attempting to retrace her footsteps would leave her more lost than ever, she'd have turned back. But it wasn't that alone.

There was something ahead, urging her on. The same feeling she'd had about the statue. Familiar. Welcoming.

More likely, she was going mad.

"Should have tried the climb," she muttered. "Now you'll die down here, and no one will ever know."

She regretted the words at once. Bad enough to suspect the fate without hearing it spoken.

"No," she said firmly. "Trelans are stubborn, remember? And you're stubborn enough for two or three. Otherwise you'd not be here, would you?"

"No," Calenne replied to herself. "Likely I'd be dead twice over."

She growled back a despairing sigh. "And now I'm talking to myself. Nothing good ever comes of that."

Feeling more alone than ever, she walked on, never glimpsing light.

Melanna emerged from the sanctum tent into the blinding sun. Her head throbbed. Her cheek stung from the balm with which Sera had treated her wounds. Her circlet was gone, mangled by the Thrakkian's axe-blow. Her broken banner had been lost in the confusion of the knights' charge. But she could yet hold a sword, and so was content ... in one way, at least.

Far to the west, the owl-banner flew on a field empty of conflict. Strife persisted on the heights, but the only Tressian banners were those above the distant redoubts.

Muffled footsteps drew close. Shadow eclipsed the sun. Melanna found herself staring up at her father.

She knelt. "Forgive me."

"For what?" he rumbled.

"I failed you. I disobeyed. You ordered me to take the heights, and instead ..."

He stooped and took her fingers in one massive hand. "And instead you saved my life. It was a brave, foolish and noble gesture. My gratitude cannot be measured. Just as my fear at the cost knew no end, Ashanal."

So saying, he raised her up and – to Melanna's surprise – drew her into an embrace. The Immortals of his guard hung back, silent and disapproving. She suspected her father's rare affection appalled them as much as *she* appalled them. Only Hal Drannic had understood, and he was dead – cut down by the man-of-shadow.

"I'm not Ashanal," she breathed. "I am Saranal, and Saranal alone."

He drew back. "What do you mean?"

She could lie. She could tell him that being his daughter meant more than any divine tie. He'd believe it, especially in that moment. But she had to tell someone. "The goddess rejected my desire for war. Her steward gifted me the sword."

He nodded, his expression unreadable. "Emperors rule despite the will of the gods, not because of it. I've no doubt that you will one day do the same."

A sliver of guilt fell away. Not quite enough, but close. "Thank you, Father."

"Emperor, soon enough." With a sudden bark of laughter, he swept his hand across the battlefield. "They are broken! Defeated! This day, the house of Saran has done something not seen for centuries! We've humbled the bloodless Tressians on their own territory. Let the Golden Court deny me my father's throne now."

"Then it is done?"

He waved a dismissive hand. "All but. Devren holds the south. Aedrun will scour the slopes. As for their patchwork fortresses? We'll crack them apart with catapults and take the survivors by spear. Are you hale enough to join me, daughter? It will be half the victory without you."

Melanna squeezed her sword and felt her strength return. Her head still throbbed. Her cheek still stung. Neither mattered. Not now.

"Of course, my emperor." She dipped head and knee in formal curtsey.

Her father bellowed with laughter. "*Now* you're prepared to behave as a woman should? Had I known a little bloodletting was all it took, I'd have indulged . . . "

He broke off at the blare of a distant horn. Not a Hadari horn. It was brighter, brassier – a triplet of low notes capped by a half-octave leap. Melanna had heard it many times during her weeks in the Southshires. The signal call that roused wolf's-heads to attack.

"It's Crovan," she said tightly. "The Wolf King's betrayed us."

Josiri ran full-tilt down the slope, careless of the treacherous ground. One misplaced boot ran the risk of injury or indignity, but he let the wild notes of the horn drive him on.

Maiden's Hollow emptied behind him. Wolf-cloaks, bandits; the downtrodden and the dispossessed. They screamed like madmen, drowning out fear and doubt. This wasn't war as Josiri had known it at Zanya – the serried ranks and the banners streaming high. The wolf's-heads formed no line and bore no heraldry. They were a mob, driven by the guilt of inaction, betrayal and hesitation. Like Josiri, they came for redemption or the Raven's embrace.

The northern edge of the Hadari line shrank inwards. Warchiefs bellowed orders. Strung out across the hillside in a battle for gulley and outcrop, they'd no chance to reform. Josiri had just enough time to worry about the balance of the numbers before and behind. Then the first shield was before him, and such concerns lay in the past.

Josiri leapt the streambed. His shoulder struck a shield and drove it aside. His sword-thrust skirted the heavy wooden rim and bit into flesh. The Hadari fell, and Josiri ran on.

Panting, he hacked down another. The first wolf-cloaks overtook him, driving deep into the disorganised foe. One died without landing a blow, ribs crushed by a war hammer's punishing strike. One of Gavamor's simarka pounced past Josiri's right shoulder and bore the hammer-wielder to the ground.

Josiri hefted his sword high. "On! On! Keep them off-balance!"

That was the trick. The only hope the wolf's-heads had. Hammer at the Hadari, keep them off-kilter. Deny them time to react. If the Hadari formed up, much less brought their numbers to bear . . .

Josiri swung at a shield bearing the likeness of a snarling wildcat. Hide tore. Wood splintered. He parried a spear and rammed his heel against the shield-boss. His opponent staggered back and lost his balance on the rocks.

Josiri ran on, leaving the man's fate to those who came behind.

"On!" he shouted, though he doubted anyone heard. "On!"

The first serious attempt at a shield wall came as the gorse of the upper slopes gave way to grass. A dozen wolf's-heads died on its spears before a pride of Gavamor's simarka ripped it apart. The next came on the steep banks of a stream. Josiri lost most of a sleeve in that clash, and damn near an eye. But a volley of arrows hissed out of the western rocks, and the Hadari melted away.

Shivering with exertion, Josiri halted for breath. Already, the madness of battle was slipping away. Memory gladly regaled him with every near-miss, every mistake and every botched strike. Harbingers of a death not yet earned.

He growled and shook the recollections away. He was alive. The details were of no account.

A woman in a high-necked naval jacket picked her way through the rocks. She held a bloodied cutlass. Her battered tricorne couldn't hide the soiled bandage about her head.

"Is that what passes for armour among the nobility?" she asked.

Her appearance struck a chord in Josiri's memory, but he couldn't quite place the tune. Josiri stared down at his torn coat and blood-stained shirt.

"One tries to stay abreast of fashion," he said evenly. "I seem to have failed."

She offered a stiff bow. "Captain Kalla Masnar. I'm rationing out this particular barrel of disaster. At least I was. Reckon that's you now, your grace."

At last, Josiri recognised her. The reeve of Ardva. She'd been at Branghall for last year's Ascension. Riotously drunk.

"What about Akadra? My sister?"

Masnar winced and shook her head. "You can see everything *I* can."

Indeed Josiri could, and he liked little of what he saw. Further down the slope, the Hadari were in full retreat, but beyond that? Saran's owl-banner was moving, the blaze of gold growing brighter as other war bands formed around it.

"We were doing fine until those witches showed up," said Masnar. "Our constructs just ... shut down. I don't know who you've got controlling your simarka, but you'd best warn them."

"I'll make sure he knows."

Josiri glanced back up the hill to where Gavamor and Anastacia made a careful descent. Gavamor because of his age, and Anastacia because, in her words, *I don't run.*

A crowd gathered at Masnar's back – one every bit as motley as his own. Tail-coated marines. Hooded wolf's-heads. Labourers with mattocks, billhooks and even the odd shovel. All of them, like her, looking to him for leadership.

Not for the first time, Josiri felt like a fraud. But what else could he do? Calenne was down there. And if he didn't fight now, there wouldn't be a Southshires much longer. He'd have failed everyone.

Masnar offered the wry smile of a woman glad to pass her problems elsewhere. "Waiting on your orders, your grace."

"Form up," he said. "This isn't over."

Kurkas squatted beside the rotten birch and peered out through the ferns. "Well, that's a sight."

The distant northern heights were alive with running battles. The mish-mash of blues, greys and murky browns were dull against golden armour and emerald robes, but they outnumbered the beleaguered shadowthorns, and they were winning. For the first time since his mad scramble from Blackridge, Kurkas felt a rush of grim joy.

Halvor followed his gaze. "Josiri. He must have talked Crovan round."

She looked a decade younger than when he'd found her. Nothing like a little hope to smooth away the years. "The duke? Had him down for a bottle-dweller."

"Mind your tongue!" She winced an apology. "We all lose our way. He's a good lad."

Kurkas stifled a smile. They were all children to Revekah Halvor. Hard to imagine one of the northern nobility sticking their necks out for their beliefs as she had, and at her age. Might be she'd more in common with Lord Akadra than she reckoned.

He pointed north-east, to the owl-banner that claimed dominance of the battlefield's centre. Remnants of the cataphracts and a sole grunda chariot flanked the marching ranks of Kai Saran's Immortals. "Dead lad, if he's not careful."

"Give Josiri some credit. Better yet, we'll give him some reinforcement. The redoubts are intact. We can scrounge up a couple of hundred . . . "

A rustle of leaves drew Kurkas' attention. He stared past Revekah, back into the forest. "Not going to happen."

"Fine," snapped Halvor. "I'll go alone."

"That's not what I meant."

Black-cloaked icularis ghosted through the trees towards them. Kurkas drew his sword.

"Calenne."

The voice jarred her from nightmares to the suffocating un-light of Skazit Maze. If there was any longer a difference. Dizziness swirled the gloom. She hadn't meant to sleep. A moment's rest. Nothing more.

"Calenne."

The voice came again. This time loud enough that Calenne knew it to be real. Not some figment of forgotten dreams. She scrambled to her feet and pressed her back against the cold stone.

"Who's there? Where are you?"

Wings fluttered past her head, invisible in the darkness.

"I'm here."

Calenne turned a giddying circle and found herself face to face with a tall, tatter-coated man wearing a feathered domino mask. She backed away, the hairs on the back of her neck prickling.

"Who are you?"

He stroked his goatee. "A friend. I saw you fall. I'd like to help."

"You'll forgive me if I don't believe that."

"Will I?" He shrugged. "Why not? But I *am* your friend. I'm a friend to everyone, in time."

Calenne felt her eyelids droop. The stranger's soft, rational manner begged for agreement. For accession. She struck her shattered wrist against the wall. The pain snapped her eyes wide open. She choked back a sob.

"There's no need for that," said the stranger. "I've come to show you a way out."

"A way out?" It took all she had not to beg. The stranger would have been discomfiting even back at Branghall. Here? In the gloom, he was a hair short of terrifying. It wasn't just a matter of him being out of place. He filled the chamber, and more besides. As if what Calenne perceived was but the tiniest part of his being. "I'll find my own exit."

He drew closer with soundless footfall. "I think not. You don't know where you are."

"I'm in Skazit Maze. Wolf's-heads get in and out all the time. So will I."

"No. Konor Belenzo sealed this catacomb precisely *so* that nothing would get out. He was *terrified* of something getting out." His words didn't invite belief. They demanded it. "Neither of us wants you to stumble onto her, believe me. But you can escape, if you accept my help."

He held out his hand.

"Tell me," he asked, his voice soft as smoke. "Do you dance? I confess it's become something of an obsession of late. We all have our vices."

Calenne felt her eyelids drooping. This time she did nothing to halt it. Even as a small inner voice screamed at her to back away – to run! – she raised her good hand to his.

The stranger's gloved fingers brushed her wrist. Something cold and sharp pressed to her skin. Warmth swept it away. Muscles tightened in Calenne's shattered wrist, grinding the bones together. She yelped in pain and glanced down.

She saw no sign of the stranger's hands, just her own. Her left, somehow free of its sling, held her dagger-blade against her right wrist. The steel was slick with blood from a nicked vein. A hair's breadth more …

"And now you've spoilt everything." The stranger's voice echoed about her, the syllables thick with disappointment and ... fear? "I wish you hadn't. Now there's nothing I can do. I'm sorry."

Invisible wings buffeted Calenne's head and arms. Harsh voices rose in croaking chorus about her. Heart pounding in terror, she hurled the dagger away and fled.

Forty-Two

Arrows hissed through the air. Leather-clad outriders scattered away from the volley, leaving dead behind. A ragged cheer went up from the southwealders' mismatched ranks. In a day of sparse victories, even the smallest counted.

"Form up!" Josiri shouted. "Lock shields!"

The cry rippled up and down the line. Shields scavenged from the dead formed a wall of mismatched heraldry. Here a phoenix. There a swan. The hounds and serpents of vanquished Hadari clansmen. Josiri pictured Makrov's disapproving expression on seeing the serpent-shield he himself carried. The image provoked a burst of cheer in an otherwise grim moment.

[[A pity no one else wants to play.]]

Anastacia gestured at the nearest redoubt. Soldiers stood silent on its ramshackle battlements. Not one had marched out to join them.

"You shouldn't be here," said Josiri.

[[None of us should be here,]] she replied. [[I want to try out my new toy.]]

She hefted a war hammer claimed from a dead Immortal. She looked ridiculously frail – as if one good swing would send her spinning off into the distance.

Josiri shot a glance at Masnar, but the captain was either not listening, or at least giving a good pretence. The same couldn't be said of the nearby wolf-cloaks who paid unabashed interest. Or possibly it was fear. Word of Vorn's death – and the manner of it – had spread.

He lowered his voice. "I don't want to lose you."

[[You won't. I'm hard to miss.]] A bitter note crept into her voice. [[Especially now.]]

Josiri stifled a scowl. Even now, she delighted in missing the point. "That's not what I meant."

[[I know what you meant. Whatever I have become, I used to be a serathi. A herald of dawn and bringer of hope.]] She raised her voice. The hollow words danced. [[And I'm *certain* I've killed more men than you.]]

Laughter rippled around him – all of it at Josiri's expense.

"Here they come!" bellowed Masnar.

Mirth dissolved into jeers as the Hadari line came about. Disciplined, overlapped shields put Josiri's formation to shame. The glittering emeralds of Kai Saran's armour exuded regal destiny. Not for the first time, Josiri gave silent thanks that battle had so severely thinned the cataphracts' ranks. As for the pale-witches – the lunassera, Anastacia had called them – and their chandirin? Or the tales he'd heard of a woman wielding white flame . . . ? The grunda?

The grunda alone was enough to break their line.

"Steady!" He shouted, as much for his own benefit as for those around him. "Didn't you hear? We've a serathi with us! She brought the sunlight! Don't let her down!"

Laughter returned, this time at Anastacia's expense more than his. She kicked his shin. [[Just what I needed to hear.]]

"You started it. Do you want to be a bringer of hope, or not?"

[[Yes.]] She stared out across the field. [[Yes I do.]]

The Hadari line quickened. The cataphracts and chandirin kept pace with the marching infantry. White flame blazed beneath the owl-banner. The grunda outstripped them all. Josiri felt the tremor beneath his feet.

"Merrik!" he shouted. "Don't let that thing reach us!"

[[No! Save your arrows for the lunassera!]]

Masnar shot a hurried glance up and down the line. "This formation's held together by good intentions and spittle. If that thing reaches us . . ."

Anastacia dropped her shield. [[It won't.]]

"Ana!"

Josiri grabbed for her too late. She strode purposefully across the field, the hammer's head raking the dust as it dragged behind. Josiri moved to follow.

Masnar seized his shoulder. "You want to kill us all? Hold the line!"

Josiri shrugged Masnar's hand away. Throat thick with worry, he gripped his shield until his fingers ached. *Do you want to be a bringer of hope, or not?* How he hated those words now.

He hoped Anastacia knew what she was doing. The chances of that seemed slender as her doll's body before the charging grunda. She didn't run – of course she didn't – but strode with purpose, shoulders bowed. The charioteer's whip cracked. The grunda picked up speed. Anastacia halted and planted the hammer's butt in the ground. In the moment before impact, she shied away, hands flung up to ward off the inevitable.

A thunderous, hollow *thud* shook the sky. Anastacia and grunda vanished in a cloud of dust.

"Ana!" A scraping, grinding sound drowned out Josiri's cry. It rose in brief crescendo and fell away to nothing. The dust cloud blossomed, stinging his eyes. Then the wind gusted, bringing revelation.

Anastacia's boots sat planted deep in twin furrows stretching back towards the Hadari lines. Her outspread hands – the war hammer's handle still grasped between them – were braced against the beast's massive snout. Churned soil and wheat-stalks matted her dress.

Even as Josiri wondered at the strength it had taken to bring the grunda to a halt, the beast reared up. Leathery feet flailed at Anastacia's head.

She stepped back. Her grip shifted on the hammer's haft and she swung it in a full, dizzying circle. Metal cracked against the grunda's upraised head. The beast gave a final, empty bellow. Wrenching free of the chariot's spars, it toppled sideways in a spray of dust.

Disbelieving cheers rang out from the Tressian line. They grew in volume and stridency as voices caught up with evidence of eyes. Josiri joined them, his throat thick with relief.

Anastacia strode up the grunda's armoured flank. She seized the charioteer by the throat and hoisted him high above the ground. Then she cast him aside and raised the war hammer in triumph.

The cheer redoubled in volume. For the very briefest of moments, Josiri glimpsed a ghostly echo of black-feathered wings at Anastacia's back. He blinked, and they were gone.

Careless of the oncoming Hadari, Anastacia dropped from the grunda's back and rejoined the line.

[[Told you I'd a lot of repressed anger.]]

"And now?" he asked, almost laughing with relief.

[[I've barely scratched the surface.]]

Horns urged the Hadari to the charge.

Calenne ran until her legs were jelly and her lungs burned. She gave no thought to what lay ahead, only the horror behind. Doubled over and panting for breath, she strove to make sense of what she'd seen.

The Raven! The Raven was *real*. The thought set her trembling again. She spun around and stared back into the gloom.

Nothing. No sound. No movement.

Dizziness returned. With it the doubt she'd seen anything at all. Had the "Raven" been anything more than fevered imagination? She glanced at her bloodied wrist.

"He was there," she breathed. "He *was* ... Wasn't he?"

Calenne pinched her eyes shut and tried to ignore the buzzing in her head. Water. She needed water. She opened her eyes as her breathing steadied, and noted something new.

Light.

It wasn't much. A soft, yellowish tinge where the passage forked. Warm, even inviting. A hint of sunlight. And the Raven had said there'd been no way out ... More than ever, Calenne grew convinced that she'd experienced a hallucination. Despair did strange things to the mind.

But not now. Not with the possibility of salvation. Even a glimpse of the sun would help ... even if the opening was too high for her to reach. Even if a cohort of Hadari blocked her way.

There were no Hadari around the next turning. Nor was there a glimpse of the sky. There was only the light, which grew brighter with every step. A spill of rubble blocked her way, the end of a snapped lintel protruding from the mound of discoloured rock. Calenne scrambled over the stones and pressed on in search of freedom.

Beyond, the character of the walls changed. No longer smooth, they bore bas-reliefs of half-height figures. Calenne ran her fingertips across the stone, tracing faces and the outlines of shields.

No two were the same. Some wore the short tunics and banded armour of early Tressia. Others the precursor to the robes and scales she'd seen too often that day. Then there were thicker-set figures, decked in furs and plaited beards. And through it all, the same stylised motifs. The sun and the moon. A blazing fire and a foam-flecked wave. A thorned rose and . . . and a raven.

Calenne suppressed a shudder. Still she caught no sign of the light's source, only the reflections it scattered across the polished black stone. She gave no thought to turning back. Better the perils of the light than the uncertainty of the dark.

The passageway opened into a high-vaulted chamber, twice the size of her room at Branghall. At the very centre, a ring of iron-caged torches blazed – not with fire, but with golden light. Within the ring, there was only darkness. A darkness that was somehow more welcoming than the light.

The darkness swirled like windblown smoke as Calenne drew closer. Though it never broached the threshold of torches, the turbulence revealed a little of what lay within. A soot-blackened plinth, and atop it a twisted, scorched skeleton whose mouth gaped wide in a silent scream. Ash lay thick about the plinth's base, shot through with gobbets of silvered metal. Bindings rendered molten by flame.

Instinct screamed at Calenne to flee. Her legs didn't respond. She felt a sense of belonging she couldn't place, much less explain.

The darkness guttered, then billowed. A womanly shape coalesced. Black vapour trailed behind in a windswept mane. She hammered at the torch-lit boundary, her thin, sharp features contorting in a voiceless scream. The air rippled like water beneath her fists. Shards of golden light flashed with each impact.

Her face flickered and reformed, likeness bleeding into likeness. Dozens Calenne didn't recognise, and others she did, faces from her childhood. Then her own. It was gone as soon as glimpsed, replaced by the sharp-featured face first worn. Then the woman swirled away, her body collapsing into formless darkness again.

At last, Calenne's legs responded. She staggered away, a hand thrust to her mouth to stifle a scream. A name echoed through her thoughts. A name from legend.

Malatriant.

*

The icularis attacked in a whirl more dance than war-craft. The folds of his cloak disguised his dirk's lunge until it was too late to parry.

At least, that was the intent. But Revekah had seen every trick under the sun. This one, she'd seen many times in preceding minutes. She'd bled for the first, but *only* the first. The cloak's edge slipped away. She stepped back, her shoulder blades pressing against Kurkas'. Her sword teased the dirk's point aside, and her riposte slit the icularis' forearm to the bone. Her backswing cut off his scream almost before it began.

A wet thud sounded behind. Kurkas grunted in pain and sank against her shoulders.

"Don't embarrass me in front of the shadowthorns," she said.

"Just getting my ... " Another thud. A scream. " ... second wind."

Revekah worried at the breathiness of Kurkas' protest, then wondered why she cared. Of the two icularis still facing her, one mistook concern for lack of focus. He died with her sword in his throat.

Kurkas groaned. His weight slipped from Revekah's shoulders.

"Kurkas?"

Revekah spun on her heel. He lay at her feet, eye closed and tunic marred by fresh, bloody rents. Another corpse to join the half-dozen icularis they'd dispatched.

Three remained. Two of Kurkas'. One of hers. Manageable odds, fighting back to back. Now?

Revekah threw herself at the nearest and bore him to the ground before he'd a chance to scream. Her sword sliced up under his breastbone. She rolled away, gaping in pain as the motion jarred her injured shoulder.

Another icularis stabbed down. Revekah struck the blade aside and staggered to her feet. A swirl of robes and the wicked dirk came again. A second parry, a third, a fourth – the timing of each cut finer than the last as her strength failed.

The icularis thrust at her heart. Revekah twisted aside, burning the last of her reserves in the process. She slammed her head forward. Cartilage crunched. The icularis yelped and reeled away, blood streaming from his nose.

Revekah plunged her sword into his back. It had taken too long. The third would finish her.

She spun around at the high-pitched scream.

The last icularis stood motionless above the prone Kurkas, his mouth agape. The hearthguard's sword was buried almost to the hilt in his groin.

Dry, wheezing laughter crackled up from Kurkas' bloodied lips. The icularis slid sideways, taking Kurkas' sword with him.

Chest shuddering with exertion, Revekah fell to her knees. "I thought you were dead."

"Not ... Not yet," he croaked. "Now bugger off and save your precious duke."

Revekah stared out through the trees towards the distant battle. Did Josiri still live? Could she even reach him in time to make a difference?

Josiri's life or death wasn't in her gift. But Kurkas ...

She swore softly, tore a strip of cloth from an icularis' cloak and pressed the bundle against the wound in Kurkas' chest. "Here. Hold this tight while I take a look at the rest." She set to work unbuttoning his tunic.

Kurkas flinched as her bare flesh touched his bloody skin.

"Madam, I must protest," he gasped weakly. "You're not even my type."

"Oh shut up."

She threw herself into the task of saving a life she'd twice tried to take.

Viktor awoke in a suffocating, sweltering world. One swamped in darkness, stinking of sweat, blood and ordure. He tried to move. The oppressive weight on his chest shifted with a scrape of metal. It slipped a hair's breadth closer to his nose, feeding sudden fear that whatever lay atop him would crush him entirely.

He twisted his head. Dead eyes stared back from an Immortal's helm. Without the Hadari's corpse to bear some of the weight, he'd have been crushed.

Scattered memories reformed. Saran. The white flame, and his shadow's scream. The falling kraikon. Trapped beneath a kraikon? It was only dumb luck that he wasn't dead.

Sights and sound trudged into shape. The distant sounds of sword on sword. The screams.

He was needed.

Slowly, carefully so as to not invite further collapse, Viktor braced hands against the kraikon. It barely shifted. He tried again, arching his back and kicking his heels against the ground.

The kraikon moved. Viktor roared as it gave. The kraikon slipped to his left, tilting as it did so. Daylight streamed in above Viktor's head, giving shape to the mangled bronze torso.

Another muscle-wrenching heave and his right arm came free. From there, an undignified wriggle freed his right leg. His chest followed, though at the cost of a torn surcoat. Viktor didn't care. He was free.

He lurched upright on rubbery legs and drank in sunlight and clean air. Or nearly so, for the stench of death lay thick on the wind. The Raven had feasted well that day. There, barely four hundred yards north, a new banquet awaited. A mishmash of wolf's-heads, militia and Lumestra alone knew what else buckling beneath the remorseless Hadari advance.

"Em'shal rae, Ashanal!"

The pale-witch came for him at a dead run, healer's tools spilling from an abandoned haversack. A shard-spear flashed to life, the blade under her hand, and the shaft running parallel to a back-flung arm.

She leapt, slashing at his face from mid-air. Viktor caught her by wrist and throat. A wrench. A *snap*. The woman went limp. The man the pale-witch had sought to treat crawled desperately away across the dead on his elbows. Viktor let him go and stared northwards once more.

For the first time since its cowardice before the white flame, his shadow demanded freedom.

So much death, and born of his pride. Viktor Akadra, who didn't lose. It was his responsibility. He was tired. But more than weariness of the body, he was sick of holding back, of hiding who he was and what he could do. If he'd drawn on his shadow from the first, the battle might have ended in victory long ago.

His boot brushed against steel. Stooping, Viktor reclaimed his claymore. The blade was battered and notched. The ribbon – Calenne's ribbon – was still knotted tight about the pommel.

What had become of her? What fate had he led her to?

Again, Viktor's shadow cried out.

Weary, sore and his heart heavy with rising anger, Viktor granted its wish. More than its wish. Even as he reached for the shadow, he touched something deeper, stronger. Buried deep not within himself, but in the soil – in the very bedrock of Southshires. It wasn't the same as his shadow, but nor was it wholly different. Unfamiliar words sung to a tune memorised long ago.

He hesitated, wary of the hidden tides swirling inches from his grasp, but only for a moment. His pride had brought about enough death. No more hiding. No more fighting what he was. What he could do.

Viktor's breath frosted in the air as the hidden power bent to his will. Ice crackled about his fists. The ground shook.

The cavern screamed. Stone split beneath Calenne's feet. She hurled herself sideways. Her shoulder struck rock. The bones of her broken wrist ground together. Darkness pulsed within the ring of light. Dust spilled from fresh cracks in stone. One by one, the torches went out. A wordless cry echoed through the air – part longing, part triumph.

Calenne scrambled to her feet and backed away across the bucking floor. Darkness surged between the quenched torches.

Malatriant's sharp-featured form coalesced a pace beyond the extinguished cage. No longer swamped in shadow, her flesh was pale as alabaster and shot through with spidery black veins. Her hair streamed behind like a dark, windblown flame. A hollow flame, bereft of texture and being. To stare upon it was to stare through the world itself, to whatever lay beyond.

"Child." She reached out a hand. Hungry eyes glittered like coal. "Come to me."

The sense of belonging returned, stronger than ever. Calenne stood paralysed as the chamber collapsed. She was content to be so, and hated herself for it.

Malatriant drifted closer. The skirts of a fibrous dress trailed behind her like smoke. Yowling faces formed in the cloth. They scattered as the threads contorted with fresh movement.

"You feel it, don't you? Our bond."

"No," croaked Calenne. "I'm Calenne Trelan, daughter of the Phoenix. We're nothing alike."

A stone slab shattered against the floor to her left. Dust stung her throat.

"The Phoenix." Malatriant chuckled. "I was there when Konor Belenzo first uttered that prophecy. He desired a legacy of light. But light flickers. It fades. Only the Dark is for ever. Only in darkness are we free. We are all one in the Dark. You feel it, don't you? It's part of you."

The worst of it was, Calenne did. She longed to embrace the apparition, and to be held in return. But she clung to the memory of the Raven. His forlorn tone when she'd seen through his enchantment. And the legends. The scriptures. To embrace Malatriant was worse than death, to be severed for ever from Lumestra's light and the promise of Third Dawn. Calenne had never truly believed, not until that moment.

Better to die, if it came to that.

"No!"

Dredging up the last of her fading will, Calenne jerked away. With Malatriant's soft laughter on her heels, she fled into Skazit Maze. The darkness swallowed her up.

Josiri lost his footing as the tremor struck. He stumbled against the line of shields, only to discover it already breaking apart. Men and women staggered, designs of death thwarted by the bucking ground. The grunt and fury of battle fell away beneath cries of alarm.

A hand closed around his tattered collar and righted him. Anastacia, inevitably, stood solid as a rock amid the tremor.

A shadow fell across the sun, drowning the field in darkness.

With Anastacia's help, Josiri regained firm footing. "Blessed Lumestra! What's happening?"

His breath frosted as he spoke. His limbs trembled with cold as much as in sympathy with the shaking ground.

She stared skyward. [[Lumestra has no part of this.]]

Uneven shadows flickered across the ground. The drums fell silent. Hadari cried out in dismay. Others clutched their eyes and fell to their knees. A few fled, tearing madly at kin in their striving. Horses reared, hurling riders to the ground.

Josiri stared left and right along his own ranks, but saw none of that madness, only perplexion akin to his own.

The tremor faded. The shadow passed in a gust of wind. Sunlight beat down with renewed splendour, driving back the cold. The Hadari line, an unbreakable bulwark of shields only moments before, had cracked like weak-mortared brick in a gale. For the first time since Josiri had come to the field, the enemy were vulnerable.

"For the Southshires!"

Other voices took up his cry. The line came forward. Not as a shield wall drilled for battle, but a mob of vengeful men and women with the scent of victory.

Anastacia splintered a shield with a hammer-blow. Stepping into the gap, Josiri beat aside the Immortal's flailing sword with his own. The man died in wide-eyed confusion, and Josiri pressed on. Two more perished to his blade before recognition dawned. The Hadari had been struck blind. Not all of them, but enough.

Masnar went howling past on his left, her cutlass a blur of bloody steel. A pack of marines followed on her heels, their short swords brutally efficient in the press of bodies. A proctor came with them, sun-stave flaring like fire as it struck shield and flesh.

A heavy shove sent Josiri sprawling. A war hammer whirled. Anastacia's head cracked back. Her shawl's hood fell open to reveal a jagged black line across her right cheek.

Josiri hacked at the hammer-wielder's legs. With a cry, he fell to his knees. Anastacia's return blow all but struck the man's head from his shoulders.

Josiri clambered to his feet. "Are you all right?"

[[I'm fine. Be more careful.]]

The deeper they pressed into the Hadari formation, the stiffer the fight. The crowd heaved and bore him from Anastacia's side. A shard-spear flashed to his left to down a moustachioed marine. The lunassera galloped on. Her ethereal steed shimmered as its straining limbs ghosted through Tressian and Hadari alike.

Josiri threw himself to the ground. A scream sounded as the spear flashed over his head.

The circle of Immortals pressed in. A wolf-cloak gurgled and died, his throat torn away by a spear. Masnar's cutlass shattered beneath a hammer-blow. She died with her hands around an Immortal's throat, screaming defiance at the faceless helm.

Josiri fought back-to-back in the shrinking knot of Tressians. He snarled as savagely as any as he fought to survive. But for every Hadari that fell, another came forward to take his place.

A war hammer battered at Josiri's sword and drove him to his knees.

Steel screeched. The Immortal shuddered. He jerked aside as if struck by the flat of a colossal hand. The mighty claymore swung again. It clove a second Immortal and swept a lunassera from her dissipating steed. Viktor Akadra stood in the widening gap, his ragged surcoat gaping to reveal buckled armour beneath. The glower on his bruised face sent a chill shuddering along Josiri's spine.

A bloody gauntlet reached forth. "Rise, brother. There is work yet to be done."

After the briefest hesitation, Josiri took the hand of the man he'd hated half his life.

The wolf-cloak twisted away, his hair ablaze and his face blackening beneath the flame.

"Ashana! Ashanael Brigantim!"

Only a handful of voices echoed Melanna's cry. Too many had died in the grip of the shadow. Melanna had felt its coils about her, the light sucked from her eyes. But then her sword had blazed anew. The shadow had bled from her sight. But it had claimed too many others.

She stared across the sea of strife, her throat souring at how little green and gold remained. Frustration burned away the heavy throb in her brow. She hammered at shield and helm. Spat and cursed until her throat was raw. But with each blow, there was less and less of her in the wielding.

Melanna's father reached her side. His cloak was torn. Uneven gait betrayed injuries concealed by gilded armour.

"Daughter, you must go. My guard will hold them long enough for your escape."

"No!"

He removed his helm and set it aside. Earnest eyes bored into hers. "You must. The redoubts are emptying. Our warriors' hearts are failing. The battle is lost. I will not lose you alongside."

Our warriors. Not his. Theirs. If only she'd heard those words in happier times.

Melanna stared out to the west, to blue tabards lining up beneath the redoubts. At the familiar shadow gathering beyond the beleaguered shields. She could do as he asked. Sera's chandirin would bear them both away. But ... "And what of you?"

"My place is here, come what may."

Death or capture. Which meant death now, or death later, his last dignity stripped away before baying crowds in the grey city. Melanna gritted her teeth against her tears.

"No! It won't end like this! I won't let it!"

Her father's tone hardened. "It is not for you to choose. As your father – as your emperor – I command you to leave. To keep our family name alive."

Thick, bitter laughter spilled from Melanna's lips. "Oh, Father ... When have I ever followed your commands?"

She pushed him away. The white flame blazed in her hand. "Saranael Brigantim!"

Tears hot on her cheeks, she ran for the shield wall.

Akadra cut a path towards the owl-banner, claymore a bloody blur. Josiri kept pace though there was little for him to do in that trail of carnage, save dispatch those the widow-making blade had merely stunned, not slain.

A line of golden shields split apart. White flame blazed, given purpose by a young woman's hand.

And Akadra? Akadra did the very last thing Josiri had expected. He shrank back, hands upraised as if to shield his eyes from the piercing light. Seeing her victory, the woman screamed like a cyraeth claiming the damned. The white flame crackled and swung for Akadra's head.

But then Josiri was there, between Akadra and the fire. His skin prickled with the heat. The edge of his blade ran molten beneath the alabaster flame. The woman screamed and ripped her sword away. The fire came again.

Again, Josiri parried. This time, he'd attention enough to note the woman's youth. Younger than Calenne. Almost young enough to be his daughter. And yet there was something familiar about her. Not her face, but her manner. Josiri had seen it enough in his own reflection that past week. Frustration. Self-loathing. They could almost have been twins – if in spirit, rather than flesh.

But . . . a woman in the Hadari ranks? And not robed as a lunassera? Josiri recalled the details of his conversations after Crovan's death. Was this Melanna Saranal, the would-be emperor's daughter?

Melanna loosed a wild flurry of blows. Josiri parried each in turn. As the fourth scraped aside, he braced his feet and rammed his shield forward.

The impact lifted Melanna clean off her feet. She struck the ground with enough force to drive the breath from her body. The sword shuddered from her hand. Fire faded as it left her grip.

She clutched her belly and lay among the dead, eyes blazing with hatred. "Kill me!"

"Gladly." Akadra pushed past Josiri and planted his foot on Melanna's chest. All trace of his earlier weakness had fled. His breath steamed as he drew back his sword.

"No!"

Josiri wasn't sure why he struck the claymore away. Was it the presumptive kinship with the beaten woman? Or perhaps he was tired of death. But whatever surprise he felt at his action, it was far eclipsed by astonishment at Akadra's lack of protest. Instead, the giant stood in place, boot pinning the woman to the ground.

"Kai Saran!" Josiri shouted. "I have your daughter! Surrender, and she lives!"

Akadra grunted, his lip curling with what might have been approval. A ragged mix of wolf-cloaks, bandits and militia formed a ring around them to forestall an attempt at rescue.

"Kai Saran!" Josiri's voice cracked. Was the prince even alive? "What is your daughter's life worth?"

Golden ranks parted to reveal emerald armour. A shield crashed to the ground. A sword followed. In sudden silence broken only by Melanna's anguished howl, Kai Saran knelt.

Forty-Three

Josiri arrived at camp long after nightfall. The perimeter guard – a mixture of wolf-cloaks and Tressian soldiers – let his horse canter past with barely a challenge. For the first time in fifteen years, north- and southwealders were as one. Not in the manner he would have chosen, and certainly not how his mother had foreseen, but did that matter? Josiri felt guilty for not appreciating it more, but his mind wandered distant fields.

[[I take it you've met without success?]]

Anastacia drew closer, a dark silhouette against leaping campfires.

"I can't find her." Josiri swung wearily down from the saddle. He hated the confession. It sounded like abandonment. "But I have to rest, otherwise I'll fall from the saddle."

The doll's mask tilted. [[It *would* spoil things if you were trampled by your own horse. I don't believe Calenne would want that.]]

"Given our last conversation, I'm not so sure."

That had been when? Only a few days ago. It felt like a lifetime. In fifteen years, they'd never been apart so long.

[[She's a Trelan. She's stubborn.]]

He nodded, fighting a fresh flood of despair. "I can't find Calenne, nor Revekah. What's the point of victory if it feels like defeat?"

Anastacia took his hands in hers. Josiri stared away to the east, to the redoubts. No longer bastions of war, they served as prisons. The remaining Hadari had limped away behind the eastern hills, watched by a sentry line of wayfarers and the sleepless malice of Jesver Merrik's band.

"Don't wish away what you've achieved," rumbled a new voice.

Josiri turned. Viktor Akadra stood a short distance away. One bandaged hand led a horse's bridle. His other cast about the campfires, and the weary men and women who hunched near to the flames. At the closest, voices lifted in the strains of "Seca's Lament", the dour notes hastened along by a fiddle's rasp. Bottles clinked. Wolf-cloaks and king's blue around the same fire. Fancy that.

"They're alive by your actions," Akadra continued. "Don't dishonour that."

"Right now, all I care about is my sister," Josiri replied. "I don't expect you to understand."

"Then you're a fool." Akadra's bruised face twisted, as one who knew he'd overstepped. "I don't blame you for feeling as a man, but you and I must be more than men. Especially now. We have to lead."

Josiri felt his cheeks colour. "If that's so, why are you sneaking off?"

"Because you're not the only one who fears for your sister's safety."

For all his effort, Josiri found no glibness in the other's tone, nor deception in his expression. Their lack irritated as much as their presence would have annoyed. "If you cared as much as you'd have me believe, you'd have been out there these past hours."

Akadra's eyes tightened. "As I said, I've had to lead. Lavirn is dead. So is Masnar. My list of subordinates runs thin. But you've returned, and so I'm free to be a man once more. In my absence, I've made it known that you are to be treated with the same respect owed to me. Rise to the challenge."

Josiri winced at the rebuke. Shame coursed hot through his veins. So much had changed, and yet he'd fallen back into old patterns almost at once.

"Lord Akadra ... *Viktor* ... " The other halted in the act of clambering into his saddle. Josiri pressed on before the courage to do so failed completely. "Do you think that we could begin again, you and I?"

"The past is not for changing, not if we're to learn from it." The dark features broke into a broad smile. "But in the future, perhaps we *could* both think better of one another."

He extended a hand. Josiri hesitated. Even now, Akadra sought equality. Only this time, it was of blame – a blame Josiri was certain was all his own. How had he misjudged this man so badly? Calenne had been right. Their mother's legacy coloured everything.

Calenne . . .

He took Viktor's hand. "We can surely try."

Viktor felt it as soon as their fingers met, though he couldn't quite describe exactly *what* he felt. It was like . . . Thunderheads on the horizon, the pressure building before a storm. Bleak. Hollow . . . Almost *hungry*. His shadow twitched in affinity. Josiri too had something dark slithering about his soul. But where Viktor's shadow was a piece of him, the darkness in Josiri felt alien . . . like a seed.

He tightened his grip. His eyes bored into Josiri's. "Are you wounded?"

"A few scrapes, and a cut from an Immortal's sword. Nothing more. I've been lucky." Suspicion bubbled to the surface. "Why?"

"You'll allow me a little concern."

Old tales of cursed blades and maledictions of spirit trickled into Viktor's thoughts. He'd never given them much credence until now. They belonged to myth, but only in the same way that swords blazing like fire belonged to myth. A cut would be more than enough.

Viktor sent his shadow snaking between them, its coils lost in the dark.

It obeyed reluctantly, exhausted from the labours of the day and from tapping the now-vanished wellspring of magic that Viktor had sensed beneath soil and wielded to turn the tide of battle. Still, the pride remained. He'd harnessed the power of a Forbidden Place – he'd touched the face of the divine. Elzar would be hungry for the details.

Viktor shook the thought away and focused on the moment at hand. He'd never attempted something of this kind, but his relationship with his own shadow had shifted ever since he'd returned to the Southshires, particularly since the conjuring at the battle's climax. It wouldn't be right to describe it as *tamed*, but there was a new calm between them. Perhaps that same accord allowed him to see deeper into Josiri's core?

He released Josiri's hand and stepped back. His shadow probed the seed in Josiri's soul.

And just like that, it was gone. Devoured.

Josiri blinked and stood straighter than he had before.

Viktor drew back his shadow. It felt heavier. Content. How much good had he previously left undone through restraint? Something to think on.

"Forgive me," he said. "But I must go. I *will* find Calenne if she's there to be found. My tent is yours."

He clambered into his saddle, wincing as the motion pulled on recently stitched wounds.

Calenne was still out there. She had to be.

Josiri watched until Viktor was lost to sight, and the rhythmic thump of hooves faded beneath the sound of drunken carousal. The world suddenly seemed brighter – as if pressure had lifted from behind his eyes. What was it his father had always said? *A heartfelt apology is good for the soul.*

Turned out it might be true.

He felt Anastacia's eyes on him. "You're unusually quiet."

[[What would you have me say? That I'm proud? Or I can mock you, if you worry over a swollen head.]]

Josiri gazed out across campfires far sparser than they should have been. How many lives could he have saved by joining with Viktor from the first? "No danger of that. I've made too many mistakes."

[[If you live to see two hundred years, perhaps then you'll match my tally, but I doubt it.]] She paused. [[Viktor's right. The past's not for changing. But the future is what we make of it.]]

She drew closer. The tattered shawl twitched about her shoulders. Black eyes gleamed in the perfect white-gold face. A witch's eyes, as they were so often called. How terrifying she should have seemed to him, and to the superstitious soldiery. But Josiri had no fear of her, and word had spread as evening wore on. Of the porcelain woman who'd felled a charging grunda. Whoever Anastacia had been before she'd come to Branghall, she'd made herself a legend, if only for a day.

"I love you."

Her head twitched in irritation. [[Josiri . . .]]

"No. You're not bound to Branghall any longer. Not now. We're free. There's nothing to keep us apart."

Her fingers brushed his cheek. [[Oh, my dear heart. There'll always be something to keep us apart. I'm a daughter of Lumestra. My light may be fading, but it'll shine long after you're dust.]]

"But that's tomorrow. Or the day after. Or the day after that." He took her smooth fingers in his, again surprised at the warmth of what should have been cold. "The moments we have together are what matter."

[[You're not going to give up on this, are you?]]

"I'm a Trelan. I'm stubborn."

She offered a hollow echo of what might once have been a sigh and embraced him. [[I *do* love you, Josiri. Insofar as I am able.]]

Josiri felt his mouth twitch in what was surely an idiot smile. He felt no shame, only relief. "That's all I ask."

He closed his eyes and put his arms about her. For a long moment, he forgot Calenne; forgot the bloody horror of the day and the challenges that would come with the dawn.

"Sorry, your grace. Can't let you in."

The northwealder set a hand on his sword and shot a sidelong glance at his fellows, clustered around the nearby fire. A ruffianly bunch, and neither a friendly face nor a wolf-cloak to be seen. It seemed that Viktor Akadra's promise of shared authority didn't extend as far as the prisoners. That, or the guard didn't care. Probably the latter.

Josiri didn't much care either. Not with a span of broken sleep behind, and a surfeit of unresolved worries ahead. Even the clothes he wore were not his but borrowed from Viktor's possessions – there'd been no saving his own garb. They were by no means a good fit. Even cinched in by a belt, the shirt felt like a sack.

"And I'd rather be sleeping," he snapped. "Major Keldrov sent me. One of the prisoners requested a meeting."

"Don't see her with you, your grace."

"She's resting."

Work parties had dug Keldrov out of the ruin of Blackridge Farm at dusk. Even stitched and bandaged up she looked more dead than alive. Josiri hadn't found it in himself to drag her broken bones the quarter mile from the camp. Instead, he'd ordered her to sleep.

"Leaves us at an impasse, doesn't it, your grace?"

"Not at all," said Josiri. "One of two things is about to happen. Either you let me inside, or I send a herald to Lord Akadra. Which would you prefer?"

The guard beckoned towards the fire. "Dasari? His grace is going inside. You're his escort. Rest of you, give me a hand with this bloody door, would you?"

The space within was thick with hunched or sleeping men, and others for whom slumber had become something deeper and irreversible. It stank of blood, sweat . . . and despair most of all. It brought to mind the desperate hours after Zanya where he and his uncle Taymor had waited for word of his mother. Just as he now awaited news of his sister.

Josiri shook the memory away. No distractions. There were no weapons in sight, but desperate men didn't need them.

The gate slammed shut.

"You are his grace, the Duke of Eskavord?"

The speaker was an older man, with accented speech and grey hairs prominent in a dark beard. It also revealed the slightest quiver. Not of fear. Josiri would have bet long odds against that. Anger. Shame. Distrust. The speaker didn't know what the dawn would bring. Not for himself, nor for those he served.

Josiri inclined his head. "I am."

The watchful eyes eased. "Thank you, *savir*. My name is Aedrun. If you follow me, I will take you to the Lady Ashanal."

Aedrun led Josiri around the perimeter, threading a path until they reached a wood and canvas lean-to set beneath the rampart of the palisade. It wasn't part of the original construction, as the garrison had no need of cloistered spaces. Melanna Saranal plainly did.

A quick-fire exchange of Hadari came as the group approached the canvas curtain. A woman's voice from within, and Aedrun's from without. Josiri understood nothing of the melodic speech, though Aedrun's unhappiness lurked beneath the words.

"You may go inside, *savir*," Aedrun announced. "But you alone."

Josiri passed into a blanket-strewn space barely large enough to lie down in.

"So you are Josiri Trelan."

The voice was younger than Josiri had expected. But then only her eyes were old. He wondered how much they'd aged that day.

"And you are Melanna Saranal. Or is that Ashanal?"

"The former." She spoke the words hurriedly, then calmed her pace. "It is as my father's daughter that I speak to you. I believe you understand the duties of an heir."

"Not as well as I'd like."

"You must forgive Aedrun's manner. For him to leave me alone with a heathen is a weighty burden – let alone to leave us within arm's reach of one another."

"Lady, I'm weary. My soul is stretched thin. I have kin and companions unaccounted for. If you've something to say, let's have it."

Melanna raised an eyebrow. Calm. Collected. Josiri envied her poise. He couldn't have done the same. "My sympathies for your missing blood. A brother?"

"My sister. The Phoenix."

"We crossed swords. She fought well . . . "

Josiri's pulse quickened. Crossed swords. Was he even now speaking with Calenne's murderer? "Where is she?"

Melanna's lip hooked. White teeth gleamed. "Hear my petition, and I'll tell what I know."

Josiri swallowed away his impatience. "I'm listening."

"Why did you fight for your oppressors?"

The unexpected question took Josiri off his stride. "That's why you asked to see me?"

"No, but I'm curious. I've spent many weeks in your lands. I've seen first-hand how your people are treated. And yet you fought for them, as Crovan always said you would. Your kin in the north will keep taking from you until you've nothing left worth stealing. Because they can. Because you let them. My father stood ready to give you everything you wanted."

"Is this the same father who threatened of children enslaved and croplands sown with salt?"

"A lie!" Her eyes narrowed, making her look twice the serpent she had before. But the words were too defiant. Too rote. She believed.

Josiri shook his head, glad to have shivered her confidence. The threat had made his skin crawl when Gavamor had spoken of it. "No. Though I'd made my decision long before I learned of that."

"Then why?"

"Because my mother's war is fifteen years in the past. Mine's here and now, and it's not the same."

He fell silent. It really was that straightforward, wasn't it? Strange how the simplest concepts took longest to comprehend.

Melanna's mask of unconcern slid back into place. "Never trust a shadowthorn, is that it? I know what your priests teach. That we take root in tainted soil. That we wear the corruption in our souls as proudly as heraldry."

"An abhorrent belief. One I don't share."

"Enough do."

"Those same priests preach that my folk are both rebellious and shiftless," said Josiri. "Where we find the energy for the one if we're the other, I don't know."

"Did you ever wonder what came first – the hatred, or the lies? Or perhaps we fascinate? Nothing breeds hatred like desire."

He winced. "I've answered your question. Tell me about my sister."

"Not yet."

Tired of her games, Josiri reached for the canvas flap. "Then I'll wish you good night."

"No!"

For the first time, a note of desperation crept through. Josiri halted.

"I asked you here to propose a trade," said Melanna softly. "My father took wounds in the battle. He sleeps feverishly elsewhere."

"You want me to send a physician?"

"I want you to set him free."

Josiri laughed. "Your father's responsible for more deaths than I can tally. How much pity do you suppose I feel?"

"He harmed no one who didn't oppose him under arms. That should count for something."

"Perhaps. But not enough."

She stared at the rutted, straw-strewn floor. "You'd have the architect of today's battle face justice?"

"Not I. The Council."

"And we all know Trelans always do as the Council demands."

With iron will, Josiri kept his face expressionless. She knew too much of him, and his mood. "On this occasion, our interests align. There must be a reckoning."

"And there will be. But I'd spare my father the humiliation of being paraded through your streets. And the indignity of the noose."

"I doubt he'll get the noose," said Josiri. "They'll probably burn him alive."

Melanna met his gaze, her eyes afire. "And you'd call that justice?"

"It doesn't matter what I call it. You're heathens. Heathens get the pyre."

She shuddered and with visible effort brought herself under control. "My father is not the architect you seek. I am."

Josiri frowned. "I don't understand."

"Aedrun called me Ashanal because I bear the favour of the goddess. With her blessing, I swept aside those in our path. I brought us to the cusp of victory. Let my father go."

Josiri wasn't sure how much to believe, or even *if* he should believe. Hadari womenfolk never took to the battlefield, so Melanna was already unusual. As for the rest, Josiri had woken from the arms of a serathi-turned-spirit, turned . . . well, he wasn't sure, but it certainly encouraged him to discount little of what he heard.

"Even if what you say is true, you offer to trade with something I already possess."

She took a deep breath, no longer the proud princessa, but something vulnerable. Josiri wasn't sure which to believe, if either. In fact, he was starting to suspect that neither aspect held more than a portion of the true Melanna Saranal. He'd spent too long playing a role not to recognise the masquerade in another.

"Name your price. I will meet it without defiance," she said. "There is nothing I would not do to save my father."

Josiri took her meaning. It was impossible not to. A bride of brief moonlight, he'd heard it called. Daughters of the defeated offered as chattels. His father had called it barbaric. His mother had suggested it wasn't all that different to the principles of arranged marriage – for was that not a trade of sons and daughters? Except arranged marriages seldom ended with a slit throat.

Makrov would have accepted, Josiri had no doubt. And when the old goat was done, Melanna would have found herself cloistered as a reluctant serene – a beatified trophy of conversion and conquest, bound by word of honour given freely. If Melanna was as devout an Ashanan as she seemed, that would have been a fate far worse than death.

Yes, Makrov would have accepted. Others too.

"I'm sorry," Josiri murmured. "I cannot do as you ask."

Why did he feel such regret? Not from the offer refused. Perhaps it was because he saw an echo of his own past in Melanna's present. What would he have done had his mother been taken captive before she'd chance to take her own life? Raven's Eyes, but Melanna was practically the same age as he'd been then, tangled in a parent's honour.

Or perhaps it was because he knew all too well what lay at journey's end for both Melanna and her father.

She held his gaze a moment, then looked away. "All my life, I was taught of the cruelty of Tressians, and of their greed. Now I find that the latter is a lie, but the former unswerving."

"Your bargain would leave us both shadows of who we are now ... whatever your father's fate."

She snorted. "Such fortune have I to fall into the keeping of the only honourable man in Tressia."

"There is at least one other," said Josiri. "Lord Akadra would give the same answer."

Melanna's expression darkened. "The man who bested my father?"

"The man who spared your life."

"Be wary of him. He's awash with shadow."

Josiri frowned, suspecting an oddity of translation. "I don't follow."

"I am ... I was ... Ashanal. I carried the goddess's light. He carries something else."

The magic Viktor had used in his attempt to free Anastacia? Another path to the pyre, were that detail to reach the wrong ears. Even a week before, Josiri would have gladly delivered it himself. "He's a good man. I'll speak to him. I'll see if anything can be done for you, and I'll send physicians to your father."

"Perhaps I was wrong. Perhaps you are kinder than you are cruel." Another pause, though a friendlier one. "I don't know what became of your sister. Her horse bolted, but she was unharmed when last I saw her ... I hope you find her."

"So do I."

Melanna offered no reply. Josiri pulled aside the canvas and entered the cold, clear night.

"Blessed Ashana, I beseech you. Guide your ephemeral daughter."

Melanna rocked back and forth on her haunches. So much easier to focus on the words than dwell on her thoughts. On her father's wounds. On her failure. She didn't even know what had become of Sera.

"Blessed Ashana, I beseech you. Guide your ephemeral daughter."

Goddess, but it had been all she could do not to break down and beg. She felt certain Josiri had seen clean through her; had recognised the tangle of anger, despair and loathing that had racked her from the moment her father had laid down his sword. Worse than that, she found it impossible to untangle those emotions. They knotted about her throat so tightly she could barely breathe.

She knew only that this was her fault. Her failure. Her hubris.

She clenched her hands tighter until her nails gouged her palms bloody.

"Blessed Ashana ..." She broke off, her voice swamped by emotion. She clamped her eyes shut. "I'm ... I'm sorry." The confession, once begun, would not abate. "You warned me. I didn't listen. But please, if you love me at all, help my father. He deserves better."

"Most people do."

Melanna opened her eyes, scarcely daring to believe. The goddess sat in the opposite corner of the tiny shack, her knees tucked up to her chest and her blue eyes unblinking. One by one, the timbers of the walls peeled away like autumn leaves, laying bare the mist-wreathed trees beyond.

"Goddess ..." Melanna breathed.

She sighed. "You're disappointment enough without falling into old habits. Especially as I understand you've taken to calling yourself my daughter."

Melanna swallowed. "Yes, lady."

"*Ashana.*"

"Yes, Ashana."

A small, sad smile. "Better. Do you know why I'm disappointed?"

"Because I ignored you. Because I sought battle, and failed."

"No. For that, I'd be angry. Fortunately I'm a goddess, and above such things."

"Truly?"

"No." She shrugged. The folds of her shining dress rippled. "But I'm working on it. You're not the only one with much to learn. For example, I need to keep a closer eye on my steward. I tell you, the men in my life are never more dangerous than when they think they're helping."

Melanna winced. "You've punished him?"

"We had a ... conversation. I taught him several new words. Certainly I used a few he never expected of me. A Thornhill mouthful fit to wither a forest. I've a horrible feeling I sounded like my mother." She shrugged. "But words only. I'm not a monster, Melanna. At least, I'm trying not to be. I've something of an idea how that will turn out."

"I'm glad. He only wanted to help."

Ashana arched an eyebrow. "Did he? Still, I suppose this was inevitable. Some lessons are learned only by thrusting your hand into the fire. Have you learned yours?"

Melanna longed to answer in the affirmative. Instinct warned her against. "I don't know."

Ashana nodded. "Better. So why am I disappointed?"

"Because I accepted your steward's help."

"I shouldn't say this, but *that* actually impressed me. Convictions are nothing without courage to back them up. I wish I'd had your spark so young."

Melanna blinked at the unexpected compliment. "Then ... No, I don't know. I'm sorry."

"It's not enough to be sorry. You have to understand."

"Then tell me!" Melanna caught her tongue, aghast at her tone.

To her surprise, Ashana grinned. "Better. How long have we been having these little conversations, Melanna?"

"All my life."

"And in that time, you've wanted only one thing. To rise above the position tradition demanded and be treated the equal of a son."

"Yes, godd ... Ashana."

"So what did you do just now, faced with a challenge not easily overcome? You did what tradition expected and made yourself a commodity. You sought a trade that would have been accepted only by a man unworthy of the offering. Would a son do that? Would an empress?"

Like so many truths once revealed, this one blazed fit to blind.

Melanna closed her eyes. "What else was I to do? My capture brought defeat. My father should not pay the price."

Ashana sighed. "You're not a fool, so don't behave like one. The battle was long since lost when they took you. And your father set this war in motion, not you."

Melanna gritted her teeth. "You'd have me abandon him?"

"I'd have you be smarter. We are none of us the folk we seem in the light. Not me, not you and not your father. It is in the darkness, when all seems hopeless – that's when your true self stands revealed. That's when your decisions matter most."

She hung her head, more lost than ever. "Then perhaps I'm no empress after all."

Ashana rose to her feet and gazed down in a not unkindly manner. "Or perhaps you merely need to think like one. You are not one woman alone. You speak for a people. That's no small coin of trade, and can buy a great many things. You might find it already has."

She turned in a whirl of effervescent skirts and walked away towards the tree line.

Melanna shook her head. "I don't understand."

Ashana halted. One palm pressed to the trunk of a silver birch, she shot a small smile back at Melanna. "Then you should work on that. But I do wish you hadn't lost my sword. I was fond of that sword."

Then she was gone, lost to the trees.

The mists rose, and the dream fell away.

Viktor rode until his limbs were weary and his skin chafed. Until he no longer felt jolts of pain from jostled wounds. But unfamiliar desperation grew with every tussock and crag that passed away beneath his horse's hooves. Unfamiliar, and unwelcome.

The irony wasn't lost on him. He'd lectured Josiri for acting as a man, and not as a leader. But it was all hypocrisy. For all that Viktor told himself he sought Calenne out of a leader's responsibility – after all, he'd encouraged her to take the field of battle – he was forced to admit that the concern driving him was entirely other. He sought Calenne not out of duty, but from fear for her safety. From the knowledge that her loss diminished the vibrancy of his world.

Why? A hard question to answer. Viktor's best guess was that though she'd better reason than any to fear him, Calenne did not. He admired her for that – no less for the courage and forthrightness she'd shown in other matters.

Respect had grown between them, and Viktor couldn't now judge for certain if he'd have made half of his recent efforts without her by his side. He hoped so, but unpicking motivation in hindsight was ever an uncertain chore. In a few short days, Calenne had inveigled her way into his life, though only the prospect of her loss had made that truth apparent.

So easy to see how Kasamor had been ensnared. Viktor only hoped that he too had not perceived affection where none existed. And that the span of years between them would not prove an obstacle all its own. Arranged marriage often bridged decades, but seldom with warmth. But those troubles, at least, could wait. The man remained enough the leader to recognise that Calenne's life, and not the burden of her heart, mattered most.

And so Viktor rode far and wide. He walked among the dead. His heart quavered with every glimpse of a phoenix tabard, only to settle before the cold face of a stranger. He spoke with wayfarers, sentries and the fitful stream of wounded making moonlit return to camp on stretcher or wagon. Though many recalled the Phoenix, none had seen her.

The first pre-dawn light found Viktor weary, heartsick and saddle-sore. It also drew his attention to commotion some way south, at the forest's eaves. The south wind bore angry voices, though it stripped them of words. Ignoring the creak in his bones, Viktor turned his horse about.

Three men and a woman stood around a crude pyre assembled from wind-fallen timber. Two men had the third restrained. The former wore wayfarer's tabards. The latter, blackened chainmail and scorched leathers. His face was raw and burnt, his beard and hair singed.

As Viktor slowed his horse to a standstill beside a trio of restless steeds, the woman – also garbed as a wayfarer – clambered uncertainly onto the pyre. Boughs and branches clattered away from her boots. The entire construction teetered alarmingly.

"What's this about?" he asked.

"She deserves burial," said a wayfarer. "Not a burning. This one has other ideas."

"Let her alone!" bellowed the captive. "She must go to the forge before dawn!"

He struggled vainly. Boots slipped on the uneven ground. Arms still pinioned, he fell to his knees with a keening wail.

But the guttural voice had told Viktor all that the man's dishevelled appearance had not. "Armund? Armund af Garna?"

"Lord Akadra?" Armund turned his ravaged face. Sightless eyes stared up. "Call this pack of *rakkyg* off me! They won't let me tend to my sister."

Viktor took in the huddled bundle atop the ramshackle pyre. More questions answered. Another slain ally, if one he'd but briefly known. It didn't escape his memory that the twins had served as Calenne's guard.

"Let him go," he said.

"He means to burn her," the wayfarer protested. "It's a sin."

"Do I strike you as one who needs a lecture on the nature of sin, lad?"

The wayfarers shared a worried glance and let Armund fall.

"Go," growled Viktor. "Be about your business."

The men withdrew to their horses. After a moment's hesitation, the woman clambered down from her perch and followed. Hoof-beats rang out.

"I heard you were dead," said Viktor.

"Damn near was," growled Armund. "The witch took my eyes. Her handmaidens nearly had the rest. Lucky, if you want to call it that."

Viktor leaned forward in his saddle. "And Calenne?"

"I don't know. Astor strike me for a cinder, but I don't." He hung his head. The scorched remnant of his beard brushed against blackened chain. "I hope she found a good death. Skinny thing, but she'd fire."

"She lives." Viktor heard more hope than certainty in his own voice. He turned his horse about to ride away. "I'm sorry for your loss."

"Then help me." A most un-Thrakkian note of pleading crept into Armund's voice. "I don't need eyes to know that dawn's coming. If I don't set Anliss free before then, the Raven'll have her. My sister died well. She deserves the forge, not the wandering of the mists."

Viktor stifled a scowl. Never a dedicated adherent to the Lumestran creed, he still found ... something ... intolerable at the prospect of burning the dead. Let Thrakkians believe what they wished about freeing the soul to feast in Skanandra – fire was the very bleakest fate. At least where Tressian law reigned.

Between the wayfarer's attempts to climb and the flaws born of Armund's sightless construction, Anliss' pyre stood on the verge of collapse. Once the flame took it, the body would as likely tumble away as burn. A strong, sighted man could have fixed it in a span of minutes. Armund remained the former, but the latter? Viktor was astounded he'd accomplished as much as he had.

The urge to keep searching for Calenne had a tinge of madness to it now. It was almost desperation. But even through the weariness, Viktor knew it a false spur. He'd promised Josiri to return at dawn. That time was all but spent. And for all he knew, Calenne had already reached camp, delayed by happenstance. Or she was dead. Had been for hours. Were that true, what right did he have to solace if he denied Armund the same? The leader had a duty, and so did the man.

He swung from his saddle. "Very well. Tell me what you need."

The fires caught as the first pre-dawn light touched the distant mountains. It gripped the bone-dry timber as tight as a miser's fist about coin and roared at the brightening skies. Hollow booms rippled across the skies. Distant thunder grew near. Or perhaps, Viktor mused, it wasn't thunder at all, but the strike of hammer on anvil, chiming to guide the dead to their reward.

Thus passed Anliss af Garna to the Halls of Skanandra – her axe upon her breast, and her eyes as open to the journey as her brother's were not.

Viktor watched from what he deemed a respectful distance. It wasn't how he'd hoped the night to end, but a life of soldiering had taught him that you took what victories you found. Calenne's fate remained hidden, but he'd spared a comrade's spirit the listless roaming of Otherworld's mists. That counted for something.

And tomorrow the search could begin again. The battle for the Southshires was done. It was over. He was free to do as he wished, and Lumestra help anyone who stood in his way.

Armund rose heavily from his knees as the fires slackened. "I need your eyes again, my lord."

Viktor drew nearer. His flesh prickled in the heat of the flames. "What can I do?"

The Thrakkian turned a tear-stained face to the pyre. "Her axe. Her spirit's gone. She doesn't need it any longer, and I'd carry a piece of her with me while I can."

Viktor eyed the flames without enthusiasm. "You'd have me burn alongside?"

"So the Lord Akadra *does* know fear?"

"The Lord Akadra fears more this night than he has for many years. Moreover, he is not fireproof."

Armund chuckled. "Hush your whimper. I only need your eyes – my hand will do the work. Show me where I need to stand."

Viktor set his hands on Armund's shoulders and guided him until he stood level with Anliss' withering corpse. "Here. The flames are still fierce."

"A Thrakkian doesn't fear flame. He masters it."

So saying, Armund thrust a gloved hand into the fire. The leather steamed and smouldered. Flames flared about chain as the padded undershirt charred anew.

Armund grunted. His fingers groped for the axe's haft, closed about it and heaved it clear. He let it fall on the trampled ground and patted urgently to smother the small fires flickering across his arm.

Viktor stared down at the axe. At the fading ember-glow in the runes of the blackened haft. His shadow twitched, uncertain. It hadn't done so before – not in Armund's presence. Then again, his shadow had felt different ever since the battle's ending – or at least his perception of it had shifted. The bounty of acceptance? Or maybe there was more to the ritual than Armund had admitted?

He was about to ask when a new sound joined the distant thunder and the crackle of flames. Hoof-beats. A great many of them.

He shifted his gaze eastward, towards the rising sound. Towards the ravaged field and the remnant of the Hadari camp. Dark shadows against the dawn – riders leaning low over their steeds and drawing closer with every breath.

"What is it?" asked Armund.

"I don't know," Viktor replied. "But they're headed this way. You should hide."

Armund spat on the ground. "Clink-rot take that."

"You can't see, and I can't protect you. Not against a dozen riders."

He squatted, his hand patting the ground until it found the scorched axe. "I'm not feared of fire, and I'm certainly not feared of a few Hadari horsemen."

Viktor let the matter drop and drew his sword. Death was one thing. To die while bickering was unseemly.

The riders were yet two-score paces distant when Viktor recognised the uniforms as Tressian. At a dozen paces, he recognised the leader's face.

"Governor Yanda? You pick a strange hour to ride. The battle is done. It's over."

She blinked away her surprise. Then she sawed on her reins and wheeled the horse to a standstill. The other riders – a mix of wayfarers and knights in Prydonis colours, shuddered to a halt around her.

"Lord Akadra? I expected to find you at camp."

"And I expected aid from Kreska," he said as evenly as could be managed. "As for the victory, that belongs to Josiri and Calenne Trelan, not I."

She scowled. "I'd soldiers ready to march. I was ordered to hold my ground."

"Ordered? The Southshires are mine to govern. Its armies mine to command."

"Not any longer. The Council has revoked your authority."

Viktor's blood ran cold, even in the heat of the fire.

He'd been wrong. The battle for the Southshires wasn't over. It had merely changed form. "In whose favour? Yours?"

She gave a bitter laugh. "Who else? The archimandrite. He's coming back. And I doubt any of us will much enjoy his arrival."

Lunandas, 7th day of Radiance

Savour your time in the light, for darkness is
jealousy unbound.
  And like jealousy, it always returns.

from the sermons of Konor Belenzo

Forty-Four

"Revekah."

The breathy whisper echoed about her. The Dark knew her name.

Revekah froze, her thoughts trapped in nightmare, but unable to awaken. The ground beneath her feet was hidden in rushing, swirling blackness. Yet she knew the precipice was there, just out of sight. Maybe one step. Maybe two. Maybe she was already falling.

"Revekah."

Heart thundering, she spun around. "Who are you?"

Her foot pressed down on emptiness.

She fell. Fingers scrabbled vainly on a slick surface. Her second foot joined the first in emptiness. Unseen hands clutched at her calves and thighs – a hundred insistent fingers drawing her into the abyss.

She wanted to scream. She couldn't. Her throat was parched as the dust of a Midsommer field. Instead, she redoubled her efforts, searching for a handhold in the world without substance.

"Lay down your burdens. Come home."

Her hips slid across the precipice. With a silent scream, she fell.

Revekah jerked awake into the rising dawn with a scream ringing in her ears. Her scream.

She clambered to her feet. She made it as far as her knees before her stomach spasmed. She doubled over. Hot, sour bile rushed over her tongue and spattered against rock.

"Nice," said Kurkas. "And here I was just getting used to the place."

He sat propped against the cave mouth, his wan features dappled by grey dawn and tangled briar. His right leg lay bent beneath him; his bloodied left bar-straight in front. His words were scarcely more substantial than the voice from Revekah's dream.

"Don't make me regret saving your life," she growled. "Bad dreams, that's all."

"Had a few myself. Most of 'em about a demoness sawing off my other arm, if you must know. Drives a man to drink." His head fell back and his eyes closed.

Revekah wiped her mouth on a filthy sleeve. "I don't want to talk about it."

She couldn't. Whatever had startled her awake had vanished from memory. Only the shadow of helpless terror remained. That, and limbs that quivered like jelly.

"You shouldn't be moving about," she said instead.

"Someone had to keep watch. You needed a bit of shut-eye."

"Much good it did me." She rubbed at her eyes and peered out through the brambles masking the cave mouth. Trampled crops were just about visible through windblown branches and seething rain. "How's the world looking?"

"I *think* we won. Leastways, there's more of our lot riding about than theirs. Hooray for us."

Our lot. Strange how that now encompassed the very people she'd been fighting half her life. "Then it's over."

He snorted. "It's never over. There's always another battle. We can't help ourselves. The shadowthorns aren't fighting nobody, are they? Ain't no lasting peace this side of Otherworld."

"That why you became a soldier?"

He shrugged. "Better a wolf than a sheep. You?"

Revekah stared down at her palms and strove to recall a day before callouses and wrinkles. "These hands of mine have never been much good for anything else."

"You don't have to tell me." He sniffed. "Reckon my left leg's hanging by a thread. I'll be walking with a stoop for the rest of my life."

"Keep talking, and that won't be a problem for long."

Kurkas grinned wearily. "Charmer."

There was little force behind the jibe. Despite her best efforts, Kurkas was already halfway into the mists. He'd lost too much blood. He needed warmth, food and a better class of care than she could provide. But he couldn't walk, and she couldn't carry him. Getting him to the cover of the cavern had been touch and go. Yes, someone would happen by sooner or later, but that wouldn't be soon enough for Kurkas.

"You planning on staying this side of the mists if I fetch help?" she asked.

He waved a lazy hand. "Can't say the Raven holds any appeal, but . . ." He paused. His good eye narrowed as he stared through the trees. "On second thoughts, I'd rather you stuck around."

In the distance, what had been an empty field was thick with marching soldiers. And at their head, scarlet robes on a white horse. "Makrov's back?" said Revekah.

"Looks like. Holy fervour and a thousand halberds. Fun and games."

She shook her head to dispel growing unease. "Why? What's happening?"

"Both of them excellent questions, Captain Halvor. Alas, the eye with which I read minds was the one you plucked out." He sighed. "But I'll warrant you don't want to be anywhere near that lot."

"I thought Lord Akadra had the Council's authority."

"Sure. But only if he's still living."

Revekah swore under her breath. Kurkas was right. But what was the alternative? Leave Kurkas to die? Nothing easier a week ago. There'd even have been joy in it. Now?

"You need help."

"So I'm painfully aware," he said. "But I see little point in risking your life for mine."

"I won't let you die."

"Good," he said wearily. "Then we need another option."

Commotion broke through Josiri's dreamless sleep. Urgent shouts, bellowed oaths and running feet. All of it drowned in the fierce patter of rain and the howling wind.

He opened his eyes onto the musty confines of Viktor's tent. Anastacia stood by the flaps, staring motionlessly into the camp beyond.

"What is it?" he asked.

[[You should get up.]]

Hastened by the clamour, Josiri pulled on his borrowed clothes. Had the prisoners escaped? Some quarrel between his people and the north-wealders blown out of control? He shook his head. Enough speculation. He left the tent, Anastacia on his heels.

And entered into a scene from hated history.

Wolf-cloaks and phoenixes snarled from within rings of shields and drawn swords, penned about the smouldering campfires by king's blue soldiers. Wayfarers cantered hither and yon, corralling fugitives for capture. A lone kraikon loomed silent over all like an inscrutable judge of old.

Some southwealders fought, weapons to hand or no. Isolated and outnumbered, they had no chance. Even as the tent flap fell from Josiri's numbed hand, a phoenix sprawled in the mud, run through by a wayfarer's spear. Her sword hadn't even cleared its scabbard.

A wolf-cloak hurled himself at shields and broke through. A north-wealder tackled him and both men went down. Angry voices sounded as comrades joined the quickening brawl.

The world fell away beneath Josiri's feet. Akadra had lied. He'd looked Josiri right in the eye, spun promises of freedom and friendship, and all the while he'd planned this betrayal. The bitterest core of Josiri's soul – the echo of a young man orphaned by civil war – exulted in vindication. The larger part could have wept for the betrayal.

Both kindled to rage undimmed by the downpour.

"Ana, I need a horse."

[[Gladly.]]

A wayfarer splashed past, spear lowered. Anastacia's hand closed around the trailing reins. Her boots skidded in the mud. As the steed whinnied in alarm, she plucked the struggling young man from his saddle and tossed him aside.

[[Horse.]]

The wayfarer made to rise. Anastacia's boot connected with his temple, and he slumped.

Josiri scrambled into the saddle and turned his stolen steed about, searching for a brawl closely balanced enough that one righteous man might make a difference.

That was when his gaze fell across Major Keldrov, propped up on crutches at the entrance to the physicians' tent. The one eye visible beneath the soiled bandage flickered back and forth. Her pallid face lacked Josiri's fury but held every ounce the confusion.

If she didn't know ...

For the first time, Josiri realised she wasn't the only one. There were two groups of northwealders within the camp. The first, weary and dishevelled, looked on with uncertainty as the second group – travel-stained but otherwise unsullied – wrought capture and oppression. Maybe this wasn't Akadra's work. But if not his, then whose?

[[Josiri!]]

Anastacia screamed – a sound so pained and desperate he didn't at first recognise the voice as hers.

He turned. A proctor dangled from Anastacia's grip. Three others converged, sun-staves held ready. Golden light flared. She cried out and fell to hands and knees. The captive proctor scrambled free. Anastacia strove to rise. Another jab – another golden bloom – and she collapsed anew.

[[Get out of here! Don't let them take you!]]

"No!"

Josiri screamed his voice raw and thrust back his heels. His horse surged forward. A proctor made desperate parry, and his sword skittered away. A sun-staff blazed, drowning the grey morning in brilliance. Off-balance and blind, Josiri fell sideways from the saddle.

Muddy water rushed up his nose and into his mouth. He spat it out and grasped for purchase in a splotchy blue-black world. Something cracked against his wrist, jarring the sword from his hand. The butt of a staff thumped into his back, driving him to hands and knees.

"Stay down," growled a proctor. "Or you get the other end."

Josiri spat a bitter mouthful into the puddle and stayed down.

"Bind her!" A new, strident voice cut through the tumult. "Fetch silver! By the Holy Dawn I'll have her back in Branghall where she belongs."

Blinking furiously to clear his vision, Josiri stared up at a vision in scarlet robes, his fleshy face twisted in satisfaction. Makrov. Of course it was Makrov.

"What is the meaning of this, Makrov?" Josiri demanded.

"The meaning, your grace?" The archimandrite spoke with feigned surprise. "The Council would very much like you and your co-conspirators to answer for your crimes."

"You mean now we've won the victory they could not?" Josiri laughed without humour. "And you wonder why my mother rejected your advances? You're a coward, Makrov. A feckless, honourless . . . "

Makrov gestured. The staff thumped home. Josiri prised himself free of the mud.

The archimandrite leaned low over his horse's neck. "You are a traitor, a troublemaker and an embarrassment. You've sought solace in the arms of this . . . this . . . demon . . . "

[[Oh Arzro,]] whispered Anastacia, [[does this mean we're not friends any longer?]]

She convulsed as a sun-staff's tip touched her shoulder. Her low, hollow moan set Josiri's teeth on edge and his heart racing. Makrov's eyes gleamed beneath bushy brows.

"Stop it!" snapped Josiri. "Let her alone!"

Makrov nodded. The light dimmed. Anastacia's moan faded. She gazed up at Makrov, eyes brimming with murder.

[[Play . . . Play as rough as you like. I've a long memory.]]

A pair of king's blue soldiers scuttled forward, a coil of silver rope in their hands.

"As have I," said Makrov. "And I'm sure silver will hold you as well in this form as it did in your other. As for you, *your grace,* declining the Council's invitation would be a poor choice. I'm certain that bandit Merrik would tell you so . . . were it not for the fact that he's dining with the Raven even as we speak. The disgraced Proctor Gavamor too."

Josiri offered silent prayer for his fallen comrades. They deserved better. They *all* deserved better. Even Melanna Saranal, whose fate he was now to share.

Summoned to Council. Just like his father. So easy now to understand why his mother embraced the Raven. Had Josiri a knife to hand, he'd have taken the same course then and there – though he'd have taken Makrov's throat first, sun-staves or no.

Thunder rippled across the sky. Josiri caught a glimpse of his sword, just out of reach.

[[Next time,]] Anastacia murmured, [[just run.]]

"No," said Josiri. "Never."

He tensed, a shiver running up his spine as the folds of his sodden clothes shifted. One last deed before the mists took him.

The soldiers paused, Anastacia's wrists still half-bound. Josiri glanced up. A giant loomed through the rain behind Makrov, his face grim as death.

"Arzro Makrov!" bellowed Viktor Akadra. "I would have words."

For one joyous moment in the hissing rain, Viktor thought Makrov might fall from his saddle in surprise. Alas, the archimandrite steadied himself on the cusp of no return and turned his steed smartly about.

"Lord Akadra, a pleasure to . . ."

"Enough." Viktor's fury, building ever since Yanda's warning, threatened to spill over into unwise action. He buried it deep and gestured sharply at Josiri and Anastacia. "Let them up."

Makrov flinched but held his ground. "They are malcontents of the first order and will be treated as such."

"The Council granted me a warrant of pardon," growled Viktor. "For Josiri Trelan and all others I deemed worthy." He let his voice carry through the rain. "I proclaim all who fought yesterday to be worthy! Anyone who breaks this decree will answer to me! In private, and with a sword in their hand!"

The sounds of battle faded. Fitful stillness overtook the camp. Southwealders eyed Makrov's soldiers uneasily and were regarded with suspicion in return. Those northwealders who'd shed blood alongside those Makrov had come to claim stood frozen – uncertain and apprehensive.

Stalemate.

"Major Keldrov!" Viktor shouted. "Kindly escort the archimandrite from the camp. He and his men are leaving. Everyone else stays!"

Keldrov didn't move. Of course she didn't. She was too young. Too wary of the archimandrite's authority. Kurkas would have done it. He'd have dragged Makrov out by his heel without a second thought. Yanda *might* have done it. But Kurkas was gone, and Yanda was back in Kreska, purposefully insulated from whatever acts Viktor needed to perform.

Makrov removed an envelope from his saddlebags. "You have a warrant of pardon. I have a warrant of arrest. One that specifically overrules yours, I might add. The demon goes back to her lair, and the named persons are to stand trial for treason. This is the will of the Council, Viktor. It is not for you or I to break."

With stiff stride, Viktor closed the distance between them. "Let me see."

Makrov's lip twitched. "Gladly."

Viktor unfurled the scroll and began to read. With every line, his heart sank a little further. All was as Makrov had claimed. Though the ink was already beginning to run, the names upon the warrant sprang clear. Josiri Trelan. Calenne Trelan. Drakos Crovan. Revekah Halvor. Anastacia Psanneque. The list went on. And the seals of the Council at the base. No surprise to see Ebigail Kiradin's mark present, but his father's black swan . . .

He fought temptation to tear the letter to shreds, his breath frosting in the air as his shadow coiled free. Destroying the document would be nothing but petulance. Makrov would have a copy. He'd won one battle but lost another without knowing the clarion had sounded. For the first time in a dozen hours, Viktor was glad Calenne wasn't there to see him humbled. The accusation and hope brimming in Josiri's eyes was bad enough.

Calenne . . .

The flames of an idea flickered.

"You may have those named on this list. I've no doubt the Council will see their mistake soon enough." The hope faded from Josiri's eyes until only accusation remained. "All others are to be released, at once."

Makrov scowled, but he surely knew the warrant back to front. The wording allowed him to claim named ringleaders – it did nothing to gainsay Viktor's broader powers of pardon.

"Very well," he said, with fragile huffiness. "Out of respect for you, Lord Akadra, and for your victory, I'm sure the Council will approve a little . . . clemency."

He gestured at Josiri and Anastacia – the latter with her hands now bound. Viktor winced at the sight. Silver and magic were a poor mix. He could only imagine her discomfort.

"Bring them," said Makrov.

Viktor let the soldiers get the pair to their feet before clearing his throat. "Apologies, eminence, but where are you taking that man?"

"Josiri Trelan is mine, as agreed."

"He is indeed, if you can find him," said Viktor. "The man you hold is an Akadra. Calenne Trelan and I were married at dawn yesterday. She petitioned me to adopt her dear brother, and I gladly agreed."

Taking advantage of Makrov's sudden descent into apoplexy, Viktor embraced Josiri.

"My brother. I'm glad to see you unharmed." He dropped his voice to a whisper. "Forgive me. I can conjure no other solution."

Josiri returned the embrace, if stiffly. Over his shoulder, Viktor made eye contact with Anastacia, who gave the slightest of nods.

"And where is the Lady Trelan ... forgive me, the Lady Akadra?" asked Makrov.

"Missing." Sorrow tugged on Viktor's heart as he spoke. "No other fought harder for the Republic than she."

"And the priest who married you?"

"Dead." Viktor shrugged. "He didn't fight so hard. But what can one expect of a priest?"

Laughter rippled around the camp. Makrov scowled.

"If you don't believe me," said Viktor, "you need only ask around. We made no secret of our betrothal."

Makrov shot a glance at Keldrov. She nodded without hesitation.

"I'm taking this man," he snapped.

Viktor folded his arms. "No, eminence, you are not. The sins of the kith do not jump family to family, and your warrant is quite clear. Josiri Trelan is yours to claim. Josiri Akadra is not. This is the will of the Council, Arzro. It is not for you or I to break."

Makrov scowled at the repetition of his own admonishment. "And if I choose otherwise?"

"You've known my father long enough to know better than to come between an Akadra and his kin."

Makrov fell silent, his face thunderous as the sky. He clicked his fingers. "Bring her."

He trotted away, entourage of soldiers and proctors in his wake.

Anastacia, her wrists bound on a silver leash, strode in their midst, shoulders back and head held high.

Viktor watched them go, partly to ensure Makrov made no attempt to take others to whom he was not entitled. Mostly because he couldn't face Josiri.

At last, the gate cleared. Weary, worn and still abuzz with a fury he dared not express, Viktor beckoned to Keldrov. "Major? I have a task for you, if you're feeling bold."

She limped over, eyes wary. "Sir?"

He set Makrov's precious document in her hand. "Armund af Garna you'll find on the field, beside his sister's pyre. Korsov and Drenn, I don't know. Find them. Warn them. Carefully. The archimandrite's wrath is not to be taken lightly."

Her lips pursed, then relaxed. "At once, my lord."

He watched her go, glad and proud. Perhaps there was hope for the Republic after all.

And then the moment could be put off no longer. Josiri had to be faced. Viktor strode through the mud with a certainty he scarcely felt, not wanting to be thought diffident or reluctant.

Josiri met him with bleak stare. "A fine token your friendship bought, Viktor."

"I know." He strove for words to express the knot about his heart. "You've no reason to believe me, but I will *not* let this stand. I've allies on the Council. Makrov will be stopped."

He broke off, the full consequences slamming home. That meant leaving. Leaving meant abandoning Calenne. As ever, the desires of the man and the duties of the leader walked divergent paths.

"You'll have to come with me, brother."

"Back to Tressia?" Josiri snarled. He stared back through the rain towards the gate. "I'm going nowhere. Ana needs me. Calenne needs me. And my people. The people you and I betrayed. They need me." He punctuated each point with a jab of a forefinger to Viktor's chest.

"If you stay, Makrov will kill you," said Viktor. "In the north, I can protect you. The pardon restores your family's seat on the Privy Council – a full vote, not the half-measure I once commanded. We can use that to change things."

He turned away and stared at the sky. How swiftly happiness turned to ash, triumph to defeat. How could intent count for so little? "I'm … I'm sorry that it's come to this."

Hearing no reply, he turned. Josiri had gone.

Josiri staggered through the rainswept camp, heartsick and seething. Once again, he'd lost everything. Calenne. Revekah. Anastacia. The others.

He suspected – as Makrov surely suspected – that there had been no marriage between Viktor and Calenne. And to be named an Akadra? He couldn't even begin to express his distaste. But he admired the cleverness of the ploy. It had preserved those who'd fought under his command and in his sister's name.

Better than that, it gave him a chance to hurt Makrov as he had been hurt. He paused for breath in the lee of a supply wagon. The rain hammered down, fit to match his mood. No. Not as he had been hurt. He could never repay Makrov so completely. But there had to be something. His mother would have known how to twist the knife.

He thought of their last day together, as he had so often since waking. Her last advice. *When enemies are your only recourse, choose the one with the least to gain.* Katya had surely not meant the words as he now took them, but wasn't that the nature of legacy?

He cast around with renewed purpose and took his bearings. Gavamor was dead. But if his possessions remained, one last act of retribution could yet be managed.

Melanna gazed out across the prison stockade, her mood bleak as the skies. Perhaps half her fellows had survived the night. The rest had succumbed to their wounds, quietly or with din fit to wake the heavens. At least the rain served to wash away the smell, though she was sure it would return soon enough.

"So that uproar wasn't Devren coming for us," her father grunted. He was pale beneath his wounds, his breathing shallower than she cared for.

"It seems not." Melanna had hoped that Ashana might relent and send the Huntsman for her. But no. This mess was of ephemeral make. It was for ephemerals to resolve.

"A pity. I'd have preferred to die with a sword in my hand."

"I'll find you one." She shivered and drew her cloak tighter. "I promise."

Not that she knew how such an oath was to be kept.

The soft rumble of her father's laughter broke off in a coughing fit. Blood spotted the back of his hand. He wiped it away on his fur. Melanna pretended she hadn't seen.

"This wasn't your fault," he said. "All war is a gamble. Had the Tressians threatened a son, I'd have laid down my sword as readily. But I imagine of no son serving his father more faithfully than you have me."

Pride fought melancholy for purchase on Melanna's soul. Fought, and lost.

Her father shivered and drew deeper into the cramped lean-to. "I've instructed Aedrun to make parley. If there is trade to be made, you'll go free."

"I spoke with the Duke of Eskavord while you slept," she said. "The Tressians want nothing from us."

"Nothing?"

Her cheek twitched at twin memories of rejection and admonition. "Nothing at all."

"Then we must put our faith in Devren," her father grunted. "He's loyal."

He was indeed, Melanna allowed, but he was also cautious. She was about to say as much when a chorus of alarm broke out beyond the walls.

Her father straightened. "What is that?"

Melanna frowned. "I don't know." She strained her ears. "They're saying something's out of contr—"

A hollow boom split the air. Halfway to the gate, the palisade wall shuddered. Another strike followed hard on its heels. Then a third. And a fourth.

Across the compound, men staggered to their feet. Some scrambled away. Others jabbed wary fingers at the wall. Cries of consternation rang out.

A section of wall fell inwards. Rain spattered off a sleek, bronze hide. Blue and white paint gleamed dully above a feline maw.

"Defend the prince!" bellowed Aedrun.

A ring of bodies pressed around Melanna and her father as more of the wall toppled inwards. They crowded so close she could barely breathe. She clawed at Aedrun's shoulder.

"Let me see!"

"*Savim . . .*"

Think like an empress. Behave as one. "Do as I command, warleader!"

His cheek twitched. "Yes, *savim*."

Aedrun drew hesitantly aside. Melanna stepped into the gap. A dozen simarka sat at perfect attention directly ahead. Not a limb moved, nor a tail twitched. All bore stripes of blue paint across their eyes and muzzles.

Josiri Trelan stepped out of the rain, his raiment so filthy that Melanna didn't recognise him at first. He held an amulet about his neck as tightly as a castaway clutching driftwood, and his eyes were wild.

"Stay back!" Aedrun bellowed in accented Tressian. "You'll not harm the prince while we live!"

Josiri threw his head back and laughed. Then he gave a formal bow and stepped aside. "Go. You're free. The guards are attended to, but there'll be more coming. The simarka won't harm you. I give you my word as a Trelan."

He seemed to find this last uproariously funny, for he laughed again.

"This is a trap," hissed Aedrun.

Melanna's father pursed his lips. "If so, it's an exceedingly strange trap. Daughter? You've spoken with the man."

She considered. "What have we to lose?"

He chuckled. "We should make that the family motto."

Aedrun frowned. "My prince . . ."

"Enough. The decision is made."

Melanna's father at their head, prisoners threaded through the unmoving simarka. Slowly, at first, but with growing confidence as the constructs made no reaction.

"Head north for the forest." Josiri shouted to be heard over the rain. "You can cut east from there."

Aedrun shot him a suspicious look and clambered through the breach. A heartbeat later, he beckoned back for Melanna's father. "Come, my prince."

Melanna hung back. She ignored the rain pooling in her collar and stared at Josiri. "Why?"

"Because you were right. They'll never stop taking from me, whatever I do. But this victory? The battle I won? The prisoners I took? That my sister likely died for? These things, I can take from *them*."

Melanna gazed at him, unable to untangle the swirl of sorrow and glee he wore like a cloak. "I'm sorry."

"Ashanal!" shouted Aedrun. "We must go."

She lingered all the same, recalling Ashana's words. *You're an empress. You speak for a people.* That sword cut both ways, didn't it? In vengeance, and in unsought kindness.

"I owe you for this, Josiri Trelan," she said. "The house of Saran owes you. Ashana watch over you and your kin."

The last of the joy slipped from his expression. "Go."

Melanna vanished into the rain. Josiri, abuzz with defiance and fear, let Gavamor's amulet fall at his feet and propped an elbow on the nearest simarka.

"Well, that's that," he said softly. "Makrov will be here soon. Viktor too, I shouldn't wonder. And then someone will think to send you after them. Can't have that, can we, Samias? Do you mind if I call you Samias? You look like a Sam."

The simarka offered no opinion. Like cats of all stripes, what wisdom it had it kept to itself.

Josiri brought his boot down on the amulet. Golden light flared under his heel and dissipated into the grey. With a sigh that stretched all the way to his toes, Josiri sat down alongside the simarka and tilted his face towards the rain.

"What a miserable day."

Jeradas, 10th day of Radiance

Folk praise me as a saviour.
  Is the wolf thought righteous for siding with
the sheep?
  Perhaps, had he not slaked his own hunger first.

from the sermons of Konor Belenzo

Forty-Five

No one spoke. At least, no one uttered words loud enough to draw notice above the creak of the wagon's axle and the rumble of wheels. After two days on the road, no one had anything much left to say. The escort even left marching songs unvoiced. But for the tramp of feet, Josiri might have believed they'd parted ways somewhere in the Tevar Flood.

Josiri squeezed his interlocked fingers tight and strove to restrain his worries. For himself. For his companions. For Anastacia . . . and for Calenne most of all. The absence of news was a hungry void that gobbled up all around it until only despair remained.

The cart shuddered to a halt. A soldier parted the canvas flaps. "Lord Akadra, your presence is requested."

Lord Akadra. Josiri rose on numbed legs and shuffled out into the open air. A bleak afternoon sliding into nondescript evening. Grey fading black. If there were a more apt metaphor for his life, he couldn't grasp it.

The soldier led him around the wagon's front, past the double column of northwealders. Most were arrayed in the king's blue of the 12th, though the foremost wore the Akadra swan.

Viktor sat at the head of the convoy, unarmoured but garbed in black and silver. A riderless horse waited beside his own. Far to the north, beyond the rolling, windblown meadows and huddled villages, the white stone of Tressia's outer wall waited.

Viktor gestured to the empty saddle. "Join me, brother."

Josiri scowled, but obeyed. "I wish you wouldn't call me that."

"We do not live in a world of wishes. You of all people should know that by now."

With a flick of his reins he set the horse in motion.

Josiri did likewise, and the convoy rumbled on. "No. I live in a world where a man's wishes ... a man's words ... mean nothing."

"I ... " Viktor broke off, the angry rumble beneath his words subsiding. "My every dealing with you has been in good faith."

"And much good it has done!" snapped Josiri. "Or do you suppose Makrov shares your noble sentiments?"

The air grew colder. Far colder than an overcast Sommertide's day should manage.

"I know your pride's hurting. That's why you set the prisoners free. For that act alone, Makrov wanted you hanged. The Akadra name you loathe so much is the only reason you're alive. Josiri Trelan would be crow-food by now."

"They were *my* prisoners," Josiri bit out.

"I recall playing no small part in their capture. But yes. They were *your* prisoners. And for whatever it's worth, I understand why you acted as you did. I might even have aided the endeavour, had you trusted me with your intent."

"I've trouble believing that."

"We'll never know, will we?"

"Your manner tells me enough. I placed your enemy beyond your grasp."

To Josiri's surprise, Viktor laughed. "You think that's why I'm angry? Kai Saran's fate isn't worth a brass shilling to me. His wildcat daughter's far less. But I would have parleyed their deaths into freedom." The laughter faded into bitterness. "Instead, I must seek another path, when every bone in my body calls me southwards to search for Calenne. I am riven by duty. Worn down by it. And in great part the fault is yours."

Josiri cast about for a rebuttal. To his dismay, he found none. "The princessa ... I wanted to spare her my burdens."

"Compassion for your enemy, brother? I fear Ebigail Kiradin will never approve of you. But compassion isn't enough. Not if we're to spare our people Makrov's cruelty."

Our people. Viktor was far easier to loathe from a distance than in person. "You believe that's possible, even now?"

"Makrov, Ebigail ... even my own father. They mistake bigotry for the tinder of great days gone. They scry the past for comfort but are blind to its lesson."

"And that is?"

"That if those in power refuse to change, others will take the decision from them."

He spoke with laconic, deliberate passion. The sentiment, aggrandising in another, offered only an ascetic's humility.

Josiri's cheeks warmed with shame. "I'm as trapped as any of them. As my mother once was."

"Not so," Viktor replied. "Even at the end, when she'd nothing more to lose, Katya couldn't bring herself to trust me. To hope for something better. We needn't agree on everything, you and I. But from here on out, we must work together. Everything we love lies in the south. That alone should bind us."

Calenne. Anastacia. How was he to help them now? "I'll not be your puppet."

"No, but if I'm to shoulder the aftermath of recklessness, I'd at least partake in the joy. Can you make me that promise?"

Josiri hesitated. His mother would have warned him against. But Viktor was right. The past was the past, and Viktor Akadra – of all people – was the only source of light in a bleak feature.

"Yes."

A double line of soldiery waited among the bustling crowds coming and going from King's Gate. A full company of the 7th, but not arrayed as an honour guard, as Viktor might have expected. Drawn weapons were held ready, not shouldered in respect – a detail that explained why the milling citizenry gave them as wide a berth as the roadway's confines permitted. The knot of grey-garbed provosts struck a further jarring tone, as did the pair of kraikons hunched beneath the gateway.

But none of this, unexpected as it was, troubled Viktor half as much as the woman who stood at stiff attention a dozen paces before the blockade. The stranger who wore the face of a friend.

Viktor brought the convoy to a halt with a closed fist.

Josiri straightened in his saddle. "What's happening?"

"I don't know," Viktor replied. "I'll attend to it."

"Shared recklessness, remember? That promise goes both ways."

"Reckless deeds could not be further from my thoughts."

"And from theirs? I've spent my adult life a prisoner, Viktor. I know a cage when I see one."

Viktor grimaced. So Josiri read the situation the same. It had to be Makrov's doing. A swift herald could have overtaken them on a different road. But why? To shake Josiri free of the haven Viktor had arranged? It made no sense. If anything, the protection of the Akadra family name was stronger within the city walls, where there were hearthguard aplenty to back words with steel.

"Very well," he said. "But please let me do the talking."

Josiri nodded. With a twitch of reins, they walked their steeds closer, the crowds parting before them. The woman on the roadway didn't advance. She didn't smile – didn't even offer a word of greeting.

"Rosa," said Viktor. "It's been too long."

"Lord Akadra."

She looked older. No, that wasn't right. What Viktor perceived was not an aging of the body. It went deeper: a hollowness of spirit, conveyed more by his shadow than any ephemeral perception.

"Josiri, I present Lady Roslava Orova, Knight of Essamere and my friend. Rosa, this is Josiri Akadra." He ignored the twitch of Josiri's brow and pressed on. "My brother by right of law, and of adoption."

Josiri inclined his head.

Rosa offered a rigid bow. "By right of law?"

"Of marriage, to his sister Calenne."

Her expression grew bleaker still, sparking fresh unease. "And the Lady Calenne? She is not with you? Some ... misfortune, perhaps?"

"The Hadari took her from us in the hour of victory." The words did not come easily, but they came. "It's my hope Lumestra will return her to us."

"I'm sure." Rosa spoke flatly. "A tragedy, so soon after her betrothed perished on the road. But people die so easily within your orbit, Lord Akadra."

Enough was enough. Viktor swung down from his saddle. "Rosa, what is this?"

A muscle twitched in her cheek. For the briefest of moments her blue eyes softened. But only for that moment. "Lord Viktor Akadra, you stand accused of crimes against the Republic. Treason. Corruption. Murder. Witchery. Surrender yourself."

Viktor felt the world slip away. Had his father revealed their demon's bargain? That would explain the witchery charge. But not the others.

"Rosa. What is this? Name my accuser. This is a—"

Rosa's gut-punch sucked his words into a wracking, gasping void. Another blow snapped his head aside. Red flared behind his eyes. His knee jarred against stone.

The crowds shrank back in alarm. Murmurs of outrage and worry rippled through the air. A merchant brought his cart to a clattering halt beneath King's Gate, not wanting to be caught up in the unfolding commotion.

Viktor spat a mouthful of blood onto the roadway. Rosa's emotionless facade fell as her body quivered with rage. Her eyes blazed with it. A sight he'd not seen since their first meeting, when he'd dressed her down for the idle, privileged brat she'd been.

"Bad enough that you've been in the Crowmarket's pay all this time! But Kas would have died for you!" she spat. "And you murdered him!"

Kasamor? Pieces of the puzzle were coalescing, but too slowly to be of use. Not that Viktor imagined facts had much purchase on Rosa at that moment. There was too much anger in her blood. Though somehow the cause of her wrath, he suspected she barely saw him. "Rosa, you're not making any ..."

This time, he rolled with her punch. It still set his teeth rattling.

Commotion broke out behind. Hearthguard hurried forward, their words murky in Viktor's ringing ears.

Rosa backed away. "7th! To me!"

The king's blue line surged forward. The last of the passers-by withdrew, streaming back beneath the gate, or making for the open fields of the city approach.

Viktor opened his mouth. Words vanished into the black clouds about his thoughts. He didn't have time for this. Calenne missing. His honour on the knife-edge of betrayal through unseen circumstance. And now someone had set the cornerstones of his life crumbling?

His shadow roared for freedom. The roadway felt cold as ice beneath his fingers. But this was one problem it couldn't fix. One glimpse would unmake him. And he didn't want to hurt Rosa. She was as much a victim as he. She had to be.

"Stand back!" shouted Josiri. "Sergeant, hold your ground!"

The hearthguard drew back. Rosa clasped a fist, and the 7th halted.

Josiri dismounted in front of Viktor, his back to the line of drawn swords. Rosa glowered and backed further away. Her lips thinned almost to nothing, and her jaw muscles went taut as mooring ropes. She knew she'd overstepped. A good sign among the bad.

"Your friend seems nice," said Josiri.

Viktor grimaced. Taking the proffered hand, he rose. "Something's wrong."

"I'd worked that out." He shot a glance over his shoulder. "What can I do?"

The matter-of-fact tone banished a little of the cold gnawing at Viktor's thoughts. Nothing forged friendship as readily as a common enemy. If only that enemy had not also once been a friend.

"Have Sergeant Brass take you to Malachi Reveque. He'll protect you." He offered a wry smile. "I don't imagine you can expect a warm welcome from my father."

The corner of Josiri's mouth curled. His eyes shifted restlessly. "Your friends thus far inspire little confidence."

"If you return to the Southshires, Makrov will seize you as a fugitive. You can't help Calenne or Anastacia if you're dead."

"Nor can you."

"They'll want a confession about the witchery. That will take time." Viktor eyed the provosts. He knew too much of their reputation to believe it would take *much* time. "I imagine it will hurt, but I'll survive."

"See that you do." He offered a lopsided smile. "With Calenne and Ana gone, who else will I quarrel with?"

Viktor nodded. Wrists held out before him and heavy heart weighing his steps, he approached Rosa's line. The provosts hurried forward, robes trailing in the dust, and bound his hands with silver rope.

Forty-Six

The cottage door creaked open. Warmth howled out into the miserable afternoon and the crisp scent of rain rolled in. Kurkas set his hand of cards on the table and drew his blanket tight. The motion pulled on the torn flesh of his gut, lending irritation to breathy words.

"Close the bloody door, would you?"

Halvor heaved it shut and set the latch. "So he's still in a foul mood?"

Across the table, Ardel grinned and ran a calloused hand through thinning hair. "Can't help that he's losing."

Kurkas glowered at one, and then the other. He sighed and flipped his cards face up. The Queen in Twilight, the Soldier, the Three of Moons and the Eight of Ravens. Worthless hand anyway.

"I don't like being cooped up. I'm not poultry."

Halvor shook off her cloak and hung it on a peg beside the door. She didn't look right without the battered phoenix tabard. Kurkas knew a thing or two about divesting parts and pieces of one's body. A missing arm or eye should have trumped a scrap of ratty old cloth, but Halvor just didn't seem whole.

"Any word on Lady Trelan?" asked Kurkas.

A small, sharp shake of the head. "No. Either she's lying low, or ..." The words faded into a weary growl.

"How is it out there?" asked Ardel, all levity gone from his weathered face.

Halvor pulled out a chair. "Granfield's a mess. Soldiers on the streets. Door-to-door searches."

"What're they looking for?"

"Same thing as in the other villages: opportunity," said Kurkas. "Makrov's tidying up before the wind changes."

"He's right," said Halvor. "They'd prisoner wagons out front. They weren't empty, neither. Two lads and a lassie. One of them more banged up than Kurkas here. Anyone suspected of being a wolf's-head is dragged up to Cragwatch. Word is that most who survived the Hadari are up there too." She brought her fist down on the table. Her face scrunched tight. "It wasn't supposed to be this way."

Kurkas knew better than to meet her gaze and settled for meeting that of the Queen in Twilight. "Lord Akadra will put it right."

He felt the fury of her gaze fall on him. "Can't put right the dead, can he?"

"Wouldn't be a popular fellow if he could. Different kind of trouble, that."

"Can you not spring the wagons?" asked Ardel.

"With who?" Halvor replied. "What's left of my phoenixes have scattered. Running for the coast or the Thrakkian border, if they've any sense. Everyone else too, I shouldn't wonder."

Kurkas chuckled. "So, what do we do?"

"You're staying here. I'm a fugitive, but you're a loyal servant of the Republic. Ardel found you on the battlefield and nursed you back to health. Try not to die on him. It'll raise questions."

Halvor's story wasn't too far from the truth. Only Ardel hadn't "found" him – Revekah had fetched Ardel from his tiny hilltop farm.

Kurkas sniffed. "I'm feeling much better."

"Feeling better?" Halvor replied. "How far can you walk without that stick?"

Kurkas patted the crudely padded and cut-down spear-staff resting against his chair. "Reckon that if Lumestra meant us to walk unaided, she'd not have given us the idea of crutches."

"You're impossible."

"And *I'm* hearing a lot about what *I* should be doing, and nothing of what you intend." He shrugged. "If you don't trust me, just say so. I can take it."

She tipped forward, head falling into her hands. "What I want to do more than anything is pull the ground up over my head and sleep. I feel like I've barely closed my eyes in days."

Kurkas couldn't deny that Halvor had lost a good deal of her spark. She looked every bit as grey and miserable as the weather, and with about as much prospect of sunlight breaking through. She'd almost killed him a few days back. Now, a determined field mouse could have given her a stiff challenge. It was upsetting, and not just because that same field mouse could have settled him with two paws tied behind its back.

Why was he thinking this way? He was a soldier. Halvor was a traitor. That circumstance had flipped her back and forth across that line wasn't supposed to matter. Smart thing to do would be to walk away, maybe even report to Makrov. Problem was, there were two kinds of loyalty in the world. One to the rule-makers and the other to comrades. The one was not equal to the other. Couldn't be, could it? Or he'd have seized the retirement Akadra had offered him after Zanya, taken a steward's position with a noble family and lived the easy life.

Slippery slope, friendship. Might even tempt a man to treason. Still, treachery *was* the Southshires' perennial crop. Maybe there was something in the air …

"What would Katya have done?" asked Ardel.

"She'd have looked for another way forward," said Halvor. "But I don't see one. It took years to gather support. It's all gone. *They're* all gone."

"Not entirely," said Kurkas. "Didn't you tell me they'd taken the duke's doxy back up to Branghall?"

Halvor raised her head and fixed him with a scowl. "Her *name* is Anastacia."

He stifled a smile, glad to see a little fire in her eyes, but knowing better than to say so. "Didn't say it wasn't. Point is, I've still got my ward-brooch, and I'm betting you've still got yours. If you're lacking for inspiration, I'll warrant she's an idea or two."

"What if Anastacia's not there? What if Makrov's had the enchantment altered?"

"Reckon he's been too busy for that. Not a man for details, our archimandrite." Kurkas shrugged. "And if he has? Well, I shouldn't rightly say this, what with you being a traitor and all, but my mother set a lot of store by retribution. If Anastacia's beyond reach, you might find Makrov pleasingly close to hand."

Reluctance sharpened to suspicion. "And you'd stand by and watch while I ripped out his fat throat?"

"Madam, please!" Kurkas scratched at his eyepatch. "I'm a soldier of the Republic. Moreover, I do have some finer feelings. I'd turn around first."

She laughed her acceptance. Kurkas shook his head and wondered again about what it was about the Southshires that tempted honest souls to treason.

The dray cart's reins hung loose in Revekah's hands. She hadn't wanted to take the cart at all – the only thing worse than walking in the rain was *sitting* in it – but Ardel had insisted. And it wasn't as though Kurkas could have made the journey on foot. Glib remarks about Lumestra's holy crutches aside, the man still had as much trouble walking as keeping his fool mouth shut.

She didn't even know she could trust him, not really. And here she was, rumbling soggily into harm's way at his suggestion. But despite it all, Revekah was glad of the company. Even if that company was given to tuneless whistling. After a third breathy iteration of "The Maid of Kilver", she could take no more.

"Will you *please* give it a rest?"

Kurkas leaned back on the bench seat, shoulders slumped. "I liked you better when you were trying to kill me."

"I *definitely* liked you better when you were unconscious."

He flicked the tail of his sodden cloak and drew the rest in tighter. "You want to tell me what's eating you? You've had a face like a flooded gutter all day."

"I've failed my oldest friend in every possible way, and you want to know why I'm unhappy?"

"Don't give me that. You've fought ever since Zanya. Don't reckon you'd give up now."

"Why do you care?"

"I'm the sympathetic sort, ask anyone."

Revekah grunted. She'd caught her reflection that morning. Or at least the reflection of an old woman who looked like her. She'd never thought of herself as *old* before. Just old*er*. But these past days she felt the tally of years in every creaking joint.

"I've not slept well," she said at last.

"So you said. Guess it must've been thunder I heard last night. Maybe a wild pig broke in and passed out beside the fire."

"Will you stop with that?" she snapped. "There's a difference between sleeping and sleeping *well*. It's the same as exists between having been bred and having good breeding."

"That an insult? Because I never had much tutoring, so I ain't one for erudition or loquacity. And don't get me started on similes. Pass me by like a leaf in a gale, they do."

Revekah shot Kurkas a suspicious glance. He stared dead ahead, with his good eye out of sight. Aggravating man.

"Bad dreams, is it?" he asked.

"I never remember them."

"Might be it's better that way."

She shook her head, again trying to piece together the scattered details. There were no images, only feelings. Of yearning. Of coming home. "All I know is that my thoughts feel heavy all the time. Like I could curl up and sleep at any moment."

"Then why don't you? Plenty of room in the back. I can manage the cart for a spell."

"Won't help," she said instead. "I'll just feel worse when I wake."

"No way to live, that. Makes my skin itch just thinking on it."

"You asked."

Another prolonged silence, broken only by the hiss of rain and the mare's plodding footsteps. Eskavord became a grey smudge on a rain-swept horizon. To the north, firestone lanterns blazed beneath dancing heels on Gallows Hill.

Revekah glanced away. It wasn't supposed to have ended like this.

"Why are you here?" she asked. "Why help me?"

"Why'd you save my life instead of going to your precious duke?"

"Can you not *once* give a straight answer?"

He grinned. "Maybe. Why'd you patch me up? Me, a fearsome northwealder."

Why indeed? But there was really only one answer. "We were comrades back then. We're not any more, so I'll ask again: why are you helping me?"

He shrugged. "I like having my debts paid off good and prompt. Figure this might set us even. Besides, Makrov's a boil on the Republic's arse. My lads and lasses fought for something better than his pride."

It was all a mess, Revekah decided. He owed her. She owed him. Over and over, tallied in wounds mended and foes fought. Perhaps it wasn't the greatest foundation for friendship, but she'd had worse.

She listened close to the rain, and fancied she heard Katya laughing at her.

The sentries at Eskavord's east gate waved the dray through with only the most cursory of searches. Kurkas guessed few of his fellow north-wealders had much stomach for their current duties, especially in the rain. Only away to the west, where Branghall stood dark against brooding clouds, was there the suggestion of sun and clear skies.

Halvor stabled the dray and they set off through the streets. Here, at least, the rain was a blessing. With so many folk swathed against the weather, Halvor's hooded cloak wouldn't draw notice, let alone suspicion. In fact, no one seemed eager to pay them any heed at all.

Tressian patrols marched past with the determined speed of soldiers who believed they could stride between raindrops. Southwealders shuffled about like folk on the brink of exhaustion, eyes downcast and dull. The whole town stank of malice and despair.

It was such a bloody waste, thought Kurkas. Criminal, really.

He staggered as Halvor's shoulder thumped into his. The crutch skidded across cobbles. Kurkas scrabbled for a handhold but found none in the press of the crowd.

Strong hands righted him before he fell entirely.

Halvor grimaced. "Lost my footing."

He set his crutch back in place. "Raven's Eyes. If you like patching me up that much, just break a few bones while I'm sleeping. Spare me the excitement of the fall."

"You've had your apology." Her breath steamed in the cold. "Everyone's heading to the marketplace."

"Want to bet Makrov has something planned?"

"No."

They joined the shiftless procession, which in truth wasn't all that much faster than Kurkas' crutch-bound pace, and joined the crowds packed in the shadow of the reeve's manor. Taking up position towards the rear – but not so far back as to seem unwilling – Kurkas glanced around. He took in dispirited face after dispirited face; the ring of king's blue soldiers at the periphery and the one broken-down kraikon salvaged from the battle.

Hard to believe the marketplace had rung with cheers just a week before.

The crowd should have been rife with discontent – mutters loud enough to carry, but not so loud as to identify those who gave them voice. There was nothing, just the drum of raindrops on wattle and timber – the swish of boots traipsing across waterlogged cobbles.

"Don't know why they're bothering with the soldiers," muttered Kurkas. "This lot look ready to lie down for just about anything. So much for the unruly south."

The expected protest from Halvor never arrived. Kurkas turned about to find her staring distantly at the reeve's balcony. As a man with few friends and no family beyond the one offered by the hearthguard, Kurkas knew he'd never really understand the depths of Halvor's losses. Sure, Zanya had cost her, but there'd been hope things might change. Now? Now she was fifteen years older. If Akadra couldn't set things right, she'd more chance of seeing the mists of Otherworld than a free Southshires.

"Nothing lasts for ever," he said softly.

Halvor blinked and stared at him with fleeting confusion. "Did you say something?"

"Nothing. Nothing at all."

Branghall's clock chimed for six. Heralds appeared on the balcony. Buccinas blared their brash chorus. Even in the deluge, Makrov couldn't resist pomp and ceremony.

As the notes faded into the rain, the archimandrite appeared on the balcony, scarlet robes bright in the gloom. Yanda stood a little to the side, her expression only a shade less dour than the assembled southwealders. A trio of veiled serenes stood in silent attendance behind.

"People of Eskavord!" Makrov's querulous tone was a poor match for the rain. The more he strove to overcome the din, the more his voice cracked and broke. "Blessed Lumestra despairs how you have strayed from the Council's authority! I will guide you back to the light. Lumestra's radiance may once more grace this town. But it must be earned!"

If Makrov hoped to fan the flames of fervour, he'd sorely misjudged his audience, who regarded him with the same sullen indifference they'd earlier reserved for the rain.

"There can be no hope of redemption while you harbour traitors!" shouted Makrov. "I know these were once your friends, your family, but they have renounced Lumestra's light, and the light of the Council! Their deeds have left us all with empty bellies! They bring punishment down upon you out of selfishness, and out of pride!"

There should have been something by now, Kurkas decided. Some rumble of discontent. Some protest. Had the tumult of recent days broken the folk of Eskavord so completely?

Makrov braced his hands against the balustrade and leaned out into the rain. "But I understand loyalty. I do. I served in the Republic's army. I stood the line on the border. I know that swords drawn together are the highest loyalty. So I'll make this offer: whoever brings me Calenne Trelan or Revekah Halvor will receive clemency for themselves, and all their kin! They'll earn exemption from rationing, and the gratitude of the Council! I know I ask much. I know this is a sacrifice. But the Republic was built on sacrifice!"

Beneath the balcony, one soldier dipped his head to another's ear. A finger pointed across the crowd. Shoulders hunched, they made their way into the marketplace, parting onlookers with sharp gestures and the flats of swords.

"This was a mistake," muttered Halvor.

"Let's not make a scene," Kurkas replied.

The soldiers drew nearer.

Kurkas blotted out Makrov's diatribe and swept his gaze around the marketplace. The ring of soldiers was tight, but not unbroken. Through the gap, beyond the fountain and an empty wagon, an alleyway beckoned. A potential escape, for someone light enough on their feet. *If* she could get through the crowd. *If* the soldiers didn't block her retreat in time.

If a lot of things.

"Hold, you!"

Gloved fingers tightened around the shoulder of a woman a dozen paces in front of Kurkas. The soldier spun her around and ripped her hood back. "Thought it was you!"

The woman struck the challenger in the gut. Golden hair spilled free as she made to run. The second soldier reeled her in and cuffed her about the head.

"Hands off, northwealder pig!"

The second soldier clapped his hand over her mouth. He snatched it back with a cry and cuffed her again. She collapsed into the first soldier's waiting arms, eyes glassy.

Halvor stiffened. Kurkas gripped her wrist in warning. "No scene, remember?"

Makrov's invective faded. Brow furrowed, he stared down at the interruption.

"What is this?"

The first soldier straightened. "Wolf's-head, my lord. Snagged a wagon of provisions meant for Cragwatch just yesterday. Killed two of my company and wounded a third."

"You know her?" murmured Kurkas.

"Elbi Semmer," Halvor replied through gritted teeth. "She's a phoenix. One of mine."

Makrov raised his voice and flung a hand in Semmer's direction. "You see? They're still among you, inviting punishment! Stealing from those who defend you against the eastern barbarians!"

A scuffle broke out. A soldier staggered away, a hand cupped to his face.

"I fought the Hadari!" shrieked Semmer. "Where were you? Where were any of you?"

Makrov gestured. Three more soldiers started out across the crowd. "Where are the stolen supplies?"

"Gone," spat Semmer. "Gone to feed the hungry."

"And your compatriots?" Makrov shook his head and leaned low over the balcony, elbows propped on the balustrade. "Give me their names, and where they can be found. Your sin will be forgiven. You'll go free."

She spat. "I'll tell you nothing."

"That too I doubt. Take her away!"

The soldiers dragged Semmer from the marketplace. She fought and kicked at every step, her heels splashing through the filthy puddles.

"Help me!" she shouted at the crowd. A few glanced away. Most gave no reaction at all. "We fought for you! Why won't you help me?"

Then she was gone, dragged into the streets beyond. Makrov resumed his tyrant's sermon, though Kurkas spared it little attention. His one good eye he spared for the woman at his side, her manner rigid as a serpent coiled to spring. It was easier that way. Easier than reconciling his own thoughts. He'd celebrated victory at Zanya as much as his ravaged body had allowed. But this? This made him want to scream.

At last, Makrov tired of hearing his own voice. With a last heartfelt cry of *Praise Lumestra* – one almost nobody echoed – he withdrew from the balcony.

Yanda lingered a moment longer, her eyes sweeping the crowd. Before Kurkas had a chance to look away, her eyes found him. Recognition was as mutual as it was instant – the sidelong glance she shot Halvor as unexpected as the tight, respectful nod that followed.

Kurkas braced himself for the accusation and the call to alarm. Neither came. Yanda simply turned her back and passed inside.

"She knows," muttered Halvor as the crowds began to thin.

"Yes, but I don't think she'll say anything," Kurkas replied. "We're not all like Makrov."

She stared across at the reeve's manor. "Enough are. Enough that killing him won't change a thing."

"Might make you feel better."

"You're an odd one, Kurkas. Even for a northwealder, you're odd."

He stared gloomily across the thinning crowd. "I'll take that as a compliment, under the circumstances."

He hitched his crutch closer and hobbled for the alleyway. The cold and wet had seeped into his bones. Branghall seemed a long way off. Two paces distant, he turned back the way he'd come. Halvor hadn't followed. She stood in the empty marketplace like a child cut adrift from her parents in the rain.

"Can't you feel it?" she said.

He winced and lurched back towards her. "All I feel right now is ice in my bones and a yearning for a crackling hearth."

Where he was to find the latter, he wasn't sure. Ardel's cottage was a good three hours' ride back across the fields, and he was certainly in no state to go clambering about over Branghall's walls, ward-brooch or no.

Though Halvor's eyes met his, Kurkas had the strangest feeling that she hadn't seen him.

"Don't come apart on me now, yeah?"

"The Dark surrounds me," she murmured, "and there's no light to show the way."

Scripture? Now? Kurkas revised his assessment of his companion's grip on reality.

"A soldier makes his own light. Just needs something to burn."

Her eyes widened in recognition. "Kevor? Kevor, is that you? Just wait until I tell Katya. We thought you were dead."

Kurkas felt a chill that had little to do with the weather. This went far beyond exhaustion. "Snap out of it, Halvor. I can't drag you out of here by the heels, much less carry you."

"I've no need to leave." She frowned and sat down in the wet. "I'm home. I can lay down my burdens."

Brilliant. Absolutely bloody brilliant. What was he to do now? Smart thing would be to leave her to it. Maybe find a way of reaching Yanda without Makrov catching wind. But he wasn't that smart, was he? Smart folk didn't leave pieces of themselves on battlefields, much less stomp into occupied territory with a fugitive.

He cast about the marketplace. A few knots of southwealders remained, eyed warily by a handful of soldiers. No one seemed to be paying them any heed. So far.

"Captain Halvor," he hissed. "You need to pull yourself together right bloody now, you understand me?"

She stared past him, expression brightening. "Elda."

Elda? Who in the Raven's name was Elda? Kurkas glanced back over his shoulder. A stocky woman stood in the alleyway mouth, rain trickling across a crow's-footed face and iron-grey plaits. He'd seen her before, though she'd not seen fit to waste her breath on him. Calenne's foster-mother.

Boots splashing through filthy puddles, Elda closed the distance. "Revekah? It's me. I'm here." She glared at Kurkas as if seeing him for the first time and sniffed. "Oh, it's you. The captain who left filthy boot prints across my hallway. What have you done to her?"

"What have *I* done?" Fraying patience snapped. "Now you listen to me ..."

"It can wait." Elda straightened, suddenly all business. "Let's get her inside."

Kurkas glanced from one to the other, the hairs on the back of his neck prickling with uncertainty. But what were the options? Leave Halvor out in the rain?

"Have it your way."

Forty-Seven

For nearly twenty years, the city of Tressia had held dual identity in Josiri's memory, his childhood recollections muddied and distorted by a man's resentments. A place of alabaster towers, fluttering hawk-flags and gilded statues, it was also the place his father had come to die. Where hundreds – even thousands – of southwealders laboured in servitude, having committed no crime other than to have lost.

Strange, then, that the streets were neither so glorious as Josiri remembered, nor as horrifying as he'd feared. The white city of his dreams and nightmares had grown grey through neglectful years. The flags streamed not from proud towers, but from walls surrounded by rubble, brick-spoil and sweating labourers. Statues bore powdery stains that marked them as gull-roosts. But then nor did Josiri catch signs of the slavery he'd feared. The labourers worked unfettered, and the streets were empty of the shuffling columns of oppressed he'd conjured in his mind's eye.

Tressia, bastion of glory and oppression, was merely a place, neither intrinsically good nor irredeemably evil. It simply ... was.

It was also oddly empty. In the long walk from King's Gate, Josiri and his five-man escort passed perhaps a thousand souls. The marketplaces, which should have been bustling even at that hour, were but sparsely attended. The church doors were sealed tight, their congregations and preachers cloistered inside, their hymns echoing out into the open air. The taverns and hostelries of the deeper streets, which should have been thick with drinkers celebrating the dying work day, played host to but a few huddled inebriates. But for all that, Josiri felt eyes upon him from every alley-mouth and window. Empty though the streets might have been, the people were still there.

Kraikons stood silent sentinel at the confluence of major thorough-fares. It took Josiri a moment to recognise them for what they were. Steel armour and polished bronze flesh gleamed in the waning daylight, giving them the aspect of gods, and not the broken-down old field-hulks Josiri knew. But their stance was familiar. Watchful. In this, if nothing else, Tressia reminded him of Eskavord, and he wondered why that should be so.

They began the curved descent towards the harbourside and the Silverway River. Battered kraikons loomed alongside silent, moored ships. Josiri spotted a woman dragging her child along. The girl, oblivious to her parent's wishes, lingered at arm's extent, gazing up at a kraikon in wonder. What was a familiar sight in Eskavord was apparently not so in Tressia.

"Is it always so quiet?" he asked.

Sergeant Brass pondered, as steadfastly laconic as a cow chewing cud. "No."

Josiri waited for him to expand on the answer. After a dark, silent tavern fell away behind, he realised no such expansion was forthcoming.

"Do you know what's going on?" he asked.

Brass quickened his pace. "No."

Josiri fell silent. The wary look and the hastened tread told him plenty. Something was badly wrong, and Brass knew it.

By the time they reached the intricate wrought-iron gates of Abbeyfields, the further thinning of the crowds and the increasing prevalence of constabulary tabards allowed him to put a name to circumstance. Curfew. Not yet begun, but soon. Apparently he'd brought at least *part* of the Southshires with him.

Four guards watched the main gate. Brass made a lumbering beeline for the woman who shared his sergeant's stars. After brief conversation, Josiri was beckoned through into the gardens. At the mansion door Brass hauled hard on the bell-pull. Shortly after, the door creaked open to reveal a rotund, grey-clad servant whose harried expression spoke to labours interrupted.

"Yes?"

"'The Duke of Eskavord to see Lord Reveque." Out of nowhere, Brass possessed a crispness of voice and manner that had earlier been lacking.

The servant's brow furrowed. Josiri felt disbelieving eyes boring into him. Jack o' Fellhallow and an entourage of thornmaidens would have been only a fraction less surprising a houseguest – and he'd have managed better garb than Viktor's borrowed clothes.

At last, the fellow nodded. "Very well. If you'll wait inside, your grace?"

"You'll have to forgive me. This is a lot to take in."

Malachi topped off both glasses and returned the decanter to the dresser. He handed one glass to Josiri Trelan – it seemed odd to think of him as Josiri *Akadra*, even given the explanation for why he should do so – and reclaimed a seat at Lilyana's side. Her glass remained untouched.

Josiri nodded his thanks. "Easier to hear it than to live it."

"You're certain the Hadari won't return?"

"Kai Saran is wounded, his army broken. The Hadari are no longer a threat." His tone darkened. "They never were. Not the one I should have heeded."

Malachi nodded. "I wish I could say that Ebigail and Makrov's arrangement came as any surprise. But Viktor arrested? And by Rosa? Time was, she'd be first to defend him."

It at least explained why she'd moved out that morning. Was she protecting him, or avoiding confrontation? The former would have been very much in character.

"People change," said Lily. "Rosa's been through a great deal. She may not be the person you knew any longer. Or perhaps Viktor never truly was."

Malachi scowled away a flash of irritation. "I can't believe that. I won't. They're my friends. The world's gone mad."

"The world was always mad," said Josiri, his tone edged with steel. "I don't blame you for not noticing. It's easier to look away than to fight."

Malachi flinched. "Josiri . . ."

Lily rose in a swish of skirts and fixed Josiri with a cold stare. "You've no idea how my husband has sacrificed – how he's fought. I don't expect gratitude, but you might show respect!"

"Lily, please. Josiri's . . ."

" . . . behaving like a poor guest." Josiri's posture softened. He ran a hand through his tangled blond hair. "I apologise without reservation. It's easy to fall back onto firm habits, and history has tempered mine hard as steel. Still, that's no excuse."

He approached the leaded window and stared across the dusk-shrouded garden. Lily scowled and reclaimed her seat as Malachi sipped from his brimming glass and gathered his thoughts.

He couldn't say what he'd expected of Josiri Trelan – a man he'd never met save through the dry distance of written report – but the dishevelled individual whose outsize garb more suited a beggar than a nobleman was certainly not it. He'd hoped they'd meet, of course, once common sense prevailed at council. In his folly, he'd expected confluence of mind and opinion. Brotherhood born of common cause. Soft words of thanks dismissed with dignified grace.

The reality was sadly lacking, as reality so often was. He'd have been blind not to recognise the resentment and worry underlying Josiri's every word and gesture. How well Malachi knew those feelings. And yet he worried only over one friend – maybe two, given Rosa's part in unfolding events. Josiri had family, loved ones . . . even an entire people at risk.

"You're with friends," he said at last. "Apologies are unnecessary."

Josiri gave a wry snort. "If I've learned one thing of late, it's that apologies are more necessary between friends than elsewhere."

Lily's scowl receded into thoughtfulness. "Actions are better."

"I agree, but what would you have me do?" He spoke without turning.

Malachi shook his head. "She's talking to me. My dear wife defends me, Josiri, but her appraisal of my efforts is eerily similar to your own. I think too much, and act too little. I rely on Viktor's support where I should have learned to stand alone. Now he – and you – rely on me. I shall not be found wanting."

"Thank you—" Josiri broke off. When he spoke again, it was with quiet mirth. "You should know that there's a mass of water-slime making its way up the garden path. I think there's a child at the heart of it."

Lily growled. The sitting room door slammed behind her. Malachi joined Josiri at the window. Constans indeed looked more nightmare than child, with thick green weed trailing behind like some vile bridal train. White teeth hinted at a broad grin beneath the mud.

"You don't have children, do you?" asked Malachi.

"My life's complicated enough."

"They have a way of simplifying matters. I'd die for Constans and Sidara. Without hesitation."

Lily appeared in view, her face brimming with incipient thunder. Constans hooked his hand into claws and spun gleefully towards her.

"Then you'd best hurry," said Josiri. "I fear you're about to lose a son."

"There are limits to all things," Malachi said airily. Lily stalked back up the garden path, her hand tight about Constans' collar. "But you're right. He'll be *my* son for the foreseeable future. I hope he learns better sense as he grows."

"The same might be said of us all. I've made poor decisions of late. I can't afford any more."

And there it was: brotherhood born of common cause. Or something so near to it that divergence didn't matter. "Viktor was right to send you to me."

"Viktor has an annoying knack for being right. Can you help him?"

"Yes." Malachi imbued the word with confidence, and hoped it was true. "Hadon may not often see eye-to-eye with his son, but I can't imagine he'll allow Viktor to go to the pyre. Given the Council's denuded state, that's no small prize."

Josiri set his back to the garden. "What's happened to the Council?"

"What *hasn't* happened? We were five, saving yourself. We're now three. Lord Tarev embraced the Raven and so, they're saying, did Lady Marest."

"You don't believe that?"

"As a vranakin tried to kill me less than a week back, no I do not. Neither do Ebigail nor Hadon." Malachi forced a smile he didn't feel. "A rare moment of unity."

"Hence the curfew?"

"Hadon's idea. Ebigail backed him. I don't blame her. Her daughter's missing. Knowing the Crowmarket, that means she's dead. But curfews don't stop assassins. They simply make everyone feel . . . safe."

"My mother spoke of the Crowmarket," said Josiri. "She sought their help, but the price was too steep."

Malachi shuddered. Given the ease with which the kernclaw had infiltrated his home, it was easy to conjure how Katya's rebellion might otherwise have ended. "Did she say what they wanted?"

"They wanted her. Obedient and blind. But my mother was nobody's puppet."

"So I understand." A newly freed Southshires would have been profitable ground for the Crowmarket. "She made the right decision."

"Did she? I think her pride got in the way. One life in sway to the Crowmarket to free thousands. It's not such a poor trade, is it?"

The skin on the back of Malachi's neck prickled. "If you thought that, you'd have made your own deal by now."

"Maybe I'm proud, too. But maybe I'm learning to put that aside. I'm hoping you'll offer a different path."

He spoke the words as simple matter-of-fact, without malice. But there was threat, all the same.

"We can do nothing tonight," said Malachi. "We'll start tomorrow, at council. If nothing else, I'd like to see Hadon's reaction when he learns he now has *two* sons."

"This is a game to you, isn't it?"

Malachi's soul ached at the accusation. "It's all a game, and one won by canny action, not passion. By the terms of your original pardon, and despite your adoption, Viktor's seat on the Privy Council reverts to you and claims a full vote. We can use that. In the meantime, my house is yours." He looked Josiri up and down. "And we'll find you some clothes that actually fit. Please. You trusted Viktor enough to come here. Trust me."

"Through here, your grace."

Josiri passed into the airy, high-ceilinged room. It wasn't anywhere near as grand as his chambers at Branghall, but it was generous enough. More generous than he deserved. He'd known it wouldn't be easy coming back to Tressia, but he'd not anticipated just how changeable his mood would become. Everything reminded him of what he'd lost – and what he yet stood to lose. Ana in Makrov's clutches. And Calenne? Lumestra knew where she was.

"You'll find a selection of outfits in the wardrobe," the steward continued. "Serviceable, but I'm afraid Lord Reveque doesn't hold fashion in high regard."

"I'm sure I'll manage," Josiri murmured. "What's your name?"

"Braxov, your grace."

"*Your* name, not your family's."

"Yan, your grace. Will you be needing anything else? Some food perhaps?"

Josiri's gut rumbled, reminding him that he'd eaten nothing since an early and frugal lunch. But he couldn't face food. The sense of displacement was almost worse than the feeling of loss. Fifteen years, always sleeping in the same bed, shackled to the same routine. Freedom brought strange fears.

"No."

Braxov offered a pot-bellied bow. "If you change your mind, I'm at your service. Whatever the hour. The bell-pull rings through to the kitchen. If I'm asleep, one of the night-maids will find me."

"I'm sure I'll not put you to that trouble."

"It's no trouble, your grace." Braxov extended his left hand and spread his fingers. The faded swirl of a rose-brand stared up from his palm. "Some things are more important than sleep."

The mark of indenturement. Josiri had attended the first brandings – he'd felt he owed the victims that much. But he'd never seen one healed before. And this one had been healed a long time.

"When did they take you?"

"I was part of the exodus, your grace. Me and two sisters. They went to the Outer Isles. Haven't seen them since. I came here. But I've never forgotten. Not where I came from, and not the Phoenix."

How old was Braxov? A few years younger than himself? Young enough to have been little more than a child when the exodus had begun. "I'm sorry."

"I'm sure you've had your own burdens." He shrugged. "It's not been so bad. I've been part of Lady Reveque's household since before she was married, and she's a good sort. You can trust her. You can trust them both. And for anything else, I'm here."

"Thank you."

Braxov bowed and withdrew.

Josiri sank onto the bed and stared at his reflection in the full-length mirror.

"You need to pull yourself together."

The reflection offered a baleful stare from behind red-rimmed eyes and four-day stubble. Nonetheless, Josiri's spirit lightened. Braxov had offered a connection to home. One tainted by guilt and failure, but a connection nonetheless.

Clothes. Clean clothes would help. Josiri clambered to his feet and examined the contents of the wardrobe. Braxov had understated the selection, and it was a simple matter to find shirt, waistcoat and trousers of a close enough fit.

He took the time to unbundle his few possessions and toyed with the idea of asking Braxov for hot water and a razor, the better to scrape away the bristling ruffian he'd beheld in the mirror. But no. That ritual could wait for the morning. He'd need all the sense of self he could muster if he were to face his new "father" and the redoubtable Ebigail Kiradin. Instead, he kicked off his boots and lay down on the bed, fully intending to collect his thoughts.

A polite knock on the door jarred him to wakefulness.

Josiri levered himself groggily upright and rubbed at his eyes. Beyond the curtains, grey skies had deepened almost to black.

"Uncle Josiri? May I open the door?"

The girl's voice was soft but insistent, not so much posing a question as forewarning of intent.

"Come in."

The door opened a crack. Blonde hair and blue eyes appeared around the frame, the latter alive with amusement. "You've been sleeping."

"Sidara, is it?"

The skirts of her dress gathered in slender hands, she bobbed a curtsey. "Yes, uncle."

There it was again. "I'm not your uncle."

"Mother says you are Uncle Viktor's brother? That's so, isn't it?"

"So I'm told."

"Then you are also my uncle. Not a *real* uncle, but near enough. Or am I to address you as Lord Akadra?"

He winced. "Uncle Josiri will be fine."

"See?" She smiled, leaving Josiri with the distinct impression he'd been outmanoeuvred. "It's very simple after all. I'm sure I'll be your favourite niece."

He couldn't help but smile at her earnestness. "As it happens, you're my only niece."

If the lack of competition troubled Sidara any, none of it showed in her expression. "Father wishes to know if you'll be joining him for dinner."

"Thank your father for his concern, but I'm not hungry."

Lips pursed in an expression of disbelief too old for her face. "I don't believe you."

"I'm truly not." Josiri wondered why he justified himself to a child. "I need rest, that's all."

"I don't believe you." Sidara nodded past his shoulder. "Neither does she."

Josiri frowned and cast a long glance around the bedroom. He saw no one. "Aren't you a little old to have an imaginary playmate?"

"She's not *my* friend. She's *yours*."

Once again, he had the distinct feeling the girl was playing a game of some kind, but there was something in her voice . . . "What does she look like?"

"She's all hollow, with dark eyes like a cyraeth. But she has beautiful white curls. I sometimes wish my hair was curly."

Anastacia. Or at least, Anastacia as she'd once been. "Can I speak to her?"

An eye narrowed in thought. "I don't think she's for talking to. She's more like . . . a memory."

"I don't understand. My memory?"

"*Her* memory. She left it with you for comfort." Sidara stared down at her feet as if suddenly aware of the conversation. "Please don't tell Mother. She'll only get upset."

Josiri blinked away his confusion. How could a memory express disapproval? Probably Sidara had invented that detail in the hopes of getting him to eat. But how had she known Anastacia's appearance? He'd been careful not to speak of her in front of Malachi and Lilyana, for fear of their reaction. What was the alternative? That Ana had indeed left a "memory" with him? An afterimage of the magic that was her flesh? It almost didn't matter. She didn't seem so far away any longer, and he no longer felt as alone.

But one thing was clear: Sidara had been blessed with magic and didn't want her mother to know.

"Uncle Josiri? You mustn't tell her. Please."

A few hours, that was all. He'd been in Tressia for a few hours, and already he was invited to intrigue. Not by Malachi, as he'd feared, but by a girl who looked very much as if the sky was falling.

"What manner of uncle would I be if I couldn't keep a secret?" he said. "Tell your father I'll be down shortly."

Viktor's shadow moaned at the touch of silver, the low, breathy wail more sensation than sound. It wasn't pain – pain he could have ignored – but a crawling, gnawing discomfort that permeated every inch of his being, ephemeral and eternal alike. It hadn't been so bad at first, but after hours in the darkness without other stimuli, it had worn Viktor ragged.

It wasn't the first time Viktor had seen the inside of such a cell. It was his first as a prisoner, stripped to shirt-sleeves and left barefoot in the dank. For more than a hundred years, the vaults had been a site of inquiry and investigation – a testing ground for those accused of demon-hood and witchery. Few examinations ended well.

He shifted position on the narrow stone bench. Beyond the barred window, waves crashed on distant rocks, howling salt-tinged cries on the western wind. Silver shackles about wrists and ankles glinted in scant moonlight. Ropes, he might have ripped free, but not chain. Most certainly not chain bolted to the rock wall. And even if such a thing *were* possible, there was still the locked door and the provosts roaming beyond.

Never mind that even an *attempt* at escape was as good as a confession of guilt. Sun-staves would sear his flesh from bone before he reached the Hayadra Grove high above. And if death didn't find him thus, simarka would be loosed to the hunt.

He could take the risk if it came to it. Better to trust Malachi to see him freed. Or maybe even his father might stir himself to the task? Probably not. He'd sever one branch of the family tree and hope no one sought rot among those that remained. No one could accuse Hadon Akadra of lacking pragmatism, least of all his son. Still, he *would* be free. He had to know what had become of Calenne. To see her again, if she still lived.

A key rattled in the lock. The door creaked open. Viktor tilted his head against the sudden brightness. A robed man entered the cell. He set a firestone lantern on a hook beside the door. He placed two bundles on the table, one of rough cloth and the other in leather binding. Two provosts came in close behind. They took up positions to either side of the door, dulled sun-staves held at guard.

The lead provost drew across a chair from the opposite wall and sat at the table. Stick-thin, he did not so much occupy space as the empti-ness between. An unremarkable man, with greying brown hair and an aquiline nose.

The door slammed.

"Greetings." The man's voice was as nondescript as his appearance. It held neither interest nor anticipation, only boredom. "I don't believe we've had the pleasure. I am Hargo. And you, I believe, are Viktor."

Viktor strove to silence his shadow long enough to form coherent words. "*Lord* Akadra."

Hargo tutted. "Not here. Here, we are all equal in Lumestra's sight. There are no ranks. No titles. There are only her servants of light and those who have strayed." He leaned low across the table, his nose almost touching Viktor's. "We are bound together, you and I. You, the mystery. I, the seeker of revelation."

"You've no cause to test me." The words came slow and heavy, dredged up from behind the implacable grasp of silver.

"So I am often told. So seldom is it true."

Hargo unwrapped the cloth bundle. "*Mysteries of the Raven*, penned by our old friend and probable pseudonym Alain Corbeau." Another followed. "Brathna's *The Undawning Deep*. I confess, I'd always thought this one the stuff of rumour."

Even with his shadow wailing, Viktor sensed the power within the pages. The first book felt cold and clammy, like a brisk sea wind on a hot day. The second ... it hurt to look at the second. No. Not hurt, not exactly. It gnawed. As if it sought to burrow into his soul. Hargo didn't seem to notice.

"What have they to do with me?" Viktor breathed.

"They were found in your chambers."

So much for any hope that this was all a mistake. Someone had planned this. Someone who'd known his secret, or suspected it. Someone who'd convinced Rosa that he was responsible for Kasamor's death. That pointed the finger of guilt at his father, and left Malachi his one hope for salvation.

"They're not mine."

"Of course not." A smile tugged at the corner of Hargo's mouth. "But it's better to be certain. The sooner the mystery is solved, the sooner I can release you back to the Council for the settlement of the more ... commonplace charges."

He stood, and unrolled the leather bundle across the table. A wicked array of spikes and blades glinted silver in the lantern light.

"The path to revelation. Let us seek it together."

Endas, 11th day of Radiance

Do we worship light for its glory, or because darkness too easily breeds suspicion?

Is a righteous man ever truly thus if none bear witness to his deeds?

from the sermons of Konor Belenzo

Forty-Eight

Ebigail Kiradin was a dark shape at the sitting room window, a serathi with a halo of brilliant sunlight. For all that, she remained cold ... distant. As if she touched the world but lightly. But Apara knew all too well that the lightest touch often wrought the greatest change.

"How goes our endeavour?"

Lady Kiradin's voice held an unusual note. Not fear – that the lady might fear anything was unthinkable – but an admission of equality, of shared desire.

"Captain Horden understands the consequences his family will pay for defiance." Even in dawn's light, the elder cousin cast a wispy, indistinct shape. More a shadow-strewn nightmare than a man.

The lady nodded. "And the chapterhouse seneschals?"

"Rother and Mannor will comply. Tassandra is proving ... intractable. The honour of Essamere."

The lady crooked a sour lip. "Honour is a sop to those without power. Have her killed. Something that will pass into rumour."

The cousin's hood tilted, reshaping the shadow beneath. "Another death so soon ... Perhaps a display of largesse would be more appropriate."

"Offer a bribe, and we admit weakness. Weakness invites betrayal." The lady sniffed. "The Republic needs strength more than I need the services of Kaleo Tassandra. Those who survive must understand the single, inflexible truth of our times: that I am not to be defied."

The cousin stiffened, his robes twitching in a non-existent breeze. Apara caught her breath. No one spoke thus to an elder cousin. More than ever, she wished she were elsewhere.

"Have a care, Lady Kiradin," he breathed. "The Parliament of Crows remembers your service, but there is a limit to latitude granted by favours past."

"I agree," the lady replied. "It is the future alone that concerns us. You will fulfil my wishes."

After brief hesitation, he nodded. "Cousin? The task falls to you."

Apara offered a bow. She, at least, knew the difference between a request and an order.

"What of the Grand Council?" asked the elder cousin.

Ebigail snarled. "Hah! The Grand Council is irrelevant. The Grand Council was *always* irrelevant. A talking shop for inbreds unfit for true responsibility. They will fall into line. Everyone will fall into line. We need only give them reason to pause."

Green eyes blazed beneath the hood. "We will not be your footsoldiers."

"I'm well aware of that. Look at you! For all your tricks, a little daylight chills you to the marrow, doesn't it?" She fixed the elder cousin with an iron stare. "The Crowmarket has always clung to the shadows. I am a creature of light, and I'll scour this city clean before I'm done. Work with me a little while longer, and we shall all have what we desire."

The shadows about the elder cousin deepened, the dawn further distant with each quickening beat of Apara's heart. If he ordered Lady Kiradin's death, Apara knew she'd have no choice but to obey. The raven-cloak whispered in anticipation. She pinched her eyes shut and blocked out its voices.

"Will there be anything else?" Ice crackled beneath the elder cousin's words.

"No ... Yes." The lady pressed a finger to pursed lips. "I'd like to retain Apara's services here at Freemont for the immediate future. For contingencies, if you will."

"She is yours."

Apara cursed softly behind an impassive expression.

"Good," said the lady. "Now if you'll both excuse me, I have family business to address."

The cell was dark, and silent but for the crash of waves. Viktor wasn't sure how long he'd hung there, his chained wrists suspended from an iron hook in the ceiling. That was the point. Let isolation work on the mind as surely as fire and silvered steel worked on the body.

Ironic, then, that Viktor welcomed the quiet. It allowed him to bend his full concentration on his shadow, which hissed and spat beneath the silver manacles like a beast before flame. It worried and wearied at Viktor's fading reserves, little caring that its freedom was the very proof Hargo desired.

And so Viktor hung in the near silence, eyes closed and torso sheeted in sweat. His skin crackled and tugged where the sun-staves had seared it. Wounds taken in battle with the Hadari had reopened under the strain, setting bloody rivulets trickling across his skin. And then there were the newer wounds – those opened by silvered needles at the points scripture taught offered access to the soul. Black blood for a black soul. Scarlet for a healthy one.

Thus far, Viktor's had tended towards the scarlet. But if his shadow seeped free, who knew what dark miracles might be wrought?

He strove not to think of past or future, only the moment at hand – and when that moment had gone, the one that replaced it. But each existed only in a haze of pain.

Through the weariness, through the pain, Viktor clung closer to Calenne than ever. He'd see her again, whatever it took.

The cell door creaked open. Viktor opened a blood-crusted eye. Hargo held his leather satchel and a firestone lantern, his escort a sun-stave.

"Good morning, Viktor." As ever, Hargo sounded overwhelmed with tedium. A man doing necessary work, all the while wishing he were elsewhere. "I thought we might renew our conversation?"

"When I get down from here, you'll wish we'd never met."

"Is that so?"

Fire blazed across Viktor's spine – the familiar strike of a sun-stave at the small of his back. Viktor sagged against his manacles. This too was a moment, no longer or shorter than the others he'd endured. This too would pass. He closed his eyes.

The sentries wore the forest green surcoats of the Knights Essamere. For a moment Josiri was back on the battlefield, lost in the shouting, striving mob – fighting beside the survivors of Calenne's charge. Less than a week, and yet more than a lifetime ago.

Malachi took Josiri by the elbow and led him away across the empty drill square.

"You've nothing to fear," he said. "Kaleo Tassandra is an old friend."

Josiri shook his head. Malachi wanted so badly to be liked, and to be trusted. While Josiri had little trouble acceding to the former, he knew the latter would come only with time, if it came at all.

"The mistress of a chapterhouse sounds like a useful friend to have."

But then his mother had thought that too, hadn't she? And at the end, every chapterhouse had betrayed that friendship.

"I'm not good enough for you?" Malachi smiled away his offence. "I'm sure introduction can be arranged. But you'll have to wait until after I've presented you to the Privy Council."

The Privy Council. Josiri told himself the frisson was of anticipation, rather than fear. He still couldn't believe this was happening. Josiri *Akadra*, Duke of Eskavord, heir to the Trelan seat on the Privy Council. A responsibility he knew almost nothing about. Strange how Viktor could be accused of witchcraft and yet his claims of adoption went unchallenged. Then again, there was so much about the city that Josiri found baffling.

"I wish you'd tutor me in protocol," he said.

"I shouldn't worry about it. What precious little there is, Ebigail will almost certainly ignore." He shrugged. "Protocol is for the Grand Council. Pique and hauteur hold rather more sway above."

"Sounds delightful."

"Follow my lead and you'll be fine."

"What about Viktor?"

Malachi's good cheer evaporated. "That's harder. He'll be in the hands of the provosts by now. If we can't persuade Hadon or Ebigail to join us in ordering his release, it won't matter if he's guilty of witchcraft or not. The provosts don't deal in innocence, only guilt. They'll keep delving until they find it, or there's nothing left to answer their questions."

"We're familiar with the technique in the Southshires," Josiri said sourly. "Only there it's applied to more than witchcraft."

"Witch or not, he's my friend," Malachi replied. "Viktor would never abandon me, no matter what the world said of my deeds. How can I abandon him?"

Josiri grimaced. "Is there nothing more we can do?"

"Perhaps. I'm not dragging you about the city for no good reason." He peered over Josiri's shoulder, back towards the stable block and the dressed stone of the officers' lodgings. "And here she is, right on time." He raised his voice. "Lady Orova! Please join us."

Josiri turned. Rosa – clad in full armour and surcoat – halted mid-step at the door to the officers' lodgings. She stifled a frown and strode to join them.

"Lord Reveque." She offered a stiff bow entirely lacking in friendliness and faced Josiri. "I confess, I don't know how I'm to address you."

"I share your confusion. 'Josiri' will serve."

She nodded. "What do you want, Lord Reveque?"

Malachi sighed. "We're not friends any longer, Rosa?"

"Not if you insist on defending Viktor. He's in league with the Crowmarket. He had Kas killed. He ..."

"I'm aware of the charges, just as I'm aware that you chose to keep them from me until it was too late." He set a hand on her shoulder. "What if he's innocent?"

She shrugged him away. "I found the proof myself."

"So Josiri told me. I wish I'd heard it from *you*."

Her eyes narrowed. "Why? So you could convince me I was wrong?"

"Because I'm your friend. Right or wrong, you shouldn't have to bear this burden alone."

It was as impressive a disarmament as Josiri had ever witnessed. A few words and Malachi had bled Rosa's hostility away. The woman left behind had neither the fire of the one who'd marched Viktor away the previous evening, nor the starchily formal manner of she who'd approached them moments before. Now, Rosa just seemed drained.

"What do you want, Malachi?"

"To talk. Only to talk. To hear, in your words, what you've found and what you believe."

"You *do* want to convince me I'm wrong."

"I want to hear your side of things. As I did after Aske Tarev died."

Josiri noted Rosa's flinch – as soon hidden as seen – and wondered what it meant.

"I have duties," she said.

He heard more excuse than substance in the reply. Judging by the wry upturn at the corner of Malachi's mouth, it hadn't gone unremarked by him either. "Tonight, then? At my home? Constans was upset that you left without saying goodbye. This will give you a chance to make it up to him."

"Did you just wield your *child* as a weapon?"

"I'm a politician," sniffed Malachi. "No tactic is beneath me."

Rosa regarded him sadly. "That's just it, old friend. You're too kind. You always have been. You're not cynical enough to see the truth."

"Then make me see. Tonight."

She hesitated. "If that's what you want."

Marek was on his feet, serving tray in his hands, before the bell stopped. He'd expected it. Welcomed it, even. How swiftly routine bedded in. Adapting to new duties was the mark of a good servant. Even when those duties left a sour taste.

An elbow's jab sprung the door, and then he was out of the kitchen and into the hall. Lady Kiradin met him there as she had in past days. As before, her expression gave little clue to the sorrow she had to be feeling. But wasn't that the mark of true nobility? To stay the course even through stormy seas?

Without waiting for instruction, Marek descended the stairs into the basement. There, he set the tray down and turned the heavy key. As the door swung open, he reclaimed the tray and stepped into the dim space beyond.

He stood for a time, waiting for his eyes to adjust. The high, frosted windows gave little light to work with, and left the sheet-draped furnishings little more than ghosts. A room of echoes, where possessions once treasured lurked beyond enquiring eyes.

The chamber's sole inhabitant sat on the narrow bed, back against the wall and one knee braced against the other. Unfriendly eyes gleamed in a filthy face. Rose-petal scent couldn't disguise the bitter stench of a slops bucket.

Lady Kiradin set the door closed with a muffled *thud*. Marek shuffled across the dusty floor and set the tray on the bedside table. The previous night's offering was still there, untouched. How swiftly routine bedded in.

"I see you're still not eating," said Lady Ebigail. "You remain a child, even after all these years."

Lady Sevaka leaned forward. The chain linking her shackled wrist to the iron bedframe went taut. "You needn't pretend concern. Or is it Marek you hope to convince?"

"Marek knows his place," Lady Ebigail snapped. "If only you'd learned yours."

"Oh, poor Mother. Your life *is* hard."

The slap echoed about the chamber. "You will keep a civil tongue!"

Lady Sevaka pressed a palm to her reddened cheek. "Or what? You'll have me murdered, as you did my brother? I didn't want to believe, do you know that? Even when Rosa told me, and I knew without question, I told myself that even you wouldn't go so far."

Marek kept a studiously neutral expression. It wasn't the first time he'd heard the accusation. Lady Sevaka had first levelled it four nights ago, when she'd burst into the kitchen, breathless and thick with fury. She'd repeated it at every opportunity since.

"Kasamor sought to humiliate us all," said Lady Ebigail. "He was weak."

"He was in love!"

"And what good did love ever do anyone?" She shook her head. "I loved my first husband, but he too was weak. Sloppy in his dealings with the Crowmarket. Bad enough that he got caught, but he'd have had me on the gallows beside him. He'd have dragged the whole family down into the mire. Sacrifices must be made."

"You'd compare accusations of treason to a marriage?"

"A *calamitous* marriage. The southwealders are unruly. Divisive. Their lands grow sedition as readily as any crop. The best thing Katya Trelan ever did for the Republic was to get herself killed. And you'd have her brat taint our great family? Our Republic? Just because your brother was smitten?"

Lady Sevaka hung her head and laughed. "Our great family? You betrayed your first husband to the Council. You ordered Kas' death. You had Marek drug me and lock me in here, which I'm sure he enjoyed more than he should have. Did you enjoy laying hands on me, you old letch? You think I've never noticed how you look at me?"

Marek's heart faltered at the venomous words. "Lady Sevaka, I swear ... I'd never ... "

Lady Ebigail cut him off with a chop of her hand. "Enough! Both of you!"

Marek plunged into humiliated silence. He wasn't sure what stung more, daughter's accusation or mother's reprimand.

"Tell me," Lady Sevaka placed each word with weighty precision, "did Father find his way to Otherworld without your help? Or was he too an *embarrassment*?"

"You wicked child! He'd be horrified to hear you ask such a question!"

Lady Sevaka met the icy stare head on. "Yes he would."

Chill silence reigned, with Lady Ebigail either unable or unwilling to speak. Marek bit his tongue, lest he fill the void with renewed protestation. Ironic that Lady Sevaka had found in confinement the courage her mother had wished for her.

"I've always known you were cruel," breathed Lady Sevaka. "I never realised you were mad."

"An accusation levied by hearts too soft for deeds."

"You can't keep me here for ever."

"I've no need. A few days are all I require. Roslava Orova has already played her part. Viktor Akadra will be exposed for what he is."

Lady Sevaka pinched her eyes shut. "I'm sure he's a good man. Otherwise you'd not work so hard to destroy him."

"Have you learnt nothing? This isn't personal. Viktor is the key to ending the divisive nonsense of the Privy Council. He'll drag Hadon and Malachi down by association, and the Republic will finally have a strong, guiding hand."

"You *are* mad if you think the people will stand for it."

"The people?" Lady Ebigail snorted. "The people are cattle. They care only for safety, and for the certainty of their next meal. They will do as instructed, and we shall return to our roots. Our glory."

"And the constabulary? The chapterhouses? The army? They'll all stand by and do nothing?"

"If they don't, there will be a regrettable period of violence. And I shall be most disappointed in the Parliament of Crows' ability to deliver on its promises."

Lady Sevaka's dry, mirthless laugh echoed about the chamber. "These are the foundations of your glorious age? Threats? Blackmail? Intimidation? It would be funny if so many people weren't to die in order to prove you wrong."

Lady Ebigail knelt and laid a hand on her daughter's knee. "You'll see the matter differently when it's over. You and I can begin again, and you will learn to be what the Republic requires of you."

"And if I choose not to?"

"I've no wish to lose you, Sevaka. With your brother gone, you're all I have left. But do not test me."

"Oh, Mother." Sevaka shook her head. "How can it be that I understand you so well, and you understand me so poorly? I'm done trying to please you."

Lady Ebigail rose, her face once more set solid as granite. "We shall see. Eat. Or I will have Marek feed you."

She strode away, wisps of dust kicking up at her heels. The door opened, then slammed.

Marek stooped to recover the first, untouched tray. Lady Sevaka's baleful stare bored into him every inch of the way.

"Why do you serve her?" she asked.

He winced and straightened. That he'd done his duty by his mistress didn't mean he was proud of his actions. But what else was he to have done? "On my life, Lady Sevaka, I did nothing that was not your mother's instruction."

Her free hand closed over his wrist. "Answer me."

Willpower melted beneath the earnest stare. "Because I love her, as I love you. You're like a daughter to me."

The words were a mistake. He knew it at once. But that was still an age too late. He glanced away, only to find himself drawn back to that stare.

"A daughter." Lady Sevaka shook her wrist. The chain jangled. "You've abused my trust in almost every way possible. If that weren't a Freemont tradition with daughters, I'd laugh in your face."

She drew him in until his face was inches from hers. Stale breath washed across his cheeks. "You heard my mother. Love never did anyone any good. You've seen how she treats her own blood. What prospects for you? Run from this house, Marek. Because if my mother doesn't kill you, I surely will."

She shoved him away. The tray tipped as Marek lost his balance. He caught the plate of meat and congealed vegetables before it slid free. Cutlery scattered across the floor. A mug shattered on tile.

Marek righted himself and gathered what he could back onto the tray. "Lady Sevaka ..."

She rested her head against the wall and closed her eyes. "Just go, Marek. As far and fast as you can."

Tears stinging his cheeks, he fled the chamber.

Forty-Nine

Eskavord's marketplace remained a drab, empty expanse, frequented only by occupation patrols and a handful of shuffling, dead-eyed southwealders. Kurkas held lonely vigil from beneath the lychgate, crutch tucked close, and cloak wrapped tight.

The soldiers barely acknowledged his presence; the southwealders ignored him entirely. At least the air was crisp beneath the overcast skies and the rain gone. More and more, Kurkas had the sense that something beyond the obvious was wrong in Eskavord, though he couldn't quite put his finger on what.

"Better to have burned the whole bloody place last time around."

"Be careful," counselled a soft voice. "The archimandrite doesn't need ideas."

Kurkas turned. Yanda stood among the skeletal yews of the outer churchyard. She looked older than he remembered.

Lot of that going around.

He shrugged. "Way I hear it, Makrov's never short of ideas. And Makrov needs Eskavord, doesn't he? It's a trophy – proof that his eminent self was right all along."

She drew closer along the waterlogged path. "Not much of a trophy."

"Makrov's not got much in the way of standards."

"You want to be careful who hears that, too."

"I can look after myself."

"That's a common sentiment hereabouts." Her tone darkened. "It seldom ends well."

Kurkas searched her eyes for a clue to her mood. "That a threat, governor?"

"Not a threat, and not a governor. Makrov holds the title now." She offered a wry, weary smile. "Captain Shaisan Yanda at your service, and his excellency has made it very clear I'm fortunate to be that."

"Compared to some, certainly."

She shrugged. "You think I don't wish there'd been another way?"

"Never been one for wishes, governor. I prefer actions."

"And what actions bring you to Eskavord?"

Again, that slight edge to her voice. Could he trust it? Better not to. "Just taking a look around. Basking in the glories of victory."

Her eyes tightened. "Will you do something for me, one captain to another?"

"Long as it's within hailing distance of common decency."

"When you see Lord Akadra – either Lord Akadra – tell him I'm sorry. I should have done more."

For the first time, Kurkas heard a note of genuine regret. "Might be you're not out of chances."

"I don't think so. Don't you feel it? This will get worse before it gets better." She shook her head. "Whatever brings you to Eskavord, have a care not to get caught."

Halvor was hunched over Elda's kitchen table when Kurkas returned, a steaming mug clasped between white-knuckled hands. Elda sat in the corner, arms folded and her expression that of a woman whose worst suspicions were coming true.

"You'd better have cleaned your boots this time," she growled.

He lifted a foot to give her clear sight of a filthy and threadbare sock. "Boots are in the hall. So's the cloak. And I'm fine, thanks for asking." He hobbled over to the table. "How about you?"

Halvor stared up at him. "Like a scarecrow left out through Wintertide."

"You look it."

And she did. Though her eyes lacked the confusion they'd held when Elda had set her to bed, they were dark-rimmed and weary – as if she could fall back into slumber at any moment. And her skin . . . so pale as to be almost grey. Just like every other miserable body lurching its way through Eskavord. At least there was a smile, or rather the ghost of one.

"You're nothing special yourself."

He sniffed and pulled out a chair. "And whose fault is that? Did you at least get some sleep?"

Halvor took a pull on her tea. "I think so, for all the good it's done."

"At least you're done mistaking this handsome face for someone else."

"Elda told me. I'm sorry. I can't explain it."

"Nothing to explain." Kurkas tapped the side of his head. "Age is a terrible thing."

Eyes closed to slits. "Say that again."

"Your ears playing up too?" He shrugged away a venomous glare. "You're sounding more like yourself. I'll take that."

She sighed and set the mug down. "I wish I felt it."

Elda laughed to herself. "There's no sense wishing for anything, nor weeping." She snorted, the derision palpable in her voice. "As if tears ever counted for anything."

Kurkas leaned back in his chair and regarded her with distaste. At least someone in Eskavord found a mote of pleasure in events. She and Makrov would likely get on like a house on fire. Now *that* was a happy thought. He'd even supply the flame.

Elda held his gaze for a long moment. Then she shuffled in her chair and stared pointedly out across the garden. "You should go."

At last, they agreed on something. Especially in light of what Yanda had insisted was *not* a threat. "Yeah. We'd better get moving . . . " Kurkas glanced at Revekah. " . . . if you feel up to it."

"You misunderstand me, young man," said Elda. "*You* should go. Revekah can stay. This is her home. This is where she belongs."

Halvor winced an apology. "Elda . . . "

"Why should I leave?" Kurkas interrupted breezily. "Everyone's so friendly hereabouts."

"Why should you stay?" snapped Elda. "There's nothing you can do. Eskavord is beyond ephemeral aid."

"Right barrel of cheer, ain'tcha? You're just as bad as Yanda."

Halvor frowned. "Yanda?"

"We crossed paths. Looks like a woman who traded her soul to old Jack and got stiffed on the deal."

Halvor closed her eyes. "Maybe she didn't have a choice."

"You believe that? With everything you've lived through?"

"No. I suppose not."

Kurkas couldn't quite put his finger on why he hated Yanda's attitude so much. Maybe Elda was right. Maybe he should leave before he found his own hanging spot on Gallows Hill. But not yet. First he'd get Halvor to Branghall. Because as much as he didn't want the life of a south-wealder rebel, he fancied Yanda's hollow-eyed and impotent stare far less.

"You ready to get out of here?"

Revekah shot Elda a sidelong glance. "Yes."

To Kurkas' mind, every step carried them further from their destination. Every inch of forest looked much the same: bedraggled and as morose as he was steadily coming to feel. It didn't help that every root and briar seemed determined to entangle his crutch. At least it was drier beneath the branches, give or take.

"You sure you know where you're going?" he shouted. "Some guide you are."

Halvor offered an acerbic stare. "We can't go marching up to the front gate. Which means we need another way in."

"Ah, the thrilling secrets of the southwealder resistance. Should I feel honoured?"

"If you like. Scratched hands and skinned knees. *If* you're up to it."

Climbing the wall. Child's play for a man with two functioning arms and legs. Not so easy for a fellow with half that tally. Not that he'd any need to cross the wall himself. Main thing was to get Revekah inside.

"I can go anywhere you can, old woman."

"Don't look so worried. There's a section to the north that's barely hanging together. It's only the enchantment keeping anything out."

At least the brightening sky offered hope. It was too easy to lose track of time within the gloom. Seemed the sun always shone on Branghall.

"Looks like we're nearly there."

Halvor nodded and propped herself against a birch tree, head resting against her forearm. The hike through the forest had done little to bring colour to her cheeks, and her chest shuddered with every breath. Not for the first time, Kurkas wondered if it would have been kinder to leave her with Elda. Whatever ailed her was taking its toll.

"Why are you doing this?" she asked.

He snorted. "Anything to get out of Eskavord. That place is a suffocating mess."

"That's not what I meant, and you know it. Why are you helping me? If Makrov finds out it won't end well."

He sank against an oak and breathed deep of the soft, sweet air. "I'm not afraid of Makrov."

"Maybe you should be. Weak men given licence are always more dangerous than the strong."

"Could be."

He fell silent, knowing he'd given no answer worth the breath, but not really knowing how to supply a better.

"I'm sorry about your arm, and your eye."

Halvor uttered the apology with such deliberate, genuine warmth that Kurkas couldn't help but smile. "A soldier's fate. If it wasn't you, it'd have been someone else. And if it wasn't me, it'd have been you. A wound or two always draws interest. Especially if the lads are impressionable."

The familiar scowl returned to weary eyes. "Do you take nothing seriously?"

"Life's too short for that, Halvor." He shrugged. "Better to die with a smile than live with a frown."

"Life's too short for anything nowadays. I thought Katya and I would change the world, and now see me." She shook her head. "Shouldn't be far. Just over the next rise. You mind taking a look? See if Makrov's got anyone patrolling the perimeter? I need to catch my breath."

Kurkas rolled his good eye and stood straight once more. "That's right, leave the back-and-forth to the cripple. Just don't fall asleep on me again. You hear me, Captain Halvor?"

"I hear you, Captain Kurkas."

Branghall's clock chimed noon. Makrov peered in the tarnished mirror and straightened his circlet of office. In Yanda's opinion, the stylised sun-disc on his brow lent an altogether cheerier air than merited, just as the rich scarlet robes lent his presence a weightier authority than deserved. As for the three robed serenes he'd handpicked from Eskavord's choir to serve as his attendants? Their downcast gazes suggested boredom more than respect. Or perhaps it was disgust.

"Are the crowds ready?" intoned Makrov.

Yanda glanced through the balcony doors of the reeve's manor. The marketplace was fuller than it had been in days – proof that Makrov's threats concerning non-attendance had taken root. Better a few minutes harking at the archimandrite's rhetoric than a gallows jig.

"Ready," she confirmed, "but I suspect not eager."

With a final nudge of the circlet, he turned from the mirror and took his sceptre from a serene. "They will learn, Shaisan. They must *all* learn."

Yanda's eyes tracked across the miserable crowd, dancing from miserable expression to miserable expression. "Are you sure this is wise?"

Makrov's cheek twitched. "Ebigail Kiradin bade me show strong leadership – the sort that *you* failed to provide. The southwealders scattered these seeds. The harvest is long overdue."

Yanda felt something break, deep inside. "This isn't strength! It's spite! If you really cared, you'd help them heal. Look at them – they're beaten! They won a war no one believed they could, and you're busy grinding them into the mud for it."

Makrov's shoulders shook. His jowls ruddied. "You've been here too long, Shaisan. You're thinking like one of them."

"I wish that were true. I lack their courage. This, and this alone, is a trait you and I share."

Impossibly, Makrov's face darkened further. He stalked towards her, teeth parted and lips atremble.

"You will stand with me for today's address," he spat. "After that, you may go wherever you wish. Ride north to your family. You can grub about in the woodlands with these malcontents you so admire. But you are relieved of duty and title, do you understand me?"

Part of Yanda heard the words for the death knell of a dying career that they were. What remained soared free on golden wings. "Oh yes, excellency."

*

Revekah slumped wearily against the birch tree. Kurkas wouldn't be long, but she needed only a little time.

She crooked her knee and slid the dagger from its ankle sheath. Kurkas wouldn't understand. He'd try to stop her. And she couldn't explain. How did you explain a feeling? She knew only that something inside her had awoken. Something that didn't belong, and yet was as much a part of her as her memories. It had been growing since the battle, but had quickened to a gallop once she'd set foot in Eskavord.

She set the blade to the pulsing vein in the side of her neck and closed her eyes. Was this how Katya had felt at the end? Fitting, somehow, that they walked the same path even now.

"So you know?"

The woman stood among the trees, dark and pale all at once. Hair danced in a non-existent wind. A tattered, fibrous dress clung close about her legs and bare feet. Her face was Revekah's own, but as it had been years before the ravages of age took their toll. The image flickered and crackled, as if she wasn't truly there. A hallucination? Or a mind's last, desperate trick as it fell under another's sway?

"I knew you were coming," she breathed.

"That's why you sent him away?"

She sounded like Elda. Like Calenne. Like Tarn. Like Katya. Even like Crovan. Like Crovan most of all. Sounded like all of them, and none of them. A hollow voice billowing with a thousand souls. A voice for which there could be only one name. Malatriant. Revekah supposed she should have been terrified to come face-to-face with a legend, but she was too cold, and too weary.

"Maybe I just wanted some privacy?" No. No lies. Not now. "He's a good man. He deserves better."

"He deserves whatever I choose."

"Why?"

"Because that *is* what I choose." Malatriant drew closer. Her stolen face melted away into Katya's likeness, her lips curling into that beautiful, long-lost smile. "Your town is built on my bones. My ash is in your blood. I know you're tired. I know you want to let go. That's why you came home to me, is it not?"

Somehow, Revekah found the strength to answer. "No."

"You're the last, Revekah. The others have embraced me. My children. My fading ash. So worn down by pettiness and jealousy. They longed for me to take their burdens. Now we are one – as all were one before the light divided us."

The dagger dipped in Revekah's hand, as if the weight of the world rested atop its pommel.

"I've fought all my life," she gasped. "I won't stop now."

"You will. We are one. We are all one in the Dark."

Malatriant knelt. Cold fingers drew Revekah into an embrace. The dagger slipped from her numbed hand.

Yanda felt it as soon as she stepped onto the balcony. The mood of the crowd was different. Sharper. *Expectant.* She couldn't see it in their faces, but it was there. As certain as the wind in the trees or the fall of night.

Even Makrov felt it. He stumbled at the balcony's edge in unfamiliar hesitation. "People of Eskavord! Blessed Lumestra has sent me before you this day! I—"

"Enough!"

The outburst cut through Makrov's affronted splutters. "Who dares?"

Yanda peered out into the crowd, straining without success to see the speaker.

"By Lumestra's light, you will show yourself!" bellowed Makrov.

"The light?" came the reply. "The light has no hold on Eskavord. Not any longer."

Yanda suppressed a shiver, though she couldn't decide if the speaker's certainty provoked the reaction, or her voice. There was something about the timbre ... something she couldn't quite identify.

Makrov leaned out over the balcony, knuckles whitening around the balustrade. "Guards! Find the heretic! She'll repent her wickedness!"

One-sided commotion broke out as the soldiers peeled away from the perimeter and entered the marketplace proper. One-sided, for no one resisted. Men and women, young and old, they merely stared up at the balcony with empty, expectant expressions.

In the centre of the marketplace the crowd parted, flowing away across the cobbles like waves retreating across shingle. A lone figure stood in the clearing – an aging woman who stood with the aid of a curved stick. Yanda scrabbled for a name in the recesses of memory. Elda Savka. An ally of the Trelan family years back, but a model citizen since Katya's death.

"They don't belong to you. They are mine, and I theirs," pronounced Elda. "You have my thanks. So many broken spirits searching for solace. You drove them back to me. The work of years accomplished in days. All that I do now, you made possible. Now we are all one in the Dark."

"*We are all one in the Dark,*" the crowd echoed. They stared up at the balcony with glittering black eyes.

Yanda's blood ran cold. "Makrov ..."

But if Makrov understood how badly things were amiss, none of it pierced his apoplexy.

"You think I'm intimidated by games?" Spittle flecked the corner of his mouth. His bunched fist strove against empty air. "I'll break you all for this! You'll beg for another exodus! Guards! I want that woman! Now!"

Elda smiled. As one, the crowd turned on the guards in their midst with clawing hands and bludgeoning fists. Steel glinted through the rain. Screams rang out. Southwealders fell, blood streaming from their wounds. Others pressed on with implacable purpose.

Yanda gazed in horror. "Do something!"

Makrov stood frozen at the balcony's edge, mouth agape in a suddenly pallid face.

"Fall back!" she shouted. "Get out of there! Mobilise the garrison!"

It was an age too late. All a mob needed to overcome its cage was selfless purpose, and the southwealders had that and more to spare. One by one, the soldiers drowned beneath a tide of bloodied flesh. Then the mob turned its attention on the perimeter. With a deep, keening growl it surged forth. Screams began anew.

Elda stood unmoving, her gaze locked on the balcony. "Do you understand now?"

Yanda gripped her sword's hilt. It offered no comfort. A cold hand closed about her heart.

The mob converged on the reeve's manor. The main door burst apart with a wrenching crash.

Makrov moaned and staggered away from the balcony's edge. "No. This can't be happening."

He ran for the door. The serenes moved to bar his way in a swirl of black silk. The eldest led the way, the younger pair matching her graceful stride in strict unison. The cultivated innocence of moments before turned stony and bleak.

"Hush, my lord archimandrite." Dark eyes glittered beneath gossamer veils. "Have dignity in your last moments."

With a garbled scream, he hurled the nearest serene aside. She struck the balustrade and vanished into the rainswept evening without a sound. The two who remained stood voicelessly aside as the door burst outward beneath the mob. Grasping hands closed about flailing scarlet robes.

"Shaisan! Help me! I order you to . . . "

Makrov's impassioned cry gave way to dull wet thuds. Screams subsided to whimpers and fell silent. His killers straightened. Coal-black eyes bored into Yanda's.

Her hand fell from her sword. What was the point?

"Who are you?" Her breath stuttered in her throat, but the terrible, paralysing fear had gone. Fear was born of possibility. It held no sway against the inevitable. "*What* are you?"

The youngest serene wiped a bloody hand on her black dress. "You know my name. Will you join them in the Dark? You are not hated as he was hated. If you ask, I will permit it."

Yanda stared skyward. She'd have given anything for a glint of sunshine. "Lumestra is my light."

The serene cocked her head. "Then you die a fool."

Kurkas lumbered wearily into the dell. Halvor, upright when he'd left her, sat between the roots of a mournful-looking birch. Her chin rested on her chest.

He swore under his breath. "Don't you do this to me. Not now."

He let the crutch fall. Torn muscles screamed in protest as he fell to his knees beside her. "Come on, Halvor. You better not have upped and died."

He pressed a hand to her neck. A pulse throbbed beneath his fingers.

"That's what I thought," he lied. "You're a tough old bird."

Kurkas caught the dagger's glint out of his peripheral vision. He threw himself aside. Steel arced past his belly. He landed heavily in the mud. Felt a hot rush as a wound in his gut tore open anew.

Stupid. Stupid. Stupid. Shouldn't have crept up on her like that.

"Raven's Eyes," he gasped. "You trying to kill me?"

Halvor rose to her feet. Glittering black eyes gazed into his. "I told you to leave."

Yes. Yes she was.

Kurkas couldn't even begin to tally everything wrong with that moment. He didn't even try. He'd been too long a soldier not to know death when it beckoned.

He shoved. She went backwards with a hollow cry and fell face-first into the mud. The dagger skidded away. Kurkas grabbed for his crutch and hobbled away, redoubling his pace as a shout rang out behind.

He'd no illusions about his chances in a fight. Not with his litany of injuries, and the renewed fire blazing in his gut. Nor did he reckon much to his prospects for hiding. As for outrunning her? Hah! He'd never been a runner, not on his best day.

Branghall was now his only hope. His lungs burned before he'd covered even half the distance. Feet skidded in the mud. Somehow he turned each near catastrophe into fresh momentum, driving him forward step by agonising step.

The trees peeled away as he reached the outer wall.

Half-blinded by the rain, Kurkas angled for the fallen oak and the spill of crumbled masonry where the tree had struck the wall in years past. Golden light sparked and shimmered across the slighted crest. Even part-collapsed, it meant a climb of some twelve feet up a surface offering sparse purchase.

Kurkas let the useless crutch fall away and clambered up the oak. His good foot slipped on sodden moss and shot away. Desperate fingers closed around a worm-eaten bole. A knee braced against a barren limb. He kept climbing.

"There's no escaping this."

The hollow timbre of the words – Revekah's voice, and yet not – washed up from below. Breath rattling in his lungs, Kurkas glanced down. Halvor stood at the foot of the oak, hair plastered across her scalp.

"No harm in trying!"

Somehow, he reached the junction of tree and wall without sliding clear. Faced with an impossible climb and death below, Kurkas did the only thing he could – he hurled himself at the wall with the defiance of a doomed man. Scratched, bloody fingers scrambled for purchase between the stones and grasped at ivy. He kicked at crumbling mortar to create toeholds.

His heart lurched every time his fingers let go and gravity dragged him outward, only to thunder back when he found scrabbled handhold. He was only ever one slip, one misjudgement, one moment of weakness from disaster.

And yet somehow, disaster never came. His straining hand found the wall's capstone. With one last, heroic effort, he dragged his heaving chest onto the crest.

The skin on his cheeks tingled as it passed through the enchantment. The crisp, sweet air beyond filled ravaged lungs. And the light! It was like passing through a waterfall's veil. Within, Branghall lay resplendent in sunshine. The ward-brooch pulsed on his chest.

Throat thickening to disbelieving laughter, Kurkas hooked a knee on the crest.

A hand closed around his trailing ankle. Kurkas bellowed as tortured flesh gained new burdens. He slid his knee off the wall and lashed out.

The heel of his boot thumped into Halvor's head. She spun away, her grip broken. With a final, desperate heave, Kurkas hauled his legs over the crest and stared without enthusiasm at the twenty-foot drop into overgrown gardens.

The cloak went taut across his shoulders. Halvor's hand closed about his wrist. His precarious balance shattered, Kurkas realised with iron-clad certainty that he was going to fall. Outward or inward were his only choices.

With his last strength, he pushed off. Halvor cried out in alarm as his weight dragged her over the crest. The thorn-laden flowers of the gardens reached up, tearing at his clothes and flesh.

Darkness rushed in.

Fifty

The chapel cellar had gone undisturbed since Nikros' judgement. The bloodstained blankets lay piled at the foot of the bed, the bright stains soured to murky browns. Her nose wrinkling in disgust, Apara gave the bed a wide berth and crossed to the back wall. The heel-marks still marred the dust, as did Apara's own footsteps from that awful night. The elder cousins had left no sign of their presence. They never did.

She laid a hand on the wall and drew strength from the roughness of cracked plaster and brick. Tangible. Real. A world away from raven-cloaks and elder cousins. From the path she had to tread. She wanted to turn back. Wanted it so badly she feared her heart might give out. But she was a kernclaw. She had duties to her cousins. If she left them unfulfilled . . .

Apara took a deep breath, filling her lungs with the musty air, and roused the spark of magic that was the Raven's gift. It rippled through her, ecstatic and foreboding. The wall fell away into a mist-wreathed arch.

She snatched back her hand. The world beyond the archway was different: gone was the ornate tomb and the ominous black walls, replaced by a narrow street whose upper storeys vanished into skies dancing with viridian light.

More importantly, there was no sign of *him*. She couldn't have gone through with it otherwise – would sooner have made a daylight assault on the Essamere chapterhouse than tread the mists with the Raven at her side. Bad enough that the washed-out streets were thick with the spirits of the dead. The chill air of the place that was no place shortened her breath even from beyond the arch.

Otherworld was no place for the living, not even for a kernclaw – much less a reluctant one. Time flowed strangely within, hours passing like minutes, or minutes like days. And the pathways were treacherous. Though the entrances to Otherworld were fixed – determined by where the walls between worlds ran thin – it was easy to run astray, lured from the path by temptation or fear. All vranakin knew that. It was the stuff of harrowing legend. But turning back meant failure. And the stark scrape of heels across the dusty floor laid bare those consequences.

Drawing the raven-cloak close, Apara stepped through the arch.

The Privy Council chamber stank of dwindling and dust. From the oversized map that proclaimed dominance of provinces long since lost, to the escutcheons of noble lines long since faded, it spoke of minds mired in a golden age more fantasy than historical fact. No wonder the Tressian Council clung so tight to tradition. It belonged more to the past than the present.

The sword in the centre of the table struck a jarring note. Melanna Saran's blade shone brilliantly even in the gloom.

"I greet you, Josiri. But I do not welcome you." If Ebigail Kiradin's voice held any more warmth than her expression, it was by the barest margin. "Your mother tore this Republic in two. We need no more troublemakers at this table."

Josiri had known Kasamor well enough to like him, and saw little of the mother in the son. She seemed perfectly in place in that chamber, a flesh and blood relic surrounded by those of wood and stone.

"I came here only to put the past behind us." He chose his words with absolute care. "Why else would I embrace Viktor as a brother?"

Hadon Akadra snorted. "To spare yourself a cage, I've no doubt."

Here at least the apple had not fallen so far from the tree. The elder Akadra was very much a greyer, worn version of the younger. He was no friendlier in manner than Ebigail, and made little attempt to conceal his dislike.

"Not so, Father." Josiri felt a surge of wild glee as Hadon's eyes narrowed at the unwanted – but entirely proper – form of address. "I'm sure Viktor would confirm that, were he here."

"So I'm Father to you now, am I?" growled Hadon. "If you'd any inkling of that bond's importance, you'd have presented yourself to me last night, and not left Sergeant Brass to bring tidings."

Malachi shot Josiri a warning look from across the table. Even before the meeting, he'd warned that Hadon might seek grounds to annul the adoption. Such efforts were seldom invoked, but not unheard of.

"I did only as Viktor instructed, Father." Again Josiri took silent revel in Hadon's distaste. Being accounted an Akadra had become bearable knowing that Hadon hated the idea even more than he. "I thought it best to respect his wishes, but I'll gladly forgo Malachi's hospitality in favour of yours."

Hadon drew himself up, a stiffness of his shoulders betraying fresh discomfort. "That isn't necessary. Though I'll of course see you quartered at Swanholt, if you wish it."

Josiri decided not to dwell on the twin meanings of the word "quartered". "I'd as soon not be a burden to you until I'm more familiar with my new home. Viktor assured me it wouldn't take long."

Ebigail's thin fingers drummed on the table top. "I'm afraid young Viktor's word is not all it was. Accusations of treason, corruption – even complicity in the death of my beloved son."

She glanced away and pressed a bunched handkerchief to her lips. The lines around her eyes softened. Then she rallied, the handkerchief tucked deftly away, and the patrician air back in full force. "I shall feel a keen sense of betrayal if it transpires that Kasamor died because Viktor was jealous of his good fortune with your sister."

Josiri bit back a flare of resurgent worry at Calenne's fate, and wished he'd taken the opportunity on the journey north to pry information from Viktor. Take Kasamor. All Josiri knew of the man's murder was what Ebigail had included in her perfunctory letter.

Hadon thumped the table, setting porcelain teacups jingling in saucers. "Dammit, Ebigail! That's my son you're talking about."

Her lip curled. "He wouldn't be the first traitor to drag his family into the gutter. And as for those *other* accusations . . ."

Malachi cleared his throat. "Speaking of which, I'd hoped we might prevail on the provosts to halt their enquiries until these other, *criminal*, matters are settled. If Viktor *is* a traitor – and I pray that he is not – then his offences against the Council must take precedence."

"I disagree," said Ebigail. "Witchery is an affront to Lumestra, and this council is an instrument of her will."

What would she say, Josiri wondered, if she knew Lumestra had perished long ago, torn apart by her daughters? "I concur with Malachi's assessment. If for no other reason than we shall all look foolish if we can't hang Viktor for a traitor if the provosts have already burned him."

Malachi shot him a look only fractionally less sour than Ebigail's. Josiri paid them both no heed. If gallows humour kept him from angry outburst, then he'd gladly indulge it.

"Father?"

Hadon shared a glance with Ebigail and stared down at his clasped hands. The elder Akadra resembled nothing so much as a greying wolf-hound whose master had just yanked his leash.

"I regret that I cannot agree," he said. "I cannot open myself to accusations of using status to protect my son."

Malachi half-rose from his chair. "Hadon ... "

Hadon's unhappy stare snapped. "Do not test me on this! I will not follow Viktor's supposed corruption with the certainty of my own. Sometimes silence is the only acceptable course. You're a father, Malachi. Pray you never find yourself in my position."

"Lord Reveque! A moment of your time."

A vision in scuffed leathers, Elzar hurried along the palace corridor at a pace seldom employed by a fellow of the high proctor's rank.

Malachi tapped Josiri on the shoulder and nodded towards the knot of hearthguard waiting nearby. "Go. I won't be long. And, Josiri? Don't be downhearted. You and I are going to change things. I promise."

Josiri withdrew with a weariness Malachi himself felt all too keenly after long hours in the company of Ebigail Kiradin.

Malachi forced a smile and grasped Elzar's proffered hand. "High Proctor. I'm afraid I've little progress to report on your ... inventory issues."

Reports aired only hours before had made it clear that the joint patrols of constabulary and seconded hearthguard had turned up only the pettiest of criminals. No stolen kraikons, no crowmarketeers, and no consensus in council as to how to proceed. Hadon had been all for widening the search, but Ebigail debated the issue with scarcely contained boredom – a stance Malachi would have found more detestable if he'd not felt similar apathy. A man had only so much attention to invest.

Elzar took his arm and steered him to an alcove sporting a stern marble bust of Konor Belenzo.

"I heard Viktor's been taken by the provosts," he muttered. "Is it true?"

Relief and renewed disappointment mingled in Malachi's veins. "Shouldn't I be asking you, *high proctor*?"

"We both know my colleagues are bound to a certain … secrecy of action. Just as we both know it's poor manners to evade an honest question."

"My apologies. I've spent much of the day in council – some of it failing to secure Viktor's release."

Salt and pepper brows knotted. Elzar's face wrinkled. "You must find a way."

"I know. A provost's inquisition never ends in acquittal. Innocence is only proven in death."

"You misunderstand." Elzar dropped his voice another notch. "They'll not kill him for what he is not, but for what he *is*."

Malachi glanced hurriedly about. "You can't be serious. Elzar, do you know what you're saying?"

"Better than you, my lord."

"You're telling me Viktor *deserves* this!"

Wrinkles reknitted into a scowl. "Do you believe that?"

Malachi's thoughts raced. Yes. No. Viktor. A witch. An abomination in Lumestra's sight. His friend. It was too much to take in. He felt dizzy with it. "I don't know."

"I told you before. A gift is a gift. It's the use that separates wicked from divine. Darkness. Light. They're excuses. Or do you hold all proctors to be paragons of virtue simply because we wield the light?" He gave a sharp smile. "The archimandrite, perhaps, for his unwavering faith?"

"What do you want me to do?" Malachi hissed. "I can't storm into the vaults and demand his release, not without the backing of the Council. And even Viktor's own father won't lend his support."

"No, I suppose not. Forgive me, my lord. I've spoken out of turn."

"I'm glad you did," Malachi lied. "At least now I know the truth of things."

So why did he feel hollow to his very marrow?

Even bloodied and blind, the knight battered at Apara with a gauntleted fist. Tightening her grip about his head, she rammed a knee into his back and drove his throat onto her claws. The lightest of pressures, the softest of tugs. His defiant bellow gasped into a stuttering gurgle.

She let the twitching body fall and slumped to one knee in the thinning mists, barely able to breathe for the hot scent of fresh blood. Her cloak, her garb – even her skin was thick with it. Her stomach spasmed, held in check only by the tatters of her fading will.

She stared at Kaleo Tassandra's corpse, lying in a dark pool strewn with papers scattered from the office desk. She didn't even remember killing the Mistress of Essamere. There was only the rush of wings, the exhilaration of slaughter. She recalled scant else of the others. Five knights, trained warriors all, and she – Apara Rann, who'd never taken a life until a week prior – had slain them all as naturally as drawing breath.

They'd not even landed a blow.

The younger her, the one who'd struggled to thrive mired in Dregmeet's myriad rivalries, would have rejoiced. The older, more seasoned woman knew better. What was she becoming? What was the cloak making of her?

Urgent voices stirred her from misery. The cloak whispered hungrily, urging her to stay. Worse, a piece of her wanted to.

Apara reached trembling fingers to the wall. A bloody handprint smeared across whitewashed plaster and fell away into Otherworld's mists.

As she stumbled into the ghost-crowded streets beyond, she felt a presence at her shoulder.

"Impressive, my dear," whispered the Raven. "Very impressive. You might have a knack for this."

Apara yelped and spun around, ghosts parting before her. But the Raven – if indeed he'd ever been more than a figment conjured from a mind sick with terror and disgust – had gone.

Head swimming with nausea, she fled into the mists.

Fifty-One

"Halvor!"

Kurkas shot bolt upright, hand flailing for support at the bedside. He bided a moment, feeling ridiculous at his outburst. Fortunately, the room was empty. And what a room it was. Faded grandeur was grandeur nonetheless, and Kurkas reckoned the furniture alone had cost more than he'd earned in thirty years.

Branghall. He had to be in Branghall. But where was Halvor? What in Queen's Ashes had gotten into her? And that voice ... Like the spaces between the slivers of the soul.

He prised himself out of bed and found his clothes – dry, but still dusty with mud – slung over the back of a chair. Dressing swiftly as injuries permitted, he stalked into the hallway. His wounded leg bore weight better than he'd expected. Still, he propped himself against the wall every few paces, leaving dusty smears against the faded paintwork.

A soldier in the king's blue of the 12th intercepted him halfway down the corridor.

"Captain Kurkas, you're awake?"

Kurkas didn't recognise the youth, though clearly his own appearance hadn't drifted so far into vagabondage that he'd gone unrecognised. Then again, he *was* somewhat distinctive. "So it'd seem, lad."

"Lieutenant Brask would like to speak with you."

He nodded. The head of Branghall's garrison lay roughly third in line of Kurkas' priorities, after Halvor and Anastacia, but you took matters as you found them. "I'm sure he ... "

"She, sir."

" . . . she does. Lead on."

The soldier led Kurkas along the hallway, down a narrow set of servants' stairs and thence into a small library with high windows. A young woman glanced up from the desk as Kurkas entered, then scrambled to her feet.

"Captain Kurkas. Glad to see you up and about. Given your injuries, I wasn't sure . . . "

Kurkas sank gratefully into a fraying armchair, its leather cool where it touched his skin. "Thought I was soft, just because I'm a hearthguard, and not a 'proper' soldier?"

Brask's lips pinched tight. "Not at all. I meant no offence."

But nor did she see fit to offer the honorific that went with superior rank. Too young to realise that the differences between hearthguard and regular army were of little account, and too arrogant to offer proper deference.

Brask stared past Kurkas to the doorway, where his escort still waited. "Dastarov? I'm sure our guest's hungry."

"Sir." Dastarov bowed and withdrew.

Brask rounded the desk and perched on its outer edge. "What were you doing climbing the wall?"

"Trying to get in."

"We've a gate for that."

Kurkas scratched at his eyepatch. Brask didn't sound suspicious, though you never could tell. "Weren't possible, given the circumstances . . . The woman. Where is she?"

Brask snorted. "The southwealder? We've turned a wine cellar into a jail, just for her. Two of my lot had to drag her off you."

"Did they now?" Kurkas stared at his feet. His last hope that he'd somehow misremembered events crumbled to dust. It shouldn't have mattered, but it did. "She seem normal to you?"

"By whose standards?" Brask shook her head. "Southwealders aren't like the rest of us. They're barbarians, little better than the Hadari."

Should he ask about the eyes? No. Better to see for himself. Just because his memory wasn't playing tricks with the broader canvas didn't mean the details were true. "I'd like to see her."

Brask folded her arms. "When we're done."

"You've something you want to say to me, lieutenant? An accusation, perhaps?"

"I just wonder why one of our own was caught breaking into a prison, and in the company of a southwealder. Especially when he's on a roster of missing. The archimandrite's had folk searching for you."

"Nice of him."

Kurkas met Brask's stare. *Now* there was suspicion. A pity she was so close to the truth. It left him only one resort. Under other circumstances, he'd have felt guilty. As it was, it'd hardly make Halvor's life more difficult.

"Her and me, we were comrades at Davenwood. Fought the shadowthorns back-to-back." He filled a scowl with chagrin. "Took me captive after. Hid me away in one of their rat-holes to use as leverage against Lord Akadra, but I escaped. The rest you know."

"She had a ward-brooch."

"Of course she did. One of the duke's confidants, isn't she? Helped win him round."

Brask gave a slow, thoughtful nod. "I suppose treachery is all we can expect from her sort."

With grand effort, Kurkas kept his face immobile. Brask was a little *too* convinced for his tastes. "Close to the archimandrite, are you?"

"I'd the good fortune to study beneath him before joining the army."

"I thought it'd be something like that. Don't suppose he's here?"

"His eminence prefers to be among the people, though he visits the prisoner each day."

"She giving you any trouble? Anastacia Psanneque, I mean."

A small, sly smile. "Oh no. We've been quite thorough."

A shiver darted along Kurkas' spine. "She up to a conversation?"

"She's in confinement. Contact is forbidden save with the archimandrite's personal approval."

"I've Lord Akadra's authority," he lied.

"Which I'm sure his eminence will be delighted to discuss," Brask said smoothly. "Anyway, she's hardly worth listening to. Just sneers and heretical doggerel. What else can one expect from a demon?"

Kurkas rated his odds of swaying Makrov as rather dimmer than the sun over Eskavord, but it had to be attempted. Strange times demanded the insight of strange folk, and Anastacia was the oddest person he'd met in years.

"He'll be here later, did I hear you say?"

A frown touched Brask's face. "As it happens, he's overdue."

Bloody typical. Some poor wretch was suffering for that, Kurkas was sure.

The door creaked open. Dastarov entered.

"Ah," said Kurkas. "Is that breakfast?"

"Yes ... and, well ... We've got a problem. At the gate."

Branghall's gatehouse possessed a modest rampart, just large enough to accommodate Kurkas, Brask and a crossbow-armed sentry. A dozen soldiers waited behind the closed gate, weapons readied, the rubicund proctor at their head clinging to a sun-staff as if it were his sole means of support.

Kurkas wolfed down a final mouthful of bread, savouring the salted butter, and tossed the rest over the rampart. It flared briefly as it passed through the enchantment, then fell away into an unnatural darkness that went far beyond the gloom of overcast skies and into the cold embrace of night.

Scores gathered in that darkness. A mass of young and old, their raiment spanned from rough farmer's garb to the black and gold silks of serenes and everything in between. Motionless, they stared unblinkingly at the gate as if willing it to open.

"I'll call out the guard," said Brask. "They'll disperse before steel."

Kurkas shook his head. "I wouldn't be so sure. How many soldiers do you have in Branghall?"

"Twenty, plus three proctors and a kraikon."

He let his gaze drift across the crowd. No, not a crowd. Crowds made noise. And their manner. The unity of posture and expression. The darkness hid their eyes just as it hid their numbers. Only close to the wall, where sunlight bled out from within, were they more than shapes. But Kurkas already knew what he'd see. Glittering black, just like Halvor's. Hundreds upon hundreds of glittering black eyes.

"It's not enough," he said softly. "The gate stays closed."

Brask glared at him. "And if the archimandrite tries to get through?"

Kurkas spat on the rampart. "I guess we'll find out how much Lumestra really loves him."

Her gaze grew every bit as frosty as the air wafting in over the crest of the wall. "*Captain* Kurkas. I don't care for your manner."

"My manner's the least of your bloody problems. Reckon this is bloody normal, do you?"

Brask bristled. "It's a consequence of the enchantment."

"Really? Winter's night out there and a summer evening in here? No. Something's badly bloody amiss. Given the state of that lot, I'll wager it's not us who've the problem. I've seen more spark in a priest's conscience."

Brask's expression flickered between pride and outrage. Neither concealed the worry bubbling beneath. "So what do you suggest, *captain*? Well?"

Kurkas offered a lopsided shrug. "We go back inside. No sense worrying until we know what we're worrying about, and we'll think better away from those dead-eyed stares."

Brask scowled but nodded. "I suppose you're right. I'll post more men, and ... "

"Blessed Lumestra," muttered the sentry.

Kurkas stared into the rain. At the far end of the drive, where the silent mass faded into the sea of downcast grey, the press of bodies drifted apart to form a clear channel.

Newcomers emerged out of the murk. An old woman, walking with a cane. Elda Savka. A Tressian soldier, his king's blue uniform bloodied and torn and his face blackened with bruises, came behind. His feet barely touched the ground, his toes scraping the cobblestones. That he moved at all was down to his two minders. A greying man and a young woman, they dragged the soldier along by his shoulders.

"Bring me the serathi!"

Kurkas recognised the voice, though it wasn't Elda's. Halvor had addressed him in something akin to those hollow, commanding tones even as she'd sought to kill him. Or maybe it hadn't been her at all, but something acting *through* her. Kurkas, never the most religious of men, felt his fingers twitching in the sign of the sun.

"Bring me the serathi, or I'll tear him apart!"

Brask stared unblinkingly at the captive. "Kasnor," she muttered. "It's Sergeant Kasnor. From the archimandrite's personal guard."

"Then I don't reckon his eminence will be joining us, do you?" Kurkas replied.

"Raven's Eyes, what do you mean?"

Kurkas didn't bother to reply. "Mother Savka? You've been misinformed. No serathi here. Maybe go back into town and check with the archimandrite?"

"Arzro Makrov dines with the Raven even as we speak."

Lucky old Makrov, thought Kurkas glumly. Getting to the feast before the crowds. "Then you'll have to take me at my word."

"Do you think I'm blind? I see the sun shining within."

Kurkas tapped his fingers on stone. At least things were drawing together to make a mad kind of sense. Not that he cared for the picture taking shape. No. He didn't care for it at all.

"I'm more interested in why it's so dark out there."

"Your queen has returned. We are all to be one in the Dark."

A name drifted through Kurkas' thoughts. He pushed it away. If he didn't think it, didn't say it, then this wasn't really happening, was it? Icy water rushed through his veins.

"If you want to be a queen, turn east and keep walking," he hollered. "No royalty in the Tressian Republic."

"You think I care for your paupers' council? I am Malatriant. This land belongs to me. You all belong to me."

Malatriant. The name he'd tried so hard not to think, now spoken plain. No putting that jack back in the box, not now.

"Should have gone north when I had the chance," he muttered.

"She's mad," murmured Brask.

"Is she, though?" asked Kurkas. "I'd as soon not take chances."

"What does she want? There are no serathi here."

"There's one. Anastacia."

"But . . . she's a demon."

"I don't think her majesty cares."

Kasnor's escorts forced back his arms. The rain beyond the walls didn't do nearly enough to dampen the dry, rotten cracks of breaking bone – nor the ragged scream. Kasnor hung limp between them.

Elda planted her walking stick between her feet. "He'll beg to die before I'm done. When he's all used up, I'll find another. And another."

"Stop!" shouted Brask. "I'll have her brought. Just leave him be!"

She turned for the stairs. Kurkas grabbed her arm. "There'll be no trade."

"As you wish."

Elda gestured. Still staring ahead, the dead-eyed woman slipped a dagger into Kasnor's armpit and wrenched the blade about. He howled.

Kurkas gestured at the sentry. "Shoot him."

"Sir?"

Kurkas snatched the crossbow from his grasp, propped it on the rampart and fired. The shot was everything he'd come to expect from his post-Zanya aim. The bolt whistled past Kasnor and struck his captor in the shoulder. The woman staggered, each person in the crowd shuddering as if they too had been struck.

The woman stared disinterestedly at her blood mingling with the rain and twisted the dagger anew.

Kurkas snarled and thrust the crossbow back at its owner. "If you don't put Kasnor out of his misery, I'll toss you over the wall and find someone who will."

The sentry's throat bobbed. Then he reloaded the crossbow, his silence stark contrast to the small, whimpering screams rising up through the rain. After what seemed for ever, he levelled the crossbow and sent a quarrel whispering away. By luck or design, it found Kasnor's heart.

Kurkas sighed and patted the sentry on the shoulder. "Good lad. Now, if she tries this again, you keep shooting until your pouch is empty, you understand me?"

The sentry's eyes pinched shut, but he nodded. "Sir."

Fighting to contain his nausea, Kurkas turned his back on Elda and her thralls.

Brask had gone.

Swearing under his breath, Kurkas lurched after her as fast as his wounded leg allowed. She waited at the base of the spiral stairs, eyes blazing hot as the sun.

"What did you do?" she hissed.

"Delivered a speck of kindness," he replied. "Might be we'll need the same before this is done."

"Why should I care if she takes the prisoner? Kasnor was one of ours. One of *mine*."

Kurkas supposed he should have applauded her loyalty, but his patience had all but dissolved in a corrosive mix of anger and terror. He grabbed Brask's shoulder and shoved her against the stairway wall.

"Because that's what she *wants*, you useless dreg. If Katya bloody Trelan crawled her way out of the mists and demanded you give her back her home and the Southshires alongside, you'd not bloody well do it, would you? So why now?"

Brask's face paled, her resistance draining with it. "Because that's the Tyrant Queen!"

"Maybe it is, maybe it isn't," Kurkas said. "But we're soldiers, and she's the enemy. Raven's Eyes, but she's *the* enemy, walked straight out of bloody legend to make our lives a bloody misery. That means whatever she wants, she can't have. You understand me?"

Brask nodded. "Yes, sir."

Sir. That was a start. Some of what he'd said had sunk in. Kurkas was glad of that, because at that moment all he wanted to do was curl up in a ball and drag the world over his head.

"Double the guard on the gate. No one comes in, and sure as Queen's . . . sure as sin no one goes out, you understand me?"

"Yes, sir. And then what?"

"Then I want to talk to Anastacia Psanneque."

Fifty-Two

Anastacia stood in a web of silver at the head of the great hall, the white and gold of her porcelain skin gleaming in the sunlight. Or what Kurkas had been *told* was Anastacia. The tatter-clothed doll bore little resemblance to the woman who'd greeted him to Branghall what seemed a lifetime ago. Another sign that the world he thought he'd known was but a shell for another lurking beneath.

A silver collar sat snug about the doll's neck, the bar-taut chains at its compass-points anchored by eyebolts in the walls. So too were her wrists bound, with the attendant chains let into the flagstones. Taken alongside the heavy shawl and ripped black velvet dress, she looked every bit the lumendoll trussed and readied for the Midsommer fires.

[[Visitors. How nice.]] At last, Kurkas found familiarity. Whatever constraints the shackles placed on Anastacia's body, they did nothing to still her tongue. Despite the hollow sing-song of the voice, there was no mistaking the barbs beneath. [[But where's the archimandrite? Do I bore him already?]]

"Set her free," Kurkas said.

Brask blanched. "Sir, the archimandrite gave strict ... "

"Do I seem in the mood for defiance? I said set her free!"

Brask recoiled and glanced at the overweight proctor lurking in the doorway. "Solas?"

Solas gave every sign of being unhappy, but he slunk towards the web, a key clasped in his pudgy hand. Eyes never meeting Anastacia's smoky stare, he unlatched the collar, then set about the shackles on her hands.

[[You remember when you set me here, proctor? You remember what I said I'd do when the chains were gone?]]

The key slipped from Solas' hands and chimed on stone. Anastacia's laughter echoed about the hall as he fell to his knees to reclaim it.

Kurkas cleared his throat. "Please don't damage him. Might yet be that we need him."

Anastacia regarded the proctor as a serpent might regard something small and furry. [[I find my needs and desires an increasingly poor fit to those of ephemerals.]]

The last chain clattered free. Quick as a whip, Anastacia plucked Solas off his feet and slammed him against a wall.

"Solas!" Brask started forward, useless sword already half-drawn.

The proctor scrabbled at Anastacia's fingers. "Please . . ."

[[So many diligent hours hoping to cause me pain. My turn now.]]

Solas fainted dead away. Anastacia uttered a sharp sigh and let him drop.

[[Boring.]] Her smoky gaze settled on Brask. [[What about you?]]

Brask shuddered to a halt.

Enough, Kurkas decided, was enough. "That'll do."

Anastacia bore down on him. Kurkas held his ground, though not without effort. The veneer of a glib-tongued society lady was as tattered as her dress, giving full view to the timeless spirit beneath. She wasn't his to tame, but she could perhaps be reasoned with.

"There's something at the gate claiming to be Malatriant." Even now, speaking the name sent a shiver along Kurkas' spine. "She's got the townsfolk twitching like a puppet theatre, and she wants you. Don't make me regret not agreeing the trade."

Anastacia faltered mid-stride. [[Then it's true . . . I felt the Dark pressing in. I thought it sorrow, clouding my mind.]]

"Why does Malatriant want you?"

[[Why else? She's of darkness, as I am of light.]]

"That's not as useful an answer as you think." But it explained why the sun still shone over Branghall.

[[Don't presume to know my thoughts.]] Shoulders slumped. The fight went out of Anastacia's voice. She gave a dry, bitter laugh. [[She hates me for what I am. It seems my prison is now my refuge.]]

"And if we hand you over? She'll leave us be?" asked Brask.

[[Am I to be expected to know the whims of every ephemeral? She's *your* Tyrant Queen. You tell me.]]

"Tell you what," said Kurkas. "Let's ask her."

Like much of Branghall, the makeshift cell had seen better days. Sunlight streamed through a crack in the western wall, casting umber shards through dusty air. Revekah Halvor – or at least whatever wore the form of Revekah Halvor – sat hunched in the corner, as far from the light as her chains allowed. Bony fingers traced eye-maddening whorls in decades-old dust.

"Vladama. Come to visit your dear friend?"

Kurkas curled his lip. Strange to hear the voice that was and wasn't Halvor's. Oh, it still held her sardonic tones, but underneath? Hollow and distant, like whatever emotion lay beyond despair. Stranger still to hear it speak his given name. It felt unearned – a violation. "You're not my friend."

She looked up. Dark eyes glittered. Jagged lines crawled outward across cheek and brow, mimicking the veins beneath, or perhaps the roots of something growing strong in its nest of flesh and bone. "Such hatred!"

"Am I misremembering the part where you tried to stick me in the guts?"

"And impertinent. Don't you know who I am?"

"I know what you want me to *believe*."

Icy waters rushed beneath the glib rejoinder, beneath his frail mask of unconcern. Malatriant. The Tyrant Queen. Crawling beneath the skin of a woman who might just have been his friend.

"Time was, I'd have had you flayed for your discourtesy."

"I bet."

"Revekah's still here." Lips parted in a sly smile. "Would you like to talk to her?"

"I want you to let her go."

"Then you aren't truly her friend."

"So you *could* let her go?"

Halvor returned to tracing in the dust. "All her life, she longed to be part of something greater. That's what you all yearn for. To return to the

Dark. To be one in the Dark. No fear. No strife. Just peace. The same peace that has always been my gift."

"What do you want?"

"To see my legacy restored."

Kurkas shuddered, a hundred tales of cruelty vying for his thoughts. The Tyrant Queen sought a legacy? She had one already. Its bleak shadow warped history centuries on.

"Doesn't sound like anything I'll much enjoy."

"You will. Once you come to the Dark."

Shadows shifted. Anastacia drew into the light. [[This is a waste of time.]]

"I want Halvor freed."

"And I told you that she is *already* free."

For a heartbeat, Kurkas allowed himself to believe that she spoke the truth. But only for a heartbeat. "I wasn't talking to you. Can you do it?"

[[Yes.]]

Anastacia strode across the cellar. Shadows retreated, the shards of sunlight flowing across the cellar like molten gold.

"Leave her be!" Panic crept into Halvor's dark eyes. She scrambled backwards on heels and hands, only to be trapped between Anastacia and the whitewashed wall.

Anastacia embraced her. The cellar blazed like fire, the stink of dust seared away by summer days. Kurkas twisted away, hand shielding his eye. An afterimage lingered, of outspread wings dark against fire. Then the light faded, and there was only an old woman, clutched tight in a doll's porcelain arms.

Halvor's eyes flickered open, the black supplanted by hazel and blood-shot white. The spidery lines ebbed from cheek and brow but didn't fade entirely. She blinked and pushed unsteadily away.

"Kurkas? I'm sorry. I couldn't stop her . . . "

"Doesn't matter." How he wished that were true. But if Anastacia could drive Malatriant out of one, maybe she could do the same for others. How that was to be managed with a whole town, he wasn't sure. But something was *always* better than nothing. "You're free now."

Downcast eyes narrowed. Her chest fluttered. "No. She's still with me. I can . . . hear her thoughts – burrowing like worms beneath my own."

So much for hope ... Kurkas glared at Anastacia. "You said you could free her."

[[And I have. But to all things there are limits.]] Fingers glinked against a white-and-gold cheek. [[Mine run a lot closer than they once did. I can hold the Dark back for a time, but that's all. She and Malatriant are bound too tight.]]

He stared at Halvor, gnawed by loss he couldn't explain. "How long?"

[[A few hours.]]

"But you can get her free again?"

[[Perhaps. I took Malatriant by surprise this time.]]

Meaning that next time would be harder. "How does this even happen? Raven's Eyes, but you see strange sights growing up in Dregmeet, but this? This takes the whole of the weasel, guts and all."

Chains rattling, Halvor set her shoulder to the wall. "She said her ash was in our blood."

"*Our* blood?" said Kurkas.

"The town's. The whole damn valley's. I can ... feel them. The others. The cold." She shivered. "She is us, and we are her."

Kurkas thought back to the gate, to the shudder of the crowd. "Do you share their pain?"

Halvor's eyes narrowed. "Why?"

"I shot one of her thralls. Didn't get much of a reaction, but the others shared it."

She laid a hand across her upper arm. "Here?"

He nodded, not sure whether to be impressed or terrified. "You felt it?"

"I remember Malatriant screaming. The babble of confusion. This ... " She gripped her arm tight. "It's like the memory of pain. I don't know if that makes any sense?"

He snorted. "Look at who you're talking to. Not a day goes by when my missing arm doesn't itch. But Belenzo *burned* Malatriant! Every child knows that! Dragged her off into the wilds and gave her to the flame! That's why we burn witches! Because it *works*."

[[Much can change, in time,]] said Anastacia. [[Truth becomes hope, and hope becomes legend. What was wild becomes settled, and fear lives on as prejudice. People remember where history forgets.]]

"My old mother always said southwealders were wicked." Kurkas shook his head. "Cheered louder than anyone when I marched down here back in the day."

Halvor grimaced, and her thin voice drifted. "When I close my eyes, I can almost ... see it. I feel the flames take root in my flesh. I hear her screams ... my screams. And we make Belenzo a promise, as he stands behind the barrier of light. We promise that this isn't the end. That the Dark will return."

Kurkas shot Anastacia a worried glance. She shook her head, her mood unreadable as ever.

"Our ashes seeped into the soil." The lines on Halvor's face reknitted in a new frown, as if she were striving to recall a dream long-lost. "Bitter seeds took root in blood, and we slept. Waiting."

"Waiting for what?"

"I don't ... I don't know." She hunched over, head in her hands. "I think I've lost my mind."

[[It's not lost,]] said Anastacia. [[But taken.]]

Kurkas glared at Anastacia. "Did you know about this?"

[[No ...]] She tailed off. Her chin fell almost to her chest. [[But I think Emil Karkosa did.]]

"Makrov's predecessor? Heard he went mad, pleading with Lumestra to send him a serathi ... " Kurkas fell silent. Karkosa had begged for a serathi, and he'd received one, hadn't he?

[[He bound me here.]] Anastacia's voice quickened with anger. [[He staked me out as a lure.]]

"Or else he hoped you'd stop her."

She laughed, the sound bitter as the ocean spray. [[All this time, I believed myself an outcast, hurled from the golden spires. But it wasn't that way, was it? Mother heard Karkosa's prayers.]]

Kurkas frowned. "Your mother?"

[[You'd call her Lumestra.]]

He'd nothing left to argue with. Not now. "Sure. Why not?"

[[She saw the Dark taking root beneath the soil. And even though her realm was riven by war, she sent a daughter. But Karkosa was cruel, and I was arrogant. The years slipped away. Now it's too late.]]

Halvor laughed softly. "You're talking like a northwealder. It's never too late."

Kurkas scratched his eyepatch. "I don't believe this. Defying the Council? That's one thing. But this? We're talking about a deathless witch who's got her claws into every poor sod for miles around." He felt himself slipping, panic at last finding purchase in flesh. "What happens when she starts plucking demons from the shadows? Raising the bloody dead? How do we fight that?"

"We find a way," snapped Halvor, her eyes alive with anger.

She sagged and sought the wall's support once more.

Kurkas rubbed his jaw. "Who finds a way? That useless lot upstairs? I wouldn't trust them to fight their way out of an orphanage. That leaves you, me and the walking plant pot over there. Unless we can count on Lumestra herself striding down from the clouds with a flaming sword and a host of serathi at her back . . . Wait. That a possibility?"

Anastacia gazed at him. [[My mother is dead.]]

He threw up his hand in surrender. "Course she is. Anything else you'd like to share?"

[[Only that you're making a *very* annoying noise, and that I could snap your neck like a rabbit's.]]

"Well, don't do me no favours." He sat heavily on an upturned wine barrel and almost slipped off the far side. A deep breath helped, so he took another. And another. "Assuming you don't put me out of my misery, what do we do?"

"We get help," said Halvor.

"From where? If Makrov's dead, you can bet Cragwatch is overrun. Your wolf's-heads are scattered, even if we could trust them."

"Then someone'll have to ride to Tressia. There must be horses in the stables."

Now *that* was a fine idea. A herald, riding light and changing horses along the way, could reach the Council. Plant the whole mess in Lord Akadra's lap. "There are, but there's no way out. Gate's sealed up tight."

Halvor nodded. "What about the wall?"

"And *how* do we get a horse over the wall?"

[[We don't,]] said Anastacia. [[I can open the hallowgate. It can trot out through a tunnel of roots and boughs.]]

"Sounds lovely." Kurkas decided against asking exactly *what* a hallowgate was. "But I had Dastarov make a circuit. We're surrounded. Not as deep at the wall as at the gate, maybe, but enough that it'll be a fight to get clear."

Anastacia stared down at her feet, then straightened. [[Then I'll hand myself over. I can be *very* distracting.]]

"No," said Halvor. "You're the only advantage we have."

"Then what?" asked Kurkas. "How do we make this work?"

Halvor slid down the wall and sat in the dust. She stared at her hands, turning them over and over as if to memorise every crease. "There's a way. You won't like it, but there's a way."

Fifty-Three

The key turned in the lock. Marek hesitated. So easily everything turned to dust. Used to be, he basked in Lady Sevaka's company. Now he couldn't bear her to look upon him. But duty performed beneath the weight of a breaking heart was the pinnacle of service. He entered the room.

Lady Sevaka watched from the bed. "Mealtime again so soon? Come to spare the great Lady Kiradin the disappointment of a dead daughter by forcing her to eat?"

Marek told himself he wasn't responsible for what his hands did at Lady Ebigail's instruction. Only what he *chose* to do counted. He had to believe that, or what was he?

Lady Sevaka hung her head. "How long before it's your turn, Marek? What mistake will see you dangling from the gibbet?"

He knelt beside the bed. She pulled away as his hand reached for hers. His was the quicker.

"Don't touch me!" She kicked at him. "Don't . . . !"

Protest fell silent as the key slipped the manacles' lock. She pulled back, eyes hooded.

"The south gardens are lightly patrolled." Marek's speech came easier now the deed was done. He'd loosed more than one set of shackles. "Climb into the street from there."

"Why?" She rubbed at a chafed wrist. "Why are you doing this?"

Marek glanced away. If she didn't know by now, then what point in telling her? "Go. Be safe."

He remained on his knees as she moved towards the door, unsteadily at first, but growing in confidence with every stride. For a heartbeat, Lady Sevaka was a silhouette frozen in the firestone glow of the corridor. Then she was gone.

Marek sighed, overcome by contentment not known in years. With good fortune, it would be morning before Lady Ebigail checked on her daughter. He'd be aboard ship by then, bound for the anonymity of the Outer Isles.

As he reached the basement door, a new shape appeared at his side – one hooded and framed by raven feathers.

A gloved hand caught the door as it closed.

The firestone lanterns of Abbeyfields smouldered low. Hearthguard were at their posts and the children in their beds – or at least, so Malachi fervently hoped. Josiri glanced at the clock for the dozenth time since dinner.

"She's late."

"She is." Malachi took a swig of brandy and gripped the glass tighter.

"She's not coming."

Lily's fingers closed over Malachi's wrist and gave a gentle squeeze. He shot her a grateful look and received a slender smile in exchange.

"You don't know Rosa. She promised. She always keeps her word."

Josiri scowled into his drink. "Then why are you so on edge?"

Malachi fell silent, his thoughts returning to Elzar's revelations. Viktor was a witch, and no amount of reason could dislodge the uneasiness worming through his gut. Viktor was a witch. No other man was as entangled with Malachi's life. His family. He'd been alone with Sidara and Constans. Malachi hated how completely his world had been set adrift. But that was the power of superstition.

"Malachi?" Lily's insistence dragged him out of reverie. "Malachi? She's here."

He rose as Braxov ushered Rosa into the sitting room and noted that Josiri did the same. Good. Some manners still held sway in the Southshires.

"Thank you for braving the curfew, Rosa. Can I offer you a drink?"

She gave a stiff shake of the head. "I shouldn't be here at all."

"Ridiculous," Malachi replied. "Whatever happens with Viktor, we can't let it divide us."

"This isn't about Viktor. Mistress Tassandra's dead."

"What? How?"

Unreality crowded out sorrow. Tassandra had been bullish as ever the previous day – larger than life. But a day was an increasingly long time in Tressia. Events turned on their head in hours.

"Murdered in the Essamere chapterhouse, four of my brothers and sisters alongside."

Malachi grimaced. "The Crowmarket?"

"Who else?" She gripped the back of a chair. "This is a warning."

Lily gathered her skirts. "If you'll excuse me, I'd like to check on the children. And that the hearthguard aren't asleep at their posts."

Now it was Malachi's turn to offer a reassuring squeeze of the hand. "Take Braxov with you."

She nodded and drifted from the room.

Rosa turned towards the door. "I must go. I came only out of courtesy."

Malachi caught her arm. "Rosa, please."

"I have duties."

"So you said before." He took a deep breath. "I could command you to stay."

"You must do as you think best, my lord councillor."

He didn't think it best at all. Formality wouldn't break through the walls Rosa had erected, though perhaps logic might. "What do you think to achieve at this hour that cannot wait until morning? Even with their mistress dead, the Knights Essamere will endure until dawn ... and I need my friend's help."

She snorted, but ice thawed from her expression. "You always were soft, Malachi."

He grinned, glad to glimpse a little of the old Rosa. "Please?"

She sighed and sank into a chair. "Very well. But not in here. I've spent the afternoon cooped up in the chapterhouse. I need to feel the wind on my cheeks."

Malachi crossed to the dresser, poured a generous measure of brandy and passed the glass to Rosa. "To Kaleo Tassandra. May Lumestra light her path."

Glasses tilted in salute, but neither of his companions echoed the toast – though Malachi suspected for different reasons.

Abandoning the attempt at ritual, he led the way out onto the terrace garden. Josiri and Rosa took up positions to either side, neither of them terribly close to him, but noticeably more distant from one another. Firestone lanterns shone through the trees, betraying the positions of patrolling hearthguard. But for all the activity in the grounds, the night remained quiet enough that he heard the rush of the river on the boundary between his gardens and the overgrown wilderness of Strazyn Abbey.

"I've never known the Parliament of Crows to be so bold," he said.

Rosa stared into her glass. "I never truly believed the vranakin existed before they murdered Kas. Viktor has made them bold."

"*Events* have made them bold," Malachi corrected. "The Council has never been more divided."

"And whose fault is that?" She didn't address Josiri by name, nor even look at him, but her meaning was obvious. "You invited this division, Malachi. You and Viktor, and your schemes to pardon the south-wealders. But I suppose that was always part of his plan."

"You mistake the symptom for the disease." Josiri spoke flatly, but taut cheeks and eyes betrayed a waning temper. "I've spent the better part of a day in council. I found only a catalogue of sneers and petty complaint masquerading as governance."

"*Because* of that division," snapped Rosa. "Weakness is like rot. Once it settles in the bones, it spreads."

Malachi sighed. "You sound like Ebigail."

"She talks a lot of sense. More than you credit. She was right about Viktor, wasn't she?"

She spat the words, but Malachi heard a crackle of self-loathing beneath the rage. He'd hoped the worst anger and grief behind her. He now realised he'd been wrong to do so. Unable to avenge Kas, she'd found a new target for her ire. Found one, or been guided by an old and canny hand. A callous strategy, even by Ebigail's standards, and one that preyed on Rosa's first love: duty.

He forced himself to meet Rosa's flinty stare, searching for a sign that some part of her knew how badly she'd strayed. Perhaps she even knew and couldn't bear the pain of the admission. Malachi of all people knew the strange comfort of being trapped – the absolution of actions taken or denied, all the while claiming events had conspired against you. He had to find a way to reach her. Not only for Viktor's sake, but hers also.

"That's what I want to discuss," he said at last. "Tell me what you know."

"Why? It'll be a matter of record once the provosts have done their work."

Their work. The butchery of a friend. How could she speak so calmly? "Because I want to hear it from you. I want to know what you know, while there's still anything left of Viktor to save. Will you do that for me?"

"Where is she?"

Marek's head snapped aside. Blood oozed up where Lady Kiradin's heavy rings had torn his cheek. A hearthguard wrenched the steward's arm behind his back and shoved his head forward, keeping him on his knees.

Apara watched with distaste from beside the hearth. Even with all the blood that had flowed over her hands, the display turned her stomach. She was grateful for that revulsion. She clung to it.

"Where. Is. She?"

A backhanded slap punctuated each word, the strikes opening fresh wounds.

"I don't know," gasped Marek. "You think I'd ask? You think she'd tell me?"

Lady Kiradin froze, her hand backswept for another blow. A low growl escaped parted lips. Then she straightened, the animal snarl retreating from her expression and a semblance of decorum returning. Stooping, she set a knuckle beneath his chin and tilted back his head.

"No. A secret's worth nothing when shared with the likes of you. I see that now." She sighed. "How could you do it, Marek? Have I not treated you well?"

"Better than I could ever have dreamed, lady," his voice shook as he spoke.

"I thought perhaps you understood what was necessary. I thought you had the strength for this." Her expression wavered, a rare moment of vulnerability glimpsed and concealed. "Lumestra damn me for a fool for ever thinking that. This isn't what I wanted for you. It's what you've chosen. You must understand that."

Marek stared at the floor and offered no reply.

Lady Kiradin straightened and fixed the hearthguard with a baleful stare. "Set the dogs on him. Cast whatever remains into the sea."

Marek offered no resistance as he was dragged from the room – not even a word of protest. Apara envied him his peace, fragile though it might have been. Another death laid at her door, even though she'd done nothing more than raise the alarm. If only she'd chanced by the cellar a minute later. Little would have changed, but she wouldn't have been the one to deliver another man to his death.

Lady Kiradin set a hand against the window frame and stared out across the night-shrouded garden. She seemed smaller, shrunken – as if for the first time she bore every one of her advancing years.

"It's too soon." The words came as a breathy, urgent mutter. "I'm not ready. She mustn't ... "

The windowpane rattled beneath the impact of a thin fist. Lady Kiradin spun on her heel, renewed fire in her eyes. "Find her."

Apara blinked at the impossibility of the request. "How? I don't know where she's going. I've never seen her face ... "

A hand swept out. A porcelain vase flew from the table top and shattered against the floor. "Must I do everyone's thinking? She'll go to Malachi Reveque! Fools always flock together! As for her face, you'll know it when you see it. Kill her, and anyone she speaks to."

"But she's your daughter!"

"Not any longer."

Apara shrank back from the lady's fury. Other worries crowded in. Sevaka had a head start. Even the raven-cloak couldn't close the distance in time. She had to get ahead of her quarry. That meant risking the paths of Otherworld. Fearful as she found the idea, it paled beside the prospect of lingering in Lady Kiradin's company.

A chorus of throaty, canine snarls split the night air. The first screams came soon after.

Sevaka fled through streets emptied by curfew, navigating by sparse streetlights and what little of the moon breached oppressive clouds. She longed only for the strength to keep moving.

Keep moving. But moving where? No one in the extended family would offer shelter – her mother had too long a reach for that. The same was true of her old shipmates – even assuming the *Triumphal* still lay at anchor.

Her pulse quickened. What use was it being free of one cage only to roam another? And Tressia *was* a cage. It waited only for her mother's cold hand to reach down and scoop her up.

Ribald voices chimed ahead, the soft mutter of bored men on lonely duty. Sevaka gathered her stolen cloak and clung deep to the shadows.

Two constables appeared at the end of the alley, one chuckling at the other's murmured witticism. She could go to them. Beg for protection. No. If she couldn't trust the navy to offer sanctuary, what hope of salvation with Captain Horden's constabulary?

The patrol trudged past, their stride that curious mix of unhurried and urgent practised by purposeless lawkeepers everywhere. Sevaka lingered in the shadows, groping tiredly for options.

Not the constabulary. Not the navy. Not family. Friends? That was a poor joke. She'd none in the city save Rosa, and she was compromised.

That left only one possibility. Malachi Reveque. He'd no reason to help her, but perhaps that wasn't the point. It wasn't really about her, was it? Even in her own life, she was a bystander. But there was still time to change that.

She sucked down a deep breath. It wasn't far. Three streets, no more.

Apara stumbled out of the mists, the portal to Otherworld already closing behind. As much as Otherworld sometimes resembled the mortal realm, it was all illusion. The slightest wavering of attention, and the mists delighted in steering you wrong. Caught between the dread of disappointing Lady Kiradin and the fear she was already too late, Apara's attention had wavered like never before.

Despite everything, she'd come true to her destination: the ruined bell tower amid the granite ribs of Strazyn Abbey. Not somewhere she'd have come by choice, even though she knew that the rumours of cyraeths and revenants owed more to the thinness of the boundary between the mortal realm and Otherworld than deathless malice lurking among the weeds.

But the bell tower offered unparalleled vantage of the nearby streets.

Of patrolling constables, and packs of ne'er-do-wells risking curfew for a dubious thrill. And there, in the alleyway to the west, a lone figure running with uneven gait, a Freemont hearthguard's cloak flapping behind.

Apara cast the raven-cloak wide, and gave herself to the wind.

Sevaka clutched at the rough brick of the townhouse wall and whooped air into heaving lungs. Across the street, the railings of Abbeyfields glinted in the flicker of a firestone lantern. Almost there. One last effort, and she'd be safe.

Pulling her hood low, she pushed away from the corner.

A bell clanged out. "Hey! Halt and be recognised!"

Sevaka threw a glance over her shoulder, gauging her chance of out-pacing the pursuing constables. Not nearly good enough. She shuddered to a halt and turned about. The constables approached with hands on swords but faces devoid of hostility.

"You're in breach of curfew," said the nearest, a matronly woman with more years behind than left ahead. "Let's have your name."

"Please," Sevaka gasped. "I must see Lord Reveque. He'll vouch for me."

The last vestiges of friendliness slipped from the constable's expression. "You not hear me, missy? Curfew. If you want to slip into his lordship's bed, you do it before dusk or out of my sight."

"Listen to me, please . . . "

"What's the point? It's the cells for you. Bind her up, Garsh. We'll take her in."

Garsh eyed his colleague without enthusiasm and reached for the shackles on his belt.

The night exploded with crow-voices. A torrent of black wings plucked at Sevaka's cloak and swept over the constables.

Garsh's wild screech gurgled into nothing. His body hit the cobbles at Sevaka's feet. Somewhere behind, steel scraped free of its scabbard, only to be drowned by a chorus of crow-shrieks and small, wet tear-ing sounds.

Blinded by the storm, Sevaka wrapped her arms about her head and ran for the railings.

*

Malachi rubbed his forehead with the heel of his hand. Even with the terrace's gloom to confuse matters, Josiri suspected his lordship was close to losing his patience.

"That's your proof, Rosa? A pair of forbidden texts?"

"It's more than enough to involve the provosts."

Josiri was well accustomed to listening to gaps in conversation. Life with Calenne and Anastacia had taught him that what was *not* said was often as important as what *was* – especially when you could practically hear the evasion rushing like a river beneath the words.

It seemed Malachi thought so as well. "But not for accusations of conspiracy," he said, "let alone murder. You know better than most that an unusual gift is no proof of blackened character."

Josiri had thought Rosa's stare couldn't get any colder. He'd been wrong.

"What do you mean?" he asked.

"Malachi . . . " growled Rosa.

Malachi set his glass down on a planter. "It means dear Rosa here is what legend once called an eternal. She doesn't bleed. She can't die. Sadly, it also seems to have rotted her brain."

Rosa sprang. One hand about Malachi's throat, she slammed him against a trellis.

"How dare you!" She drew Malachi in and slammed him forward again. The trellis rattled in its moorings. "That's not your secret to tell!"

Malachi spluttered and clawed at Rosa's forearm. Josiri flung his arms about her shoulders and heaved. He might as well have striven against a tree. A thrust of her elbow sent him sprawling, gasping for breath.

"The provosts . . . are killing my friend," gasped Malachi. "There's . . . nothing I don't . . . dare."

Rosa snarled and flung him away. He thumped into the balustrade and scrabbled for purchase on the stone. Braxov hurried out of the night, a pair of wooden-faced hearthguards looming to either side.

"Is there a problem, my lord?"

The steward's tone made it damn clear that he knew there was a problem, but Malachi waved him away. "High spirits, nothing more. Brandy's a mocker of dignity."

Braxov's expression did nothing to hide his scepticism, but he withdrew all the same, the hearthguards on his heels.

Malachi rubbed his throat. "I'm sorry, Rosa. I spoke out of turn."

She stared off into the night. "I'm sorry too."

To Josiri's way of thinking, she didn't sound any sorrier than Braxov had looked convinced. After a brief check that his ribs were still where they should have been, he clambered to his feet.

"If it helps, you've my word I'll tell no one."

"As if a southwealder's word is worth anything."

Josiri gritted his teeth. The anger in Rosa's voice was sickeningly familiar. He'd been the same back when Viktor had arrived in Eskavord. She'd made a choice, and now events were galloping away with her in the saddle. Better to hang on for dear life than risk the fall.

"Tell us the rest," he said. "What harm can it do?"

She grimaced. "You won't—"

A woman's scream echoed up from the grounds. It lingered in the night air, then faded to nothing.

Malachi went deathly pale. "Braxov! Braxov! Where are you, man?"

The steward entered the terrace at a flat run, the hearthguards in his wake. "My lord?"

"Lady Reveque? Where is she?"

"Inside. I spoke to her not five minutes ago."

Malachi nodded tersely and jabbed a finger at the nearest hearthguard. "Back inside. You stay with my wife until I say otherwise, do you understand me? Braxov, see to my children. The rest of you are with me. Rosa . . . "

Josiri turned. Rosa had already gone.

Apara let the constable's body fall and vaulted the railings, raven-cloak squalling at her heels. Two more deaths. Two more cyraeths waiting for vengeance in the mists. How many more?

She glanced up just as Sevaka vanished into the trees.

One more. At least one more.

Apara cast the raven-cloak wide. She dove through the trees as fragments of fluttering shadow, each one more than a piece but less than the whole. Her quarry's fear was sharp on the breeze, intoxicating and sickening in equal measure.

The trees thinned. Sevaka lurched to a halt on the sheer riverbank.

Arms spread wide, she steadied herself. Soil scattered away into the waters twelve feet below. Apara drew in the cloak. Her fragments coalesced and landed lightly a half-dozen paces from the cliff.

A hammer-blow cracked against her skull. Her head snapped back, vision drowned in black and red splotches.

Sevaka let another stone fly. Apara twisted away, and it crashed into the trees.

"You won't take me back!" shouted Sevaka.

Apara shook her head to clear it. "No. I won't."

She closed the distance in a single leap. Her left hand closed around Sevaka's throat. The right drove steel claws deep into her belly.

"I'm sorry," she breathed. "I truly am."

Sevaka shuddered. Her heels scrabbled on the edge of the cliff. Her hood fell back ...

... and Apara found herself staring into a mirror.

No, not quite a mirror, she realised through creeping numbness. Sevaka Kiradin was fair where Apara was dark, and younger by a good many years. But the snub nose, the grey eyes – the arc of her brow. Close enough for kin.

Close enough for a family Apara had never known.

As for her face, you'll know it when you see it.

"No!"

Sevaka's flailing hand grabbed Apara's collar. Her head slammed forward.

For the second time in as many minutes, Apara's sight danced black and red. When it cleared, she was on her knees, and Sevaka was lost to the river.

Lanterns gleamed on the lower bank, the sound of voices close behind. Apara tore her gaze from the waters and vanished into the night.

Rosa plunged into the river as the body struck. Waters surging about her waist and the soft mud of the riverbed sucking at her boots, she half-walked, half-swam to where the woman drifted like a macabre lily blossom.

Bracing against the current, Rosa hoisted her clear. Blood gushed across a torn jacket. Grey eyes fluttered open. A pale, weed-strewn hand brushed Rosa's cheek.

"Rosa?" Greenish water spilled from her lips. "Always . . . saving me."

"Sevaka?" Surprise and horror fought for command. Anger triumphed over all. It drove her back through the rushing water towards the riverbank. "I've got you."

" . . .'m sorry."

"Don't speak. I'll get help."

"Help . . . I helped her lie to you." Sevaka gripped Rosa's shoulder. "She killed him . . . She killed her own son . . . "

She fell back, pale and still but for a fluttering chest.

"Sevaka!"

Water streaming through her armour, Rosa stalked through the rushes and into the gathering circle of lantern-light. Cold, hard faces stared back. She laid Sevaka on the grass.

Malachi knelt, his eyes darting. "Is she alive?"

Rosa barely heard. *She killed her own son.* There was no mistaking Sevaka's meaning. Anger faded and left behind a cold void where her heart should have been.

"Look after her." She backed away.

Josiri grabbed her arm. "Where are you going?"

She shrugged him off. "To put things right."

Fifty-Four

Malachi swept the contents of the kitchen table onto the floor. "There. Set her down."

Water trickling across the tiles, the hearthguards bore Sevaka to the now-empty table and laid her down. The room already stank of blood, and of the riverbed. She moaned as her head came to rest. She'd not stirred to wakefulness in the trek across the garden.

He gestured blindly at the hearthguard. "One of you, fetch Lady Reveque. Quickly!"

"Lady Reveque is already here."

Lily strode into the kitchen in nightgown and housecoat, a golden halo of disarrayed hair trailing behind. She caught sight of Sevaka and her purposeful expression wavered.

"Malachi? What happened?"

"Rosa pulled her out of the river."

Lily offered a crisp nod. "No time for a physician, curfew or not. I'll do what I can. Braxov? You know what I need: hot water, clean linen ... whatever salve hasn't lost its colour. You two, get out. I need room."

Braxov, who'd entered a pace behind his mistress, vanished into the hall once again. The hearthguards followed.

"Malachi. You have a handkerchief?" asked Lily. "A clean one?"

He fished the folded cloth from his pocket and handed it over. Lily shook it open, gave cursory examination, then pressed it against the wound. Sevaka's eyelids twitched. A thin moan escaped her lips.

Lily brushed a weed-caked fringe from her patient's forehead. "Where's Rosa?"

"I don't know." Malachi shook his head. "How can I help?"

"You can stay out of the way. I don't need you fainting on the poor woman."

"What about Sidara?"

"Patching up her battered father's one thing. Death creeping in under your hands? She's too young for that."

Braxov returned, arms laden with cloth and vials. "Water's coming, my lady."

"Good. Keep pressure here while I get this coat off her."

Lily set a knife to Sevaka's coat. Malachi turned away, isolated and useless in his own house. He blotted out Lily's terse instructions and Sevaka's soft, breathy cries. Instead, he stared out into the garden, and lost himself in unanswered questions. Why was Sevaka out after curfew? Who had attacked her? Was it chance that had brought her to his door?

Only Sevaka knew the answers. Sevaka, and perhaps Rosa.

The kitchen door burst open to admit a harried and breathless Josiri.

"Where's Rosa?" asked Malachi.

"Gone. I lost her when she hit the streets."

Malachi scowled. "You should have followed!"

"Yes. I, a southwealder, should have traipsed my way through the curfew-laden streets. What could have gone wrong?"

Malachi winced, embarrassed. It had barely been a day, but already Josiri was so intertwined with Malachi's world that it had become easy to forget the weight of history and intrigue that had made it necessary. Even now, protected by the Akadra name, Josiri's freedom was more illusion than truth. Even the small transgression of a broken curfew could doom him.

"Josiri . . . "

"Bicker elsewhere," snapped Lily. "I'm trying to save a life. Go!"

Knowing better than to argue, Malachi gestured to the passageway door.

Josiri hesitated. "I'd rather help."

"This is no time for well-meaning bumblers," said Lily.

Josiri's expression cleared. His tone took on aristocratic hauteur Malachi had not yet heard him use. "Don't mistake me for a fool, lady."

Lily held his stare for a moment, then nodded. "Take over from Braxov. He has water to fetch."

By the time Apara arrived at Freemont, confusion and sorrow had given way to howling rage. Otherwise she'd never have dared take the tone she did.

"Why didn't you tell me?"

Lady Kiradin offered no reply. She had her back to the door, lost in conversation with a slight, red-haired young woman. Only the slightest tensing of her shoulders betrayed that she'd heard.

"I don't care what you have to do, Tailinn. Events are coming to a head. I need them mobile. As many as can be managed." She lifted an upturned hand to Tailinn's chin, forcing the younger woman to meet her gaze. "I've suffered too many disappointments of late. Do not find yourself among them."

Tailinn stared over Lady Kiradin's shoulder, her hazel eyes widening as she caught sight of Apara. She gave a small, hurried nod and withdrew from the sitting room.

Still Lady Kiradin didn't turn.

"Another life you're tearing apart?" demanded Apara.

At last, she turned. "That's twice you've addressed me thus. Do not make the mistake of a third."

Apara froze mid-stride. Lady Kiradin's posture hadn't changed. Not so much as a wrinkle had shifted on her face. So why did she have the sudden sense of having crossed into a wolf's lair? Anger turned cold, uncertain.

"Did you think I wouldn't find out?" she asked.

"I didn't mean for you to learn of it this way. But events ... events make a mockery of intent. A mother cannot love all her children as she wishes, especially those whose existence invites scandal."

Apara pinched her eyes shut. Sevaka stared accusingly out of memory. "You sent me to murder my sister!"

"Sevaka wasn't your sister," snapped Lady Kiradin, "any more than I am your mother. Whatever you were before, you are now vranakin, a cousin to the Raven. That was the bargain I struck for you. And how you've prospered."

"And my father?"

"Were you not listening? The Crowmarket is your only family."

Apara flicked her eyes open, rage rekindling. "Answer me!"

Lady Kiradin shrank back. "Gone, and good riddance. A charming man, but he'd a soul scraped from the gutter. He thought I'd be content to live with him in the shadows." She rallied, her tone crackling with satisfaction. "I was always meant for the light."

She stepped closer, her voice softening with remorse. "I would never have given you up, but I needed to remarry, and Samias Kiradin would never have adopted some vranakin whelp as his own. Don't you see? I protected you. Kept you safe the only way I could. Surely you believe me?"

Apara shook with anger and . . . yearning? She hated herself for a fool. More than thirty years behind her – old enough to have raised a family of her own, had life and desire coincided – and yet she trembled like a child.

"I might," she breathed. "If you'd said something these past years."

"I know." Lady Kiradin's fingers brushed the bloody steel of Apara's claws and closed about her wrist. "Oh my dear, I know. But I was afraid. Not of my reputation – that fades with age, whatever others might say – but of your judgement. That you wouldn't forgive me the mistakes of youth. And so the years slipped by. It has been torment."

Tears spilled unbidden across Apara's cheeks. Sorrow mingled with the bitter mirth of disbelief. "A woman who orders the deaths of her children *should* know torment."

"True. I have performed terrible deeds, and will yet do more, if called to. All I have done, I have done for the Republic, for she needs a mother far more than you ever did. She lacks your strength." She set Apara's unresisting claws to her own throat. "But if you cannot forgive me, then at least grant me a quick death."

Apara tried to pull away. Lady Kiradin held her close. "You'd have me kill you?"

Wasn't that what she'd determined to do the moment Sevaka's body had slipped away? She couldn't recall. Emotion had swamped motive.

Lady Kiradin's eyes brightened with tears. "If that's what you want. If that's what it takes to settle things. I promise you, I shall feel nothing."

Overcome by conflicting emotion, Apara sank to her knees. "I don't know what I want."

"Hush, child. I know."

Lady Kiradin ... no, her *mother* ... crouched at her side and drew her into an embrace. Part of Apara screamed at her to pull away, to run from Freemont and never return. But the greater part came home.

"You have done a hard thing tonight," her mother whispered, breath warm on her ear. "The hardest. I am prouder than you can ever know. If your sister had been half the woman you are, it would never have been necessary. But you are my firstborn. You are the best of me. Your sister ... she *is* dead?"

Apara flinched. "I can't be sure. Someone came. A knight of Essamere. The one who took my cousin's hand, I suspect."

Her mother sucked in a sharp breath. "A woman?"

"Yes."

A sigh. "I see. Then we had best prepare for her arrival."

Lilyana pressed the glowing flat of the dagger home. Sevaka's lips parted, drowning the sizzle of burning flesh with a breathy wail.

"I said hold her down!" snapped Lilyana.

Josiri put his full weight on Sevaka's shoulders and wondered how a woman so far gone into the mists could possess such desperate strength. At the far end of the blood-slicked table, Braxov tightened his grip on her ankles. The steward was nearly as pale as the patient, and little wonder. Sevaka's belly was a torn, gory ruin. It didn't matter how much Lilyana staunched or cauterised, there was always more.

Lilyana stifled a shriek of frustration and flung the dagger across the kitchen. It clattered off a wall and settled beside the hearth.

"It's not working!" Head hung low, she planted her hands on the table. "Must have been a serrated blade. She's all but torn apart. I can't stop the bleeding."

Josiri stared down at Sevaka. Her chest pulsed in arrhythmic, shallow breaths. Her eyelids twitched. Lilyana was right. He'd seen it before, in the stockade after Zanya. The Raven was calling her. Didn't seem fair. She was barely older than Calenne. Had life worked out differently, the two would have been sisters.

Calenne. Had the Raven already taken her? His throat tightened with the sudden, irrational belief that to lose one was to lose both.

"Keep trying," he said.

Lilyana wiped her brow, leaving behind a bloody smear. "I tell you, it's no good. We can only ease her passage. Braxov, fetch the moonglove extract. I know you keep it for the horses."

Josiri glared at her. "We don't give up until she's gone."

"It's cruel."

"It's life." He shot a glance at Malachi but found hollow eyes and no support. Northwealders. Always the easy way out. "You don't give up until it makes you."

Lilyana's fingers closed around Sevaka's. "Braxov, please do as I ask."

Josiri met the steward's gaze. What if he demanded the steward refuse? Would loyalty-in-exile carry him that far? Had he any right to invite consequences on Braxov out of some weary, farcical notion that Calenne and Sevaka's fates were entwined?

"I can help," said a small voice.

"Sidara?" Malachi hurried to the door. His hands closed about his daughter's shoulders and turned her about. "You shouldn't be here."

What a sight they must have seemed. A dying woman on the table. Lilyana bloody to the elbows, cowing three grown men with quiet fury. And yet Sidara didn't blanch. She stood there in her nightdress, granite as the hearth.

"I can help her." Certainty waxed in her tone. "I helped Father."

Malachi shook his head. "This isn't the same."

Lilyana's shoulders shook. "Sidara Reveque, you will go to your room, and you will do so this instant, do you understand me?"

To Josiri's surprise, the girl ignored her parents and stared directly at him.

"Let her try," he said.

Lilyana rounded on him. "Don't encourage her fancies. She's just a girl."

So Lilyana knew after all? Or at least suspected. "And what if they're not fancies?"

"What are you both talking about?" demanded Malachi.

Josiri kept his eyes on Lilyana. On the expressionless face that nevertheless spoke volumes. She knew. "Your daughter is blessed with light, Malachi."

He blinked. "What? No ... "

"Let her try."

Malachi blinked as a man waking from a dream ... but he let go of Sidara's shoulders.

Lilyana strode to intercept her. Josiri blocked her path. "You're a devout woman, Lilyana. I know that. What would Lumestra have you do?"

The look she gave him was filled with ice. But after a moment, she stepped aside.

Josiri beckoned to Sidara. "Are you sure?"

She gave a small nod.

"Then do what you can."

Hesitantly, but with growing confidence, Sidara reached across the table. Her face flickered with revulsion as her hand touched Sevaka's ravaged flesh. She closed her eyes.

At first, nothing happened. Then the first crack of light shone beneath Sidara's fingers. It hissed where it touched blood, then blazed into a gold-tinged white so bright that Josiri had to shield his eyes. He raised his hand too slowly. In the moment before flinching away, he could have sworn he saw winged silhouettes among the brilliance. Then he closed his eyes, and they were gone – or perhaps had never existed at all.

The light strobed and ebbed. Sidara cried out. Half-blind, Josiri caught her thin, shivering body as it fell.

"Are you all right?"

She blinked and stared at her outspread fingers. The hand was still bloody, but what remained was dry and friable. "I'm tired, and a little cold."

He smiled. "I'm sure you are."

She pushed upwards and away, her shoulders atremble.

"Sidara!" Lilyana knelt beside her daughter. Careless of her bloody hands, she held the girl tight and peered intently into one eye and then the other. "Are you hurt? Tell me."

"I'm fine, Mother."

"Don't take that tone with me."

Josiri disentangled himself from broiling domesticity and turned his attention to Sevaka. She remained dead to the world, and paler than any living body had any right to be. But her breathing was deep and steady,

and her wounds ... What had been red, seeping flesh was crusted shut
by dried, clotted blood.

"Raven's Eyes," breathed Malachi. "She did it."

"Where is she?" Rosa slammed the hearthguard against the wall. "Tell
me, or I'll break every bone in your body!"

The man scrabbled at her gauntleted fist, eyes wide with terror. Well-
trained and well-paid though the hearthguard of the nobility might have
been, they were nothing to a knight of Essamere – a fact that the trail of
bodies from the listing gate had surely rammed home. Rosa knew she'd
not so much crossed a line as bolted madly past it. She didn't care.

"Tell me!"

Another slam – hard enough to shiver Rosa's own elbow, let alone
the captive's spine.

A pained gasp burst from his lips. "The rose garden. She's in the ... "

Rosa planted a fist in his face and let him drop. The rose garden? She
knew Ebigail to be an early riser, but it was yet some hours to dawn.
Respectable folk were in their beds. Then again, Ebigail Kiradin only
pretended at respectability, didn't she?

Sword held ready, she followed the gravel drive to the rear of the house,
the pain of injuries already fading as the wounds closed. Truth hardened
into unassailable creed. Elzar had been right – an eternal's existence didn't
make her a monster. Rather, it gave her the means to *punish* monsters.
What other fate fitted a woman who'd sought the deaths of her children?
Who'd so cleanly manipulated Rosa into turning on Viktor?

Rosa's skin prickled as she approached the garden. She'd downed
what, a dozen hearthguards? There should have been twice as many on
duty, given the recent string of deaths and assaults. But then ... Ebigail
was behind those, wasn't she? What need had she of increased protection, when hers was the only life not in danger. Raven's Eyes! Why hadn't
she seen it before?

At last, she reached the terrace. The thick, sweet fragrance belonged
to secret assignations and whispered intimacies. Perhaps that was fitting.
After all, there was nothing so intimate as betrayal ... or the murder that
would wipe the slate clean. There was no proof. No leverage. There was
only the sword and the will to use it.

Rosa ignored the distant barking and picked her way through the maze of trellises. At last, there she was, stood at the centre of the terrace. A spider in a web of thorns.

"Hello, Roslava. You've come to kill me, haven't you?"

"Yes."

A gentle tilt of the head. An eyebrow arched, barely visible in the soft glow of the firestone lantern. "And for which crime have you come? For making you see a fool in the mirror? For the fate of my feckless daughter? Or have you come to avenge the death of a man who was never capable of loving you?"

The barbs ripped at Rosa's heart. "Does it matter?"

Ebigail sat down on a bench. Skirts shifted as she hooked one knee over the other. "Not to me. They're all pathetic. You're a soldier. Soldiers serve the Republic, and you have served well. A shame it must end like this. I'd such hopes for you."

"I'm glad to disappoint."

Ebigail laughed. "So many are. Am I permitted to plead for my life? To convince you that what I did was necessary for the Republic's survival?"

Rosa strode closer. Strange how knowledge altered perception. No longer did Ebigail Kiradin resemble the ideal of Tressian matronhood, but a withered, embittered old witch cackling at the world.

"No, but you may choose between the sword and a broken neck."

Ebigail folded her hands in her lap. "I can't say either of those appeal."

Something hissed out of the gloom and thunked into Rosa's chest.

Croaking for breath, she closed a hand about the crossbow bolt and ripped it free. Bright spots of pain burst behind her eyes. They passed as all pain had passed since Kas' murder. Ebigail had underestimated her. A rare lapse, no doubt.

"Did you ..." She broke off and coughed. A stream of black spittle evaporated into the air. "Did you really think that would stop me?"

"That one?" Ebigail shrugged. "No. I'm sure the rest will."

The trellis came alive in a storm of petals and dancing leaves. A dozen shots slammed home into Rosa's body. The night blazed red and black.

Hands twitching, she fell to her knees. Gasping for breath that wouldn't come, she grasped at one of the bolts. Shuddering fingers refused to close. Hearthguard filed from concealment behind the trellis.

"That how you wanted it, my lady?" asked a grizzled fellow with a captain's star on his shoulder.

"Exactly right, Captain Farran," Ebigail replied.

Recalcitrant fingers closed. This time, Rosa screamed as the bolt ripped free. Eleven to go.

Ebigail rounded on her, lips pursed in polite interest. "I imagine that hurts a great deal. I knew there had to be more to you than there seemed. A lucky woman might survive one kernclaw's assault, but two?" She snapped her fingers. "There's luck, and then there's . . . something else."

A patch of shadow shifted in a world rapidly losing its colour. No. Not shadow. A woman in a feathered cloak. A kernclaw. Keening pain, Rosa wrenched another bolt free.

Metal glinted in the lamplight as the kernclaw handed Ebigail an ornate sword. A Hadari sword.

"Josiri Trelan presented this to the Council as a trophy of his victory. The shadowthorns have such a way with metalwork. Gaudy, yes, but not beyond redemption. Take this, for example. A silvered blade. If you're what I think, it'll take the fight all the way out of you."

She took the sword in a two-handed grip, blade down. Rosa tore another bolt free. Was it her imagination, or was the kernclaw looking away? Not a good sign.

"You . . . you send me to the mists and . . . and . . . " Rosa's chest shuddered, rendering the words more croak than speech. "I'll come . . . back."

Ebigail tutted. "Oh, don't be so dramatic. You're still of use to me, Roslava. *This* is just to keep you quiet."

The sword plunged into Rosa's shoulder. Her flesh turned to fire and swept her into blackness.

Fifty-Five

Sitting in the overgrown gardens beneath Branghall's terrace, Kurkas could almost believe recent troubles were but figments of his imagination. It was only when he stared beyond the wall, to where the moon faded and darkness became suffocating and oppressive, that truth returned. He could almost *feel* Malatriant, the Dark gathered as a shroud about her.

He tipped the goblet to his lips. Empty.

"Here."

At the other end of the stone bench, Halvor tilted a half-empty bottle for a refill. Her hand shook as she poured, as much wine trickling down the cracks between paving slabs as finding its way into Kurkas' goblet. She'd deteriorated so much as evening had worn away. Tried to hide it, of course. But the weakness stood revealed in the tightness of her features.

Kurkas could only guess what it cost her to keep Malatriant at bay. But what could he say? She knew that he knew. Words would only get in the way.

"Expensive way to water the weeds," he said instead.

"Josiri," Halvor said loftily, "can send me the bill."

He laughed and stared at the empty bottles lining the bench. Faded ink on the tags proclaimed them a good fifty years older than Kurkas himself. Halvor could have laboured a lifetime and not replaced even one.

Kurkas took a mouthful. It wasn't unpleasant, but he couldn't see what the fuss was about. Maybe wine was another of those things the nobility only *pretended* to enjoy. Like honour, responsibility. All that good stuff.

"Don't make me do this, Halvor."

"There's no other way."

"Of course there's another bloody way," he snapped. "We've ammunition enough."

"And how's that better? Pain's still pain. How many will die?"

"As many as it takes."

She drained her goblet and set it down. "It won't work. It has to be something that lasts, that deepens. Something that can't be outrun or suppressed. It has to hurt, and it has to *keep* hurting."

"Then I'll lead a charge out the main gate. Take fire with me. Set 'em all burning." Kurkas hated the petulance in his voice. He felt like a child.

Halvor gave a wheezing chuckle. "Didn't you say this lot couldn't fight their way out of an orphanage?"

"*Is* there an orphanage in Eskavord?"

"No." She abandoned her goblet and swigged from the bottle. "It burned down."

"You can come with, if it makes you feel any better. Just try not to show the rest of us up."

Dry lips cracked a wry smile. "Look at me. I can barely stand."

"You can still kick my arse."

"No."

"Prove it."

"Stop, Kurkas. Just . . . stop."

He stopped.

Halvor let the bottle drop. "Anastacia set a light burning in my soul, but it's fading, and *she's* getting stronger. When she takes me again, I don't know that I'll want to come back."

"Don't talk like that."

"You don't know what it's like to be a stranger in your own skin. It's suffocating, but there's also peace." She took another swig. "Never had much peace. But I've lived free. If I get to choose, I'll die free too."

He nodded. "Didn't have much use for Lumestra back in Dregmeet. Sun doesn't shine much down there. But the Raven? Give him a coin, give him a feather, and he'd hear you, so my old man said. Death as a friend. Your *last* friend."

"Or a final bastion, when all other walls have fallen."

"I like that."

Halvor raised her bottle. Kurkas chinked his goblet against its neck.

She took another mouthful and hurled the bottle into the hedge. "You know the worst part? Even now, I don't know if what we fought for was what we thought we were fighting for. What if Malatriant was pushing us all along?"

Kurkas hesitated. "Reckon you give her too much credit. Way the Council treated you? I couldn't have taken it. Might be I'd make different choices myself, given time over."

"Vladama Kurkas, the wolf's-head. Hard to picture."

"Maybe in the next life, after Third Dawn."

"There'll be war after Third Dawn? You reckon Lumestra will allow it?"

"If Anastacia's right, there is no Lumestra, not any more. But there'll always be people, so I reckon there'll always be war."

"If Lumestra *is* dead, maybe there'll be no Third Dawn."

"Then look for me on that last bastion. We'll hold it together."

The undergrowth rustled. Brask stood on the weed-choked path, the brooding silhouette of Branghall's tower blotting out the stars. No longer the proud lieutenant of the afternoon, she had the furtive, skittish manner of an animal tempted to flight. Kurkas wished he'd the freedom to let his own fear show. But that wasn't his privilege, was it? Not until someone else took over this mess.

"It's time," said Brask. "Anastacia says she's ready."

Anastacia. Not "the prisoner". Not "the demon". Fear taught respect.

"Dastarov has my letter?"

"He does. And the swiftest steed in the stables."

Kurkas grunted. "Raven only knows what Lord Akadra'll think of all this."

"That's not our worry," said Halvor. "Our job is to make sure he gets it."

The soldier's life. You did your part and hoped others did theirs. Pivoting sideways to compensate for his battered leg, he lurched upright and held out his hand. "Coming, Captain Halvor? We can't start without you."

She gave a taut nod. Her fingers closed about his.

"Captain Halvor?" Brask's hesitant words stuttered over her lips. "I wanted to thank you."

"I'm not doing this for you," Halvor replied, her tone less acid than the words. "You're just along for the ride."

They made for a strange pair hobbling up towards the terrace, Kurkas leaning on her for balance, and she on him out of faltering strength. Brask followed at a respectful distance. Soldiers glanced away as they approached, but furtive eyes always returned. Likely they couldn't believe what was to come. A special kind of madness, borne out of cruel times.

At last, they crossed inside the ring of lanterns, and the wall of restless king's blue uniforms. All of them facing outwards.

"Still time to change your mind, Halvor."

She snorted tiredly. "And waste all their hard work? Look how pretty they've made it."

The pyre was decidedly *not* pretty. It had been thrown together from fallen boughs, spare lumber and broken furniture, then packed with twigs and leaves gathered from the grounds. And planted at the centre, a beam salvaged from the wreckage of the manor's tower.

"Then we'll wait," said Kurkas. "I'll have them pull it apart and build it up again. Lumestra knows the bloody thing looks like it'll come down with a gust of wind."

Halvor shook her head. "No. She'll be back before then, and I'll be gone."

"So what? We chained her up before. This'll work no matter who's holding the reins."

"So it won't be my choice any longer. It'll be something done to me. And I want it to be my choice, Kurkas. I want to know I *hurt* her."

He winced away his selfishness and gazed into the flickering brazier beside the pyre. Better to send an enemy to the flames than a friend, but it wasn't his choice. However deep Malatriant had her talons into Eskavord, it wouldn't stop there. Might be it couldn't be stopped at all, but that didn't mean you couldn't try.

"Brask? You heard her."

The lieutenant helped Halvor onto the pyre. Another necessity, this one borne of Kurkas' status as a one-armed and practically one-legged man. He watched as the lieutenant drew Halvor's wrists behind the makeshift stake and set the shackles in place. Could he have done the same, had he been called to it?

He hoped never to find out.

Too soon, Brask withdrew, and strode from the ring of lanterns.

"You ready, Halvor?" asked Kurkas.

"You don't have to stay."

"Bugger that. With you to the end."

So saying, he pulled a brand from the brazier. It felt heavier than it should, but he knew the weakness wasn't in his arm, but in his heart.

"For the Phoenix, Captain Halvor."

Her lips broke into a broad grin. For a moment she was again the defiant woman who'd fought so hard to kill him, and striven with equal fervour to save his life. What was that Thrakkian saying? *Enemies made the finest friends.*

"For the Phoenix, Captain Kurkas."

Swallowing the lump in his throat, Kurkas thrust the brand into the pyre.

"Father!"

Melanna sat bolt upright, heart hammering at her ribs. The distant scream fell away into the murk of scattered dream, revealed not as her father's – not even belonging to a single voice – but a chorus of strangers, howling in agony.

Shadows receded, revealing the castellan's quarters at Voldmarr Watch, Melanna's home while the dispirited remnants of her father's army gathered for a humiliating march home.

Melanna's pulse steadied, her death-grip on the blankets relaxing alongside. The nightmare had seemed so real, though she recalled nothing of it save the scream. It wouldn't hurt to check in on her father. Wounds turned sour, and the conditions in the Tressian stockade . . .

Aware that she was conjuring bleak fates from nothing, Melanna threw aside her blankets and pulled on her robes. The rampart beyond the chamber door carried the cold breath of the mountains, parting the last skeins of sleep. It was also quieter than it should have been, lacking the small sounds of the crowded courtyard.

The empty courtyard.

Melanna stared over the inner rampart into a space that should have been filled with men, wagons and horses. But there were no tents. No campfires. Fingers scratched on rough stone as Melanna steadied herself against the wall. Even her guards were gone – Sera and the two lunassera who had stood as sentries since her arrival. All gone.

She was alone.

Shifting wind drew Melanna's eye westward. Past Kreska, past the humiliating fields of Davenwood, to where Eskavord should have lain defiant beneath the stars. There was only darkness.

"You see the price of arrogance." Ashana propped her elbows on the outer rampart. The slit sleeves of her dress hung like verdant pennants against the wall.

Melanna's panic receded as she at last noted the mists curling across the hillside. "My arrogance?"

"In part. You awoke desperation in another. In that desperation he roused something better left sleeping."

Melanna's blood ran cold. "Malatriant."

Ashana nodded. "Or as near as doesn't matter."

"You're talking about the Sceadotha! How can it not matter?"

"Maybe it *is* Malatriant. Maybe it's the power she wielded, which only believes itself her. Our fears shape the Dark as much as the Dark shapes our fears. That's why it so often chooses a trusted face. I've seen it. I've lived it. The truth makes little difference."

Melanna found herself struggling to follow Ashana's words. But other details sang out. "Akadra. The man-of-shadow. He awoke this."

"He did a terrible, foolish thing for the very best of reasons. You pushed him to it, you and your thirst for battle." She sighed. "But something would have cracked, even without you. She's been twisting souls for years. Making proud folk stubborn, and petty folk cruel. That was always her gift."

Melanna closed her eyes, lost in the tales of a blazing hearth. The soft pearlescent notes of her mother's harp-strings. "She conquered the old Tressian kingdom and brought order out of anarchy. But only for a time."

"Order is never absolute," said Ashana. "Change is the paradox of perfection that keeps worlds turning and hearts beating. Unity unmakes itself. Malatriant couldn't accept that. As her realm fell away, she reached into the Dark. She forged her peace – the peace of silence, where hers was the only voice. One by one, Tressia's neighbours fell. Until all were one in the Dark."

Melanna frowned. Somehow, the goddess made a hopeless tale bleaker still. The warmth of the fireside receded, until only the chill wind remained. "And then you intervened."

"Not me. My predecessor and her siblings. They chose champions and granted them magic. The first and last thing they ever agreed on, I don't doubt. Those champions cast down the walls of Darkmere and ended Malatriant's rule. Your empire arose from those ashes, and the Tressians . . . ? What they didn't forget, they warped their histories to conceal." Ashana sighed. "And now they long for a past that never truly was. It's all very familiar. No wonder I feel at home."

Melanna opened her eyes. The mists were thicker than before, clawing at the fortress walls like besiegers. In the distance, darkness shimmered beneath the stars.

"So the legends are true. The Sceadotha met her end in the Southshires."

"There's no end in the Dark. It was here before light was light. Everything that exists is built upon its bones. One day it will reclaim what was lost, and silence will reign."

Melanna shuddered. "That sounds like a prophecy."

"Then perhaps I'm finally getting the hang of being a goddess." Ashana hunched lower over the rampart. Dirty blonde hair framed her face. She made a disgusted noise. "I'm not sure that's a good thing."

"So all this . . . It was meant to be?"

The goddess snorted with laughter. "Where did you get that idea?"

"You just said it was prophecy."

"I agreed it *sounded* like a prophecy – and that, Melanna, is a word by which we justify our deeds, or excuse their lack. Just because something's inevitable, doesn't mean it can't wait. Otherwise, why get out of bed? Why do anything at all?"

The fortress walls faded behind mist. There was only the rampart, and the goddess. "So you'll stop this?"

"I can't. I'm bound by divine law. Not much to be gained staving off Malatriant if my step-siblings fall to brawling over protocol. That too can be held off for another day."

"You . . . your predecessor . . . involved herself."

"No. Her *champion* did." Ashana straightened and struck a thoughtful expression that was entirely too guileless. "Now where would I get one of those?"

Melanna staggered back a step. "Me?"

"You *are* Ashanal, aren't you? Names are like clothes. Steal them, and you should be ready to play the part."

The mist rolled in.

After what seemed for ever, the screams died away. The stillness of night rushed back, broken only by the roar and crackle of the pyre. Kurkas, his eye stinging from the smoke and his skin raw in the backwash of the flames, watched until the shape at the pyre's heart collapsed into the flames. Only then did he turn away, and cuffed tears from filthy cheeks.

Brask approached from beyond the ring of lanterns and threw a salute. "Dastarov's away."

There should have been satisfaction in that. Joy, even. Both seemed too distant to acknowledge, much less embrace.

"Sir?" Brask edged closer, more hesitant this time. "Did you hear me? It worked."

Kurkas took a deep breath, bitter smoke swirling into his lungs. "Put it out. Put it all out. Then you bury whatever's left, and you bury it so deep that nothing can touch her until the light of Third Dawn. You understand me?"

"Of course, sir. Whatever you want. Where will you be?"

"Drunk. You can wake me in the morning." He stared back at the pyre, and hoped it had all been worth it. "Assuming there is one."

Maladas, 12th day of Radiance

Where light rises, ambition follows.

from the sermons of Konor Belenzo

Fifty-Six

Time had lost meaning for Viktor. There were only the hours where Hargo was present, and those blessed, fleeting moments when he was not. This was one such moment, to be treasured as long as it lasted. Shoulders screamed with every sway about his shackled wrists. Dull red fire blazed the length of his body. Breath rasped across a parched tongue. Even the tiniest motion sent hot shards flashing through wounds barely closed.

But Viktor knew his downfall would not come from mere pain, however cunningly wrought. No. The deeper Hargo's silver burrowed, the closer Viktor's shadow wormed its way to the surface.

If it emerged, there'd be no more questions. Only the fire.

All he'd striven for would come to nothing. He'd never see Calenne, unless chance brought them together in the mists.

The thought quickened fresh defiance, as it always did. But not enough. Viktor Akadra, who seldom admitted limits, now finally accepted their closeness.

A muffled scream jolted Viktor from his thoughts. A fellow prisoner?

Another scream quavered through the darkness. A woman's, this time accompanied by the clatter and scrape of collapsing stone.

The cell door smashed inward. Light rushed in. A robed body collapsed against the opposite wall. Hargo. A battered bronze leg glinted dully in the corridor beyond. A metal hand reached through the doorway and brushed aside the splintered remains.

Elzar shuffled into the cell, his movements incongruously

furtive for one who'd caused such commotion. Blood drained from his weathered face.

"Viktor? What have they done to you?" His throat bobbed. "Forgive an old man for taking so long to find his courage."

He clicked his fingers. The wall collapsed in a shower of dust, torn apart by the implacable strength of the kraikon hunched in the corridor beyond. Golden light crackling beneath its misshapen helm, it reached towards Viktor.

"No!" One hand locked about his control amulet, Hargo lurched into a sitting position. The kraikon ignored him. "Why won't it stop?"

Elzar's lip twitched. Fingertips brushed his own amulet. "I'd be a dull fellow without a surprise or two. Edvard operates under a different enchantment to his brothers. Mine is the only will he obeys."

With surprising gentleness, Edvard unhooked Viktor's shackles from the ceiling and lowered him to the floor. Viktor clung to the construct as the world steadied.

"He's corrupted you!" Hargo spat. "You're as damned as he!"

"Perhaps," murmured Elzar. "Can you walk, Viktor?"

"Yes." The word crackled across dry lips. "You shouldn't have come."

He snorted. "Ingratitude."

Hargo's cheeks bloomed almost to the colour of his gushing head wound. "You will burn together!"

Viktor's shadow howled. Every moment, every harm, every slice of flesh echoed back. He bore down on Hargo.

"Viktor!" Elzar glanced at the remains of the door. "We have to go!"

"This won't take long." Viktor knelt beside Hargo. Even now, the man showed no fear, only righteous indignation. A fanatic. How much blood had he spilled? "I warned you what would happen once I was free, did I not?"

"Do as you will, witch! It changes nothing!"

"On this, at least, we agree."

Wrists still shackled, Viktor grasped the provost by his jaw and by the base of his skull. The muffled scream matched the widening of his eyes. A sharp wrench. A greasy crack of shifting bone.

Viktor rose on aching legs. "Now we can go."

*

They left the house before the sun was fully in the sky: four hearthguards and two weary councilmen hastening through crowded morning streets. Malachi's eyes itched with lack of sleep. He'd *tried* to rest, but worries had crowded out the darkness.

Sevaka. Sidara. Rosa. Rosa most of all. At least Sidara seemed unharmed, and Sevaka Kiradin now had a chance, if a slender one. Both were in bed, the one watched over by an anxious mother, and the other by a maid. But Rosa? It was too easy to fear the worst.

He stifled a yawn and tripped on the cobbles.

Josiri grabbed him by the shoulder. "Easy there."

Malachi shook his head. Josiri had slept no longer than him. "I still don't know how you're functioning better than me."

"Years of a double life. You learn to take sleep when you can, and cope when you can't. I still say you should have sent a herald."

Malachi bristled. "Ebigail will want details. Better she has them from us."

Josiri's eyes narrowed. "And that's your only reason?"

"I . . . No. Sevaka's plight is sure to set her off-balance. She might even feel she owes us."

The curl of Josiri's lip made Malachi's skin crawl. "I hate this city."

"It's how things are done, Josiri. A favour for a favour, on and on and on, into eternity. I don't like it, but we have to play every advantage. There's too much at stake. For Viktor. For you. Even for the Southshires."

Josiri walked in silence for a few steps. "Which is why however today plays out, I need to leave."

"What?" The word croaked from a dry mouth. "If you go home, there's no telling what Makrov will do. Your status as an Akadra won't protect you away from the city."

"I thought I could wait this out, but I can't. I have to know what's become of Calenne. Last night brought that home to me."

Now it was Malachi's turn to walk in silence through the swirling crowds and the silent, watchful kraikon. How could he convince Josiri to stay? Indeed, did he have any right to, or was he clinging to a rare like-mind as old friends were stripped away? Kasamor. Viktor. Rosa. All gone.

As he walked, he became aware of a new sound rising behind those of the streets. Voices – no few of them – caught in a rumble of opposing conversation. Then buccinas, rising crisply above. A parade? He recalled nothing being brought to his notice, but Viktor *had* won a great victory. Patriotism birthed strange spontaneity.

"I can offer little help if we can't persuade the Council to offering its blessing," he said at last.

"I know. A horse, provisions and a sword. That's all I ask."

Fresh gloom settled on Malachi's heart. It was hopeless. Josiri was riding south into death. "Let's hope it doesn't come to that."

"Hope is a poor coin. I'll rely on it only when all else fails." He growled. "Raven's Eyes! How much further is it? We should have taken your carriage."

Malachi forced a smile. "Spoken like a man never deadlocked on market day. It doesn't take much to bring Tressia to a standstill."

He bent his meandering thoughts on the hours to come. Council first. Then, if a stop at the Essamere chapterhouse didn't turn up news of Rosa, he'd head to the constabulary barracks and have Captain Horden get word out.

"She can look after herself," he muttered. "She can."

The road widened out into the plaza. A very *full* plaza. A crowd thousands strong had gathered beneath the steps of the palace. A dozen kraikons stood at the boundary fence; as many again lurked in the confluence of nearby streets. Something about the sight niggled at Malachi's thoughts, but there was so *much* wrong with that gathering.

Two companies of the 7th barred the palace steps, swords out and shields levelled. Behind them, Ebigail Kiradin stood before the great iron-studded doors, a knot of Freemont hearthguard at her side. She stood rigid and unmoving, her ice-white dress billowing in the grasp of the same northerly wind that carried her words clear across the plaza.

" . . . your council has failed you. I have failed you. Lumestra charged us to remain vigilant against the Dark, and we have not. Poison has crept into our veins – into the very lifeblood of our greatest families! Tolerance for the shiftless and lazy! For the southwealders! Yes, even for the shadowthorns!"

Malachi watched agape. "What is this?"

"I don't know." Josiri's eyes were everywhere but on Ebigail.

"I, more than any, have paid a price for our laxness. My son, Kasamor, whom I know many of you loved, torn apart by those he trusted! His sister, taken from me this very night by those who seek my silence! But I am Ebigail Kiradin! I do not bend my knee to murderers and assassins! I will not let them do to you what they have done to me!"

The crowd's muttering swelled to a low growl.

Malachi frowned. Kasamor had been popular, not least within the 7th. As for the rest ... "But Sevaka lives! I must speak with Ebigail."

Josiri grabbed his arm. "Don't."

Ebigail spread her hands. "Our fair city. Our beautiful, glorious Republic. It is rotten to the core! Eroded from within by those in whom we have placed our trust. Last night, they came for me! But for my steward, I'd have joined my dear children in the mists."

She gestured. The palace gates swung inward. A kraikon strode out into the light, a great baulk of timber held aloft like a banner-pole. But no flag fluttered in the wind, no bright heraldic silks. Instead, it bore what Malachi at first took for a bundle of rags. But as he peered closer, he made out hands and feet twisted and bound behind the pole, and the steel glint of mooring spikes driven through green cloth into shoulder and thigh. A ragged gasp rippled through the crowd. A sword hilt projected from her shoulder.

Stone hands gripped Malachi's gut. "No!"

Ebigail cast a triumphant hand towards the macabre display. "My would-be assassin! A markhaini spirit conjured from the mists. A thing that bears the likeness of one of our greatest heroes, but which does not bleed!"

Another gesture, and the kraikon set finger and thumb to the silvered sword-hilt and twisted. Rosa slammed her head against timber. Her desperate scream ripped across the plaza. Not one drop of blood flowed.

Malachi pinched his eyes shut and fought for breath. "We have to go back."

Josiri's eyes widened in disbelief. "You can't let this continue!"

Malachi stared out across the crowd, at faces riven by fear and consternation. He heard the growing swell of outrage. At last, the kraikon let go of the sword. The scream faded to a sob. Rosa sagged against the mooring spikes. He'd accused her of falling hard beneath Ebigail's sway, but he'd been snared no less. In his arrogance, he'd seen only Ebigail's opposition to his and Viktor's ideals. But her designs went deeper and wider than he could ever have believed. And now? Now it was too late. Ebigail fancied herself a queen and reached to claim her goal.

"Don't you see what this is?" he said softly. "Don't you see where this is going?"

"And now, this very morning," Ebigail's voice cracked as she strove to be heard, "I learn that Viktor Akadra has fled the provosts' lawful interrogations! No innocent would behave so! Who knows how deep this rot goes? The Council will be cleansed! The Republic will be cleansed! The demon burns at dusk, those she had corrupted alongside! Will you stand with me? Will you give me your trust?"

The crowd roared their assent.

"Surely it's not too late," Josiri grabbed at his arm. "You can speak with Hadon. The masters of the chapterhouses ... She can be stopped."

Malachi pulled free. He wanted to shout, to break into a run. But such behaviour would only make things worse. "How? You and I, we're right at the top of her list for rooting out. And it won't stop with us. You of all people should realise that. Family is everything."

Josiri paled. "Lilyana. The children."

"Come *on*."

The roar of the crowd rumbled like thunder through Elzar's foundry workshop. Edvard stood motionless beneath the rising arch of the steeple. The hessian sack in whose embrace Viktor had been smuggled into the foundry lay draped over the kraikon's arm.

"What now, I wonder?" muttered Elzar.

"Nothing good," Viktor buttoned the borrowed shirt and winced as the motion put fresh strain on his injuries. Elzar's perfunctory bindings were no match for those of a trained physician. He remained a mass of livid flesh, haunted by agony each time he did more than draw breath. At least he was free. But the price ...

"You shouldn't have come for me."

"Viktor ... " Elzar set a gentle hand on his shoulder. "My only regret is that I left it so long."

Viktor nodded and laid his hand on Elzar's. It wasn't that simple. It could never be that simple. Elzar's life, his work, his calling. He'd thrown it all away. And all the while, Viktor's father had done nothing.

"They'll be coming."

"And you'll be gone." Elzar began sorting through the clutter of tools and cast-off scraps of metal that littered his bow-legged desk. "Don't tell me where. Better if I don't know."

"You can't stay here."

"Where would I go?" He patted the wall. His fingers left no mark in decades of impacted soot. "Forty years, this place has been my home. There's something to be said for the familiar."

"Maybe." Viktor limped to the filthy window and stared out across Tressia. "My whole life I've fought for the Republic. Now? I wonder whether I should have been fighting at all."

"That depends. Why did you fight?"

"Because those were my orders."

Elzar scratched the back of his head. "Don't give me that. Why did you fight?"

"To defend those who couldn't."

Elzar's smile was weary. "And that's your answer. Don't mistake the people for the Republic. Fighting for one needn't mean fighting for the other. But you already knew that, else you'd never have gotten into this mess."

Viktor laughed. A flash of pain dulled the mirth on his lips and he pressed a hand to his side. The fingers came away bloody.

"So much for your healing touch," he breathed.

"I told you before – it takes a rare talent to make magic lower itself to knitting flesh. *I* don't have it." Elzar sniffed and fished a rag from his desk. "But if you want to try for yourself . . . ?"

Viktor ignored the quizzical eyebrow. His shadow had been silent ever since escaping the vaults, and it certainly had no gift for healing.

"I'll give you another chance, old man. Just try to keep my insides on the inside."

"What in Lumestra's name do you think you're doing, Ebigail?" roared Hadon Akadra.

It was Apara's first glimpse of his lordship so near. She'd seen him before from a distance, giving one pompous speech or another in the Hayadra Grove. She'd always written him off as just one more arrogant noble – all wind and no fury. Up close, she realised that she'd been very much mistaken, and darted across the Council chamber to block his path.

Lord Akadra barely spared her a glance. It might have been otherwise if Apara had still worn the raven-cloak rather than the plain tunic of a Freemont hearthguard, but its presence would have invited too many questions best left unanswered.

Ebigail brushed Apara aside. "I should have thought that was obvious, Hadon. Even to you. I am giving the Republic much-needed direction."

He drew up on the far side of the table and glared daggers at her. "And what of the Council?"

"As of this morning, you and I *are* the Council. I've given orders for the arrest of Malachi Reveque and Josiri Trelan, *and* Josiri *Akadra* – we'll have no more bungling in that regard, I can assure you."

"On what grounds?"

"Their association with your heretic son. I assured Captain Horden you and I were of like mind on this issue."

He gripped the backrest of the chair so tight Apara feared it would shatter to splinters. "You lying, treacherous ... "

Ebigail cut him off with a wave of a finger. "Don't let pride lead you false, my dearest. It would be such a shame if the shadow of suspicion fell across you as well."

"The Grand Council will never stand for this."

"Oh yes, the Grand Council." Ebigail shook her head. "Never knowingly bereft of empty opinion and meaningless debate. I fear it is *infested* with traitors."

"You have proof of this?"

"Proof is for doubting minds. I have the support of Prydonis, Sartorov and the church. What need have I of proof? The constabulary are already going door to door. I expect many will not be taken alive, one way or the other, but we'll have enough left for the spectacle of a trial."

"And the pyre you're having built in the Hayadra Grove? More spectacle?"

"A lesson, scratched out in the ashes of Roslava Orova. A cleansing will do the Republic all manner of good. It will burn away our weakness and leave us stronger." She shook her head, as might a disapproving tutor. "On which side of that lesson you serve is down to you."

Hadon's expression didn't flicker. But Apara knew what many did not – that truth often dwelled in the eyes. So it was here. Hadon Akadra's eyes broke alongside his spirit.

Perhaps she'd been right all along. All wind, no fury.

"What do you wish of me?"

Apara's mother drifted around the end of the table and set a hand to his cheek. "Go home. When this is over, we'll discuss how you can best serve my Republic."

Defiance flared in his eyes. Then it was gone. "Yes, Ebigail."

Lord Akadra retreated from the chamber, leaving mother and daughter alone.

"He used to be such a vigorous man, afraid of nothing," Apara's mother said. "Even ten years ago, he'd have fought. He'd have squeezed the life out of me before making that craven display. Now look at him. Gelded and brittle. But he may yet serve some small function."

Apara cleared her throat. "May I ask something?"

A brief smile. "Whatever you like, so long as you retain a civil tongue."

"This ... All of this. Was it always your plan?"

"Only the goal. The rest ... Well, you must be flexible if you are to thrive, Apara. Fate laughs at your intentions." She paused. "Kasamor. There was no going back after that. I couldn't let his death be for nothing. He forced me to it, you know. He found out about my links to the Crowmarket, and threatened to tell the Council if I blocked his ridiculous betrothal to that southwealder. He was never more my son than in that moment, and never more a fool."

Was that bitterness? Regret? Apara couldn't be sure. She couldn't even be certain her mother was speaking to her at all. Kasamor. A reminder that she'd not merely lost a sister, but a brother too. Apara shook her head. Such thoughts belonged to the past.

"And Viktor? Lady Orova?"

Her mother sighed. "Opportunities too good to waste. Superstition has such power. Even a simpleton knows how to fear, and to hate.

Convince people that your will is actually theirs, and they'll bleed themselves dry without ever really knowing why."

"And what do you fear, lady?"

"Dying with my work undone. I intend to live on in every brick and stone."

Apara realised she could no longer put off the reason for her presence. "My cousins are unhappy, lady."

There was no outburst. No scowl. Rather, her mother laughed. "I'm certain they are. Let me guess the nature of their complaints. They're afraid my little enterprise will interrupt their own. And are livid that I have temporarily reclaimed the kraikon they accepted as payment?"

Apara inclined her head. "Yes, lady."

"Tell them not to be so foolish. Short-term turbulence is to be expected, but the curfews will not last for ever. The Crowmarket will ply profit from its sordid little trades soon enough, and the kraikons will be theirs again. They need only grow a spine."

Apara winced, the memory of the elder cousin's green eyes vivid in her mind. "I might phrase it differently, lady."

"You may phrase it however you like, so long as they understand."

Apara nodded. "Yes, lady."

A sharp knock sounded at the door.

"Enter!" snapped Ebigail.

A red-haired young woman in a proctor's robes crept into the room, head bowed. "Lady Kiradin?"

"Tailinn? I gave instructions you were to remain in the foundry in case of ... complications."

"Yes, lady," Tailinn's coastlander's lilt danced atop the words like wind on waves. "Only I thought you'd want to know – Viktor Akadra's there. In the high proctor's workshop."

Apara's mother laughed under her breath. "Elzar. Of course. I never knew the old goat had it in him. Apara? Find Captain Farran. He'll secure the foundry. Viktor is yours. I've no need of him alive."

"Yes, lady."

The door had barely opened when Lilyana Reveque, ordinarily so restrained, flung her arms around her husband. Josiri stepped aside and averted his gaze, embarrassed to witness a private moment.

"Malachi! Thank Lumestra! I was on the point of sending Braxov after you!"

"What? Why?"

"Sevaka's awake." The words came out in a gabble. "She says that Ebigail's responsible for all of this. Kasamor. Poor Abitha Marest. Viktor's arrest. She locked Sevaka up for days. What manner of mother could do such a thing?"

Malachi disentangled himself. "A mad one."

"Or one whose sanity is so tightly wound it's snapped like a rotten mooring rope. Excuse me." Josiri pushed past into the house. "Braxov? Are you there?"

The steward appeared from the kitchen at close to a run. "Your grace?"

"The children. Make sure they're ready to travel."

The unspoken question dissipating from his lips, Braxov hurried upstairs.

Sevaka stood in the sitting room doorway, her face as pale as her borrowed dress. "It's my mother, isn't it?"

Josiri nodded. "She's intent on remaking the Republic. I doubt she has any place therein for the Reveques. Can you walk?"

"I shouldn't be able to. I shouldn't be able to stand, but . . . "

"Yes or no?"

"Yes."

"Go with them. Your mother thinks you're dead. If you're found here, you will be."

Braxov reappeared on the stairs, a coated and booted Constans and Sidara in his wake. Constans regarded the assembled adults with suspicion, Sidara with apprehension.

"Uncle Josiri? What's happening?"

How much should he tell her? How much *could* he tell her? "You have to leave the house for a time. Perhaps a long time. Your father will explain."

"No!" The door slammed back on its hinges, admitting a Lilyana of very different mood to the one Josiri had last seen. "This is my home! I am *not* leaving!"

Malachi hurried in behind. "There's no choice; it's not safe."

"You're right," Lilyana snarled. She reached up behind the sitting room doorway and unhooked a battered militiaman's sword from the wall. "If

Ebigail wants my children or my husband, she'll have to go through me."

"She will," said Sevaka. "She'll have you cut down in a heartbeat and not shed a tear."

"Let her come."

Josiri stepped past two startled children and laid a hand on the scabbard. "Fifteen years ago, I heard many speak with that same defiance. They're all dead."

The anger in her eyes guttered and died. "But ... this is our home."

"And it might be again tomorrow. But for today, you must leave."

She shuddered. The sword, still sheathed, fell to her side. Slowly, she nodded her head.

Malachi shot Josiri a grateful glance. Josiri turned away. Tressia was starting to feel like home for all the wrong reasons. Why did he even care? They were northwealders, one and all. They weren't his people. What battles they had were theirs, with allies and hearthguard aplenty to fight for them. Not like Ana, or Calenne.

Hurried footsteps sounded on the gravel. A breathless hearthguard appeared in the doorway.

"My lord," she gasped. "Captain Horden's at the front gate with warrants for your arrest. He has a score of men and two kraikons besides. If they make a fight of it ..."

Josiri scowled. "Is there any chance?"

"Against a kraikon? Let alone two?" Malachi shook his head. "Thank you, sergeant. Tell everyone to lay down their arms."

She shot him a confused look and beat a hasty retreat.

Malachi pursed his lips, his expression teetering on the brink of despair. He crouched beside his son. "Constans. I need you to do something very important. Take your mother and sister through the gardens and out into Strazyn Abbey. Along that briar-path you think I don't know about. Can you do that?"

His son frowned. Then he nodded earnestly. "Yes, Father."

Malachi hugged him, then Sidara and finally kissed his wife. "Go. And remember always that I love you."

Lilyana's eyes narrowed. "Malachi ..."

"I'll give Horden part of what he wants and buy you time to escape. Sevaka and Josiri will go with you." He turned to Josiri. "Get them clear of the grounds, then head south. Find your sister. I'm afraid we north-wealders have lived down to your every expectation, haven't we?"

Josiri nodded. "Close enough."

He'd no reason to stay. He'd come north for his own safety, and to save his people. Neither goal any longer held hope. But he couldn't entirely set aside how his mother, bereft of reasons to live, had instead chosen to die. All for want of someone to share her burdens. Malachi deserved better.

"I'm staying." He met Sevaka's gaze. "You owe Sidara your life. Remember that. Keep them safe."

She nodded. Malachi kissed his wife again. Slowly, reluctantly, she shepherded the children into the kitchen. Sevaka and Braxov followed, the former already limping.

As soon as they were out of sight, Malachi slumped. "I'd talk you out of this, but I find I really don't want to."

"I know," said Josiri. "Let's get it over with."

Fifty-Seven

The distant drumbeat kept Rosa awake more than the pain. Suffocating black notes against a red sky. Her heartbeat. Why a heartbeat if no blood coursed through her veins? She hid in that bleak humour, a shield against the metal slicing her flesh and joints bent out of shape. At least someone had removed the silvered sword, for whatever that was worth.

Gusting wind turned sweat cold. Rosa's eyelids fluttered. Red sky turned blue. The thump of her heart gave way to angry, broken voices. The Hayadra Grove stretched away before her, alabaster trees yielding to crowds cordoned behind soldiers' tabards and unmoving kraikons.

Far beneath her dangling feet, another kraikon toiled, fashioning a pyre of white logs about her gibbet's base. The cloying scent of fresh sap sweetened what shallow breaths the mooring spikes allowed.

"How easily tradition fades." The man in the feathered domino mask and battered velvet jacket was less a physical presence than a stain upon the grass. Neither kraikons nor crowd paid him any heed. "These trees were a gift to Lumestra. Now they'll birth the flames to swallow you whole. I doubt the goddess would have approved."

The sun emerged from behind a cloud, and cast a vast, bird-winged shadow behind the man. Rosa's questions died on a parched throat. She'd seen him before. The dance on the autumn path. In Malachi's bedchamber. How had she forgotten?

"Are you ready to come with me?" asked the Raven. "There's so little here for you now. Immolation is not a kind way to pass, even for an eternal. I can spirit you away from the fire, and from the Dark rushing close behind. But you have to ask."

"Why?" she gasped.

He offered a low, formal bow. "Because that's how it must be."

Rosa closed her eyes, overcome by shame. Kas. What would she say if she met him in the mists of Otherworld? Could she confess how badly she'd failed him? How she'd been used?

"No."

The Raven tilted his head. "A shame. I commend the day to you. Looks like it'll be a warm one."

He vanished like a shadow in sunlight. Rosa let her eyes fall closed and retreated into the red. Where she belonged.

"I'm sorry, high proctor," said Lilyana. "I didn't know where else to go. They'll be watching my father's house. King's Gate is sealed . . . The docks are thick with soldiers. I . . . "

She broke off. Sevaka glanced across the foundry's loading yard, embarrassed less by Lilyana's distress, and more at the part she'd played in causing it. Was there anything more useless than courage found too late?

Courage. That was a joke. Only her grip on the sword stopped her from shaking. Braxov had it together more than she did. Even Sidara's watchful composure put her to shame.

Elzar locked the slatted iron gate and set a hand on Lilyana's shoulder. "Hush, lady. You've chosen the best from a series of poor choices. You shall have shelter however long I can offer it."

"Why's it so quiet?" Constans' brow furrowed in thought. "Where is everyone?"

The boy was right, Sevaka realised. She'd been to the foundry on naval business many times, and it had never been less than a hive of activity. Now, the chainways were still, the forges silent. The interior, normally so brightly lit by hissing magic, was pitch dark. Even the air felt different. No longer thick and suffocating, it held the sharp acidic tang of cooling metal.

"I sent them home. Better that way."

"Then you know what's happening?" asked Lilyana.

"Some of it. Enough to be worried."

"We won't impose upon you for long," said Sevaka. "My old ship – the *Triumphal* – lies at anchor. If I can get word to them . . ."

Elzar shook his head. "You needn't worry about me, young lady. My fate was decided some time ago." He stared briefly over her shoulder and bundled the children towards the inner door. "Inside. Quickly."

Sevaka peered back through the gate. A triple column of soldiers in Freemont uniforms were marching through the empty street. A towering kraikon kept effortless pace alongside. She dragged Elzar out of sight.

Lilyana's face tightened. "They've found us."

"That all depends on who they want to arrest first," hissed Elzar. "Go! Head for my workshop at the top of the second tower."

Lilyana ran to join her children. Sevaka lingered, unwilling to leave the old proctor alone.

A gauntleted fist hammered on the gate. "High Proctor Ilnarov! You are called before the Council on a charge of aiding a fugitive. You will open these gates!"

"You know this man?" murmured Elzar.

"Captain Farran. Of my mother's hearthguard." At last, Sevaka's thoughts caught up with her ears. "Wait. Aiding and abetting *one* fugitive. That crack about your fate being decided. That wasn't pious gabble, was it?"

"One moment, captain! I seem to have misplaced the key!" Elzar lowered his voice to a whisper. "I *may* have freed Lord Akadra from the provosts."

"Viktor? Viktor's here?"

"About four-fifths of him. I left him sleeping. He's in a bad way."

A bronze hand closed over the top of the gate. A wail of tortured metal filled the air. Elzar touched a hand to his control amulet. His scowl gave way to a horrified grimace.

"It's not working. That kraikon won't obey my commands!"

The gate's upper edge peeled back. A hinge exploded from brickwork in a shower of dust. Elzar remained rooted in place, his lips working restlessly.

"My own trick used against me! Someone's altered the enchantment!"

The second of four hinges tore free. The gate shook. Sevaka grabbed

Elzar by the collar and shoved him towards the inner door. With a last glance at the trembling gate, she limped after him.

The gate struck cobbles with a jarring clang. The kraikon lumbered into the loading yard.

"Move it!" bellowed Farran. Impatience coursed through his veins. If Marek could go to the dogs, so could any of them. Malachi Reveque wasn't the only one with a family. "Drag them out by the heels if you must!"

Hearthguard flooded through the ruined gateway, swords out. Sergeant Volarn hung back, her face haunted by reluctance.

"I saw children. What about them?"

"Malachi Reveque's brats? They're on the list. They come with us."

"She's not sending them to the gallows too?"

Farran glared at her. "Why? Do you want me to tell Lady Kiradin you were asking?"

Volarn blanched, and no wonder.

"I don't like it either," Farran murmured. "Pray the kernclaw gets them first. Kinder on everyone."

Apara clung to the soot-clogged rafters and wondered again how she was to find Viktor Akadra in the labyrinthine foundry. The place was a mass of vaults, forges and ratway tunnels – to say nothing of the stowage crates and half-finished kraikons looming through the shadows. She could search for days and still not find him.

The assault on her senses made it all the worse. Not the darkness. She was no stranger to that. The panoply of echoes from running feet, the heat rising from the seething vats. She didn't care for it at all, and the raven-cloak liked it far less. Its voices squawked and fussed at the edge of her hearing, making a difficult search far worse.

A clatter of metal echoed up from below, chased along by a child's yelp. Apara shifted position, grasping for purchase on the motionless chainway as she scoured the gantry below.

There. A smudge of filthy white cloth in the gloom. A woman hauling a young boy to his feet. And behind, a man hurrying a girl up a scuffed stairway.

It was exactly what she needed. One fugitive to draw out another.

Letting go of the chainway, Apara spread her raven-cloak wide.

Sevaka steadied herself against the wall and gulped down stifling air. Whatever good Sidara had done the previous night had been rapidly undone through exertion. The heat from the smelting pit didn't help. Even with the metal dulled to a red smoulder, it sucked the breath from her lungs and dampened her clothes with sweat.

Elzar shook his head and flailed angrily at the air. "Stealing my kraikons! Twisting their enchantment! It goes against all tradition!"

That, Sevaka decided, was the very least of their worries. "There must be *some* that'll take your commands! This is the bloody foundry!"

Voices sounded behind. Sevaka twisted around. Farran's kraikon stood silhouetted in the loading yard doorway. Hearthguards streamed past, spreading out through the maze of forges and smelting pits.

She pushed clear of the wall and limped towards Elzar. "Come on, old man. Keep moving!"

He gave no sign of hearing. Just stood there between the wall and the smelting pit with both hands gripped to his useless control amulet.

"Hold fast!" bellowed a deep voice behind.

With faltering heart, Sevaka turned about. Two hearthguard bore down.

The nearest straightened in surprise. "Lady Sevaka? But you're ... dead?"

"Then leave my corpse be."

He shook his head. "Can't do that, my lady. Orders."

"Yes. I can imagine my mother being very clear."

Dredging forth her last strength, Sevaka sprang. Steel sparked as she battered a sword aside. She hacked down. A hearthguard screamed and fell at her feet.

The second stepped over the body of the first. Sevaka threw herself under his blade, half-stumbling, half-falling as her trembling leg gave way. Her shoulder took the man in the chest, slamming him back against the smelting pit's guard rail.

A brief cry. A desperate scrabbling hand. Then he was gone.

All but overcome, Sevaka fell to hands and knees. The kraikon started forward from the doorway. Three hearthguard advanced in a loose line behind.

The ground shook, slow and rhythmic at first, but with increasing speed. A new kraikon barrelled out of the darkness. Chains scattering from its lowered shoulders, it swept the advancing hearthguard aside and crashed into its twin. Fists slammed down in thunderous blows, the impact ringing out like church bells.

"Edvard will keep his sibling at bay, but he's the only one I've got." Elzar stooped and helped Sevaka to her feet. "The rest are damaged hulks or unfinished lumps."

Sevaka coughed into her hand. Bloody spittle gleamed. "So keep moving."

A scream rang out.

The man screamed as the raven-cloak tore into him. His back struck the guard rail. Then he was gone into the gloom beyond the gantry.

"Braxov!"

Grimy white skirts swirled as the woman spun around. One hand pushed the girl behind her. The other scraped a sword clear of a battered scabbard. The point wove and dipped. Her voice held no such uncertainty.

"Sidara! Constans! Run!"

Metal clattering beneath their feet, the children broke for the far stairway.

The woman moved to block the gantry. "You'll not have my children!"

Raven-cloak swirling around her, Apara darted aside. The woman's blade hissed past. Counterblow came as instinct. Claws flashed out. The woman shrieked and fell to her knees, sword abandoned and hands clasped to her face. Blood oozed between her fingers.

The raven-cloak croaked its triumph.

Apara kicked the sword over the gantry's edge.

"Mother!"

Sidara skidded to a halt on the stairs and reversed course. The woman shuffled along the gantry, waving blindly at her daughter. "Sidara! Go! Keep Constans safe!"

Blue eyes daring Apara to approach, the girl tugged at her mother's shoulder.

A child made for a better lure. Steeling her heart, Apara beckoned. "Come to me, girl, and I'll let your mother live."

Sidara glared at her unblinking. "Raven take you first!"

Bitter laughter swelled in Apara's chest. "He already has. Now come here!"

She lunged, fingers grasping for Sidara's wrist.

The girl flinched away. A furious scream tore free of her lips. Searing golden light exploded in the dark.

Viktor convulsed. Blankets scattering, he fell from the chair. Insubstantial dreams dissipated as sore muscles hauled him upright. What had woken him? He had a sense of a bright light, or the strike of a bell. But the more Viktor reached for answers, the less certain he became.

He cast about. Elzar's workshop. Everything flooded back. Hargo. The provosts. Rosa's accusations. Truth and lies intermingled. Like everything in the Republic.

He flexed his limbs. There was pain, but pain was to be expected. But there was no rush of blood to darken Elzar's imperfect bandages. It would do.

Screams echoed up from below. The strike of metal on metal. A child's sobs. The harsh screech of birds.

Viktor's breath misted as his shadow stirred. He let it rise.

"Come along, my old friend," he murmured. "We've slept too long."

The sonorous chimes of the kraikon-battle ended with a screech of tearing metal. Golden magic arced away into the rafters. Farran's kraikon, or Edvard? Sevaka had no way to know. Barked commands and running footsteps grew louder with every passing moment, just as Elzar grew slower with every step. They'd be caught, and sooner rather than later.

Unless something changed.

Her legs buckled as she reached for the banister. Brow streaming with sweat, Sevaka hauled herself into an approximation of upright. Elzar halted at the half-landing and stumbled back down the steps. Weathered hands reached for hers. She waved him away.

"I'm slowing you down," she said. "Leave me. Find Viktor."

He stopped, bushy brows knitting with indecision. "They'll kill you."

She laughed, the sound more gasp than mirth. "You don't know my mother. She'll want to lecture me first. Go."

Elzar gave a sharp nod and fled up the stairs.

Running footsteps grew nearer. Shadows took on ephemeral shape. Sevaka cast down her sword and folded her arms. "Here I am. You can take me to my mother now."

"Get back here, gutterling!" bellowed Farran.

The boy ignored him and ran full-tilt across the gantry. Farran caught him on the threshold to the next hallway. He snaked his hand about the boy's mouth and dragged him back off his feet.

"Got you, you little ... "

The brat bit down hard on the heel of his hand. Howling in pain, Farran cuffed the boy about the head. The child hit the floor. Defiant eyes blazed through tears.

Farran grabbed the brat again – by the collar this time – and yanked him to his feet. "You want to live to see daylight?"

The sullen stare was his only reply.

Volarn stepped from the stairway. "Everything under control, captain?"

"You being funny, sergeant?"

"No, sir." Her eyes dipped briefly to the boy. "Looks a handful. The high proctor's still here somewhere. We've got Lady Sevaka. Kernclaw's playing with the rest."

Farran shuddered. Orders were orders, but just because her ladyship had commanded he work alongside the vranakin didn't mean he had to like it. Even thinking about her made the shadows lengthen. "Any sign of Akadra?"

"Not a glimpse. Maybe the kernclaw already got him."

Wouldn't that be nice? Farran tried to ignore the chill settling in his bones. All of a sudden, he longed for the daylight. "All right. We'll take this one out and leave her to it. You know Akadra's reputation. I don't want to run into him."

"Too late," rumbled a new voice. "He has already found you."

The shadows pulsed. Farran didn't even have time to scream.

*

Viktor let the bodies fall. Constans stared at him with dark, disbelieving eyes. The lad had courage, at least.

"Uncle Viktor?"

Viktor gathered the trembling boy into an embrace. "Where's Malachi? Where's your father?"

"They came for him. Uncle Josiri too. We had to run."

A swell of rage fought the cold of Viktor's shadow. So he'd only been the first? Viktor saw no need to ask who "they" were. Not with two of Ebigail Kiradin's hearthguard lying dead at his feet.

"And your mother? Your sister?"

Constans pointed back the way he'd come.

Viktor released the boy and slid the sword from the dead captain's scabbard.

"Stay close," he rumbled.

The girl was halfway along the gantry by the time Apara's vision cleared. She had her mother's left arm across her shoulders. The right still clasped a hand to an injured face.

Blinking away blue-black splotches, Apara soared across the intervening span. A thrust of her elbow knocked the mother clear. Then she had one hand across the girl's mouth, and her claws against her throat.

"I don't want to hurt you," she breathed, "but I'll slice you open if you do that again. Do you understand me?"

Sidara nodded. Her quick, shallow breaths rushed over Apara's fingers. Apara tried not to think about the threat she'd just made, and to whom. She let her hand fall.

"I didn't mean to," the girl whimpered. "Don't hurt my mother."

"Viktor Akadra!" shouted Apara. "I know you're here! Show yourself, and I'll let the child go!"

How far she'd get with the foundry full of Freemont hearthguard was another matter, but that was hardly Apara's concern.

"Well, *Lord* Akadra! What's it to be?"

The mother lowered her hand from her face. Ragged gouges ran from chin to brow across her right cheek. "Please," she begged. "Let my daughter go. You have me. I won't fight."

Apara brushed the girl's cheek. "As long as I hold her, I have you both. I'm guessing a man of Lord Akadra's reputation won't easily pass that up."

"Are you certain?" Akadra emerged from the darkness of the gantry, the boy trailing behind him. "Of late, Lord Akadra's reputation is not what it was."

"You're here, aren't you?"

"And in some demand, it would seem. What do you want?"

Apara hesitated. Akadra was most definitely not what she'd expected. The title of Council Champion carried the image of a battle-tempered brute, with as much muscle between his ears as in his sword arm. The bruised giant looked the part, but his voice lay heavily at odds.

"It's very simple." She filled her voice with ebbing confidence. "You die. They live."

He stepped closer. "No. That isn't what's going to happen."

Apara gripped Sidara's forehead. "Stay back!"

He came on another step. "Let her go, and *you* live to warn Ebigail that I'm coming for her."

The words should have sounded ridiculous. From him, they formed a promise certain as death. Apara felt the first flutter of panic. "You heard my terms."

He shook his head. "This isn't a negotiation."

"I'll kill her." Raven damn them both. Couldn't he see she didn't have a choice?

"You won't." Akadra's eyes dropped. "Sidara? Do you trust me, little one?"

"I . . . I do, uncle."

"Then close your eyes."

For the second time since entering the foundry, Apara went blind. This time, there was no searing light, no flash of brilliance. There was only darkness. Suffocating. Pervasive. Penetrating. It coursed through her, ice crackling beneath her skin – beneath her eyes. The raven-cloak shrieked in terror. Then the world fell away, and she with it.

Viktor caught the woman's falling body, his shadow soaring as it enveloped her. Fingers hooked like claws, he tore her cloak to tatters. Bird-voices screamed in agony. Feathers burst into strands of black vapour and spiralled away like fading smoke. Viktor shuddered as unfamiliar magic washed over him. Then he turned his attention on the woman once more.

The contradicting tangle of her soul unwound like yarn, fears gleaming bright and reluctance shimmering like silver. It wouldn't take much, sang his shadow. Just a gentle tug. A caress. The woman could be redeemed. She could serve a better, nobler purpose than Ebigail Kiradin's schemes.

He'd felt the lure before, in the Southshires. When Josiri had first refused him. On that occasion, he'd turned aside. How many lives could he have saved had he done otherwise? And the woman was *not* Josiri. She had the stink of Otherworld about her. A vranakin. A murderer. He owed her nothing . . .

The woman screamed and twisted free of his hands. Eyes feral and face taut with terror, she flung herself from the gantry. Viktor's fingers closed on empty air.

Viktor cursed under his breath. The kernclaw was gone. Lost. And to his surprise, the piece of his shadow that had assailed her lost alongside. He expected to feel diminished, lessened with the dwindling of himself. But somehow, he felt more complete than ever.

Opening his eyes, he faced the Reveques. Lilyana, on her feet once more, had her arms tight about her children. Her face was slick with blood and tears, but her eyes shone.

"Bless you, Viktor."

Elzar staggered out of the gloom, doubled over and a splayed hand to his heaving chest. "They're falling back." He stared down at the motionless vranakin. "Those that can. They've taken Sevaka."

Viktor frowned. Clearly the tangle of the vranakin's soul was nothing to that which had claimed Tressia. "Tell me. All of it."

Fifty-Eight

They marched across the city in a tight column, Captain Horden at their head. Two dozen constables and Freemont hearthguard for a pair of unarmed and shackled captives. Ridiculous, Malachi decided, but for the reason.

No one appeared particularly happy, least of all Horden himself. The captain had made a perfunctory reading of the arrest warrant, but that hadn't stopped him from making a thorough search of house and grounds.

"The captain doesn't seem pleased," Josiri muttered. The southwealder held his head high and shoulders back. Malachi envied his composure. "What do you reckon? Conscience, or confusion?"

Malachi sighed. "Does it matter?"

"It always matters. Just because they've made you a prisoner doesn't mean you have to think like one."

Malachi bit back an angry response. Josiri was right. He still had his wits. Better to use them. As the column drew to a halt outside the constabulary barracks, he took his opportunity.

"Captain Horden, I'd like to speak with you."

Horden stiffened and made his way back along the ranks. Malachi's escorts drew back, their newfound distance as much an illusion of privacy as it was the possibility of freedom.

"Don't make this more difficult." Horden spoke without meeting his gaze.

One vote for conscience. Perhaps. "You're a servant of the Council. Of the Republic. What Ebigail's doing ... it'll tear both apart. You're better than this, Mikel."

Horden clenched and unclenched a fist. "It is what it is."

He turned away and bellowed towards the gate. "Bring the others! They'll all hang come dusk!"

Malachi tamped down resurgent desperation. He'd always known this would end on the gallows. Treason always did, whether real or imagined. But to hear it confirmed . . .

"And what of your children?" he demanded. "What do they think of their father's deeds?"

Horden's bunched fist drove the breath from Malachi's lungs and left him a winded wreck on filthy cobbles. Malachi twisted aside as a boot stomped down. Leather grazed his scalp.

"Leave him be!" Josiri thrust himself between them. Two constables dragged him away.

"My children?" Horden squatted beside Malachi, eyes blazing. He spoke in a hushed, bitter whisper. "The Crowmarket has them. What would you do?"

Malachi found no good answer. Not that he'd the breath for one.

Horden strode back towards the gate. "What're the rest of you looking at?"

Constables averted their eyes.

Josiri, released with Horden's retreat, helped Malachi stand. "Picking a fight wasn't what I had in mind."

"Ebigail's in league with the Crowmarket," Malachi said. "That's how she's got her hooks into Horden. You can bet that's why the chapter-houses are looking the other way. Tassandra refused to play, and they killed her for it."

"Whatever Ebigail paid, the vranakin will want more."

"Hardly helps us, does it?" Malachi frowned. There *was* something there, although he couldn't quite see the shape of it . . .

At last, the constabulary gates opened. Two dozen prisoners swelled the column – members of the Grand Council, and a handful of aides. A grey-haired and neat-bearded fellow fell into step beside Malachi, his lips parted in a sardonic smile.

"Well I never. Malachi Reveque. And this, I presume, is the trouble-some Duke of Eskavord."

Malachi nodded. "Josiri? Jardon Krain, councillor for Rackan and the Outer Eastshires."

"No friend to Ebigail Kiradin, I assume?" said Josiri.

Krain's green eyes twinkled. "Friends don't have friends arrested on charges of treason, and certainly not at dawn. Most uncivilised. Would you believe she sent Prydonis knights for me? I suppose I should count that a compliment."

So Ebigail had the loyalty of Prydonis as well? The chapterhouses were more than looking the other way – they were as complicit as Horden, and likely for the same reason. However readily Ebigail cast her own family aside, she understood the power of blood.

Horden bellowed, and the column moved out.

"You know where they're taking us?" asked Josiri.

"I hear tell of the Hayadra Grove," said Krain. "A burning and a forest of gallow-trees. We should make quite the spectacle."

The road narrowed and climbed into the heart of the old town. Timber-framed houses leaned closer as if to examine the curious parade. Malachi glimpsed worried faces at leaded windows. Worried, or perhaps grateful the day's events were passing them by.

Josiri drifted closer. "If they get us to the grove, we're dead."

Malachi glanced back at their fellow captives without enthusiasm. Twenty-odd manacled prisoners – most of them far older than he – matched against an equal number of guards. Slim odds. Very slim. And that was assuming the others would fight. Most looked too beaten to consider resistance.

"You don't give up, do you?"

The column lurched to a halt before Josiri could reply.

Malachi stared out over the shoulders of the leading constables. A knight stood in the middle of the road, arms folded. Tan skin betrayed a life lived beyond the city walls, and a hunter's green surcoat proclaimed his loyalty to Essamere. This last, he shared with the double rank of men and women stood behind.

"Well, well, well," he said, the eastsider's hollow vowels and softened consonants echoing along the street. "This is a right shabby parade, and no mistake."

Horden broke ranks, his hand on his sword. "Stand aside, Izack. We're under council orders."

"Is that so?" Izack drifted closer. However nonchalant his manner,

Malachi found no levity in voice or expression. "Seems to me you've more of the Council in chains than you'll find on the hill. You sure you've the right of all this?"

Horden drew his sword.

"Clear the road," he growled. "These men are traitors."

Izack tugged the wrinkles out of his uniform. "I'm a simple soul. I don't put much stock in fancy speeches. I draw my own conclusions. When I see one of our best trussed like a hog for the roast? When I find my mistress in a pool of her own blood at the heart of our chapterhouse? Those conclusions get a mite uncharitable."

"You owe the Council your loyalty!" Horden's protest held more than a whiff of hypocrisy. But maybe that was why he sounded so angry.

"Bugger the Council," spat Izack. "We fight for Essamere, and Essamere fights for the Republic. I reckon it could use us right now."

Running feet thumped on cobbles. Alleyways came alive with hunter's green and the shine of steel. Within moments, prisoners and escort were surrounded by some fifty knights. Constables and Freemont hearthguard froze with swords half-drawn, then cast their weapons down.

Horden broke for the nearest alley, a desperate bellow spilling from his lips. A clash of swords, a shove to send a knight crashing against brick, and he was gone.

"Let him go!" shouted Izack. "Tie the rest up. We'll take 'em back to the chapterhouse. Might be they find some bloody sense along the way."

As the knights busied themselves with Horden's troops, Izack pushed through the throng and freed first Malachi's shackles, then Josiri's.

Malachi rubbed his wrists. "Thank you, captain."

Izack grinned wolfishly. "Not me."

He shared a glance with Josiri, who shrugged. "Then who?"

"You'll see."

Josiri wasn't at all surprised to find a battered and bloodied Viktor waiting at the Essamere chapterhouse. The presence of the Reveques, he took less easily in his stride – especially upon learning of Braxov's death – but the shared joy of father and family was a welcome sight.

Leaving Malachi to a heartfelt reunion in the officers' quarters, Josiri hung back in the muster yard and joined Viktor in the cool, deep shadows beside the chapterhouse well. He was once again in armour with a claymore strapped across his back, though this time the surcoat was hunter's green, not black.

"Come north, you said. I can protect you there, you said."

Viktor shook his head. "Of late, my promises have not been all they should."

Haunted eyes told a deeper tale. Josiri decided the details could wait. "What happens now?"

"Now?" Viktor arched an eyebrow. "Now, we put a stop to this nonsense."

"Just you and me?"

"And as many as will follow. We cast Kai Saran from the Southshires. Do you suppose Ebigail Kiradin more dangerous?"

"Yes."

"You should. Essamere stands with us. Alone, so far."

Icy fingers danced along Josiri's spine. "A few dozen knights? It's not enough."

"Don't let Captain Izack hear you. But yes, most are on the border. It's the business of knights to be in battle, and we're fortunate to have as many as we do. Too many follow Ebigail out of habit. I hate to say it, but my fellow northwealders lack your people's fire. They're too easily led."

"Be glad they've not had to learn defiance," Josiri replied. "It's a hard lesson."

"And one that must be taught today. Revolution is like glass. For a time it is malleable from the fire of its birth, but once it cools? Then, only destruction will serve." Viktor's gaze slackened as he stared not at what lay around him, but a future only he beheld. "I'd spare everyone that."

Josiri cast his mind back to the plaza filled with soldiers and a cheering crowd. "Didn't you say we were outnumbered?"

"I *implied* it. But there's little choice. Ebigail has woven lies to protect herself. If we pluck her from that web, perhaps events will return to their proper course. If we offer defiance, others will break from her side."

"And if they don't?"

Viktor shrugged.

"That's what I thought," said Josiri wearily. "What about the vranakin?"

"The Crowmarket has no taste for defeat. If we prove Ebigail vulnerable, they'll abandon her."

"That's a leap."

"Nothing else will serve. If we do not come for her, she'll surely come for us."

Josiri glanced about the courtyard. The chapterhouse was a sturdy enough fortress, its thick walls a throwback to more fractious times. But it wouldn't hold long against kraikons. "You're still the Council's champion. Surely you can rally support out in the shires?"

"Ebigail's had a busy morning. If Izack's to be believed, there are 'traitors' enough gathered at the Hayadra Grove to keep the gallows swinging until dawn – members of Malachi's extended family among them." Viktor shrugged. "And Rosa? Rosa is my friend. For her alone, I'd take this chance. But you? You may go wherever you wish. Home, if that's what calls you. I'll think nothing less of you. This isn't your fight. I wish it weren't mine."

The words were different to those Malachi had used that morning, but the sense was the same.

"People keep telling me that," Josiri replied. "But I don't think I can."

Viktor clapped him on the shoulder. A grin broke like sunlight from behind storm clouds. "Then let's be about our business."

Viktor watched Josiri cross the courtyard to the brutish blockhouse of the Essamere armoury. At last, there was true accord between them, but the price . . . Why did fate hate him so?

"Uncle Viktor?"

He forced a smile. "Sidara. Aren't you supposed to be with your parents?"

"They're arguing again. I doubt they've even noticed I'm gone."

"What are they arguing about?"

She pulled herself up onto the rim of the well and sat in silence for a time, heels kicking back and forth. "Mother tells me I shouldn't use my light to help people – even her. She says I should keep it secret."

Was she answering his question, or was this a different conversation entirely? Viktor couldn't tell – he'd never been good at reading children. He'd suspected Sidara of being gifted for several months, but hadn't known how to broach the topic with father or daughter.

"She wants you safe."

"But I helped Lady Sevaka. It was the right thing to do ..." Her tone wavered. "Wasn't it?"

Sevaka. What had become of her? Another fly caught in her mother's web. "Sometimes it's not enough to be right, little one."

One eye narrowed to a scowl. "That's not fair."

"No. It's not."

Sidara thought for a long moment, lips pursed and eyes downcast. "*You* use your magic to help others, don't you, uncle?"

So she *had* seen. Viktor had hoped the gloom of the foundry had kept his secret, but he supposed it no longer mattered. "Not as often as I should."

"Why?"

Why indeed? "It's complicated."

"Grown-ups always say that when they don't want to answer the question."

He smiled. "Yes we do."

She grinned back. "So what should I do?"

"What do you *want*?"

Another pause. "To help people. Mother and Father are for ever talking about duty. What if this is mine?"

She sounded so earnest. So much nobler than he had at her age. So much less twisted up with anger and loss. He squeezed her shoulder. "Then I think your mother will understand, little one, if not easily. And when this is done, we'll see what can be done about lessons."

Blue eyes widened in excitement. "Truly?"

"Have I ever lied to you?"

"Never, uncle."

Viktor was glad she thought so. Yes, a far nobler child than he'd been. A good omen for the Republic, if it could be preserved for her to inherit.

Time to do something about that.

*

"It seems failure is the tonic of the hour, so readily do you all sup of it."

Ebigail Kiradin stood before the church altar, her lips twisted in distaste at Horden's grovelling bow. Apara hung her head, knowing the criticism was directed at her as much as the guard captain. Worse, she couldn't truly recall *how* she'd failed. Lady Reveque's scream ... a burst of light, and then ... nothing. She couldn't even remember what had become of the raven-cloak, only that it was gone. Uneasiness of the consequences to come should have outweighed her sense of failure, but Lady Kiradin was close to hand, and her elder cousins were not.

"I ... I can go back," stuttered Horden, his eyes still fixed on the nave's gold-chased tiles. "If you'll lend me a portion of the 7th ... "

Lady Kiradin stared up at the eastern window. Radiant Lumestra stared back, her expression frozen in coloured glass. Inscrutable, the both of them.

"I will not compound failure, captain." Her gaze drifted to the two-score haggard prisoners at the church's rear. "We've traitors enough to serve as example. Besides, young Viktor's pride won't let him stand apart. You may atone by making preparations for his arrival. This first failure I will generously discount. Further lapses? Well, those I'll have no choice but to interpret as wilfulness. And the wilful do not prosper in *my* Tressia."

Apara judged it no accident that Lady Kiradin's iron stare took in Mannor and Rother, masters of the Prydonis and Sartorov chapterhouses. Lord Karev, commander of the 7th, had earlier been despatched to take charge of the city's gates.

The citizenry might follow Lady Kiradin out of patriotic fervour, but the soldiery required guidance. And the soldiers' commanders required ... motivation. Motivation Apara's cousins had provided through the seizing of loved ones. She wondered at the future Lady Kiradin sought to build on such foundations. Rother's venomous glances suggested his leash had already stretched almost to breaking point. He was surely not alone.

"Are you struck by wilfulness, Captain Horden?"

"No."

"Good. Do your duty."

Straightening, Horden marched stiffly past the hushed choir of serenes and out into the grove.

Soft, bitter laughter echoed around the nave. Apara's heart sank.

Ebigail turned slowly about, her expression cold as it fell upon her youngest daughter. Of all the church's unwilling congregation, only Sevaka seemed without fear. Her hands bound and her face haggard, she hung from the arms of her hearthguard captors as one without the strength to stand. But still she burned with defiance.

"You find something amusing?" snapped Ebigail.

The laughter faded. "Don't you see? The firmer you grip, the faster everything falls apart."

Apara wordlessly pleaded her sister to silence. That Sevaka had survived was the only shaft of sunlight in troubled skies. She'd hoped the younger woman would have the wit to hold her tongue – that Lady Kiradin might stir herself to forgiveness. Those foolish hopes faded as Sevaka warmed to her theme.

"So certain in your strength," she sneered. "The proud Kiradin matriarch. The rocky shore upon whom the waves of history break. But you're blind. Too blind to see the lesson."

"And what lesson is that?" Lady Kiradin advanced a pace with every crisply enunciated word.

"That the weak only need one another to be strong. I hope they tear you apart."

Lady Kiradin trembled, her composure scattered to the winds. "My daughter is dead!" she screamed. "Set this prizrak on the pyre. I want to see it burn!"

Josiri emerged from the armoury, already cursing the sweltering afternoon sun. Only lingering memories of near-misses at Davenwood prevented him from having the layered steel plates and padded jerkin peeled back off. And so he remained, a crab roasting in a shell not his own.

He counted seventy knights, and perhaps fifty hearthguard in a mix of Reveque, Krain and Akadra livery. Scarcely more than a hundred blades, and Ebigail Kiradin had a city.

Viktor remained unyielding as ever, Malachi distracted. An older man stood close by, his fingers tapping idly on a control amulet. He reminded Josiri of Gavamor, now dead at Makrov's order.

"Now that's a sight," said Izack. "A southwealder in full armour. Shouldn't you be in the shadows, readying a knife?"

Josiri spoke before Viktor could offer rebuke. "Maybe later. It'll give you time to whip up some support. I've never known north fight south without at least ten to one advantage."

Malachi looked at the flagstones. Viktor's lip curled in amusement. Izack stared. Josiri grew uncomfortably aware that Izack had his ten to one odds close by, and then more if he chose.

Izack threw back his head and roared with laughter. "Oh, I like him. You're not hiding any more hereabouts?"

"We'll have to make do." Viktor nodded at the old man with the amulet. "Josiri, this is High Proctor Elzar Ilnarov. He'll assist us with the kraikons."

Josiri's ears pricked up at the guarded reverence. "As easy as that?"

Elzar shook his head. "I'm afraid not. I've already fallen foul of a kraikon with a corrupted enchantment. There are bound to be more. Lady Kiradin's been stealing them for months."

"Hang about," said Izack. "Stealing kraikons? Are you telling me she had a bunch sitting around in a warehouse, just waiting for this?"

He bristled. "Not exactly. I had a chance to examine some remains. The alterations are subtle *and* remain hidden until triggered. I expect Lady Kiradin had a tame proctor set them loose in the city until they were needed. Who'd notice? Who complains about too many kraikons?"

Josiri cast his mind back to Eskavord, the silhouettes of the bronze giants dark against sunshine. "I could have managed with fewer, these past years."

"So might we all today," said Viktor. "We've no way to know how many are Ebigail's, and how many aren't."

Izack scratched the back of his head. "I just hope you're right about folk coming to their senses, otherwise it's going to get very lonely up there." He threw a salute at the assembled soldiers. "All right, lads and lasses. Time to be heroes."

The captain at their head, the soldiery filed into the street.

"Go," said Malachi. "Try not to do anything foolish."

Josiri snorted. "Too late. You're not coming?"

"I'll only get in the way. My weapons are words, not swords. Remember?"

He nodded. In many ways it was the correct decision – the practical decision. So why then did Josiri have the sense that something else lay hidden behind Malachi's eyes?

Viktor beckoned. "Come. Time grows short. Be well, Malachi."

The other nodded mutely and waved them to the gate. "Go. Carry my greeting to Ebigail."

A heavy tramp of feet. A swirl of dust in the parched courtyard. Then they were gone. Malachi's grimace, so long held back, stole across his face.

Lily arrived at his shoulder. Her face was pale save for her livid, crusted wounds. His heart went out to her, as it had from their first reunion. The Essamere physician had done her best to stitch them closed, but Lily would bear those marks as long as she lived.

"Are they gone?" she asked.

"They are." He braced himself for an argument renewed. It wasn't that Lily didn't understand. Goddess, but she understood better than he did. But understanding was only ever half the battle. "I should go too."

Her face fell. "I wish you didn't have to do this."

"So do I. But what else is there? Who else is there? Krain?"

"Then *I'll* go."

"We both know that won't work." He took her head in his hands. "How many times have you told me to do better?"

Her eyes glistened. "Just once."

"And how often have you *wished* that of me?"

Her shoulders trembled with reluctant laughter. "On more occasions than I can count."

A tear trickled down her cheek. In that moment, he wavered. It would be so easy to remain at the chapterhouse, in the company of his wife and children. To let others fight battles that were his.

"If I'd listened before, maybe none of this would be necessary." He smoothed a thumb across Lily's cheek, brushed the tear away. So many years wasted on coldness and quarrel, and now it was too late. "The fault is mine ... but my heart belongs to you."

Sorrow hardening to determination, Malachi let his hands fall and strode purposefully to the gate. He halted at Lily's call.

"I'm proud of you, Malachi Reveque. Come home to me."

Lily stood framed in the archway, burdened but unbowed. Without a word, he pressed on into the streets.

Fifty-Nine

Josiri heard the low, close-harmony dirge of hymns soon after leaving the chapterhouse. Though distance made the words impossible to sift, the melodies were plain enough. Ridiculous at first, they made disturbing sense on further contemplation. Ebigail intended great change. The hymns offered ties to the past and a promise that the future would not stray.

"Halt!"

The cry rang out from a line of toppled wagons. King's blue uniforms and worried faces lined the timber crest. Banners fluttered limply overhead, the numerals and spread-winged badge of the 7th Regiment barely visible. Two kraikons stood silently behind, swords held at guard.

Viktor quickened his pace.

"Stay back!" The challenger's voice rose in pitch. "Stay back!"

Crossbows appeared along the barricade and on the rooftops behind. Enough to rip the heart from any advance.

"Drakonback!" bellowed Izack. "Form drakonback!"

The Essamere ranks closed tight about Josiri, his shield locked tight between Izack's to his left and another knight's to his right. The sun turned dark as the second rank hoisted their shields high. And all of it without a missed step.

Only Viktor advanced alone. He hadn't even drawn his sword.

"I know that voice!" His words echoed along the cramped street. "Moldrov! Is that you?"

An older man in a major's uniform appeared on the barricade. He raised his hand, fingers skyward – the precursor to the signal to loose. "Don't make me give the order, my lord!"

"A long time since we held the Ravonn together."

"I remember it well."

Viktor halted. "Then you know the only way to stop me is to shoot. You know what's about to happen. Is that what we fought for on the border?"

Finally catching up to Viktor, the drakonback slowed to a stop. Josiri's arm ached from holding the shield level. His shoulders were raw from the press of ill-fitting armour. Every breath tasted of metal-tinged sweat, and the sour exhalations of his fellows.

"They're traitors!" shouted Moldrov. "And I hear you're a witch."

"Then where is the trial? Where is the proof?" The claymore scraped clear from its slings. "Shoot if you must. Otherwise, get out of my way."

Josiri caught his breath. The overlaid shields of the drakonback would stop most quarrels. But Viktor . . . ?

Moldrov's hand dropped. "Let them through."

Josiri sighed his relief. Izack gave a grim chuckle.

"Bring him down!" A new voice rang out from the barricades. A Freemont hearthguard appeared on the crest. She pointed a quavering finger down at Viktor. "Bring them all down!"

Crossbows levelled anew in uncertain hands. Moldrov's expression, suffused with reluctance a heartbeat before, grew hard. "I've made my decision."

"Akadra's a witch! Those with him are traitors!"

"Then they belong in the grove, with the other witches and traitors, don't they?" He turned away, no longer addressing the furious hearthguard, but his soldiers. "They go through."

Izack tutted. "Shields down! It's gone awful boring out here!"

The drakonback unfolded. Sunlight flooded in, bringing a welcome breeze to Josiri's skin. Viktor started towards the barricade.

"No!"

The hearthguard rounded on the nearest kraikon. Her hand went to her control amulet. The bronze giant crackled to life. Soldiers scattering before it, the kraikon mounted the barricade.

Izack's sword came up. "Until Death!"

"*Until Death!*" The knights surged forward, Josiri with them.

Behind the barricade, the second kraikon awoke. Letting its sword fall, it vaulted the barricade. Without slowing, it closed one hand about the first kraikon's neck and planted the other in the small of its back.

Glass, brick and timber gave way with a splintering crash as the first kraikon struck the nearest house. With a mournful rumble, the roof collapsed, burying both constructs. Golden light crackled across exposed brick and leapt skyward.

"Oh dear," muttered Elzar, hand falling from his own amulet. "Two more to repair."

Josiri grinned with relief and stared up at the barricade. The hearthguard was on her knees, a sword at her back. Moldrov slipped the amulet from her neck and tossed it into the street.

"How can we help?" he asked.

"Hold this street," said Viktor. "If this goes badly, we'll need a line of retreat. Can you do that?"

Moldrov nodded. He raised his voice, staring up and down the barricade. "Lady Kiradin'll call that treason, so if anyone wants to leave, now's the time."

No one moved. Moldrov nodded in satisfaction. "Lumestra be with you."

Malachi edged down the stairway. Even with the sun blazing bright, this portion of the dockside lay heavily in shadow. Ramshackle buildings leaned in like forest eaves. Crooked chimneys clawed skyward like bare branches. Here, as in the old town, the streets were deserted, but they were deserted in a different way. The eyes dogging Malachi's footsteps weren't fearful, but predatory. Curiosity held them at bay, but curiosity wouldn't last.

Heart hammering harder with every step, he descended deeper into the knot of alleyways. The stench made his throat gag and his eyes water. There were no sewers down here below water-level, no rush to carry away the gutter-mulch.

Handkerchief held to nose and mouth, he pressed on, heading always downhill. Sun-motifs on lintels and cornerstones gave way to serpentine swirls, themselves half-hidden beneath crude daubings of spread wings. Not the wings of a serathi, but a crow, or a raven.

Not for the first time, he wished he'd listened to Lily. Most didn't leave

Dregmeet the same as they entered. Some didn't leave at all. The hopes he'd entertained faded. Behind, they left only the prospect of a slit throat and a grave among the grime.

At last, the alleyway opened up onto a narrow square. A marble fountain sat at the very heart, its waters limp and clogged – the cheeks of its statue stained by black tears. Woman from the waist up and snake below, her face was curiously bereft of malice. Wings spread behind, the mass of uneven wooden spars and rotting feathers bound to the stone by fraying rope. What other art the fountain had once borne was long since lost beneath generations of scrawl.

Beyond, a church sat sullen and dark. Its squared-off bell towers were of a design that had passed out of use long before Malachi's birth – before even the Republic had risen from the ashes of Malatriant's rule. Broken windows leered like narrowed eyes. Bowed walls strained between the weight of black ivy. Mist trickled between the worn headstones and headless serathi of the tiny churchyard.

Struck by sudden dizziness, Malachi stared up past jettied timbers. He caught no sight of the sun, only distant cracks of blue sky. He was truly down in the dregs. That he'd come willingly was no consolation.

"Malachi Reveque." A patch of gloom about the fountain shifted form. Green eyes gleamed beneath a grey hood. "You are a long way from home. This is a place for those that have no place."

"I . . ." He clenched his fist to quell its tremors. "I come to petition the Parliament of Crows."

"Is that so?" The figure drifted closer. "And what do you offer?"

Hairs prickled on the back of Malachi's neck. He glanced over his shoulder. There were grey shapes in the alleyway, and feather-cloaked kernclaws amid the chimneys. Watching. Waiting.

He turned his attention back to the fountain – to the elder cousin who waited silently for an answer.

"That's for the Parliament's ears."

For a long time, the elder cousin said nothing. A bell tolled, low and mournful. The church gate yawned back into mist-wreathed darkness.

"They will hear you." The elder cousin drifted away. "Come."

After only the briefest hesitation, Malachi followed him into the mists.

*

Rosa jerked awake, roused by the clamour of battle. Bleary eyes strove to make sense of what she beheld. The panicked crowd fleeing from the hilltop. The buckling cordon of king's blue uniforms on the grove's edge. Kraikon trading blows to shake the sky. And in the thick of it, a wedge of green uniforms, glittering in the sun. Had the Hadari come? Was Tressia invaded?

"Rosa?" The voice scraped like sand on skin, but savage glee shone beneath. "Hold on, Rosa!"

Sevaka?

Rosa twisted her head. Ravaged flesh tore anew on mooring spikes. It *was* Sevaka, bound and tied – not nailed – to a second gibbet set within the pyre. Like Rosa, her feet sat mere inches above the stacked timber. Dozens more gibbets stood in the outer ring of trees. Empty nooses spoke to purpose unfulfilled. A knot of bound prisoners within a ring of swords made that purpose plain.

A little further distant, Ebigail Kiradin stood in a knot of hearth-guard, staring out across the chaos with a rigid expression.

Rosa stared again at the carnage. The green was not that of the Hadari, but of Essamere. Her Essamere. Her comrades. And there at their head. Viktor. The friend she'd betrayed. He'd come for her. And now he'd die for it.

All her fault.

"You mustn't think badly of yourself." The Raven sat cross-legged beneath her feet, fingers drumming idly on logs. "Everybody dies, sooner or later."

Was she really so transparent? No wonder Ebigail had twisted her so easily. "Why?" she croaked. "Why . . . are you . . . here?"

The Raven cracked a smile. "Why not? It promises to be an interesting afternoon."

The line of king's blue broke. Viktor didn't blame them. Most were constables, trained for keeping peace and for containing crowds of the sort that tore and clawed at one another as they sought to escape the grove. Holding firm against the Essamere onslaught was another matter entirely.

"Hold!" he bellowed. "Stay together!"

The Essamere wedge shook itself back into shape, hearthguard moving to fill gaps emptied by ill-luck.

"Run back to her ladyship!" Izack shouted at the retreating line. "She might have spines you can borrow!"

"A little decorum, captain," said Viktor. "These are our people."

Izack shrugged. "Should have the sense not to fight, shouldn't they?"

Viktor nodded. "Redress the ranks. Knights to the fore. Everyone else behind."

Izack clasped a hand in salute. "Gladly, my lord."

Truth was, the constabulary had held longer than he'd expected. Long enough for a new line to form. A stiffer proposition, thick with the red of Prydonis and the blue wolf of Sartorov – to say nothing of the kraikons waiting silently behind. Viktor counted a full dozen waiting on the steps of the pyre. Enough to batter his tiny army apart. Elzar had salvaged three kraikons of his own from the initial battle. It wasn't going to be enough.

If nothing else, they'd robbed Ebigail of her audience. What had been a muster of thousands had quickly reduced to a few hundred curious or macabre souls. *And* the hymns had fallen silent. Viktor had never cared for hymns.

Josiri drew up in bloodied armour. "I'm surprised Ebigail's still here."

Viktor cast his gaze to the knot of figures on the pyre's steps. "Why would she flee? Our deaths set her ascension hard as iron. How does it feel to live your mother's dream?"

"Waging war against the Council on their land, not ours?" He flashed a weary smile. "I fear we'll end as she did."

Deep down, deeper even than his shadow, Viktor shared that fear, but he dared not say so.

"Thank you for standing with me, brother."

Josiri stared off across the hilltop. "You stood with me first. I just wish this had ended better."

"That's not for us to choose. We do all that we can, and hope our labours are equal to the task. But I think Calenne would be glad to see us fighting together."

"Perhaps."

Viktor stared back at his dwindled army and let his shadow swell. Just a little. Enough to know it would come when called. Even a glimpse of his magic would make truth of Ebigail's lies. But the time for discretion was rapidly falling behind.

"We go in hard. We go in fast. Essamere leads the charge. You come behind. Free as many prisoners as you can, and get them away."

Suspicion gleamed in Josiri's eyes. "And you?"

"I fear I shall have to do something ... provocative. But I would not see it wasted. Can I trust you with this duty, brother?"

The play of Josiri's expression told Viktor he at least *suspected* the truth – that the request sprang as much from giving Josiri a fighting chance at survival as any other factor. But he nodded all the same.

The church was as decrepit inside as out, with cracked tiles underfoot and pews sagging like mooring rope at high tide. Rubble skittered away from Malachi's feet as he drew near to the altar.

Mist hid the walls from sight more often than not. At times, they were narrow tile. At others, rotten plaster or crumbling brick. The world drew back with every step, leaving Malachi abandoned in a place that was no place.

The elder cousin held up a hand as he reached the altar. No other had crossed the church's threshold. A bell tolled. The mists ebbed, and three black marbled thrones stood revealed beneath a vast iron chandelier; preachers' pulpits left for centuries in sodden dark, their stalactite-crusted flanks lending stone the waxy appearance of dying candles. No two were on a level, nor shared more than the simplest of shapes. Dark clung to the hollow beyond, though Malachi made out a deeper gloom within, given shape by the backwash of gleaming green eyes.

The elder cousin sank to his knees in the mist. Malachi stood firm, though his own knees strove to betray him.

"You have a petition," said one, her voice dry as dust.

Malachi sucked down a deep breath. It didn't help. Nothing helped. Nothing in the chamber felt real, save for the scrap of ground upon which he stood. "I do."

"Do you speak for yourself, or for the Council?" asked another.

"Or for your family?" asked a third.

"I speak only for myself, Malachi Reveque."

Dry laughter echoed through the mist. "So say they all."

"Will you hear my petition?"

The shadow within the shadow shifted. "We will hear it."

"What do you desire of the Crowmarket?" said another.

Only directness would serve, Malachi decided. Strip away the supernatural, and this was a negotiation like any other – and a negotiation from a position of weakness was no negotiation at all. So he told himself, and so he almost believed.

"Withdraw your support from Ebigail Kiradin. Return those you have stolen."

"Ebigail Kiradin has long been a friend of the Crowmarket," said one.

"You have brought only persecution," said another. "Why should we accede, Lord Reveque?"

There was challenge in his voice, but curiosity also. The Parliament were at least prepared to listen. It was more than he'd expected.

"Because Ebigail is bad for business," he said. "She knows loyalty to no one save herself. She killed her own son out of pride. How long before she turns on you?"

Shadows shifted about the central throne. Ridged, ivory fingers steepled. "She will not."

"She cannot threaten us," said another. "Nor can you."

A bleak answer, but one Malachi had expected and prepared for. "Ebigail prizes order above all. Her fist will close so tight about the Republic that even down here you'll find it hard to breathe. Do you think she'll abide your smugglers slipping in and out of harbour, bleeding her domain of wealth? Do you believe she'll tolerate the 'influence' you've spread? The blackmail you levy? The petty crime upon which your vranakin thrive?"

"She has before," said one.

"She *needed* you before," said Malachi.

His words faded, dampened by mist. No reply came. Had he, by directness, broken protocol? He glanced about the mist. Even now, a kernclaw could be drawing nigh, talons readied to repay insult.

A dull rumble arose in the distance – the rhythmic, growling grumble of a runaway wagon, running at the gallop. A dozen such wagons, with some howling beast swept along behind. The ground shook beneath

Malachi's feet. Wax-crusted feathers drifted lazily down from the chandelier. He closed his eyes, expecting the floor to open up and swallow him. That moment never came. The rumble faded to nothing and the floor ceased its dance.

Pallid fingers grasped the outer edge of the rightmost pulpit. "Your petition is understood."

"What do you offer as payment?" said another.

Somehow, Malachi found his voice. "A return to normality."

"Then you offer us nothing."

"I offer certainty."

Dry, rasping laughter echoed through the mists. "You offer what we already have."

"How much is Ebigail Kiradin worth to you?" asked another.

"Fifty thousand crowns. Paid once the taken are returned."

"Insufficient."

"One hundred thousand, then." He winced. Such a sum would leave him and Lily nearly penniless – unless sanity returned to Tressia, and with it a councillor's access to the city treasury. He doubted that the Parliament would take payment in promises. "I've nothing more to offer."

"Look around, Lord Reveque," said one. "Drink in our glory."

"What use do you suppose we have for gold?" said another.

"We are not fledglings, distracted by baubles," said the third. "Your petition is rejected."

"You may go."

The bell tolled anew. The elder cousin rose and gestured.

Thoughts crowded by failure, Malachi held his ground. "What do you want of me?"

The thrones remained dark and silent.

"Their decision is made," said the elder cousin. "You must leave."

Malachi remained rooted to the spot. How had this happened? What more could he offer? What had Ebigail offered? What was worth more to the Crowmarket than a lord's ransom in gold?

Only one thing came to mind.

"I'm sorry, Lily," he whispered. He thrust his head back and stared up at the silent thrones. "I have a new proposal."

Sixty

The Essamere line came forward in a wild barrelling run more suited to the barbaric tribes of old than the flower of Tressian chivalry. Apara hunched her shoulders tight and drew deeper into the fitful shadow of the nearest hayadra tree.

"They're coming, lady."

Captain Horden made the pronouncement in a flat, disinterested tone. He and Lady Ebigail stood a half-dozen paces to Apara's front, in the bright sunlight of the outermost ring of hayadra trees. Apara suspected his thoughts lay more with the dead than the living. Essamere had certainly made a butchery of his constables.

"What a perceptive fellow you are, captain." Teeth parted, Apara's mother stared across the field of mournful stumps and felled trees. "Young Viktor was always a brute. Tailinn? You may send in the kraikons."

Golden robes whispered at Apara's side as the red-haired proctor set a hand to her control amulet. Metal screeched into wakefulness. The hillside shook. The kraikons strode away, picking up speed.

Apara stared uneasily through the trees. "Are you sure this is wise, lady?"

"They will break. They always do. A firm hand, and they will crumble." Lady Kiradin gestured to a nearby hearthguard. "Tell Rother and Mannor that I want prisoners for the gallows once the kraikons have done their work."

The hearthguard scurried away through the trees, towards the motionless ranks of scarlet and blue. Torvan Mannor stood still as a statue among the Prydonis ranks, though out of discipline or from denial, Apara couldn't readily judge. By contrast, Markos Rother had long abandoned stillness in favour of pacing back and forth.

Apara stared at the giant leading the Essamere charge. Viktor Akadra. Her legs turned to jelly at the thought that her mother might send her against him a second time. And yet . . . once her eyes settled, she found she couldn't look away . . . as if something called her.

"Apara!"

Lady Ebigail's command brought Apara up short. She spun around, disoriented. Her mother and Captain Horden now stood several paces behind. In the outer grove, the first kraikon struck the Essamere line. Bodies and broken shields cartwheeled through the air.

Her mother strode forward and took her none too gently by the elbow.

"This is no time for spoiled pride," she snapped. "I know the humiliation burns, but I need you here. You may have whatever remains of Viktor once the battle is done."

Apara blinked the fog from her memory. "Of course . . . Mother."

She gave a sharp nod. "And Captain Horden? Light the pyre. Let them burn."

The kraikon's sword crashed down. Shields buckled. Screams rang out. Swords chimed against bronzed flesh but found no weakness. Jag-headed maces found better fortune, but first had to crack layered armour plates and thick corrosion. Soldiers' wisdom was that you never knew the strength of a foe before you had to face him yourself. For the first time, Viktor truly appreciated the valour of those Hadari who'd gone willingly into a kraikon's path.

"Keep on! Keep on!"

Even as he bellowed, Viktor knew the command would do no good. His advance had stalled. Even if they made it to the line of Prydonis and Sartorov shields, they'd do so in laughably piecemeal fashion.

It needed something else. Something provocative.

The ground shook beneath a kraikon's lumbering tread. Viktor threw himself aside. A down-thrust sword churned the turf. Three knights hurled themselves at the construct, hacking and hammering at its legs. A massive hand swept them aside.

The kraikon blotted out the sun, sparking memories of Davenwood – where one had almost crushed him flat. But there was something else, wasn't there? Something about that battle ...

"Viktor!"

Josiri's impact bowled him clear out of the kraikon's path and into the trunk of a willowy hayadra. As the construct turned about, a second kraikon thundered past from behind, magic crackling from a wounded shoulder. It struck the first with the hollow boom of a ship slamming into a quay.

Viktor pushed away from the tree. A glance behind revealed that Josiri was not alone – the hearthguard had come with him. "You were to wait until we'd cleared a path!"

"There's no more time. That's the last of Elzar's kraikons. If you've something planned, we need it!"

But there wasn't a plan, was there? Only an idea, half-glimpsed amid the motionless kraikon of the lunassera charge. A tactic of desperation.

"Viktor!" Josiri cried again.

Two more of Ebigail's kraikons descended on Elzar's last, embattled construct. Fists rose and fell as they pummelled their estranged brother.

Pushing Josiri's impassioned pleas to the back of his mind, Viktor let his shadow slither free.

Captain Horden strode through the weeping and huddled prisoners. Constables set as guards shied away from his approach. They didn't want to be there. They didn't want to be part of the unfolding madness. Horden didn't blame them.

He reached the base of the pyre and drew a brand from the brazier. Flames spluttered impatiently. Two more deaths to join the constables he'd sent against Essamere, not knowing Lady Kiradin had held back the blades of Prydonis and Sartorov. All to save his sons.

"You'll never be free of her," gasped Sevaka.

Unable to meet the accusation in her eyes, Horden glanced away. "It's almost over."

"Not for you. You broke. She'll break you again. And she'll despise you more each time."

On the far gibbet, Roslava Orova stared down at her feet, lips twitching in the silent speech of addled wits. Horden had spent too long on Dregmeet's boundary not to know that demons existed. For all he knew, she was something worse. But Sevaka? She'd done nothing more than defy her mother. A good man would have recognised that. But Horden had no illusions to being a good man. Sevaka had to die so that his sons might live.

"I'm sorry, I've no choice."

He raised the brand.

A brisk wind sprung up across the hilltop. The air came alive with crow-voices. The brand's flames flickered and rushed back brighter than before. His blood cold as ice, Horden spun about, but saw no sign of the screeching flock. There was only the clutch of prisoners, the battle raging beyond the outer ring, and the remnants of the crowd on the western roadway.

A crowd at whose forefront now stood Malachi Reveque. At his back stood a dishevelled, filthy mass of men, women and children, familiar faces among them. Lady Adrias Rother, wife of Sartorov's master. Hawkin Darrow, whose marriage Horden had attended only a week prior. And at Malachi's side . . .

Horden stared at his distant sons. Perhaps there was still time to be a good man. He thrust the brand back into the brazier and began to climb.

Viktor closed his eyes and let his shadow soar. The lunassera had brought the kraikons to a standstill. Proctors had failed to restore them at battle's end, claiming that some other, heretical magic had doused the light within. And what was his shadow but anathema to the light?

Through the shadow he saw not constructs of steel-clad bronze, but shards of light on a hilltop buffeted by shifting greys. One such blaze flickered and died – the last of Elzar's kraikons torn apart by its brethren. Others remained. Could he quench the light as he'd absorbed the Dark in Josiri's soul?

He dove down into the light.

His shadow screamed.

It was a moment before Josiri realised the bellow of pain had been Viktor's. By the time he turned about, the other man was on his knees, sword abandoned and hands clamped about his head.

"Viktor?"

He rocked back and forth. A low, thin moan – more the growl of a wounded animal than a man. Frost whitened his surcoat and gathered in the stubble of his beard. One eye on the kraikons, Josiri crouched beside him.

"Viktor?"

Mist curled up from Josiri's mouth and danced briefly in the sunshine before fading from sight. How many times had he imagined the hated Lord Akadra laid low? How often had he prayed for it? But not now. Not like this.

The victorious kraikon turned from the remains of the vanquished. Golden eyes fixed on Viktor as if they sensed his weakness. White leaves scattered from branches as they bore down.

Josiri gave a fruitless tug at Viktor's wrists, and then abandoned the attempt. He raised his sword high. "Essamere! Essamere to Lord Akadra!"

Knights and hearthguard alike took up the cry. The space beneath the branches filled with running feet. Not all of them belonged to friends. In the middle distance, the scarlet and blue of Ebigail Kiradin's knights started forward.

"What is that fool doing?"

Her attention snapped from the battle by her mother's exasperated shout, Apara stared back at the pyre. Horden, moving with the ponderous care of the heavyset, clambered onto the raised platform beneath Sevaka's feet. A log slid away beneath his boot.

"I've no patience left for the man," muttered Lady Kiradin. "Deal with him. He can burn with them for all I care. Don't disappoint me."

Apara ran for the pyre.

Fresh despair crowded Rosa's heart as the mingled Prydonis and Sartorov line came forward. The green of Essamere was a shrunken blob among the trees. Surrounded, outnumbered. Doomed.

"You needn't watch," said the Raven. "Say the word, and we'll be gone."

"Why . . . do you care?"

A bitter note crept into the gravelly voice. "Because I'm a friend. Sooner or later, I'm everyone's friend. So why not sooner, if only for the change of pace?"

"You think ... I'd believe that?"

He scowled. "Fine. You were supposed to be mine. You've worshipped me so completely, and with no expectation of reward. You know how rare that is?"

Rosa shot Sevaka a sidelong glance. The other woman paid them no heed. Likely she couldn't even see the Raven. Rosa still wasn't convinced he was anything more than delusion.

"I've never ... served you," she croaked.

"But you have, and so readily." He stared up at her. Black eyes twinkled beneath the mask. "The Reaper of the Ravonn. Service is service, no matter how it hides its face. Would you like to see your offerings? They are legion."

Rosa swallowed a grimace. "No."

"Modest too. I like you all the more. Let me set you free. Embrace me. You'll not regret it."

Embrace the Raven. A euphemism for bearing life's burdens no longer. But his voice warned of a deeper meaning. One that set her shivering.

"You ... You did this to me."

"Not I." Wounded innocence softened the words. "For years I've courted you. Watched you as your life slowed. And then my little sister stole away your soul. She thought she was helping. She has *so* much to learn."

No. That couldn't be. "My soul ... belongs to Lumestra."

He chuckled. "Lumestra is in no position to gainsay the stake. When the fires catch, you'll go to the Evermoon." He gestured at the moon, ghostly pale against the brilliant blue sky. "An eternity of repose beneath starlight, surrounded by the spirits of your ancestral enemies. I hope you enjoy poetry and contemplation, otherwise you'll be *terribly* bored. And I promise that the light of Third Dawn will never find you. Not in Ashana's halls. Better to bind yourself to one who appreciates your talents, eh?"

Weary beyond words, Rosa slumped against the mooring spikes. Why not indeed? Perhaps it was better to embrace the Raven than face eternity in Ashana's service, like some shadowthorn drab who'd never known battle. If she was to be denied the glories of Third Dawn, did damnation's form truly matter?

She met the Raven's inky gaze.

The rope frayed and split. Sevaka fell forward against Horden's arm. As she strove for balance, his dagger slit the last of the ropes. A hot, prickling rush swept through extremities too long denied. It felt *good*.

"Here."

Horden thrust a canteen into her twitching hand. The contents spilled across parched lips. She spat a mouthful away, and gulped for more.

"Can you stand?"

"I can stand." Hearing the tremor in her own voice, Sevaka clung tight to her pain, let it blossom to anger and hot-edged truth. "I can fight. But Rosa. We have to free Rosa."

"Look at her! Even if we could get her loose, she's away with the feylings!"

Sevaka snatched away his dagger and shoved him aside. Timber rocked under her feet as she stumbled towards the second gibbet. "Rosa! Rosa! Can you hear me?"

"Rosa! Rosa! Can you hear me? I'll get you free. Just stay with me."

Sevaka's urgent cry flared like lightning through the murk of despair. Acceptance of the Raven's offer faded into a croaking sigh.

Rosa stared at her through blurring vision. The world seemed distant, smeared beneath grease and molten tallow. Even the light seemed strange, tinged with greenish-white.

"Ignore her." The Raven looked Sevaka up and down and tutted fussily. "She doesn't understand. How could she? You've betrayed your friends, your comrades – even the memory of the man you loved. Can you really make that right? Why would you even want to make amends? We both know you haven't the strength."

He stared at her, head cocked. Somehow the question in his tone was not quite the same as the one he'd given voice.

Sevaka's dagger parted the ropes about Rosa's wrists. Her hands fell free.

The Raven extended a gloved hand. "You don't belong here any longer. It's time to leave."

"Yes," said Rosa. With the decision came peace. "It is."

Horden's cry of pain faded to a gurgle. Sevaka spun around, the dagger slipping free from the bonds about Rosa's ankles. A lithe woman in Freemont uniform held the captain's dying body at arm's length.

Sevaka didn't recognise the kernclaw at first, not without the cloak of feathers. But the poise, the self-assurance – those betrayed her. And the face. The face that was an older, darker mirror of her own …

The kernclaw let Horden's body fall. It bounced a bloody smear down the outer face of the pyre and struck the brazier. Hot coals scattered across timber. Sap spat and crackled.

"Come with me." The kernclaw's grey eyes pleaded as she spoke. "I'll beg our mother to spare you. She'll listen, I swear it."

She advanced as she spoke, timber rocking under her boots. Sevaka stared, transfixed by the face that was hers, and yet was not. Another of her mother's secrets. "You don't know her at all, do you?"

She drew closer. "Please. I don't want to hurt you. We're family."

"I don't have any family! Not any more!"

Sevaka lunged, her dagger flashing at the kernclaw's eyes. It missed. Her balled fist did not. It struck the kernclaw's jaw with a fleshy thud. Her head snapped aside, and she skidded back a pace across the logs.

The first flames licked up from below.

"Not so impressive without that cloak, are you?"

"Didn't you hear me?" said the kernclaw. "I don't want to hurt you!"

"I don't give a damn what you want!"

Flames raced hungrily up the pyre. Sevaka's boot sent a log skittering across the pyre. It smacked into the kernclaw's leg and pinwheeled away. But even that small gesture left Sevaka's legs leaden. The kernclaw was holding back. She had to be. As soon as that changed …

The kernclaw sprang through the greasy smoke. Timber bucking beneath her feet, she closed the distance in two graceful strides.

Sevaka swung. The kernclaw ducked beneath the dagger and rammed a fist into her gut. Sevaka retched desperately in the inky smoke. Her knees struck timber.

"Don't make me do this." The kernclaw's breath washed warm over the nape of Sevaka's neck. "I beg you."

Smoke swirled up around the Raven, hiding Sevaka and the kernclaw from Rosa's fading sight.

"Take my hand," said the Raven.

"I'm not coming with you."

"Ah. Then the Evermoon it is. The easy way out."

Again that knowing smile. Rosa hated it.

"I'm not . . . going anywhere." She gritted her teeth. There was another choice, beyond Ashana and beyond the Raven. And strange though it was, Rosa could have sworn he'd wanted her to see it. "My friend . . . needs me."

Straining fingers found the gibbet's upright. Heels dug against timber. Gathering her last strength, Rosa arched her back.

The mooring spikes in her torso turned to molten fire. It seeped through every torn fibre and every lesion, setting nerves wailing and muscles atremble.

Rosa screamed, and found strength in the sound. Metal scraped past bone. Flesh tore free. Every inch was a scarlet eternity. She closed her eyes, blotting out the Raven, the fire, the smoke. There was only the molten metal in her chest and the hope of redemption.

And beneath it all, the sound of gravelly laughter, and soft applause.

The scream was like nothing Sevaka had ever heard. It rose to a raw, jangling pitch and then was lost to the rush of flames. Rosa was gone. Choking down a sob, she rammed back her elbow. The kernclaw shifted her grip and the blow struck empty air. Vice-like fingers closed about Sevaka's weapon-hand, striving for mastery of the blade.

Talons pressed against Sevaka's throat. "Drop it! I won't burn, not even for a sister."

The kernclaw yelped. Her hand slipped from Sevaka's wrist. A heartbeat later, the talons followed. Sevaka staggered away, legs buckling as she sought footing. Through stinging eyes, she stared back toward the gibbet.

A smoke-stained figure stood amid the leaping flames, soot streaked in her tangled blonde hair, and the edges of her ravaged clothes curling with smoke. She had one hand about the kernclaw's throat. Another about her wrist. A mooring spike deep in her left shoulder confirmed the impossible.

"Rosa?"

Arms convulsed. The kernclaw vanished into the smoke with a thin cry. Rosa stepped through the rising flames and toppled. Sevaka caught her.

"It's not fair." Tears of sorrow and joy mingled on her cheeks. "It was my turn to save you."

"I saved you?" Even with Rosa's lips practically touching her ear, Sevaka barely heard her reply. "You saved me first . . . Gave me something to fight for."

She sagged. Sevaka held her tighter, as if to bind spirit to abused body. The smoke swirled. For a moment, Sevaka glimpsed the outline of a thin, dark man, tipping an imaginary hat in salute. Then the smoke shifted, and the vision was gone.

Gritting her teeth, Sevaka dragged Rosa away.

The shadow's scream bled away. Viktor reknitted his scattered thoughts. Every inch, every scrap of his being, throbbed with pain beyond reckoning. As if he'd plunged into the heart of a forge and the depths of an ice-crested caldera all at once.

His body was a distant presence on the edge of perception. The muted greys of the shadow's existence were all. Dark. Bleak. And afraid of the light.

Arrogance had all but unmade him. The same arrogance that had failed Anastacia. The same arrogance that had led him to believe he could end Ebigail Kiradin's ambitions with a handful of willing blades.

To all things there was a limit.

The greys of the grove coalesced. A ring of shields, Josiri and Izack at their heart. Viktor felt Elzar at his side, one hand clutching a sword he did not know how to wield, his lips moving in silent prayer. Two tiny figures emerging from the blazing pyre, the one dragging the other. A lone rider galloped from the west. Infantry bore down from the east. And the golden light of the kraikons, relentless among the grey as they smashed Josiri's shield ring to broken matchwood.

Tomorrow. He could learn his limitations tomorrow.

Viktor drove his shadow against the nearest kraikon. How plainly he saw it now. The kraikon's light blazed almost as bright as Anastacia's soul, and was not for him to tame. But there: gossamer strands of golden light, puppet strings twitching among the grey, and all of them tying back to a small, brilliant speck at the very heart of the grove.

With a rush of jubilation, Viktor hurled his shadow at the speck of golden light.

Heat flared beneath his shadow's folds. But this time it was not the seething majesty of the sun, but the flicker of a candle flame. Like a candle flame he smothered it.

Cold rushed in. Too late, the puppeteer realised her danger. Her panicked cry rose to a terrified shriek, then shattered like glass.

The slap rocked Apara's head back on her shoulders. Flesh burned raw by the heat of the pyre's flames throbbed anew. She spat a mouthful of soot-black sputum onto the grass and glanced down, unable to meet her mother's fury head on.

"Escaped? Can I trust you with nothing?" Lady Kiradin threw her hands to the sky. "Has anything ever failed me so completely as my own blood?"

Apara kept her eyes downcast. Much as she wished it otherwise, her mother was right. The failure seared her spirit as readily as the flames had seared her skin. "Horden is dead. As you commanded."

"And Roslava Orova is free! My treacherous Sevaka is free!" She gestured around the circle of hearthguard. "I should adopt from the gutter. At least they'd have gratitude enough to display competence. Queen's Ashes, but I . . ."

Her vitriolic splendour drowned beneath Tailinn's desperate screech. The proctor released her control amulet as if burned and threw hands up to shield her face.

In the time it took Apara to catch her breath, Tailinn changed from a vibrant, rose-cheeked young woman to a corpse fished from the northern floes. Tears froze to icy droplets on her cheeks. Freckles vanished beneath a patina of impossible frost. Exposed flesh paled, cracks snapping across skin like a pane of glass beneath a mallet.

Something beneath the robes gave way with a tortured, squealing snap. An ankle. A knee. Perhaps a thigh. Apara leapt back as the body fell, a backwash of icy air brushing her feet as the lifeless remains shattered into a dozen pieces.

The kraikon ceased. Josiri, caught mid-flinch from a sword-blow he'd thought certain to take his head, stared up at the motionless construct in disbelief.

"I don't believe it," breathed Izack. "Praise Lumestra, but it's a bloody miracle."

Josiri glanced about. The remaining kraikons were every bit as immobilised; battered statuary looming large beneath alabaster trees. And beyond, advancing in the pyre-light, Ebigail's loyal knights, coming to finish what the kraikons had begun.

"We're not done yet."

Izack laughed. "That lot? I'd take those preening Sartorovs alone after what we've just lived through."

"Not alone," croaked a familiar voice.

With Elzar's assistance, Viktor groaned and clambered to one knee. Josiri hauled him the rest of the way upright. Izack was halfway right. A bloody miracle it was, but not of Lumestra's doing. What would Izack say if he knew? What would any of them say?

"I thought you'd gone to the Raven," said Josiri.

"Not yet." Viktor stared across the grove, at the dancing flame of the pyre. Dark rings beneath his eyes spoke to flagging reserves. "One last bout. Then I can rest. Then we can all rest. Essamere! Until Death!"

"*Until Death!*"

Shields came forward to form a ragged line beneath the trees, their wielders bloody and wearied, but unbowed.

Josiri's heart swelled. This was not the Republic he'd hated all his life. Across the grove, sheltering in a ring of Freemont hearthguard while good men and women died for her ambition? That was where his hate belonged, with Ebigail Kiradin and those like her. There were worse causes to die for, and worse comrades to die alongside.

The scarlet and blue line picked up speed. Josiri counted six hundred, at least. And every blade fresh for battle.

"Well," he said softly. "At least we made a fight of it."

Buccinas sounded. Boots thundered across the hilltop. Josiri's fingers tightened about his sword. He wondered at Anastacia's fate. If she'd understand why he'd died so far from home in a battle not his own.

A rider galloped out of the west, jolted around like a miller's sack tied to the saddle more than a man sat upon it. Sawing on his reins, he skidded to a halt between the battle lines. Josiri at last saw that what he'd taken for one rider was actually two. A white-haired woman whose expensive dress offered stark contrast to her filthy appearance, and ...

"Malachi?" Viktor's consternation matched Josiri's own.

Oblivious to the oncoming knights, Malachi swung from the saddle and helped his fellow rider down. At the very centre of the Sartorov front rank, a man in golden breastplate and blue velvet cloak silenced the buccinas with an agitated wave. The line stuttered and slowed. Not so the woman, who stalked onward with all the furious certainty of a serathi in a pit of sinners, fraying plaits bobbing behind her like serpents.

"Markos Koschai Rother," she snapped, finger jabbing as mercilessly as any spear point. "Thirty years of marriage. Thirty years, I've abided your nonsense about honour! And now look how readily you throw it away! Your brother would be ashamed!"

"Adrias?"

Rother blanched, his face momentarily torn between chagrin and surprise. But only for a moment. Breaking ranks, he cast down his shield and threw his arms about his wife.

The Knights Sartorov lurched fully to a halt. The Knights Prydonis, riven by consternation, slowed also, their line breaking apart as individual knights fell out of step.

New hoof-beats brought more riders from the west, some in constabulary tabards, others in clothes as ragged as Lady Rother's.

Viktor's laughter rolled like thunder beneath the trees.

Lady Kiradin's shoulders shook. Cold eyes blazed disbelievingly from a bloodless face. "What have they done?"

Apara tore her gaze from Tailinn's frost-sheathed body and stared across the grove. Knights knelt before their foes, heads bowed in contrition. The battle, such as it had been, was done.

"The Parliament," she said. "They have betrayed you."

"Betrayed?" Lady Kiradin rounded, hands hooked to claws. "Betrayed?"

For a moment, Apara feared her mother meant to attack her, so mad was the gleam in her eyes. Then with shuddering breath Lady Kiradin drew herself in, her fingers working feverishly against one another.

"And you?" she snarled. "Where does your loyalty lie?"

Apara blinked away the question. "We can't stay here, Mother. Your enemies will be coming. Please?" She held out a hand.

Rage slipped from Lady Kiradin's expression. For the first time, she seemed old, her fire faded and her steel rusted. Her fingers closed around Apara's and clasped them tight.

"Dear Apara. You were always my favourite." She stared blindly across the grove. "Take me from this terrible place."

Sixty-One

The gates of Freemont yawned wide beneath dusk's ruddy wings. Kneeling hearthguard waited on the drive, heads bowed and hands clasped to the backs of their necks. Viktor scarcely spared them a glance and hobbled on. If he'd learned but one thing that day, it was that Captain Izack knew his business.

"She inside?" he asked.

Izack grunted. "Hard to be sure where the vranakin are involved. They come and go as they please."

"And now they've gone. Lady Kiradin is on her own."

"Look ..." Izack broke off. "Don't take this the wrong way, but you're fit to drop. Happy to handle this for you, no questions asked, if you follow?"

Viktor shook his head. "This is my responsibility."

Izack nodded. "And this sorry lot?"

"Lock them up with the others. The Council will decide their fate."

A darkened hallway beckoned. Firelight clawed fitfully beneath the sitting room door. Viktor pressed on beneath disapproving gazes of Kiradins long dead. His shadow, every bit as weary as he from the labours of the day, coiled restlessly about his soul.

The sitting room door fell open at the slightest touch. Ebigail Kiradin stood at the hearthside, a brimming brandy glass in her hand. Nary a hair on her greying head nor crease on her crimson dress was out of place.

"Young Viktor. I thought it'd be you. Won't you come in?"

*

"Josiri! Please come in."

Hastened by Malachi's greeting, Josiri stumbled into the Privy Council chamber. As he did, the other man wrinkled his nose. "What is that smell?"

Josiri was aware more than ever that he stank like something three days dead, and possibly regurgitated. "That smell is what happens when you fight in full armour at Sommertide. I don't recommend it."

Malachi took his place beside jumbled papers and quill. "I imagine not. You're otherwise well?"

"Nothing that won't mend. You?"

A wintery smile. "Time will tell."

"Lilyana was asking for you."

"I'm sure she was. And it'll be longer still before I've a chance to see her. Ebigail is in hand, but she's not without her supporters." He rubbed at his brow with ink-stained fingers. "I've no choice but to draw up a few lists of my own."

"Then it's over?"

"I think so. With Horden's death, command of the constabulary passes to Vona Darrow. Given that her wife was part of Ebigail's leverage, I'm less concerned with Vona letting fish slip through the net than I am her gutting, frying and devouring them whole. I've asked Krain to provide restraint. Between that and some *very* penitent knights patrolling the streets, well . . . "

"Sartorov and Prydonis? Are you certain you can trust them?"

"Reasonably so. After all, I have their families."

"That had better be a joke."

A small smile. "The last was escorted home just a few minutes ago. My apologies. Lily's for ever warning me about my sense of humour, and I think it may have warped under the strain."

Josiri eased himself into a chair. *His* chair, although he still couldn't bring himself to think of it as such. The wood dug into bruised muscles. "Mine's taken a knock or two as well. As for the rest, it all seems so . . . I don't know if easy's the word."

Malachi nodded. "Ebigail had orders ready, drawing troops back to the city. Some, I've intercepted. Others? Well, I've sent heralds of my own. Those officers too deep in her pockets will be removed. What we've done here would have been impossible even two days later. Viktor was right. Again."

"Perhaps. But the triumph is yours." Josiri planted an elbow on the table and propped a weary head on his hand. Stubble pricked at his knuckles. "How did you do it?"

"I once asked Viktor much the same question. He and I were determined to help your people, but we needed one more vote to break the deadlock. Viktor went into a room with his father – who was *not* sympathetic. When they came out, we had our vote." Malachi spread his hands like a conjurer at the close of a trick. "I asked Viktor how he'd managed it. Do you know what he said?"

"Something gruff, I imagine."

"You'd be right. *I got what we wanted. That's all that matters.* His words."

"And you let it go at that?"

"I did."

"And you'd like me to do the same?"

"Ideally."

"Letting things go isn't really what I do."

Malachi sighed. "No, I suppose not. I entreated the Parliament of Crows. Pointed out to them that Ebigail was fixing to bring all manner of trouble down on their heads. They concurred."

"As easy as that?"

"No, but I got what we wanted ... "

" ... and that's all that matters?"

"See? Sometimes it really is that simple."

Simple. Hundreds dead, either in Ebigail's purges or the skirmish at the Hayadra Grove, many of them simple folk who'd been caught up in something complicated. And as for Malachi? He looked five years older. Josiri himself felt a good *ten* years older. Viktor was indestructible. Mere mortals aged badly in his shadow.

"All right," said Josiri. "So what happens now?"

At last, Malachi smiled. "I thought you'd never ask. Assuming this doesn't all come crashing down around our ears, or Jack doesn't come storming out of Fellhallow with a host of wood-demons at his back ... Well, I thought we might take the chance to make things better. Ebigail wasn't entirely wrong. My entire life, the Republic has been paralysed by squabbles at council."

Josiri cut him off. "Malachi, I'm tired, I stink. Above all I want to journey home with the express purpose of feeding Arzro Makrov to something ferocious. I'm glad that I was in a place to help, truly I am. But my people are suffering, my sister is missing, and my love is doubly a prisoner. I've no time for intrigues."

Malachi's smile broadened to a grin. "You'll want a part of this one, trust me."

"I will? Why?"

The door slammed open. Hadon Akadra stormed into the chamber. "Gentlemen. I am not accustomed to being summoned at this hour, and certainly not by . . . "

"By the men who likely saved you from a gallows jig?" Malachi's gaze dropped to the pile of papers, the ink still wet. "Or were you bound so close to Ebigail that you'd no need of fear?"

Hadon's scowl deepened a notch. "I'd no part of her plans. Bring her before me and I'll hoist the hag myself."

"I'm sure that's true," said Malachi smoothly. "So let's not discuss the past. We three are all that remains of the Council. The future is ours to shape. Let us see what can be done."

The grey world that passed for sleep peeled away. Murky lamplight granted shape to the sparse furnishings of her chapterhouse quarters. Limbs creaked as Rosa tested them against the weight of blankets. There wasn't any pain, not as such – just the abiding soreness of old wounds.

"So you *are* alive?"

Muscles protested as Rosa pushed herself upright. Sevaka sat at the bedside, her face bruised and blonde hair almost grey with ash. But her eyes shone brighter than ever.

"Ask me again in an hour." Every breath carried the bitter taste of soot.

"I don't understand. You should be dead thrice over. When they said you didn't bleed, I thought it was some trick to gull the masses. But it's not, is it?"

The words shaped accusation, but Rosa found only curiosity in Sevaka's face.

"Something happened to me when Kas was murdered." She felt sick just thinking about it. "It's kept me alive since."

"I see." Sevaka stared down at her feet. "So the night we were attacked?"

Beneath the blankets, Rosa clenched her fists. The night she'd beaten Aske Tarev to death. "She ran me through. I should have died."

"What *are* you?"

There it was. The note of fear. The newfound distance.

"I don't know." Rosa stared at Sevaka, willing her to listen – to *understand*. "I've made so many mistakes since Kas died. Sometimes, I feel so lost I want to scream. But I'm still who I was before. It's just that I'm something else as well."

"You were named a demon."

Something withered in Rosa's soul. She'd lost her. Sevaka, who'd anchored her enough that she'd found the strength to reject the Raven, now set her adrift once more. "Maybe it's true."

Fingers gripped the rough weave of the blanket tight about hers.

"I don't care," said Sevaka. "You're my friend. Let the rest go hang."

It took a moment before Rosa heard the words for what they were. She felt a grin steal across her face. "Thank you."

"We can always burn you if I change my mind."

Rosa winced at a new concern. "Or if the physicians tell the provosts about me."

"The physicians haven't seen you. They wanted to, but Josiri got involved, which meant that Captain Izack got involved." She waved a lofty hand. "So I need you up and about. I expect to earn *quite* the reputation for your miraculous recovery, what with me nursing you back to health."

Relief bloomed to a fit of giggles. When had she last laughed? Truly laughed? Rosa couldn't recall, and didn't care. Sevaka shook her head in mock disdain. Then infectious mirth swept her away alongside, until eyes ran and abused muscles ached anew.

It passed too soon, as all happiness must, and Rosa's thoughts were drawn to a familiar, grey world. "What of your mother?"

Sevaka's smile soured. "Lady Ebigail Kiradin has retreated to Freemont and burrowed in like a tick. Viktor's gone to dig her out."

Rosa winced. "You didn't want to be there?"

"I don't wish to set eyes on her again." Sevaka's eyes narrowed to match the venom in her voice. "I've already hurt her more than she's ever hurt me. She doesn't know it yet, but she will."

Rosa slid her hand free of the blankets and held Sevaka's tight. "You're free of her now."

"I know." Sevaka shook her head as if clearing it of cobwebs. "So, ready to move about? I've a reputation at stake."

That meant facing Malachi, Viktor ... even Josiri. So many amends to make. So many apologies.

A new strain of laughter reached her ears, gravelly and sardonic. And beneath it, the harsh cry of bird voices. She bit her lip.

Sevaka frowned. "Rosa? What is it?"

Rosa smoothed the scowl from her face. "Nothing. Will you leave me to hoist myself out of bed? If I'm to fall flat on my face, I'd as soon as not do it with an audience."

"Of course."

She waited until the door was closed and Sevaka's footsteps echoed on the stairs beyond. "You might as well show yourself. I know you're here."

The shadows twisted and the Raven stood in the far corner of the room, his shoulders pressed against the wall. "I'm not accustomed to ephemerals addressing me with such irreverence."

"You had me. I was ready to give up, and you gave me reason to fight. Why?"

He ran a gloved finger along the top of the footboard and stared at it with disdain. "Does no one ever dust in this place?"

"Does the Raven ever answer a question?"

"You're very bold."

"I've reason to be."

He gave a dry, gravelly laugh. "Do you know how many unwilling servants I have at my beck and call? Thousands. Desperate sorts who'll do anything for a little hope." He sighed. "Ah, hope. Where would we be without it?"

"Serving the Tyrant Queen."

"You should be careful whose name you take in vain." The Raven straightened. "But to answer your question, I don't need another woebegone lickspittle. When you come to me – and you *will* – you'll be willing, even glad. Otherwise, you'll not really be *you* any longer, and what's the point in that?"

Rosa grimaced. "It'll never happen."

He tugged at his goatee. "*Never* is a very long time. And you and I are here for all of it. Take my advice: don't over-invest in ephemerals, no matter how sweetly they smile or how readily they laugh. Eternity is better unsoured by grief."

"I'll do as I choose."

"Why of course you will. Haven't you been listening?"

The lamplight flickered, and he was gone.

Viktor stepped into the room. A glance confirmed that Lady Kiradin was indeed as alone as she appeared. Heavy drapes and scattered furnishings offered little scope for concealment.

"Ebigail."

"Can I offer you a drink, young Viktor?" She waved a lazy hand at a decanter on the mantelpiece. "The Rothlin '78. There's so little of it left. But greatness has ever been finite."

He inclined his head. "I must refuse."

"Hah." She arched an eyebrow. "Afraid I'll poison you?"

"The thought is unthinkable. But then, you've laboured hard to re-define that word."

She took a sip. Maudlin eyes gave way to close-lipped bitterness, and thence to furrowed anger. "You really are nothing like your father. His fire faded so long ago. Yours, I think, will burn as long as you draw breath. Maybe longer. The desire to change the world, and the will to see it through. If only you hadn't chosen the wrong cause."

"I might say the same to you."

She brushed his words aside. "We are lions, you and I. Lions among bleating sheep. I wish I'd realised that long ago. A wasted opportunity."

"To have me killed?"

The corner of her mouth twitched. "Not so foolish, are you? Tell me, do you suppose the bleating masses would cheer for you if they knew you've one foot in the Dark? Oh yes, I know your secret. Tailinn whispered it to me months ago. She'd have made it public herself, but for the price it would have cost that foolish old proctor."

Viktor forced a studiously neutral expression. So his father hadn't given him up? It shouldn't have been a surprise. Betrayal took courage. How had he wronged Tailinn that she'd found that courage? How had she known? Perhaps Elzar had spoken more freely than was wise, or had she simply seen or heard more than she should. It was easy enough to imagine – in hindsight, he and Elzar aught to have been more circumspect. Viktor supposed it was pointless to speculate, and even more so to distress Elzar by speaking of it with him. Tailinn was dead, and the matter done.

"Secrets don't make one evil, Ebigail. Only the cause to which they are harnessed."

"Hah." She shook her head in derision. "Have you come to kill me?"

"You'd deserve it. No trial. No podium from which to spit your venom."

"So you *haven't* come to kill me?" She snorted. "You should."

Viktor couldn't help but feel grudging admiration. Even now, her back to the wall and the howls of the hunt all about her, Ebigail was immovable.

"Fifteen years ago, the Council had me crush a woman for her dreams. I offered mercy. When she refused, her death opened a doorway onto all manner of suffering. I make you that same offer."

"Mercy?" she sneered. "What use is mercy?"

"It grants opportunity to atone. You said it yourself, Ebigail. You're a formidable force. One that could still serve the Republic."

She gave a low, mocking laugh. "You dare compare me to Katya Trelan?"

"Not lightly. Katya Trelan was loved."

"And I am a Kiradin. We raised this Republic out of Malatriant's ashes. Parade me through the streets or throttle me here and now. But spare me your weakness." She glared at him. The old, familiar stare that stripped flesh from bone to reveal the thoughts beneath.

Viktor shrugged. "Malachi said you'd refuse."

"Oh yes? And did the high and mighty Lord Reveque have anything else to say for himself?"

"Only this." Viktor stepped closer. "That if you refuse, the Privy Council will remove all trace of the Kiradin family from governance, and from history. You and your forebears will be forgotten. When your spirit looks onto Tressia from Otherworld's mists you'll see a Republic devoid of your reflection. You'll no longer exist, not even as a cautionary tale."

She drew back with a sharp intake of breath. "You wouldn't dare . . . "

"Why not? History isn't fact, Ebigail. It's what we choose to remember . . . and what we choose to forget."

"My line will go on," she snapped. "My name will go on. Or do you intend to erase Sevaka?"

"Sevaka took the name Psanneque earlier tonight. Whatever betide, the Kiradin line is ended. Whether it is remembered, and *how* it is remembered, falls to you."

Ebigail's brandy glass shattered. Shards scattered onto the carpet. Shoulders quivering, she stabbed a bloody finger at the air between them.

"You made my daughter an exile?"

"She chose it for herself." In his mind's eye, Viktor still saw Sevaka's earnest, smoke-blackened face as she made the declaration. "She hates you more than anyone."

Ebigail grasped the mantelpiece. Ragged breaths slowed as she fought for control. "The way of guarded smiles and watchful tears. She's learned more than I thought."

She laughed, though Viktor heard little humour within.

"She's made her choice," he said. "Yours remains. I must have your answer, Ebigail."

She straightened. When she spoke, her voice was again steady as stone. "And you shall."

The wall dissolved into writhing mist. A dark shape sprang clear, steel flashing in the firelight.

Viktor flung himself aside. The lunge meant for his belly thudded into an armchair and tore free in a spray of goose-down. His shadow wailed. He staggered back, one hand clasped to his head to blot out its distress.

Melanna Saranal's sword. The kernclaw from the foundry. A dangerous combination. So much for the Crowmarket having wholly abandoned her cause.

"You'll not have my mother!" shrieked the kernclaw.

Mother? That explained part of it. Now he saw her in the light, the resemblance to Sevaka was undeniable.

Viktor hurled another armchair by the headrest. The kernclaw dived back and it shattered against the wall with a crash. But it had bought time. Viktor dragged his claymore free of its slings.

The kernclaw darted in, sword flashing. Viktor's shadow screamed fit to wake the dead. What should have been a simple parry became a desperate, scraping block. The kernclaw's shoulder took Viktor in the chest and sent them both crashing across a table. Already off-balance from his shadow's scream, Viktor sprawled across the floor, claymore abandoned.

The kernclaw landed atop him, knees on his chest and silvered blade at his throat.

"I'm glad it was you." Viktor barely heard Ebigail's words over his shadow's distress. "Malachi wouldn't have come alone, but you've always been proud, young Viktor. Always so certain of yourself. But even the strongest man has a weakness."

Viktor strove to blot out his shadow's wail. One last miscalculation in a day filled with them. Only this time there'd be no one to rescue him from arrogance.

"I *will* be remembered." Ebigail stooped over him, eyes alive with amusement. "But not by you. Apara? Stop toying with him. It's time to go."

Viktor pinched his eyes shut and wrestled with his shadow. It spat and seethed, coiling away. But something else answered. Something the same and yet not – a piece of himself he'd forgotten in the tumult of the day. Viktor gripped it tight, his command more unvoiced instinct than intent.

The weight on his chest shifted. A wet, tearing rasp choked away a distant scream. Warm red rain spattered Viktor's face.

Gasping for breath, he opened his eyes. Ebigail and the kernclaw stood locked in a motionless embrace, the daughter with her arm tight about her mother's back, and the mother with her face buried in the daughter's shoulder. A touching tableau, but for the sword buried deep in Ebigail's belly.

His shadow finally a distant ache, Viktor sensed a cold, umbral tether binding him to the kernclaw – to the scrap of himself he thought lost in her escape from the foundry. He stumbled to his feet. As he rose, the unseen bond ebbed. The kernclaw jerked – a woman awakening from nightmare into something far worse. Ebigail and sword slipped free into the spreading stain.

"No!" Her voice racked with mewling, stuttering sobs, the kernclaw backed away. She raised a bloody hand to her face. Eyes widened in horror. "What have you done to me? What did you make me do?"

On another day, Viktor might have felt sympathy for the woman, or even disgust at his own unwitting actions. But not this day.

Lost in grief, the kernclaw never saw the blow that struck her clean into unconsciousness.

Sixty-Two

Outriders preceded the convoy, shields slung and banners furled. A column of Immortals marched at the heart, a blaze of gold around a wagon draped in green silk – the wagon in which Melanna's father rested as his wounded body healed.

She should have been with him. It was a daughter's duty to be close at hand if the worst befell. But her thoughts lay not to the east, where her father's procession squeaked and rumbled along the uneven road, but to the west whence a cold wind plucked at her hair.

"It's time, Ashanal," said Sera. "The lunassera march with the next convoy. If you do not leave with your father, you should do so with us."

Melanna stared away into the west. The horizon lay hidden beneath brooding cloud, as if the sky itself wrestled with matters weighty beyond her comprehension. The darkness of the dream lay hidden within, if it existed at all.

"What if I choose to stay?" she asked.

"That would be unwise." Sera's careful reply gave a hint to the expression hidden beneath her mask. "The eastern road lies thick with opportunity."

"The goddess commands . . . " Melanna cut herself off. If she'd learned only one thing since coming to the Southshires, it was not to overplay Ashana's intent. "The goddess implied I should stay. The Dark has arisen in the west. It wears the shape and intent of the Sceadotha."

The lunassera, normally so fluid and graceful in motion, went still as a rabbit in a wolf's gaze. "Are you certain you understood her? You will be empress one day. Is it wise to risk your life on girlish fancy?"

It wasn't so much the words that brought Melanna up short, as the tone. The same tone she'd faced all her life, when she'd pleaded for lessons in archery and swordplay. When she'd insisted on riding astride a steed, rather than side-saddle. The tone that spoke to arguments exhausted, and her own patience close behind.

She set her back to Sera, determined that the other woman not see her anger. In the courtyard below, a handful of Immortals, stripped to the waist, laboured to make a cairn of abandoned weapons. Seen from above, as she viewed it now, steel and spear-staff blossomed outward like the petals of a flower. A traditional offering to the victor, granted in defeat. That it was raised beside the defenders' graves – dug just as willingly by Melanna's countrymen – only added to the poignancy.

It was strange, thought Melanna, how something so horrific as a sword could become part of something so beautiful. But that was the contradiction of war, and the contradiction of warriors. No order had been given for the cairn's construction. The men simply knew to salute their opponents even while they mourned their own loss.

Glory in victory, fortitude in defeat, and honour always.

"Do you think I'm prone to delusion, Sera?" Melanna said.

"I would not have put it so, Ashanal."

Again, that tone. "How *would* you put it?"

"I fear that your heart is sick with failure. That you are impatient for new battles. I fear that it is not the goddess you hear, but your own pride. Have you spoken of this with your father?"

Melanna pinched her eyes shut and gave an angry shake of the head. "He wouldn't understand."

"Or do you fear he'd understand too well? This defeat rests as poorly with him as it does with you." She drifted closer, head dipping respectfully. Close enough that the heady scent of sanctum-incense danced on the breeze between them. "The lunassera will fight for you, Ashanal. We will die for you in need, as so many of our sisters already have. But as I stand with you now, I cannot be certain that need is upon us."

"The goddess believes it *is*," snapped Melanna. "She stood with me on these stones and spoke of my responsibilities."

Or the responsibilities of the Ashanal. A name she'd stolen. But even now, Melanna couldn't spur herself to that confession. The shame went too deep.

Sera spread her arms wide. "Then where is her sign? Where is the fire and the moonlight?"

Melanna had no answer. Certainly Ashana had granted her no weapon and no magic. Perhaps because she had no more to lend. Or perhaps Sera was correct. Perhaps she *had* imagined it all. Perhaps the dream had merely been a dream – a reflection of sundered pride.

No. She couldn't think that way. If she was to amount to anything at all – if she was to become an empress fit to guide her people – she had to have faith in herself. She'd lived for years knowing that to be true. Why was it so hard now? Why was her chest so tight she could barely breathe?

That answer, at least, was obvious. Sera had believed in her, and now she did not.

"Why are you so against this, Sera? Are you afraid?"

"If the Dark has returned, we should all be afraid, Ashanal."

"Then we fight to take away the fear, as is our way."

"And if you fall, the lunassera will be returned to their cages. We will be healers, priests and courtesans once again, for there will be no banner to which we can rally."

Melanna caught her breath. It *was* fear, and it *was* pride, but neither of them hers. She'd given the lunassera freedom, and her death threatened to return their shackles.

"What if I head west," she asked, "and seek the truth of my dream?"

"I beg you not to." Sera reached out as if to take her hands but thought better of it and withdrew. "Come home to Tregard. If the Dark reaches out for the Empire, confront it from a position of strength."

"And how many will die in the meantime?" Melanna shouted, her hand flung westward.

"Does it matter? They're Tressians."

Melanna scowled. The obvious answer. The easy answer. Had her Tressian opponents lived by such precepts, her father would have died in the stockade. She'd be dead, or else a trophy.

The sun emerged from behind cloud as the last offering was set in place in the courtyard below. Polished steel blazed like fire, and Melanna realised that the Immortals hadn't crafted a flower, but a sun – a sun with a halo of stylised rays. An acknowledgement that radiant Lumestra had prevailed over her argent sister.

The soldiery had made their tribute, but what of the empress to be?

I owe you for this, Josiri Trelan, she'd said. *The house of Saran owes you.* Josiri had gone north under guard, at least so Haldrane had reported. Melanna didn't pretend to understand the politics, but only a child would believe the mercy he'd shown her had not worsened his situation. Who now fought for the land he'd saved? Who'd hold the Dark at bay?

The pressure about her chest dissipated, dispelled by the peace of revelation. In the end, it didn't matter if she'd imagined Ashana's command. If she did nothing, she betrayed Josiri's kindness and thus the only thing that brought beauty out of war.

Glory in victory, fortitude in defeat, and honour always.

Always.

"I will go west, Sera," Melanna said. "I will see for myself the truth of my dreams. I make no claim on you, or on your sisters, but if you wish to stop me, you'll have to drag me away in chains."

Eyelids fluttered closed beneath the mask. Hands pressed together, palm to palm and fingertip to fingertip. "Then I pray Ashana keep you safe."

"Pray for us all, Sera. For if I'm right, we're not yet done with sorrow."

Tzadas, 13th day of Radiance

Concord decays, riven by selfishness or the mere mundanity of boredom. It is in the nature of ephemeral labours to fall apart, and our duty to gather the pieces and forge them anew.

from the sermons of Konor Belenzo

Sixty-Three

Surprises, Viktor's mother had once told him, *are to be cherished as gifts from Lumestra*. For Alika Akadra, relegated to the custodianship of Swanholt at her husband's insistence, even small changes in routine were welcome. Viktor preferred predictability to surprise. Surprises got folk killed.

He breathed deep and steepled his fingers. "I'm honoured to have the Council's confidence, but I must decline."

Malachi, Josiri and Viktor's own father shared curiously alike expressions. The parted lips. The furrowed brows. Men suffering through an unexpected veer in the road.

Predictably, Malachi recovered first. He rose and set his back to the Council chamber's great gilded map. A clever bit of presentation, lending the Republic's weight to his words.

"Please reconsider," said Malachi. "The Republic needs better leadership. The position of First Councillor will provide that leadership while keeping the foundation of our Republic intact."

"I don't disagree," said Viktor. "It's your choice of candidate with which I take issue."

His father stirred. "You're the unanimous choice, Viktor. Have a little civility. Accept."

"Then perhaps the Council will have the civility to explain. As has been pointed out several times in this very chamber, I've little experience of politics. And now you'd have me govern our nation?"

"Lead," said Malachi, "not govern. Both councils will remain, but you'll have authority over both."

"None of which answers why it should be me."

"It's simple," said Josiri. "You're the only one we all trust."

He leaned forward in his chair. Viktor knew the Southshires were calling him home. He too felt the pull. Calenne had been his touchstone throughout his torture. In victory, comfort had turned to unease, and unease to guilt. He had to know what had become of her.

"Even you?"

"Even me."

How far they'd come. If only it hadn't cost so much. "I must still refuse."

His father scowled. "I raised you better than to turn your back on duty."

In fact, Hadon Akadra had barely raised his son at all, but Viktor elected against saying as much. "Duty aside, how do you suppose the Grand Council will react to the Republic being handed over to a witch?"

"Those accusations are done with," said Malachi. "Between Ebigail's actions and Rosa withdrawing her charges, there's no longer any case to answer. This council has already acknowledged Provost Hargo as one of Ebigail's conspirators . . . "

"And was he?" interrupted Viktor.

His father gave a bark of laughter. "It hardly matters."

" . . . and High Proctor Ilnarov has been granted our full support for retrieving you from the provosts' vaults," Malachi continued. "There's nothing left to offend the Grand Council's sensibilities."

"Except for the truth," said Viktor. "The fact remains that I *am* a witch. Were I to accept, and that knowledge became public . . . ?"

Viktor's father thumped the table, setting decanter and glasses rattling. "The Republic needs leadership."

"That it does," said Viktor. Could they not see the disaster they invited? But that was the nature of compromise, was it not? Malachi and Josiri were likely honest in their dealings, but his father . . . ? No. To Hadon Akadra, his own son was merely the least worst option – one through which he hoped to levy influence. "I propose the position of First Councillor be given to Malachi."

Again, the silence. The curious similarity of expression.

Viktor pressed on. "Malachi has the experience, the ability and the courage the position requires. If the Republic is to move forward, it requires a quieter form of strength than mine. It needs someone whose first instinct is to talk, not fight."

Josiri nodded. "Viktor's right. We need look no further for the proof than yesterday. While Viktor and I battered Ebigail to little avail, Malachi found a solution."

Lips pinched, Malachi grasped the back of his chair and said nothing. There were secrets there, Viktor felt sure, but who was he to judge? A conversation for a calmer time.

"It occurs to me," Viktor's father said stiffly, "that this entire conversation may be premature."

Josiri narrowed his eyes. "What are you proposing?"

"Only that we hold off on the elevation of a First Councillor until such time as empty chairs about this table are filled. That we prevail upon the Tarev and Marest families to embrace their responsibilities. As to the others? We can open the remaining seats to application from the Grand Council. They have, after all, been empty too long."

Viktor sighed inwardly. "You wouldn't be seeking to weight the balance in your favour, Father? If you consider yourself a candidate for First Councillor, you should say as much."

He bristled. "I've more experience than any of you. If you refuse the honour, then I see no reason why I shouldn't embrace it."

"Save for your closeness with Ebigail Kiradin, of course," Viktor replied with a studiously blank expression. "Half of Tressia knows of it, and are probably wondering why you're still free."

"As Rother and Mannor are still free?" The first puce of outrage touched his father's bearded cheeks. "They committed armed revolt, and you suggest I should be censured for mere association?"

"Rother and Mannor acted under duress." Josiri drummed his fingers on the table top. "When freed of it, they made amends. Where were you, Hadon?"

"Where was I?" The reply came low and dangerous. "I shed my blood for this Republic long before you were born. Before even your wretched mother entertained her first treasonous thought ... "

"Enough! Please!" Malachi silenced the diatribe mid-flow. "The position of First Councillor has little merit if it causes further division, and so I must remove myself from candidature."

He reclaimed his seat – not with the dejection that he would have done but a few weeks prior, but with careful dignity. First Councillor or no, Malachi had found his heart, and his strength.

"Clearly this topic requires more ... discussion ... than I thought," Malachi went on. "I suggest we adjourn until tomorrow. The clerks assure me that the documentation regarding the Southshires will be ready by then. You'll be free to leave us, Josiri. I assume you'll accompany him, Viktor?"

Viktor nodded. "Indeed."

Which meant leaving his father and Malachi at loggerheads for however long he was away. Days? Weeks? However long it took to find Calenne. To find her – and if necessary to mourn her.

Malachi nodded. "Then if we've nothing more to discuss, perhaps you'll excuse me."

Malachi stared across the sunlit gardens. At least his house remained an island of familiar calm. Could he convince Viktor to change his mind? Quite possibly not. Opportunity lost through poor timing. Such was the way of the Republic. Still, one defeat was but a slender catastrophe under the circumstances. For the first time, he'd matched Ebigail's dance, and bested her. A shame he wasn't sure whether to be proud or horrified.

"It didn't go well?"

Lily slipped her hands about Malachi's waist and rested her head on his back. He shut his eyes, blotting out the sun in favour of her embrace.

"Am I so easily read?" he asked.

"There's a gargoyle on my father's stables that looks exactly as you do at this moment."

"So he's a handsome fellow?"

"If one lusts after enormous teeth and a scowl fit to curdle milk."

"Viktor refused the position."

The weight vanished from his back. The hands remained. "And you're angry with him."

"Yes ... No ..." He sighed. "I can't be. I turned it down too."

He braced himself for the inevitable criticism. To his surprise, none came. Things really had changed between them. Slipping free of Lily's hands, he turned around. He brushed his hand against her veil, careful to avoid the torn cheek beneath.

"You don't have to wear that around me."

Pale lips twitched a sad smile beneath black gossamer. "It's not for your benefit. I just ... want a little distance from the world."

"You look like a serene."

Sorrow turned wry. "Serenity is not my foremost trait at this hour."

"I wish you'd let Sidara help you," he said. "She brought Sevaka halfway out of the mists. I'm sure she could do *something*."

"I don't want her to." Lily's fingers closed about his wrist and pulled his hand away. "We've been too complacent, you and I. The scars will serve a reminder. Did Viktor truly kill Ebigail?"

"He says not. He says the kernclaw turned on her at the end."

"Do you believe him?"

A harder question. Viktor would face no sanction either way. At worst, he'd saved the hangman's fee. And yet Malachi still felt as though his friend hadn't been entirely truthful. Then again, evasion *was* the order of the day.

Ebigail Kiradin was dead, her mortal remains sealed up in the family vault without ceremony, and without prayer. She'd face Lumestra come Third Dawn, and Malachi had no doubt that meeting would end poorly.

"I actually don't care," he said at last. "Ebigail is dead. I'm concerned about the living. Sidara, for one. What she did for Sevaka – for you – I've never heard of even a proctor wielding so much light. The church will want her for the foundry."

"No. My daughter will *not* toil away in darkness."

"It's the law," he said.

"Then change it."

"It isn't that easy."

"It would be if you were First Councillor."

How easy to see in hindsight the road along which she'd led him. Not for the first time, Malachi wished their positions reversed. "I can't do it. Please don't ask me again."

Lily tilted her head. Eyes narrowed to slits beneath the veil. "They'll take her away. They'll take our brilliant, radiant daughter and drown her in grime. Is that what you want?"

"Of course it isn't, but . . . " He swallowed back a rising sense of frustration. "If you'd told me she was gifted, I'd have had time to address this in council."

"If you'd been home more, you'd have seen for yourself." She drew up, face wrinkling in distaste. "There's much we both could have done, but didn't. And now our options are limited."

"I know."

Malachi embraced his wife, as much to hide his torment as in reconciliation. Lily was right. As First Councillor, he could protect Sidara from hidebound tradition. But what Lily wanted was impossible. And the worst of it was, he daren't tell her why.

"I'll talk to Viktor," he said. "He'll change his mind, and I'm sure he'd want to help. After all . . . " He bit his tongue, remembering just soon enough that Lily wasn't privy to Viktor's secret.

"Perhaps I'd have more success," she said. "Sometimes it's easier to refuse a friend than a stranger."

"We'll see. At least Constans isn't a problem." He drew back from the embrace. "Unless you're hiding something from me on that score."

"No. Constans is Constans. He, at least, can be a child a little longer." Lily lifted her veil and kissed him on the cheek. "Speak to Viktor."

"I will."

A vision in black silk, she retreated across the terrace and vanished inside. Malachi tried to remember the last time he'd changed Viktor's mind. Still, there had to be a first time, and given the consequences of failure both for the Republic and for his daughter . . .

He took a deep breath and held it until his lungs burned. Mist gathered about his feet, cold in the noonday sun.

He froze.

"Your wife is correct."

Malachi spun around. There, in the shadow cast by the swaying boughs of the silver birch, the hazy outline of an elder cousin. There was no one else in sight. Fear gave way to anger, and he bore down on the vranakin.

"This was not the agreement," he hissed. "My home is off limits."

Green eyes gleamed beneath the grey hood. "The Parliament of Crows wish you to accept the position of First Councillor."

Which was *precisely* why Malachi had refused. "They'll survive their disappointment."

"True." The elder cousin crossed to the balustrade, her form becoming ever more indistinct in the sunlight. "Disappointment passes. Much like life."

Bright laughter rang out across the grounds below as Constans ran past, a dark blur against the grass. Ada ran behind. The tutor had her skirts gathered in one hand and the other extended in fruitless beckoning.

"My family, like my home, is off limits," Malachi bit out. "I promised a sympathetic ear on the Council and an easing of patrols around Dregmeet. That's all."

"Indeed. And a First Councillor's ear is worth far more, wouldn't you agree? A bargain was struck. Straying from its terms will have ... consequences." The elder cousin reached up and snapped a branch from the tree. "By all means, think on the matter. Consider your priorities."

"It can't be done. Hadon will never support me."

"Then perhaps we should help you with that."

Malachi stared down at his feet. He'd always known he'd regret his bargain with the Crowmarket, but for that regret to blossom in less than a day ...

"Go! Leave me in peace!"

He glanced up to find himself more alone than ever.

The gloom of the foundry matched Viktor's mood to perfection. Better reflection in welcoming darkness than out in the glare of sunlight. Better Elzar's company than Josiri's, or even Malachi's at that moment. Elzar placed no expectation on him.

"Life used to be simple," he said. "Now the journey grows harder with every step."

"Life's never simple." Elzar perched on his desk and folded his arms. "Just looks that way when you glance behind. In five years you'll stare back at this moment and curse your younger self's easy life."

Viktor turned from the soot-smeared window and took a deep breath. Even the air wasn't right. Gone was the thick, suffocating rush that flooded lungs and set the skin prickling. With its furnaces cold and silent, the foundry felt like a tomb.

"Perhaps you're right. The church conclave has given you no trouble?"

"A few suspicious glances, but the backing of the Council has dealt with the rest. The archimandrite will have a word or two to say upon his return, but ... "

"Makrov will have his own troubles by then." The thought alleviated a little of Viktor's dourness. "He has them now, though he doesn't realise."

"Planning to put him in his place, are you?" Elzar nodded. "Then I doubt I've reason to worry."

Viktor had known him too long not to recognise the note of reserve. Truth was, the surviving provosts wouldn't forget. One false step, one whiff of questionable behaviour, and they'd have Elzar in their clutches – all in the name of vigilance, as far as anyone else was concerned.

"You shouldn't have become involved," said Viktor.

Elzar sniffed. "And if I hadn't? Lilyana would still have fled here, which means Ebigail would still have sent her thugs. You might at least thank me for my trouble."

"I thought I had."

He grinned. "Wouldn't hurt to do it again. You know what my memory's like."

Viktor offered a low bow. "Then, thank you High Proctor Ilnarov, for saving my life. And my apologies for putting you behind schedule."

Elzar gave a dismissive wave. "This place will be up and running again by the end of the week, though I don't know how I'll manage it without Tailinn."

Tailinn. Ebigail's tame proctor. The passage of time had done little to dull the memory of her death. The first time he'd used his shadow to kill. The memory felt better than it should. "I'd say you'll manage."

"True enough. What about you? What will it take to scour the misery off your face?"

"A miracle."

"Then I'll get accustomed to that grimace. Miracles are in short supply ... Unless we make them ourselves."

"And how do I do that? Malachi wants me to solve everyone's problems." He plucked a scrap of cloth from Elzar's desk and turned it over in his hands. King's blue. Like the ribbon Calenne had given him the last time they'd spoken. A lifetime ago. "I'm a soldier, not a politician.

Worse, I've been overconfident. Arrogant. It nearly cost me everything just yesterday ... It may already have cost others more."

"I see." Elzar raised a bushy eyebrow. "What's her name?"

There was no arguing with that stare. Viktor took another deep breath of the stale air. "Calenne. She rescued me from a mistake. Steadied me when everyone else begged me to fail. And in the end, she took up an unfamiliar sword and fought in a cause she hated, all because I asked her to do so. I have to know what's become of her."

"Then find her."

Viktor set the scrap of cloth aside. "And if I do, my father will drag the Republic back into the mire. He'll twist Malachi's intent into his own ascension. He'll not be as bad as Ebigail, but nothing will improve."

"So what?"

Viktor blinked his surprise. "I don't follow."

"How long have we known each other?"

"Too long."

"Heh. And in all that time, I've never known you put desire before duty. Perhaps it's time you started. Put aside the soldier's burden for a time. Lumestra knows you've earned it."

Elzar's advice, the reverse of what Viktor had so recently given Josiri, coaxed forth a dry smile. "And what if my father makes trouble?"

"What if he doesn't? And what manner of leader can Malachi be if he's nothing without your support? What manner of support can you offer if your body's here but your mind's away to the south, turning over every rock and stone in search of this Calenne? I think the Republic will manage without you for a time."

Ordinarily, Viktor would have agreed. Though the Privy Council had always divided along roughly similar lines, that same division – the *possibility* of shifting allegiances – had stopped anyone, even Ebigail, having things her own way. Only now the numbers had thinned almost to nothing was lasting change possible. They'd thin further the next day when Josiri headed south. And if the architect of that change was Hadon Akadra and not Malachi Reveque ...

Viktor turned again to the filthy window, to the tangle of streets that led away to Dregmeet and the harbourside. Tressia had never felt more fragile.

Elzar had counselled him to put desire before duty – to stop being a soldier for a time. But that wasn't the solution, was it? The soldier saw the situation plainly. His father was a clear threat to the Republic – whether he intended it so or not – while Calenne offered no certainties, only questions that might never be answered.

Viewed from that angle there was only one solution, though even the soldier in him was loathe to embrace it. But love, especially of a distant and uncertain kind, was as nothing compared to duty. Sometimes one had to be sacrificed for the other.

It had cost Apara most of the morning and a good deal of the skin on her wrists to get free of the manacles, but get free she had. Most of that she owed to a perfunctory search that had divested her of talons and daggers but had somehow missed the cotter pins stitched into the hem of her tunic.

Not that she'd gotten a deal further once the shackles were off, not with the cellar door barred and bolted. She'd been over every inch of the filthy stone, searching for a way into the mists of Otherworld. She'd found nothing. But freedom was like death – it often came sliver by sliver.

At times, she wept. At others, her eyes grew so dry they stung. Each time she closed them, the afterimage of her mother's face loomed, the eyes alive with horrified accusation.

She'd killed her.

She'd not meant to, would never have believed herself capable of doing so. But then had come that cold, suffocating presence in her mind, like fog rolling in off the sea. And for one, brief moment, unanswerable desire had swallowed everything. The sword had come alive in her hand, and . . .

Nausea crowded Apara's thoughts. She wasn't a fool. She knew her mother deserved death. But to be the one who'd dealt the blow? Even if she'd been helpless to do aught else?

The scuff of heavy boots dragged her back to the dingy present. Her captor was returning.

Swallowing back the last of her nausea, Apara took the shackles between her hands, and stood to one side of the door. Metal scraped as bolts were withdrawn. Hinges creaked.

A spill of grey light cast a long shadow into the room.

One step. Two. Apara sprang.

The world slipped sideways. Black fog swallowed her thoughts.

When it receded, she was on her knees, trembling like a woman lost three days in a blizzard. She tried to rise. Part of her – the part still embroiled in the black fog – didn't want to. Its contentment only quickened her nausea.

"You should have known that wouldn't work."

The gloom took familiar shape. Akadra. The part of Apara caught in darkness sang to see him. The rest trembled with fear.

"What's your name, kernclaw?"

She fished around for a lie. Lucialle Trast. The cousin who ran the lower docks. That would do. Lucialle was a selfish spirit.

"Apara Rann," she replied. The air was cold. Why was the air so cold?

It was only then she realised she'd given him her real name. The fog-bound part of her laughed for joy. The rest screamed.

"And Ebigail Kiradin was your mother?"

"She said she was." Again, the answer came without the decency of consent.

Akadra grunted. "You're better off an orphan."

"How ... How are you doing this to me?"

Akadra crouched before her, his handsome, scarred face demonic in the long shadows. "Did you kill Kasamor?"

"I ... I took the commission." Apara swallowed, desperately trying to assert control over her wayward voice. "I didn't kill him. I didn't know he was my brother!"

She screamed those final words – the only ones she'd chosen.

Akadra ran a thoughtful hand across his chin and rose to his feet. "I offered your mother atonement. With her passing, I offer you the same. Do you take it?"

The black fog retreated. Breathing became easier. Thinking became easier. "Why should I?"

"To earn back your life. By rights, you should go to the gallows or the pyre. And from there, to the Raven's keeping. I understand he's *most* jealous of the souls bartered to his care."

Apara closed her eyes, remembering Nikros' last moments. Lost in a storm of black feathers. She hadn't chosen the kernclaw's path any more than she'd chosen to kill her mother. Seemed she hadn't chosen much of late. Was she truly being offered a choice now? Or would the black fog coax her to whatever answer Akadra desired?

"What ... what must I do?"

The river gushed away into the gloom, its inky surface ungleaming in the glow of the firestone lantern. The flickering stalactite-cast shadows gave the sense of breathless spirits watching and waiting wherever the light faded.

Like the shambles of Dregmeet and the hollow halls of Strazyn Abbey, Coventaj cavern was a shunned place. Unlike them, it was avoided even by the vranakin. It hadn't always been so – at least, not judging by the lissom, nymph-like statues, whose stone glowed white in the lantern's backwash. The remnant of an earlier age, remembered only in rumours of Tressia's third, forgotten river. So legend told, its headwaters sprung from a land of giants, and vanished into Otherworld without ever reaching the sea.

Viktor had never been one for legends, and remained so at that moment. He cared only for privacy, and Coventaj offered that more than any other place within the city's bounds.

The air changed, the cold caress of anticipation fading into crackling, searing chill. Mist curled across the mottled stone to weave a blurred, inconstant doorway, offering sight of Coventaj's mirror beyond the mists. Viktor glimpsed a spectral host paying homage at an altar, a chalice brandished high, and then two figures filled the entranceway.

"He's yours, as promised."

Apara kneed her captive in the small of his back. Blinded by the hood tied over his head, he fell awkwardly against a stalagmite.

"I'll have your head for this, gutter-scum!" the hooded man rasped.

Viktor allowed himself a moment of sympathy, even admiration. Courage should always be acknowledged, even when bluster more than valour.

"Were you seen?"

Apara's lips tightened. "Please. The mists swirl thick about Swanholt. A child could have brought him."

The prisoner stiffened. "Viktor? Viktor, is that you?"

Apara struck him behind the ear. He grunted and fell to his knees.

"I did what you asked." She stared down at her feet, the picture of obedience. "Is my debt repaid?"

Such desperate yearning. Viktor supposed that was always the way with predators, once teeth were at their throat.

"You've made a good start," he said. "I'll call for you again."

Hope gleamed in her eyes. "How will you find me?"

He focused his thoughts on the tether that bound them and tugged. Not much. Not enough to cloud her will. Just enough to remind her of its existence. "I'll find you."

Apara shrank away at the words. But then her manner shifted. The cold, frightened shape at the back of Viktor's mind grew warmer. "Then I want his rings."

"You're in no position to make demands."

"The Parliament have marked him, and I want the bounty." She looked up, fresh resolve in her grey eyes. "I'm more useful to you if I have their confidence."

So his father had roused vranakin ire? He could leave the Crowmarket to its business, and that would be the end of the matter. No one need know. Except ... *He'd* know. The memory of that weakness would stay with him far longer than the guilt.

"Take them and go."

Apara crouched beside the prisoner. He fought, but he fought blind and groggy, and a second blow to the head stilled his last resistance. Hands gleaming with silver and gold, Apara retreated into Otherworld. Mist flooded the doorway and boiled to nothing, leaving the men alone.

Viktor unbound the captive's hood and tore it free. Bleary eyes stared up from a haggard face.

"Viktor?" gasped Hadon Akadra. "So it is you. What is this?"

"This, Father, is our last conversation."

His father staggered upright. Desperate eyes flickered about the shadows. "Where in Lumestra's name are we?"

"Coventaj, where men once sought absolution for their sins."

Eyes widened. "This place is forbidden."

"Mother told me stories of how they'd bathe in the waters, lured by siren song. Those whom the spirits found worthy were permitted to leave. All others, they dragged beneath the surface, never to be seen again." Viktor lowered himself onto a slab of rock. "Tell me. How do you suppose you'd fare?"

His father scowled. "Your mother filled your head with a lot of nonsense. It's little wonder you turned out as you did."

"As a witch?"

"As a fool. A muddled fool who lacks all sense of priority. Whose veneer of courage peels away at every sob-story." His eyes narrowed. "I raised you to be strong. All your mother ever gave you was weakness."

Viktor shook his head. He'd wondered what he'd feel at this moment. Sorrow? Dread? Anger? But there was nothing. Just a yawning chasm filled with spent memories.

"You lecture me about strength, Father? It's been years since you found the courage to stand for more than self-interest."

Now there was anger. Not at his father, necessarily, but at the waste of everything his father could have been. Hadon Akadra, General of the Republic and Defender of the Ravonn. He'd seemed a giant when Viktor had been young. No. A god. How times changed.

"But you're right, Father. I've been weak. I've asked others to make hard choices – choices that have cost them everything. And all the while, I've shied away from my own. No more. You belong to the past. It's time you took your place within it. You'll not be found, and you'll not be missed."

His father straightened. His manner, no longer furtive or afraid, belonged to the muster fields he'd not trod in decades. Perhaps just enough of the soldier remained to know that this last battle could not be won.

"I'll not beg."

Viktor rose. "I never thought you would."

His father sprang. They fell, rolling over and over across the cavern, hands locked about one another's throats. A flailing boot struck the firestone lantern. Glass shattered on stone. The golden light died, replaced by the soft phosphorescence of the cavern walls.

And all the while, Viktor's father grunted and snarled, loosening his grip only to pummel his son about head and body, hammering at old wounds and opening new.

Viktor let his shadow flow free.

Darkness gathered his father up as it had at Freemont a lifetime ago. Heels bounced off stone and skittered back towards the river. Then Viktor was on him once more, his weight bearing them both down at the river's edge.

His father's head slipped beneath the inky surface. His body jack-knifed, and he broke spluttering for air. Viktor planted a palm beneath his chin and forced him below once more.

His father thrashed, clawing and punching. River water drenched them both. Through it all, Viktor had the strangest sensation. That the statues' eyes watched with approval – almost with hunger. He held on as his father's struggles faded, his own lungs aching in sympathy. Then Hadon Akadra's desperate vibrancy turned limp and dark.

Sodden garb clinging to his skin, Viktor slid away onto the stony bank and waited for the rush of guilt. It never came. There was only purpose, and a sense of freedom. For he *was* free. Free to ride south without fear of what would happen in his absence. Free of his father's selfishness and scorn.

"Goodbye, Father. May the Black River carry you to wherever you most deserve."

Closing his hand about his father's belt, Viktor tipped the body into the water. The current dragged Hadon Akadra out of sight and into history.

Sixty-Four

Josiri read the letter for the third time in hope that its contents might somehow differ from readings one and two. They remained every inch as impossible.

He let the paper fall and stared across the Council chamber. Weariness, held at bay by anticipation of homecoming for much of the night, returned as vengeful as a Thrakkian lost to a blood-debt. The only bright note was that Kurkas' account made no mention of Calenne, though the omission was hardly grounds for hope. And Revekah ... Gone, and by the cruellest road.

"This isn't real," he muttered. "It can't be."

Malachi stared at the letter much as one might regard an empty vial of poison beside one's equally empty wine glass. Viktor's expression gave no clue to his thoughts.

"Beg your pardon, my lord, but it's true. Every word." The travel-stained soldier did his best to stand to attention as he spoke but wavered with exhaustion.

"Every word?" Tiredness and worry added bite to Josiri's tone. "You know this for certain? That my home – my people – are overtaken by the Tyrant Queen of myth?"

He wanted to laugh, but too much of him *believed*. That was the fate of the Southshires, after all, for hope always to sour. With all mortal enemies exhausted, why should it seem strange that Immortal peril had descended?

"I can't speak to that, my lord. I only know what Captain Kurkas said.

But the Dark? I've felt it. Like spiders creeping on the skin. I'm glad to be out of it."

That much, Josiri believed. The soldier was deathly pale, and the catch to his voice went beyond exhaustion.

"What's your name, lad?" asked Viktor.

"Dastarov, my lord. Guardsman Dastarov of the 12th."

Viktor nodded. "The Council thanks you for your service. Get some food, and some rest. Your horse will be seen to."

Dastarov made an unsteady bow and withdrew. It seemed to Josiri that he took the last vigour with him, for the three men remaining looked suddenly old before their time. Three, not four as it should have been.

"Where's Hadon?" Josiri asked. Easier to dwell on mundanities than tackle the issue at hand.

"My father hasn't been seen since this evening," rumbled Viktor. "I don't doubt that with Ebigail Kiradin slumbering beneath stone he's found a warmer bed. I've hearthguard out searching, but we'd be fools to expect him before dawn."

Malachi nodded wearily. "Viktor's right. We can't wait."

Josiri looked from one to the other. Neither of his companions looked wholly at ease, but that was hardly surprising. If even half of Kurkas' letter was founded in fact, Hadon Akadra's absence was the least of their concerns. But still, he had the sense of something unsaid – as if the two shared a truth they couldn't bear to give voice. Under other circumstances, he'd have pursued it. As it was . . .

"Kurkas is your man," he said to Viktor. "Do you believe him?"

"Yes." The reply came without hesitation.

Malachi flinched. "But *Malatriant*? She's a myth. A name to curse by."

"And is Rosa a myth?" rumbled Viktor. He turned his gaze on Josiri. "Is Anastacia? The Crowmarket and their kernclaws? For that matter, am I? Or Sidara? Myth is merely a word for history half-forgotten, and our history is malleable as clay."

"Kurkas must be mistaken," insisted Malachi.

Josiri stared at the second signature – this one inked in a flowing, elegant hand. Its presence reduced myriad possibilities to a single, horrific certainty.

"I can't imagine Ana lending her name to a document against her will."

Malachi scowled. "It hardly matters. We can't take the chance." He leaned back in his chair, eyes gazing roofward, as if seeking guidance from his stony predecessors. "Is it wrong of me to wish that Ebigail were still here?"

"Yes," said Viktor. "Because she'd have gambled Eskavord's fate. You won't."

"You're right, of course. You're always right." Malachi planted his elbows on the table. A little of his weariness fell away. "Under the circumstances, I think it best I assume the position of First Councillor ... with your assent, Josiri."

"Hadon is sure to object," Josiri replied.

Malachi sighed. For a man on the brink of power unseen since the time of kings, he seemed inexpressibly unhappy, but also seized of purpose. Josiri knew the latter feeling well. Not all victories were happy ones. In fact, both Malachi *and* Viktor seemed uncomfortable, but then Josiri had despaired too much at his own reflection that morning to hold them to higher standards.

"A problem for tomorrow, or the day after," said Malachi. "Whether I like it or not, I have to deal with the situation before me, which is that my only two allies will ride south as soon as they leave this chamber. If I'm to spend the future arguing with the elder Lord Akadra, I'd sooner do so from a position of authority." Malachi offered a wan smile. "Honestly, I'm surprised you're not already out the door."

The words, doubtlessly meant in support, only deepened Josiri's despondency. "If Malatriant really has taken Eskavord, haste on my part will change nothing."

"But a little urgency on ours might change everything." Malachi's tone hardened. His posture set like steel. "My first declaration is that all accusations levied against the Trelan family are dismissed and all crimes pardoned. You may be Josiri Trelan again – and not Josiri Akadra – without fear of consequence. My second decree is that Lord Viktor Akadra, the Council's champion, has full authority to requisition whatever forces he believes necessary to address the situation in Eskavord."

"Good," said Viktor. "Saves me being declared traitor twice in one week."

Which meant, Josiri decided, that he'd already determined to take such a course. "Thank you."

"For nothing," said Malachi. "If this *is* Malatriant, what has begun in Eskavord will cross the Tevar Flood soon enough. Besides, you've stood with us twice, though Lumestra knows we've given you every reason not to. We stand with you now. Isn't that so, Viktor?"

"Without a doubt."

Malachi nodded, his gaze falling upon Josiri. It was a curious stare, laden with hidden intent. As if he'd more he wished to impart but could not find the words. "Whatever comes next, Josiri, you are my friend. You'll always be welcome in this city. I hope to see you again, without need of armed men to drag you north."

A wry smile coloured his last words – one Viktor mirrored, if darkly.

Finding no words to match the burden of his heart, Josiri rose and embraced Malachi. How strange to find a brother – an equal – in a place he'd hated so long. How gratifying to do so. If only his mother had lived to see it.

"Goodbye, First Councillor Reveque," he said at last. "Don't let the power go to your head. Ebigail was enough."

"I doubt Lily will let that happen."

With a final bow – a bow no duke or duchess of Eskavord had offered a northwealder in five generations – Josiri left the Council chamber.

Rosa took the last flight two stairs at a time and tugged her surcoat back into place. Unsteady with wine taken and yawning wide, Sevaka had left at midnight, bound for the *Triumphal* and the hope of a naval career renewed. For her part, Rosa felt neither aftermath of drink nor the burden of sleeplessness. The blessings of an eternal's constitution.

The bruised sky promised at least an hour until dawn. Izack's summons suggested her duties would begin sooner. Rosa was glad. It meant she was still a knight, and not some curiosity to be studied, or an abomination to be tested. More than she deserved, given how readily she'd allowed Ebigail Kiradin to lead her astray.

Returning the sentry's salute, she passed beneath the escutcheoned arch and into the master's quarters. Izack glanced up from the desk – soon to be *his* desk – and clambered to his feet. Dark circles beneath his eyes spoke of sleep lightly taken. It wasn't a feeling Rosa missed.

He cracked a dour smile. "Well, well, well. Don't you look disgustingly cheerful, sister?"

"Just glad to be alive." And for the first time in weeks, it was true. She'd mistakes to atone for, but she'd all the time in the world in which to do so. "You've orders for me?"

"Not me." He hooked a thumb towards the far end of the room. "Him."

The shadows shifted, reforming around a battered man garbed in black and silver. A scarred face Rosa knew as well as her own. A friend she'd betrayed.

Viktor.

Her cheer, so carefully husbanded, slipped away. "Izack, I don't . . . "

"Well, that's me off," Izack interrupted. "Apparently the Council reckons we're not stretched thin enough as it is, so I'm away to drag that treacherous bastard Rother out of his bed and share the joy about a bit. *She's* all yours."

Retrieving his helmet from the desk he struck out for the door, a jaunty whistle trailing in his wake. The door slammed, cutting off both whistle and boot-treads.

Viktor neither moved, nor spoke. In a flash, Rosa was transported back a decade, a lowly squire called to account for recklessness. She still felt an echo of that fear. But she wasn't that callow young woman any longer. She'd own her mistakes. Even if that meant losing her spurs, and the brotherhood of Essamere.

"Lord Akadra, I owe you an apology." Realising her eyes had dropped to the floor, she forced her head back to meet his gaze. "I let grief colour my actions. I allowed myself to be deceived. And I betrayed your trust. If you've come to bring me to account for that, I understand. I'll offer no resistance."

He stepped out of the shadow and into the dancing lantern light. "Viktor. To you, Rosa, I'll always be Viktor. We've been friends too long. As to the rest? Kasamor wouldn't wish us to fall out over his mother's actions."

Forgiveness gleamed, bright as sunlight and sweet as honey. But she couldn't accept it. "I let Ebigail use me. I knew what she was, and still I let her use me. I should have known better."

He gave a lopsided shrug. "All any of us can hope for is to do what seems right at the time, no matter how hard."

"And if we choose the wrong path?"

"Then we should not make the same mistake again."

Rosa had the sense that the words were no longer meant for her. "You sound as though you've learnt that the hard way yourself."

"Perhaps. There's something you can do for me, if you're willing."

She clasped her fist to her chest in salute. "Anything."

"There's trouble in the Southshires."

"When isn't there?"

Viktor attempted a smile but fell short. "This is different. Malachi's scraping together as much of an army as he can. He wants me to lead it, but I'm asking you to go in my stead. I can't leave it to Josiri. He's a good man, but he's a southwealder and we can't afford old suspicions. I need *you*."

So that was what Izack had meant. Rosa nodded, heart too full almost for words. *Now* she could accept forgiveness. Now, she'd prove herself worthy of it.

"You have me. Body, soul and sword." She paused, at last unpicking the detail hidden in his words. "And you? Where will you be?"

"Riding a swifter road."

Lunandas, 14th day of Radiance

The Dark is always with us.

from the sermons of Konor Belenzo

Sixty-Five

The roadway shifted beneath Viktor's feet. Faces leered out of dancing vapour, only to dissipate as stumbling steps drew him on. Cobbles gave way to stark black soil and desiccated vines. Buildings crumbled to ruin as he drew near, stones cracked to rubble and woven through with the pale fronds and withered leaves. And always that piercing cackle of birds, and the thrum of beating wings.

The passage of the mists, though terrifying, might have been bearable but for his shadow, which reeled drunkenly about his soul. Even when the road ran clear through the green-white skeins, Viktor was beset with such nausea that it was all he could manage not to lurch headlong into the shifting tides of spectres long dead.

Viktor clung to the memory of Calenne. As within the provosts' cells, she offered anchorage where mortal senses offered none. At times, Viktor thought he saw her beside him, her being as pallid as all else in that accursed realm – her face pleading as she reached for him with insubstantial fingers. But only a fool trusted to his senses in the Raven's kingdom.

At last, he could bear it no more. Legs buckled, and then gave. Viktor fell to his knees beside a shallow pond of water that was not water. A face pale as parchment gazed back from the reflection. *His* face, or a bleak approximation thereof, with hollow cheeks and cruel demeanour. More like his dead father than himself.

A hand closed around Viktor's collar. His bellowed challenge died beneath a smother of bird-voices. Dredging up his last strength, Viktor thrust a hand into the mist and pivoted about cold stone.

The weight on his collar vanished. Off-balance, Viktor sprawled into mud. Darkness rushed in. Not of sleep, but something deeper and more pervasive. But even that vile, discomfiting sensation was as the sweetest wine after the numbing mists.

Mud oozing between his fingers, Viktor rose on unsteady legs. Already the mist-wreathed portal was fading into the brick of the farmhouse wall. Apara stood beside it, shoulders propped against a crumbling buttress, the white streak in her hair vivid in the oppressive dark. Her expression fell a hair short of sullen superiority.

"Why?" Viktor wiped a clump of mud from his chin. "You could have abandoned me. You'd have been free."

"And if you'd found your own way out? Would you have forgiven that betrayal?"

Viktor spat the last of the sourness from his mouth and nodded. "You *may* yet live to pay your debts."

Her lips tightened. "And when does that happen?"

"When I consider them settled."

Apara pushed away from the wall. Sullenness gave way to worry. "If the Parliament of Crows learns I've taken an outsider into Otherworld, I'll not live to eat another meal, let alone pay my way clear of you. Perhaps I *should* have left you there."

Viktor hauled hard on her hidden tether. She fell to her knees, hands splayed for support.

"Do not mistake my kindness for weakness," he said.

Her defiance beneath his shadow burned like a hot coal under his hand. It would be so easy to smother it, to snuff out the last vestige of the woman. Viktor wasn't certain what that would leave behind. Something biddable, certainly, but he sensed a precipice, and an abyss beneath. That one, simple step would be a step too far.

What good of reunification with Calenne if he'd made himself the monster she'd once feared? He stooped and raised Apara from the mud.

She shied away. "So who have you brought me here to kill? I assume that's what you want."

Viktor unhooked the lantern from his belt and coaxed it to life. Light rippled across the flooded courtyard, picking out the farmhouse's hunched eaves.

"Where have you brought me?"

"Where you wanted," said Apara.

"I *wanted* to be brought to Branghall."

"It doesn't work like that. The mists run where the mists run. Eskavord should be a few miles south-east. Whichever way that is. We weren't in the mists that long. It should be dusk."

"It *is* dusk. The Dark has smothered the sky."

"What *are* you talking about?"

He crossed to the nearest window. The drapes hung open behind the leaded frame. Three bodies lay slumped across the table. A father and two children. Their eyes gazed emptily across half-eaten meals. No blood. No sign of struggle. A peaceful tableau, but for the flies swarming like fractured shadows beyond the glass.

And everywhere the echo of magic. A familiar magic, like to Viktor's own shadow, but deeper ... so much deeper. He'd touched it before. At Davenwood. In that one, desperate moment when all had seemed lost, and anger had slipped the shackles of reason.

"Malatriant is making Eskavord her stronghold," he said. "Those she can't control, she kills."

"Malatriant? You've been too long in the mists. It's scattered your wits."

"No. If anything, I'm seeing clearer than ever."

Apara joined him at the window. Her face twisted in revulsion. "Poison. Blue spittle's a giveaway. Moonglove, most likely."

"And the fourth plate. Untouched. The mother's. Malatriant whispered in her ear and she poisoned her family, never knowing why."

"No. You're mistaken. There are a dozen reasons she might have done such a thing."

He lowered the lantern, glad to let the scene sink into gloom. "You shouldn't judge all mothers by the standards of your own."

Apara answered his bleak humour with a bitter look. "Nothing could make me do that to my own kin."

He snorted. "I could. I *did*. Malatriant once bent whole nations to her will. This ... This is nothing."

Apara glanced about. "Do you suppose she's still here?"

"I doubt it. I understand she keeps her thralls close. They have Branghall besieged."

"Sounds like you need an army."

"I have one. But I wanted to arrive sooner. There's someone I have to find."

He broke off. There'd never been much chance that Calenne had survived the Battle of Davenwood. What hope he'd allowed himself floundered in the darkness.

Apara snarled a short, bitter laugh. "Can it be that you actually care about someone?"

"I care about everyone. Even you." He fished a coin purse from his belt. She caught it smoothly, despite evident surprise. "For your service. Should I need you again, I'll find you."

Eyes narrowed in suspicion. "As easy as that? You don't want me to stay?"

"I've distractions enough without worrying about a knife in the back. Go home."

She hefted the purse. "This doesn't excuse what you've done to me."

"I don't mean it to. If I don't return, you may consider your debts paid, and a new life earned. Do better with it."

She gave a slow nod and backed away. One eye ever fixed on him, she traced her fingers across brick, coaxing forth the mists. Greenish-white light spilled into the courtyard. For a time, it vied with the glow from Viktor's lantern, a curious darkness flickering as a barrier where the two met. Then Apara was gone, and a gust of wind scattered the gate to nothing.

The walls of Cragwatch sat silent. Neither lantern nor flame graced the battlements. If anything moved within it did so hidden from Melanna's sight. Like the Eskavord road, it seemed wholly bereft of life. Kreska at least had shown signs of activity, if furtive and fleeting.

At first, she'd told herself the quiet of Kreska was merely the aftermath of battle. That, or the fruits of whatever quarrel had broken out between the Tressian factions. But then she'd noted the wreath of bramble and black ivy nailed to the gate. The bonfires raging on the battlements, the sweet notes of duskhazel and fleenroot soured by burning flesh. Charms to ward off witchcraft, and fire to cleanse those suspected of the crime. And fear. Fear above all.

It had taken Melanna every scrap of willpower to press on into the Dark, but she had done so, through fields empty of workers and houses bereft of tenants. Before Kreska, she'd travelled with bow slung and daggers sheathed. After, she did so with arrow nocked. The silver arrowhead, blessed in the crystal waters of high temple, glowed with soft moonfire. Just as well, for she'd never have found her way through the trees without it.

And now she knelt on the ridge above Cragwatch, aged by every whisper of movement and scurry of claw on branch. Eskavord yet lay miles to the west, but already Melanna's heart had almost failed her on more occasions than she could readily count.

She wanted to turn back, to flee to the border and the embrace of kin. So why was she seized with a desire to slip inside the silent fortress? Was it curiosity, or simple defiance? Proof to herself that the Dark hadn't turned her into a fearful, timid creature as it had the folk of Kreska? Or perhaps she hoped for a sight so horrific that it would grant licence to turn back, to endure Sera's certain chastisement?

So it was that without really knowing why, Melanna descended the root-woven hillside and ghosted across Cragwatch's dry moat. There was no cover to be had in the ditch, but she kept low and moved at a bandy-legged run, all the while expecting to hear challenge from the wall, or else the heart-stopping thump of a bolt in her belly.

Neither came.

She scrambled up the sheer bank to where the weathered stone bridge met archway. Silver arrowhead bobbing before her like a hallow-wisp, she approached the iron-braced timbers of the gate. They sat ajar.

The stench hit Melanna as she passed inside. Soft and sweet; rotting meat leavened by dawnblossom. Kin to the bonfires on Kreska's walls, and yet different. Sour where the other was smoky. The stink of death left unburied.

Cragwatch's courtyard lay thick with corpses; scores, even hundreds. They lay in groups, beneath stones smeared with blood and half-sunk in filthy puddles. Most wore the king's blue of the Tressian army – the rest a hodgepodge of garb drawn from all walks of life. The latter struck Melanna as almost peaceful in repose. Not so the former, who had the look of men and women set upon by rabid wolves. It wasn't war as Melanna knew it, but desperation. The stones practically shrieked with terror.

And the citizenry ... Torn fingernails and blood crusted about their lips. Their wrists shackled. And their eyes ... glittering black, with spidery vein-work running across flesh like cracks across parched land. And the wagons standing empty. A prison convoy? Southwealders bound for servitude in the north until ... Until what? How could folk furious enough to contest steel with bare hands seem so serene in death?

They couldn't. Not unless the will driving them was not their own.

Sera was wrong. The dream had not been a dream.

The boggy field sucked at Viktor's heels, clinging to his boots with the determination of a street-keelie to a nobleman's stolen purse.

Viktor pressed on, head bowed into the wind, hewing as south-westerly a course as the muddy fields allowed. If anything, his mood was blacker than his immediate surroundings. They, at least, had the lantern to lend contrast. He'd done this. He'd loosed the Dark in a moment of pride and fury. The land he'd sought to save from the arrogance of his countrymen was now humbled by his own.

He had to do better. He *would* do better.

The fault, he deemed, lay not with his actions, but that he'd been driven to such desperate means in the first place. If the Council had granted him soldiers with which to oppose the Hadari, he'd never have been forced to reckless use of his shadow. Poor strategy birthed desperate tactics. It was obvious with hindsight. Indeed, if he'd slain his father back when all this had begun ...

Even now, Viktor felt no remorse. Whatever love he'd felt for his sire had faded long ago, replaced by creeping disappointment at his failures, and contempt for his deeds. More than anything, Viktor resented the waste – that a great man could be so overcome by selfishness. The real Hadon Akadra had died long ago, drowned in comfort and privilege. Viktor could conjure no shame for ridding the world of his remnant. Whatever stain it placed on his soul he'd bear gladly, knowing that Tressia was richer for it.

Viktor came to a squelching halt. Thus far he'd navigated not by sight – for he could make out little, even with the lantern's aid – but by instinct. He could *feel* where the Dark thickened away beyond the field – beyond the forest's edge. He felt its lure, and the pull it exerted on his shadow. If that was Malatriant, and Malatriant had taken Eskavord, then that at last had given him some idea of where Branghall could be found. Now, the paling sky rising above the treetops confirmed it.

He had to start at Branghall, to bring word that help was coming, and to learn of Calenne's fate, if anything were known. Viktor knew that wasn't entirely rational but was at a loss how else to proceed. One man alone could do little for Eskavord, but if fortune was with him, he could yet find Calenne.

Undergrowth rustled. An old woman in a heavy woollen shawl stepped out onto the path ahead. Viktor halted, his free hand at the hilt of his claymore. He knew the face.

"Mother Savka?"

The woman straightened, and Viktor recognised the right and wrong of his challenge. The body was Elda's, or at least it had once been so. Now her eyes glittered darkly in black-webbed sockets, as if the flesh beneath had shattered, and some unspeakable darkness had come crawling out. Her shadow belonged to a much taller figure and flickered where the light did not.

"So you've come. I knew you would."

The voice was older even than Elda's leathery face, and dry with the rasp of the tomb. When Viktor looked on her through his shadow's eyes rather than his own, he saw a faint echo of . . . something . . . at her shoulder. A cadaverous figure whose hair coiled to entwine the old woman's misshapen shadow.

"What is your name, my child?"

"You knew I'd be coming, but not my name?" Viktor forced bravado into his voice. There *was* fear, but distant. He felt the yearning more. A need. Even a kinship. "I expected better from Queen Malatriant."

Filth-matted plaits danced as Elda tilted her head. Her lips hooked an old smile. "We have no need of names, you and I."

Brambles crackled. A dozen shapes emerged from beyond the lantern light. A man in frayed proctor's robes. A young girl, her hair still bound in fraying plaits. A woman swathed in a wolf-cloak. An older man in the silk scarf and weskit of the well-to-do. Most wore the homespun cloth of farmers. Two carried swords. Others bore labourers' tools: mattocks, baling forks and shovels. All shared Elda's glittering eyes.

"I've waited so long for this moment." Elda extended her hand. "Come with me."

The others formed a loose ring, as Ascension dancers gathering about a lumendoll. A piece of Viktor wanted to go to her. More than a piece. Desperate for an anchor, he stared into the lantern. It helped. Yearning flickered to vapour in the golden glow.

He slid his claymore free of its slings.

"I regret that I'm needed elsewhere."

Elda laughed. The notes scraped across Viktor's thoughts like steel on slate. "The needs of others are of no concern."

The ring of thralls closed in.

Lantern still gripped tightly in his left hand, Viktor sent the claymore arcing towards the merchant. There was little threat in the clumsy, one-handed blow, but still the thrall stumbled away. Viktor hurled himself at the opposite side of the circle, angling between sword-point and mattock.

His shoulder struck a labourer's ribs, driving the man back. The proctor moved to take his place, his sword held more like a ceremonial candle than a weapon. Viktor battered it aside with his own steel and lunged for freedom.

Sword abandoned, the proctor threw himself onto the claymore's killing point. A scream parted pale lips. Others echoed the cry, as if his pain were their own. The man grasped at the crossguard and drew himself inch by bloody inch onto the blade. Giving voice to a last gurgling whimper, he sank to the soil, dragging the sword from Viktor's grip as he fell.

Viktor backed away from the surviving thralls. Weaponless, he did the only thing he could. He called for his shadow.

It refused him. There was no fear, no reluctance ... not even malice. It simply sank into his soul and did not rise.

Viktor scrambled away uphill. Only Elda hung back from pursuit, a knowing, ancient smile frozen on her lips. A mattock's wild swing smashed the lantern. The forest drowned in hungry darkness.

Blinded, Viktor fled. Boots snagged on tree-roots. Branches ripped at his cheeks. His right shoulder slammed into a bough.

"There is nothing to fear," intoned Elda. "We are all one in the Dark."

Yearning returned. Like calling to like. Only this time there was no lantern-light to sear temptation away. Instead, Viktor clapped his hands over his ears. It helped. But it also meant he didn't hear the hoof-beats until the rider was almost on him.

Viktor threw himself aside. The horseman galloped past, a dark presence against a black sky, given shape only by Branghall's distant glow. The horse wheeled about. Viktor tensed for a pounce. Better to die in pursuit of freedom than surrender.

The rider slowed. The juddering pulse of hooves faltered to nothing. A cloak's folds parted, and lantern-light blazed forth.

"Viktor?" Calenne's lips parted, torn between laughter and surprise. "I might have known. What in Lumestra's name are you doing out here?"

Viktor fumbled for a reply and found none. Undergrowth crackled on the slope behind.

Calenne straightened in her saddle and gazed over his head. "Tell me later ... Unless you'd rather stay here?"

There it was. The smile he'd yearned for and feared never to see again. "No."

For a moment, Viktor forgot the Dark, forgot the Tyrant Queen drawing near through the trees, and lost himself in that one, unlooked-for moment of perfect joy. Then he swung onto the horse behind Calenne and let her bear him far away.

Sixty-Six

The flame shrank back from the gloom of the empty barn. Or perhaps, Viktor allowed, the fault lay not with the fire, but with him, for his own emotions were such a whirl that light and warmth held little of his attention.

Calenne watched him from across the flames with shadowed eyes. She looked . . . different. Leaner. Sharper. It suited her. But beneath the grime, beneath the fraying plaits and weather-stained ribbons tied through her black hair, she remained Calenne more than she did not. As if hardship had peeled away the last shreds of a pampered cocoon to reveal her truth.

All this and more Viktor longed to say, but he instead retreated into practicality.

"Are you certain the fire won't give us away?" he asked.

"They never come out this far. Not now."

The weary voice matched Calenne's appearance. Still unquestionably hers, it was hollowed out by hardship; adrift on a grey ocean with no shore in sight. Viktor couldn't imagine the lessons she'd learned to change her so, and wished he'd been able to spare her the tutelage.

Calenne poked at the smouldering ash with her dagger. "First couple of days were different. They came marching in from the surrounding villages. Horrible to see. Then the rain stopped and the Dark flooded in. Now they only leave Eskavord with a purpose. Like when an idiot northwealder comes plodding about with an unshielded lantern. You must be special. I've not seen Elda beyond the walls since this started."

Viktor winced. "I suppose that *was* foolish."

"You're lucky I found you."

"And you've been fortunate to stay free."

She nodded, thoughts plainly elsewhere. "Yes, that's me."

"What about the others?"

"There are no others." She closed her eyes. "Not outside Branghall. Malatriant's thralls are ringed about those walls three deep – so many that Eskavord's deserted. I've found no one else. And I've looked, Viktor. Every farm and village, one edge of the Dark to the other. It's horrible. Simply horrible. And it's all my fault."

He frowned. "How do you conjure that?"

"After my horse bolted, I fell deep into Skazit Maze – maybe even *below* Skazit Maze. I saw her. Bound behind walls of light. The memory's so hazy, but I ... I know I set her free. I've been running ever since." She jerked upright, eyes taut with sorrow. "And now look what's become of my home."

Guilt crowded Viktor's thoughts. "You're not to blame. Someone erred. Someone so desperate for victory that they didn't stop to consider the cost."

Calenne's gaze hardened. "That Hadari witch."

It would be so easy to lay the blame on Melanna Saranal, to free Calenne of her guilt and his. But he'd been nothing but truthful with Calenne from the moment they'd met. How could he now be otherwise? Better to lose her trust through honest mistake than wilful deception.

"No," he murmured. "The Hadari had no part of this."

She gazed at him, expecting more. Then her throat bobbed and she stared down into the fire. "I see."

Silence reigned, broken only by the thin crackle of the flames. Viktor breathed deep of the bitter smoke and scrabbled for an explanation. But truth was he'd little more to say. Pride had loosed great evil. All else was evasion.

Calenne's lips thinned. "So where do we go from here?"

"We destroy Malatriant."

She snorted. "Just us?"

"No. An army is coming."

"I thought the Council didn't care about the Southshires."

"A great deal has changed, and for the better."

"And my brother?" Her tone held no concern, only polite interest.

"Rides at the army's head."

She laughed, none too kindly. "So Josiri finally slipped from under his mother's shadow?"

He shook his head. "I'd say rather that he's found purpose."

Viktor laid out all that had occurred, sparing only his personal dealings with Apara and his late father. "I told you much had changed. And it began here, with you and I."

She leaned forward, a glint of mischief in her eyes. "Have you nothing more to say to me?"

"I don't follow."

"You've spoken of the city, the Council, my brother. Your eyes have shone with the joy of it. So I ask again, have you nothing more to say to *me*, the woman who is to be your wife?"

Fragile defiance came into her eyes, a need to hear words expressed, but too proud to speak plainly. Viktor rose. Skirting the flames, he held out a hand. After a heartbeat, she took it and stood before him. He faltered, apprehensive of a woman half his size. But his earlier determination to speak only truth carried him through.

"Only that you have been my anchor through strife and torment. That there has not been one moment where I did not yearn to see you, to know that you'd come safely through the madness." He faltered, unused to speaking at such length, and entirely unaccustomed to speaking from the heart. "That's how I know Malatriant can be beaten, because I have more to fight for than ever."

"We both do."

She took his head in her hands and drew him down into a kiss. Looping his hands about her waist, Viktor lost himself in their closeness, in the taste and scent of her. For a long, glorious moment, the world beyond no longer existed. Not the Southshires, nor the Republic as a whole, nor even the Tyrant Queen he'd roused to ruin. There was only Calenne, and a joy he'd never known.

Then he felt it. A seed of darkness buried in Calenne's soul. Bleak. Hungry. Like to that he'd sensed in Josiri after the Battle of Davenwood, in the manner that a raindrop was like to the storm. The same, yet vast in scale. He'd missed the connection before, even with Kurkas' letter before him. To think, he'd believed it a Hadari curse. Now there could be no doubt. His shadow, quiescent since before he'd come to the barn, growled its curiosity.

He broke contact and pulled away.

"Viktor?" Calenne kept pace. "Viktor, what is it?"

Truth, he reminded himself. Only truth. "There's something . . . inside you. Something dark. A piece of Malatriant."

He'd expected horror, revulsion. He saw only sadness. "I know. I think it's always been there, waiting, goading . . . whispering through my dreams. I hear her sometimes, calling me as she did back in her crypt. A voice so honeyed and welcoming that it's all I can do not to listen. But it doesn't matter. We are all one in the Dark."

"How do you keep her at bay? How do you stay free?"

A wan smile. "I'm a Trelan. I'm stubborn."

He nodded, struggling to hold horror at bay while he digested the new information. The shadow on Calenne's soul dwarfed the one he'd found in her brother's. If it had grown so vast in a week, it would soon overtake her.

"Let me help."

"How?"

"I drew the Dark from your brother. I can do the same for you."

She shook her head. "No. I can't let you take that risk."

Calenne made to turn away. He gathered her into an embrace, their faces so close as to be almost touching, his eyes fixed on hers. "I have borne a shadow all my life. I will gladly bear yours."

She gave the smallest of nods. "Thank you."

As his shadow made contact with the dark seed in Calenne's soul, Viktor briefly worried at the scale of the task – that some piece of Malatriant's will might yet hold sway. The fear that he'd again rushed into the matter conjured further doubt, but he could no more leave Calenne beset in this manner than any other. Taking a deep breath to steady himself, Viktor enfolded the seed and made it his own.

Blackness washed over him. With it came sights and sounds of a world he'd never seen, a world with a sunless sky and a broken, grinning moon. Lupine howls echoed beneath twisted, skeletal trees, while men and women cowered beneath the stones of hollowed-out, crumbling halls. And everywhere that sinking, gnawing instinct. That his skin was not his own, but a mask to slough away and run free wherever the light was not.

Viktor's vision cleared into flame. He trembled on hands and knees, a brackish taste in his throat and umbral flecks dancing before his eyes. And his shadow? His shadow exulted. Viktor knew that he could never again do what he had done for her, not without losing himself.

"Viktor?" Calenne shook his shoulders. "Viktor! Thank Lumestra. You went so still, I thought . . . "

Viktor took her hand and set his shadow prowling once more. The seed was . . . gone. Instead of Malatriant's darkness, he saw only an echo of his own, like gazing at a reflection in the rushing waters at Coventaj.

He squeezed her hand tight and cleared his throat. "How do you feel?"

A tremulous, uncertain smile parted her lips. "Like I can breathe for the first time in my life."

It had worked. It had pushed him to the brink, but it had worked. With that realisation came purpose. Malatriant could be diminished – maybe even slain, if the blow were levelled at the right point. Of the thralls who'd sought to cage him, only Elda had spoken.

"You say Elda never leaves Eskavord?"

"I said I've not *seen* her leave Eskavord."

She *was* feeling better to quibble so. Viktor clambered upright. "And you know a way inside?"

"I didn't say *that*."

"Calenne . . . "

She rolled her eyes. "One of the exits from Skazit Maze comes up in the churchyard. It's where I finally clambered out. It's that or swim the Grelyt. What's on your mind, Viktor?"

"There may be a way to end this without anyone else getting killed. If Malatriant *has* taken root in Elda . . . "

She shot him a look as old as the hills. "You said Josiri was bringing an army. Wait for it."

"This started with my mistake. I have to try."

"And if you're killed?" She scowled. "You haven't seen Eskavord. There are bodies in the streets. She's made a throne of corpses in the market-place! You'd already be dead if I hadn't found you. And now you'd give her a second chance?"

"One life wagered to save hundreds, maybe thousands. I count for little set against that."

She folded her arms. "Not to me."

Viktor finally understood some of Malachi's spousal frustrations. It was no easy thing to argue with someone who sought only to save you from yourself.

"Please don't make this difficult."

"On one condition only."

"And that is?"

"I'm coming with you."

"Calenne ... "

She jabbed a finger into his ribs. "Maybe this is your fault and not mine, but this is still my home. And you need a guide."

That much made sense. "Very well. But only as far as Eskavord."

"Hah! As if I'd agree to that." She grinned and kissed him again, this time holding him so tight that Viktor feared there'd be no way to free himself without breaking her arms. "Where you go, I go."

With no other option to hand, Viktor accepted defeat and gave himself to her embrace.

The rustle of ivy sent Melanna scurrying for cover behind what had once been a stone archway. She set a hand around the arrowhead, muting its glow to a pale white sheen.

Someone *was* there. Away past the crude altar and its smattering of peasant offerings. Out past the ring of young trees that nestled between the tumbled walls. A towering shape, identifiable as such only when motion split it from impenetrable gloom. The first such shape Melanna had encountered since entering the unnatural dark. She'd seen nothing larger than a fox since leaving the charnel of Cragwatch, and that beast had possessed the good sense to scurry away as soon as noticed. The woods had otherwise been silent, as if birds and beasts held their breath.

The rustle came again. Dark moved against dark. Melanna sank back behind stone.

A lantern's warm glow spilled across the overgrown temple, the sight of it so sudden, so welcome, that Melanna almost laughed to see it. But only almost. There were plenty of reasons for a Hadari to be afraid with Eskavord's walls so close.

A grunt. A grinding, jarring rumble of stone moving on stone.

A hushed, basso whisper, couched in dry humour. "Ladies first."

Melanna knew that voice. The man-of-shadow.

She craned back about the arch. It *was* Lord Akadra, if a goodly bit more bruised than when she'd last seen him. But there was no mistaking the coils of dancing shadow. Of his companion, she saw nothing. The empty void beneath the altar, now revealed in the lantern-light, explained why. Another wolf's-head tunnel. She'd used many herself.

Akadra stood with his back towards her, hands still tight about the slab he'd dragged clear. Melanna eased her arrow onto the bow-string. The man who'd crushed her father's dreams. Here. At her mercy. She could put a shot in his throat, and he'd never see it coming. Never know who'd sent him to the mists. Debts owed to Josiri did *not* apply to the man-of-shadow.

Melanna shook her head, disgusted. Perhaps they didn't, but an assassin's arrow was unworthy of her. Glory in victory, fortitude in defeat, and honour always.

She sank back again as Akadra turned, her breath staling in her throat. A dozen frantic beats she held that breath. Then the vines rustled again, and the lantern-light faded.

A glance confirmed he'd gone. But gone where? Into the tunnels, certainly, but with what destination? For that matter, why was he here at all?

The sharp snap of a broken twig halted that line of thought. Footfalls followed. Three pairs. Maybe four. All closing at a pace neither swift enough for immediate concern, nor slow enough for comfort.

Melanna risked a little light. The silver glow gave shape to four Tressians, advancing from the direction of Eskavord. Melanna hastily covered the arrowhead, but not before black eyes glittered. Just like the dead citizenry at Cragwatch.

Their approach made Melanna's decision for her. Heart in her mouth, she slunk away.

*

"What do you think?" asked Kurkas.

Brask peered out over Branghall's gatehouse. "I don't know. I can't see anything."

"Fat lot of good you are."

He gave the gate approach the full benefit of his one-eyed stare. It was no good. Within the wall, the evening sky had darkened to starlit night, but everything beyond the gatehouse lanterns remained black as pitch.

"Could be they're hiding," said Brask. "Maybe the light hurts them."

"I don't think we're that lucky," said Kurkas gloomily. "That were the case, we'd polish them up with a handful of firestone lanterns and a bit of cold steel."

[[They're gone,]] said Anastacia. [[At least, I can't see any between us and the town.]]

"Guess she's got more in mind than seizing a serathi after all ..." Kurkas frowned. "Wait. You can see through that muck?"

[[Of course.]]

"You might have said something," said Brask. "We could have used you on watch."

[[I'm not a scarecrow, however much I'm dressed the part.]]

Sensing another argument, Kurkas stepped between them. "Right then. We're leaving."

Brask blinked. "You're sure that's a good idea?"

"Don't know about you, but starvation rations of wine and horseflesh are only half appealing." Kurkas nodded, warming to his theme. "And I don't fancy marching down into the town, so we'll use the hallowgate and head north. We get lucky, we'll run right into whatever help Lord Akadra's sending."

"Assuming Dastarov got through," said Brask.

Kurkas slapped her on the back. "Cheer up, lieutenant. It's only the end of the world."

"Fine." Brask jerked a thumb at Anastacia. "But she stays here, otherwise come sun-up those thralls'll know exactly where to look for us."

Kurkas rubbed a bristly chin. Raven's Eyes, but he looked more a vagabond with every passing day. "She's got a point. Have you tried *not* being a little ray of sunshine?"

[[Have *you* tried not being a fool?]]

"I thought I had," he said mildly. "The quest continues. Changes nothing. We all go, or we all stay."

"This is a mistake," said Brask.

Kurkas sighed. "What this is, lieutenant, is an order."

Brask opened her mouth, thought better of it, and stalked towards the stairs.

[[She might be right,]] Anastacia said. [[Perhaps I should stay.]]

Kurkas propped his back against the outer rampart and stared down onto Branghall's terrace. The pyre was long gone and Halvor's blackened remains buried, but the starburst of ash remained.

"I'm already leaving too many behind. It's all of us, or none."

Viktor pressed his shoulder to the trapdoor's sagging, rotten timbers. It bucked, giving him space to slide one hand off the rusting ladder and onto the cold stone beyond. Another heave, and he climbed out into the sepulchre. A crack of light from Calenne's hooded lantern gave shape to a choir of weeping serathi, their marble features silted from a leak in the ancient roof.

"Come on," he breathed.

Calenne ghosted up the final span of rungs. Viktor drew his sword as she set the trapdoor in position. A farmer's blade, half-gone to rust, but it would serve. It would have to. Experience warned it was foolish to rely on his shadow.

"I wish you'd go back," he whispered.

"Only if you come with me."

It was, Viktor allowed, the opposite problem as with Apara. The kernclaw couldn't be trusted near him; Calenne, he feared, couldn't be trusted out of his sight.

"If I ask you to go, you must promise to do so."

"Viktor ..."

"Please, Calenne. I swear I'll demand nothing more of you as long as we live, but I must have your promise." He breathed deep, exhausted once again from speaking from the heart. "I nearly lost you once. I can't bear to do so again."

"All right." The gloom shifted, and he had the impression of her looking down at her feet. "You won't lose me, but all right. But afterwards, no more demands."

"Thank you. Douse the lantern."

The sepulchre door opened with a screech of tortured metal, but there was no sudden commotion in the churchyard, no hollow voice raised in greeting. That only left the problem of how to navigate.

"Give me the lantern," he hissed.

"Don't be a fool," she replied. "I used to play hide-and-seek around these tombs. I can get us to the road."

Viktor slipped his hand in hers. "Lead on."

To his relief and surprise, Calenne struck a faultless path through the shrouded graveyard, guiding him by gentle – and increasingly not-so-gentle – tugs on his hand, and hissed warnings. Hazy grey murk spilled across the cobbles beyond the lychgate. Somewhere in Eskavord, there was light.

Calenne at his side, they headed west, crossing the bridge where he'd fought Katya Trelan so many years ago. With every step, the Dark receded. He almost wished it hadn't. What before had been indistinct masses at the roadside were revealed as huddled bodies. Some had the black vein-work and glittering eyes of thralls. Most did not. The stench of death hung heavy on the still air.

Viktor gritted his teeth and pressed on. He'd heard so many stories of Malatriant, both as a child and in the years since. Some fanciful, others starkly real. The Abdon Temples, where ritual coaxed forth demons with the scent of innocent souls. Children stolen and raised to be their parents' executioners. The blood tithes levied against every family, some taken as conscripts, others in service of the darkest gluttonies. How she'd poisoned her husband, but dragged his bodiless spirit back from the mists to console an irredeemable conscience. By the time they reached the marketplace, he believed them all.

Calenne had warned him Malatriant had made herself a throne of the dead. Reality transcended bleak imagining. The mass of corpses rose out of what had once been the fountain, a hummock of souring flesh and broken bone pinned in place by timber spars. So twisted and jumbled was the mound that Viktor could seldom tell where one victim ended, and the next began. The rich scarlet of an archimandrite's robes brought no satisfaction. Some fates, not even Makrov deserved.

That Viktor made the detail out at all was possible only because of the single firestone lantern set at the summit, resting beside a wooden chair anchored among the dead. Viktor couldn't see the occupant, for the chair faced west towards Branghall. But he'd no doubt of her identity. Elda Savka, or at least the old woman's puppeteered body.

"I knew you'd come." The hollow words echoed about the market-place. "Did you really think I wouldn't?"

The gloom of alleyways parted. Thralls flooded into the marketplace. Scores. Hundreds. Only the road to the church remained open.

"I thought you said they were all at Branghall?" said Viktor.

"They were!" Calenne hissed.

Irrelevance. The gamble had failed. Only one last throw of the dice remained. He stared at the implacable tide. Too many to fight. But that didn't mean he couldn't try.

"Go! Find your brother! Tell him everything!"

"I won't leave you!"

"Keep your promise!"

She glared at him – glared at him with a hatred he'd never seen in her face before. Then, tears streaming down her cheeks, she fled.

Viktor hefted his sword and ran headlong for the throne.

A thrall veered into his path. Viktor sprang aside. Two more bore down, others rushing close behind. Viktor angled towards the leftmost. The first cut knocked the man's sword aside. The second opened his arm to the bone.

The crowd convulsed. A babble of pained voices split the cold air. Just as they had earlier that day. What one felt, all felt – if all were not *already* one.

Good. He could use that.

Viktor forged on through the crowd, sword lashing out not to kill, but to grant pain. A slice at a farmer's belly setting the mass of thralls shuddering. A lunge at a proctor's leg loosed a ripple of movement as others stumbled in unwilling sympathy.

Hands grasped and tugged. A yank of Viktor's surcoat dragged him back, then ceased as his sword bit into flesh. Cloth tore. Filthy nails scratched at his skin. But no sword came for his throat, no dagger stabbed at his spine.

He tore free, bellowing as the action left a hank of hair tight in a thrall's grasp. A lowered shoulder barged another aside. A bunched fist felled a third. Then he was at the base of the charnel throne, scrambling for the summit.

Elda rose from her chair, the motion as regal as ailing bones allowed. "I'm starting to wonder if you're worth the trouble."

Fingers locked about Viktor's ankle. He twisted about, expecting to see that a thrall had followed him onto the slope. None had. Men, women and children waited at the foot, beyond wooden spars and the fountain perimeter.

The pale, waxy hand belonged to the dead.

A second burst from the corpse-pile, pulling on the cloth at Viktor's thigh. Fighting for balance, he backswung his sword, severing fingers and splitting bone. His leg came free, but more hands burst from the mass of dead, pinning his legs anew. Others closed about his arms, holding him fast. Fingers dug into his wrists and twisted the sword from his hand.

"It's done, Viktor. Let it go."

So she *did* know his name. "I will not yield!"

For every hand he tore free, another took its place. The ground beneath his feet shifted, his boots sinking as if into a mire. Viktor glanced down. The carpet of corpses peeled apart like wriggling petals. His lungs filled with a rancid copper-stink. Slack faces and pallid eyes stared up to meet his.

His boots sunk beneath the surface, then his knees.

"Hush." Elda tapped her stick against the foot of the throne. "We'll talk when you're less excitable."

Viktor's shoulders slid beneath the surface. With a last surge of effort, he tore his right arm free and clawed at the pit's edge. The last thing he saw was Calenne atop the bridge, lantern held high above her head as thralls closed in about her.

Dead hands heaved anew and drew him down into their clammy embrace.

Lumendas, 15th day of Radiance

If all else fails, put your faith in fire.

from the sermons of Konor Belenzo

Sixty-Seven

Minutes crept by at a foetid crawl. Shards of red framed Viktor's vision, scant glimmers of firestone light worming through the cage of bodies. He struggled against his bindings, but the embrace of the dead remained tireless and unflinching. Muscles faltered and Viktor hung in the stinking void, lungs straining for what sustenance the confines allowed.

Through it all, Viktor's shadow lurked beneath the surface, at once closer than ever and yet beyond reach. Malatriant's doing, he was sure. But how? Why was he even still alive when she'd made no bones about wreaking slaughter on Eskavord?

Focusing on Calenne made matters both easier and worse. Easier, because it set his mind adrift. Worse, because his thoughts delighted in conjuring the very worst outcomes. What hope had she of reaching Josiri and Rosa? A few hours reunited, and then he'd led her straight back into danger.

After uncertain eternity, the cage of dead shifted. Wan firestone light drowned Viktor's vision, leaving him blind to all else.

A bony hand seized him by the chin, stronger than its appearance allowed. "Yes. You look more manageable now."

"Where's Calenne?" he croaked.

Elda's wrinkled visage gathered from the shadows of his clearing vision. Behind her, a circle of thralls watched with blank stares.

"Perhaps she's dead. Perhaps she died days ago, swallowed by the darkness of Skazit Maze, all the time wondering why you never came for her."

"You forget. I've held her in my arms."

"And she led you here? Are you sure that's how it was? Perhaps what you thought Calenne was but a snare, set to draw you to this place. She belongs to your past. Leave her behind."

The callousness was all the worse coming from the lips of the woman Calenne had considered her mother. A lie crafted to break him. Let her try. Viktor clung tight to the memory of Calenne's embrace and met Elda's abyssal gaze.

"Let her leave, and you may do as you wish with me."

A lie, for he'd no intention of lasting cooperation. Whatever it might cost him.

She let her hand fall. "How reasonable of you."

Strength returned, replenished by sated lungs. Viktor pulled at his bonds, but the lifeless jailers held him fast. "And what does the Tyrant Queen know of reason?"

"You might be surprised, if you permit yourself to listen."

"What you've done here offers me little encouragement to do so."

"I had to be certain of your attention."

Distantly, Viktor acknowledged that he should have been terrified. That he was not . . . ? He told himself it was anger – his determination to see no harm come to Calenne. But there was something else. Something harder to parse. There was a likeness. A bond. Even . . . a kinship? His shadow certainly seemed to believe so. Sated on the darkness he'd earlier drawn from Calenne, it rumbled like a contented kitten.

"Why?"

"Because you are to be my heir."

"Slow down some, plant pot. Have sympathy for a war hero."

Anastacia halted. Ahead, the loose column of soldiers and servants pressed on along the road, beneath trees made golden by molten dawn. Branghall was but a memory, lost to murk. There was only the circle of light and a world lost to shadow.

[[What did you call me?]]

Kurkas fidgeted against her shoulders. "This goes on, you'll pull my damn arm off and leave the rest of me behind."

[[I can carry you?]] Sarcasm dripped like venom.

"Feel bloody ridiculous, wouldn't I? Just … not so fast."

[[Your Lieutenant Brask sets the pace.]]

"She's not mine, and she won't get ahead of you, will she? Not if she likes seeing where she's going."

Kurkas tried not to think on the consequences of Anastacia's presence pushing back the Dark. It was as good as lighting a beacon. Pursuit would be coming. That it wasn't on their heels already suggested that Malatriant had been distracted from claiming Anastacia, but Kurkas knew better than to trust to that lasting long. Being carried would soon become the least of his problems.

The gold-and-white head dipped. [[As you wish. But it's Anastacia, or Milady Herald of the First Circle, *not* plant pot.]]

"My mistake."

A new sound rumbled beneath the birdsong and the swish of leaves. Hoof-beats. Kurkas' heart quickened. Sound travelled oddly in the Dark. Pursuit from Eskavord, or aid from the north? The way his luck had run of late …

"Close up!" Brask's cry echoed back along the road. Three long strides took her up the root-woven embankment. "Shield ring! On me!"

Kurkas nodded approval. Maybe Brask wasn't so useless. The slope and closeness of the trees didn't offer much shelter against cavalry, but it was better than an open roadway.

He was about to say so when the world lurched and the ground rushed away. Anastacia struck a brisk walk, leaving his objections trailing on the crisp morning air. Fifty bone-rattling paces later, she set him down in the heart of the shield ring.

Brask's eyes brimmed with amusement.

"Something funny, lieutenant?"

"No, sir."

Kurkas shook his head, struck by the unmistakeable feeling that Halvor's spirit was laughing at him from the mists.

The hoof-beats grew louder. Kurkas cast an eye about the make-shift formation. Twenty knackered soldiers, five terrified servants and Anastacia. It'd not be much of a stand.

A dozen riders peeled out of the northern darkness like oil separating from water. All carried naked swords and wore green surcoats blazoned with white stars. All save one, arrayed in the same black and silver uniform as Kurkas – if one far less worn.

[[Josiri?]]

Leaving Kurkas grasping at a tree for support, Anastacia parted the misshapen shield ring and ran – actually *ran* – onto the road. Josiri hauled his steed to a halt and dismounted into an embrace so heartfelt it warmed even Kurkas' sorry soul.

Brask's shoulders slumped. The shield ring softened. The lead knight walked her horse around the oblivious couple and removed her helm. "Captain Kurkas?"

"Lady Orova." Kurkas grinned. "Nice to see a familiar face."

She nodded. "How long has it been? Two years since that squabble at Ardovo?"

"About that. This is worse." He stared back along the empty road. "Tell me you've more coming."

"Two regiments, and three brotherhoods. Plus every proctor, simarka and kraikon that could be spared. We saw the light and rode ahead."

Kurkas grunted. "All that on the word of a hearthguard captain? Council must be going soft."

Lady Orova's lips tightened. "Let's just say you've missed a lot."

Words and tone practically screamed to be questioned. Instead, Kurkas stared at the remaining riders. "Lord Akadra not with you?"

Josiri disentangled himself from Anastacia. "He said he'd find his own way here. You've not seen him?"

"Not a whisker. Not that we've been looking."

Josiri's brow wrinkled in thought. "Maybe he never left Tressia."

"No." Lady Orova spoke with flat certainty. "He said he'd be here, and by a faster road. He'd not break that promise."

[[Then where is he?]] asked Anastacia.

"I've seen him."

A new shape emerged from the eastern trees, a dark-skinned young woman clad in Hadari travelling leathers. She had a bow slung across her shoulders, and a hand near to – but not touching – a scabbarded dagger. Kurkas had only ever seen her at a distance, and then in the full scale of an imperial Immortal, but there was no mistaking that combination of willowiness backed by steel.

"You're looking for Lord Akadra?" said Princessa Melanna Saranal. "I know where he is."

Viktor hung in the cage of hands, unsure whether to laugh or to weep. "Your heir? You've been dead too long. It's rotted your wits."

Elda regarded him with disdain, the lid of one glittering eye narrowing to a slit. "Is that so very strange? We all of us long to leave something of ourselves behind – a testament to our deeds when flesh and spirit fail."

"You have that already. Your name is reviled."

She shook her head angrily. "Myth. Rumour. Belenzo tore me from history's pages and unmade my achievements. Now I'm nothing but a name."

"Achievements? You enslaved thousands. You murdered thousands more. And for what? For power? For a throne from which to rule the world?"

Elda's eyes blazed. "You see the world through a child's eyes. We were falling into chaos, two-score petty kings and queens driven mad by the light and battling for supremacy. Those who fell in my cause did so to build something greater than themselves. You must see that."

"I might, had they been given a choice."

Her low, hollow chuckle swept over him. It was strange how readily the mannerisms of today matched those of the woman he'd met before. How much of that irascibility had actually been Elda's? How close to the surface had Malatriant been that whole time? Had Elda ever truly existed?

"Do I hear the bleat of Belenzo's democracy? Where foolishness is forgiven and suffering ignored, so long as principle is followed? What matter the means if the ends are the same? Or have you never taken action out of need, even while the world condemns you?"

Viktor's shadow hissed. Faces rose out of memory, their souls long loosed into Otherworld. His father's chief among them. "Only to save lives."

"There. You do understand." Elda gave a small shake of the head. "If only you'd seen the world I was born into. Strength was the only law, and I had little of my own. So I delved into the Dark and there found not only strength, but truth and purpose. Much as you have done."

"You and I are nothing alike."

She scowled. The pressure about Viktor's limbs grew, as if the fingers were maggots determined to burrow clean through his bruised flesh. Pain trickled a sharp hiss across his lips. Elda nodded, and the dead relented.

"We possess the will to do what others cannot. We see things unshrouded by fickle morality. Where we differ is that I learned to tame the Dark. You, Viktor? You were born of it."

"I was born to Hadon and Alika Akadra." Strange that his sire was now a source of pride. Even tarnished metal shone in the Dark. "I'm mortal. Ephemeral."

"Of course you are. But you're also something else. Something blessed, as all the greatest witches ever were before madness took them. You carry the primal Dark, a sliver shattered by the light of First Dawn." Withered lips cracked a faraway smile. "Once, all were one – equal and unchanging in the Dark's embrace. But then selfish Lumestra brought her light, and parity was lost. Dark is equal. Eternal. Light never falls the same twice, even upon twins. It brings division. Jealousy. Uncounted minuscule differences that shatter order."

"Lumestra freed us from the tyranny of the Dark." The words, learned by rote under Makrov's tutelage, came readily enough. "Her light gave us this world, and the will to tame it."

"The second part, at least, is true," said Elda. "The Dark is power. It is the foundation of everything. Lumestra and her siblings indulged their fancy. They created worlds over which to rule, and laws to govern every facet of life, from the first breath to last gasp. Evermoon. Astarria. Vaalon. Eventide. So many more. They sought a new order to replace the one they'd destroyed. But the gods too had been changed by the light. Now they had names, faces, forms – things they'd never needed in the Dark – and they grew every bit as jealous and divided as their worshippers. Such is the burden of light. Only in the Dark is there order. Only in the Dark is there peace."

"Shadowthorn!"

The shield ring clashed tight. Three knights peeled from the road and spurred into the trees. Melanna stood stock still, ignoring the voice in her head that screamed at her to run, to draw a blade. She'd taken the light in the sky as a sign from Ashana. Too late, she realised it wasn't so.

"Wait!"

The knights slowed at Josiri's shout.

"I'm alone," said Melanna, the unfamiliar Tressian falling harshly on her ears. "I'm not here as an enemy, but to discharge my debt."

The horsewoman exchanged a glance with Josiri and nodded. "Test her words!"

The knights closing on Melanna spurred away east into trees where darkness yet held sway. Hands raised, Melanna drew closer to the road.

"I swear by the goddess and my father's life, I come as a ... friend."

Only now did she recognise the knights' leader – the same woman she'd laboured to save all those nights ago. But Melanna dared not rely on the woman's memory of that time.

"Josiri." She offered a bow of equals. One warrior to another. "I offer my help."

Within the shield ring, the one-eyed man stirred. "Reckon your lot have done enough."

"Enough, captain," said Josiri.

Encouraged, Melanna stepped closer. The horsewoman's eyes never strayed from her. Nor did the peculiar hollow-eyed mask of the woman at Josiri's side.

"You've seen Lord Akadra?" asked Josiri.

"In the grounds of a ruined temple, out to the east. He had a woman with him."

"Calenne?" Josiri started forward, restrained only by a tattered black glove on his arm. "Calenne was with him?"

The missing sister? "Perhaps. I didn't see her. I only heard their conversation."

Urgency overtook his voice. "Take me."

Melanna shook her head. "There'd be no point. He entered the tunnels."

He nodded. "I know them. So he's inside Eskavord?"

[[He's confronting Malatriant.]]

The hollow voice dragged Melanna's attention to the woman at Josiri's side. If she *was* a woman. She was cloaked in light as Akadra was cloaked in shadow. It clung to her.

"Always the show-off," muttered the one-eyed man. "Can't leave him alone for five bloody minutes."

"But he needn't do it alone." Josiri remounted and reached down for the masked woman. After a brief hesitation, she clambered up behind him. "How long ago?"

"I can't be sure," said Melanna. "Hours, certainly."

"Then he might already be dead." The horsewoman frowned and turned her attention to the one-eyed man. "Kurkas, how many blades does Malatriant have?"

"Hundreds," he replied gloomily.

"And I've a dozen. We wait for the army."

"And if matters were different, Lady Orova," said Josiri, "would Viktor wait?"

She scowled. "Captain Kurkas?"

The scruffy soldier offered a sharper salute than Melanna could have imagined. "Milady?"

"When the vanguard arrives, have them surround the town. Nothing in, nothing out. If we don't return, the command is yours."

"Yes, lady."

"And you?" Josiri asked, his eyes on Melanna. "What do you intend?"

She could leave. Debt discharged, she could head east to the safety of her own kind. Or could she? Was anything ever that simple? "I'll ride with you, if you'll have me."

Lady Orova's scowl deepened. "We don't need a shadowthorn's help."

"We need all the help we can find." Josiri spurred forward and put a hand on his sword. "Before I left Tressia, I had a dream, the kind that vanishes into mist as soon as you wake. I recall only two things. An owl, and ironclad certainty of a burden I should bear southwards. I told myself it was tiredness and brandy."

He drew the sword. Silver gleamed in the sunshine as he reversed the blade and held it for Melanna to take. "This, I think, is meant to belong to you again."

She closed a shaking hand about the grips. Her sword. Perhaps the light had been a sign after all.

Viktor cast a long, significant look at his cage of corpses. Another at the dull-eyed thralls gathered in the flickering firestone light. So many. Drawing the Dark out of even one would destroy him.

"This? This is your idea of peace?"

"This is desperation. You don't know what it's like, to have yourself scattered to a thousand pieces, each yearning for the whole. Then fifteen years ago, I felt it. A soul steeped in the Dark but not yet driven to madness by it. Your soul."

Fifteen years. The aftermath of Zanya. When he'd used his shadow to defeat Katya Trelan. Bitter seeds, planted long ago.

"I could have wept with the joy of it, had the traitor Belenzo left me eyes with which to do so. Do you know how long I've felt myself slip away? Part of me trammelled in a cage, and the rest dwindling as bloodlines perished or thinned? Another generation, perhaps two, and I'd never have found the strength to assert myself – to stir a conflict that would lure that brilliant, dark soul back to me. The Hadari were . . . unexpected, but Drakos Crovan and his wolf's-head uprising would have given me everything I needed."

Viktor grimaced. There was little consolation in the fact that he couldn't have known. Elda was correct on one score. Konor Belenzo had done too good a job of turning history into myth. "And in my arrogance, I set you free."

"As I knew you would. It was fate, Viktor. You were born to the Dark. Embrace it. Accept my gift. Wield it as your own."

"And should I choose otherwise?"

"I am fading, yes, but I am still bound to Eskavord. To its people. I will cling to every rock and stone, every scrap of flesh and every spark of soul." She spoke softly but with needle-like precision, the old woman falling away as the ancient spirit within rose to the surface. "I will blaze with Dark one last time and birth an age of horror and destruction such as you cannot conceive. I will have a monument of blood and bone to ensure I'm never forgotten. And all because you were afraid of your nature. Because you lacked courage."

The last words formed a sneer, cold and unforgiving, calculated to shrivel. But Viktor had endured the sour tutelage of Arzro Makrov, and hours in the company of Ebigail Kiradin. A thousand years beneath that sneer and he would have remained unwithered.

"At least I know my own mind," he said. "You speak of serving order in one breath and threaten destruction in the next. You're every bit as capricious as the gods you despise."

"Because I've had to be. Because selfishness gave me the power to grasp the Dark. I fought to claim it, offered up countless souls to lure it forth, but you? It's already part of you, and you of it." Elda spun about, outstretched hand encompassing the gathered thralls. "You can save them all. Not just these wretches, but every child who cowers from a soldier's cruel fanfare. Every family caught between the clash of egos and a wall of spears. Is that not what you want?"

Viktor stared across the marketplace, at the horde of gathered thralls. "What I want is a world free of you. A world free even of your memory."

"Then make one. The legacy I offer is one of magnitude, not intent. I was a tyrant because I allowed times to shape me thus. For centuries I brought an end to war, to suffering. An Age of Dark, where all were one and wanted for nothing."

"Save for want itself?" growled Viktor. "Or do your puppets retain desire? Have they any hope of freedom?"

Elda dipped her head and cast a sidelong glance at the nearest thrall: a young lad, barely of recruiting age. "Belenzo stripped that away when he set my ashes dancing on the winds. In betraying me, he also betrayed those he wished to save. Hold your anger for him."

"He couldn't have foreseen what would happen!"

"So his intent matters, where mine does not?"

She shrugged. Melancholy stole across her features. For the first time since his return to Eskavord, Elda Savka resembled a frail, old woman.

"I'll not deny that I was afraid. That I could have handled matters differently. It will be different for you, if you let it." With that, the vulnerability passed and calculation filled the void. "I know you feel the lure. Your shadow has grown so vibrant. I feel it throbbing beneath your skin. I know you long to embrace it."

"That's not true." Viktor didn't even convince himself.

"Then why have you sought to call on it so many times since arriving in Eskavord?"

"Out of need. I've only ever used my shadow out of need."

"Are you certain? Or is that simply what you tell yourself? Did you never wonder why you so often get what you desire? Even sealed in Belenzo's cage, my whispers shaped the Southshires, pushed men and women along paths they would never have trod without me. Are you certain you haven't done the same?"

Elda's words burrowed into Viktor's thoughts like maggots. Apara. Bound to him by strings of shadow. A woman who'd killed for him, kidnapped for him, and none of it by her own will. And Josiri. At that first meeting. He'd almost done to him what he'd done to the kernclaw. But still, that wasn't so bad. There was justice to Apara's servitude, and he'd stopped short of binding Josiri. He remained a moral man, for he'd overcome temptation.

But no sooner had that thought formed than doubt slithered coldly in. Comments once thought innocuous took on fresh significance. *Akadra the charmer*, as Vladama Kurkas had taken to calling him behind his back. Malachi's good-natured complaints that he was "always right". The easy authority he'd taken for granted all his career. The reason of a rational man, or something ominous? Josiri. Revekah. Anastacia. Malachi. He'd convinced them all to go against their better judgement. And Calenne . . . Lingering on that thought was like thrusting his hand into a fire.

"You," he growled. "You did this. You've manipulated me."

"No. You've simply acted according to your nature and your desires. We all yearn for life to unfold as we wish, and the Dark gives us the power to make reality of our dreams, whether we command it to or not. To make the dead walk and the living kneel. To make memory substance. And you *have* manipulated those around you. Even your sainted Calenne. How else could a woman love a monster she'd feared her whole life?"

"No!" He pulled fruitlessly at his bonds. "That's not how it is!"

Calenne. Who'd lived in terror of the Black Knight and was now as infatuated with him as he with her. And she'd embraced more than Viktor himself. Her family's hated heritage. The mantle of the Phoenix. Her desire, or his longing finding unconscious lease?

He'd never considered himself a "good" man. He couldn't, for war didn't allow such certainties. But he'd always held firm to the idea that he was dutiful – even righteous. Now, lost in the Dark and his every recent deed open to appalling question, Viktor's certainty slipped.

"You are a child of the Dark, Viktor, and the Dark is power. It wants to be used, and will seek to control you if it is not. It could drive you to madness . . . but it does not have to. Drink from me. Learn from me. Be the heir I've longed for all these years."

"To return the world to your peaceful Dark?"

"That choice falls to you. If my legacy is to be a shining realm of privileged squabbles, with you as its champion and Calenne at your side, then so be it. I wish you the joy of making it so. I will sleep well in the mists knowing that my legacy lives on, and that my efforts were not wholly wasted."

A shame that Ebigail and Malatriant had never crossed paths, for they would have found much to admire in one another. History. Legacy. Strength . . . The strength of a hand clamped tight about the throat.

Viktor took a deep breath, and strove to ignore the thick, heavy pulse of his shadow. It, at least, approved of Elda's proposal . . . but that was increasingly a reason to be wary. Where before it had been distinct from the Dark he had drawn from Calenne, now he couldn't tell them apart. Had he poisoned himself by saving her? Had Malatriant planned matters to enfold thus?

A stray memory clicked. Playing jando with Kasamor during a lazy border watch. Kas had taken every hand, courtesy – as it transpired – of a marked deck. This felt the same way.

If he refused, Malatriant would make good her threats of terror and destruction. If he accepted, he ran the risk that her promises were lies. That Malatriant sought only to possess him as she had so many others and bind his shadow to hers.

But if Malatriant did indeed seek to possess him, that she hadn't simply done so suggested she needed a measure of cooperation, which in turn offered a chance of resistance. If it came to it, could she do more damage alone than bound to him, with him resisting her every step of the way? There was no way to know.

In accepting, he at least saved Calenne. Even if her love was but a selfish dream, it changed nothing of his own feelings. And he'd save others too – all those who'd otherwise perish in the Tyrant Queen's last act of spite.

And what of him? He'd been sliding ever since he'd returned to the Southshires. Little by little, he'd used his shadow as it wished to be used – to control, to harm, and even to kill – and perhaps lost pieces of himself along the way. What if Malatriant truly was the only thing standing between him and madness?

Come to that, what if every word she'd spoken was the truth?

The cards were marked. He'd been playing – and losing – all his life, and never known it. Now there was one last hand to be wagered, and the deal had come due.

"Very well," said Viktor. "I accept."

Sixty-Eight

The cage of hands released him. Viktor fell forward, righted on the slope of dead by Elda's outstretched hand. Not the grip of an old woman, but something ancient, unshackled by mortality.

"Now," she intoned, "drink of me. Embrace my gift."

The Dark flooded over him. Through him. His shadow rose to greet it; cold, coiling and exultant. They were bound, he the river and she the sea. The one impossible without the other.

With that knowledge came fulfilment, and with fulfilment, understanding. The Dark was more than power. It was alive, as his shadow was alive. Viktor found no point at which it ended and Malatriant began. Weapon and wielder were as one.

In that moment, Viktor recognised the lies couched within truth. Yes, the Dark was a tool, capable of miracles untold. But to join with it – to grant it full rein – was to give away the pieces of yourself that no longer belonged. Duty. Honour. Love. These had no place within the blooming shadow, and sloughed away like dead skin.

Viktor felt them go and cared nothing for the loss. He was of the Dark, and the Dark was of him. He lost himself in a black sea of possibility.

Golden sunlight blazed through the stifling murk, white fire blazing in its wake.

He heard voices. The clash of steel. Screams. The wet roar of ragged flesh. Sounds from another life, at once yesterday and for ever ago. And above the tumult, a single voice clear as a clarion.

"*Ashanael Brigantim!*"

*

Eskavord's north gate had held firm against bandits, a farmer's revolt, belligerent Thrakkians and the floods of '76. But its stalwart timbers were as nothing beneath the impact of Anastacia's shoulder. On the third strike, the crossbar split with fury worthy of a storm from winter skies. Sunlight flooded the benighted streets, the fires of Ashana close behind.

They struck at the gallop, twelve riders on twelve horses. Ten Knights Essamere, a princessa of Empire, and a duke returning in sorrow to a slighted home. Josiri alone slowed his steed on approach, and then only long enough for Anastacia to regain her station behind his saddle. By the time she had done so, bodies lay thick about the gateway and the battle had moved on.

Familiar faces gazed up from blood-slicked cobbles. The folk he'd conspired and fought for his whole life.

"This is *not* how I imagined my homecoming," said Josiri. "These are my people."

[[Not any longer,]] said Anastacia. [[Now they are Malatriant. You cannot help them. You can only set them free.]]

Reluctance to draw blood faded with the first desperate parry. His backswing opened the thrall's filthy scalp to the bone. The shudder of shared pain parted the press of bodies long enough for his horse to barge a path.

"Ashanael Brigantim!"

White fire blazed at the Highgate crossroads where Melanna Saranal fought from her borrowed horse. Thralls shied from the holy light.

"*Until Death!*" came the bellow of Essamere.

Death had already found one of their number, who lay in the gutter's grime, surcoat torn bloody. Another fell from her saddle, dragged by grasping hands. Steel gleamed silver in the backwash of Melanna's sword, then crimson as the blade bit deep. A serene fell, other thralls echoing her hollow cry. Then the knight was gone, swallowed by a surge of the crowd.

Rosa stood tall in her stirrups. "Don't stop! Stop, and you're dead! We're here for Lord Akadra, not martyrdom!"

The mass of green divided. Knights galloped east and west along Highgate, the firestone lanterns upon their saddles a precaution should their search lead them too far from Anastacia's light. Melanna spurred west, Rosa east and Josiri straight across the tollway.

He hauled hard about an abandoned cart. Hooves skittered on cobbles. Fingers hauled on Josiri's leg. He hacked down, and the pressure vanished.

Even the Dark itself fought back. It spat and crackled on the edges of Anastacia's light, flowing through the streets like blood from a wound, only to hiss into vapour. The hollow screams of thralls howled beneath the eaves like ill-tidings on the bleakest wind. Josiri caught snatches of other voices too: Melanna's strident cries, Rosa's bellowed orders.

Darkness retreated over the Grelyt bridge.

[[There!]] said Anastacia.

Josiri stared at the marketplace fountain, and the hummock of dead raised upon its stone. And at its foot, kneeling with his eyes closed and hands pressed to his temples ...

Dark billowed around Viktor like black flame, the shrunken frame of Elda Savka barely visible at its heart. More thralls gathered in a circle, black eyes transfixed.

Fear winnowed its way through Josiri's coursing blood. Until that moment he'd not truly believed. He dug back his heels. The horse sprang forward.

"For the Phoenix!"

He crested the bridge, thralls scattering before his blade. Anastacia cried out. She struck the cobbles with a clatter and clambered to her feet.

Josiri twisted in his saddle. The strike of Anastacia's palm drove a thrall over the parapet and into the Grelyt's seething waters. Others thickened the street behind.

[[Go!]] A sword skittered along Anastacia's arm, shredding her sleeve. [[Get Akadra!]]

The words weren't the same, and the women worlds apart, but for an instant Josiri was fifteen years in the past, watching his mother throw her life away. He hauled on his reins, desperate to bring his horse about.

"Ana! Come on!"

[[I'm not your mother, Josiri. I've no plans to die in this squalid little town. Go!]]

She leapt into the mass of thralls. As he had at Davenwood, Josiri had a brief impression of black wings unfurling behind her, more dream than substance. Then she was gone, and for the second time in his life he rode from Grelyt Bridge and left a piece of himself behind.

Viktor wandered in the Dark, the sensations of battle lost in a maze of eddying shadows. He heard the battle cry of Essamere. He felt the fire of Melanna Saranal's sword, the welter of pain from bodies not his own. The confusion to find a Hadari fighting alongside Tressian knights. But more than anything, he felt the cold of his shadow. His true self.

Doubt remained, but it guttered with every step. Stripped of pretence, this was what he was – a vessel of primal Dark.

At Davenwood, with Calenne missing and his army routed, he'd sworn to fight his nature no longer. No more lies, even to himself.

The maze of suffocating Dark – *his* Dark – fell away into a vortex. A precipice beckoned.

He'd used everyone around him, bent their purpose to his own. Josiri. Malachi. Calenne. Others. He'd twisted them as Malatriant had twisted Eskavord. The man he'd believed himself had been a lie. He'd always been of the Dark. This wasn't transformation. It was truth.

A woman's form coalesced on the edge of the abyss. Her features danced, curling soot-laden smoke into mimicry of Calenne's subtle beauty.

"This is who you are." She even sounded like Calenne. "This is what you deserve. Claim it. Begin anew."

Yes, Viktor agreed silently. *This is what I deserve.*

He took her hand.

The thrall reeled away from the fire, hands clutched to his face. His scream echoed from a dozen mouths. Melanna galloped on past the west gate and back towards the heart of the town.

She fought by rote, no thought given to her blows. Worry grew to desperation with every clattering hoof-beat and crackle of flame. She felt her strength slipping away, her courage alongside. What had she truly hoped to achieve? What could a mere dozen do against the Sceadotha?

The street widened into a marketplace. The tide of thralls ebbed, and Melanna found herself without opponents. To the east, a slight figure framed by the memory of feathered wings held the bridge's crest. Nearer to, Josiri cut a path to where Akadra knelt in a torrent of dark.

Through the light of her sword, Melanna saw what was hidden from eyes alone. The tendrils that bound the man-of-shadow to the greater darkness. He couldn't be saved. Twice, she'd had the chance to slay him, twice she'd failed or turned aside. She could not afford a third.

She sheathed her sword and unslung her bow.

Josiri would never have seen the draw of the bow but for the glint of moonlight on the arrowhead. Only a blind man could have missed Melanna's intent. The arrow was meant not for Elda, but for Viktor.

"Melanna! No!"

The distance between them swallowed his shout, or else she paid no heed. Her horse picked up speed, galloping hard about the marketplace's perimeter. She leaned back over the saddle, the bow-staff crosswise across her chest and the arrow's nock touching her cheek.

"Melanna!"

Josiri urged his horse to redoubled effort. Not towards Melanna, who he knew he'd never reach in time, nor even to Viktor. Instead, he drove hard for the point between.

The bow sang. Moonlight gleamed.

Fire struck Josiri's shoulder and twisted him about. Blood rushed hot and cold. His numbed fingers slipped from the reins.

Josiri's cry echoed through the Dark. Viktor halted on the precipice. In his mind's eye, he saw Josiri fall with a black-fletched shaft deep in his shoulder. Emotion he'd thought sloughed away boiled up anew. Viktor clung to those scraps. Lies melted into new truths.

Lost to the Dark, he'd not seen the arrow, nor the doom it promised. Josiri had made his sacrifice willingly, unurged. Their bond was born not of the Dark, but of friendship hard won. And if he was worthy of that friendship, Viktor realised, he was worthy of more besides. It didn't matter that he was born of the Dark. It mattered only what he chose to be. And if he chose to be a man, and not a monster – the choice that had always been his – then he could be so.

He drew back his hand and stepped from the precipice. The Dark receded, the cold alongside.

Calenne's face dissolved into sharp, haggard features. "No! What are you doing!"

She lunged for him, fingers hooked like talons. Viktor caught her wrists. His own anger rose in reply, bringing with it pieces of himself he'd thought lost to the Dark. Duty. Purpose. The cornerstones of the life he'd made. He bound them as a cage about his glutted shadow, and flung it howling into the depths of his soul.

He drew Malatriant close. How weak she seemed now.

"I may have been born to the Dark, but I choose to walk in the light." Malatriant shrieked.

The Dark broke apart. Viktor found himself on his feet in Eskavord's marketplace. Elda fell away, her black eyes glassy and cold. Her body shattered as it hit stone, scattering across the cobbles as thick, black ash.

Thralls stood motionless all around. Not frozen, simply . . . inert. Like kraikons awaiting commands. But beyond the sunlit whitewashed walls, darkness reigned. He'd not destroyed Malatriant, only her vessel. She'd regather herself. And now he'd rejected her, there was nothing to hold back her last act of malice. Or almost nothing. There was a third path, though its price was almost too high to contemplate.

Ignoring complaints from stiff limbs, Viktor vaulted from the soiled fountain. He fell to his knees beside Josiri. His heart was a lump of stone, and grew heavier as he took in the pooling blood.

"I have you, brother."

Furtive eyes stared out from a pale face. Blood trickled between the cobbles. "And . . . Calenne?"

"She's here." Viktor took his hand. "I'll find her, I swear. See that you're here to greet her."

Josiri's eyes slid closed. The weight about Viktor's heart grew heavier still. Josiri's friendship had saved him – had maybe saved them all. For him to die . . .

"Ashana Brigantim!"

Lost in despair, Viktor noted too late the galloping hooves for what they were. Then Melanna was upon him, leaning low in the saddle as her sword hacked down.

At Davenwood, Viktor had been paralysed by his shadow's terror. Now, with his shadow consigned far from the light, he knew no such constraint. One hand sought Melanna's wrist and the other her belt. With a grunt of effort, he swung her from the saddle and pinned her to the ground. The horse galloped away.

"I am not what you think," he growled, his face an inch from hers.

She thrashed beneath him. "You are of the Dark!"

"Are you sure?"

Uncertainty crept across her features. "No. It's . . . Why is it gone?"

Viktor rolled clear. "If Josiri dies, there is no fortress, no army, no godly blessing that will save you. Am I understood?"

Melanna clambered warily to her feet. Her face fell. "I didn't mean for this."

[[Josiri?]] Anastacia pushed through the motionless thralls and collapsed at Josiri's side. Cradling his head in her hands, she glared up at Melanna. [[What happened?]]

"A mistake," said Viktor. "Nothing more."

He glanced at Melanna and wondered why he lied. Perhaps because the princessa was as much his saviour as Josiri. Shading his hand against the sun, he stared east across the bridge and a trio of Essamere uniforms riding closer, Rosa at their head. Good. Someone he could trust.

The nearest thrall twitched. Not by much. A spasm of the hand. Malatriant was almost done licking her wounds.

Viktor snagged the bridle of Josiri's steed, masterless since his fall, and drew the beast to Anastacia's side.

"Take him. He'll live if his wounds are tended."

She swung into the saddle. With the aid of a contrite Melanna, Viktor eased Josiri into her arms.

[[You're staying?]]

"I can't leave without Calenne."

"Then Essamere stands with you." Rosa walked her horse to a halt alongside. Her eyes darted warily from one thrall to the next. "We've lost too much coming this far. We'll not abandon you now. *I'll* not abandon you."

"You must. Has the army arrived?"

"Should have the town halfway surrounded by now."

Viktor closed his eyes, part of him wishing the answer had been something other. Friendship had saved him, but now he had no choice other than to cast it away. He was almost glad Josiri had one foot in the mists.

Viktor waited beneath the fountain long after the last rider departed. The firestone lantern in his hand held the Dark at bay, though he no longer feared its coming. He barely felt his shadow squirming behind the cage he'd made for it. His shadow, and the Dark he'd taken from Josiri and Calenne.

Only when lightening skies to the north showed that his allies were beyond the town wall did he pick his way through the streets. Weary feet traced a route learned in happier days, when invasion and betrayal were all he had to fear, and his standing in the Council all he had to lose.

Part way along his journey, the thralls finally awoke. Viktor wasn't entirely sure when it happened, for they made no move to stop him. They simply watched with cold, dead eyes. Indeed, the only act of resistance came as he approached the weather-beaten apothecary's cottage that had been Elda's house and Calenne's home. A double line of men and women waited outside the door, a barricade of flesh and bone.

Was Calenne still within? Viktor was certain he'd felt a flicker of her presence when Malatriant entwined him – a glimpse of her sitting at the kitchen table, motionless and alone, the Dark thick about her. And it made a strange kind of sense – one last shard of Elda Savka wanting to keep close the child she'd raised. But all was a gamble now.

"I suppose you think you've won?"

The question came not from one of the thralls blocking the door, but a young man seated on a bench beneath the gable. Twenty years old, or thereabouts. Younger even than Viktor had been when he'd first come to Eskavord during Katya Trelan's rebellion. Viktor read no hostility in voice or manner, just resignation and a hollow timbre too old for his years. Perhaps there was even a shadow of regret.

"Look around you." He sat down on the wall opposite. Fifteen years ago he'd left Eskavord on its knees. Today would be worse. "No one won today. We are all losers."

"You could have been a king."

"I would have been a monster. The choice you offer is no choice at all."

"It is all you have."

"Let you wreak havoc, or inherit your madness?" Had Malatriant always been cruel? Viktor wondered, or had the Dark made her so? "There's a third choice."

Amber light flickered on the northern skyline. Hungry tongues of flame leapt skyward. Others arose in the east, and then to the south. A distant crackle, like leaves tramped underfoot, billowed with the first skeins of smoke.

The lad stared past Viktor's shoulder, dark eyes aghast. "What have you done?"

"I'm finishing what Belenzo started," he replied. "By now, Eskavord is surrounded. You may be in every root and leaf, every scrap of flesh and every spark of soul. One by one, I will take these from you. I will render them dust. No spark of life will remain. No meadow will be left unsalted. Eskavord will pass into history, and you with it. You will have no heir. No testament. Only the fire and a legacy of ash."

To the west, fresh flames leapt across Branghall's gatehouse.

"It will mean the deaths of thousands."

"They're not alive now. Not in any way that counts."

"Few will believe that."

"So be it. I've no need to be remembered as a hero, or even at all. All that matters is what I do, here and now. And in this moment, trapped between light and dark, between fire and shadow, I reject you."

To his surprise, Malatriant laughed. "So this is why you risked the fires. To taunt my failure?"

"I came for Calenne." He shrugged. "The rest is ... what it is."

The lad waved a hand. The thralls parted and bled away, leaving the door unguarded. "You'll find her within. If that's what you truly want. But I spoke true before. She belongs to your past."

"You'll not stop me?" Viktor asked, surprised at the sudden accession.

"What would it change?"

"Nothing."

"Then I'm right to choose nothing in return," the lad replied bitterly. "Believe me in this: opening that door will bring you only misery."

"I'll take that chance."

The hungry roar of flames growing all around him, Viktor approached the cottage. He hesitated at the door, haunted by Malatriant's promise of misery yet to come. What if Calenne was dead? What would he do then? And even if she still lived, how could she ever again look on him as anything other than a monster? Could he live with that?

He'd have to.

Viktor grasped the door handle. In the distance, the first screams began.

Josiri jerked upright into bitter gloom, all but tipping himself from the tent's narrow bed. Numbness and thick bandages about head and shoulder sapped him of what little coordination he had left. Only the intervention of slender hands stopped him striking the floor.

"Have a care," said Melanna. "You'll be unsteady until the bethanis tincture wears off. When it does, you'll wish it hadn't."

Jumbled memories fought for dominance. "What happened?"

She eased him back and turned away. "I did something foolish. Then you did something foolish. And then Lord Akadra ..."

"Viktor? Where is he? Where's Anastacia?" And what was that damnable smoke? It grew thicker with every breath. "I want to see them."

He swung his legs clear of the bed, only to overbalance a second time before his bare feet touched the floor. Again, Melanna came to his rescue.

"Did you hear nothing?" she snapped. "The tincture has your wits. You'll fall before you get a dozen paces."

"Then you'll have to help me, won't you?"

She pinched her lips together. "I won't make it even half that far."

Josiri forced blurry eyes to focus and at last saw the rope binding Melanna's hobbled ankles to the tent's central pole. "I see."

"It has been made clear to me that another rope awaits me, should you die." She forced a thin smile. "So please, no foolishness."

[[I'll take you wherever you want to go.]]

The tent flap parted, leaving Anastacia silhouetted against an amber sky.

A little of the tension in Josiri's chest faded. "Ana. You're all right."

[[Naturally.]] Something in her hollow voice sounded amiss.

With Anastacia's help, Josiri hobbled from the tent and into the commotion of a camp half-set. King's blue uniforms vied with the green of Essamere and the scarlet of Prydonis. Horses, men, the beginnings of a ditch and palisade. The army had finally arrived.

In the middle distance, Eskavord burned, black plumes of smoke looping into the clouds. There was no darkness, only the midday sun stretching from Branghall's fire-wreathed tower to the uneven rampart of Eskavord's east gate. The only home he'd ever known, caught in one last, all-consuming inferno.

"What . . . What has he done?" Josiri breathed.

"What I've always done," rumbled Viktor. "What was needed."

He stood in the lee of the unfinished palisade, forearm propped against timber and eyes staring southwards. His torn surcoat was filthy with soot. It seemed to Josiri that he needed the palisade's support every bit as much as Josiri required Anastacia's.

"This was the only way," Viktor continued. "The old way. Fire to kill a witch, and send her spirit howling into the Raven's embrace. Every house. Every field. Every soul she ever touched."

Still Josiri didn't turn. He could almost *see* the ghosts of the dead crowding the ashen fields. So many lost to the flames, and all of them staring at him with accusing eyes. And one above all, dearer to him than all the rest, though he'd never truly told her as much.

"And Calenne?" asked Josiri. "Where is my sister?"

Seconds scraped by, accompanied by the distant crackle of flames and the desperate double-thump of Josiri's heart.

Viktor straightened. His arm fell to his side. "I'm sorry."

Without another word, he strode away, a black shadow against an amber sky, leaving Josiri amid the remnant of his shattered world.

Tzadas, 20th day of Radiance

A phoenix shall blaze from the darkness.
   A beacon to the shackled;
   a pyre to the keepers of their chains.

from the sermons of Konor Belenzo

Sixty-Nine

The fires raged until there was nothing left to burn. For five days, flames haunted the horizon, consuming field and forest, hearth and home. The dead. The living. Everything in between. All gone in a conflagration worthy of fable. Of what had once been the jewel of the Southshires, only charred stone remained. Acre upon acre of ashen wasteland unfolding across the Grelyt valley. The Southshires would go on, but Eskavord and its neighbouring hamlets were no more.

Even Kurkas, no stranger to the cruelties of war, had sought every excuse he could not to look upon the sight while the fires raged – while living and dead were offered up to the flames. Hundreds of thralls, motionless and sightless, shepherded into cleansing coruscation. They hadn't screamed, hadn't uttered a sound. That was almost worse.

Only now it was over had Kurkas gathered the resolve to make the long, stumbling walk up Drannan Tor, and fulfil a promise given to an old enemy.

[[He doesn't want to see anyone. I thought I'd made that clear.]]

Anastacia emerged into the sun-dappled glade. The tangled plaits of her wig would never be the same again, but she'd patched the worst of the tears in her dress. Still, the tatterdemalion aspect remained, lending her the air of a vagabond queen more than a well-to-do lady.

Kurkas drew to a halt, glad of the respite. Pain he didn't mind – it meant the parts and pieces were still there – but the stiffness? That couldn't fade fast enough.

"Pretty clear, I'd say, plant pot." He paused. "Sorry. *Milady* plant pot. You didn't have to toss that herald down the hillside. Poor lad was only doing his duty."

Gold glinted as she prowled nearer – a simarka stalking prey. [[And you suppose I'd not do the same to you?]]

"Reckon you'd do it with a smile, if those lips'd let you." He rubbed at his eyepatch. "We both know he can't hide for ever. Let me talk to him, *then* you can throw me down the hill. Call it a pleasure deferred."

Anastacia withdrew. Taking it as invitation, Kurkas followed.

To his relief, the slope lessened as it neared the old watchtower. A campfire smouldered on the lee side of the sole remaining wall. Josiri sat beneath canvas strung between windblown trees, staring out across the ashen waste. Staring but not *seeing*.

"Captain Kurkas." He spoke without turning. "If you've come on Viktor's behalf, you might as well save your breath."

"Sah! 'Specially after that climb. His lordship's worried about you."

"And what good did Viktor's concern ever do anyone?"

Kurkas limped closer. The gusting wind set white petals dancing over the ashen wastes below as proctors scattered duskhazel and fleenroot to cleanse the last of Malatriant's taint. Superstition, as far as Kurkas was concerned. But he also believed in taking no chances.

"Reckon he did what he had to. There wasn't any saving them."

Josiri glared up at him. "And you know that for a fact?"

"She knows it." Kurkas jerked a thumb in Anastacia's direction. "And I'll bet you a year's wage that she's tried to tell you. I get it, my lord, I do. You feel you've failed 'em, which is why you've stood vigil. One last duty, and all that. But that time's passing. They'd want you to move on . . . your sister more than any."

Josiri sprang to his feet, a wild look in his eyes. "And you speak for the dead? Calenne, with her throat cut in a final act of spite? What does she have to say?"

Kurkas stared straight ahead. The old muster-field trick that deflected many a noble's wrath. "Don't claim to speak for anyone other than myself, sah." Bracing himself against the crutch, he tugged the battered envelope from his belt. "And I reckon she'd give me hell if I did."

Josiri stared at the envelope as if waking from a dream. "Revekah?"

"Halvor ... *Captain* Halvor made me promise to deliver this. Don't go making a liar of me now."

Hesitantly, Josiri took the letter. "Why now?"

"Because I'm riding north tonight. Think I've earned a bit of peace and quiet."

"Thank you, captain."

Kurkas shrugged. "I keep my promises where I can. In the end, that's all we can do. Just ask the plant pot over there *not* to toss me down the hill, if you'd be so good."

Josiri watched Kurkas go with tired eyes then turned to look once more upon the land he'd failed. Five days with too little food, and less sleep. He knew they'd taken their toll, that reason ebbed as low as his spirit, but the walk back down Drannan Tor seemed so long as to be impossible.

He turned the envelope over and over. He dreaded what he'd find within, and for a moment longed to crumple the paper into a ball and hurl it away. He slit the envelope before temptation could take hold, and read.

> *Josiri,*
>
> *If you're reading this, then it's over. I can only imagine the cost. I hope you can save something of the Southshires. As for me, that witch has her claws so deep that I'll never be free. But I can hurt her, and that will have to do.*
>
> *For as long as I've known you, you've been trapped by the past. I've been your jailer as much as anyone. In that I've served you poorly, and I hope you can forgive me. If you'd honour my memory, I beg you not to spend your life fighting old battles, or in penance for what cannot be changed. Give me this, and I'll walk the mists content.*
>
> *Remember me well. I'll look for you come Third Dawn.*
> *Revekah*

He lost track of how long he stared at the scratchy handwriting, the hilltop breeze threatening to tug the paper from his hand.

"She knew," he whispered. "She knew how this would go."

Anastacia slid her arms about his waist and laid her head on his shoulder. [[She suspected. We talked, she and I, that last day. One out-cast to another. She saw only a dark road, filled with regrets. She didn't want that for you.]]

"You . . . You knew about this?"

[[Of course. Why do you suppose I didn't throw Kurkas down the hill?]]

"Why didn't you tell me?"

[[Because you wouldn't have listened. Sometimes it's better to let the dead speak for themselves.]]

Josiri let the letter go. It danced away on the wind. "And what do you think?"

[[Does it matter?]]

"More than anything."

She hesitated. [[Then I think you should honour Revekah's request. Neither she nor Calenne would want you to wither away up here, or anywhere else, agonising over a guilt not yours.]]

Calenne. Josiri fought back sudden tears. Their arguments now seemed pettier than ever. Wasted moments that would have been better spent on anything else. "I've made a poor job of keeping my promises, haven't I?"

[[You see?]] Her tone grew stern. [[That's precisely what Revekah meant. And you've only broken one. Eskavord may be gone, but the Southshires is free. Not just from Malatriant, but from the Council.]]

"But for how long?"

She pulled away. [[If you persist, I'll throw *you* down the hill. You have a seat on the Council. Even friends, if half of what you've said is true. Use them.]]

"You mean . . . leave the Southshires for Tressia?"

She shrugged. [[Why not? You're hardly the Duke of Eskavord any longer.]]

Josiri winced at Anastacia's bluntness, but her wisdom shone bright even through sorrow. With Malachi's help he could do more – far more – for his people than he could as the master of a scorched ruin. Grief was a privilege he'd not earned.

"And you'd come with me? Life's different in Tressia. You'll be on display in a way you've never known here."

She slid her arm through his. [[Let them stare. I'm worth it.]]

*

Viktor set his pack to his shoulder and stared back across the deserted camp. Most of the soldiers had gone. Those who remained were out in the ashen fields, aiding the proctors in their labours. It was better that way. He'd never been one for fanfare and ceremony, and never less than today. The dead of the pyres would stand witness. He doubted their eyes would ever leave him.

He looked up and found Rosa staring at him. "What?"

"Nothing. It's just that I don't remember the last time I saw you out of uniform."

He stared along the open road and offered no reply. It felt no less strange to him. The travelling leathers didn't ... Well, they didn't *feel* right. But uniforms were for soldiers, and he wasn't a soldier any longer.

"You've freed Melanna Saranal?" he asked at last.

"She left at dawn," Rosa replied stiffly. "I let her have the sword, but not the bow. I still say we should have kept her. A princessa is a valuable bargaining piece."

"Josiri would only have let her go. Better I take the blame for that, too. You have my written orders?"

Rosa nodded tersely. "I do."

"And you'll present them to the Council?"

"I will not. We took this decision together."

He laughed under his breath. Did guilt or friendship lie beneath her defiance? "There's no point us both becoming pariahs. Let the blame fall on me."

She folded her arms. "I can't do that."

"You're a good woman, Roslava Orova. The Republic's fortunate to have you."

"To have us *both*."

He grunted. She'd change her mind once she was back in the city, and learned he'd already sent a herald north with documentation absolving her of Eskavord's razing. However justified their actions, the Council would never forgive, and nor should they. But they would need Rosa, whether she liked it or not. The Hadari would come again. They always did. And the Republic needed a champion to stand against them.

"Where will you go?" asked Rosa.

"Someone needs to keep watch in case a piece of Malatriant survived. Blood travels far."

"One witch to catch another?"

He grimaced. "I imagine so."

Viktor didn't feel like explaining the rest. That even with his shadow now locked deeper than he could ever recall, he didn't trust himself. Better he was away from folk until he did. Rosa wouldn't understand. Or perhaps she would. After all, her own being was at least as muddied as his own.

"Farewell, Rosa."

She clasped a fist to her chest in salute. "Until death, Viktor."

He set out through the gateway. A lone figure waited on the roadway. One Viktor had both hoped and dreaded to see.

"Brother."

"Don't call me that." Josiri scowled and glanced away. "So it's true. You're leaving."

"I think that's for the best." Viktor hesitated. Five days since they'd last spoken. Five days in which to find words for the terrible burden of his heart. A wasted search, for he'd no more notion what to say now than then. But still he tried. "I wish things had ended differently."

"That's not enough. It'll never be enough. You came to me as a friend, but you've taken more from me than an enemy ever could." He sighed. "To think, you were the Phoenix all along."

Viktor blinked. "I don't follow."

"*A phoenix shall blaze from the darkness,*" quoted Josiri, his voice thick with emotion. "*A beacon to the shackled; a pyre to the keepers of their chains.* It was never my mother; never Calenne. But you. The man who killed them both."

Viktor closed his eyes. He'd never considered that. Never thought to place himself in prophecy, but he *had* brought fire out of darkness, and freed Malatriant's slaves.

But not all freedoms were equal.

"I'm sorry," he said. "I wish I could bring her back to you."

"You didn't even bring me a body to mourn."

The urge to ease his anguish flared. Viktor forced it back. "There was nothing to save." He cleared his throat. "I understand you're leaving too. I'm glad. Malachi will need all the help he can find."

"Even from a southwealder?"

"In my experience, there are few things finer than a southwealder's friendship, and few losses weightier."

Josiri's brow flickered. His mouth opened for a response, then stone slabs fell down behind his eyes. "Goodbye, Viktor."

Two words. Two words would ease his heartache, but to speak them meant breaking a promise, and Viktor had so few left intact.

"Be well, my friend."

Leaving Josiri behind, Viktor struck out southwards, walking the road that had once joined Eskavord to the distant Thrakkian border. Fields smouldered to either side, dull orange slumbering among the lifeless greys. The bitter notes of yesterday's blaze melded with sweet duskhazel and the sweat of the soldiers sent to tend the razed crops. To the west, beyond motionless kraikon silhouettes and the remnant of Eskavord's wall, the stones of Branghall yet stood – a lonely, charred reminder of the world as it had been a week before.

At last, Eskavord passed away behind him. An hour later, ash gave way to golden wheat, promising harvest yet to come. The once empty road thickened with travellers.

The sight went some way to raising Viktor's spirits. Life would go on. The Southshires would go on. So too would Josiri, though their brief friendship was as ashen as Eskavord.

As dusk slid into night, he left the road entirely. He set off into the hills, losing himself in the trees and the fragmented ruin of ancient days. At last, he arrived at the statue – Ashana and Lumestra back-to-back on a crumbling plinth. The one with a crescent moon in her hands; the other hooded, with a lantern held outstretched.

"It's done," he said. "I wish you'd let me tell him the truth."

Calenne emerged from the trees, her dark hair cut short to disguise her rank. Her cold hands took his and held them tight.

"It's kinder this way," she said. "Josiri would see me remain a Trelan for ever. He'd make us both miserable with his demands. Better a clean break. He can mourn me in memory, rather than hate me in the flesh."

Viktor's discomfort returned with her bitter words. "I think you misjudge him."

She smiled, though not unkindly. "And *I* worry that you love my brother more than you do me."

He grunted. "No. Never that."

"Good." Holding tight to his hands, she rose onto her toes and kissed him. "We are one, Viktor. Light or Dark. Now and for ever."

Careful not to set the leaves rustling, Melanna let the branch fall back into place. She'd followed Lord Akadra from Eskavord, hood drawn low to hide her shadowthorn features. She hadn't been sure why at first – save perhaps a vague notion that she owed him thanks for her release – but by now trusted her instinct far more than her judgement.

Now, hearing him speak in earnest tones to an empty clearing, Melanna knew without doubt that her instinct had the right of it. Her shoulders itched with the feeling of an unwelcome presence she couldn't quite see.

Akadra turned this way and that, the soft baritone of his words losing their form long before they reached Melanna's position among the trees. Then he gazed briefly up at the twin statues of Ashana and Lumestra, and strode deeper into the forest. Alone, save for the Dark billowing about him like a shroud.

"Goddess," she breathed. "It's not over."

She felt the presence before the soft glow of moonlight reached her eyes. Turning about, she saw Ashana standing a pace behind her. And further back, a heavy cloak, an antlered helm, and blazing green eyes.

"No," said Ashana. "It's not over. It has barely begun."

Acknowledgements

You made it! All the way to the end. Or rather, all the way to the end of the beginning. I hope you'll stick around for another couple of hundred words, because there are thanks to be made. If you need to grab a cup of tea first, go right ahead. I need one myself. Writing about intrigue, gods and battles? Easy. Talking like a human being? Much harder.

Let's see how I go.

First of all, a heartfelt thanks to my agent, the estimable John Jarrold, not only for his unflagging support, but also for weathering my storm of questions, worries and outright nonsense. Likewise, my editors at Orbit, James Long and Priyanka Krishnan, for helping the story shine all the brighter.

Beyond that, I'd like to offer my gratitude to the friends and family who have offered encouragement along the way. Special mention should go to Mum and my good friend Greg Benedict, who have never met, but are allied in abject horror when I sometimes spell like an American (look, sometimes it's just *clearer* that way, guys). To Mark Latham, who keeps me a good deal saner than he might suspect. And of course to my wife, Lisa, who doubtless longs for the days when we could make car journeys unaccompanied by soliloquys of fractured narratives and character arcs as I unpick the mess I've gotten myself into the day before.

As for the cats, to whom I am but a humble servant? They need no thanks. They know all and see all.

extras

about the author

Matthew Ward is a writer, cat-servant and owner of more musical instruments than he can actually play (and considerably more than he can play *well*). He's afflicted with an obsession for old places – castles, historic cities and the London Underground chief among them – and should probably cultivate more interests to help expand out his author biography.

After a decade serving as a principal architect for Games Workshop's *Warhammer* and *Warhammer 40,000* properties, Matthew embarked on an adventure to tell stories set in worlds of his own design. He lives near Nottingham with his extremely patient wife – as well as a pride of attention-seeking cats – and writes to entertain anyone who feels there's not enough magic in the world.

Follow him on Twitter @TheTowerofStars

Find out more about Matthew Ward and other Orbit authors by registering for the free monthly newsletter at www.orbitbooks.net.

interview

*Legacy of Ash **is an epic story, featuring multiple characters
who are all pursuing their own goals. What was the starting
point for the story – was there a specific character that you
originally built the plot around?***

Viktor's always been the heart of *Legacy of Ash*. Unusually (for
me, at least) I knew how his story ended long before I understood how it began. Most of the other characters came into
being through digging into Viktor's journey, and the rest of the
book coalesced around them.

*Did you have a favourite character to write? And were there
any that you found particularly challenging?*

Be it books, films or comics, I've always loved the folk who
dwell at the edge of the narrative more than the protagonists.
As a writer, I'm drawn to them even more, because they've
more freedom to affect the tone of the story, rather than the
plot. Characters like Anastacia, Kurkas and the Raven are a joy
precisely for that reason.

Of the others, Josiri was probably the hardest to write. He

falls further than anyone before he gets his second wind, and it's a careful balancing act. Leave him in misery too long, and you lose all reason to hope he gets through it. Cut it shorter, and redemption loses its power.

Your world-building is particularly rich and possesses a tangible sense of history, which lends your world real depth. How much background work and research did you do when creating the world of Aradane?

Consciously, very little – dull stuff like "Is this a reasonable distance to march in a day?" But folklore, history and culture have all left their mark on Aradane. I'm fortunate to have a memory that holds onto stray facts and concepts and spits them out when needed. The main thing I try to keep in mind is how history casts a shadow over the present. Tradition, superstition, folklore and religion all arise out of tangible reason, even if it's distorted by the passage of time.

But I do like to walk old or abandoned places. York (to which the city of Tressia owes a debt), parts of London, the Scottish Highlands, Snowdonia . . . You can feel old stories, real and imagined, echoing through them – especially when night falls or mist comes down. It's that feeling, more than anything, that I wanted to instil in Aradane. For it to be a place where history and folklore overlap, and truth is tangled.

The battles in* Legacy of Ash *are particularly visceral. What's the secret to writing a good battle scene?

Keep things brief, keep them moving and always make sure your characters have something at stake beyond mere victory or defeat.

The simarka and kraikons are a striking feature of the world – was there a particular inspiration behind these magically fuelled metal constructs?

Honestly, I've no idea at this point. The simarka have been rattling around my head for years (although the name was relatively recent), and the kraikons are an extrapolation of the same concept. Part of it's probably that I have a lingering fear that I never put enough "fantasy" in my fantasy stories. And they certainly lend a horrifying, faceless texture to the oppression of the Southshires.

***Speaking of inspiration, what would you say were the main influences for* Legacy of Ash?**

So many go back to childhood – stories and settings that made fantasy of the mundane. In terms of books, that's Tolkien (I'd read *The Lord of the Rings* by age seven), Narnia and other bits and bobs along the way. TV offers up influences like *Doctor Who*, Richard Carpenter's *Robin of Sherwood* and, years later, *Babylon 5*, which hooked me with its character work (especially its supporting characters), and the sheer *scope* of the narrative.

Tonally, my writing style owes a lot to Alistair MacLean and Timothy Zahn, and my battles to Bernard Cornwell, who remains the absolute gold standard when it comes to the clash of armies.

Legacy of Ash *is something of a door-stopper, weighing in at around 230,000 words. How long did it take to write, and what does your writing process/routine look like?*

The core idea (Viktor's journey) has been kicking around for years and years, although I was never quite certain how to do it justice. When I finally gave it a go, it quickly became apparent that this was going to be *big*, and a bit of a gamble besides. I knew it had the potential to be great, but that I wasn't likely to know if it was for months.

What's now the first 30,000 words took probably a month and a half to get nailed down. Adding Ashana to the cast was the turning point – it answered a load of questions I'd not yet thought to ask. It also ripped the roof off the world and made everything *bigger*. Afterwards, everything got a lot easier. As the crow flies, it took around six months writing full-time, from empty Word .doc, to 285,000 word first draft, to polished manuscript.

My routine's pretty much a 9ish to 5ish day, punctuated by many, many feline interruptions.

Finally, can you give us a hint at what we can expect in the next book, Legacy of Steel?

History doesn't end with the turn of the final page – there's always more to gain, and more to lose. I don't think Viktor, Josiri and Melanna understand that yet, but they will.

I've also been itching to bring more of the divine pantheon into play, so it's a good bet that we'll be seeing at least one of Ashana's siblings following her into the ephemeral world. There are crowns to be claimed, wrongs to be righted, mysteries to delve, moments of desperation and the promise of joy.

I guess what I'm saying is "consequences". Lots and lots of consequences.

if you enjoyed

LEGACY OF ASH

look out for

THE GUTTER PRAYER

by

Gareth Hanrahan

The city of Guerdon stands eternal. A refuge from the war that rages beyond its borders. But in the ancient tunnels deep beneath its streets, a malevolent power has begun to stir.

The fate of the city rests in the hands of three thieves. They alone stand against the coming darkness. As conspiracies unfold and secrets are revealed, their friendship will be tested to the limit. If they fail, all will be lost and the streets of Guerdon will run with blood.

PROLOGUE

Y ou stand on a rocky outcrop, riddled with tunnels like the other hills, and look over Guerdon. From here, you see the heart of the old city, its palaces and churches and towers reaching up like the hands of a man drowning, trying to break free of the warren of alleyways and hovels that surrounds them. Guerdon has always been a place in tension with itself, a city built atop its own previous incarnations yet denying them, striving to hide its past mistakes and present a new face to the world. Ships throng the island-spangled harbour between two sheltering headlands, bringing traders and travellers from across the world. Some will settle here, melding into the eternal, essential Guerdon.

Some will come not as travellers, but as refugees. You stand as testament to the freedom that Guerdon offers: freedom to worship, freedom from tyranny and hatred. Oh, this freedom is conditional, uncertain – the city has, in its time, chosen tyrants and fanatics and monsters to rule it, and you have been part of that, too – but the sheer weight of the city, its history and its myriad peoples always ensure that it slouches back eventually into comfortable corruption, where anything is permissible if you've got money.

Some will come as conquerors, drawn by that wealth. You were born in such a conflict, the spoils of a victory. Sometimes, the conquerors stay and are slowly absorbed into the city's culture. Sometimes, they raze what they can and move on, and Guerdon grows again from the ashes and rubble, incorporating the scar tissue into the living city.

You are aware of all this, as well as certain other things, but you cannot articulate how. You know, for example, that two Tallowmen guards patrol your western side, moving with the unearthly speed and grace of their kind. The dancing flames inside their heads illuminate a row of carvings on your flank, faces of long-dead judges and politicians immortalised in stone while their mortal remains have long since gone down the corpse shafts. The Tallowmen jitter by, and turn right down Mercy Street, passing the arch of your front door beneath the bell tower.

You are aware, too, of another patrol coming up behind you.

And in that gap, in the shadows, three thieves creep up on you. The first darts out of the mouth of an alleyway and scales your outer wall. Ragged hands find purchase in the cracks of your crumbling western side with inhuman quickness. He scampers across the low roof, hiding behind gargoyles and statues when the second group of Tallowmen pass by. Even if they'd looked up with their flickering fiery eyes, they'd have seen nothing amiss.

Something in the flames of the Tallowmen should disquiet you, but you are incapable of that or any other emotion.

The ghoul boy comes to a small door, used only by workmen cleaning the lead tiles of the roof. You know – again, you don't know how you know – that this door is unlocked, that the guard who should have locked it was bribed to neglect that part of his duties tonight. The ghoul boy tries the door, and it opens silently. Yellow-brown teeth gleam in the moonlight.

Back to the edge of the roof. He checks for the tell-tale light of the Tallowmen on the street, then drops a rope down. Another thief emerges from the same alleyway and climbs. The ghoul hauls up the rope, grabs her hand and pulls her out of sight in the brief gap between patrols. As she touches your walls, you know her to be a stranger to the city, a nomad girl, a runaway. You have not seen her before, but a flash of anger runs through you at her touch as you share, impossibly, in her emotion.

You have never felt this or anything else before, and wonder at it. Her hatred is not directed at you, but at the man who compels her to be here tonight, but you still marvel at it as the feeling travels the length of your roof-ridge.

The girl is familiar. The girl is important.

You hear her heart beating, her shallow, nervous breathing, feel the weight of the dagger in its sheathe pressing against her leg. There is, however, something missing about her. Something incomplete.

She and the ghoul boy vanish in through the open door, hurrying through your corridors and rows of offices, then down the side stairs back to ground level. There are more guards inside, humans – but they're stationed at the vaults on the north side, beneath your grand tower, not here in this hive of paper and records; the two thieves remain unseen as they descend. They come to one of your side doors, used by clerks and scribes during the day. It's locked and bolted and barred, but the girl picks the lock even as the ghoul scrabbles at the bolts. Now the door's unlocked, but they don't open it yet. The girl presses her eye to the keyhole and watches, waits, until the Tallowmen pass by again. Her hand fumbles at her throat, as if looking for a necklace that usually rests there, but her neck is bare. She scowls, and the flash of anger at the theft thrills you.

You are aware of the ghoul, of his physical presence within you, but you feel the girl far more keenly, share her fretful excitement as she waits for the glow of the Tallowmen candles to diminish. This, she fears, is the most dangerous part of the whole business.

She's wrong.

Again, the Tallowmen turn the corner onto Mercy Street. You want to reassure her that she is safe, that they are out of sight, but you cannot find your voice. No matter – she opens the door a crack and gestures, and the third member of the trio lumbers from the alley.

Now, as he thuds across the street in the best approximation of a sprint he's capable of, you see why they needed to open the ground-level door when they already had the roof entrance. The third member of the group is a Stone Man. You remember when the disease – or curse – first took root in the city. You remember the panic, the debates about internment, about quarantines. The alchemists found a treatment in time, and a full-scale epidemic was forestalled. But there are still outbreaks, patches, leper colonies of sufferers in the city. If the symptoms aren't caught early enough, the result is the motley creature that even now lurches over your threshold – a man whose flesh and bone are slowly transmuting into rock. Those afflicted by the plague grow immensely strong, but every little bit of wear and tear, every injury hastens their calcification. The internal organs are the last to go, so towards the end they are living statues, unable to move or see, locked forever in place, labouring to breathe, kept alive only by the charity of others.

This Stone Man is not yet paralysed, though he moves awkwardly, dragging his right leg. The girl winces at the noise as she shuts the door behind him, but you feel an equally unfamiliar thrill of joy and relief as her friend reaches the safety of their hiding place. The ghoul's already moving, racing down the long silent corridor that's usually thronged with prisoners and guards, witnesses and jurists, lawyers and liars. He runs on all fours, like a grey dog. The girl and the Stone Man follow; she stays low, but he's not that flexible. Fortunately, the corridor does not look out directly onto the street outside, so, even if the patrolling Tallowmen glanced this way, they wouldn't see him.

The thieves are looking for something. They check one record room, then another. These rooms are secure, locked away behind iron doors, but stone is stronger and the Stone Man bends or breaks them, one by one, enough for the ghoul or the human girl to wriggle through and search.

At one point, the girl grabs the Stone Man's elbow to hasten him along. A native of the city would never do such a thing, not willingly, not unless they had the alchemist's cure to hand. The curse is contagious.

They search another room, and another and another. There are hundreds of thousands of papers here, organised by a scheme that is a secret of the clerks, whispered only from one to another, passed on like an heirloom. If you knew what they sought, and they could understand your speech, you could perhaps tell them where to find what they seek, but they fumble on half blind.

They cannot find what they are looking for. Panic rises.

The girl argues that they should leave, flee before they are discovered. The Stone Man shakes his head, as stubborn and immovable as, well, as stone. The ghoul keeps his own counsel, but hunches down, pulling his hood over his face as if trying to remove himself from their debate. They will keep looking. Maybe it's in the next room.

Elsewhere inside you, one guard asks another if he heard that. Why, might that not be the sound of an intruder? The other guards look at each other curiously, but then in the distance, the Stone Man smashes down another door, and the now-attentive guards definitely hear it.

You know – you alone know – that the guard who alerted his fellows is the same one who left the rooftop door unlocked. The guards fan out, sound the alarm, begin to search the labyrinth within you. The three thieves split up, try to evade their pursuers. You see the chase from both sides, hunters and hunted.

And, after the guards leave their post by the vaults, other figures enter. Two, three, four, climbing up from below. How have you not sensed them before? How did they come upon you, enter you, unawares? They move with the confidence of experience, sure of every action. Veterans of their trade.

The guards find the damage wrought by the Stone Man and begin to search the south wing, but your attention is focused on the strangers in your vault. With the guards gone, they work unimpeded. They unwrap a package, press it against the vault door, light a fuse. It blazes brighter than any Tallowman's candle, fizzing and roaring and then—

—you are burning, broken, rent asunder, thrown into disorder. Flames race through you, all those thousands of documents catching in an instant, old wooden floors fuelling the inferno.

The stones crack. Your western hall collapses, the stone faces of judges plummeting into the street outside to smash on the cobblestones. You feel your *awareness* contract as the fire numbs you. Each part of you that is consumed is no longer part of you, just a burning ruin. It's eating you up.

It is not that you can no longer see the thieves – the ghoul, the Stone Boy, the nomad girl who taught you briefly to hate. It is that you can no longer know them with certainty. They flicker in and out of your rapidly fragmenting consciousness as they move from one part of you to another.

When the girl runs across the central courtyard, pursued by a Tallowman, you feel every footstep, every panicked breath she takes as she runs, trying to outdistance creatures that move far faster than her merely human flesh can hope to achieve. She's clever, though – she zigzags back into a burning section, vanishing from your perception. The Tallowman hesitates to follow her into the flames for fear of melting prematurely.

You've lost track of the ghoul, but the Stone Man is easy to spot. He stumbles into the High Court, knocking over the wooden seats where the Lords Justice and Wisdom sit when proceedings are in session. The velvet cushions of the viewer's gallery are already on fire. More pursuers close in on him. He's too slow to escape.

Around you, around what's left of you, the alarm spreads. A blaze of this size must be contained. People flee the neighbouring buildings, or hurl buckets of water on roofs set alight by sparks from your inferno. Others gather to gawk, as if the destruction of one of the city's greatest institutions was a sideshow for their amusement. Alchemy wagons race through the streets, carrying vats of fire-quelling liquids, better than water for dealing with a conflagration like this. They know the dangers of a fire in the city; there have been great fires in the past, though none in recent decades. Perhaps, with the alchemists' concoctions and the discipline of the city watch, they can contain this fire.

But it is too late for you.

Too late, you hear the voices of your brothers and sisters cry out, shouting the alarm, rousing the city to the danger.

Too late, you realise what you are. Your consciousness shrinks down, takes refuge in its vessel. That is what you are, if not what you have always been.

You feel a second emotion – fear – as the flames climb the tower. Something beneath you breaks, and the tower sags suddenly to one side, sending you rocking back and forth. Your voice jangles in the tumult, a sonorous death rattle.

Your supports break, and you fall.